THE YOUNG CHESTERTON CHRONICLES

VOLUME TWO:

THE EMPEROR OF NORTH AMERICA

© 2011 by John McNichol

Published by
Bezalel Books
Waterford, MI

www.BezalelBooks.com

The choicest first fruits of your soil you shall bring to the house
of the Lord, your God.
~Exodus 23:19

Printed in the United States of America

Cover painting ©2011 by Edward Shuman
Along with the artwork from Deacon Lawrence Klimecki
(Lawrence@GryphonRampant.com) as appears on The Young *Chesterton
Chronicles: Volume 1, The Tripods Attack!* by John McNichol

ISBN 978-1-936453-07-8
Library of Congress Control Number 2011911793

The air was cold, crisp, and smelled of icy rocks. The snow had pooled in hollow areas on the hillsides and crannies in the mountain stone. Clouds the color of slate covered the morning sky like a rough, frigid blanket, hiding the sun from any living thing below as it had for centuries.

The ground looked much like the sky above it. It was a monochromatic rainbow of grays, blacks and whites. Even what passed for grass in this part of the world had somehow become a gray shade of green. The only bright color for miles around was the blood of the dead mountain cat at the base of a freshly turned mound of ancient earth. And the only movements made were those by the black crows on the dull shaded dirt. Dozens of the dark birds swarmed over the animal's body, busily carving, snapping and squabbling over any available tidbit clinging to the large cat's fur and bones.

The birds had been pecking at the cat's corpse for days. In truth, it was the best meal the crows of the region had had in many generations. And while the concept of generations of life was wholly beyond the birds' comprehension, the idea of a free, plentiful meal was not.

The birds continued to gobble and feed, so intent on their feast that when the winding, whirring sound began above them only a few birds gave even the slightest notice of it, and even these paused for less than a second from their fevered mission of indulgence.

The noise above increased. After a few more seconds, something happened that the eldest stone in the valley could not have remembered, had it any memory at all. Several hundred feet above the swirling mass of scavenger birds, the clouds suddenly parted as water parts when a stone breaks the surface, letting the first peek of actual light in centuries hit the valley floor and scattering the greater mass of crows from their meal.

But no stone had split the clouds. Instead, a metal sphere had dropped out of the sky. It was attached to a long dark rope that extended from the sphere itself in an almost straight line up into the sea of clouds above it. The whirring that had barely disturbed the crows' breakfast had come from the top of the sphere, as more and more of the thick-fibered metallic rope unwound from a rapidly spinning winch on the sphere's roof.

The metal sphere landed on the ground with a slam, loud enough to startle the birds into flying away with hundreds of angry *caws* sounding in the wind. Free now from the presence of chattering scavengers, the sphere sat quietly—a metal ball perhaps eight feet in diameter, with a single, small porthole and lines of rivets criss-crossing it in concentric patterns across its surface. After a few seconds there were several frantic clicks inside the sphere, followed by a loud clang and a rusty squeak as a door to the sphere opened.

The man who stepped out was dressed in white overalls, and in no mood to be slowed down. Breathing heavily and quickly, he balanced both feet on the lower edge of his curved doorway and leapt from the sphere that had carried him down from the clouds. His tightly-laced rubber boots crunched on the gravel and old grass as he hit the ground in a squatting position. He quickly straightened his body, found his balance and ran down the rough path he'd eyed from a distance for many months.

"C'mon ... C'mon ... C'mon," he mumbled to himself rhythmically as he ran. He was tall, a little past middle-age with gray temples, but lean and fit. He'd run at an even pace for nearly five minutes when he heard the whirrings in the air above him.

His eyes bulged and his pace quickened. There were several rock outcroppings in the misty distance, but as he neared them they became more mountains. He slowed, trying to reconcile the impassible rocky formations in front of him with the gentle, sloping hills he'd seen in the maps.

"Must run ... Must run ... Must run ..." became his new refrain. He hit a downslope and began almost leaping in an effort to put more distance between himself and the sphere he'd left behind him. He gave a quick look behind, and his heart sank as he saw the clear footprints he'd left in the crunchy, dying grass. If he could reach the rocks ...

"Clank!" Though several hundred yards away, the metallic sound hit his ears with the zeal of an assassin's bullet. Two more "Clanks" sounded in rapid succession. They'd found the sphere! The rocks—his only hope!

Whimpering in fear for the first time in his adult life, he reached the first of the rock outcroppings. The rock walls were too sheer to climb; another thing the maps hadn't told him! Blast! He ran along the side of the walls as the echo of grinding metal and hissing steam sounded in the distance.

He couldn't spot a causeway, a cave, or even a large enough pile of rocks to hide behind. His legs were tiring. No, please, God in Heaven, it couldn't end like this! Frantically, he searched in the mist for any place in the rocks he could hide, or at least lift his feet from the incessantly crunching gravel beneath his feet. Something, there must be something! Anything to give him the slightest advantage! He'd heard of a master rock climber that could raise himself with one-fingered chin-ups. He would try anything now, if only he could find a ledge or a dead tree!

The sound of gears grinding, rhythmic pounding and steam blasting became louder, and he realized with a fresh new sense of panic that the rock walls were curving him back towards the path he'd left. Instead of escaping through a series of mountains, he was trapped in a small box canyon. Were the maps wrong? Or had he miscalculated? Where was he? Could he slip by them, or ...

The sounds of machinery swelled suddenly nearby, and stopped. He turned and saw they had arrived at the crest of the hill behind him. There were three of them, watching him with neither noise nor visible emotion.

He swallowed, wondering if the few tens of yards would give him enough room to run around them, doubling back the way he came. Before he could decide, the leader gave a single, piercing blast through an air horn.

From high in the clouds, the distant sound of another air horn answered in two, short blasts.

"No," he said softly, backing away from the dark shapes silhouetted on the hill as gears began to grind, engines blasted black smoke, and three machines began moving towards him without any hurry.

"No!" he screamed, turning and running futilely at the high rock face. They spread apart to ensure his capture. A casual observer would have noticed that every scream and step he took brought them in a tighter alignment, pointed in his direction.

They didn't begin until they had pinned him against the rocks, and the last noises he heard were his own screams mixed with the pulpy sound of metal against his own flesh and bones.

They took their time. He screamed, and screamed, and ...

Chapter 1

"Journalism is popular, but it is popular mainly as fiction.
Life is one world, and life seen in the newspapers another."
– GKC, *All Things Considered*

Gilbert's scream blasted through the closed door of his hotel room and bounced on the walls of the hallway beyond. Herb Wells, being both in the hall and Gilbert's best friend, sprinted at the sound. He slammed through the unlocked door into Gilbert's room ready for a bruising fight, and was completely unprepared for what he saw.

A year and a half before, Herb and Gil had survived the Martian invasion of Earth. They'd also each managed to survive several instances of direct contact with the Martians, something only a handful of people in England could claim. Herbert had seen his friend Gilbert lose friends and face death relatively coolly, which made the sight before him all the more bizarre.

Seventeen-year-old Gilbert Keith Chesterton, world-renowned journalist and reputed killer of either one or three full-grown Martians, depending on how you counted, was screaming in frustration at his own reflection in a mirror. His hair was askew, his eyes were wild, and there was a bunched-up, shapeless blob of fabric at his neck that was failing utterly at being a properly knotted tie.

"Gil," Herb said in an annoyed voice, his face red from running, "are you mad, or just acting that way to impress the scientists?"

"This ... this ... this TIE, Herb! I've tried twenty times to tie the thing, and ..."

"Wot, it won't tie around your neck?"

"No! It does that just fine! But it keeps looking awful! Worse each time! And even if I could tie the thing right, then I'd have to try and make these clothes look ... look ..."

"Dashing?"

"Yes!"

"Well, Gil, they're not." Gilbert was dressed in a plain tweed jacket, white buttoned shirt and coarse black trousers. He was dressed normally for Gilbert, really. Something was up.

"I know that!" Gilbert said. "They make me look sharp as a wooden spoon! I've tried changing my clothes six different ways, and I might as well be polishing a dunghill! I look lousy, Herb, and I can't change that!"

"Gil, we're journalists," Herb began, sitting on Gil's hotel bed. Gilbert didn't respond, but kept huffing and puffing while pacing in front of the small mirror in his hotel room.

Herb continued, "They don't give us a huge bank account. Half our pay is the warm glow we get inside from seeing our names in print. Besides, you don't look any worse than any other journalist here in Berlin. Well, none here at the World's Fair anyway."

"That's the point, Herb! This is the World's Fair! People from all over the globe are here for this, and they're all going to be at the ball in the *Himmelpalast* tonight. Hundreds of them, Herb, in that floating airbase they've converted into a giant dance hall! Wealthy industrialists, world leaders, diamond merchants and university professors, all dressed up in all their finery and looking like they light their cigars with hundred-dollar bills. And then there's me. Next to them, Herb, I'll look like some little tramp that wandered into the wrong place looking for the bathroom and a warm fire."

"Well, Gil, it could be worse."

"How?"

Herb paused. "It could be me instead of you."

"Herb!"

"Gil, I'm sorry, but I just don't see what's eating you about this thing. You've never gotten upset over a dance before. And I know you hate dressing up. So why the change?"

Gilbert inhaled, started to speak and then stopped himself. Then started again.

"Herb, those bigwigs at the dance tonight—some of them ... some of them and their families are from England."

Herb waited. "And?"

"Remember six months ago? That time we were in Paris? Where you actually set me up on a blind date with a girl whose eyes didn't turn me into stone?"

Herb thought. "Oh, yes! I matched off with the blond, the one who went to some boarding school with a nun as the headmistress, and you had the brown-haired one."

"The blond and the brown-haired ... Herb! Don't you at least remember the names of the girls you go out with?"

Herb leaned back on the bed and stared at the ceiling with a whimsical look on his face. "Names give me a problem. Hair, now, or a pretty pair of eyes, those I never forget."

"Well, the brown-haired one was named Frances, Herb. And she was ... she is an intoxicating woman!"

"Hm! I knew something was up. When we've gotten together over the last few weeks since Paris you've had this relaxed look in your eyes. You're making me miss the insecure, jumpy Gil I knew who was always afraid of getting caught at something. Is it all over this Frances girl? Did you two hit it off? When ... Madeline! That was her name. When Madeline and I saw you two walking off in the drizzle together, we thought we'd let you two alone. Did something happen?" Herb leaned forward with a slight grin.

"Herb, you're not hearin' me! Frances, she's ... well, remember what you said about me talking philosophy with girls?"

"Gil, I told you that was pointless. Girls don't care about anything besides how much money you have in your pocket."

"But Frances isn't like that, Herb! Not only is she beautiful, she's smart! We stayed up the whole night talking on a bench just outside her door."

Herb's brow furrowed. "Talking? About what?"

"Well, we started talking about her life as a wealthy diamond merchant's daughter. And then about my life as a clacker ..."

"Gil ..."

"And then we talked about how the industrial revolution was affecting the family unit, and what that could mean for the morals of society ..."

"Gil ..."

"Next we started talking about religion, the Catholic versus the Anglican faith ... did you know she didn't know about the whole Henry the Eighth thing? Anyways, Herb, after our night together, she wants to turn Catholic! She wants to join the Church, Herb! Isn't that amazing?"

"Gil!"

"What?"

"Gil, I'm going to ignore the whole thing about religion for now and get back to you screaming at yourself in the mirror and giving me a heart attack, 'kay? No, don't answer yet. First, you're all addled in the head over a dance, which is unlike you. Specifically, you're upset because you've nothing to wear, which is also unlike you. And when I ask you why you're agitated over things you normally don't care a whit about, you begin telling me about the night you met a smashing young lady, your June night in Paris together, and how the pair of you talked history and philosophy all night. Which *is* like you, though unbelievable for anyone else.

"So, Gil, if I keep hounding the trail of this fox, can I assume this Frances girl is going to be at the dance tonight?"

Gilbert's face fell. "Yes! And her folks and siblings are gonna be there, too. I've gotta make a good impression, Herb! We've been writing each other all the time, and I ... I've never felt this way!"

"Hut, tut tut tut! No more sap, Gil. You'll give me diabetes. Now, to the point: You need a suit, and I need something to do besides drink with a bunch of socially challenged science journalists tonight. Come along with me—how long 'til the ball begins?"

"Two hours, Herb."

"Good. We'll fix your wardrobe problem, and just have time for a pint after. Let's go."

Chapter 2

"Marriage is a duel to the death which no man of honour should decline." – GKC, *Manalive*

Gilbert ran his index finger under his collar for the third time. The waistcoat, trousers, overcoat, cufflinks and polished black shoes made him look more sophisticated and feel more uncomfortable than he'd ever been in his life. "Herb, how do they dance with these collars? The thing's going to cut my throat."

"That's the point, old bean. Upper-class twits are always uncomfortable in what they wear. It helps weed out the surplus population who can't afford to be anything but relaxed, wrinkled and content."

Gilbert was too busy trying to adjust his waistcoat for the fourth or fifth time to argue. "Are you sure this is the right size, Herb?" he asked.

"Gil, you saw the guards. We didn't have time for a full fitting. Not without a few more pounds out've my pocket anyway."

"Where'd you get the money to flash in front of the guard, anyway? And why was he guarding a room full of dress clothes? "

"Hanged if I know why it's guarded, Gil. I saw them loading the place with clothes earlier today, and when I saw guards there tonight I did what I usually do when I want to get inside someplace with guards outside of it: I barked a few words in the local language, flashed my press card, and pressed the local equivalent of a five-pound note into his palm. Works nearly every time."

"You didn't answer my first question, Herb."

"You want to put the clothes back? That sport coat you had back at the hotel would look lovely at a homeless men's club."

"Herb!"

As they rounded the corner, two enormous Zeppelins were hovering several hundred feet in the air. Suspended between them was a long, wide platform. In the middle of the platform, lit from within by thousands of lights, was the *Himmelpalast*, or the *Sky Palace*. It was a large, round building three stories high with a multi-faceted glass dome on top. The spotlights from inside the palace lit up the night through the dome, projecting kaleidoscopes on the chilly clouds above them.

The sight had awed them when they'd first come to Berlin, but less so as days passed. The whole apparatus was tethered to Earth by a thick array of cables that ended in a series of enormous winches. A glass windowed box that looked like it could hold fifty people was attached to one of the cables by a number of iron rollers on its roof. A line of people grew steadily behind the box, waiting for a ride through the air to the floating dance hall despite the night's chill. The winch was rolling steadily, and as Gilbert neared he could see that there were, in fact, several boxes moving to and fro across the expanse of air on their own cables. How many people did they expect at this thing?

Gilbert looked at the size of the palace hovering in the air and felt a little nervous. In the battle with the aliens, he'd seen a similar contraption lit afire by the Martians' heated rays. It had crashed in a fireball with all hands lost. And even though the nearest live Martian was back on Mars, Gilbert still found himself scanning the Berlin skyline for the mobile, three-legged towers the squid-like creatures had used to invade Earth.

"Gil, do you have your press pass?"

Herb's voice brought Gil back to reality. "Yep," Gilbert answered. "Nice that we won't need tickets."

"Makes sense," said Herb. "The Germans' advances with the aliens' trinkets are the main reason they got to have the World's Fair this time around. They'd want the world's newspapers talking about their scientific marvels as much as possible. I'm surprised they won't check our passports, though. That usually happens to foreigners at these things."

"True, but not this time. Did you have any trouble getting into the country?"

"Not a whit, Gil. The German border guards just want to make sure you aren't going to overthrow the government, and they'll wave you in to spend your money. You Yanks have the toughest country to get into, you know."

"How so?"

"Other countries just want to make sure you won't make trouble. If you're a foreigner going to America, they ask if you're an Anarchist. Or a polygamist. Or five or six other kinds of '-ists,' or otherwise a danger to the moral order of things. Very annoying."

They took a place in line behind a well-to-do couple in their fifties. Though both Herb and Gil were shivering in the cold, the husband and wife wore fur-lined longcoats and could easily ignore the freezing January night air.

"Gil, tell me something, would you?" Herb said, his teeth chattering slightly despite the warm, borrowed coat he was wearing.

"This pretty little sweet of yours, Frances, right? Why bother? Your stuff on the Invasion was published all over the country, and even back in the Americas. There's a lot of girls who'd be willing to step out with you. Why are you so mad-as-a-cut-snake over this Frances girl?"

"Herb, when you find someone special, you'll know why. There's a lot of pretty women in the world, true. But I found out real quick that even though a pretty face ropes you in, it can't keep you."

"But that's the point, Gil! You're seventeen! You act like you're already looking for a wife!"

"Well, why else step out with someone if there's no chance of that? Herb, I've been through enough that I don't wanna give my heart to someone who'll dance a hoedown on it. And I don't want notches on my belt, either. I want someone to love forever, and who'll love me back just as much. Anything else is just using someone and wasting our time."

"But Gil," began Herb, who was quickly interrupted by one of the six or seven glass boxes touching Earth with a loud clank as its winch unwound. Gil, Herb and the other spectators watched in soundless fascination while several large men secured the giant windowed box to the ground with a series of smaller cables attached to the ground by large iron rings. They worked with an efficiency that was almost machine-like, and when the operation was complete they stood in a line with feet apart and hands behind their backs. Their eyes faced forward, all still save for one man who was slightly older, larger and slightly better dressed than the rest. Obviously their leader, he walked forward to the head of their line.

Gilbert saw that the passengers were separated from the fastened glass box by a thick, velvet rope bracketed by two brass posts. The dockhands' leader unhooked the rope from the right post, smiled, and began waving people through. People were reaching into coat pockets and producing papers with ornate writing on them. Were they invitations, perhaps? Better get his own press pass out! These dockhands looked like they could be dangerous to anyone who didn't belong. When it came time for Gil and Herb's papers to be inspected, the chief dockhand's face wrinkled slightly at the sight of Gilbert's press pass. "I am a reporter," Gilbert said slowly and just a bit louder than necessary, "for the London Times."

"I know what you are," the Chief said in German-accented English, giving the impression that Gil's presence at the event would be tolerated, but just barely. "Enjoy your evening, sir. Next, please," he said with no expression, looking quickly at Herb's pass before waving him through as well.

Gil felt a small but potent shot of anger go through him at the treatment he and Herb had just received. He wanted to bark at the porter, but there was a surge of waiting people behind him and he decided to bite his tongue for now.

The remaining dockworkers directed them to the inside of the windowed box. It was arranged very much like a train, complete with cushioned seats and a center aisle way.

"First class!" whistled Herb softly as they took their seats. "No wonder that chief ogre treated us like pond scum," Herb said with a small chuckle. "He probably feels we did nothing worth earning this!"

Gilbert stayed silent, pouting. Herb may find the whole thing funny, but Gilbert didn't. They were sitting just behind the couple in the fur coats that had been standing in front of them in line. The husband was powerfully built with wide shoulders, while his wife was a full head shorter, with brown hair under a thick, mottled fur hat.

Through the windows the brawny, overall-suited dockworkers scurried to free the box from its mooring, moving in patterns that were practiced, efficient and nearly perfect from the boys' perspective. A large clank sounded above them as the winch prepared to wind its way to the heavens with its human cargo.

A voice to their right began speaking German. They turned and saw an attractive blond woman in a trim uniform addressing them in German. Her speech was short, and at its end she presumably started the speech over again in French. "Ladies and gentlemen," she said at the end of her French speech, shifting her voice to English, "Please remain seated during our journey to the Himmelpalast tonight. If anyone here is afraid of heights, they are advised to disembark now or keep their eyes firmly shut during the course of our ascent."

"You're missing out on thrills, Gil," said Herb as they began ascending. "Don't you see? There's nothing like the thrill of a smashing looking girl sitting beside you, and knowing she's there because she thinks you're handsome."

Gilbert sighed while their car rose high above Berlin. Herb never let a conversation about girls go once he started it.

"Are you loving her, Herb, or yourself when that happens?"

"Why should I worry, if we both know it's only for now?"

"So if you're both just using each other, that makes using each other like a piece of furniture fine and dandy? Whoever she is, you're both worth more than that, Herb."

"Why? Because you say so?"

"No; what I say doesn't matter. It's because the same God made you both. Remember that auction a few weeks back, where some fellow paid millions for a few drawings by DaVinci? Well, if a few scribbles by a human master are worth millions, how much more is a human being worth, crafted by the architect of the universe? Treating a person that way is like using the Mona Lisa to wrap fish."

Herb looked befuddled. "Now, hang on a second, Gil ..." he said as he struggled for a reply. "But if you ..." Herb began, only to be interrupted by the clacking and shuddering of their transport as it neared the end of its journey. A crew of workers nearly identical to the group they'd seen on the ground moved with clear purpose and sure movements to their appointed places and secured the air car to its moorings. Gil heard several clanking gears sound off, hissing as a set of gear-driven, floor-bay doors ground shut beneath them. They descended to the floor within a minute, gently touching the floor where the workers secured them with clamps and tightly wound steel cables.

Once they stopped moving, Gilbert, Herb and everyone else stood and waited. Once the door opened, they followed a river of people out the door and into a cold hallway made of Roman pillars. They were a few dozen feet from the large open double doors at the end of the hallway and the beginning of the dance hall when Herb looked back at Gil and raised one eyebrow. "Ready to dance, Gil?"

Gilbert swallowed and looked at the floor.

"Aw, Gil, no!" said Herb, exasperation raising his voice to a whiny pitch. "Gil, it's the first ball to be held in the air, and you couldn't be bothered to learn to dance?"

"Well, Herb," Gilbert said, "you really can't use the kind of dancing you learn on a farm at a ball like this. Besides, I wasn't really thinking about dancing. I was hoping to catch Frances and talk for the evening."

"Gil, maybe she really is different from every other woman in the universe. Maybe she really won't care about how well you can do the waltz. But can you really chance that?"

"Are you offering to give a lesson, Herb?"

"No! No, you ..." Herb was interrupted briefly as his press pass was checked for a second time.

Herb's face brightened with a sudden idea. "Gil, you know what?" he said.

"Uh oh."

Herb stopped in the river of people gently being herded through the labyrinth of hallways. He put his hand on Gil's shoulder and looked in his friend's eyes. "I know how to help you, Gil. What's more, I know *why* I'm going to help you."

Gilbert's voice took a very cautious edge, and he looked at Herb with eyes that held the slightest hint of fear. "Herb," he said, "what exactly are you planning to do? And why?"

"Gil, leave it all to me. And as to why I'm doing it, well, remember when we were making merry over in London after the whole kerfuffle over the vivisectionist chap? The one with the island?"

"The way I remember it, you were making merrier than me."

"You're right Gil. I ignored your warnings and made poor choices. So poor, in fact, I was in no shape to leave my room the next day. Let alone write and file my story. I could've lost my job over a party I couldn't bring myself to leave.

"But a funny thing happened, Gil. When I slunk back to the Telegraph to get my comeuppance, I was half-expecting my editor to meet me with a large board with nails sticking out of it. I was ready to get sacked, Gil. But you know what happened next?"

"Do tell," said Gilbert, smiling.

"He gave me the biggest smile, shook my hand, thanked me for working so well under pressure, and said a few more pieces like that would land me a corner office."

"Did he?" said Gil, his interest peaked.

"Yeah, but I muffed the next few jobs, so that went out the window. The point is, mate, you covered for me. You could've scooped the *Telly* and made yourself look twice the reporter, but you didn't. You filed your story, changed your wording 'round a bit, and then filed it again with my boss, saying your story was mine. You saved my neck, Gil. And while I'm not always the nicest of blokes, I always pay my debts.

"And besides: I'm doing it because I have a purpose in this world. Remember that fellow, Kipling? He talked about the white man's burden?"

"Herb, we're both white. And when you smile like that you scare me."

"Gilbert, old bean," said Herb, putting his arm around Gil's shoulder and walking with the crowd, "Kipling thought it was England's job to bring the rest of the world to its level. Well, I've been gifted with looks and a silver tongue, and you've been gifted with a pure heart and a quick mind. Right now, my job is to bring you up to my level of grace and savoir faire, and later your job will one day be to bring me to yours in the written word."

"What about the pure heart thing, Herb?"

"One thing at a time, chum. No need to rush things."

"So you've got dashing con-man's burden, and I've got naïve clacker-man's burden?"

"Gil, I've just offered to solve your problem about dancing with Frances. Are you looking a gift horse in the mouth?"

"Beware of gifts borne by Greeks, especially if they look like giant wooden horses. Beware even more if they're part of a dashing-con-man's burden."

"Touche! See, Gil, one day, you've got to teach me how you come up with bits just like that. Girls love a wit."

"When I'm around girls that's only half right."

"Don't call yourself a half-wit, Gil. Remember: confidence."

"What do you expect? I'm nervous. If Frances is here and I mess things up, I won't get another chance."

"Right, Gil, look here."

The crowd had been passing through a tunnel that had a solid floor but walls made of glass, reinforced by iron bars and steel frames. Outside, the night clouds floated aimlessly, the city lights winked behind the clouds, and the two gigantic Zeppelins floated ominously on either side.

As he spoke, Herb's hands suddenly removed Gil's glasses, then gripped Gil's shoulders and pivoted his body so that Gil faced the window. The soft lights inside turned the glass wall into a low-powered mirror while still allowing them to see outside.

Gilbert looked at his reflection. Tall for his age, he was just a shade over six feet. He was still skinny, but he'd filled out some since he'd switched from being a wage-slave clacker to a journalist and started eating better. His eyes didn't always need glasses now that he didn't have to stare at tiny holes in punchcards all day, and without his spectacles his face no longer looked thin or sallow, especially with his hair shorter and combed. Added to the nice suit Herb had procured for him, Gilbert realized he looked better than he'd ever looked in his young adult life.

"Now, Gil, before the next wave of people come by, keep your eyes on that reflection and answer me this: who killed a Martian in the

Woking sewers with a six-shooter?"

Gilbert looked into his own eyes' reflection. "I did," he said slowly.

"Right. Now, who saved my life when a Martian tried to grab me, right before they all traveled up to the choir invisible?"

Looking into his own reflection, Gilbert realized he'd been slouching. He straightened, so slightly only he and Herb could have noticed. "I did," he said, his voice getting stronger.

"And," continued Herb, "who grabbed that worthless spy the Doctor, back when we were captive inside the Martian collector basket? Who rattled him around so much that he ended up speechless, probably for the first time in his miserable life?"

Gilbert stood erect, his voice confident and certain for the first time in days. "I did!"

"That's the stuff!" roared Herb, clapping Gil on the back without concern for who could hear him. "That's my mate Gil! Now," he grabbed Gil's shoulders and spun Gil around to face him, replaced Gil's glasses and looked him in the eye. Still holding him by the shoulders, Herb shook Gilbert slightly for emphasis as he continued speaking to his taller friend. "Go out there," Herb said, "look that lovely little brown-haired thing in the eye, and ask her for a dance."

Gilbert looked over Herb's shoulder at the shining white room with lace curtains draped at the corners of the enormously high entrance. For a second his face started to fall. He was just about to say to 'No' when Herb's fingers grabbed Gilbert's collar with an iron grip, a grip which quickly became an irresistible force pushing Gilbert forward.

"Ow!" Gilbert yelled. "Herb! Lemme go! You're gonna wrinkle my collar!"

"Better you get your first dance with a wrinkled collar than not at all."

"You're not my mother and you're not cupid, either. Now leggo!"

"Fine." Herb answered with a smile, gently releasing Gilbert.

Gilbert shrugged off Herb's hand, adjusted himself and looked around to get his bearings. He realized he was standing in the great hall.

The hall had been designed to strike awe in a person as soon as they entered, and it did its work well on Gilbert. High above his head, the ceiling was a curved dome of intricate glass work. He saw stars and the bright, full moon clearly through the transparent panels, all of which were at least a hundred feet in the air. The glass ceiling was surrounded by dimmed lamps made of glowing globes, and detailed with artwork of various heroes of German mythology engaged in combat, various arts or other pursuits. The whole thing was held high by four thick white stone pillars that ended on the floor, marking the four corners of the biggest ballroom floor Gilbert had ever seen.

"Herb," he said quietly, "... I can't walk in here, Herb."

"Oh you can't, can you? Gil, d'you see those strutting peacocks over there?"

Gil looked in the direction that Herb had pointed. Several well-dressed young men, all his own age or not much older, were standing in a rough circle with drinks and cigarettes in their hands. They were chatting with each other about subjects Gilbert instinctively knew he knew nothing about and wouldn't be able to converse on. "I see 'em. I just hope they don't see me."

"Gil, could you picture any of them walking through a sewer with a wounded leg, or foiling a hungry Martian by sealing shut the door of their own prison with an improvised welding torch? If any of those nancy boys had a Martian mollusk facing them, what would happen, hm?"

Gilbert looked again at the group of privileged young men. Now they looked like spoiled children playing a game with each other that was silly and pointless. "Y'know, Herb," Gil said, thinking, "as soon as one'a those guys saw a Martian squid up close, I bet they'd go yellow as a dandelion."

"Not as yellow as their knickers would be after they soiled themselves. Now, if they can strut in here having done nothing worthwhile in their lives, how much more do we belong here, when we helped save the world? Now, where's this Frances girl of yours?"

Gilbert looked around the hall, quickly searching each face attached to a ball gown. After a few seconds, he inhaled quickly and his eyes widened.

"Where, Gil?" Herb said, "Where is she?"

"Over there. See the one in the light green dress and the white trim?"

Herb looked, then gulped. A brother, mother, and two sisters surrounded the only young lady matching Gilbert's description, all together in a closed group. They looked forward while walking purposefully to the other end of the hall, except for Frances, whose eyes were searching the crowd just as Gilbert's had a few seconds ago. The family, though, hadn't made Herb gulp. What had done that was the outer ring of bodyguards that surrounded Frances and her family.

An outer ring made up of six broad-shouldered, clean-shaven men with close haircuts, dark servant's clothes and very large hands. "Who're the sides of beef guarding the girls, Gil?"

"Frances' dad is a diamond merchant. They say he listened to some investment tip by a difference engine, and ever since he's had money coming out of his ears. He's probably off in a back room somewhere doing a little business, and the family's been told to have a good time or else. The bodyguards are there to make sure they only have a good time with the right people."

"A diamond merchant?" Herb said. Gilbert nodded his head. Herb whistled low. "I missed that bit before. Good job your girlfriend has a few sisters, Gil. Introduce me, won't you?"

"Herb, with those bruisers in place it's not likely I'll get to introduce myself, let alone you. I got the impression from Frances' last letter her dad isn't too keen on her seeing a clacker."

"You're not a clacker anymore. You're a journalist."

"That's not exactly a step up in her world. More like a wobbly-shuffle sideways."

"And you think those blokes'll make trouble if you go up to say hello?"

"I know they will. Since Paris my face might as well be on a wanted poster in her house. Don't ask me how she's been getting my letters."

Herb thought a moment, and then looked excited. "I have a plan!" he said, reaching into his jacket pocket.

"Herb, no bribery."

Herb frowned, paused, and closed his eyes for two seconds. "I have another plan," he said, his eyes open wide again. "What's her last name?"

"Blogg. Why?"

Herb made no answer, but only nodded and strode off towards the ring of bodyguards.

"Herb!"

"Just stay here," Herb said, turning around briefly, "and make your move when I have the thugs distracted."

Gilbert watched Herb make his way across the crowded floor. The musicians were apparently taking a break. "Saint Raphael," Gilbert whispered, hoping the patron saint of sweethearts was listening to him, "Herb's heart's in the right place. Look after him and don't let him get us both thrown overboard."

Chapter 3

"Do not enjoy yourself. Enjoy dances and theaters and joy-
rides and champagne and oysters; enjoy jazz and cocktails
and night-clubs if you can enjoy nothing better; enjoy
bigamy and burglary and any crime in the calendar, in
preference to the other alternative;
but never learn to enjoy yourself."
– GKC, *The Common Man*

The guards closest to Herb singled him out as a threat the moment
he started towards Frances' family. Being among the best paid
bodyguards in the whole of England, they assumed everyone
approaching their employer's family was a potential kidnapper,
assassin, or (worst of all) a panhandler begging for charity.

Herb was forty feet from Frances when a bald guard with a thick
black beard fixed his eye on the young, clean-shaven dark haired man.
Before Herb took five more steps, the bald guard had signaled with
slight hand movements for two other guards to join him in meeting a
potential threat. *Blogg*, thought Herb as he closed in. *You'd think a
bloke who has that much tin in his pocket could buy himself a better
last name.* By the time Herb finished this thought, three of the largest
men he'd seen outside of a sailor's bar stood in his way. Two were
blond, clean-shaven, and could have been twins. The dark-haired,
bearded one in the middle approached Herb with a smile full of gold
teeth, and eyes flicking from Herb's face to his hands, breast pockets
and shoes.

"Can I help you, sir?" said the bearded bodyguard, moving forward
with more grace than Herb had expected to see in such a large man.
Cripes, Herb thought, this bloke was at least six-foot-four and full of
twenty stone worth of muscle. The guard's accent was flawless British
upper-class; he was either a fallen member of the upper crust, or a lout
who'd been instructed ruthlessly in the art of high society etiquette.

"Herbert Wells, sir, from the London Telegraph." Herb flashed his
press pass quickly enough for the Telly's symbol to be seen on his
identification card, along with the portrait of him that the Telly's
analytical engine had stippled from a photograph. A quick peek, and
then back into his breast pocket. "Are you gentlemen in the employ of
Mister Blogg?"

"Mister Blogg has no interest or reason to speak with journalists at this time, Mister Wells. Now, if you will please allow his family their privacy ..."

Herb smiled. "Gentlemen, I completely understand. But I have no interest in interviewing Mister Blogg, either. I want to interview *you*."

Gilbert watched as each step brought Herb closer to the bodyguards surrounding Frances and her family. Good luck getting past them, Gilbert thought. Herb could fight, but against those guards? He'd have a better chance taking down a Martian tripod with a popgun. He stared longingly at Frances, hoping to catch her eye. He was still trying to slide around the family and evade the bodyguards when his and Frances' eyes met.

Most moments in a person's life pass without consequence in a boring and never ending line of banality. But some moments in a young person's life mean so much that they can never be forgotten, nor their impact ever lessened regardless of the passage of time.

For some these moments are times of humiliation or trauma.

For others they are events of triumph and joy.

For Gilbert, it was the instant that Frances' eyes met his over a distance of fifty feet with a multitude of well-dressed people between them.

For to Gilbert, Frances' gaze was the entire world, and though every person in the enormous hall seemed determined to walk between them at that moment, Gilbert couldn't care less. He walked towards her as if in a dream, and the spell was only broken when she suddenly turned and began speaking to a girl slightly younger than herself, though dressed just as opulently.

What the ...

While Gilbert watched, all but one of the bodyguards moved away from the family and began talking to Herb. Herb stood with his notepad, his pencil flying across the small slips of paper, struggling to jot down the words dictated to him by each excited guard.

"Alright, so, you all like working for the Bloggs, then?" Herb said.

"Well, gov, you didn't hear this from me," said the dark-haired one with the beard, "but he's a hard man to work for."

"Yeah, Bill," said one of the twins, "but 'e pays us well. Better than you were making working for yer last boss."

"Yeah," spoke up the other twin, "an' he only makes us work a ten hour shift. Better than pulling twelve or fourteen hours as a steam monkey in some factory!"

"Or," said the first twin, "running some game where the coppers might swoop on ye any second. I likes workin' where I don't have to look over me shoulder every minute for the long arm of the law."

"Alright boys, alright," barked Herb suddenly, "slow it down. I'm not a typing engine. So only one of you is dissatisfied working for one of the richest men in England?"

"Now, look, I never said I was ..."

"Hard man to work for. Weren't those your exact words?"

"Yeah, you said that Bill. You sure you want to keep that in print?"

"Now look you ..."

Gilbert looked back at Frances, whose eyes were still on her sister. Gilbert kept watching as Frances pointed to Gilbert with her fan. The sister looked at Gilbert briefly, looked back at Frances, looked at Gilbert a second time and smiled.

Now Frances' sister ran to the elder woman in their group. Frances, now alone and free of family and almost all bodyguards, looked at Gilbert. She opened her fan, rested her free hand on her right cheek and smiled again.

Crimony, thought Gilbert. He remembered that the position of a lady's fan communicated how interested she was in someone. An open fan? What did that mean again? Well, she was smiling. Probably a good sign. *Just asking her for a dance is like the negotiations at the end of the Civil War,* he thought. *Am I gonna need a lawyer and a diplomat when I ask her to marry me?*

Gilbert started walking forward again, but Frances suddenly looked serious, her eyes jumping to her left. She shook her head at Gilbert and closed her fan with a snap.

Gilbert stopped, just in time to see the last guard stand between Gil and Frances. Suddenly, off to Frances' left, the older woman of her group snapped her fingers, grabbing the last guard's attention. He looked at Gilbert for a second, but then turned away and walked several steps towards Frances' mother. Once the guard was close enough, she started giving him a series of rapid-fire orders and quick hand movements, leaving the way clear for Gilbert.

Gilbert swallowed and stepped forward, trying with everything he had to be silent, quiet and completely invisible. Twenty feet, ten feet, five, and ...

Frances was in front of him. Her blue eyes were bright, quick, alive and perfect, just as they had been the night he had met her in Paris, six months, three weeks and four days ago. Gilbert had rehearsed this scene in his mind a thousand times or more, and each time he had become more dashing, more handsome, and a more perfect man for her than in the fantasy before.

Now, Gilbert's throat felt like it had closed, his tongue far too big for the rest of his mouth. *Say something, fool,* he thought to himself, *what would Herb do?*

No, scratch that. Scratch it 'til the paper tore through. Herb's way of doing things wasn't the right way here.

"Hello, Frances," he said, trying to control his breathing and keep his smile from being too wide. Never appear too eager, his father had once told him. That always kills a deal.

"Hello, Gilbert." She said, giving him a smile that made his heart do a happy flip-flop. "I've missed you." She offered him her hand.

"And I've ... I've really missed you, too," he said, giving the back of her hand a small peck from his lips. He hoped they still did that in England.

She stood, still looking at him. After a few awkward seconds Gilbert realized she was waiting for him to do something. He looked to her right and saw the mother and sisters looking at him with wide smiles on their faces. "Is ... are those your family members, Frances? May I meet them?"

Frances, a good foot shorter than Gilbert, leaned closer to him on her tiptoes and whispered in his ear. "Later, Gilbert. My father may be here soon. My mother has given me permission to speak with you without her present, though she's still keeping an eye on me. Do you know of a place quieter than this? I can barely hear you above the din."

She had a point. The debate between the bodyguards over the benefits and drawbacks of their profession was rapidly escalating. In the heat of arguing with each other, their polished high-class accents had quickly given way to lower-class cockney. They hadn't even noticed that Herb had slipped away.

Gilbert turned back to Frances. "I just got here, myself," he whispered. "Is there an observation deck or something? Somewhere we can talk without the posse remembering they're supposed to beat up guys like me?"

"Yes. I've seen several people use it. Come, follow me."

Frances tiptoed lightly as she could in her heeled shoes, holding Gilbert's index and middle fingers so gently in her hand that a casual observer would not have suspected that she was directing his path. After a stealthy walk through the crowd of people dressed almost exactly like Frances and himself, she pushed open a glass door and stepped through into a darkened hallway. He followed, and as the door shut quietly behind him the general din of the partygoers in the hall was shut out as well, leaving them in silence.

With the dance hall now behind them, Gilbert walked forward at a slow pace. He could see Frances' silhouette against the cloudy night sky. There was a thick pane of clear glass separating her from the frigid night air outside, and as he neared her he could see her face in the glass, faintly lit and reflected from the city lights below.

He stood beside her, feeling awkward in the silence. Should he put his hand on her shoulder, or would that be too forward? Should she ask him first? Maybe instead he should talk. Talk was safe.

"I'm ... well, I'm really glad to see you again, Frances."

She turned to face him, and her smile and sparkling eyes made his heart do the happy-little-flip-flop thing again.

"I feel the same way, Gilbert. I've thought of little else the past few months except the wonderful night we spent in Paris."

"I loved your letters," he said, trying hard to keep the words from spilling out in a flood. "Every time I got back to London, my postbox at the office was the first thing I checked."

"And whenever I saw a letter from you in mine, dear Gilbert, I'd, well ..."

"I'd get so carried away inside, Frances, just seeing that you'd written me again."

"When I held your letter, Gil, I could've made the greatest fool of myself in the world and not cared a whit."

"When I got your letter saying you'd be here, I did make a fool of myself. I jumped on the nearest desk and danced a hoe-down."

"I squealed like a little girl when I found out papa was taking us here, and you'd be here, too. My sisters say I've been quite insufferable for the last few weeks. But what's a hoe-down?"

"Nothing. Never mind. It's a little dance Yankee farmboys do when we're happy the work's done. Look, Frances," he said, gently taking her hands in his own.

He was heartened that she didn't flinch at his touch. As he held her fingers and looked into her eyes, several movements caught Gilbert's peripheral vision. He turned and saw several of the Blogg family bodyguards walking with large, purposeful strides directly across the dance floor towards the door they had exited from.

Uh oh, Gilbert thought. Herb's ruse had run out. Was there a saint in Heaven who could protect a journalist from being thrown over the side of a floating party hall?

When Herbert had seen Gil and Frances leave the hall through the glass doors, he'd told himself at first that his job was done for the evening. If Gilbert was a typical, red-blooded member of the male species, he'd try for a kiss at the first opportunity. And if Frances was a typical, red-blooded female, she'd accept the offer as something wonderful, romantic and unforgettable.

After he extricated himself from the bodyguards, Herbert couldn't keep from smiling. Like many young men of his age and times, romance was seen as the key to all happiness. Maybe, just maybe, if he saddled Gil with a fine little maid, he might even come 'round and leave the silly religion he'd got mixed up with last year.

Herb suddenly paused in mid-stride. Could he *really* trust Gil to do what most men would do? After all, this was the same fellow who had a millionaire-heiress to himself for the whole of a June night in Paris, and had spent it talking to her about religion, history and philosophy until the sun came up.

Worse, she'd actually *listened* to him the whole night.

Worse than that! She'd kept up the conversation. A girl like that might drive Gil deeper into his religious twaddle, instead of away from it!

Now Herb walked slowly, deep in thought, whispering to himself and ignoring the crowd as his mind darted through strategies of love and romance with a speed and skill worthy of a chess grand master. Only instead of Pawns, Knights and Queens, his thoughts were focused on Gil, Frances, and the delicate arts of matchmaking.

"If I were to somehow dash their hopes, perhaps drive a wedge between them? No, no. That's too callous. Gil would never forgive me if he found out. But if they stay together I'll be a third wheel in their romantic penny-farthing. I might lose my best friend, and Gil won't know what he's lost until it's too late. What to do?"

Herb was now so wrapped in thought that he gave little notice to the other party goers or the odd looks they were giving him. Most of the guests soon looked elsewhere, having assumed Herb was drunk or batty.

One pair of eyes, though, lingered on Herb for a while, eyes that were green and set in a cool, pale, female face framed by dark, perfectly styled shoulder-length hair. Still focused on Herb, she swigged the last of her drink and followed him from a safe distance.

Herb broke out of his reverie when his foot hit the base of the bandstand. He looked up at the band. The musicians looked ... odd, somehow. It took him a few seconds to realize that the movements of the three female singers and five male musicians were stilted and stiff, like marionettes or dolls. The three singers were identical in every way except for their red, black and blond hair colors. And the male musicians could have been a set of repetitively moving, identical quintuplets, distinguished only by the instruments they played.

In less than a second Herb had it figured out: they weren't people at all, but animated figures that looked like people, with hinges and pivot points where their creators had wanted them to move. What looked at a distance to be a band and several singers were actually parts of a complex machine that could play music.

Music.

Music stirred emotions. And emotions turned heads and hearts better than any argument, philosophy or theology.

"Don't want to lose my friend," he said, "but what if I ... make them both a little more worldly? Then I'll have a place in their lives. If I could get them to ... That's it!" He nearly shouted these last two words. Several pairs of eyes turned to look, while their owners tried hard to seem disinterested in the odd, single fellow by the bandstand.

Herb waited patiently for the artificial musicians and singers to finish their song. There was a conductor to this unique music group that was most definitely human. With a slicked-back head of gray-tinged hair, he went through a series of repetitive movements on an analytical engine in front of him, all the while pushing a set of black-framed glasses up over the bridge of his nose.

No time to lose, thought Herb. As the mechanical singers' voices and the musicians' instruments faded with the end of the song, Herb quietly mounted the stage. As Herb neared the conductor, he saw him fiddling with several sets of carefully arranged punchcards. Much as he'd seen Gilbert do when pressed to work with such an engine, the bespectacled man lifted punchcards up to the light, made adjustments to them with odd little tools, and then slid them into one of a half-dozen slots in the top row of the analytical engine's control panels. The globes of the electric ceiling lights shone off of his cheap black suit, but the conductor seemed far too intent on his machines to be properly embarrassed.

"If you will please," the man spoke loudly to the audience of dancers before him, speaking English with a discernible German accent, "my children and I are in need of a short respite. During this time, please to amuse yourselves and converse with one another, and I will prepare them for their next series of auditory delights."

Herb slipped onto the stage. His last two years as a reporter had given him much practice in getting into places he shouldn't be in, and even more skill in staying in such places until he'd gotten what he wanted.

"Excuse me, *Mein Herr*," Herb said, trying to use the kind of voice that would command much obedience and little unwanted attention.

The conductor turned to look at Herb with expressionless eyes behind the sizable lids of his glasses. Herb sized him up instantly: the conductor was working, he had people to impress, and little time to trot around with small talk. Since he'd called the mechanical performers his children, he was likely not only the operator, but the inventor of the bizarre machine as well.

"Mein Herr," said Herbert, "your machine here is most impressive. I may know of some buyers for such a device, if that interests you."

"I will be willing to discuss such matters after the show, young man. For now, I am more than quite busy. Is there anything else?"

Herb opened the left side of his jacket, his right hand digging for a moment in his inner breast pocket. When it emerged it held a wad of bills nearly an inch thick. Herb watched the eyes of the inventor closely, relieved when they widened and the inventor's jaw dropped just a little.

Herb chalked up another victory for himself. For the past year there hadn't been any kind of trouble that a thick wad of bills couldn't smooth over or get past.

"I ..." the inventor started, "I should like to discuss with you, young man, but I have many cards to arrange for the next song. If I do not play tonight and satisfy this audience, my children might never play again."

"Sir, I completely understand. And so, here ..." said Herb, peeling off a German five mark note and placing it on the conductor's podium, "is something for your time listening to me. And trust me, I will be brief. For now, please look through that open glass door. Do you see the two young people through it?"

The inventor peered through his glasses at Gil and Frances, holding hands and staring into each other's eyes. "You mean the pretty, brown-haired one and the beanpole with the spectacles?"

"Precisely. My good man," said Herbert, smiling while putting his left hand on the inventor's shoulder and carefully keeping both their attentions on the young lovers, "that beanpole is my best friend in the whole of the world. And that young lady is the only woman in the world, I think, who can truly understand and appreciate him. Now, if you could get your children here," he swept his hand behind them, directing attention to the mechanical band and singers, "to sing something so romantic that my friend has his first dance with a lady tonight, I am prepared to give you another five marks for your time and trouble. If he gets his first kiss by the end of the evening, I'll make it twenty."

The inventor paused, looking at the two young people with a slow gaze filled with longing. His eyes misted over as long forgotten memories and wishes surfaced.

"You say, young man, that Herr Beanpole over there has never danced, never kissed a *fraulein* in his young life?"

"That is the way of it, I am afraid."

"Young man," said the inventor quietly, "you truly do not know the forces you have helped unleash upon this Earth."

"'Scuse me?" said Herb, keeping his eyes on his quarry and only letting his smile falter the slightest bit.

"Young man, in my youth, I chased foolish dreams and neglected much. Now that I am older and wiser, all the wishes, hopes and prayers for a different life must be directed towards two things: the joy I take in assisting a chaste pair of lovers, and the opportunities afforded me by the cold, hard paper your marks are printed on." The inventor paused to kiss a small, shiny oval disk attached to his shirt sleeve.

"What's on that, anyway?" Herb asked.

"Ah! Saint Genesius, young man!" the inventor paused in his feeding the cards to the analytical engine to flash the disc on top of his ring to Herbert. It held a picture of a young man holding a lute in both hands by a Roman pillar, his eyes pointed upwards. "The patron saint of artists, actors and musicians. Very useful for a man who creates out of love for God, music and man."

Herb paused. "You really believe that stuff, then?"

"Of course! And if you wish your friend to have his first romance," the inventor continued, "you'd best find a way to get him back into the hall. He and his lady left through the north door."

"The north door?"

"Yes. Followed by two very large gentlemen who appear to be

equally interested in this fact."

Herb followed the thumb that the inventor had jerked over behind his back. Two of the Blogg family bodyguards were indeed making their way to the door to one of the enclosed observation decks. Enclosed or not, Gil was in trouble. Those thugs didn't look in a mood to play around. But they were too far across the room for Herb to get there in time and try to bluff Gil out of harm's way.

"What to do?" Herb thought, "What to do?"

Herb looked at the center of the stage, and back at the inventor. The inventor had finished with his cards and was now adjusting the works connected to the artificial musicians of his contraption.

"'Scuse me again, sir. What's your name?"

"Friedrich," said the inventor without looking up, "Friedrich Bartimeus Gatz."

"Well, Freddy old sport, think you can toss a request up to your saint friend for me? I'm going to do a spot of acting."

When Gilbert saw the large men in identical suits start across the dance hall towards him and Frances, his first instinct was to leap at his foes with the kind of wild abandon that Robin Hood would have used to impress Maid Marian. He'd give two quick punches to the jaws of the hulking guards, make a mad dash across the floor, sprint over a series of delicacy-laden tables, then escape with a daring leap from a second story balcony using chandeliers and curtains as a series of improvised trapeze ropes. And all would end with a blown kiss to his lady love as the cabled car spirited him away from his pursuers.

One look at the guards' eyes and reality hit hard. There would be no dashing race for the exit, and no pretensions to being Robin Hood. These boys weren't simple sides-of-beef in suits. They had the stride and in-step cadence ex-military men fall into when focused on a mutual goal. Fight them? Nuh-uh. It didn't take a Philadelphia lawyer to figure if these louts got close enough, they'd politely escort Gilbert to a dark corner and turn him into dog food before the next song was over.

"Frances, I think we're about to be interrupted." Gilbert said, using a voice he hoped concealed his fear.

"Gilbert," she said, "follow me. Sometimes if I rush them head on, they become confused and obey me instead of my father." She turned and quickly moved through the glass door, out of the twilight of the observation deck and into the brightly lit and now quite warm dance hall.

"Sometimes?" Gilbert said, obediently following her. *Jeepers*, he thought. *Even the* back *of her head looks gorgeous!* "What happens if they don't?"

"I don't know," she turned and whispered as they closed in, "you're the first boy who's ever evaded them this long."

Gilbert swallowed. Running away and melting into the crowd right now would have been easy, but it would have meant looking like a yellow-bellied coward for the rest of his life in Frances' eyes.

In two seconds, the bodyguards were on him. They completely ignored Frances, walking around and ignoring her words with the ease of liquid mercury flowing around a bump on a polished marble wall.

Then they zeroed in on Gilbert with the intensity of a sniper's bullet. Before Gilbert could reach for his press credentials, the faster guard had his hands on Gilbert's collar, physically lifting him up on his tiptoes.

"Excuse me, *sir*," said the man. He was shorter than Gilbert by a few inches, but his biceps seemed at least as big as Gil's thighs. There wasn't a doubt in Gilbert's mind that his new captor could shake him around at will like a Mastiff dog with a rag doll in its teeth.

At one point in his life, Gilbert would have met the situation like most bullying victims, taking his beatings quietly in the hopes that his current tormentor would get bored and move on to easier prey.

In the past year, though, Gilbert had undergone a number of life-changing experiences that altered forever how he dealt with unfair aggression.

When Earth had been invaded by the Martians last year, Gilbert had very nearly tried to use the 'hide-until-they-leave' method against an alien chasing him in the sewer, until he'd realized it wouldn't work. Not this time.

The only thing that had worked was directly confronting his assailant. And although he'd walked away with an injured leg, he *had* walked away. The same couldn't be said for the Martian he'd fought. It had blown itself up in an effort to kill Gilbert by sneakiness when brute force wasn't an option.

Force.

Gilbert stared his attacker in the eyes, letting his anger flow like boiling water from a furious pump.

"Alright, buddy," Gil barked, "I'm a reporter for the London Times, and unless you think your boss would like to see his name splattered all over tomorrow's front pages, get your mitts off my neck!"

"Sir," the guard said with mock politeness. Gilbert could smell cheap tea on his breath and see a gap in his front teeth. "If you truly knew who my employer is, you'd realize that you're in no position to threaten or negotiate. Now, my associate is at this moment returning Miss Blogg to her family. And my employer thanks you to keep your distance from her from now on. That is, if you prefer your head to face the front when left to its own devices, instead of being forcibly turned the other way. You follow me, gov?"

Gilbert bristled. Frances had already wrestled her arm away from the other guard and was visibly arguing with him.

"I know exactly who your employer is, fella," Gil said, "and he wouldn't be happy about his name getting dragged through mud from Germany to America, all because you got a little over zealous protecting his daughter from a good lil' Catholic boy like me."

The thug blinked, but only once. He wasn't used to people standing up to him, but that wasn't going to slow him down much, either.

Suddenly, Herb's voice boomed over the crowd, distracting them both. Another recent piece of technology modified from scavenged alien gadgetry, its Belgian inventor had called it a "Vocal Magnifier." As a gadget it was beloved by those who had to speak to crowds, and hated by those who preferred quiet countrysides.

"Ladies and gentlemen of the world," said Herbert into the magnifier, pausing to let the nearby translators catch up, "we at this lovely celebration of mankind's achievements, are fortunate to have among us tonight one of mankind's greatest heroes. Our warmest thanks are due to one of the few men confirmed to have defeated a Martian in single combat, and contributed with me as assistant to Father Brown in his sacrificial victory against the invaders. Let us show our heartfelt appreciation to ..."

Gilbert's bravado melted away like ice under a Minnesota summer sun. Like most young men his age, he couldn't quite handle having the attention of a very large roomful of people without wanting to hide his head under the nearest table. He'd spoken to groups of people about his adventures, true, but that had been in a much more controlled environment. Usually on a stage, clearly separated from the audience.

But this was very, very different. The attentions of the world's wealthy and powerful were now trained on him, and all while he was in the grip of a man capable of snapping Gil's spine. Gilbert spent a very long quarter second begging God to silence Herb before he could say

Gilbert's name aloud.

I'm in the middle of a crisis here, Gilbert thought frantically. *I'm either going to be made a fool of in front of the most important people in the world, or beaten into something you feed to old cats. Or I'm gonna get flying lessons, sink-or-swim style. I don't wanna be humiliated in front of Frances, her family and the world, so please, God, just don't let Herb say ...*

"My very dear friend,"

Don't say it.

"...winner of the first ever, recently established World Prize for Journalism ..."

Don't say it.

"... a shining example of courage and virtue ..."

*Don'tsayitdon'tsayitdon'tsayit*pleasedon'tsayit...*

"Gilbert Keith Chesterton!"

The bodyguard suddenly let go of Gilbert's collar, smoothed it over and quickly backed away. Melting back into the crowd as the applause began, he gave Gilbert a glare that said they weren't finished with each other yet.

The applause grew louder. A thousand pairs of eyes fixed on Gilbert, and he swallowed hard. He tried to stay calm and looked around, hoping to see a familiar face...

He felt a touch at his hand. Gilbert looked down. There was a delicate, shapely, white-gloved hand placed in his own. Attached to the shapely hand was an equally shapely arm that ran up to a delicate, perfectly formed shoulder. And the shoulder was just beneath the loveliest and most beautiful of all faces in Gilbert's world.

"Frances," whispered Gilbert under the thundering applause, "how'd you get past your guards?"

"Shh," she said, smiling at him and putting a finger to her lips. "Just look up and smile for now."

"Look up? Why?"

Just as Gilbert spoke, he looked up and was instantly blinded by the spotlight as it blasted down on him.

"Trust me, darling, smile." Frances' breath was warm in his ear as a tropical rainforest, and sent a tingling thrill all the way to his feet.

Gilbert smiled widely, but not only because of her instructions. She'd called him 'darling!' Him! Darling! The Four Horsemen of the Apocalypse could have galloped through the ballroom ceiling and it couldn't have taken the smile from his face! The only things in the universe that mattered were the soft sense of perfect joy in his heart, and the touch of her four, perfect fingers against his palm.

"How's this?" he said, not caring so much if he was smiling well as to give her a reason to speak again. Maybe even call him "darling" a second time!

"Wonderful, dear …"

(SHE CALLED ME DEAR! SHE CALLED ME *DEAR*! SHECALLEDMEDEARSHECALLEDMEDEARSHECALLEDME *DEAR! DEAR! DEAR!*)

…she whispered, "but give a little wave. Trust me, I've been in this situation many times before."

Gilbert, still smiling, raised his hand and waved to all the cheering voices in the room.

"What do I do next?" he said out of the corner of his mouth.

"If there's a pause, say a few words. If not, let your friend do the talking."

"Now, gentle folk," continued Herb, "as this is a special occasion, I will introduce to my fellow Europeans a new form of dance sweeping the Five Americas even as we speak. Elegant in its simplicity, it is called the 'slow' dance by its adherents. Gil and his dancing partner, the lovely Miss Frances Blogg, will demonstrate. Won't you Gil?"

Gilbert smiled. If he smiled any wider, his face would split like the Red Sea.

"In this dance," Herb said, "the young lady places her right arm on the bent, left elbow of her partner, while the gentleman places his free hand upon her waist. Yes, Gil, that's it. Notice how the lady's hoop skirt leaves room for the Holy Spirit, as Father Brown might've said," said Herb as other young people began following Gilbert and Frances' example. "And, gentlefolk, when the music begins, the dancers move slowly in a circle, looking into one another's eyes."

Herb looked back. Friedrich the inventor flipped two or three switches and his mechanical 'children' sprang into action as steam hissed and a bellows began pumping air on the side of the stage. Mechanical musicians began playing their instruments, and mechanized singers began hitting perfectly pitched notes from the pipes in their throats.

"Now, ladies and gentlemen, before anyone becomes scandalized, note the ability the young lovers now have with regards to conversation, all under the watchful and protective eye of their parents. Good job, Gil. Just don't get her father angry." Gentle laughter sounded through the hall. Herb had them eating out of his hand like tame squirrels! "Now as the music plays," Herb said, "the dancers may either marvel in each other's loveliness, or discuss anything from each other to the price of Belgian ginger."

Herb paused. Several dozen other couples had begun dancing just as he had instructed Gil and Frances to do, their bodies swaying romantically to the gentle strains of music in the air. While the inventor's mechanical 'children' sang backup and harmony, the human voice of the inventor began crooning the actual lyrics of an American song in tones slightly tinged with a German accent:

"Is it wrong to kiss?" asked a timid maid,
Of the shim-mer-ing sands that bord-ered the deep,
No answer she got, save the wavelets that played,
Around and gay, as they kissed her feet.

Herb wasn't sure whether to feel flattered or insulted. He'd successfully hijacked the party, but done so well at introducing Gil that everyone now ignored Herb. *Blast it all*, thought Herb as he climbed down to the floor from the stage. *Couldn't that Kraut have at least picked something with a slower tempo?*

"Have you room on your dance card for me?"

Herb looked behind him, and saw a familiar pair of green eyes set in a lovely dark-haired face staring into his own.

"How did you get in here, Margaret?" he said, crossing his arms and turning away from her. *Even her American accent bothers me these days*, he thought as he faced the young lovers he'd set in motion.

"Oh, Herbert," she said in mock sadness, "why ever are you so cruel to me? Whatever have I done except for falling madly in love with you?"

"Love?" He crossed his arms, still focused on Gil and Frances with a frown on his face. "You don't know the meaning of the word."

"Au contraire, Herbert! I've never given a kiss in my life that isn't sincere."

"That makes you the sincerest person in the country, Margaret. Maybe the continent. If I kissed you tonight I'd run the risk of catching a cold from at least half the men at this shindig."

"Flatterer."

They stood in silence for a few moments. Herb noticed her fingernails were hidden behind thick coats of that new shiny fingernail lacquer some French chemistry firm had been showing off. *All the power of the analytical engine at our fingertips*, Herb thought, *and we use it to make pretty paint for fingernails.* There was a lesson there, he was sure, but he didn't want to think about it.

"They make a sweet couple, don't they?" she said, almost innocently.

"Margaret, you never drop into my life just to make small talk. Give me the envelope and I can get back to pretending for the rest of the evening that I never got mixed up with your lot."

She produced a white envelope from the folds of her dress. Herb gave it a sideways glance and stuffed it inside his tuxedo's inner breast pocket.

"You'll find the payment for your last assignment higher than originally agreed. Our employers have been most pleased with your performance lately."

"You may convey my humble gratitude," he said, looking away from her and focusing on the dancers. "Now sod off."

Margaret looked at Gil and Frances on the floor, swaying slightly in their slow dance while looking deeply into each other's eyes. "Who are those two, anyway?"

"My best friend in the world, and the girl he loves."

"What? Is he a journalist, too?"

"What of it?"

"A journalist with ... is that one of the *Blogg* girls? How on Earth did that flagpole with glasses ever get a dance with her?"

"They talked about philosophy on a June night in Paris."

Margaret was quiet. "Well, there's no accounting for taste, I guess. Would you dance with me, Herbert?"

"Only if you doubled my fee."

"I'll put in a good word for you with the number three man in the circle."

"Let's go."

Herb and Margaret strode out to the dance floor, Margaret leading him by the hand to a chorus of titters by the ladies along the wall and on the floor.

"Who on Earth is that?" asked Frances, the general whispering distracting her for a moment from Gilbert's eyes.

"My best friend in the world," said Gilbert, "and his girl of the hour. Actually, they met last year at a costume party, when Herb was chasing one of her friends."

"Do you know why she's leading him onto the floor, instead of the other way around? I can hear the scandal mongers already!"

"He'd follow a pretty girl straight to the gates of Hell, I think. Then right through it. Then down to the ninth circle and have a pint with Judas, Brutus and Cassius."

"You have interesting friends."

"I've had an interesting life."

"Would you follow me that far, Gilbert?"

"Only if I could do the Orpheus thing and bring you back out again. Hell's not a pretty place this time of the epoch."

"Our Anglican minister said last week that no one really goes to Hell, since no one in their right mind would truly choose it."

"I dunno about that. Plenty of kids I grew up with knew how real the schoolteacher's switch was. But that didn't stop them from misbehaving, or the teacher from swatting them with it."

Frances laughed. "Are all the boys in America like you, Gilbert? My sister wants to know."

Gil looked at her eyes again. "No. None of us are. Not even me. I'm only like this when I feel this way. And I only feel this way when I'm with you."

Frances looked up to Gilbert and breathed in deeply. Her brown eyes reflected the lights of the chandeliers and shone like constellations on the prairie. The just-parted-lips of her smile could have melted the heart of the cruelest Czar in the middle of a winter war.

Now or never, thought Gilbert, while the music swelled in the background. Strike while the iron is hot!

> *She asked the wind as it came from the south,*
> *the self same question the answer came*
> *For a zephyr sprang up and kissed her mouth,*
> *Till her cheeks and her lips they seemed aflame*

"Frances," Gilbert whispered in a hoarse voice, the stars shining through the window surrounding her head like a beautiful crown, "would you mind it ... would it please you if I ... well, could I kiss you?"

Still looking radiant, she nodded her head and stretched up to him.

Gilbert hadn't really thought about how much taller he was. That her forehead was level with his breastbone wasn't much of an issue for him at the time. He bent his neck and his body slowly, wanting to draw out this moment and remember it forever. He was only dimly conscious of the music and singing in the background as he drew closer,

> *She asked a youth who chanced a-long,*
> *And the moral question was solved in a trice,*

For he answered Oh, maid-en, it may be wrong,
But, here he proved it 'Tis very nice,
Ve-ry nice,
Ve-rrrrrrry niiiiice.

My first kiss, Gilbert thought, *and it's not going to be wasted on a dare or a game of spin-the-bottle. It's going to be with someone I want to love forever!*

Though every cell in Gilbert's head was exploding in anticipation of the moment, he still miraculously had enough control to count the dwindling distance between his own lips and hers, (eight inches) compose a prayer thanksgiving to almighty God, (six inches) and create the opening stanzas of an epic poem of love and appreciation for Frances, her parents and her ancestors on both sides (that took a while; two inches left), and a general, silent scream of delight and happiness that this would be shared with her, and no one else. One inch, a half-inch, a quarter inch, and …

Gilbert was in a state of such blissful anticipation, such pure and unadulterated love and joy, that he hardly noticed when the ceiling exploded.

Chapter 4

"If their cities soared higher than their flying ships, if their trains traveled faster than their bullets, we should still call them barbarians…barbarism is not a matter of methods, but of aims. We say that these veneered vandals have the perfectly serious aim of destroying certain ideas, which, as they think, the world has outgrown; without which, as we think, the world will die."
– GKC, *The Barbarism of Berlin*, 1914

Utterly lost in the rapture of the moment, Gil probably wouldn't have noticed the end of the world, much less the exploding ceiling. Frances, however, was by nature more practical than romantic. She heard the explosion and screamed at the shards of glass falling from above like daggers of the gods. Gilbert, still deaf to everything but the singing of cupid's arrow, paused for a split second where Frances' lips had been.

"What …" he began, but was cut off by a shrieking, shoving wave of people stampeding towards the exit doors. The mob jostled and bumped Gilbert so hard that he almost let go of Frances.

Gilbert, still hanging on to the faintest glow of his canceled romantic moment, gripped her waist with a protective arm as pieces of glass began falling around them.

"Ow!" screamed a woman behind him as a falling shard sliced her hand. Another man yelped as his forehead split down the middle and began flowing with blood.

"Gilbert, what's happening?" shouted Frances above the din.

"I don't know; stay beneath me!" he said. He tried clumsily to stand over her and shield her from the falling glass while the mob pressed around them in a surging human tide towards the exit.

To his right in the midst of the confusion, Gilbert saw the large bodyguards he'd tried to elude. They surged towards him and Frances through the panicked crowd, staggering in the face of the fleeing party goers like a tenderfoot pioneer forging an angry river, tossing people right and left like bundles of rootless sagebrush.

"Frances, your bodyguards are coming. Go with them."

"I won't leave you!" she yelled, as a large screaming woman in a tan dress barreled into the biggest bodyguard, knocking him to the ground and trampling over him.

"You'll be safer with them than with me, now please, g—"

A very large hand clapped on his shoulder.

Uh oh.

Gilbert barely had time to think those two short words before he was torn from Frances and thrown backwards. By now the stampede had largely petered out and he stumbled backwards into open space, his arms spinning like pinwheels in a twister while he tried to regain his balance.

He failed miserably, staggering eight or twelve feet before landing on his back with a heavy thud, rattling his teeth and stabbing the back of his head with a white-hot jolt of pain.

Though hurt, Gilbert still wasn't about to let some lout rip him out of Frances' life forever! He was already struggling to get up when his eyes met the ceiling and saw what had caused the explosion overhead.

Near the end of the Invasion, the British forces had used a series of secret war machines on the Martians. Considered pure marvels of human ingenuity and accomplishment, they had destroyed exactly three Martian Tripods before the Martian heat rays had destroyed the whole bunch of them.

Among the ill-fated inventions was a squadron of a half-dozen flying machine-harnesses that looked as if they had flown from the dreams of Leonardo DaVinci. Lying on his back, stunned by both the fall and the sight above him, Gilbert saw no fewer than four people in the air, each held aloft by a winged, propeller-powered harness very similar to those he'd seen fighting the Martians nearly a year ago in the British countryside.

And as he watched, two of them dove to the floor. He heard a typewriter in the air above him, and the floor near his head erupted as the bullets tore into it.

Chapter 5

"The true soldier fights not because he hates
what is in front of him,
but because he loves what is behind him."
– GKC, *ILN*, January 14, 1911

Gilbert looked only for a second at the column of splatting explosions in the patterned marble floor charging towards him. "Woah, woah, WOAH!!!" he yelped, rolling over sideways and up into a crouch as the bullets tore a furrow into the space where he'd been.

One of the harness-flyers sped over him, missing Gilbert's head by only a few feet. "Gilberrrrt!" yelled the pilot as she flew by, her high-pitched woman's voice mixed with the whine of propellers and the chuffing noise of the machine's mini-steam boiler engine. A second machine followed her in hot pursuit, this one so close that Gilbert could see the murderous expression under the pilot's goggles as he followed the flying girl. Lining up behind her, the pursuer fired another volley of bullets that missed the girl, instead smacking and shattering several statues along the top tier of the hall.

Whoever she is, Gilbert thought, *she knows me and they're shooting at her!* He watched helplessly at two more machines fired on her, missing as she pirouetted her flyer in a swooping motion.

Bullets flying everywhere, and me out in the open! Gilbert looked around and saw no one else in the hall—they'd all made for the exits. Good. Frances and Herb were safe. He ran behind one of the four pillars in the hall and watched the deadly aerial ballet continue between the girl and her three attackers. *I could see Herb telling me to run,* thought Gilbert, *but she knows me somehow. If they get her I might never know.*

There was a sudden movement above, a twist or a sudden trick the girl had pulled. She'd reversed direction so quickly that one of the goggled men had lost control, and …

The North pillar sheared off the wing of his machine, and the pilot screamed as he hurtled out of control towards one of the stained glass windows. His shriek echoed through the hall, interrupted by the howling wind as man and machine broke through the observation deck's window and fell out into the night.

As the two remaining pilots circled the hall for another pass, one screamed something in another language. The other had his face twisted into a deadly sneer, his black-gloved hands adjusting the levers on his harness in an effort to line up with the girl again. She tried several more of the looping maneuvers that had sent the last pilot sprawling, but this time to no avail. These guys were good!

There must be something he could do! Gilbert looked at the ground, hoping someone or someone's bodyguard had dropped a pistol, a knife, a *bread* knife ... anything that could be used as a weapon! But there was nothing but a bunch of confections and other finger food flattened by the mob's retreat, along with a single serving tray.

The tray!

Another volley of gunfire interrupted his thoughts, this time punctuated by more breaking glass and another powerful blast of wind across the dance floor. A blast of icy air slapped his forehead so hard he nearly lost his balance, and he quickly bent to a crouch again to keep from being noticed as a target. With two lower windows smashed open, the air could fly freely from the hole above as a crosswind, turning the dance hall into a giant wind tunnel. It made walking difficult for Gilbert and flying a huge challenge for both the girl and her attackers.

Gilbert watched her curve around the side of the hall again, the small engine on her back chugging rhythmically and spouting tiny clouds of black smoke like a small locomotive. Her every flying curve was dogged by short bursts of two or three bullet rounds fired by the pilots behind her. More shattered plaster and broken glass hit the floor as they missed. But then she flew through the crosswind just above Gilbert's head level, slowed her engine and ...

Gilbert blinked. She was suddenly floating in midair? How? Fighting the headwind just enough, she had somehow slowed her machine to where she could hover in space. Not an impossible trick; Gilbert had seen birds do it many times back home in Minnesota. But to do it with a heavier-than-air machine must require some great expertise!

Less than a second after she'd stopped mid-flight, one of the pilots interrupted Gilbert's musings as he streaked past her at full speed, yelling what could only be a string of foreign curse words.

The next pilot behind the foul-mouthed one wasn't so lucky. As he shot past her, their flying machines somehow entangled. Yanked from her position, both her and the last pilot now fought in a frenzied mid-air tussle in an effort to regain control.

Still wheeling around the hall in circle after circle, the girl looked like she was punching the wings of the entangled pilot below her. As she and her captive pointed themselves in Gilbert's direction, he saw the other, free pilot with the foul mouth line himself up for another pass with his guns.

There's nothing I can do, thought Gilbert. *But what if* ... his eyes rested on the serving platter on the ground a dozen feet in front of him. He sprinted across the ruined marble tiles, grabbed the tray and saw the free pilot line up the girl and his partner in the sights of his guns.

No, Gilbert whispered silently, *please, no!*

The pilot's thumbs came down on the triggers with such force that the levers, which were apparently used to steer as well as fire the guns, made his craft wobble slightly in the air. But only three bullets fired, followed by a quick and steady clicking noise. He was out of ammunition!

Gilbert's joy was short lived. The pilot had made his last three shots count, puncturing the delicate right wing of the girl's flight harness. The wing broke apart, pieces flying in all directions as her gloved hands tore frantically at the buckles on her chest.

Suddenly, she was free. Suddenly freed himself, the pilot she'd been yoked to lost control, spinning to the left and crashing outside his field of vision. She, on the other hand, tucked and rolled like a maddened ninepin ball for a full second before hitting the base of one of the pillars. She splayed out and laid still.

"No!" yelled Gilbert, his voice drowned out by the engine of the remaining pilot's harness and the howling of the higher-altitude winds. The pilot flew over her, wheeling around in the crosswinds in an effort to touch down on the dancing floor.

Gilbert later found it difficult to explain exactly how the pilot landed. It seemed that as he'd flown close to the floor, he'd arched up like a bird alighting on a branch, the flight suit's propellers suddenly slowing as they pointed his head up to the ceiling instead of parallel to the ground, bringing him up, then down as he touched the floor with his feet.

If I rush him, thought Gilbert, maybe I'll sink a punch or two before he recovers. Then maybe some partygoers might come back in and lend a hand ...

Gilbert, now standing, was about to launch himself with his silver platter as an improvised weapon when the pilot tapped a spot on his chest and turned a small crank. The wings, which had a span of at least a dozen feet on either side, folded up in the space of two full seconds into the pilot's brass-colored backpack beneath its engine. The propellers folded in as well, though the machine guns still pointed up to the ceiling.

What the ... ?

Gilbert had seen no shortage of scientific wonders in the last year, but a pair of wings disappearing into someone's back?

Gilbert was still gaping as the now-wingless pilot reached into his vest and pulled out an ugly-looking pistol with a long barrel.

Gilbert finally snapped to, realizing he was worse than useless in saving anyone if he didn't move. He brought the tarnished platter up towards his chest—maybe if he reflected light in the pilot's eyes, he could buy a split second or two, and then ...

But there was no then. The pilot spotted Gilbert and ran the few steps to him, delivering a vicious kick to Gilbert's leg. Gilbert felt a slam against his left ankle so hard he was swept off his feet. His right ankle followed suit, and Gilbert spent the next half-second falling a second time instead of saving the girl.

He fell hard, smacking the floor on his elbow. The pain was immense and instant—so much so that he wanted to roll over on his side and scream like a kindergärtner who'd been beaned by a brick.

But he didn't get the chance to yell. A leather-gloved hand grabbed him from behind, roughly hauling him back up to a standing position, the tray still dangling uselessly from one of his hands.

"What ... what the ..." Gilbert sputtered then stopped, as the pilot tightened his grip on Gilbert's hair and pressed the gun barrel to Gilbert's temple.

Chapter 6

"The act of defending any of the cardinal virtues has today
all the exhilaration of a vice."
– GKC, A Defense of Humilities, *The Defendant*, 1901

Gilbert said a quick, meek prayer to St. Michael the Archangel
for any help he might be willing to give. He still held the tray,
but what to do with it?

Then, behind him, he heard the sound of thick leather on gritty
ground.

The girl! Gilbert wasn't the target—it was her! Whoever she was,
she knew Gil's name! And her voice sounded familiar ...

The pilot heard the same thing Gilbert did, and swung himself and
Gilbert around to face her. "Fraulein," said the pilot, using one of the
few German words Gilbert knew, "give back what you've stolen," he
continued with a German accent, "or I will blast a hole in this boy's
body big enough to see the next sunrise through."

She spat back something in German that Gilbert couldn't
understand.

When her hand moved towards her own vest, Gilbert felt the pilot's
gun move for a second from his own head, the barrel pointing instead at
her.

Gilbert pushed his feet against the floor, lunging backwards at the
male pilot without thinking, knowing instinctively that he had less than
a split second to distract him before he fired.

Gil yelled, flinging the tray's side edge at the barrel of his captor's
gun while trying to duck.

There was a pop. An invisible fist slammed the tray from Gilbert's
grip, and he heard and felt a sound like crunching granola in his head as
the world spun into a series of dancing lights.

Chapter 7

"The riddles of God are more satisfying
than the solutions of man."
– GKC, *Introduction to the Book of Job*, 1907

There was a pungent smell in Gilbert's nostrils, a mixture of sulfur and a forest fire. He spluttered and tried to rise, but a pair of shapely, black gloved hands held him down gently but firmly by pressing on his shoulders.

"Gilbert," a voice asked, "can you hear me?"

He opened his eyes. The girl was there in front of him. Though her leather cowl was still in place, she'd pushed her goggles back, revealing two beautiful, china blue eyes and several wisps of red hair.

Red hair?

"You!" said Gilbert. "It's you again!"

"Gilbert, I'm sorry, but you'll have to listen to me."

"How did you find me? I remember you from London when I got my reporter job. And on the train to Woking when the aliens landed, and back in Paris the day I ..."

The girl flicked Gilbert's upper lip with her finger, causing a surprising amount of pain for so small an action. Gilbert yelped, but she placed her index finger gently on his now-sore lips, silencing him. "I'm sorry, Gilbert. I am grateful, really. Your trick with the tray saved my life and bought me some time. But I'm still being pursued."

Her eyes flicked to Gilbert's right. Gilbert saw the other pilot lying on his side. A pool of blood was growing without any hurry beneath him, a frozen sneer twisting his unmoving face. The thick metal tray lay on the floor, a metal dimple poking out of one end where the pilot's bullet had tried and failed to enter either Gilbert's brain or the girl's body. Another dimple, wider and shallower, showed where the tray had spun and smacked Gilbert's head when the bullet had slammed into it.

"Listen, Gilbert. I'm going to give you something. You must keep it hidden any way you can. Do you understand?"

"Understand? I just saw three men die! And that was after they crashed through a glass ceiling and spoiled what would have been my first kiss! And you ask me if I understand?"

She curled her forefinger in front of Gilbert's lip again, holding it back with her thumb.

"Okay!" Gilbert said quickly, "Okay! Yes, I understand!"

"Here," she said, bringing her hand down and reaching into one of the many pockets of her flight suit. She drew out a ridged, thick disc about as wide as Gil's outstretched thumb to his little finger. "Keep it hidden at all costs. The sight of it will drive some to a mad pursuit, as you've seen."

"What is it?"

"The less you know the better. Keep it secreted on your person," she said, slipping it into his inner jacket pocket. "It won't be safe anywhere else. It opens with my love."

"But what does your love have to do with..."

"No, *my* love, not ... oh, hang it all! I have to go," she stood and looked at the doors where a number of the party goers had started to timidly file back in.

"But wait, wait," Gil called out, standing and making as if to chase her. "Wait, I don't even know your name! You can't just stick me with this ... this ... whatever it is!"

She turned and looked at him with now goggled eyes. "I'm so sorry Gilbert," she said, and turned again towards the far wall of the dancing hall. She took a running start, and hit her upper chest with an audible slap. The small propellers unfolded from her pack, resting near her shoulders. The delicate dragonfly wings sprouted again from her back, spanning with hardly a sound. The rhythmic *Chuff! Chuff! Chuff!* of the small engine began to drum up a tempo, and the buzz of the propellers sounded barely a second before she jumped in the air and was aloft.

Small puffs of black smoke followed her as she flew less than ten feet off the floor, turned in the air and rose near the ceiling. The few who had dared enter the hall after the fighting had ceased gasped again at seeing the contraption and its pilot as she circled up to the open hole in the ceiling where she'd entered.

When only a few feet from the hole, the flying machine made a sudden dip, pointed nearly straight up and disappeared into the inky blackness above. Gilbert swallowed, his hand moving to touch the small token she'd left him in his jacket pocket as the sound of her engine faded into the night.

He stood staring at the hole in the ceiling, and would have remained lost in his thoughts if Frances hadn't walked into the room and stood behind him.

"Gilbert," she said, in a quiet but won't-be-ignored voice, "is there something you would like to tell me about your ... friend?"

Chapter 8

"Comradeship is quite a different thing from friendship..."
– GKC, *ILN*, May 19, 1906

Gilbert's father had made the occasional trip to the saloon in town when on an errand, but ceased the practice when he'd come home with a bruised cheek and a small cut on his hand. He'd talked to Ma about the incident long into the night, but not to little Gilbert at all. The following week, Gilbert spent a blissful five days at school that were bully free, since several of the more aggressive children's fathers had all been afflicted with broken arms, legs and other ailments that required their sons to stay home and shoulder the workloads of their injured parents.

Predictably, Gilbert hadn't thought to connect Pa's slight injuries with the thrashing of the other fathers in town. All he knew was that his father steered clear of the saloon after that, and a number of the larger men in town would walk on the other side of the dusty street when his Pa neared them. The message Gilbert received was as clear as it was unspoken: we do not frequent places involved in the sale of alcohol to potentially unpredictable people.

Still, after the incident with the flying men, Gilbert was left feeling a bit depressed. Plus the night was somewhat young, and Herb claimed he knew just the thing to lift Gilbert's spirits. Gil had thus followed Herb to the kind of place Herb could find no matter which city he found himself in. A place where the drinks were cheap, the company kept to itself, and the conversations were usually subdued enough that a man could wallow in his misery without having it interrupted by joy at the next table, or vice-versa.

"Herb, are you sure about this?" Gilbert had asked as they'd walked in.

"What can we ever be truly sure of in this life, Gil?"

"Aw, crud."

"Gil, what's the matter?"

"The only time you get philosophical is when you wanna throw me off the scent. That's the matter."

They took their seats. Herb ordered while Gilbert fidgeted. "Why do you always have to find a hole in the wall, Herb?" he said after the waiter left. "I've seen bigger living rooms in the Rookery, and it's so smoky it's like having a drink inside my father's pipe."

Herb bristled. "Look, chum, if you don't like this place, go find your own. It's not like I couldn't find other company tonight, you know."

"I'm sorry, Herb. I'm just a little down."

"Why? I thought things went well? I mean, as well as they could've gone, anyway."

"Herb, I told you. I came this close to my first kiss tonight," Gilbert said, holding his fingers an inch apart, "and I got it all blown away by a bunch of guys in flying suits. I've been shot at tonight more than when I was covering the last batch of Luddites trying to firebomb the Paris trade show on difference engines. Worst of all I've spent the last two hours talking about those insane five minutes to a bunch of policemen who have a vocabulary of about thirty words of English."

"Well, it could be worse."

"How?"

"I thought Frances was still dizzyingly in love with you, mate?"

"Well, she's a little confused. Seeing a woman drop out of the sky and talk to your beau will do that sometimes."

"Still, did she throw you over?"

"What's that mean?"

"Did she say she doesn't want to see you again?"

"No. In fact …"

"Go on."

"I told her the truth. That the red-head was someone I recognized from before, but it's difficult to be certain."

"So you did know her!"

"Herb, if it's the same red-head who's been popping in and out of my life for the last year, I really can't say I knew her. I don't know anything about her, other than that she shows up when weird stuff is about to happen. Or has happened. Or is happening."

"Gil, stop conjugating. You'll make me think I'm back in Latin class. Now, did you tell Frances what you just told me?"

"No, not everything. I would have, but I didn't have time. I just told her that I think I knew her from a story I'd done before, and she seemed to know me, too."

"Bravo! Don't let little Frances know that she has no competition. Not yet anyway."

"Competition? What're you talking about?"

"Gil, Gil, Gil! Look, if your lady friend thinks she's got you all sewn up, she'll start to ..."

The waiter interrupted Herb by silently bringing them their drinks, a clear liquid for Herb and cola for Gil. Gil didn't remember ordering, but was too wrapped up in Herb's latest treatise to argue.

"Where was I?" Herb asked.

"Me getting sewn up by Frances."

"Right. Look, Gil, Frances seems like a nice little thing. But if she's human, she might get bored with you once she thinks she's got herself a bird in the hand. If, on the other hand, she knows that some lass is out for you as well, you'll look that much better in her eyes."

"Herb, I don't like playing chess games with anyone's heart, much less hers."

"Are you two married yet? Then all's fair, friend! Look, what's the worst that could happen?"

"She'll feel inadequate next to red-heads with wings, and bow out."

"Gil, look, she may have been a bit nonplussed back there, and I'll guarantee she'll fret about it a little."

"Do you think so?" Gil asked nervously.

"I know so! And stop looking so worried, Gil! A little fretting on her part is a *good* thing! Now that you're the kind've bloke who makes women drop out of the heavens to have a spot of tea and gunplay, she'll dote on every letter you write her twice as much! She won't believe that this fellow who can get women like that would actually deign to court little, brown-haired Frances Blogg. D'you see?"

"So ... when she sees that other girls like me, that'll make her like me twice as much?"

"I knew you'd get it, old bean. Nothing looks so good as when it's not quite yours and you know other people want it. Now drink your drink."

Gil slurped down his cola. "Y'know, it was a lot easier back in Minnesota. Quite a few people there met their wives and husbands when they were kids. For a lot of 'em love didn't seem to enter into it so much as knowing and feeling comfortable with a person."

There was a pause. Gil looked into the distance, while Herb searched for the next words to say.

"Gil, how long have we known each other?"

"Long enough to outlive most other friendships I had. And long enough to be around when I killed a couple of Martians. Why?"

"I know you're upset that you won't see Frances for a while, but ... well, Gil, you're not half as awkward or bad looking as you were when we first met."

"What are you getting at, Herb?"

"Look, I guess it seems you're trying very, very hard to be, well, faithful to Frances, when you're nowhere near to being married. Some might question whether you've got a shot at being married in the next few years. With all the beautiful girls in this world, and you traveling all over, don't you think you'll regret it if you pass all of them by for this one girl?"

"Are you suggesting I cheat on Frances, Herb?" Gil's voice had gotten very quiet.

"There you go again. It's not cheating, Gil, if you're not married. Blazes, Gil, even if you are married, there's a number of freethinkers today who'd suggest that since you only go around once, you should feel free to, well, look around a bit and smell the roses, y'see?"

"Herb, you're my friend. God willing, you'll always be my friend. But if you ever suggest something like that again, I promise you with everything I can that I'll unseal a tin of whooparse on you that you won't forget in a dog's age."

"Fine, fine. It's your youth, after all. Waste it if you wish, I wash my hands of the whole thing. It's just going to make double-dating that much more difficult when your only acceptable date is a few thousand miles away with a ring of muscle-bound monkeys around her, that's all."

"Well," Herb said, his voice changing to a more casual tone, "there's at least one bright side to tonight's craziness! I finally got to see that little red-head you've been talking about! I have to ask, by the way: you two looked fairly chummy before she flew off. Did she slip you something?"

Gilbert looked at Herb, whose voice had just a bit more of an edge in the last sentence he'd spoken. "I don't have her address, Herb, if that's what you're asking."

"Gil, Gil! I was only wondering if she gave you ... ah ... well, a love note, or a ... token of some kind."

"Herb, why are you asking me this?"

"Never mind, Gil. You were just looking a little droopy about Frances, and I thought I'd cheer you up by helping you ... what did Benvolio call it in Romeo and Juliet? Examine other beauties. That's all."

"You're jealous, Herb."

"Don't talk nonsense."

"You can't believe that I have a steady girl, one who's not only beautiful, but rich, too, while you bounce from girl to girl like a birdie at a badminton match."

"I thought being rich didn't matter to you?"

"No, but it matters to you."

"Drink your drink, Gil, and let's get back to the hotel. I'm getting tired already."

"Fine by me. By the way, Herb, Frances and I both noticed that brunette who had you on her arm earlier in the evening. Anything special with her going on?"

"Oh, Gil. You must mean Margaret. Where do I begin with her?" Herb took a swig from his glass. "Some people, Gil. They're like, well, like Turkish Delight to a person whose teeth are on their way to rotting out. You know they're bad for you, but for some reason you just can't say no even when everything in you says it'd be the smart thing to do."

A haunted look passed over Herb's face and he drained his glass. Gilbert was just about to ask what was the matter when a shadow fell on both of them, blocking the already dim light from the ceiling bulb.

"Good evening," a voice said from the shadow, "Mister Chesterton."

Chapter 9

> "It is not merely true that a creed unites men.
> Nay, a difference of creed unites men–so long as it is a
> clear difference. A boundary unites ... that is the beginning
> of a good quarrelsome, manly friendship."
> – GKC, The New Hypocrite,
> *What's Wrong with the World*

The silhouette above them was man-shaped and of medium build, but still looked intimidating.

Gilbert instinctively feared for his safety. In his experience, people who approached him in unlikely places after the sun went down were either bringers or causes of bad news. As his eyes adjusted to the sudden change of light, Gilbert saw the tall man was dressed in a dark tweed jacket and trousers. What Gilbert thought was a bald head quickly resolved to a black, domed bowler hat. A split-second more and Gil could see the man also sported a set of eyeglasses whose lenses had been tinted. This last detail unnerved him; he liked seeing the eyes of someone who could be a threat.

"Who wants to know?" Herb looked at their new guest with the barest hint of menace in his voice. Dominate the pack, he'd once said to Gil, or someone in it will dominate you.

The man in tweed turned his glance from Herb to look directly at Gilbert.

"Mister Chesterton," the man spoke in a flat, crisp voice devoid of a British accent, "your presence is required outside."

"Really?" Gil said, "and why might that be?"

"Mister Chesterton, it involves a Miss Frances Blogg. There has been an accident, and your name was brought up as one whose presence could benefit her in her current state."

"Frances?" Gilbert asked, halfway around the small table before he'd fully risen from his seat, "Where is she? Is she alright?"

"Gil, wait a minute, I'm not sure about this."

"Herb, this isn't one of your girls-of-the-moment! Where is she?" he said to the large man.

"Follow me, please," said the man in tweed, whose voice and straight posture had never wavered since the conversation had begun. He turned on his heel and began a broad-strided walk to the door of the cheap bar.

"Gil, I'm coming with you."

"No problem with that, Herb," said Gilbert as he walked through the door out into the night. "I think I might need a friend before this night's through, if this is as bad as I think."

"I hope it's not, Gil. In more ways than one."

Gilbert was in no mood to ponder the last part of his friend's cryptic sentence. He was only interested in following the dark-clothed man to find Frances, whatever her state.

There was a motorcar a few feet from the entrance to the bar. Gilbert's full attention was focused first on the man leading him, and then on the car that would take him to his beloved. He tried to sort out in his mind the dozens of questions that jabbed into his head when he heard Frances' name connected with an accident. Was she hurt? How badly? Who was involved? Would she live? Would she walk?

The thought of Frances sitting in a hospital bed calling his name silently would have sounded romantic in a kinotropic film or a nickel novel. But being faced with the reality of an injured loved one blasted away every dreamy bit of the foolish fantasy. Gilbert becme so focused on the man in black tweed, the car and his own thoughts that his normally sharp sense of self-preservation was quite dulled. As such, when Herb was grabbed from behind and silenced by a chemical-soaked rag shoved onto his face, Gilbert didn't even hear Herb's angry, futile struggles or his shoes scuffing on the sidewalk before they twisted limply and were still.

The large man in tweed reached over with a black-gloved hand and opened the motor-car door. "Inside, sir. Please move over to the window."

"Thanks, now about Fran ... Hey!"

Gilbert yelped as a pair of powerful, viselike hands grabbed him from behind, one on each of his biceps. He kicked hard backwards at where he thought the legs of his assailants would be. But his right heel only met air with the first two swings, and on the third try smacked painfully against what felt like an ironwood tree stump. Gilbert yelped in pain, and as soon as his mouth was open something filthy and fibrous was shoved into it. He smelled fumes that made him think of a gutter quack that had lived down the street from him in the rookery in London.

I'm being chloroformed, Gilbert thought. He tried hard to keep his eyes open, focused on the man in tweed who'd led him here. The man now stood impassively beneath the gaslight of the street, looking with a straight face at Gilbert behind the tinted lenses of his glasses, his gloved hands folded in front of him while a much larger, different set of hands held him, and a third set was smothering him with chemicals.

Got to stay awake, Gilbert thought slowly as he tried to struggle. *Got to!*

But thinking had become like swimming through thick mud, and his limbs grew farther away each second.

Chapter 10

"Our society is so abnormal that the normal man never dreams of having the normal occupation of looking after his own property. When he chooses a trade, he chooses one of the ten thousand trades that involve looking after other people's property."
– GKC, *Commonwealth*, October 12, 1932

Hellooooo! Hello there! Wakey wakey sunshine!"

The voice was cheerful, and tinged with the slightest hint of a U.S.A. Western twang. It also sounded a million miles away, but closer with each syllable. A blurry bright light shone in Gilbert's eyes and would not let him sleep again, any more than the voice would.

"Here, boys," the voice said, tossing a shout over its shoulder like a football pass, "I think he's coming 'round again."

The smiling face had short, straight blond hair atop of it. As Gilbert peeked out through the haze, he saw the smiling face's head was attached to a dark-suited body.

"Now, Mister Gilbert, sir," the face said, speaking with a level of excitement more appropriate for telling a group of children that ice cream and cake was on the way. "We're just pleased as punch to meetcha! We haven't had a real celebrity like you here for a long time, oh no sir!"

"Enoch, back away a bit. Let me see our new friend a bit, hm?"

Another voice, this one sharper and more businesslike than the last, jabbed hard into Gilbert's ear—it was familiar... that voice! It was the man in tweed from the bar!

"Aw, gee whiz, Phineas. You always hafta spoil my fun!" Enoch of the happy voice wasn't so happy now, standing up and yielding his seat to ... what was the name again?

"Good afternoon, Mister Chesterton," said 'Phineas,' seating himself in Enoch's chair in front of Gilbert. "My name is Phineas. You're just now coming out of a nasty little chemical-based surprise we gave you. Speaking should be a problem for you, but if you can understand me, please nod your head."

Gilbert paused, then nodded with a groggy air.

"Good. I knew I hadn't mixed the batch with too much chloroform, no matter what my brother said."

"He still took too long to come to," a third voice said. It was slower, peevish. Used to being pushed around but not liking it.

"My brother, Shimei," Phineas said, almost apologetically. "He's always trying to find fault with me and Enoch. Sad really, when you think of what we've done for him. Well, onto business!"

"Umph-mumph-mumph!"

Gilbert had tried to speak, but something fuzzy and foul still stuck in his mouth.

"Mister Gilbert," said Phineas, standing straight while adjusting his tinted glasses, "before we proceed there are a few things we need to go over. First, my brothers and I are professionals. We have kidnapped you for a pre-arranged sum of money. Your arms and legs are bound to your chair in such a fashion so as to cause you maximum pain if you try to break free.

"Now, we'd like to remove the gag in your mouth. But you must understand that if you scream for help, two consequences will result: First, you will receive no help since our location was chosen for its isolation from any human being who would be inclined to give aid. Second, my brother Shimei will punch you in the face. Hard. Do you understand me?"

Gilbert nodded again. Phineas, the businesslike one, nodded to smiling Enoch, who nearly bounced forward as he tugged at Gilbert's gag with a happy flourish.

"Okey dokey, now," said Enoch, "open wide, and I'll take this out... there!" he said, taking the rag out of Gilbert's mouth, "Izzat better?"

"Can I bash his skull now?"

"Maybe Shimei," said Phineas. "We have to see."

Gilbert looked at his interrogators. All three were dressed in identical dark tweed suits, with ties and bowler hats. Phineas was blond-haired like Enoch, though slimmer. Shimei was a large, hulking mountain of a man who sat in a nearby corner, brooding at the wall and playing with something between his ankles. Gilbert couldn't see exactly, but from the sound it made against the concrete floor he could tell it was made of metal.

"Now, Gilbert," said Phineas, the dim overhead light glinting off the tinted lenses of his glasses, "our employer hires us at a significant expense to do the occasional bit of work for him. We had a small bit of reluctance to take on this job since you are one of our countrymen, but then ..."

"Then he doubled the price! Wasn't that swell?" Enoch's happiness appeared to know no bounds as his shining face appeared beside Phineas'.

"Er, yes," Phineas said, straightening his glasses with his left hand. "Well, times are hard. Always have been, always will be. Now, since our employer was willing to pay us handsomely, we did the job. We're waiting for him to arrive here, Gilbert, but we want to caution you about something."

"Our boss can be really mean," Enoch said, gritting his teeth and bugging out his eyes.

"There have been times," said Phineas, "when we've had to make things decidedly unpleasant for our prisoners."

"We've hadda just . . zip, pow 'til they bled."

"Somebody say bleed?"

"Nope, Shim. I said bled. Past tense. Like that Papist last week."

"Aw him. Guy couldn't take a punch."

"No, the guy who couldn't take a punch? That was the heretic, the one who thought that Joe junior should have been the…"

"What my brothers are trying to say, Gilbert," said Phineas, trying to regain control of the conversation, "is that we are usually very nice people. But when we accept a contract, I'm afraid things can go very hard for you unless you cooperate. Do you understand?"

"Feh," said Gilbert. His tongue felt several sizes too big for his mouth.

"He gets it! Great! Now we won't have to be mean, and we can just take out money and have fun, fun, fun 'til the Hansom cab takes us all away!"

"Oh, we'll see he gets it alright, Enoch. Now Gilbert, when our employer arrives, you'll be a good boy and do what he says. He's got no love for you, and his word might bring down a degree of doom on your head that'll make a blood atonement look like a Sunday school picnic. Understand?"

"Feh."

"Yippee!"

"Silence yourself, Enoch. Here he comes."

Gilbert looked at the sound of a creaking door. The silhouette of a man with a top hat, cloak and cane stepped into the room.

But when he stepped into the light, he looked hardly a man at all, not much older than Gilbert himself. His overcoat and cloak were thick and well woven, with the slight gloss that came with the more expensive accouterments this year. Gilbert had covered his share of rich people's events in the past year, and he could tell no weaving engine had created this fellow's clothes. Only a very expensive master tailor could've done work like that.

"So, this is the chap, is it?" The newcomer's brisk voice matched his clipped, direct stride. He walked directly towards Gilbert, never taking his eyes off the captive in the chair.

"Yes, yes sir! This is him!" Enoch was even happier than usual at the sight of his boss, nearly dancing around the room at his approach. "He gets it, he said so himself, sir! Just give your request and we can head home!"

"Can we, now?" The younger man moved to a slight crouch, bringing his face within inches of Gil's. "Tell me, sirrah. Do you really understand the degree of trouble you are in?"

"Meb ... Mebba ... Mah-Bah ..."

"That means maybe, sir," Enoch supplied helpfully.

"Quite." The rich boy stood straight again, tapping the head of his walking cane in his hand while Gilbert regarded him dully. Gilbert's mind felt awake, but not able to do much. His body buzzed and tingled like a great, big foot that had fallen asleep and never wanted to wake up. His face felt especially numb, and he could smell his own spit dribbling down the side of his cheek.

"Now, Mister Gilbert, you need to know who I am. My name is Fortescue Williamson. My father, Arthur Williamson, is an old Eton school chum of one Mister Phillip Blogg. Who is, you may know, the father of a lovely young lady with the name of ..."

"Fan-ses!" said Gilbert.

"He means ..."

"Yes, Enoch. I know. Frances. Do stop finishing his sentences for him. I find him far more entertaining as a dribbling idiot. Now, Gilbert, my father's business interests and Mister Blogg's have been working well in concert for some time. So well, in fact, that when Frances was born a few scant years after I was, they hit upon the idea of ... shall we say, making the merger a bit more permanent once we reached a certain age?" Fortescue interlocked his gloved fingers. "Do you see what I mean?"

Gilbert did his best to glower at Fortescue. The more the pompous dandy talked, the less threatening he became. "You ... wan ... ta ...marrah ...hah ..."

"Yes! Marriage. You do understand! And who says Americans have no sense of subtlety?"

"Fah hah money!" Gilbert finished, spitting out the last word with a sizable amount of drool. A few drops of it managed to end up on Fortescue's shoe. *Very nice shoes*, Gilbert thought. Probably a piece of work that could have been designed, cut and sized by hand in some foreign land for more money than Gilbert made in a year.

Fortescue Williamson stopped and looked slowly at the three drops of spittle on the toe of a shoe that a serving man had likely spent several dozen hours of his life polishing.

"Enoch," he said quietly as his good humor evaporated, "bring your brother here and show this overgrown toothpick why he should keep his bodily fluids to himself."

"Excuse me, Mister Williamson," said Phineas, "but are you asking us to engage in actual bodily harm of this young man?"

"What do you think I paid you gentlemen for this evening? To play cribbage with him?"

"I'm sorry, Mister Williamson," said Phineas, using a voice that could have been employed in haggling for a set of trousers, "but we agreed for the standard rate of kidnapping and detainment. Which, I might add, hasn't yet been paid. Contracting us now to do bodily harm carries with it a substantial difference in scaled fees and rates. Do you wish to charge by the blow, or only for effects? The rate for reducing a grown man to tears is substantially different than, say, reducing them to a compliant puddle of metaphorical jelly."

"Yeah, an' watcha mean Americans got no sense, fancy boy?" Shimei had stood erect, the length of chain in his hand clinking menacingly as it grated slowly on the floor.

Fortescue swallowed once, holding the much larger man's gaze with eyes that had widened slightly, though his voice betrayed hardly any fear. "I mean, my good man, that so many, ah, *other* Americans are so used to living a hardscrabble life that they can't understand any ideas that aren't slapping you in the face."

"Oh, we know a few things about face slappings, dandy boy." Shimei's large jaw hardly moved when he spoke. He was moving slowly now, taking quiet diagonal steps towards Fortescue with a glare that made the richer, younger man take a step back.

"Er, what my brother means, Mister Williamson," said Enoch, stepping between them, "is that we're more than willing to keep workin' for you, but we're gonna need to be paid for our last job first. You understand."

Shimei had stopped when Enoch had risen and stood between him and Fortescue. Now Phineas stepped in beside Enoch, facing Fortescue and blocking Shimei's advance. "If, of course, you'd wish to renegotiate, that would be more than acceptable. But we'd need to settle our previous arrangement."

Fortescue pursed his lips together. "Fine," he said. "How much is still owed?"

"I prefer to conduct business away from prying eyes and ears, Mister Williamson. If you'll follow me over here, we'll have a seat on this small outcropping of boxes and complete our transaction."

Fortescue and Phineas walked to a corner of the building. Now further out of his drugged haze, Gilbert saw they were all in a warehouse lit by small lanterns. The building floor was several hundred square feet at least. Glowing warmth came from Gilbert's left, and piles of old crates stacked in neat piles of various sizes stood all around them. And some of the crate piles were so high they made corridors and hallways of creaky, rotting wood.

Gilbert looked left. The brothers had set up a potbellied stove near them.

"You like that? Warm, innit? Cost a little more than back home, but it's worth it." Enoch again. Gilbert wondered if the fellow still kept that unending smile on his face when he had to bash some poor fool's face in.

"We've been doing just a swell business out here in Europe," Enoch continued. "But when Phineas told me we'd have to beat on a fellow American? An' not one-a those Confeds from the South, or a Papist from the Californias, but an honest-injun American from the You-Nited States like us? Well, I just 'bout turned down the job, you oughta know. More than that—this is the Gilbert Keith Chesterton, the one who helped kill all them squids from Mars! 'Now how,' says I to Phineas, 'how can we take a job like this when it's a hero from our own shores? What's the good and right thing to do? Because if there's a good and right thing to beating on Mister Chesterton, I sure as flint on an early morning campfire don't see it, no sir."

"Really," Gilbert rasped. He was thirsty, more than he could remember being in over a year. "What changed your mind?"

Enoch looked at the ground. "Well, 'twarnt easy. But we gotta eat, Mister Chesterton. And when Mister Williamson over there just doubled our fee, well, I have to say, there's very few men in this world what are made of stone. 'Course, when I heard that you'd done gone and be a Papist, that helped soften things a little. But still."

"You mean you wouldn't have taken the job if I'd been a Presbyterian?"

"A what?"

"Never mind. Where's my friend Herb?"

"Oh, the limey? We got him trussed up a few aisles over. He don't matter one bit to me. Closest I ever seen anyone breakin' outta my knots, let me tell you! But don't you worry about him, Mister Chesterton. I don't think you an' him are in much danger. That rich feller don't look like he's gonna come through on his end of the deal, and if'n he doesn't, well, we get to cut you loose and do a little number on him instead. Won't that be fun? Shimei's Ma, now she knew how to make examples of people. An' she taught Shim all she knew!"

"Shimei's mom? I thought you three were brothers?"

Enoch looked like a little boy who had told a family secret by mistake. "It's ... well, it's complicated. Look, Mister Gilbert, the point is this: maybe you and your friend won't have to suffer anymore tonight. But if you do, well, please don't be angry with us. We gotta make a living, same as anyone."

"Sure, Enoch. Just you remember that when some trooper locks you up for breaking polygamy laws. They're just doing their jobs, too."

Enoch went pale, and his smile vanished. "There's no need for that. No need at all."

"Yeah, and maybe no need for you boys back home, either. Is that why you're knocking heads over here in England? They already have enough bulldogs patrolling the vineyards back home? Did all the pretty girls get snapped up by your leaders and their sons? Papists may not be perfect, but I never heard of one sent packing just to get rid of the competition."

Enoch swallowed. "You're making me angry, Mister Chesterton. Nobody likes me when I'm angry."

"Enoch, Shimei!" It was Phineas' voice. Enoch, his face now swept clean of its former joy, stood up, turned from Gilbert and walked away while mumbling something.

Shimei walked with a slow and purposeful gait in the same direction as Enoch, his hands tightening and loosening on the chain as he moved.

Gilbert swallowed. Maybe that hadn't been the best time to try and convert someone.

"Gil!" whispered a voice.

"Herb?"

"Gil! I think I'm in the next aisle over from you."

"Can you get free?"

"Still trying. I heard your little conversation there. Did that little happyjack say there was a stove near you?"

Gilbert paused. "Herb, why do you care if there's a stove?"

"Oh, I don't know. I could do with a spot of bacon and beans ... Gil! Think, man! Stoves are hot! And your hands are tied by ...?"

"I'm already on it. Hang on."

"Like I could do anything else."

"Don't get sarcastic, Herb," Gilbert grunted, trying to push his chair closer to the stove, "this isn't going to be easy."

"Yeah, well, getting beaten into bloody little pieces by those three mismatched brothers won't be a platter of tea and crumpets either, if we don't get free somehow."

"Hang on, Herb. No, on second thought, keep trying to ..." Gilbert suddenly gave a reverse hiss, sucking in air quickly as his wrist touched the stove.

"Um ... you found it then, Gil?"

"Herb," Gilbert said between gasps, "just keep quiet and keep trying to wriggle out of your bonds while I work on mine."

"Fine. Just don't barbecue yourself in the meantime."

Gilbert inhaled and pressed his wrists against the stove, careful this time to keep the cords that bound them between the flesh of his wrists and the heated metal.

"Gil, how long d'you think this'll take?"

"Don't know. I've never tried to burn through cords before by putting them on a stove. I don't think anything's happening, though."

Gilbert was right. The stove wasn't red-hot, although it was hot enough to make human tissue sizzle. Ropes, though, weren't going to be worn through by the potbelly's heat before their captors returned.

"Is there something sharp enough to cut on, Gil? C'mon, you're the imaginative one! Isn't there a ghost or something you Catholics can ask to help you find things in a pinch?"

"Anthony is a saint, Herb, and you ask him to help you find stuff you've lost. And don't start, okay? Have you seen the size of those louts out there?"

Herb was quiet, but only for a second. "How big?"

"The biggest one carries a chain, and he's named after an Old Testament guy who killed six hundred people with an ox goad. The littlest one's named after someone who stuck two people through the gut with one spear shot. Worried yet?"

Herb was quiet for a full second longer than last time. "Is there a saint for escape artists?"

"Maybe Genesius. Herb, are you looking for a way to get out while you're busy talking to me? Because you cou—YEOW!"

Gilbert had turned to speak more clearly to his friend, forgetting for a second that he had a hot metal object less than an inch from his hands.

"Gil? Gil are you alright?"

Gilbert inhaled slowly, controlling the urge to yell a number of things he'd have to go to confession for. "Fine."

"Good. Now get back to escaping. We probably don't have much longer."

Gilbert bit his tongue and got back to work. By now it was more fear of alerting the brothers than offending modesty that kept him quiet. He went back to work, trying to find a spot hot enough on the stove to burn through his bonds.

He stopped working when he heard a pair of shoe heels walking on the concrete floor towards them.

Herb was right—they didn't have much longer at all.

Chapter 11

"The whole truth is generally the ally of virtue; a half-truth
is always the ally of some vice."
– GKC, *ILN*, June 11, 1910

E noch had grown up in circumstances unusual to most people,
even Gilbert. Raised in a renegade sect of the Mormon faith as
the fifth child of fifteen in a polygamous family, he'd accepted
as normal the life he'd been given. When he, Shimei and Phineas were
told it was necessary for them to leave the enclave of their little farming
community, he'd been upset and blamed himself and the many mistakes
the elders named as the reason for his dismissal.

But, he'd mused, things could have been worse. He could have
been set adrift alone in a cold, cruel world instead of alongside half-
brothers as strong as Shimei and as smart as Phineas. Still, as their little
enterprises progressed towards the dark realm of illegality, Enoch had
found himself having doubts about the wisdom of their local prophet.
Why cast them out, he thought, when none of them had committed
serious sin? Why send them out without skills needed outside their
community or means of support, when it forced them to perform
criminal acts in order to live? Phineas had said it was okay, since they
would only steal from or hurt unbelievers. But still!

Worst of all for Enoch was the nagging fear that his brothers saw
him as unnecessary. Redundant was the word he'd heard used in a
whispered conversation between Shimei and Phineas that had stopped
as soon as Enoch entered the room.

Now, worried that he wasn't pulling his weight, Enoch looked for
every available opportunity to prove himself useful to his brothers.
True, he couldn't fight like Shimei or keep track of things like Phineas,
but by gosh he was gonna prove he could do everything else just jim
dandy! From that day forward, nearly six weeks ago, he'd watched
Shimei closely as the big fellow had twisted and broken limbs, listened
carefully to Phineas when he'd made deals and kept track of their
monies, and in general tried hard to learn all he could.

Which was why when he heard Gilbert make a bit of noise, Enoch
realized he'd not paid enough attention guarding his charge. Failure
meant he was useless, and that would mean ...

No. He couldn't bring himself to use the word alone.

Enoch had dutifully walked toward Phineas when called. But when he heard Gilbert holler after burning himself, Enoch had turned and walked back to Gilbert so quickly his thick-soled shoes could probably have been heard a quarter mile away on a quiet night.

And it was quiet in the warehouse. Very quiet. With the whispered sounds of Phineas and Fortescue Williamson dwindling behind him, Enoch moved with as much focus as the escalating stress in his head would allow him. *Don't run*, he thought. *Running would show something's wrong. And we don't want to show there's something wrong when outsiders can hear.*

He turned a corner and was greeted by what had been Gilbert's fairly old and not-well-built-to-begin-with chair, mashed into several pieces on the hardened stone floor.

Oh, no! He thought with silent horror, an icicle of fear shooting through his guts. *Oh no!* He inhaled at the sight of a few small smudges of dirt leading away from the dismembered chair and around the corner of piled crates. Launching himself like a drunken torpedo, he rounded the next corner in time to see Gilbert struggling with the knots on Herb's wrists. Gilbert stopped working at the sight of Enoch.

"Oh, Gilbert," Enoch said with sweet relief. "Now, let's get you right back into another chair." He spoke deliberately, stepping slowly towards Gilbert.

Herb, still sitting and bound to the chair, kicked out and down. "Run, Gil!" Herb shouted as he and his chair fell in an arc towards the floor.

Gilbert needed no encouragement. He ran down the corridor made of stacked crates, lit only by small lamps and dim moonlight shining through the high windows. *Got to lead him away from Herb*, Gilbert thought. "Hey, smiley!" Gilbert taunted Enoch, "Think you can catch me?"

Had Gil enough time to plan his action like a chess move, he likely wouldn't have chosen to leave Herb behind. But in the fear of the moment, coupled with Herb's barked order, even Gilbert's muddled brain saw that a fight with Enoch would bring only his own recapture, and possibly a loss of life for them both. Right now, the best bet Gilbert could see was to lead Enoch and his brothers away from Herb, then either get help from the local police or possibly circle back and cut Herb's bonds while the brothers were distracted.

Fortunately, though Gilbert's mind wasn't firing on all of its gasjets, Enoch was stressed enough that taking Herb as a hostage literally never entered his mind.

Enoch, different from most in the hired muscle profession, still thought that if you were nice and likable to others, they would, nay ought, to respond with heartfelt gratitude. From Enoch's perspective, here was a case of a captive escaping and making trouble for Enoch. And all after he'd tried so very hard to be reassuring, and make Gilbert as comfortable as possible under the circumstances.

And that made Enoch angry.

Very angry.

So angry that when Gilbert ran from Enoch, anger at his perceived betrayal quickly overtook any fear of his error being discovered. He launched himself after Gilbert, so blinded by emotion that he passed the still-trussed Englishman on the floor in pursuit of Gilbert, not stopping until he had run a full twenty or thirty steps past Herb.

Breathing heavily, Enoch looked around the dimly lit warehouse. Walls made of large crates of long-forgotten merchandise formed makeshift hallways, and spread out from him in many directions. Gilbert could have taken any one of them in his dash for freedom.

Now, Enoch thought, *if I were Gilbert Chesterton, where would I ...*

Enoch's eyes fell on the windows, set high in the wall near the ceiling. Getting to them would be difficult, but not impossible. Not if you could find the right pile of boxes to climb.

Off he went, looking for a stack of crates that would seem inviting to a scared seventeen-year-old.

He didn't have to go far. After only a dozen more sprinted steps he spied a kind of crate-staircase to his right. Whether it was the deliberate result of an enterprising workman or a happy accident mattered little to Enoch at the moment. What truly mattered to him was that the dust on these containers had been disturbed with smudged, telltale footprints.

Enoch looked up and smiled. He'd been right. Making as little noise as possible, Gilbert was climbing the mountain of crates. He was only a dozen feet above his pursuer, and gave no sign that he'd been spotted.

Chapter 12

"In the struggle for existence, it is only on those who hang on for ten minutes after all is hopeless, that hope begins to dawn." –GKC, *The Speaker*, February 2, 1901

Gilbert knew his flight was doomed if he didn't put space between himself and the brothers. He ran at first without concern about noise, until he realized that he'd no idea where the building's exit was, or if it would be guarded once he got there. Pausing for only a second to take his bearings, the light of the full moon through a high window caught his eye.

Windows! Windows meant a way out! Another look and he spotted a small pyramid made of crates, likely stacked by workers trying to make their job easier.

At the top of the pyramid of crates was the bottom of a long, dangling ladder that led up to the ceiling. It was a long shot, but it beat being caught! Gil hopped up onto the first 'stair' crate, very nearly needing to swing his leg up and over in the process.

The going wasn't much easier on the second, fourth and sixth steps. He was just about to leap up past the eighth when he heard the scraping of a shoe on very old wood below him.

He turned—it was Enoch! Only three crates back, and still smiling that blasted grin he'd used since Gilbert had woken up with a smelly rag in his mouth.

"Ah, Gilbert," the bigger man whispered, "look, if you come down now, I'll tie you to a different chair, but I won't make the knots too tight like I did last time, I promise!"

"You're new at this aren't you?" Gil grunted as he hefted himself up and overtop another crate, the tenth. "Most guys in your line o' work just say 'get back down here, punk! Or I'll break yer kneecaps!'"

"Would that get you back down here?" Enoch asked, as he climbed up and over the seventh crate.

"Nope." Up, over the eleventh crate, another five or six from the top of the heap.

"What if I told you I'd let your limey friend go?" Up, over, eighth crate.

"No good. You're not the piper calling that tune, Enoch." Jump, heft, up... slip! Gil slipped and yelped as his chin smacked onto the edge of the twelfth crate.

"I could put in a good word in for you, Gilbert." Up, over the ninth crate.

Gilbert waited until he was on top of crate fourteen before he answered that one. "I'd rather trust a Martian, Enoch. Now shove off, if you know what's good for you."

As he finished the last sentence, a chill ran through Gilbert's spine and his nose hurt.

"Oh, Gilbert," said Enoch, distracting Gilbert from the already fleeting pain, "you're starting to hurt my feelings again." He hefted up and onto number eleven. "You know what happened to the last feller that did that?"

Hup, jump, onto sixteen, "No," said Gilbert in a loud whisper, "and I don't give a rip!" Fear pushed him up two more crates in seconds.

Gil stood at the apex of the eighteenth and topmost crate and looked as best he could at his surroundings. He was actually at the top of a pyramid, with a ladder dangling a few inches above his head.

"Funny you should say 'rip,' Gilbert, 'cause that's just the sound he made when I got my brother to tear his arm off." Up, over, must be on the twelfth or thirteenth step now, Gilbert thought.

Gilbert reached up and could just barely touch the bottom rung of the ladder—the workmen must have purposely piled the goods up to this height and then used the ladder to reach the catwalk that was higher up still. If Gilbert stood on his toes, he could just curl his fingers around the bottom rung. Maybe if he jumped?

"Now, mind you," Enoch said, still climbing and grunting below, "that fellow really had it coming. He was a really mean to his wife and kids." Enoch sounded another grunt as he lifted his body weight up and over the fourteenth crate. "But we wouldn't have been called in if he'd just paid his debts."

Gilbert jumped, trying to clap his hands and arms together around the bottom rung. He slapped the rung on the ladder, but slid down off of it. His feet made a hard thump as he landed on the crate below, and his hands wheeled while he tried to keep his balance.

Gilbert heard another step and huff from below. Enoch must be on the sixteenth box.

"Look, buddy," Enoch said, "can't we just get you back to the chair, an' we'll let bygones be bygones?"

Gil leaped straight up, and this time grabbed the bottom rung. He didn't answer, but grunted as he pulled himself straight up and to the next rung. His foot left the top of the eighteenth box only two and a half seconds before Enoch's hand reached up and slapped the space Gil had been standing on.

"Where'd yuh ... aw, gee whiz, Gilbert! I'm getting to where I'm willing to paste you one good!"

Gilbert, a dozen or more rungs up the ladder, looked down at the face that had been smiling at him only a seconds before. Enoch's face looked winded now, and more than a little irked.

"I've got a better idea, Smiley," Gilbert said between rungs on his ladder. "How's about you go back to your brothers, drop the leg breaking angle, and open up dry goods store or something?"

Gilbert could almost hear Enoch bristle at his comment. Enoch jumped up, grabbed the ladder by the bottom rung and tried to pull himself upwards. But his arms were more used to punching than lifting his own bulk, and it took him several tries to heft his weight up high enough to where he could grab the second, and then the third rung up.

Gilbert, meanwhile, had climbed to the top of the ladder and reached the catwalk, an elevated metal walkway near the ceiling. Running his hand along the side, he could feel the railings and used them to stand straight. No time for witty comments, now! He almost took off running across the ramp, but thought better of it. If Gil understood rightly, Enoch's brothers didn't know that Gil had even escaped, and alerting them to the fact couldn't do any good. Instead, Gil tiptoed as quickly as he could, hoping that he could put a pile of distance between himself and Enoch without giving anyone below a good reason to investigate and/or do damage to Herb.

Step, *tap*, step, *tap*. Gil's shoes made small noises despite his best efforts on the metal walkway, high above the warehouse floor but still a dozen or more feet below the ceiling. At least there hadn't been any squeaks yet from the metal itself. Now, how to get to that window ... ?

CREAK! went the walkway, shaking a little beneath Gil's feet as Enoch reached the top of the ladder and dropped his full weight onto the aging, rusting metal.

"Enoch?" Phineas' voice carried up from below. Its tone was filled with both inquiry and menace. "Enoch, is everything alright?"

"Uh, yeah, Phineas! Just jim dandy! Sorry, I musta tripped or something. Now, Gilbert," Enoch's voice suddenly dropped from its jovial, happy tone to a whispered and menacing one, "I'm gonna ask you nice just one more time, and then, *then* I'm gonna twist that skinny little neck of yours and snap it like you were a sick chicken. You get me?"

"You're gonna have to catch me first, Smiley," Gil whispered. "And if you come to much closer, I'm gonna have to jump up and down on this here bridge, and your big brothers'll know just how bad you messed up watching over me."

"They already know," a voice growled behind Gil.

Gil yelled and ducked. Shimei's powerful arms just missed him in the gloom. How'd that oaf climb this high so fast and quiet?

Staying low, Gil scurried forward just out of the bigger man's reach. But Enoch was less than fifty feet in front of him, a look of triumph on his face as he walked slowly towards Gilbert.

Gilbert looked back. Shimei was coming towards him with the same slow, measured steps, his large right hand flexing open and closed while his left hand steadied him on the railing of the catwalk. The walkway began to creak and bend, groaning with the extra weight.

Weight ... Wait!

"Don't move!" Gil yelled at the top of his lungs.

Shimei and Enoch both stopped. More than once before they'd cornered a quarry in this way, but folks in this situation usually either begged for mercy or began to panic and blubber incoherently. A victim shouting at them was a decidedly odd turn of events!

"Gilbert," said Enoch, "this is your last chance, now! You bought yourself a few seconds, but you're not gonna ..."

Gil jumped.

Straight up and down.

Nearly four feet into air, and back down again.

The catwalk creaked and bent a little more, making snapping noises in several places.

"Every hear the story of Horatio at the bridge, boys?" Gilbert shouted. He kept glancing in both directions, trying to keep an eye on each brother at the same time.

"Story, shmorey," grumbled Shimei, taking another step. Gil jumped again, this time making the bridge bend just a little more in the shape of a downward-pointing arrowhead.

"Horatio saved his friends, boys," said Gilbert, "because he was willing to drop himself along with a whole bridge full of his enemies. Now if I drop all three of us, I won't be kicking up my heels anytime soon. But you two won't be tap dancing on my face either. And I like my friend Herb's odds against that adding engine of a brother of yours down there a heck of a lot better than with you two."

Shimei tried to move closer with a slow step. Gil jumped again, but this time he pulled his legs up to bended knees, let himself drop until his head was within three feet of the bottom of the walkway, and then kicked both his legs straight down. The catwalk groaned and buckled further in a sudden jerking motion that threw all of them off balance.

"Okay, Gilbert, sir, we understand, now." Enoch's voice, no longer trying to be quiet.

"Do you?" Gil said with an angry voice. "Fine. One of you get off this bridge, and untie my friend."

"How's about we both ..."

"Nuh-uh! This only works for me while I've got a sword of Damocles hanging over at least one 'a your heads."

The brothers paused. "A what?" Shimei said slowly.

"Never mind," barked Gilbert. "Enoch, you get down, and just you. Shimei, if you so much as twitch one 'a those meathooks of yours in my direction, I jump again and we'll both find out if you're fast enough to grab one of those railings before I snap this thing."

Shimei glowered at Gilbert. His thick jaw ground back and forth as if powered by thoughts of chewing on one of Gil's limbs.

"Okay, Mister Chesterton," said Enoch. His smile was trying hard to keep himself and everyone else around him calm. "Okay! I'm backing up and getting down now. See? I'm going to slowly back away, and when I get to the ladder, I'll get down slow and untie your friend."

"You do that, Smiley. And if one of you is thinking about taking a potshot at me with a pepperbox pistol, just remember that a dead body hits a creaky catwalk just as hard as a live one."

Gilbert kept his eyes locked with Shimei's angry glare as Enoch's shoes made tiny tapping noises that faded back along the catwalk and down the ladder. Thirteen, fourteen, fifteen, sixteen taps and then a heavy *thud* as the stout man dropped to the crate at the ladder's base.

A very long few minutes passed. Gilbert held Shimei's eyes in what he hoped was an intimidating stare.

"You know," Shimei said quietly, "you shoulda took Enoch's offer. That fancy-pants down there probably won't pay up. If you'd just let us tie you back to your chair, we wouldn'ta been mean to you."

"How about now?"

"Now? Soon as I get the chance I'm gonna break both your arms, then both your legs. Then, if Phineas says it's alright, I'll think of something special for ya. Maybe tie a little rope to your ankles and dangle ya in the river a little."

"If my legs are broken, I'll be making a little noise, don't you think?"

"This isn't the kind of neighborhood where a little screaming gets too much attention from anyone, kid."

"Thanks for the warning."

"You won't be needing it, Mister Chesterton," said a voice from below.

Gilbert risked a quick look down. Phineas was down there, wearing his black tweed coat, round-topped bowler hat and staring up at Gilbert with his dark-tinted eyeglasses. Herb was standing beside him, rubbing his wrists.

"Herb!" Gil yelled.

"I'm all right, Gil," Herb called up to his friend. "You can come down now. Things have changed substantially."

Gil looked warily at Shimei. "Define 'substantially,' Herb.'"

This time, Phineas spoke up. "The dandy boy who hired us, Mister Chesterton, is now tied up in Mister Wells' place. It seems he thought that he could negotiate from a position of strength without a foundation of money to stand upon."

"What," Shimei roared, "he didn't pay up?"

"Worse, brother. He threatened to hire a different set of professionals to rough us up if we didn't cut our losses and forget the sum he still owes us. I decided to settle that score another time. It's getting very, very late, and I want us to be rested and tip-top for our next job tomorrow afternoon. Enoch is already out in the coach, and you will allow Mister Chesterton to leave his post without assailing him in any way, shape or form. He'll be all the retribution we need on Mister Williamson, if I guess my men right."

Shimei looked at Gil, who tensed to jump again. "Gilbert Chesterton," Shimei said, looking at Gilbert as if planning a satisfying form of vengeance, "They say you kin write, an' that yer brave. But I say yer a skinny little sap who's gonna get broke on someone's wheel soon as yer luck runs out," the big man said in a practical voice. "Me, I just hope I'm around to see it."

"You won't," Gilbert said, swallowing and relaxing. His legs suddenly ached and he knew he was going to be sorry for this little adventure in the morning.

"Mister Gilbert," continued Phineas, "while you may not wholly believe this, I wanted you to know it was indeed an honor to meet you and Mister Wells.Tonight, you both fully lived up to your reputations. I only wish that we could have met under more pleasant circumstances."

Gilbert listened to Phineas' speech while Shimei began his decent down the iron ladder. "That makes two of us," said Gil. "You said you were leaving?"

"Yes, we were and are. Do stop by and say hello to Mister Williamson on your way out, won't you?"

Gilbert was silent, and watched the two, dark-clothed brothers as they made their way back into the shadows of the building. A minute more and the sound of a squeaky door on rusty hinges announced their departure as it opened and closed. A few more seconds, and the distant clopping of horses' hooves sounded into the warehouse as the coach Phineas had spoken of pulled away.

Gilbert waited, continuing slowly to three-hundred after the coach had left before he began walking across the catwalk towards the place where Shimei had presumably climbed up after him.

"Gilbert," Herb called, "are you coming down?"

"I'm on my way, Herb. I found a ladder. Any sign of our friends down there?"

"If you mean the brothers, no. But there's still something I think you should see."

Gilbert found the ladder, swung his leg around and began to climb down. A wound in his lower leg near his ankle, long healed since a dying Martian stabbed him over a year ago, began to throb in pain as he descended.

"Herb, is Williamson there? Phineas said something about him as he was leaving."

"That's just what I mean, Gil. C'mon over here, and you'll see what he meant."

Gilbert climbed down fifteen or so rungs on the wrought-iron ladder, stuck his foot downwards and felt the solid, hollow hardness of the packing crate beneath him. He scampered down the crate pile to the warehouse floor, ignoring the pain in his leg. Once on *terra firma concreta*, he walked at a brisk pace to the dim lantern light around the corner of one of the crate walls.

Gilbert saw Herb when he rounded the corner. He was still wearing the slightly dirtied sport coat he'd had earlier in the evening, along with a smirk on his face. Less than ten feet away from Herb sat Williamson, a rag stuffed in his mouth, and his body tied to the chair so securely that his top hat hadn't even come off for all his writhing.

"Well, Gil," Herb said, "it looks like our friend Mister Williamson tried to be something he's not, didn't he?" Herb's eyes never left

Williamson during his speech. "In fact," Herb continued, "he tried to be a little *jemmy legs*, didn't he? Know what that is, rich boy?"

Williamson, his eyes narrowed in hatred, gave no movement or response.

"It means a smart, dishonest fellow. You thought maybe you could convince some rough characters from Gil's shores that you had a good enough line of credit to do a job for you for free, isn't that right?"

More silence from Williamson.

"Well, Gil, I guess we owe our new American friends a little favor, seeing how they left us one of Mister Williamson's party favors to play with."

Gilbert watched Herb's speech to Williamson. True, Williamson was not the first useless rich person Gilbert had ever seen. Nor was he the first bully Gilbert had ever encountered.

But Williamson was the first person to be both a bully *and* powerless in front of Gilbert.

And that made something dark and angry inside Gilbert start to stir and twitch.

"Gil?"

Gilbert turned, the spell broken. "What, Herb? What'd you say?"

"I said, what do you think of it?" Herb said as he handed Gil something.

Gil took it and looked it over. It was a black rod, maybe a foot long and nearly an inch in diameter. It had been ornately designed—the black wood was polished ebony, and there were Chinese-styled demons holding a long lightning bolt etched on the shaft. Gilbert turned it over in his hand; already sensing what it was before he found the telltale button on its underside.

"I think it's a ..." Gilbert said as he pushed the button. The top part of the stick snapped back, revealing a pair of sleek needles with small rods and filaments surrounding them.

"A shocking nancy," Herb said under his breath. "Some call it the portable lightning bolt. Remember the Doctor? He had one of those. It's a nice little toy for scaring away cutpurses or surprising street urchins. Those things put enough of a jolt in you to knock you clean flat, but they're not much good against the likes of Phineas and his lot, eh, Williamson? Not if they know enough about fighting to take it away from you."

Herbert was clearly enjoying goading the trussed up fancy-pants in the chair before them. Fortescue could only glare at them both.

"No, Herb," said Gil, his voice quiet as he turned the rod over in his hands. "The ones they made a year ago knocked you flat, or maybe start your heart up again if it stopped. One of these could carve a nice, big burn hole in your chest. And even if you live, you'll twitch for a week and probably never be the same again."

Herb looked at Gil. There was a look on his friend's face he couldn't ever remember having seen before. Gil's eyes looked like he was about to pull the wings off of a fly that had been pestering him for far too long.

"Well, ah, Gil, I guess we'd, um, better be going? We can just leave this chap here, now, you know. Just, you know, leave him behind? Just walk away, leave him and his little shocking wand? We don't have to take him with us, you know. And I don't think he'll be bothering us again. Will you, Willy?"

Under normal circumstances, Fortescue Williamson would have challenged anyone who called him Willy to a duel of pistols at dawn. Instead he nodded his head, vigorously as he could without losing his high hat.

"See, Gil? All's well. So, just put down that little electric pigsticker, and we'll go back to the hotel and sleep off this awful night, hm?" Herb tried to ease Gil's elbow in the direction of the exit with his right hand, and tried to gently remove the shocking nancy from Gil's hand with his left.

All to no avail. Gilbert kept looking at the rod in his hand with narrowed eyes. He showed no sign of his having heard Herb or anything else but his own private thoughts.

Gilbert suddenly looked up, his eyes focused on Williamson.

"Pigs," Gilbert mumbled under his breath, and took a step towards Fortescue. His movement was so sudden and smooth that Herb couldn't rightly say he'd seen Gilbert move at all, much less could have stopped him. Gilbert had become a phantom, a gliding beam of purpose whose sole anchor in reality was the wealthy, helpless young man tied down in the chair in front of him.

"Gil? Gil, what are you ... Gil!" Herb yelled, now moving himself, trying to catch up with a friend he suddenly didn't recognize. "Gil, answer me, what're going to—whoa!"

With no movement other than a flick of his wrist, Gil had swung the wand in an arc. The timing of the swing was perfect, ending just a foot in front of Herb's face where it discharged a bright bolt of blue sparks. The effect was quick, planned and unavoidable. Herb stopped and backed away several crucial feet, his hands brought up to his face palms-out, as bright sparks assaulted his eyes in the near-darkness of the warehouse.

"Gil!" Herb yelped, "What're you doing?"

Gil didn't answer, but took the last few steps toward Fortescue and stopped.

The shocking nancy was still sparking. A small blue thread of electricity danced with a happy, deadly twisting motion between the small poles at the tip of the rod. Herb saw only Gil's silhouette, illuminated by the sparking light of the rod in his hand.

Lost in thought, Gil spun the rod twice in a slow arc. The light traced a blue double-circle in the air that held Herb's gaze.

Fortescue's view was, of course, much, much worse.

Fortescue's life to this point was not unlike that of most in his social strata. Raised in opulent homes, educated by private tutors, he'd been explicitly taught that a life of honor, dignity and attention to duty was the only life truly worth living. He'd also been taught in a thousand implicit ways that the rules of honor, chivalry or dignity did not need to be applied to anyone beneath his social station who stood no chance of crawling up to it. In Fortescue's world, Gilbert and his ilk were little better than roaches. And when roaches tried to crawl out of the toilet, the proper thing to do was flush them down again. Or squash them, if you could without getting your own shoes dirty.

And yet, a young man little better than a mudlark from the gutters now held Fortescue in his power. That Gilbert was more accomplished in his life at seventeen than Fortescue would likely be at sixty-five made little difference. Being tied up with one of the roaches of the world holding the upper hand was a situation that Williamson's life hadn't prepared him for at all.

"Pigs," Gilbert muttered again, glaring at the bound young man in front of him. "Know what a fella like you used to call me and my family back in Minnesota?"

"Mmph," said Fortescue, trying to form words around the rag in his mouth.

"There was a fella like you back where I lived. When my Pa spoke at a town meeting and got all the farmers on his side against having a railroad barrel through the town, the richest fella got all sore at him and called him and the rest of us a bunch of pigs at the table. Dogs in the manger. And a few worse things besides. His boy Luther never let me forget what his Pa had called mine. And he reminded me about it at school every day when he rubbed my face in the dirt. Or kicked me in the shins. Or the gut. Or punched me in the nose.

"And there was nothing I could do to stop him. Luther had the finest house in that whole, little town. And he made a point of inviting the biggest, strongest boys over for ice cream every Sunday after Sunday services. Soon he even pulled what friends I had away from me and the swimming parties we used to have. He had them all in his hand. And then he had them as his guard dogs, in case me or any of his other victims ever tried to fight back.

"You forgive for a long time. You might even be friends again if it'll stop the beatings. But then when you see that won't happen, you get to living in fear, angry all the time. Living with a hard knot of hate building up over what you'd do to all of them, if you got the chance."

Gilbert's voice had dropped in volume, and now was little more than a whisper.

"Mister Fortescue Williamson," Gil said, "you know what I have in my hands? Do you really know?"

Fortescue froze. His eyes were wide, jumping like frightened birds back and forth between Gilbert's glowering eyes and the bright blue of his stolen shocking nancy.

"What I've got here, Fort, is that chance I used to dream about. School's in session, rich boy, and you're sitting in my classroom."

"Gil, what do you plan to do, exactly?" Herb asked in a quiet voice. Sweat beaded on his forehead and his mouth felt dry. For some reason he knew it was a very, very good idea to keep his distance from the tall, menacing stranger his friend had become.

At the sound of Herb's voice, Fortescue *mmph!*ed several more times, trying to look around Gilbert's blue torch and make eye contact with Herb through the flickering azure light.

"Oh, now don't look to me for help," Herb said suddenly, his fear vanished at the sight of the cocky rich boy's eyes begging for his aid. "You're the reason for this mess. Gil, look," he said, looking at Gilbert again and talking in what he hoped was a normal toned voice, "this little toff isn't worth the time it would take to jolt him. He'd be a lot more humiliated if some dockworkers came in tomorrow and found him trussed up. His kind hate having to accept help from anyone without a manor home on the downs and at least five digits worth of pounds in the bank."

Gilbert acted like he hadn't even heard. His eyes were narrow black chips of anger, and he walked with a slight limp closer to

Fortescue.

"Seventeen years, *Fort*, I've hadda take it from the likes of you. My whole life, I've had to see pretty boys like you get everything handed to 'em, while I deal with the short end of the stick. You follow me?"

Fort opened his eyes and nodded slowly.

"No, you can't follow me, Fort, 'cause people like you can't walk in my shoes longer than it takes for you to get tired of slumming. Until tonight, you've never known what it's like to be the plaything of someone more powerful than you'll ever be. Am I right?"

Gilbert whipped the rod close to Fortescue's face, the blue sparks shimmering like angry blue imps around the captive boy's face. Fort closed his eyes and whimpered.

"That's it!" Gil crowed. "That's how it is for your victims, Fort! That's what it's like, not knowing what'll happen next! Or when it'll end, or what to do to make it stop. Now you know, Fort! Now you know! And now, more than anything, I want you to remember this:" Gilbert leaned into his victim's ear and whispered, "remember that it was your failure, your mess up, that put you in the power of a little nothing like me. Always remember that I held the cards because you were a big enough fool to drop the hand."

Gilbert straightened up, still holding the sparking wand beside Fortescue's flinching face. "Before I go, Fort, remember this, too: If Frances doesn't want to marry me, that's fine. It'll break my heart, but I'll live.

"But Fort, if she rejects me because of your interference, I'll know about it and I'll hunt you for the length of my days. I will find you, and after I'm done you'll still spend the rest of your wealthy, privileged life with a face that looks like you stole it off of a Notre Dame gargoyle. You get me?"

Fort swallowed, nodded.

Gilbert breathed, straightened up and let the wand fall. Its glow was already fading as its powered cells began to run down.

"Gil," Herb said, "can we go now?"

"Fine," Gil's voice sounded tired. As he breathed, his tense frame relaxed. "We'll call the coppers, Fort, and tell them the whole story. I hope you don't mind, but I don't really feel good about untying you right now. And I think you don't want to be seen in this neighborhood this hour of night anyway, not dressed in those kinds of clothes without a police escort. You get my meaning?"

Fortescue nodded slowly, as if unsure as to whether or not he was hearing another round of fake concern.

"Fine. C'mon, Herb, let's go."

They left, their steps sounding very loud on the concrete floor. The door creaked open as they pushed it, and closed with a bang.

"Cripes, Gil, why the noise?"

"I want to make sure that the thing locks tight. I don't want some dock rat to go in there, gnaw the pretty boy's face off and give me the blame for it." Gilbert jiggled the door slightly, to see if the lock had fallen into place.

"Two minutes ago you were ready to burn his face off with an electric torch, and now you're worried about him getting hurt?"

"Never mind, Herb." Gilbert looked himself again, but very tired.

Gilbert turned to go. Herb followed, shivering from more than just the chilly air. For tonight he'd seen something he'd never expected to see in a million years. Not on a London street, not anywhere.

"You want to talk about what happened back there, Gil?" Herb's voice sounded hollow, almost muffled by the fog which had gotten several layers thicker since they'd begun walking, hiding the stars above from all view.

"Maybe," Gilbert said, staring at the ground with his hands in his pockets, trying to ignore the fading pain in his lower leg.

"Well, what happened?"

"What's to tell, Herb? I gave a low-down sidewinder a case of what-for."

"Gil, giving someone 'what-for,' if I read my American slang right, means giving him a solid thrashing, straightening your hat and walking with a confident swagger off into the night. Well, you didn't give him a thrashing in any kind of a fair fight. In fact, for a second I thought you were going to seriously disfigure that poor bloke. And you're not walking with a swagger; you're walking like it was you that took the beating tonight. Y'see?"

Herb had said his little speech while trying to catch Gilbert's eye. Gil's own face was pointed at the ground, not looking up or caring if he was headed the right way home or not.

"I guess I surprised you," Gil said in a quiet monotone.

"Surprised isn't a word, old bean. You did something I didn't think was possible tonight. You made me feel sorry for some tosser from the upper crust."

"Huh."

"Gil ... look, where did that come from? I've never seen that in you. I've never seen you hurt someone and actually like it. Me, alright. I could've done that to Fort back there, perhaps. But you?"

"Herb, you ever been bullied? Do you know what it's like to feel like every recess period is another ten minutes of torture for the fun of someone bigger or stronger than you?"

"Oh, back to this again. No, Gil, I don't. My folks were well to do enough that they hired private tutors for most of my life, except when I went to public school and was taught by Doctor Huxley."

"Well, Herb, tonight for the first time I really had a chance to bully a bully. Tonight he learned that he's not going to be able to do it to me. Never to me, Herb, without getting his pampered hide burned so bad he won't sit down for a week."

Herb watched Gil's face as he talked. A small edge had returned to his eyes and voice. An edge that troubled Herb a great deal, because normally Gilbert was the sort who would very nearly always look for the most peaceful solution to a problem, usually out of fear for his skin as much as for religious reasons.

But tonight a different and more unpredictable side of Gilbert had shown itself to Herb Wells. And Herb only liked unpredictability when Herb was unpredictable.

"So you bullied a bully and you liked it. Now what?"

Gilbert stopped at looked at a point a thousand yards away. Though his eyes were tilted to the heavens, they might as well have been turned inwards. "I'm going to go back to the hotel and sleep for ten years, Herb. There's something in me that wants to jump on a ship and conquer the world, but the bigger part of me feels like a wrung-out dishrag."

"Fine. That's the most sense you've made since we've left the warehouse. Come on, I know a shortcut."

"I thought this was your first time in Berlin?"

"Dock and warehouse districts are the same the world over, Gil. If you play your cards right, you'll always find a shortcut from there to the upper crust district. That's how the lower-class hoodlums stay in business, and the upper-class find hoodlums to do their dirty work."

"How did I ever get along in life before I met you, Herb?"

"You didn't. But don't worry, I won't hold it against you. How smart can you get growing up on a prairie?"

Chapter 13

"...I believe in getting into hot water. I think it keeps you clean." – GKC, *Illustrated London News*, 1906

T he World's Fair was huge. *No*, thought Gilbert, mentally tearing up the sheet of script in his head. Huge didn't do it justice. How about ... *immense*? *Enormous*? *Gargantuan*? He rummaged through his slightly-addled brain for an adjective that fit what he had seen in Berlin, but kept on emerging with the verbal equivalent of a bucket going down into a dry well and coming up empty.

The World's Fair was … sprawling? No, that sounded too chaotic. The thing had been incredibly well-organized. All-encompassing? No, he could see its borders on a clear day, if he had to. As he trudged though the mid-winter chill on the concrete of the London sidewalk, he fiddled and shuffled words in his head that just wouldn't arise or fit in a satisfying way.

Gilbert walked slowly through the glass and wooden door that opened to the street. He'd been back in London for two days and hadn't left his modest flat in all that time, trying to re-adjust his body both to the ticking of a clock a full hour removed from London time, along with the difficult adventure he'd lived through.

The elevator opened in front of him, the metal screen unfolding with a spidery clack and grind. Gilbert stepped in and tried to remember the thrill he'd had traveling on one of these for the first time. He couldn't put his finger on it, but he'd been feeling steadily grouchier as his time back in England had progressed.

A few more seconds and he was out of the elevator and onto the deserted main office floor. This floor of the newspaper building was nearly always busy, except for Friday afternoons when everyone left for a few hours. Even winning awards for his reporting hadn't kept him from being buffeted about like a toy boat in a monsoon on his first day in the actual newspaper building. He'd grown used to it, but never truly liked it.

"Hey, Chesty!"

Gil paused and closed his eyes, hating the most hated nickname anyone had ever invented for him.

"What," he growled while his eyes remained closed.

"Chief Eddy wants you in his office, Chesty, post-haste!" The voice belonged to Uriah, a former clacker colleague, now a hungry new reporter. He was also one of the many who'd made it his mission to take Gil's high place on the journalistic totem pole, gained a year and a half ago for his reporting on the Invasion. Gil turned to look at Uriah, and a brief fantasy shoved its way into his head of the electric wand being shoved into Uriah's bucktoothed mouth. Or burning off his fiery, unkempt mass of red hair.

"Thanks for the warning, Uri. I'll talk to him in a bit."

"You'll talk to me *now*, Chesterton," commanded another voice.

Gil swallowed. The last voice hadn't been high pitched and annoying like Uriah's; it had been deep with a resonant boom that stopped all foot traffic on the floor each time it sounded. The voice had belonged to Edward Edwards, Chief Editor of the floor, and 'Chief Eddy' to all beneath him in status.

No one in living memory had used his nickname to his brown-bearded face.

"Right, Chief," Gil said without missing a beat, spinning on his heel and trying hard to ignore the leers of Uriah or the heat rays that seemed to blast from Chief Eddy's eyes.

Gilbert followed the Chief into his office, closing the door behind him. His shoes sounded very loud on the Chief's wooden office floor. The Chief circled his desk, then pulled his chair out and sat down in a pair of clipped, well-defined movements.

Gilbert kept standing in front of the Chief's desk and tried not to think about the cushioned seat behind him. He felt very much like a naughty schoolboy in front of the headmaster.

"Sit," the Chief said. Gilbert sat. The chair creaked under him.

The Chief lifted a piece of yellow paper from his desk. The sunlight shining through the Chief's window illuminated it, and Gilbert saw the words on the paper were typed, not handwritten. Someone had wanted to be very official.

"Gilbert Chesterton ... " the Chief began, still staring intently at the paper. "How long have you worked for this establishment?"

"Nineteen months, sir. Two years and three months if you count my time in the basement, making punchcards for difference engines."

"And how many assignments have I sent you on?"

"After they reassigned my first editor to someplace in Canada, and transferred me here? I stopped counting after you sent me on seven or eight. It's maybe a dozen outside of England, a few dozen here in London."

"True. I am sending you on another assignment right now. One that shall take you back to your American shores, to the city of Richmond in the Confederate States of America."

Gilbert was silent for a moment. "I appreciate that, Chief. But I was really hoping you'd give me a few weeks off to testify over in Italy about Father Brown's canonization."

"Testify? Why, what's he done? He's dead, isn't he?" Chief Eddy asked. The Chief was no friend of the Catholic faith, and instinctively suspicious of anyone who wished to draw closer to any part of it for any reason.

"They're beginning the process of Canonizing Father Brown, declaring him a saint not only for his sacrifice during the Invasion, but all the other parts of his life."

"But I thought he *died*."

"If you're going to declared a saint of the Church, Chief, dying is something of a prerequisite."

Chief Eddy drummed his fingers on his desk, looking at his wall. After a few seconds, he inhaled and looked at the boy across from him. "Gilbert," he said, "you are a true enigma to me; a fellow very difficult to figure out completely. I usually can size up a man in a very short space of time. After a few minutes I almost always can know with confidence what he's about, what jobs he's suited for, and even the kind of woman he'll marry and how he'll get on with his in-laws. When I first laid eyes on you, I thought to myself: 'Here's a fine fellow who has just won a barrel full of awards for his reporting. We can expect great things from him. He will achieve much and make his name known among men in the British Empire. Most important, he'll sell a ridiculous number of newspapers for this firm, causing our competing newspapers to be thrown in the dustbin of history.'

"And yet, in the last two days," he continued, gently laying down one telegram and picking up another, light green telegram from his desk, "I have received two telegrams regarding your actions on your assignment to the World's Fair in Germany." Here the Chief's eyes flashed from the paper, boring into Gilbert's own. "What do these telegrams say, Gilbert?"

Gilbert tried hard not to swallow or show any outward sign of nervousness. "I'd like to think they gave a stirring account of my incisive journalistic style, noting the bravery with which I managed to fight off a small horde of men in tweed armed with cudgels and chains. Not to mention saving the heiress of the Blogg family fortune from a bunch of glorified flying monkeys with wings and machine guns growing out of their backs."

"And I'd like to think that His Highness the King will invite me to a game of whist," the Chief interrupted, "but the odds of that are slim at best. No, Mister Chesterton, these telegrams are anything but positive in their descriptions of your conduct among our noble cousins over the Rhine."

"What? What did I do?"

"First, I'd like to hear your side of things. Among your assignments to cover was a presentation on Eugenics. Now, just why were you so rude to the presenter?"

"I wasn't rude, Chief. If anything, *he* screamed at *me*."

"And why was that, pray tell?"

"First, he insisted that there were too many people in the world. That if we didn't take steps to reduce the number of people being born we'd be standing on each other's shoulders and resorting to cannibalism by the year 1920."

"And your response?"

"I asked him if he'd actually done the math. It doesn't take a Zeppelin scientist to figure out that if you gave all one billion people in the world five square feet of space, they'd fit in downtown London. Proving overpopulation is a farce isn't hard, Chief. I did the calculations in two minutes on my notepad. Heck, if we had *six times* that and gave them an acre of land each, you'd fit everybody in Australia and leave the rest of the world for farming and cattle ranching."

"And his response?"

"He screamed something about the need to remove with all possible speed what he called the 'human weeds' with undesirable traits. And I asked what those traits were. Then he spluttered, as if everyone should know what undesirable traits were. So I tried to help him by asking if some of those traits were baldness, obesity, poor eyesight, nasal deformities or chronic stuttering."

Chief Eddy stared at Gilbert.

"Well, Chief, just because he was bald doesn't mean I was talking about him specifically."

"And the fact that he's fat and sports a pair of thick-lensed eyeglasses didn't affect your choice of words at all?"

"You forgot the large mole beneath his nostril."

"Gilbert ..."

"Have you seen it? The thing's so big it should have its own moon."

Chief Eddy just stared at Gilbert. Gilbert stared back.

"Last, Gilbert," Chief Eddy finally said, taking the second telegram, "your name came up in a little kerfuffle that happened with the son of a very wealthy man."

"Yes, and I sent you a report over the wire as to just what that son of a very wealthy man did to both Herb Wells and me."

"Gilbert, he was found trussed up in a locked warehouse in a dangerous part of town."

"I wasn't the one that trussed him up. His own thugs did that when he wouldn't pay them for working us over."

"Gilbert, are you admitting involvement with the situation of young Fortescue Williamson?"

"That's a bit like asking a mugging victim if he's admitting to being involved in a robbery, but yes."

"Did you threaten him once the tables were turned, Gilbert? Did you hold a live shocking nancy to his face and threaten him?"

Gilbert paused. "In my country, this is where we say 'I take the fifth.'"

"You're not in your country, Gilbert. Even if you were, I doubt that invoking the Fifth Amendment of your Constitution would keep any man the likes of Fortescue Williamson's father from hiring a series of more expensive thugs to rearrange your innards."

"Maybe. Are they scarier than Martians?"

"To you, Gilbert, yes. The Martians are in your past. I know what may lie in your future. These are evil men you're dealing with."

Gilbert stuck out his chin. "I can handle them."

Chief Eddy's eyes were no longer angry, but still very serious. "No, Gilbert, you can't. Look," he said, opening a drawer and pulling out a file folder that had been wrapped tight with a string.

Gilbert, realizing that he wasn't going to be fired, relaxed visibly, but tried not to roll his eyes. After dealing with bloodsucking aliens, every danger on Earth that could come from a human source held little worry for him.

Until he saw the pictures.

Chief slapped half-a-dozen sheets of white paper on the desk and knocked them towards Gilbert with a flick of his finger. "Look at those carefully, young Gilbert. The Yard gave us the highest resolution they could muster. If I printed these I'd likely have a riot on my hands for being negligent and publishing indecent stipplographs, but they will hopefully awaken in you a sense of the danger you now face."

Gilbert leaned forward and picked up the sheets. He looked them over and nearly dropped the first one.

Gilbert was no stranger to unpleasant sights. At the tender age of sixteen, he had seen hundreds dead at the tentacles of the aliens, with most of the victims in a pile of blood-drained corpses over a dozen feet high at the aliens' base crater.

But in many ways the picture on the sheet was worse. It was not a genuine photograph, but a *stipplograph*, a photo taken by a police detective that had been run through a calculating engine, and its details fired over radiographic wires. A machine called a *stippler* had reprinted the photo with hundreds of needles dipped in tiny drops of ink, and spit it out at the newspaper offices. While a messenger tube would have done just as well, many journalistic houses were converting to stipplers for the novelty as much as the slight convenience. For some reason, a stark, slightly blurred stipplographed picture carried more weight with the populace. More important, they sold more papers.

The stippled photo in front of Gilbert was quite graphic, even if he ignored its blurred edges. It was of a man in a suit with a tie flung to the wind. His furrowed brow and gaping mouth were visible in the lines of printed dots, along with a large dark stain where his neck should have been.

"That first one was the worst, Gilbert. Perhaps their hired knife was a tad new at the game still," said the Chief, rising from his desk and walking behind Gilbert. He reached over and began to move through the pictures, since Gilbert looked very reluctant to touch them. "Most the victims were adult males, though the last ones were a father and his son. That one," the Chief pointed to the top picture, "was a barrister. And that one was a businessman of significant railway holdings. That one was a journalist like yourself, but for our rival paper, the *Telly*. And that one was a humble porter who, rumor has it, looked at a message he shouldn't have. Men of varying backgrounds and professions, all but two from the middle-class. Each one had only two things tying them together: they had their throats cut from ear to ear, and each had gotten between Fortescue Williamson senior and a lot of money."

Gilbert looked quietly at the stipplos in front of him. "Do you think that derailing a marriage of fortunes between his son and the daughter of a diamond merchant could count as 'getting between?'" he asked quietly.

"I can think of nothing else that would fit the bill more nicely, Gilbert. I know you had your heart set on going to Italy to testify on behalf of this priest chap. But do you see why I'd rather you took this assignment I am about to offer you, in the other direction? Williamson's tentacles reach far, but not so far, I think, as across the Atlantic."

Gilbert looked again at the pictures. What would Father Brown have wanted? Before the trip to Berlin, everything in Gilbert had been directed at telling the world the kind of good and holy man Father Brown had been, and how his faith and choices had saved Gil, Herb, and the whole of the world.

But looking at the pictures … they did more than just frighten him. They made a pulse of terror shoot through him that was so complete he felt more like an animal in the path of a machine than a person.

Gilbert swallowed slowly, putting a hand to his throat. "Suddenly, going home looks real good, Chief," he said, once the feeling had passed.

"I thought it would," the Chief answered, patting Gilbert on the shoulder in an unexpected act of fatherly kindness. "Go up to your desk, get what you need, and be back here in a half hour. I'll send a message through the tubes to have a punchcard made up for your expense account. You'll be taking an airship to America, and once there you'll meet your contact and learn the rest of your assignment."

"Meet my contact? Am I a spy now? "

"Not in the least. You're a fact-finder, nothing more. There's a lot of chatter going through the pipes about meetings taking place in the American city of Richmond. Diplomats from each of the Five Americas are meeting there—even a few Canadians are coming by, looking for scraps. When this many men with their noses in the air travel to the same place, something big is always afoot and I want you to find out what it is."

"How will I know my contact?"

"Once you arrive in New York, you'll dock for a few hours for the ship to refuel. During that time you'll meet your contact, Mister Kelly Ewing, a reporter for the New York World. He'll give you an envelope with the details of the rest of your assignment—names, locations, people whose sons to avoid upsetting and the like. After that you'll leave on the same ship for the city for Richmond."

Gilbert stood up quickly and extended his hand. "Thanks, Chief," he said.

"Don't thank me yet, Gilbert," the Chief said, taking Gil's hand in a firm grip. His face was grim. "I'm doing this to save the paper's skin as much as yours. If we couldn't protect our own reporters from the terrors of man's world, soon all of our best and brightest would leave the London Times like rats from a sinking ship. Protecting you not only lets me sleep at night, it also helps me convince talent from other papers to come and work for us. Talent like your friend Wells, for example."

"I've mentioned it to him, Chief, but he won't budge. I think he's a little worried what jumping ship might do to his reputation."

"More than that, likely. Competition can kill a friendship, whether over girls or gold. Well, another matter for another day. Get yourself gone, Gilbert. Time is of the essence."

"You make it sound like Williamson already has a bounty on my head."

"Each of those poor souls in the stippling pile had no warning, Gilbert. Off you go! Don't even stop for lunch until you're on board that ship!"

Gilbert went, leaving the office through the slightly creaking door. It made a light slam behind him, and he walked with a quick stride to the hallway that held his office.

Walk hard, he thought, *but don't run.* The last thing he needed was someone ambushing him to find out what was the matter. Stopping to explain to someone like Uriah would not only delay Gilbert. An enemy could use Uriah's loose lips to learn that Gil knew he was being pursued.

And right now, Gilbert's biggest advantage lay in hoarding as much information from his enemies as possible.

He arrived at his office. Well, Gilbert didn't exactly have an *office.* A luxury like four walls and a door only came with a combination of brilliant reporting, unassailable seniority, and impeccable family connections.

Well, he liked to think he had *one* out of those three. It was a start, anyway.

After winning the awards for his stories on the Martians, he'd been given a space on the floor of the paper with four walls... but no roof and no door. A cube with no top face, and within was his desk, a typewriter, a stack of blank paper next to the typewriter, and a pneumatic messenger tube poking up from the floor to a space beside his desk. For the few months he'd actually been at the desk to write, Gilbert had typed out the draft copies of his stories, edited them, re-typed them, then sent them off into the tube with the proper name and destination on the canister.

The exact workings of the London's tube system had been a complicated affair to begin with. Essentially, it was a series of pipes built into networks which had branched out, expanded and merged into other tube networks as needs had grown. After the Invasion it had been smashed to pieces, then hastily cobbled together in ways more haphazard than before. By now it was so contrived and difficult it was conceivable that no one in the entire city truly and completely knew how the system worked.

For Gilbert, the most important part of the tube system was that when he slid a card with a name on it in the address slot outside of the canister, Gilbert's words were in the paper the next day for thousands to read. *Magic*, Gilbert had thought to himself more than once. *We can dress it up in scientific finery, but it's magic, no more or less than the sun coming up or a daisy opening to greet it every day.*

Gilbert opened drawers and started pulling out small mementos and knick-knacks that he had collected over the past few months. A shark tooth, a St. Christopher medal, the latest in a long parade of St. Michael the Archangel holy cards mailed to him by well-wishers, and several letters from Frances that he had accidentally left behind on his last trip and hadn't stopped thinking about his whole time away. He'd just finished stuffing everything into his pockets when he spotted the small, red rock in the corner of his drawer.

Gilbert paused. He wasn't an organized person by any rational standard, but a lone red rock in the corner of his cheap wooden drawer stood out like ... well, like a rock in the corner of a drawer. Gilbert picked it up and held it in his hands. It was smooth and worn on one side, porous like pumice stone with a hundred little holes on the other. Gilbert had just slipped it into his pocket when the messenger tube beside his desk whistled, popped open its door and dropped a small cylinder of paper onto Gilbert's desk.

A part of Gilbert told him that it would be wiser to ignore the paper, the rock, and anything else he might need from his desk and run like a man with his shoes on fire. But he had an insatiable curiosity, so he naturally unrolled the paper. It held only six words, but they chilled Gilbert's insides like nothing had in the last year:

G. GET OUT! it said, THEY ARE COMING!

Chapter 14

"It is perfectly obvious that in any decent occupation (such as bricklaying or writing books) there are only two ways (in any special sense) of succeeding. One is by doing very good work, the other is by cheating."
– GKC, The Fallacy of Success, *All Things Considered*

T he young man sat quietly at his station, counting under his breath. His fingerless wool gloves hovered over the multiple pipe openings in front of him like a runner poised at the starting gun. At his feet was an unfurled piece of paper with a message written in curt, near-perfect, handwritten print on very official-looking stationary. Beside the message was a trail of several other sheets of paper, all with stippled pictures taken from various observation points in the city. The paper trail led to a very odd looking machine, a cobbled-together piece of equipment that remotely resembled a stipplograph. A thick cable wound from this near-blob of wire, brass, glowing bulbs and hissing steam jets, disappearing through a sizable crack in the grimy brick wall upwards to the outside.

It was the message at his feet and these stippled photographs that had motivated him to scrawl messages to Gilbert so hastily and send them flying through the pneumatic messenger tubes.

" ...Twenty-one, twenty-two, twenty-three ..."

The young man, no more than nineteen, looked nervously as his machine chattered, hummed and spit out a stippled photo. It was understandably blurred, but undoubtedly one of Gilbert hunched over his desk reading the paper that the boy had sent exactly twenty-five seconds ago.

"...Twenty-six, twenty-seven, twenty-eight ..."

More chatter from the machine. More stippling. Another piece of paper drawn with stippled ink dropped in the young man's lap.

He grabbed it and scanned it, still counting. This time, the picture was of Gilbert's desk. But instead of Gilbert, a tall, thickly built man stood over the desk, wearing a longcoat. He also wore a bowler hat, glasses of some kind, had a clean-shaven face, and one arm was visibly larger than the other.

Good job, Gil, he thought, though his mouth still counted aloud.

"... Twenty-nine, thirty!"

He opened a small sliding door on one of the tubes, and a loud whistling of air sang through his grimy underground cell. He slipped one of the rolled-up pieces of paper into the tube, closed the door with satisfaction, and began counting again.

"One ... two ... three ..."

The man had entered the headquarters of the Times at a quick pace, but not in a hurry. He'd been briefed earlier in the day, and knew just where to look for his quarry. He'd found the desk with surprising ease, but the open drawers and disturbed dust on the desk told him he'd missed his prey by scant seconds.

And a combination of training and instincts that had been honed over many years told him his prey would not return, but had to be pursued.

And that made his hunter's heart happier than it really should have.

He turned and walked quickly. After a few steps his foot hovered a moment over the mat at the exit door. Logic told him to step over and head for the docks. Instinct said to search the building one more time.

Being a predator by both experience and training, instinct won. He turned to his left and stalked down the aisle of desks and clacking stations. His walk was the slow, quiet pace of a hunter so sure of his prey that stealth need not even be pretended.

And as he walked, his right hand flexed inside its black leather glove with soft clicking sounds.

Gilbert had hesitated for only a few seconds when he'd gotten the note from the messenger tube. He almost bolted for the exit, but realized that running would only draw attention to himself. And if this message was genuine, attention was the last thing he wanted right now.

Out the exit to the street? he thought quickly. *No, if I wanted to catch someone that's the place I'd look closest. The back alley? No, that'd be next. Then where?*

The basement! Someone had once mentioned at lunch that no one ever went to the lower floors, except the janitors who worked on the boilers!

Gilbert swallowed and peeked around the corner. Seeing nothing, he walked with quiet, quick steps down to the end of the hall and the back stairwell door.

He entered the stairwell, shut the heavy wooden door without a sound, and started down the stairs. Like virtually every building in London, its back stairwell hadn't been properly cleaned or maintained since the building had first opened up several decades ago, and it creaked like the early morning thoughts of an old man. While the man with the black gloves was debating which way to follow him, Gilbert was creeping down the stairs, wincing with every creak they made under his feet. Hopefully, even if that message was genuine and someone was after him, he'd escape the building unobserved, then board his airship. After that he could count on a safe and sound trip to America, untroubled by anymore trousered apes like Shimei or either of his odd brothers.

But first Gilbert had to get out of the stairwell. Still stepping, stairs gently creaking, Gilbert tried to move down as quickly as he could. After three floors, his heart jumped as he spied the dark door that led to the alleyway behind the building.

Gilbert reached out to the doorknob and turned it slowly. The rusty knob shrieked like a woman in pain, sounding louder than Gilbert ever remembered any doorknob sounding.

The hinges on the door, thankfully, had little in common with the doorknob, only offering the slightest squeak in protest as Gilbert swung them open.

Gilbert began a sigh of relief. But as he opened the door, his sigh stopped short.

There was a man in the doorway, wearing a brown longcoat and a brown, round-topped bowler hat. He stared at Gilbert from a pair of shaded eyeglasses similar to those Phineas had used. A breeze from the alley tugged at a stray wisp of brown hair over his ear.

He raised his black-gloved hand as he stepped towards Gilbert.

Chapter 15

"Once abolish the God, and the government becomes the
God." – GKC, *Christendom in Dublin*

Herb sat at the large table and tried very hard not to fidget. His parents had been relatively simple people by the standards of British polite society. His father had listened to a difference engine's stock tip given out as a party trick, and made enough from the investment to have Herbert raised in his formative years by a succession of exhausted nannies. Later, Herbert and his siblings were schooled in etiquette and refinement in the company of one's betters.

Herbert had driven a number of the teachers in this area to distraction as well. But though he'd avoided many lessons, he had always remembered that fidgeting in the company of the powerful could result in his expulsion from their ranks. Thus, he was semi-consciously trying to get all his fidgeting done now before his lunchtime companions arrived.

But his urge to twitch, jump and parade around the room while screaming nonsense at the top of his lungs was worsened by his surroundings; the restaurant was silent. Herb was the place's only diner. It was well lit, but not by the bright sunlight from outside. There were no windows he could see, only dim beams of light from unseen ports nestled between the roof beams of the ceiling.

Fool, Herb thought. *Such a fool.* He was a fool to accept the invitation, but if he ran now, escape was ... well, not exactly possible, but perhaps do-able, for a while. If he left the room right now, he could perhaps ... No, impossible, said another thought, more insistent than the first. There would be no escape, no more than for a fox that could evade a pack of hounds. He could only run and dodge until he made a mistake or grew exhausted. No escape was possible.

No escape.

No, but ... *profit*.

Now, *profit* was a definite possibility. And he could look forward to profit without any dread at all.

A door opened behind him, and he turned to look. A well-dressed manservant walked in, his feet making soft pads on the carpeted floor. Behind him, Herbert saw the fattest man he had ever seen.

The large man was at least twenty stone... no, more like thirty stone heavy! That'd be four hundred pounds, as Gil counted weight!

The large man walked slowly, with a gait that was almost-but-not-quite waddling. He was dressed in an immaculate waistcoat and trousers, with shoes that were equally huge on massive feet that were attached to his swaying, tree-trunk legs. When he moved, a great slosh of flesh rolled from one side of his body to the other. His arms were encased in the sleeves of black fabric that almost absorbed the light around the rather than reflected it. And his chin! An amazing thing, he had ... no, yes, Herb looked again, two chins! And his waist! He was a meter across from hip to hip, at least! Herb's view of life had been largely one of workers who rarely got enough to eat to fill their bellies on a regular basis. But even the most pampered child of privilege couldn't have packed on the fat this chap was sporting without some serious effort!

Herb had been staring so intently at the man's incredible girth that he almost missed seeing Margaret behind him. Not surprising, Herb thought to himself. You could miss seeing an army behind the chubbs on this bloke! Still, she looked magnetic in the dress she was wearing.

"Ah! Mister Wells, I presume," said the fat man as he extended his fleshy palm to Herb. Herb did his best not to squirm as his hand disappeared into the huge man's enormous grip.

"I'm terribly sorry," said Margaret, "I forgot my introductions. Herbert Wells, this is Lord Musgrave."

"Good to finally meet you, sir," said Herbert, "Margaret has talked a great deal of you to me."

"Likewise, I am certain," said Lord Musgrave. "In fact, I've desired to make your acquaintance for some time now." A waiter materialized and placed a chair in behind Musgrave that could have seated two normal sized men. "Margaret here has been effusive in her praise of you and your abilities, Mister Wells."

"Thank you, sir, I'm sure," Herb said. He took his seat after the large man began to seat his ponderous posterior. Margaret sat in between them, seating herself with dainty poise, tossing her hair back quickly in a long, black wave.

Lord Musgrave sat with a long grunt and rested his left hand on the smooth glass knob of his black walking cane. "Wilfred," he said to the waiter without looking at him, "bring us a carafe of the house wine, would you dear boy? And three glasses too. Or, do you not drink, Mister Wells?"

"I most certainly do," said Herb. Herb had gotten used to thinking of himself as a man-of-the-world, the sort who appreciated sophisticated tastes better than most. But something about the ponderous man made Herb feel like a rube, country bumpkin and little-boy-about-to-be-schooled all at once.

"Excellent," said the large man, producing a cigar case from his inner jacket pocket. He popped it open with a flick of his thumb, and the scent of tobacco wafted around both Herb and Margaret. "And, do you smoke as well?" Lord Musgrave asked, looking at Herb.

"Most assuredly," Herb answered, taking a cigar from the offered case. He bit off the nub and, unsure for a second what to do with it, watched as Lord Musgrave did the same and spit it soundlessly into a napkin that he'd brought to his lips. Herb followed suit.

"Good," said Musgrave after he'd lit his and Herb's cigars and taken a few puffs. "I'm glad you are willing to indulge in a few pleasures, Herbert. I never trust a man with no vices. They're so hard for me to predict."

Herb wasn't certain what Musgrave meant by that, but smiled anyway behind the cigar as if he was in on the joke.

"Herbert, the reason I have called you and Margaret in on this little luncheon is because we have a new mission for you, one that requires the utmost commitment and discretion. We have been impressed with both your knowledge of the various circles of London society, as well as your, ahem, flexibility in accepting assignments."

Herb smiled. Circles were good. Inner circles were better. This was the number three man in the circle, Margaret said. Not just *a* circle, but *the* circle. The center circle of *all* the circles!

"Yes, well, I do aim to please," said Herb, "and your group has proven most generous with regards to compensation. How could I give it anything but my best?"

"Of course," the large man said with an icy tone. Herb got the message quickly; when the fat man spoke, it could be flowery as the fat man desired. If Herb spoke to him, it would have to be stripped down to avoid wasting the man's time.

Herb waited.

"Herbert, you are aware of some of the rewards that await those who prove their loyalty to us? Beyond simple exchanges of money for services, that is."

"I ..." Herb began. Margaret's leg brushed up against his. A thrill danced from his knee up to his spine and all the way to his neck, which suddenly felt very, very warm. "I'm aware of some of them, yes."

"Good. There are, in fact, rewards available that even your

imagination would have trouble conceiving. But all in due time."

Musgrave paused, sucking on his cigar and exercising his amazing double chin like an accordion. "We have been preparing you for a great while now, and we believe your time has come. All that remains before your full admittance to our, *ahem*, group, is a test of your loyalty. We need to know that you will not, *ahem*, decide to join with another group whose views may seem momentarily attractive. To that end, we feel that a small assignment or two will show that you are both loyal and useful to us. Does this make sense to you?"

"Perfectly. What's the job?"

Musgrave smiled, and tapped his ashes into an ashtray.

"The first task I will give you, Herbert Wells, is a simple one. Here, take this." Lord Musgrave dug a large hand into his coat pocket, produced a small white envelope and spun it towards Herbert across the table.

Herbert caught it one-handed and looked inside.

It held a small, illustrated card. Drawn on the card was a picture of the Crucifixion, with a dying Christ looking to Heaven and a crucified thief on either side of him. Storm clouds had gathered over Jesus' head, and Mary, Mary Magdalene and John the Apostle were weeping in various poses at the foot of the cross. At the sight of the eyes of Christ, something in Herbert shifted unpleasantly.

"What d'you want me to do with this, then?"

"Destroy it, Mister Wells."

Herbert looked at the picture, and sniffed. Ignoring the discomfort he'd felt a moment ago, he tore the picture once, twice, then three times into eight little pieces. "Is that good enough for you?" he asked, dropping the pieces on the table by his dish.

"Quite, Mister Wells. You see, we had been given to understand that your loyalties might lie with the Church of Rome. There is a distressing rumor that in a moment of weakness, you actually accepted the sacrament of Baptism from that misguided little cleric, Father Brown."

A shot of white-hot anger fired across Herb's face. "Father Brown died saving my life, Lord Musgrave. I'll thank you to keep any unflattering opinions of him to yourself."

"Herbert, darling," began Margaret, her voice cool as silk buried in tundra, "no one is questioning Father Brown's loyalty or bravery. Only his misguided beliefs in the Church of Rome."

"Those beliefs saved my life, Margaret."

"Yes, and ended his. He's dead now, isn't he?"

"But ..."

"Herbert," she said, caressing the back of his neck and looking deeply into his eyes. "He's dead. And you're alive. Just because you benefited from a misguided ideal, doesn't make it any less misguided, does it?"

Herb paused, absorbing Margaret's words while the little, insistent voice in the back of his head that had said he should leave got quieter and quieter.

"Herbert," Musgrave again, "we are given to understand that you have among your own circle of friends a certain young man. One mister Gilbert Keith Chesterton."

"Gil? What about him? If you want me to turn on a friend, you can take a long walk off a short dock, post haste!"

"Why, no, young Herbert! Nothing of the sort! No, not to turn on him. You have only to ... shall we say, turn him *to us*."

"Come again?"

Musgrave smiled again. He sucked the air out of the suddenly brightly lit cigar a second time, and tapped the dead ashes into the tray. "Herbert, you and Mister Chesterton are both of an age when a young man's head can be turned in a variety of directions. We wish to ensure that two young men of superior talent and breeding such as yourself and Gilbert are turned squarely towards our ideals, and fixed there."

"You want me to recruit Gil to your little circle?"

"Yes, now you see."

Herb paused. "Lookahere, Lord Musgrave, when Margaret here introduced me to your little group, I only had to get you a few bits of harmless information. Then you had me sign my name to a few documents as a ghostwriter for a piece of scientifiction that some woman wrote and would likely never be published. I haven't minded being your pawn, since I've been well paid and no one's gotten hurt.

"Now, with the way you're talking, it's sounding less like a harmless game between wealthy men, and more like a game of choosing sides. And now you want me to bring the best friend I've ever had into this little chess game of yours, on your side. I'm just not sure it's the right thing to do."

"Mister Wells, have I mentioned the words right or wrong all afternoon? Men such as we do not bother with such petty concepts unless it suits us. When you've had to walk back and forth the blurred line between right and wrong as often as I have, one ceases to pay attention. We live in a very large jungle, Mister Wells. Not of trees, vines, apes and tigers, but steel, concrete, money and steam. In a jungle, right is only whatever allows you to live for another day. If there are two apes and only one banana, shoving the weak out of the way to take the food becomes the *right* thing to do. You see?"

Herb waited, thinking. "I once said that to Gil on a train. But he said ..."

"He said the same kind of blithering rot that he likely writes about in his columns, didn't he? All about God, fairies, stars and similar twaddle. Herbert, you know how highly we think of you in our organization. You have tremendous potential—far more than you know! You and your friend both could be tremendously *useful* assets in our enterprises. If you would both join us, there are a number within our circle who see near *limitless* potential for the pair of you."

Herbert looked first at Musgrave, then at Margaret. A thought had been brewing for some time in his head, but he'd been reluctant to pay attention to it before this.

"Lord Musgrave, are you the folks who employed the Doctor?"

Musgrave smiled. "The Doctor ... hmmmm... I do have a personal physician at my disposal. Are you feeling ill lately, Herbert?"

"Please don't be coy with me, Lord Musgrave. A little over a year ago, I was running about in the sewers, trying to avoid becoming a dinnertime treat for mollusks. Although he was edited out of my stories, one of my companions was a top-hatted fellow who called himself the Doctor. He knew a lot more about the aliens than anyone I've met before or since, and was privy to a lot of other information as well. One of things he said that I've never been able to confirm is that he worked for an organization called the Special Branch, a group that makes it their business to direct the world through conspiracies and Eugenics, among other things.

"Now, a year or so after I saw him get plucked out of a tripod's collector basket and presumably et by one of the Martians, Margaret here approaches me at a party. Now, through her I've met you, and you've used several phrases the Doctor was also fond of, such as assigning value to people based on how *useful* they are to your organization."

Musgrave raised his amazingly large and flabby hand and batted two of his sausage-thick fingers while looking at Herb. Behind Musgrave, Herb saw their waiter move into action.

"Mister Wells, if I understand you correctly, you are insinuating that there is a secret group of conspirators running the world, that they employed this 'doctor' to aid them in their plans, and with his demise at the hands of the Martian mollusks we have come to recruit you?"

"In a nutshell, yes."

Musgrave smiled and looked at Margaret. Herb couldn't tell from where he was sitting, but Margaret's face twitched slightly, as if she was winking at Musgrave with the eye of hers that was hidden from Herb's vision.

The waiter arrived and placed a chessboard on the table, clearing away glasses, plates and silverware where needed. He next began placing a series of diabolic-looking black chessmen on the board, facing a series of angelic-looking white pieces.

"Leave us," Musgrave said to the waiter in a curt voice, "we will complete this task on our own. Delay our meal a few minutes until I signal you." The waiter nodded and walked away.

"You mentioned pawns, Herbert. Do you play chess?" Musgrave asked, leaning forward with his head over the table and the board.

"I do all right. I can move the pieces, but I'm really not that good."

"Chess," continued Musgrave, giving no sign of hearing Herb's answer, "is a game based upon the medieval form of combat. One wins not by decimating your opponent, but by cornering him and leaving him without options. And in the fray, the lowly pawn is often forgotten and abused, quite often the first piece sacrificed in the pursuit of victory."

Herb's patience was evaporating faster with each word and gesture. When was this fellow going to get to the point? "I understand chess, Lord Musgrave, but I don't see how this little chess clinic answers my ques—"

BOOM! went Musgrave's ham-hand as it grabbed a pawn and slammed it down on the board, making Herb jump in his seat. "The pawn, Herbert. In the hands of an amateur, it is an inconvenience and often thrown aside. But what can a truly skilled player do with a pawn, Herbert? If that pawn continues to move forward and avoid capture as it does its job, what will happen to the pawn?"

Herb had started when Musgrave had grabbed the chess piece. The fat man had moved far quicker than expected.

"If ...," began Herb, hesitantly, "if the pawn keeps moving forward, and isn't captured, then it gets to the end of the board and is promoted. Usually it becomes another Queen, the most powerful piece on the board."

"Yes, Herbert. Precisely. It becomes a Queen—a piece without equal. Except, of course, for the other Queen or Queens. Now, Herbert, what would a player do if a piece were to suddenly develop an independent streak? A tendency to move, say, a square to the right or left of where you put it, when the piece thought you weren't looking?"

"You'd remove it and put something else in its place."

Musgrave leaned back and sucked his cigar again. "Yes, Herbert," he said, puffing clouds of smoke in the air, "you would remove it, with all available speed." Musgrave paused to take another pull on his cigar. "You have a good sense of the game, Hebert. Margaret is indeed a good judge of your character.

"As for the Doctor, Herbert, he did work for us once. Unfortunately, he forgot that in our little game, he was a pawn. He, in fact, believed he had been promoted to the rank of Queen when such had simply not been the case. There is only room for five men of such rank, five Queens, if you will, in the game we play. One day it is possible that you will be one of them. But, if you prove to be unreliable, or no longer useful to our ends," Musgrave gave the slightest flicking motion of his hand and sent one of the expensive chess pieces tumbling to the ground. An indentation shaped like a crescent moon was left where Musgrave had slammed the expensive piece into the dark-colored square.

"I will give you no illusions, however. While the pay will be excellent, and our compensation will not be exclusively of a monetary nature, your work will often be tedious. At times your assignments will be quite unpleasant. But the rewards will be substantial for those who produce desirable results."

"But Lord Musgrave," said Herb, "I'm confused. You still haven't told me exactly who or what it is that I am working for. Nor do I know your aims. Only that they're willing to sell hundreds of ordinary lives to get them."

"Herbert, our aims are simple. We wish to remake the world, and remake it in the image we prefer. We see a need to ensure the best possible future for our race, and are willing to do what is necessary to bring this world about. We envision a world where people are happy, without the needless guilt and anxiety that comes from religion or royalty. Such people are easy to control and manipulate. For they will hold us, their rulers, to no standard of behavior, other than the standards we choose for ourselves."

"I thought religion made people easy to manipulate."

"No, Herbert, no, quite the contrary, in fact. Truly religious people can be quite annoying, in that they insist their leaders live by a frustratingly high standard of personal, moral and ethical conduct. If we wish to do as we please, we must remove religion as a force in society, or at least ensure that religion remains a purely private affair, and ridicule or remove those who would suggest otherwise."

"And how do you propose to do that?"

"In order to effectively manipulate a people, Herbert, it is vitally important to ensure that they feel they are not being manipulated. They must first be convinced that slavishly following our dictates will give them true freedom. Second, they must be told from a very young age that the one religion that could free them from our yoke is, indeed their freedom's greatest enemy. We must convince them that freedom from us would be the worst kind of slavery, and that slavery to us, and us alone, is freedom.

"But I digress. To bring about a well-ordered, tidy world where we are not threatened, sacrifices are necessary. As one cannot obtain a good omelet without breaking a few eggs, so sometimes sacrifices of the ordinary must be made in order that the aims of the extra-ordinary can be realized. And you, Herbert, are most assuredly among those extraordinary persons, or we would not be having this conversation. You not only survived the Invasion, but also prospered. You and your dear friend Gilbert are sterling examples of what can be accomplished, given the correct application of experience upon proper breeding.

"Which returns us to your assignment," said Musgrave, giving another signal with his fingers. The waiter reappeared and removed the chessboard, chessmen and the fallen piece from the floor, whisking them back into the kitchen with almost no sound at all. He returned moments later carrying two steaming plates of food in his hands, with a third balanced on his arm.

They were silent as the waiter set the plates on the table. Herbert, Margaret and Musgrave each had omelets, though Musgrave's was twice as large.

Musgrave fell on his food, devouring it with the fervor of a condemned man eating his last meal. "Now, young Herbert," rasped Musgrave in between bites, "It is my understanding that during your adventures last year, your young friend Gilbert demonstrated a level of resourcefulness and ability very nearly equal to your own."

"In fact," purred Margaret, indexing her body away from Herb slightly and looking off into the distance, "I heard he killed a Martian in the sewers, the same kind that the Doctor, you, and that ridiculous little priest all had to pool their resources to eliminate. Isn't that right?"

Herb bristled. "Now hold on, before you begin singing his praises. Gil's a good chap, but he couldn't fight his way out've a wet paper bag that'd been half-torn up by a rabid rotweiller!"

"Herb, dear ..."

"And you'd probably have to glaze the bag first ..."

"Herb ..."

"With bacon fat!"

"Herbert Wells!"

"Margaret, I'm just sick to death of everyone talking about what a great Martian killer Gil is! Do you know how he and I met? *I* saved *him!* A bunch of alley thugs were turning him into street haggis when I came along, and he'll be the first to admit it! If he's having a honest day, that is!"

There was a slightly awkward pause. Herb realized he'd raised his voice, and his pulse was racing. There was a slight, red haze in the air of the room Herb hadn't noticed before. His breathing was coming in quick bursts that he struggled to control. He closed his eyes and took a breath, humiliated that he'd lost his temper.

And yet ... Herb noticed a funny thing about the reactions of Margaret and Lord Musgrave. Usually when Herb went off like that, people were either embarrassed or fearful.

But instead, Margaret and Lord Musgrave were smiling.

Margaret leaned in, and kissed Herb on the cheek.

"Did I upset you, darling?" she whispered into his ear. A chill danced down his neck and the length of his spine. "I hope you can forgive me."

"Yes, Mister Wells," grunted Musgrave, temporarily ignoring his omelet and tapping the ashes into the ashtray again, "it would seem there is a certain, shall we say, good-natured rivalry between you and your friend?"

"He might not realize it, but yes," Herb said.

"And there's the rub, Mister Wells, is it not?" said Musgrave, slicing his omelet and stuffing more huge bites in his mouth. "In any relationship, one must dominate the other. One exists only by shoving aside another and taking what nature has deemed is yours by virtue of your superior talent and drive. You were perfectly happy to be the dominant player in your partnership, but now young Gilbert has taken that position."

"Or worse, Herbert darling. He was given the glory that ought to have been yours. Not very fair, is it?"

"Now, Herbert," said Musgrave, quickly stuffing another piece in his mouth and swallowing it almost without chewing, "if Gilbert were to come in to our little group, he'd soon learn we're not the bad lot the Doctor made us out to be, and that life with us is truly an adventure. The kind every lad dreams of having."

"A life of adventure," said Margaret, "in the public eye! We can see to it your goals of writing scientifiction are made a reality, dear Herbert."

Herb stopped, looked at the two of them and then at the table. The wine glasses had been smaller than Herb was used to, and the waiter had somehow filled his glass with a dark, presumably alcoholic liquid that looked very, very inviting. He grabbed the glass and quaffed the drink in one gulp, feeling the expensive wine slosh down his throat and burn his gullet down into his stomach.

"I don't think what I'd like to write is the sort of stuff people will accept," he said after a small gasp.

"I've heard of your writings from Margaret, Mister Wells. Frankly, I think it will suit our goals quite nicely. People are more willing to read about intelligences from other worlds since the Martians invaded. And, with a tweak and a twist here and there to the story, you can have men of certain ... principles prevail, and thus influence the culture in certain desirable directions."

"You mean Eugenics? You think the people will actually pay money to buy stories about men with no religion who succeed because of their ancestry and breeding?"

"Mister Wells, you underestimate the willingness of the public to devour that which entertains them. In our case studies, we've found that even the most religiously raised child is not only willing to read about, but cheer for heroes who are liars, murderers, brutes of all kinds, or even students of diabolism. They will do so without question, so long as the story *entertains* throughout."

"Wealth and adoring fans, Herbert dear, and a life of adventure! What more can anyone ask?"

"Well," said Herb hesitating slightly, "what about Gil?"

"Mister Wells, your membership in our little circle will be assured, if you will complete this test of loyalty and usefulness."

"So, before I can walk through the doors you can open, I've got to get Gil on board with me?"

"In a manner of speaking, yes, Mister Wells. Convince him, and I will believe you can persuade strangers as well."

"A life of adventure," mused Herbert aloud. "The kind all men dream of having."

"That all men dream of," said Margaret, her forefinger twirling Herbert's hair, "but so few ever really have."

Herb's eyes closed and he inhaled, his hand dropping unconsciously and unnoticed onto the ripped pieces of the holy card on the table before him. "Margaret," he said as he exhaled, "why do I just know I'm going to regret the chance that had us meet at that silly costume party?"

"Silly boy," she whispered in his ear, "haven't you understood anything? Nothing is ever left to chance. Not even chaos."

"I take it then, Mister Wells, that we have a deal?" Lord Musgrave's voice had become more gravelly as he neared the end of his cigar.

"I'll get Gil to look at you folks."

"Excellent! And, as a secondary objective: I believe Margaret has already told you, that we believe Gilbert received a token of sorts when on the Sky Palace from one of those Vinci-suited pilots. It is a small, fat disk with a series of circles and letters surrounding its center. When you have brought Gilbert aboard, it is imperative that you retrieve this disk and give it to Margaret or myself."

"But what if Gil won't come aboard? What then?"

"What, indeed?" said Musgrave as he ground the remains of his spent cigar into the ashtray, reducing it to dark ashes with so little concern that Herb was only a little frightened at the hint's meaning.

God help me, thought Herb, more in desperation than a sense of prayer, as he felt Margaret's fingers worm their way into his hair. *I'm in it now. In it up to my lip, and a wrong move will drown me.*

Chapter 16

"It is always simple to fall; there are an infinity of angles at which one falls, only one at which one stands." – GKC, *Orthodoxy*

When Gilbert saw the black-gloved man in the doorway, he brought up his hands and tried to back away a step. Quicker than Gilbert had seen almost any move, the man had raised a black-gloved hand and reached with it towards Gilbert.

Not good.

A year or so before, Gilbert's first instinctive reaction would be to run away as quickly as possible, hoping to elude his pursuer in the maze of the office building and its working staff.

But since then, Gilbert had learned some very, very useful moves to get out of a fight. And he'd learned them all from a Chinese train porter named Chang.

Father Brown had mentored Chang before meeting Gilbert. After the Invasion and Father Brown's death, the two young men had been drawn together to learn about the Faith, while Gilbert had taught Chang to better his English, and Chang had taught Gilbert to better his fighting skills.

Unfortunately for Gilbert, Chang had been accepted into the seminary soon after Gilbert began his lessons. Gilbert thus had been taught only and exactly three actual martial arts moves.

First, Gilbert learned how to block a punch, kick or attempted hold, and then how to turn the attack back onto the attacker. Gilbert had used this on Herb during a half-playful fracas they'd had in a Paris cafe right before Gilbert had met Frances.

Gilbert tried to use that move now, his left hand flying in an arc at the gloved hand.

Gil's hand hit his assailant's hand with a solid thunk, and…

And the gloved hand didn't move.

Gilbert paused, his hand and the gloved hand frozen in place.

The gloved hand was solid; hitting it had felt like backhanding a block of granite.

This is going to hurt, a rational part of Gil's mind said as the pain began singing through his hand and down his arm, making him wince.

"Hello, Gilbert," said the man with a tone that sounded more like a hunter finding his quarry than in any form of greeting.

Then, the fingers of the man's gloved hand bent backwards.

Backwards?

In his shock at how solid the hand felt when he'd hit it, Gilbert had unwisely let his hand rest against the back of the black glove. Gil cried out in surprise as the dark fingers bent backwards, curling over Gil's digits in a viselike grip he knew would be unbreakable.

No, pulling away would be impossible, but there was one other trick.

Gilbert bent his knees and dropped straight down, pivoting his fingers in the iron grip of the black-gloved man. He indexed his body sideways, so that his free left hand could hold him on the ground. He then bent both his legs and shot them out again, surrounding the legs of his captor. All this happened in a quarter second, and Gil brought his right leg against the knees and his left leg against the ankles. If done right, his opponent would fall like a brick from a window ledge.

But for the second time in this fight, Gilbert miscalculated. He didn't kick the precise point behind the knees, and his opponent didn't fall.

But he was hit off balance! He let go of Gilbert and began waving both his hands in a search for equilibrium. Gilbert was free! But he had three seconds at most before he'd be in danger again. He yanked his feet towards his body into a crouching position, and then sprang away from his former captor while the black-gloved man spun his arms like a windmill in a monsoon.

Gilbert ran back up the stairs. Getting out that way wouldn't happen now! He'd first have to lose his pursuer, and there was no way to do that in a stairwell. Gil flew up the steps two at a time, trying to pump his legs even faster when he heard the clomp-clomp of Black Gloves' feet chasing him from below. Gil found the door to the next floor, opened it in a fluid motion and ran down the carpeted floors past a number of work cubes.

The floor was deserted—where were his co-workers? Then Gilbert remembered: Friday afternoons right after lunch were often deserted for an hour or more, as the weekly staff ran out for meetings, to chase a story, or (much more often) out to the local pub for a drink or two before going home or out to another weekend assignment. Maybe if he could get back to Chief Eddy?

He'd have to wait to put that plan in motion. This wasn't his floor, and Gilbert didn't yet know the building like the back of his hand. In the year and change he'd worked for the firm as a journalist, he'd been away on assignment as often as in the building itself. He knew the path to and from the street entrance to his desk; beyond that he had only rumor, common sense and instinct.

Instinct said he should find a way down before Black Gloves caught up with him. Gilbert tore around the corner, thoughts of escape whirling through his mind like torn paper pieces in a hurricane. *Stay calm*, he thought. *Remember, fear kills your mind. You've got to think straight, or this fella with the weird fingers is gonna snag you!*

Gilbert had just rounded the corner when a hellish trick of the carpeted floor snagged his toe and made him fall to the ground with a resounding *thud*! *No*, he thought, *if I don't get up ...*

And then, three things happened:

First, Gilbert heard the door behind him swing open, followed by the velvet-soft sound of feet crushing soft carpet. Black Gloves had arrived on the floor, and was looking for Gilbert.

Second, a moment after Black Gloves began his walk towards the very prone Gilbert, there was a metallic *clink* from the other side of the room.

The footsteps paused and waited. Gilbert didn't dare breathe, knowing he'd be noticed as easily as a herd of elephants if he tried to rise or run. Gilbert's patience was rewarded as the sound of retreating steps still made their way to Gilbert's ears. Black Gloves was walking *away!* The noise across the room had drawn his attention, and Black Gloves was walking away from Gilbert!

And then, the third and most curious thing happened.

When Gilbert fell, he'd ended up at the foot of a line of pneumatic messenger tube openings—thirty or forty in all, lined up like open brass mouths. The openings ranged in size from as wide as his head in the far corner to an opening narrow as two fingers next to his head on the ground.

And it was in one of these smallest of openings that Gilbert saw a small message drop with nearly no noise at all, only the slightest whisper of air.

Gilbert risked a look—it had a crude 'G' scrawled on it in ink. He pulled it out of the holder, careful not to make a sound while giving a furtive look over his shoulder.

The message, unlike virtually everything else that was transported by the whooshing air of a messenger tube, had not been placed into a cylindrical metal container-cell. Container-cells protected messages from potential damage, kept together multiple pages or notes, and made a loud *clank* noise on arrival to let recipients know something had landed in their pneu-mail slot.

But this message was different. Gilbert looked at the paper he'd just pulled out of the tube—it was rolled like a scroll, no ribbon or wax to seal it shut. He unrolled it and found a hastily scrawled message:

G,—STAY DOUN, CRAWL FWD, THREW DOR, UP + DOUN!

Well, the writer couldn't spell. But Gilbert wasn't in a position to quibble! He crawled softly towards the open doorway in front of him.

'*Chink! Chink! Chunk!*' There were three separate metallic sounds across the room away from him as three container-cells, two small and one large, slammed into the bottoms of their messenger tubes. Gilbert heard several slamming sounds as his pursuer stamped his foot or brought his surprisingly solid hand down where he'd thought Gilbert would be hiding.

Whoever my helper is, thought Gilbert, *he knows how to lead this black-gloved fellow away from me.* Gilbert tried to remember some of the adages that his Pa had said about hunting—how did animals escape hunters, again?

But Black Gloves thwarted Gilbert's attempt to remember. Even as Gilbert tried to creep away, he heard Black Gloves' voice carry over the workstations.

"Mister Chesterton?" The voice had the lilt of a cockney accent that tried hard to be more mainstream British, "I'm terribly sorry if I've injured you. You startled me and I fear I reacted poorly. What say we start over again fresh, hey?"

Ignoring the offer, Gilbert inched forward, ready to rise and sprint if he had to. An open doorway to a different set of stairs stood no more than eight feet in front of him, but Gilbert knew he needed patience. He'd been caught as a child at too many games of hide-and-seek when he thought he was home free, and wouldn't chance it now.

Slam! Another noise, so loud that Gilbert almost started from his hiding place. Sounded like a pipe hitting metal—was the guy armed now? "Mister Gilbert, it would appear you have aroused the interest of some very influential gentlemen," said Black Gloves, "and such gentlemen do not like to be kept waiting. I'm not sure how you're keeping a few steps ahead of me as much as you are, but y'see (*Clang!*... pause...) my employer pays my firm by the hour, and the more hours it takes, the more we're paid. Too many hours, an' we're cast off for another firm wot finds people. If you don't come with me, our client'll likely hire people far more brutal than me an' me mates."

Keep talking, you big black-gloved ape, thought Gilbert as he crawled quickly and soundlessly across an aisle, now only five feet away from the open doorway through which another staircase waited. *Why did the message tell me to go up,* Gilbert thought, *then down? Down to the basement?*

"Mister Chesterton, I grow tired of this game! You can't escape me—I've been doing this for years, now!"

And all you've learned is how to beat yer gums too much! Gilbert thought, turning left and crawling to the stairwell. Black Gloves, wrapped up in his frustrated monologue, kept talking until Gilbert was halfway up the stairs.

Suddenly, Gilbert heard stomping feet behind him. He stopped any pretense at being quiet and launched himself up the stairs, around the stairwell and through the next door at the top.

He burst through the door and quickly shut it behind him, thanking every angel in Heaven that it had a bolt on his side. He slid it into place and got out of the way of the door. He'd heard too many stories of street toughs who thought themselves safe from police behind a locked door, only to learn too late that most locked doors were lousy shields against the average bullet.

As he pressed himself against the desks that lined the aisle in an effort to stay out of the doorway, Gilbert heard another loud whirring noise as a nearby stippling machine began belching out steam and small dark clouds of coal smoke. A piece of paper had just finished coming out of the stipplograph, and Gilbert tore it along the metal bar that held newly printed papers with reckless speed.

G., it said, —GO E TO OTHER STAIRS TO BASMNT—NOW!

Still holding the paper in his right hand, Gilbert looked up to the windows. The rays of the afternoon sun were shining through some of them, and Gilbert ran to the door opposite them, stuffing the paper in his pocket without taking the time to fold it. Behind him a series of dull, rhythmic thuds fell on the bolted wooden door, until a loud crack sounded, followed by the sounds of splintering wood. Gilbert looked back. There was a hole in the door behind him, with Black Gloves' dark hand shoved through it, groping for the bolt. The black glove had been torn, and the brass fingers beneath it shot a brief, bright reflection into Gilbert's eyes ...

Brass?

Uh oh.

The hand pulled back through the hole, splintering the wood

further. Gilbert opened the next door behind him, ran through, slammed and bolted it as he had done to the other door. Hopefully that would delay Black Gloves even longer!

Gilbert kept running, now across the room and through another door. He slammed it shut, then pulled a desk in front of the door to barricade it. He heard the other, unbroken door he'd run through splinter and break under his pursuer's metal hand. Gilbert heard a muffled curse when Black Gloves tried the door handle and found it bolted shut, too.

Gilbert ran across the office room past more rows of desks, opened the next door and found another stairwell.

Down I go, he thought, shutting the stairwell door behind him as the barricaded door splintered and broke. He sped down the stairs, leaping two, three, four at a time.

Will I be safe? thought Gilbert. Things were pretty calm this past year. Will I be running for my life again? Gilbert scampered down one flight, then another, then another. A few more, and Gilbert guessed he must be somewhere near the basement, at a level even lower than where he'd started as a clacker drudge over two eventful years ago.

Then the stairs ran out. There were no more levels to descend, only a large metal door with no visible handle, knob or other means of opening from the outside.

Gilbert breathed, the silence above giving him his first sense of security since being called into the Chief's office. He tapped on the door hesitantly with his knuckles, hoping for an answer from the other side.

A very long minute passed.

The door stirred, then ground open with a scraping, metal-on-metal noise. The seam between door and doorway widened with agonizing slowness, moving only a millimeter or two at a time. *Come on*, Gilbert thought. *That desk isn't going to hold someone Black Gloves' size forever. Come on, come on ...*

Upstairs, a now familiar, *bang* sounded as Black Gloves slammed open the stairwell door.

And after that, Gilbert heard a set of heavy, clomping feet charging down the stairs.

Chapter 17

"The world will never starve for want of wonders, but only
for want of wonder."
– GKC, *Tremendous Trifles*, 1909

The crack between the door and doorway widened by an inch,
two inches, then five inches as Gilbert tried to stuff himself into
the widening, but still too small, doorway.

"Open up faster! He's coming!" Gilbert yelled to no one he could
see. The footsteps were getting louder by the second—Black Gloves
must have been barely a flight above him by now!

"Are you inside yet?" a voice called to Gilbert. It was male, and
not much older than Gilbert himself.

Gilbert finally popped through the doorway like a cork out of a
bottle. "Yes," he called out, with a voice that was partway between a
yell and a grunt. "Close it! He's right behind me!"

"Already done, Mister Gilbert," said the voice again. Gilbert
squinted—the room was rather dark, lit by a small gaslight bulb. The
words had come from a shadowy figure a few feet from Gilbert that
darted back and forth along the wall, throwing levers and twisting
knobs.

The door behind Gilbert had already begun grinding again, and as
Gilbert turned, he saw that the door he'd come through was at least a
foot thick, shaped like a giant pie-wedge with a pivot set into the small
end, and controlled by a huge, motorized piston that pulled and pushed
the massive wood and metal contraption with sounds of hissing steam
and the steady crunch of well-oiled metal on metal.

The stomping of feet became louder than ever, as Gilbert's pursuer
reached his level and ran for the shutting door. The brass-colored
fingers, peeking through the torn leather of the glove, popped through
the narrowing doorway and gripped the door tightly, as if trying to hold
it firmly and force it open.

Gilbert could tell in five seconds that it was a losing battle.
Although the brass fingers curled around the door jam, dug in and
actually slowed the inexorable progress of the door, it was only for a
second.

The door pushed on. Gilbert watched with a horrid fascination as
the door closed on the shiny fingers. No scream sounded from the
fingers' owner, only a dull scraping of metal on metal. As the door

The Young Chesterton Chronicles

crushed the fingers, the leather surrounding them split, and the gaslight glinted off more dull brass. The fingers were amputated in less than a second, falling to the stone ground with a sound like heavy copper coins.

Gilbert didn't move until the door had stopped. There was no sound from his pursuer from the other side, no roars of anger, no attempts to bash the door in. After several quiet seconds, Gilbert moved in close to the fingers and poked them with his shoe.

All four of them began to buck, jump and flail around like landed fish. Gilbert jumped, yelped, and backed up rapidly, just turning to run when he plowed into the shadow who'd been standing in the room with him for the last minute of his adventure.

112 | P a g e

Chapter 18

"For there is but an inch of difference between the
cushioned chamber and the padded cell."
– GKC, *Charles Dickens*, 1906

The room was stone-brown, clean, and had the window blinds raised just enough to let the rays of the afternoon sun shine in, while keeping the sun out of the eyes of the man seated on the white stone chair.

He was an old man. That much was obvious to all who saw him. But his bright, alert eyes and quick movements would make it difficult for most people to pin down his age, even to the correct decade. He had a full, shaggy head of white hair that still sported a tinge of gray at the very top. His forehead consisted of healthy peach-colored skin, and was raised high over his thick, white eyebrows. His eyes, which remained a defiant six inches above the level of the sunlight in the room, were piercing blue. He'd cultivated that gaze over a lifetime, and could count on the fingers of one hand the people who had not succumbed to the full power of his eyes when he'd demanded someone's information, agreement or confidence. They were eyes that could dance with the bright blue joy of an animated toddler, or fire a glare that could intimidate the angriest of lynch mobs or the most determined of lawmen.

His beard was white, neat and trimmed within an inch of his chin. He wore a blue general's uniform, though the badges, medals, epaulets and other decorations on it would have been quite perplexing to any student of historical conflict. Here on his right breast was a Purple Heart from the American Revolution. On his shoulder were the golden twined ropes and tassels more akin to a South American generalissimo than any army on the North American continent, and his hat was a defiantly simple kind of blue pillbox variety worn by United States infantrymen during the American Slavery Wars, or the Civil War, or the War of Northern Aggression, depending on which side you fought, lived or died on. Above his left breast were a series of colored stripes that, were they accurate, were from the American Civil War, the War of 1812, the American Revolutionary War, the Texarcanan Secession Wars, and a host of other conflicts he would have had to be well into his twentieth decade to have fought and bled in.

He brought his right hand to his mouth and gave a deep, inhaling pull on his cigar with a slow, deliberate motion, one timed to make the underling before him squirm inside. The cigar flared with brief ember light and then hid behind the cloud of smoke. After flowing from his mouth, the cloud climbed lazily into the air in a delicate ballet of transparent purple strings and circles.

"And, y'say the lad is on his way?" he intoned with a drawl. The underling looked behind him at the twenty or so flunkies that were dressed in similarly opulent military costumes. Each of them regarded their colleague with stony silence; happy it hadn't been themselves who had been called to give an account of the Emperor's latest project.

"Our report," began the underling, trembling in his military longcoat, the sun shining in his eyes and reflecting off the gold-rope epaulets on his shoulders and the white mane-plume on his ceremonial sea-captain's hat, "from our spy in the London network states that he, ah, or rather his editor was to, ah, give him the assignment of covering life in the Confederate States, Emperor. Though I've no word as yet whether he has, erm, actually *accepted* the assignment as of yet, you see."

Another pull on the cigar brought another cloud of smoke. This wasn't going well. "Anything else, Commissar?"

"Er, well, yes. It would seem the lad has managed to incur the, um, ire, or wrath, as it were, of a rather prominent British businessman. One with a reputation for, well, *rash* actions, your Lordship."

A pause. Not even a pull on the cigar. The Commissar, as the Emperor had named him, began to sweat. Commissar Toadpipe's demotion and execution had begun with a pause just like this.

"Is our boy, then, in jeopardy, Commissar? And if so, what arrangements can we make to ensure his safe delivery?"

"I am not certain of the particulars, Emperor. But he has proven resourceful. He's already eluded one set of thugs set upon him in Berlin, and avoided taking revenge on the Williamson heir for it."

"Hurm. A young man with an eye to avoid vengeance. Well, we can work with that. Gentlenobles of the North American Aristocracy," the old man said, raising himself from his seated position, now ignoring the relieved Commissar, and instead looking briefly at his seated assistant. She was busily copying his every word for posterity's sake. "I chose each of you myself. And each of you agreed to sign yourselves to my service for the rewards I promised you, once I fulfilled my goals. Am I correct?"

The fifty Commissars, all identically dressed, all spoke as one. "YES, EMPEROR!" they bellowed.

"Sad to say, some of you would like to obtain said rewards a little prematurely."

No one in the room said anything. Silence was the highest form of approval available in the royal chamber, as the Emperor had decided this week that he despised applause.

He strode to the open window and stared at the snowy mountain range in the distance.

"If history serves, gentlenobles, I have perhaps another ten years at most on this Earth to make my dreams a reality. As I have so few sands left in my hourglass, you'll pardon me if I seem more than a little intolerant at being misinformed or outright failed by any of my Commissars."

He placed his hand on the significantly sized flintlock pistol tucked into his waistband. He then enjoyed a private smirk as the Commissar who had finished his report flinched, preparing to fall to his knees in the traditional and prescribed pose for begging mercy.

"But, as I see it, you haven't failed me yet, Commissar Elksbladder."

The Commissar relaxed, rising back up to his full height of five-foot-one, which allowed his saber's scabbard to dangle an inch off of the floor again.

"But then again, you might feel I am traveling to and in possession of a one-way ticket to that warm, happy, place known as senility-ville. Rest assured, if that were the case, gentlemen, I would not have known of the unsubtle plot hatched against me by my most recent protégé. Instead, my mind fully retains all its faculties, my will fully retains its ability to act, and I fully retain my seat of power. An excellently well-cleaned seat, I might add. Ensure that my compliments reach the cleaning staff."

The court of men nodded sagely. The Emperor's assistant, nearly invisible until now, made a note. Her eyes looked intently at her notepad through the large lenses of her glasses, her exquisite fingers directing the pen to make notes in flawless, calligraphic script. The Emperor was right, as usual. The chair hadn't the slightest whiff of blood or cleaning solvent. No one would have known that a young man had been murdered while sitting in it only that morning.

"However, I've been wondering where my latest young ward got it into his head that he or his friends could sit in my chair without consequence. Or that he could enter my throne room unannounced, with only a contingent of five lightly armed workers to do so. Where, I say, where did such a callow youth get it into his head that I was so weak that a band of tiny-minded fools had a chance of usurping me?"

The Emperor's gaze flitted from nervous face to nervous face. No one was willing to admit that they had inspired such a feeble attempt.

"Obviously, first suspicions fall on Commissar Dreeble, as he was charged with showing my ward, Victor, how the city worked. Dreeble, however, hasn't had an original thought in his head since the Slave Wars. Correct, Commissar?"

"What?" asked Dreeble.

"Precisely," answered the Emperor without missing a beat. "Now, as you know, I'm not entirely opposed to attempts to take my throne. I am in fact of the mind that a good assassination attempt keeps a leader's mind healthy and active, to say nothing of how having a heavy caliber weapon pointed at you gets the old ticker thumping. However …"

The Emperor drew his pistol, put it to the head of the nearest unsuspecting Commissar, and pulled the trigger. Half of Commissar Greedleberg's head disappeared in a flash of red mist and bone fragments. The weapon was well designed, however, and true to its function, it propelled all portions of its target directly forward, without soiling the uniforms of the Commissars on either side of Greedleberg.

"Commissar Elksbladder," said the Emperor, holstering his weapon and taking another pull on his cigar, "you will ensure that young Gilbert Chesterton will be brought safely to my throne room within the week. As for the rest of you ..." The forty-eight remaining Commissars held their breaths, though none dared close their eyes.

Greedleberg's body, finally realizing it was dead, fell and hit the floor with a heavy *thud*.

"An' the next time any of you have thoughts of revolution in your economized craniums," the Emperor continued, "you just remember your recently retired comrade here. If you must make attempts on my life, at least make them interesting. Greedleberg's attempt on my life through young Victor bored me. And I only shoot people when I'm bored."

He stalked back to his chair and sat with a flourish, waving his cape to a space where it would not be too wrinkled when he sat down.

"That's all, gentlemen."

They turned and filed out obediently, in a single file and in step.

When they were gone, the Emperor turned to his assistant. "Was that excessive, do you think?"

She turned to him and adjusted her large-rimmed glasses. "By definition, nothing the Emperor does can be excessive, since he sets the standard by which all actions in his kingdom are judged."

"Good girl," he said, staring off into space and smoking the cigar.

After a few minutes he stood again. "I'm going to inspect the city. On my own. See if the last batch of workers we got has any potential replacements for Commissar *Horizontalus* down there."

"Yes, Emperor."

"And have the cleaning crew come in and take care of the mess here."

"Yes, Emperor. Experience breeds excellence."

"Nice little aphorism, Galatea. Did I make that up?"

"Yes, Emperor."

"I knew it. Crackerbarrel, I'm a genius."

He walked out the door and slammed it behind him. The assistant swallowed and grabbed the nearest speaking tube, called for the cleaning crew and waited.

After they left, she choked back the vomit that wanted very, very much to leap out of her gut after the unexpected violence she had just witnessed. But she was a well-trained professional, and instead only wept two tears. She then inhaled and went to her next duty of the day, tucking back the single lock of her red hair that had come out of place.

Chapter 19

"Progress should mean that we are always changing the world to fit the vision, instead we are always changing the vision."
– GCK, *Orthodoxy*, 1908

W ho are you?" Gilbert asked, ready to fight.
"Gilbert," said the dark silhouette in front of him, "I know it's been a while, but I didn't think it was that long. You really don't remember your old workmate?"

Gilbert looked closer, as the speaker stepped under the dim light of a gas globe. First his new friend's glasses looked familiar, then his face. But the hair should be ... scragglier?

"Wiggins!" shouted Gilbert happily! "Wiggins, what are you doing here? I haven't heard anything about you since that run in with the Grey Mare Boys."

Gilbert and Wiggins had both suffered through a purgatorial few months, working in the clacking room for a tyrannical overseer named Mr. Philandron, and when Wiggins had been fired, Gilbert had been unfairly painted as a workplace snitch. Wiggins had later joined a street gang called the Grey Mare Boys, the leader of which had very nearly beaten Gilbert to death over Wiggins' alleged 'firing' just before the Invasion.

"Come on," said Wiggins, beckoning Gilbert to follow him as he stepped down a stairwell lit by gaslight lamps. "I'll tell you the story on the way down. Follow me!"

The stairwell looked like something out of a medieval castle, with stone steps descending in a steady curve lit by the lamps' pale light. "Quite the setup you have here, Wiggins," Gilbert said as they descended. "It's deeper and darker than the clacker room was, but I bet Mr. Philandron isn't around to make anyone's life miserable."

Wiggins smiled. "That's the truth. How I got it is a story in itself. After that run-in with Ed Pearse and the Grey Mares, I tried all over to get a job to keep the roof over our heads and food on the table for the wife an' new baby. But in the end I had to settle for running messages for rich blokes, and that didn't do much but keep hunger at bay while all the wolves I owed money to kept chomping at the door. 'Course, things got even leaner after the Invasion, what with so much of London broken into little pieces all over.

"But then a day came when it was so cold you could feel the jets of freezing air like they were knives in your ribs—augh! That day I saw one a' them messenger tubes overhead. It'd cracked from the cold, or some street urchin throwin' a rock at it or somthin', and one 'a the container cells was just sitting there, half out've the tube, pressurized air hissing out next to it like an angry snake.

"'Well,' says I, 'where there's a container from a pneumatic tube, there's usually something in it! And even an empty container could be sold for a few coppers if you know the right buyer.' I scampered up the drainpipe on the side of the building closest to the break in the tube, made the break a little wider with the knife I carried then to keep me safe, and the cell slid out like a baby on a butterslide.

"I dropped down, opened the cell, and what do you know? It was a set of instructions for a firm's business concerns how they were gonna wreck their rivals!"

"You knew the firm?"

"I'd been runnin' their pieces of paper back an' forth for months after the Invasion. I went to the rival firm, managed to sneak into one of the mucky muck's rooms, and flashed the plans to his face before he could call the local muscle to toss me out. I went home with a half-a-crown in my pocket for my troubles, and a bright idea to become a man of independent means.

"I knew I had something special. I watched while they built up the messenger tube system up again, piece by piece. I watched where every pipe went, and where every tube an' every pneumatic air pump and steam-driver was installed. I jotted things down on paper, my hand, in my head, everywhere I could until I found out they were done. And then I had this ..."

Wiggins had just reached the bottom of the winding stairwell, and pointed to the largest wall in the stone basement room. On it was drawn a crude map of the city of London, with pieces of charcoal, pastel, ink pencil and other dark-colored implements that barely showed up to Gilbert's eyes in the dim light on the dirt encrusted wall. Drawn over the map, though, in bright white chalk were a series of long and interconnecting lines, presumably the network of pneumatic tubes that businesses used to send and receive information throughout the city of London.

"Tweren't easy," Wiggins said, "but the more everybody gets to using analytical engines to get things done, the more information they need to feed the beasts. And whoever controls that information and where it goes can get quite rich doing so."

"You mean you make money doing this, Wiggins?"

"I make a nice piece of flash. Look, Gilbert, I don't mind showing you, since I'm feeling it's like I'm making up for that beating you got from Pearse and the Grey Mares. But before I say anymore, I want your word as a Christian you'll not tell anyone else what you've seen or heard here today."

"Not a word, Wiggins. And don't worry, I won't split hairs about what you told me when. Everything down here is between you and me alone. Just don't ask me to cover up anything illegal or immoral, deal?"

"Deal, Gilbert. That's the best part of this—there's no law written about it at all! I can't break a law if there's no law to break, y'see? Look, over here," Wiggins said, drawing Gilbert over to a bizarre mechanical invention that appeared to grow out of the stone wall itself.

A very large, slightly tilted table dominated the apparatus. Set about waist high, its tilt against the far end of the wall meant that that anyone seated could easily reach or read the dozens of dials, levers, dials, gages and other gadgets various controls set on the board's face.

Gilbert looked at the array and felt a vague sick feeling in his stomach. He couldn't quite figure out why he felt so awful, until he realized that looking at Wiggins' setup reminded him of how dwarfed he felt by his horrible clacker job under the watchful eye of their old overseer, Mr. Philandron.

"Boy, if old Philandron could see you now, hey Wiggins? I bet he'd feel bad for how he fired you."

"Meh," said Wiggins, taking a seat in front of the control panel. "I know just where he's working now. They've got him watching over a bunch of older men doing sums with adding machines in a different basement office. I keep tabs on the bloke, and I think he's beginning to figure out that when he treats his people bad, a lot of his stuff gets lost in the tubes and doesn't reappear until he's made amends."

"You devil," Gilbert said, smiling.

"Oh, it's a tough job, but someone's got to do it. Seriously, Gilbert, if you need information, let me know. If things keep going as they are, I'll be able to find anything you need from Fleet Street to the Rookery."

Gilbert gave a low whistle. "That's amazing," he said. "How does the whole thing work anyway?"

"Two parts, really. First, I've got a few little fellows around town who'll run messages and overhear things at businesses who use the pneumatic lines. Second, when I know something special is going to be coming down the pipe, I pull a bunch of levers here and there, and send a few signals to my boys. Then at key places in the pneumatic tubes around town, tracks get switched, little messenger tube-sized doors open and shut, and in minutes rivers of information flow into my office here like poor boys to a rich young widow. I read it, note it, and send it on its way to its destination with no one being the wiser. And if it's worth knowing ..."

"You promise to keep it quiet or offer it to a competitor, all for a price."

"Precisely."

"Aren't you worried? Not just from a legal but a moral standpoint? Some folks might call this stealing."

"I thought of that. If the stuff I was looking at were truly secret, they'd send it by foot messenger or deliver it themselves. And I don't keep the information—just look at it as it goes by. What I have is like a bunch of little ears that overhear conversations in the men's room, at the lunch table or near the workstation. If you were truly worried about something, you likely wouldn't speak about it with a voice loud enough to be overheard. Thus, my conscience is clear. Besides, Geke old boy, it helped me find out about that little visitor you had today."

"First, please don't call me Geke. They used to call me that in debating club, and ... hey, how did you know that, anyway?"

Wiggins, still seated and looking like a cat who'd just eaten a very, very tasty canary, patted the nearest lever of his machine.

"Now you are starting to scare me a bit," Gilbert said. "Seriously, though, Wiggins, who was that fellow with the metal fingers, and how did you find out about him?"

Wiggins reached into one of his desk drawers and pulled out several sheets of paper. "I first saw your name when I was doing a little eavesdropping on the Williamson estate. This paper was an order to transfer a nice little sum from Daddy Doubleyew over to a set of brothers in a Utah bank. Your initials are mentioned here several times here, with a bunch of explanation points beside them."

"Yep. Herb and I ran afoul of Daddy's boys in Germany. They got sore when junior asked for more services from them and he wasn't willing to pay up."

"Well, no matter now. I found out about your little four-less-fingered friend back there almost by accident from a different bank. See these?"

Gilbert looked at a new pair of papers. "This looks like another bank statement. What's this other one? It looks like the kind of memo I get at work when I'm in trouble."

"That almost went out to the trash with a stack of laundry lists," Wiggins said. "I remember it clearly: 'Funds have been transferred,' it began. Well, that kind of thing always gets my attention. 'Deposit made in full from B Estate. Awaken the P and send him after GKC. Try his workplace at the Times first. He just returned & is seldom at home.'"

Gilbert felt a chill up his spine. How did they know his workplace, home, and personal habits? "These fellas have been watching me for a while," he said quietly.

"And they have quite a few resources, too, Gil. I knew trouble was headed your way when the stipplograph cameras saw your new friend enter the building, especially when I saw he had one arm bulkier than the other. See these fingers?" said Wiggins, holding up the severed brass digits that his wall had amputated from Gilbert's pursuer.

"American made," continued Wiggins, as Gilbert turned the now-still fingers over in his own hands. "These have been cropping up more and more since the Invasion, Gil. The Swiss had a few models like this, designed by their own analytical engines and cobbled together by master craftsmen. Sometimes they could take a whole year to make one. But their innards were all clockworks and gears, and had to be wound up at the day's end.

"These, on the other hand, these fingers are all wires and hinges, using some of that alien technology they adapted since they pulled apart the Tripods. And see here, how they're curved over the knuckle joints? And made of a brass alloy? German ones have a much more fancy design, with wavy spikes and etched designs. American ones are made to be mass-produced. And though all the craftsmen wag their tongues about it, these kinds of artificial limbs are going to be quite commonplace in the next war we have. Anyone who invests in them can count on making a great deal of money. Oh, it's done stippling. Now, look at this," Wiggins said, grabbing a piece of paper as it slowly fed out of the stipplograph. He was by now so excited that he pulled it out before the machine was finished, and tore a jagged edge at the end of the piece. The ripping sound was very loud in the silent basement.

At the sound of the tearing paper, something jabbed Gilbert from inside his head. His mouth went dry and he twitched, his head snapping slightly to the left. It was slight and sudden, but not so subtle that Wiggins didn't notice.

"Is everything alight, Gilbert? You've gone a bit pale."

Gilbert nodded, swallowed and continued, his voice sounding normal as he looked at the picture of an artificial, metallic hand.

"Sorry," he said to Wiggins. "Something about tearing cloth always sets me off a bit. Getting back to the arm, here: I could see why a government would like something like this," Gilbert said, trying hard to sound normal. "A soldier gets hit and loses an arm or a leg, and there's no need to send him home with a pension. Just fit a shiny metal hand where the stump was and he could be firing a gun again in a week."

"Or running on a brass leg. There's a firm in the West end that's all ready to unveil it after a few more trials ... but I've said too much already. Your boy comes from across the pond, or at least his arm did. You've got a knack for making people angry at you, Gilbert!"

"Well, I am a writer, and a Christian. These days there's no better way to get a whole pile of folks upset with you from both sides of the aisle. Whoever this 'P' fellow is, do you think he's another, more expensive assassin from Williamson?"

"That I don't know. I'd say it's likely, considering that you were attacked just a little bit ago in Berlin by that fancy-pants' thugs. 'Course, if he were interested in killing you, there would have been very little I could've done about that. One blast from a pepperbox pistol, and you'd have been all over the wall."

"Good point. Maybe making myself scarce isn't such a bad idea after all. They could probably canonize Father Brown without my help in Rome. Besides, I've never traveled in an airship before."

"Oh, yes, about that. You might find there have been a few changes to your accommodations."

"What?"

Wiggins smiled. "Let's go to the docks. You'll see."

Gilbert turned over what Wiggins said in his head as Wiggins blindfolded him, then walked Gilbert through a door and started leading him further through his bizarre maze of underground tunnels. He quickly lost track of his path, and the experience reminded him uncomfortably of his adventures in the sewers a year before.

After several minutes, Gilbert felt a breeze on his cheeks. The dank air of Wiggins' dungeon/office faded away, replaced by the comparatively pleasant smell of the London Rookery slums. A few more minutes of walking, and Gilbert's blindfold was removed. He was in an unfurnished room with one door, whose blackened wooden beams looked like they had been placed sometime during the American

Revolutionary War.

"This is where we part ways, Gilbert, my friend. You'll have to find your own way to the airship port before your flight takes off in two hours."

"Two hours? I thought I was leaving at six."

"That was when you were traveling in the Tiger Moth, a Zeppelin that isn't much better than a tin can strapped to a child's circus balloon with bailing wire. It has all the comforts of home, if you were raised by bilge rats."

"You're kidding, right?"

"Your chief did the best he could on short notice, which is no good at all in the world of airship travel. I, on the other hand, found you much better accommodations on an earlier flight for roughly the same amount of money."

"Define 'roughly.'"

"The same number of digits. And drawn so deviously from so many different places in Mr. Williamson's accounts that he won't know he's bankrolled your ticket until your trip is long over, if ever."

"Well," said Wiggins, patting Gilbert's shoulders with both hands, "I've got to go, Gilbert. Enjoy the ship, and enjoy New York and San Francisco. Oh, and don't leave until you've counted to a hundred. Count slowly, please, by ones." With that, Wiggins left the room and Gilbert began counting. When he reached a hundred, he opened the door, left the room, went down two flights of rickety stairs and found the dirty, filthy street.

He had a little money still from when he left his rented room this morning, and hailed a four-wheeled growler cab once he'd left the building and seen just how unpleasant a neighborhood he'd been left in. Gilbert was no stranger to squalor; he'd lived in the Rookery himself during his time as a clacker. But since then, the city of London had been smashed and broken in swaths and was as of yet only partially rebuilt. Travelling on foot around here dressed as he was made him a rather obvious target.

Gilbert entered the growler and passed a few coins to the cabby, trying to ignore the many eyes of the locals. Gilbert shut the door quickly and waited for the cabby to leave. So intent was Gilbert on not attracting attention by returning stares, that he failed to notice a small boy who had watched Gilbert's entry with interest, and then scampered off.

He rode to the docks without incident, leaving the carriage and blending in with the multitudes of passengers bound for the American shores through the wonder of air travel.

It would be a good quarter mile of walking before he got to the docks themselves, but the airship was so large it already filled the sky before him.

Though he'd wanted to get on board quickly, Gilbert stopped at the sight of the gigantic airship and whistled low. He had never traveled in one, but had heard it was very similar to riding in a ferryboat if you ignored the hundred-of-feet-in-the-air part.

But what hovered before him in the setting sun was more than a Zeppelin. Held aloft by two enormous dirigibles attached side by side and a rear-mounted triad of enormous propellers, the vessel that Wiggins' string-pulling had gotten Gilbert onto was far more than a standard transport vessel. More like a giant ocean liner, or perhaps a floating battleship. The passenger gondola alone was at least half the size of the Titanic. If you counted the engine room, steerage levels open-air decks and dirigibles, the ship was at least a thousand feet from stem to stern.

Yes, lad, Gilbert thought to himself, *hard work pays off. But sometimes it most certainly does pay to know the right people, too.*

Gilbert began the short walk to the gangplank, a long metal walkway attached to both the dock and the underside of the vessel that swayed just slightly in the gentle afternoon breeze.

Gilbert had a thought as he walked up towards the plank. *I'll have to make sure Chief Eddy gets a telegram from me, letting him know I'm still on the job, even though I'm not on the airship I was supposed to be on.* Traveling on a luxury liner high above the Earth was an experience to remember, but would be a lousy story to tell if it ended with him losing his job! Still, if Williamson were truly in pursuit, Gilbert would be better off not mentioning which ship he was on. If he sent his message to the Chief from the docks instead of the ship itself, there'd be no way to trace him. His traveling arrangements would remain happily unknown to all but him and ... just what would you call Wiggins' profession, anyway? He wasn't a clacker anymore. Since he worked with pneumatic tubes, maybe a ... pnacker? With a silent 'p'?

Halfway to the gangplank, a colored bowling pin flashed in front of him, surprising him out of his thoughts and making him take a step back.

A juggler, dressed in a black frock coat and a battered, grey top hat, was tossing the colorful ninepin, a rubber ball, a handkerchief and a knife into the air, while a small pet monkey climbed up and down her body, using her arms and even her hair as swinging bars.

Gilbert smiled. This was a friend of Herb's that he'd described, but that Gilbert had never actually met. Aldonza the Magnificent was the name she used, and she juggled for coins on the street when she wasn't pick-pocketing the wealthy, or jimmying the locks on their homes.

"A coin!" she said, her spirits apparently unaffected by the cold, "A coin for a woman willing to entertain those waiting for the ships?"

Gilbert smiled, and dug into his pocket. He had a shilling, and tossed it to her, as Herb had once told him he should if he ever met Aldonza. Just as Herb had described, the monkey swung off her outstretched arm at the sight of the glittering coin, did a little summersault in the air, grabbed the coin and kissed it as he landed with both hairy feet on the ground.

"Thank you, sir! God save you!" she said, and began facing another, well-to-do couple with her juggling tricks.

Gilbert sighed, remembering happier times with his mother. Gilbert had learned things from his parents that at the time did not seem in the least bit unusual. As was and still is the case with most young people, normal is whatever you grow up with.

But Gilbert had since learned that his parents had been anything but ordinary. The odd thing was that unlike the other parents he knew, Gilbert's folks were unwilling to teach him their best skills. Pa showed him how to shoot, but never using his special rifle with the dials, pipes and adjustable magnifying glasses set on top of the stock. And Ma would never let young Gilbert into the kitchen when she was preparing any game Pa brought home, especially when she used her special, long knives that she liked to spin in her hands before she used them.

But eventually, that had changed. Ma had taught Gilbert one of her more unusual skills, though he'd found out about them by accident.

It had been a hot day in June when seven-year-old Gilbert had come home early from a long walk and heard the noises coming from the barn. Noises that sounded a bit like the tire swing at the pond behind his house—the sound of rope moving across wood.

Gilbert had crept up to the door of the barn and peered in through the crack between the large double doors, and was horrified by what he saw.

His mother was in the barn.

And she was swinging; hand over hand on a series of ropes hanging down from the ceiling.

She also wasn't wearing the housedress she usually wore when doing chores. Instead, she was in an outfit that looked like something he'd seen an acrobat wear two summers ago, when he'd been five and the circus had come to town.

But that acrobat had been smiling, wearing a star-spangled costume and doing high jump kicks and twirls in the air to the 'oohs' and 'ahs' of the audience under a huge tent on a fire lit Saturday night. Today, Ma was wearing an outfit that was form fitting, but dark-colored. The acrobat's suit had caused a minor scandal among the older townsfolk for leaving her shoulders exposed, but Ma's outfit was a bit more modest. It ended just above her elbows and knees, though her feet were bare. And the one time he glimpsed her face, she didn't have a performer's smile. Instead, her face had a look of total, serious focus, with no thought of an audience whatsoever.

Indeed, she was so focused that if Gilbert hadn't sneezed, she might have completed her routine without ever knowing he was there. As it was, a stray particle of dust floated without any hurry up his right nostril so precisely that when Gilbert sneezed, he doubled over with a sound like a mucousy cannon shot. His head slammed with a loud retort against the barn door.

But Ma didn't look at him or call his name. When Gilbert looked up through the door crack again from wiping his nose, she was gone.

Gilbert pushed open the door. It creaked like an old woman screaming in purgatorial torment. He took a few cautious steps forward, looking around as if an attack could hit from any direction.

"Ma?" Gilbert whispered, half-hoping that what he'd seen wasn't real. Children of any age do not like seeing parents doing something unexpected, and Gilbert was no exception.

"Ma?" He'd called louder this time after moving forward a few more feet, hoping he would hear her footsteps coming from the house.

"Gilbert," her voice sounded behind him. He yelped, jumping forward and twisting around to see behind him in a single, uncoordinated motion that had him flat on his side in two heartbeats.

He looked up. She was still wearing the black outfit. Not precisely a bathing suit—it had no frills. And it had ... legs?

Ma was wearing *pants?* He hadn't been sure before, but now he could see them clearly. Tights were weird enough, but pants?

"Ma, what're you doing?" Gilbert asked, standing up from the floor.

"Exercising," she said, pulling her face into an unconvincing smile.

"This is an exercise suit your aunt gave me long ago from ... Timbuktu. They all wear them there, and I thought I'd try it out. Do you like it?"

Gilbert stared at her warily. She was trying too hard to sound normal. "No," he said. "And since when do you exercise like a monkey in a tree?"

Her face lost its smile. "Go inside," she said. "And don't speak of this to anyone."

Gilbert looked at his mother. Love and sense of duty clashed with a now insatiable sense of curiosity. "You can't stop me from speaking, Mother," he said, jutting his chin out as he'd seen the class bully Luther do to his teacher.

Mother crossed her bare forearms in front of her, her legs visible below the knees, and her bare feet planted shoulder-width. Gilbert had never seen his mother dressed like this, and as such he'd never seen how taut and well-defined Ma's muscles were. Did farm work alone do that, or had she been practicing longer than he'd thought?

"I can stop you," she said. Her voice was quiet yet firm, like a rock outcropping in the sea that would break any ship that dared to challenge it.

Gilbert held his mother's gaze until something behind her eyes frightened him. He turned and hiked back to the house. He never told. Not even Pa.

Two weeks later, Ma had rung the bell in the yard of the barn. The hired men were gone for the day. Gilbert had been studying his lessons (Ma liked to teach him in the summer), enraptured in translating the Iliad of Homer from Greek to English when the summoning bell had sounded. He'd sighed, decided he'd have to wait to learn the fate of the Greek hero Ajax, and ran down the ladder from his room, and stairs to the ground floor and through the hallway to the outside.

There was no one at the bell. Ma was usually here at this time, but she was nowhere to be seen. But the barn door was open—why? That normally never happened! Gilbert ran into the drafty wooden barn, looking for his Ma. Ma was there in the center of the floor. She was wearing her 'exercise outfit' again, standing with her bare feet apart and arms folded, standing in a pose that looked both relaxed and ready for ... well, for what Gilbert couldn't exactly say. But she looked ready for something, nonetheless.

"Here," she'd said simply, tossing Gilbert a dark shape that rustled as it flew to him.

Gilbert reached for it, trying to catch it in midair. He fumbled, and the gift fell to the dusty ground below. He knelt and picked it up, running his fingers over it as he brushed the dry dirt off the dark cloth.

It was another exercise suit.

He was halfway up the gangplank to the ticket checkers when a voice shouted his name from the lower end of the gangplank, interrupting his musings.

"Gilbert!"

He turned and looked.

Back at the lower end of the gangplank stood a beautiful, brown-haired girl and a little street boy.

How had she known where he was?

Did it matter?

"Frances," he whispered, and ran down the plank.

Chapter 20

"It's not that we don't have enough scoundrels to curse; it's that we don't have enough good men to curse them." – GKC, *ILN*, March 14, 1908

The office wasn't really small, just crowded. Its walls and floor were made of sturdy plank wood, the kind usually found in a well-to-do house on the American frontier. No one who entered the office could honestly describe it as small, exactly. To be fair, though, a number of those who entered the one-room office left with blood pouring out of their noses, mouths, ears or other wounds, and were in no shape to recall the room's size or decor. Some who entered and emerged uninjured would later say the room's main occupant was so good at holding your attention that the rest of the room went unnoticed.

One wall in particular held the kind of artifacts expected of a man who'd gone looking for trouble, given it a sound beating and dragged it back in chains for a trial. Here in one trophy case was the gun of a train-robbing desperado. Under a glass dome on a table was the beloved smoking pipe used by a hardened kidnapper. And in yet another corner of the room a specialized belt used by a spy in the SoCal-Texarcana conflicts to smuggle any number of secrets to both sides of the fight.

The man himself who owned this office and the trophies therein was, indeed, an imposing figure. His snow-white hair had seen its share of sun and rain in the sixty-something summers he'd spent on God's Earth. Those who met him for the first time often mistook him for a rotund man, reaping a fat-bellied reward for a life spent behind a desk. He knew they thought this, and never missed a chance to stand once their first impressions had set and cooled. For when he stood, the pot-belly disappeared, revealed to be an intentional illusion of bunched-up clothes and visitor's assumptions. Not only was his stomach a flat-bellied envy of most men his age, his shoulders were broad, his arms thick and muscular, and his face had the craggy smile of a man who knew he could break you in moments if he chose to.

None but the most foolhardy had ever thought to tangle with him in a contest of strength or wills once he stood straight and displayed his physique. Fewer still tried to run when he flashed his badge while he was wearing his lawman's long coat and wide-brimmed hat. These days, it was a rare quarry indeed that hadn't heard the lawman's name, usually whispered with fearful reverence at a poker game or campfire of law enforcers or lawbreakers.

Most times, though, he had no need to live up to the tall tales that had grown up around his exploits. Usually his sheer physical brawn, alert eyes, large hands and dual automatic pepperbox pistols in his hip holsters made the argument for surrender more eloquently than any amount of reputation or negotiation ever could.

In front of his desk sat a chair of polished wood. A second man already sat in it, dressed in a vest, tie and long dusty coat. He was quiet and had a dark mustache with a few streaks of gray in it, and his eyes hid behind a set of tinted glasses. The second man didn't speak but sat quietly, bringing a cigarette slowly to his lips now and again.

The door to the office opened, and a familiar sound of hardened boot leather and spurred heels sounded against the floor.

The first lawman waited behind his desk, not looking up until his visitor had paused and caught his breath.

"Well, Joe, how'd it go?" the lawman asked as he shuffled a few papers on his desk, his voice a mixture of gruff insistence and merriment.

"We got him," the standing visitor said quietly, his young, clean-shaven face largely hidden under his own hat. "Money's in the bank, or so the army says."

"Good to hear," said the seated lawman from his desk, still looking at his papers. "How's the new one working for you?"

The standing man slapped his right thigh without taking his eyes off of his boss. A hollow metallic sound went *thong* beneath the pants leg. "Fair and well. The li'l secret spot inside can hold a pistol better n' the gunbelt ever did. The new button slips the shooter into my hand smoother 'n silk an' faster than a happy jackrabbit. I just carry the empty holster on the side to warn folks I've got a gun on me, someplace."

"Good man, Joe. Ready for your next one?"

The standing man, Joe, paused. "Colonel, I know you've got a lot on your plate, but I'm a little surprised you'd have me hit the road again this soon."

"Joseph Harper, you and I both know how much you hate having nothing to do. Besides, this'll be easier for you. You won't be in charge of this mission. I will."

Joe gave a low whistle. The boss hadn't personally commanded a mission in nearly six months. "This one comes from the top shelf, then?"

"Yep. So high up I don't think even the boys in Washington could dust it with a ten-foot pole. Take a seat."

The newest and youngest member of the entourage pulled over another chair from against the wall. He sat in front of the boss lawman's desk and beside the quiet one with the cigarette still drooping a bit between his lips. As the younger lawman sat, his right leg made faint clicking and hissing sounds.

The boss stood as Harper sat, sweeping a sheaf of papers in a fluid motion from the top of his desk and walking over to the two men seated in front of his work desk.

"Gentlemen, we have little time, so I'll be brief. The analytical engines over at home base in Washington have recommended you for your skills and experience. To be fair, I'd already handpicked you, and was ready to throw out the box's orders if they'd gone against mine."

"Not to mention that we've all demonstrated an uncanny knack for putting up with your propensity for pointless heroics," said the older, smoking man, his face unreadable behind his glasses.

"I'll ignore that this one time, Doc. Next time you sass me, that fancy hand of yours and my blacksmith hammer're gonna do some talkin'." The standing man had made his threat while smiling.

Doc leaned back in his chair and chuckled softly. They'd worked too many missions together to get upset at idle threats.

"As I was saying, gentlemen," he said, regaining their attention with two words and the slightest change of posture and vocal inflection, "both me and the machine picked you because you truly are the best we've got. 'Course that means I've stated indirectly just how pathetic the Agency That Never Sleeps has become."

"So what poor, unfortunate soul has merited our attentions today, Colonel?" said the older seated man. His hands were lying in a relaxed position on the table, the cigarette burning with a slow curl of lazy smoke rising between his fingers. The left hand was tanned, having seen more than its share of the sun in the past few weeks. The gloved right hand held his cigarette.

"The job," said the Colonel, passing out several sheets of rough, pulpy paper, "is an American who's been living in the British Isles for the past couple of years. He's on his way home, however, having already eluded capture from one of our agents in London."

Each of them stared at the papers. The older man lifted his tinted glasses, revealing a large, bulbous metallic orb with a round glass lens that seemed to be growing out of his left eye socket. He touched a small wheel on the side of his temple, and a small column about a half-inch in diameter extended from the orb. The effect was that of a child adjusting a microscope.

"Colonel," said young Joseph Harper, "are you sure you've got the right fella? This guy's a kid."

"The neophyte does have a good point, Colonel," Doc said.

"I'm no neophyte!"

"Are you cognizant of what that is, Corporal Harper?"

"I ain't no cogni—watsit either!"

"I should hope," said Doc, as his eye looked at the portrait on the nearest page, "the outfitters will at least equip us with an extra set of diapers to take Joseph here home in. I'd hate my new coat to run the risk of soilage from him."

"I thought the diapers were for you so you don't soil our campsite in your sleep, old man."

The boss' eyes flicked to each speaker in turn for the next few minutes as they'd tried to outdo one another. After snide comments about their ages, they moved on to how easy the job was going to be. His gaze finally rested on Joe.

Joe had finished talking, and picked up the stipplograph. He looked at it like a dish of near-rotten fish served to him in a congealing sauce. "Colonel, you mind telling me again why you round up two of Pinkerton's finest, just so's we can run after some skinny kid with a big jaw and a pair of sodapop-bottle eyeglasses? How old is he, anyways? He don't look more 'n sixteen."

"Seventeen, to be precise," said the boss, now standing under the skylight to emphasize his impressive height of six-feet and two inches. "Gentlemen, the stippled portrait displays our quarry, one Gilbert Keith Chesterton. As to why our new clients want him, alive and preferably undamaged, our lords and masters in Washington have graciously left that information *out* of their most recent communications to us."

"Whatta surprise," Joe grumbled.

"A most unwelcome, if expected action on the part of our so-called superiors," said Doc.

"Don't fool yourself, Corporal Harper," said the Colonel, cutting the carping short. "That boy lived through the thick of the Martian invasion over in England. Word is he took out one of those squids with a Colt .45. That alone was a feat worthy of David beating Goliath with a peashooter. But then he went on to kill another with a little Derringer, along with a third one that he and a friend crushed with their own cage after the squids caught him. He's a slippery one, alright. And, like I said, he got past one of our agents over in London, an agent outfitted with a Pincher for a hand."

There was a short moment of silence while the boss let that one sink in. Usually a quarry crumpled in fear or a fit of madness when they saw a Pincher's ability to bend its fingers backwards.

"What're we gonna get for him?" Joe asked.

"Again, Mr. Pinkerton conveniently forgot to let me know in our last official communication. But I've been informed on the Q.T. that the fee is enough to float a British battleship to Mars and back."

Corporal Joseph Harper Jr., longtime associate of the Colonel in front of him, whistled low. "Sounds like this boy's wanted powerful bad by some powerful people," Joe Harper said in a subdued voice.

"Happily, this is entirely none of our business. Gentlemen," the Colonel said, looking at three older men, "we leave thirty minutes from the time I dismiss Corporal Harper. Doc, your first stop is the equipment room downstairs. Test out yer stuff, make sure it's up for a meet, greet and grab, then after that, off to the station. We're booked on the next train to New York City. Corporal," he now looked at Harper, "I'll have some matters to discuss with you when Mister Holiday here leaves."

"Yessir."

Doc stood, tipped his hat and left the room. The Colonel didn't speak again until no feet sounded in the stairwell.

There was a brief pause while both the Colonel and Corporal Harper thought about their new assignment. Grabbing famous people against their will was often a very tricky business.

"Think this is gonna be a tough one, Colonel?"

The much larger and older man looked at the brass deskplate that declared him to be

COLONEL JAMES "H." FINN
SUPERVISOR, PINKERTON SECURITY SERVICES
EAST COAST DIVISION

"Corporal Harper, how many years have I known you?"

"Since 'afore I was knee high to a grasshopper, Colonel. 'An you knew my daddy at least twenty years 'afore that."

"That's right. And have I ever given you a reason not to trust me in all that time?"

Harper made a pretense of searching his memory. "Hmm, nope," he said quickly.

"Then lemme be honest with you again. You know what a Tar Baby is?"

"My momma told me the stories. Br'er Fox makes a baby out've tar. Br'er Rabbit gets all mad at it one day an' takes a swing at its nose. He gets stuck, an' everything he does to get free just gets him more stuck than before."

"Right. When I got handed this," he held up Gilbert's picture, "I got a sick little twist in my stomach, like when your Pa, Senator Sawyer and I were kids and we'd smoke cheap tobacco together. This looks easy, alright. The kid's not famous over here. He's an orphan, so there's no family to hide him. He's no one's idea of an athlete or a soldier. Plus, we've got Doc's eye for scouting, his arm for fightin', your leg for runnin' and me for ..."

As if on cue, there was a steady report of several bullet shots, followed by what sounded like a loud belch. At the sound of the belch a cheer went up from the men followed by a smattering of applause.

"In short, Corporal Harper," continued Colonel Finn, "this grab looks simple. But I gotta feeling this boy Chesterton is gonna be a Tar Baby for us, one that could make the Slave Wars look like a bar room brawl."

"When giving treats to friends or children, give them what they like, emphatically not what is good for them." – GKC, *The New Age*, 1908

Gilbert was almost finished with the rosary, a set of prayers Father Flambeau had introduced him to a few months back. While he had never experienced a blast of white light or a pillar of fire from Heaven in answer to a prayer, among many other benefits he found the rosary soothing and calming when his spirits were addled. Pausing between decades, Gilbert stretched a little in the comfy chair with his beads securely in his hand and realized, now that he was calm, how truly wonderful his life had become in the last few days.

Of course, the past week had been rather busy. He'd been shot at by flying men, kidnapped by thugs in tweed, and nearly grabbed by a fellow in a bowler hat and a longcoat whose hand could bend backwards. After that, most people would be a little skittish.

And Gilbert *had* been skittish. Days ago, back at the docks in London, he'd been so skittish that anyone else calling his name would have made him run into the bowels of the airship in fear.

But he didn't. Because the only person who'd called his name then was Frances!

"Gilbert!" she'd called, her voice carrying across the docks where people had just begun to gather, and all the way up the gangplank.

Gil had turned. She was running towards the docks, a boy of the streets leading her. Such children abounded in the streets of London's poorer quarters, and often sold information to interested parties. Somehow this wonderful, wonderful little miscreant knew Frances would have liked to hear news about Gilbert Keith Chesterton, and had brought her to him!

Frances!

Now Gilbert ran down the gangplank, blowing past the few other people in line who'd gathered behind him, his thick shoes making hurried, hollow noises down the long wood and metal ramp as his long legs ate up the distance between them. Frances ran too, as quickly as her afternoon dress would allow her. She was taking an awful risk being unprotected in this part of town. Some cutpurse could see her and do her harm!

Frances clasped him in a warm embrace, interrupting his thought.

He could feel her hands through the fabric of his sport coat, and it sent a thrill up his back and down his arms all the way to his wrists.

It was unusually warm here in London for late January, but having Frances nearby made it warmer still.

"Frances," he exclaimed, "what're you doing here? How did you find me?"

She looked at the young boy who had accompanied her. "This boy found me in the marketplace. He told me you were departing on an airship soon, and offered to bring me to you."

The boy looked up at them and smiled. "It's 'ard to keep a secret from a Wiggins boy," he said, and looked at Gilbert. "But you knew that already, didn't you Mister Gilbert?"

"There's something for you," Frances said, handing several coins to him, "oh, and here's more! Thank you so much!"

The lad looked at the bounty in his hands. By his expression, it was likely he hadn't seen that much money in quite a while! "Thank ye kindly, miss! Mister Wiggins was right, Mister Gilbert! You surely do 'ave a good taste in the ladies! God bless!" The boy disappeared into the gathering throng of people. Wiggins had outdone himself, Gilbert thought! Not only had he gotten Gilbert a very improved ticket out of England; he'd even found the one person Gil truly wanted to see before leaving!

After the boy had run off, Frances pulled back to look at Gil, her eyes a mixture of joy and anger. "Now, Mister Gilbert Keith Chesterton! May I ask you just why you're running off, and where to? Barely any time after you've arrived back in London, you're about to leave again! And without so much as note to me!"

"Well, I didn't even know you were back yourself, not yet! More important, I'm ... well, Frances, I'm ... aw hang it. I can't lie to you. It looks like I'm in trouble. It seems I've made some really, really bad people angry with me, and my editor has sent me on this trip to get me gone until the heat's off."

"But ... I thought you were going to Rome! To testify on behalf of Father's Brown's canonization!"

"I know, but ... well, there's enough folks can do that, I think. I hope, anyway. I mean, I don't think they need me that much. And besides, like I said, I need to lay low."

Frances paused. "Gilbert, I have to ask: Is this about Fortescue?"

Gilbert hesitated. Should he tell her the whole story?

Stop. Inhale. Exhale. Now talk.

"Frances," Gilbert said evenly, "I know Fortescue is a longtime family friend of yours, so what I'm going to say may not be easy to hear."

She looked at Gilbert, waiting for him to continue.

"Frances, he hired a bunch of thugs to rough up Herb and me in Berlin. And when he wouldn't pay them, they trussed him up. I gave him a pretty good scare, and left him there for the coppers to find. My chief said that folks who upset Fortescue's dad tend to turn up dead, and we both thought it'd be smarter and safer for me and everyone else around me if I disappeared for a while."

"Gilbert," she said, "listen: Fortescue believes he owns me. He's believed that ever since we were little and our parents planned our union. I feared after meeting him that you wouldn't want me, believing I was spoken for."

"Oh, Frances! No! Never!"

"But Gilbert, that's not all I've worried about."

Gil paused. "What else, Frances?" he asked.

"When you say you were 'roughed up.' Gilbert, I believe you. But ... Gilbert, did you try to maim him?"

Gilbert looked at Frances and swallowed. Something told him that a great deal depended on how he answered this next question.

Breathe. Above all, tell the truth.

"Frances," he said, "I've been bullied a lot in my life, everyone from schoolyard chumps to squids from Mars. But when Fortescue's own men trussed him up and left me there with a Franklin rod, I had to really pull the reins back on myself. I ... I did threaten to do to him what he paid others to do to me. But I didn't, Frances. I just put a scare in him. Then I left him in the warehouse and called the coppers when we got back to the hotel. And that's the truth."

Gilbert waited. Now it was Frances' turn to breathe deeply before she went on. "I feel better hearing that from you, Gilbert. Fortescue has been to every tearoom he can get his driver to take him to, claiming you tried to maim him with the rod. In his version, he foiled and disarmed you, and it was only because Herbert hit him from behind that you avoided a gentleman's death. But Fortescue never has been brave in his life without his father's money to give him courage. Besides that, I know you're not that sort of person.

"There's more, though, Gilbert. I'm afraid you might now think that the only reason I have declared any feelings for you is because I am looking for a means to escape a marriage to a monster like

Fortescue Williamson." She turned from him, walking a little and speaking as much to herself as to Gilbert. "I know, Gilbert, that I have struggled with that question myself, but ... oh, bother! Why does this all have to be so difficult!"

"Frances," he said, walking behind her and putting his hand on the small of her back, "Frances, if it helps I ... I never thought that. I always hoped you felt, well, for me the way that I do you."

"Gilbert, do you truly love me?"

The question hit him like a thunderbolt. It was an easy one to answer—of course he did! But when presented so suddenly, with fear in her voice, Gilbert's tongue tied itself into a knot and his throat went all mushy and filled with misgiving.

"Frances," he said, "I've seen pretty girls before. Even talked a few up. But there's no one else in this world I could spend just hours with and not notice the time go by. When I thought I'd just have to settle for having Herb's female leftovers for the rest of my life, well, there you were in Paris, and it's been all over for me ever since."

Being so open and honest with Frances changed something inside him, changed him so radically that he could feel it in his gut. He no longer wanted to be the kind of dashing lover he had seen in movies or the strong, silent type in the nickel novels, but something else. He wanted only to be something totally, and only himself.

He'd been standing beside and a little behind her, but now he moved gently in front of her and clasped her hands. "Frances," he said again, his voice sounding animated; excited, instead of fearful, "Frances, you asked if I love you. Now, if love means I think you're the most amazing woman in the world, if love means I ache when you aren't with me and I'm in total bliss when you are, if love means I could climb the highest mountain just so I could shout that you were mine and I were yours, if love means I'd be willing to take on ten Fortescues, with them all having Franklin rods and me just a little walking stick to beat them with, I'd take 'em all on! Every one of 'em! Along with anyone who wouldn't admit you are the most beautiful woman in the world! And if love means ... aw, hang it! Do you see what I'm getting at?"

"Gilbert," Frances whispered, her eyes shining like dark, starlit pools. "You ... you really think I'm ... I'm that beautiful?"

"Milady," Gilbert said, taking her by the waist and walking beside her with the swagger of a swashbuckler who'd brought down Blackbeard, "I am of the esteemed opinion that if a woman of your beauty and virtue taught just one Sunday school class to a group of imps from Hell's ninth circle, the little devils would take one look at you and melt in the face of the most glorious, virtuous and noble woman to walk the Earth since the day the Devil tempted Eve."

"Now you're just flattering me," she said, still smiling.

"No, seriously. That's why they wouldn't let devils into your Sunday school. They'd turn back into angels for you inside of six lessons. Hell'd be emptied within the year, and what would Satan do for drudge labor then?"

"Gilbert!"

"Well, he is a hard worker. But remember: he did need a third of the angels of Heaven to get his dirty work done. Think about it."

Gilbert's swagger was interrupted by the blast of a horn from the enormous Zeppelin that drew both their attentions.

"They're calling me on board, already? I thought I had two hours!" Gilbert said, more than a little frustration entering his voice. He'd been so enthralled by Frances, he hadn't noticed the crowds gradually milling towards the gangplank and at the docks.

"Oh, they have to call you on early for an overseas trip, it's always something about checking you through customs. Gilbert, darling, when will you be back?"

"I don't know—it won't be long, I hope. But when I do …" A pause hung in the air between them like a large, silent balloon.

"Yes?" Her eyes were shining.

"Frances I—well; I've never felt this way before. Not about anyone. I don't know that I ever could about anyone else, not ever."

"Not even red-headed girls who fly through ceilings?"

"Who? Oh, her. I don't even know who she is. But look, Frances, you're the only girl I've ever thought of asking to say 'I do' with someday. But right now, things are …well, they're crazy. And they're crazy for both of us. I've got to go until it's safe again, and you, well, you've got your own battles to fight with the likes of Fortescue. I don't want to ask you to marry me in the middle of a filthy dock right before I jump across the Atlantic. That wouldn't be right, and you deserve better. But would you wait for me? Wait until I'm back? And if you still feel the same and I could support us, well, would you … would you consider it?"

Frances smiled, stood up on her tiptoes and kissed Gilbert on the cheek.

He felt a wave of warm air envelop him, coupled with a firecracker going off in his head and a cherry bomb exploding in his heart.

"Remember me by this, Gilbert dear," she whispered in his ear, "I'll wait for you until the sun stops setting, if that's what it takes."

Another blast from the horn, shouts from the gangplank. Gilbert fought the urge to sweep Frances into his arms, carry her up the plank and demand that the captain marry them as soon as they were in the air.

"When I return, Frances. When I return, then, if you still want me, if you want us to be an *us*, I'll ask your father's permission for your hand! I promise!"

The departure horn made another long blast.

"Frances I've got to go now!"

"Will you wait for me, too, Gilbert?"

"Until the sun stops setting!"

They walked back and held hands for a moment at the edge of the plank. Hundreds of people had collected at the docks now, waving handkerchiefs, shouting well wishes, and saying tear-filled goodbyes. No one else was boarding the airship. "Time, Sir, please," the steward said in a kind voice from the top of the gangplank. Gilbert clasped Frances' hand in his own and kissed her fingers. *Some things are worth the wait,* he thought. He then let her go and walked up the gangplank.

Once on board, Gilbert hurried to the barred deck and began waving to Frances, instantly picking out her shining face from the rest assembled.

"I'll be back!" Gilbert shouted at the top of his lungs, trying to drown out the sudden roar of the engines and the shouts of the people on board with him and on the docks. An odd look suddenly crossed Frances' face, and she shouted to Gilbert over the din of the other well-wishers. "Did he find you? Did he find you?" she seemed to be saying.

Gilbert, unsure of what she meant, smiled and waved. They could clear it up when they could write to each other again.

That all had happened days ago. After Gilbert had said goodbye and the airship had left the docks, Gilbert had waited at the railing until Frances, the crowd, and the shoreline had disappeared behind the horizon. He'd then gone through the whole rigmarole of customs, answering some of the silliest questions he'd ever been asked, and by dinnertime Gilbert had found his cabin on the ship with the help of an obliging steward.

After he shut the door, Gilbert darned near cried his insides out. After a while, he thought he'd gotten control of himself, but then another wave of sadness hit him and he started tearing up again. He wondered if this was hitting Frances, too, but after the third or fourth wave, he felt stable enough to be outside his cabin again.

Being away from Frances was going to be no Sunday-school picnic. He knew that right off. He'd read and re-read every one of the six letters of hers he'd brought with him to help cheer him up, to no real avail. But, he reasoned, he could be in worse places to pass the time until he could return to Merrie Old England. He'd started today by walking the length, height and breadth of the ship. No small feat—this thing was five floors deep, at least half as long as the Titanic, and took a good half hour to walk up from stem to stern when you counted staircases, people and other obstacles. He eventually found a comfortable chair at one of the indoor observation decks and let himself sink into its luxury while looking at the stars.

Funny how life can be, Gilbert thought, as he twiddled the rosary beads in his hand. Twice in his life, now, things had begun in a fairly normal way, only to have a number of crazy events line up and turn his life topsy-turvy. He was still wearing the brown, laced shoes, dark stockings, brown, low weave tweed pants and sport coat he'd worn that morning to the offices of the Times. His glasses, the same pair he'd worn since his frenetic adventures over a year ago during the Invasion, still held to his face with the comfortable, padded hooks that fastened them to his face securely behind his ears. A wave of fatigue hit him unexpectedly, but a rational part of his brain said it was only natural for him to be feeling a little dreamy after that game of down-the-rabbit-hole he and Wiggins had played with Mister Black-Gloves-Brass-Hand.

He had just begun a dream where he was painting a picture of himself that Frances and Father Brown kept trying to erase, when he heard the voice at his elbow.

"Excuse me, sir?"

Gilbert opened groggy eyes. He saw a well-dressed little boy, nine years old at most. He was chubby with thick-lensed glasses and dressed in the shirt, sweater, tie and shorts that were common to English boys who were attending private boarding schools.

"Can I help you?" Gilbert asked sleepily.

"You are Gilbert Chesterton!" the boy said, "The one who wrote about the Tripods!"

Gilbert smiled. "You might be right, friend, but if I was him, I don't think I'd be talking about it right now, because I'd be on vacation." Gilbert settled back into the comfortable chair. Then an insistent point jumped in his head: he was supposed to be hiding out during this trip. A chatty little boy could give just the kind of tip to Gilbert's pursuers needed.

"On second thought, little fellow, let me clarify that. I'm not –"

"Oh, but I'm certain you are!" said the boy, moving closer. "You have the same kind of glasses that intrepid reporters wear, the ones with the hooks in the back to keep them from falling off when you have your amazing adventures. I'm your biggest fan, you know. I've read your entire editorial series, and I've read everything that's been printed about you in the British Empire, I think. I haven't gotten to see the newspapers that are written in Hindi yet, but once I get that language down I plan to read that, and the major myths of that culture too! And then I'll see what they had to say about the Invasion, and Father Brown, the first Papist priest who finally did something useful and ..."

At the mention of Father Brown, Gilbert's beloved mentor who'd died after an all too short period in Gilbert's life, and the word 'Papist' in the same sentence, Gilbert realized that it didn't matter that his new inquisitor was either nine years old or his biggest fan. What mattered was that Gilbert felt the familiar tingle in his neck and ears that usually signaled he was ready for a rip-roaring argument. And, if he wished to avoid any notice, an argument with a precocious and more than a little annoying nine-year-old with an upper-class British accent was something he couldn't afford at any price.

Gilbert rose and began walking. "I'm sorry, young fellow," he said, offering to shake his hand. The boy pumped it vigorously, and Gilbert had to work himself free. "I've just remembered an appointment I have right now with a man of some importance."

"Oh, never fear, Mister Chesterton," the lad said, following Gilbert and speaking at a volume that seemed designed to bring the attention of half the passengers to them. "As a reporter for a prestigious publication like the *London Times*, you're likely on a secret assignment, hiding among the regular people of the world just as Odysseus' men escaped the Cyclops by hiding beneath the goats! I understand, Mister Chesterton! Are you after that Member of Parliament, Mister Marconi? My father said he was crookeder than Hannibal's pass through the Himalayas, and twice as dangerous to footle with. But fear not, Mister Chesterton! As silent as the Norse god Vidar was when he defeated the wolf Fenris with his stealth and cunning, and so avenged his father's death at the battle of Ragnarök, so too will I be with ..."

For the first time in his life, Gilbert realized he could strike a child with the full force of his anger, and feel totally free of the need to attend confession for it afterwards. Was this kid ever gonna be quiet?

"Oh, look!" said Gilbert, passing the smoking room, "Here's where I have to go for my appointment!"

"Mister Chesterton! You'll be meeting your contact in a smoke-filled bar? How very much like the nickel novels you professed to like in your editorial three weeks ago!"

Gilbert stopped and looked at the little boy in front of him. The kid stared back at Gilbert, eyes filled with the kind of adoration reserved for the mythic gods the kid wouldn't stop talking about. If he *was* the kind of fan Gilbert had been warned about, the little fellow would follow Gil everywhere, making a chattery nuisance of himself. Eventually he'd begin quoting Gil's written works better than Gil himself remembered them, changing in Gilbert's eyes from a quirky child to a creepy little creature in the space of a few sentences.

Being blunt or outright cruel was the way Gil had seen some famous people deal with unwanted fans. But Gilbert couldn't be cruel to a child who had likely endured much cruelty in his own life already. Gilbert knew from painful and personal experience how unkind children could be to overly intelligent peers, especially if they were poor at sports and had annoying personalities.

"Look, um, tell you what. Where's your folks right now, little man?"

"My father has sent me on an adventure across the sea and into the Americas. I am to attend school at a proper place of boarded education in the American West. If it's suitable enough, my brother Warnie will join me next semester."

"Okay, I get it. You're going to boarding school," said Gilbert. Scratch the first option of ditching the kid; there were no parents to foist him on to. "What's your name again?"

"I never told it to you. My name is Clive Staples Lewis. But my friends call me Jack."

Gilbert paused. "How did they get a nickname like Jack out of Clive?"

"I've not the foggiest idea. Oh, could I get your signature on some of your editorials? I keep my favorites in my pocket, here," the young boy reached into his coat pocket and pulled out several sheets of thin newspaper clippings. Some of them caught on his pocket, and tore down the middle with a long, steady ripping sound.

Gilbert paused again. The look on this kid's face was the worst. Gilbert couldn't tell from it if he was trying to be obnoxious, or was only that way by accident. A kid who kept editorials in his pocket?

Worse, though, was the tearing noise as Jack pulled the papers from his coat. Gilbert winced at the sound, and bit the inside of his cheek. "Okay, Jack?" Gilbert said after the unpleasant moment passed, "You said your name was Jack, right?"

"Actually, I stated before it was Clive ..."

"Yeah, yeah, I got that. Look, Jack, Clive, whoever. I've had a very difficult week, and I really need to be by myself for a while, all right? I'm sure we'll bump into each other again on this trip, so we'll just say our goodbyes for now, and sign your pieces later 'kay? I really need to ..." Gilbert looked further down the deck and saw something he'd not seen since he'd left New York nearly two years ago.

In the parks of New York City, an enterprising soul had set up a number of stone chessboards. On a sunny day, seats at the boards were always filled with men, young and old, playing the game with noisy or quiet attitudes.

In a room just off the deck of the airship, Gil could see through an open door that a number of similar boards had been set up, though here the players were very nearly always very *quiet* with each other.

Gil had a small flash of reason: Jack seemed to thrive on conversation. Maybe a *quiet* game would eventually drive the little fellow away, leaving Gil to slink off to his cabin unseen.

Nearly all the tables in this room were filled with players and onlookers. Only one table wasn't filled up, and even it had a player looking intently at a complete and unmoved set of pieces.

As Gilbert entered the chess room and drew closer, he could see the lone player was sitting in a wheelchair.

"Excuse me," said Gilbert, "do you play chess, sir?"

The man in the wheelchair looked at Gilbert and then at Jack with a twinkle in his eye. He had trimmed white hair, a thick, salt-and-pepper beard, and was a tad overweight. He had suspenders, a white shirt, cream-colored trousers and a matching fedora. The arms of the wheelchair-bound man rested on cushioned armrests, and Gilbert spotted a small steam boiler under the right one. An odd number of mechanical rods were folded like an accordion next to the boiler, and Gilbert also saw one of the newer, more compact analytical engines installed beneath it. Several tubes and cables attached the devices to each other, and Gilbert realized uncomfortably that he had been out of circulation in regards to the technical world. At one point, Gilbert would have been able to tell the make, model and capabilities of nearly any model of analytical engine found on British shores. Not anymore. Now the French, Americans ("International Babbage Machines" was the main company producing them there), Germans, Swiss, and even the Japanese were getting into the A.E. game.

"Young man," said the wheelchair-bound adult, "I would delight in a game. Many people won't approach me because of my chair. I am Samuel Wilks, surgeon, lecturer, amateur inventor and survivor of all pratfalls befalling the paraplegic. And your name would be?" His head alone moved as he spoke, while his right hand twitched slightly.

"Gi ... George Edwardson, at your service, sir."

Jack nudged Gilbert and winked conspiratorially.

"Well," said Mr. Wilks, still smiling, "Please, do join me. Have a seat." The fingers on his left hand pointed to indicate the cushioned seat across from him. Gilbert sat, happy to have an adult to converse with for a change. If their talk crowded out Jack for even a little while, it would be time well spent!

After Jack made a series of ardent promises to be quiet during the game, Gilbert held two pawns in his hand. Wilks pointed to Gilbert's left hand, which held a white pawn. Gilbert would be playing the black pieces for this game.

"If you would indulge me for a moment, while I calibrate my engine, Mister Edwardson," said Wilks. His left hand turned a few knobs on the control panel in front of it, and a hiss and a gentle hum came out of the A.E. boxes behind him that were attached to the wheelchair.

Curiouser and curiouser, thought Gilbert.

"Stranger and stranger," whispered Jack aloud as a thin bunch of gears and rods unfolded into a mechanical arm from beneath Wilks' armrest. A small beam of light shone from the arm's tip onto a point in the corner of the chessboard. Wilks' left hand adjusted a few more knobs until the light beam was focused in the very center of the chessboard's square. "An inconvenience for my opponents, to be sure," he said, "but in the end, far preferable to breaking everyone's concentration by instructing others where I want my pieces moved."

Gilbert blinked as the contraption moved. The hinged, insect-like arm vaguely resembled a Martian Tripod's mechanical tentacle, bringing back more than one uncomfortable memory. "I'm afraid I don't understand," said Gilbert, "how does a light involve calibrating your machine? And what does calibrating it have to do with our chess game?"

"Watch and learn, my boy," said Wilks, turning more dials and pushing a button. While his arms were largely paralyzed, his fingers and hands could move enough to manipulate the controls on his machine.

Another arm, longer and with more segments than the first, extended from the same place as the previous appendage. It unfolded, piece by piece as needed, until it had extended itself over the chessboard and nearly reached the two ranks of white pieces in front of him. A last segment snipped out without any warning, unfolding quicker than the others. Three small pincers popped out at the end of the new arm segment, which then swept down, tightened around the top of the White King's pawn, moved it and then set the piece down exactly two spaces forward.

"Pawn to King Four," said Wilks. "I believe it's your move, Mister Edwardson."

Herbert sat in the uncomfortable chair, looked at the notepad on the coffee table to his left and loathed it. He decided that he loathed the table, too, along with the last three people who had tried to engage him in conversation. He loathed the captain of the ship, the ship's cabin he was sitting in, and every single member of the crew. Even the ones he hadn't met yet.

Herb was in a foul mood for several reasons, not the least of which being that he'd embarked on this voyage across the Atlantic in an airship classified as "comfortably inexpensive."

Herb almost chuckled. The phrase really meant that the food was awful, the cabins smelled like a football-team's locker room, and what heat there was in the cabins at this altitude quickly bled out to the outside world from ten-thousand little leaks in the ship's hull. If the balloon part of this airship was as leaky as its human quarters, it was a miracle on the level of the Loaves and Fishes that the thing stayed aloft at all.

Herb had been told with complete assurance as their lunch concluded that Gilbert was meant to be on this flying boat—or so some reservation clerk had told Margaret. After learning this, Musgrave and Margaret had handed Herb a forged ticket. "It is on that ship," Musgrave had said, "that you may begin your task of opening young Gilbert's eyes to the world of possibilities that awaits him. Even greater opportunities will be yours, Mister Wells, if you continue succeeding at the rate you have already demonstrated."

"A practical question," Herb had said as the last of their dishes were cleared, "what happens if I decide that I'm not up for bringing the job 'to completion' as you put it in there? What keeps me from jumping ship on you lot?"

"Mister Wells, have you ever heard of Bartolmeo Longo?"

"No. Has anyone?"

"Precisely my point. Poor Mister Longo was a lad of tremendous promise. Had an interest in spiritualism. Also had a keen and perpetually active mind for investigation. Most people go into that maze of spirits and conspiracies and either wander forever, give up in frustration, or sometimes kill themselves out of madness, despair or a fit of mysticism. Mister Longo did the one thing almost no spiritualist ever does: he began to look for truth, the *real* truth of the thing. Which spirits were real or fake, which rituals truly conjured or controlled spirits, the very nature of spirits to begin with, and so on.

"In any case, the boy peeled back layer after layer of falsity, wondering just where the whole thing began. Eventually he found the road led not to Asia or Atlantis, but to our little circle. We'd been encouraging the whole movement with funds and support for speakers, events and press coverage in respectable journals for a number of years, and he found us out by following the trail of money."

"But why push spiritualism? Why not Mohammedanism, or Popery? They're already established with millions of followers."

"I'm surprised you haven't discerned this yourself, Herbert. Today, people want something that is both new and malleable. They want to make God in their own comfortable image, one that won't threaten their choice of lifestyles or level of charitable giving. The problem with the Popish or Mohammedan faith is that both believe in an objective right and wrong, and their codes are so ironclad even their own hierarchies can't violate it without eventual consequences. Such creeds are completely unsuitable to our needs.

"Well, we tried first to buy the Longo lad off. Works nine times out of ten, but this time it didn't take. Tragic waste, really. He worked well for a while as one of our operatives, believing he was working for a secret society or some such rot. But eventually he realized he didn't have the belly for his more, ah, *demanding* duties, and decided to, as you say, 'jump ship.' Someone put him on the job of discrediting the Popish faith, but he ended up *converting* to it instead. Never one for half measures, he apparently went mad and lives in some wilderness in Spain, assisting the surplus population there."

"He went mad?"

"Is there any other explanation? Why would any man give up everything for nothing? Pure madness. They weren't even able to get word to him when his parents died at the hands of a burglar."

Herb was silent.

"So, dear Herbert," said Margaret, her hand snaking up over his back and up to the back of his head, where her index and middle fingers began to play with his hair, "If you're thinking about quitting, like Bartolomeo, know that doing so might drive you mad, to say nothing of the accidents that can befall loved ones without a strong, virile son to protect them." Her hand had stopped caressing his head, and now subtly turned it to face her own dark eyes.

"Well ... yes ... that is ... I can see your point."

"Of course you can, dear lad," said Musgrave, smiling, as the waiter returned to the door and waited silently, looking at Herbert. "Of that I have no doubt. Now, look, your hansom cab must be here. Off you go. Do let us know when you have had your success, won't you?"

Herbert left the eatery, and entered the cab after receiving a quick but memorable kiss from Margaret. While driving to the docks, he'd felt jumbled inside, like a child who had tried several ways to make a puzzle's pieces fit right but couldn't, despite all assurances that they would. He'd arrived at the docks in time to see a huge, luxury-liner Zeppelin leave the shores. The beauty and opulence of the last airship made him feel that much more queasy as he boarded the Tiger Moth, a cheaply built airship with dirt and grime in every crevasse he looked at.

He'd walked up the gangplank still in a state of confusion, a little voice inside telling him to run. Run anywhere, even if the way out was hard to see. And hours later when the ship cast off without Gilbert on board, Herb resigned himself to the failure of his mission, halfway happy that there was no way he could have succeeded.

Unless...

Unless he could find Gil. Perhaps he'd been on the other ship?

After all, if Herb just accepted failure, he'd lose not only his new ... acquaintances (he couldn't bring himself to call them friends), but also lose all the opportunities they had promised him. Not to mention the veiled threats that Margaret had made against other people in his life.

Could he find Gil? Could he get Gil to join him? And if so, could they still be friends?

"Could we?" Herb mumbled, looking outside at the clouds and

stars. He repeated the words once, twice, then over and over like a mantra. It was a fairly clear night, but the moon was nowhere to be seen. He could only see an inky blackness with swaths of dark clouds and occasional pinpricks of light, going on forever and ever.

It was very late when the voice inside was finally quiet, and Herb felt well enough to go to bed.

Chapter 21

"Angels can fly because they can take themselves lightly" –
GKC, *Orthodoxy*, 1908

Whoever after due and proper warning shall be heard to utter the abominable word 'Frisco,' which has no merits, either linguistically or geographically, shall be deemed guilty of a High Misdemeanor ..."

Joshua Norton the First, self-declared Emperor of North America, walked at a brisk pace, thoroughly engaged in his favorite part of the day. The daily inspection of his city typically took him a half hour, if he gave it the usual amount of attention. To his usual entourage of a half-dozen Commissars, the inspection was a cursory one. Norton only appeared to give short glances to the city workers and nobler classes, and paused at generators and machines only long enough to ensure that they were making well-functioning humming noises.

Emperor Norton's able, red-haired assistant knew better, of course. Though old, Norton's mind snapped up details like a steel trap. At the end of his walk, mistakes were punished, errors were corrected, and potential usurpers were either executed or met with horrible accidents, all on Norton's orders.

" ... and those guilty of said misdemeanor shall pay into the Imperial Treasury as penalty the sum of twenty-five dollars ... you gettin' all this down, darlin'?"

"Yes, Emperor," she said. She had been copying his every word in a quick and indecipherable code, which she would translate and dictate to a wax-cylinder speakwrite machine every night after he fired her. When he had his usual change of heart in the morning and rehired her, she had her words were printed out and bound into books by the most efficient of the blind workers who labored in the industrial section of the city. Thus far, not a single page had been put in upside down. Not one, their supervisor liked to crow. Better than when they had put the sighted on the job.

" ... and, having been asked the question, 'where are we going, Emperor?' by my esteemed lackey, Baron Bilgewater the Third, currently my right hand man but increasingly in danger of losing that position due to the putridity of his breath."

Commissar Bilgewater clapped his hand over his mouth and moved to the back of the group. "Now to answer the question made with such horrific halitosis, I must ask in reply, what does he mean 'we,' when *I* am the Emperor of North America and Protector or Mexico, and *he* most assuredly is not ..."

A colorfully costumed boy ran up to the Emperor, genuflected with his head bowed, and offered the Emperor a letter on a red velvet cushion.

"Well, bless my soul," the Emperor said, stopping his march, "it's refreshing to know that someone in this infernal city remembers the proper protocol for interacting with its benign dictator." Norton picked the letter up off of the cushion, and drew a long dagger from its sheath, an action that made all around him except his assistant wince in fear.

"Nothing to worry about, gentlemen. A message is seldom boring when delivered to me during my morning constitutional. Lately they've been warning me of assassination attempts, and warnings of that nature always sets my blood pumping, even if the attempts themselves have lately been disappointingly amateurish."

Norton sliced open the envelope, unfolded the letter and passed it to his assistant. She had already tucked away both her notepad and quill pen with flawless efficiency, and plucked the letter from his hand as soon he'd raised it in her general direction.

"To His Royal Majesty," she began, adjusting her glasses, "the most excellent and benign Monarch, Joshua Norton the First, Emperor of North America and Protector of Mexico, greetings and salutations.

"It is of course understandable that the relationship with the government of the United States of America and your own eminent domain has been tenuous at best for a variety of reasons, not the least of which is the current inability of any of the governing bodies of the Five Americas to admit to your existence, much less enter into more cordial relations with it..."

"Skim the milk, would you, honey? Just give me the cream. I'm not in a mood for flowery diplomat talk this morning."

His assistant nodded her head and smoothed out one of the ruffles in her white blouse. Her eyes darted back and forth behind her horn-rimmed glasses for nearly three seconds before she raised her head and looked at the Emperor.

"They say that they are aware of your interest in a certain American of recent British residence. They furthermore state you should be aware of others' interest in him as well."

"Makes sense to me," Norton said, puffing on his cigar and staring out into space while listening to her. "If a man of my genius and influence wishes to obtain someone, certainly there will be those who imitate my actions. Pray continue."

She nodded, looked at the letter and straightened her glasses with a free hand. "It finishes by stating that, um, 'They Who Do Not Sleep' have been engaged in a similar pursuit of your quarry. I am afraid I don't know who that is, Emperor."

Norton's entourage looked to him, unsure how they should react to the news. Norton still stared off into the distance, his cigar burning quietly while he pondered. His left eye twitched once, then twice. He then smiled, bringing smiles to the other six brightly costumed men surrounding him. When he chuckled, they followed suit. By the time he took the cigar out of his mouth and turned to face them, he was engaged in peals of full-blown laughter, and each of the entourage was trying to manage the difficult trick of being the loudest laugher of the group while not laughing louder than the Emperor himself.

After a full minute of this, Norton suddenly went red in the face. "Get outta my sight, you filthy vultures!" he roared, dismissing them with a wave of his cigar-holding hand. "Get outta here, afore I have some real men throw you over the side!"

The advisors and the messenger scurried away, disappearing with a rapidity born of fear and practice. In five seconds, Norton was alone in the hall with his assistant. She stood dutifully, letter in her right hand with her left hand at her side, the fingers straight.

"Galatea, my dear, do you truly not know who the letter refers to, when it talks about them that don't sleep?"

She shook her head.

"Back in the days of the War of Northern Aggression, oxymoronically called the Civil War by our brothers to the North and across the pond, it was the job of a former police detective named Alan Pinkerton to find information on enemy troops. His initial efforts were quite successful, but Lincoln's assassination put paid to his career as a master of governmental spies."

"What did he do then?"

"He went into business for himself, starting a private investigation firm called, appropriately, Pinkerton's. Its symbol was an eye that never closed, their motto, 'nos nunquam somnus.' That's Latin, my dear, Latin for 'We Never Sleep.' Someone wants our boy as badly or more so than we do, milady. And they've gone to the most ruthless and efficient band of boys in the civilized world to do it."

"And," she added, "the government of the United States is also interested in you learning about this fact."

"Sho! Very true m'dear. I love how your brain works. The thing sparkles so much it could make a constellation out've a coal mine. Now, the U.S. Gov'ment wants me to know that the Pinkertons are after the same young man that I'm after. Which means that one of a couple of things are true: One, they may want me to pick a fight with the Pinkertons, and they'll swoop in and take us both down while we're busy pecking away at each other." He paused, weighing other options in his head for a few moments. She spoke up in the break of his speech.

"Option number two," she began hesitantly, "they could greatly desire this boy to be caught by *anyone*, either to safeguard him from harm by other, less congenial folk, or to keep him from foiling plans of the government he might threaten. Telling you someone else is after your prize could be a move to make you step up your efforts to secure him."

"Excellent as always, Galatea." He was just about to begin walking down the hallway again, satisfied that he had arrived at the answer to his question, when he stopped in mid-stride. By the look on his face, she could tell that another thought had risen, and he'd gnaw on it like a puppy with an old shoe until he was done.

"Unless," he said, "Unless this isn't from the United States Gov'ment at all. If this instead were from ... one of the *other* six kingdoms... one of the four Americas, or the Canadians or the Mexicans ... hm, not the Canadians. They're trying too hard to be Europeans to do something smart like this. Not the Mexicans, since they only care about getting Texas back. The Papists in California couldn't care less what happens East of the Sierra Mountains ... I'm down to the Confederates or the crazy fools in the Texas republic. Darlin', let's say this was a fake, where would you say it came from?"

She took the paper without the slightest tremor in her hand and studied it intently.

"The calligraphy is too fine to be of standard Northern stock, and the paper is cream colored. United States paper is typically made of pine or oak pulp, which has a more coarse feel to it. Californians use redwood, with has a dark reddish tinge to it that needs a significant amount of dye to remove. Texans typically import anything derived from wood products from California or the United States territories. This paper is smooth, and doesn't rub off any pigment on my fingers. The coloring and texture has more of a feel akin to the Confederate region, where the appearance of gentility is akin to currency."

"Hm. Didn't we just have a ship come in from those parts?"

"Two, actually, in the past week."

"Hot dang! That's it! This here letter's a fake, an' prob'ly from the CSA! I'll have to get trackin' it."

"All mail from the governments who know of your existence arrives through the use of carrier pigeons, Emperor."

"Just makes for a better challenge is all, darlin'. Someone in this city is tryin' to do the ole' divide and conquer bit, get me distracted while they swoop in and take over. Now I know I've got me a clever adversary for a change, it makes me feel like singin' again! Yeah, must be them Confederates again—they've never forgiven me for escapin' their little tar-an-feather party back 'afore the War of Northern Aggression."

He walked over to a door, pulled a remarkably large lever, and stood close to the railing as it swung outwards. Galatea held her brown skirts in place with one hand and her glasses with the other as a wind of incredible coldness and ferocity blasted through the hallway through the open door.

There was a safety bar set up outside, and now the Emperor leaned on it, looking out at the white building and snow-covered mountain peaks below his vantage point. "Nothing like this, is there, darling?" he shouted, facing the outside, "Nothin' in the world! Good job, keep up the good work, or I'll fire you again by dinner."

"Yes, Emperor," she shouted back, her voice barely sounding over the roaring wind. He didn't hear her; he was already singing an aria from an opera so obscure even she couldn't recognize it.

After he left, she wiped her forehead with the palm of her hand. He'd come closer than ever that time to figuring out that she, and not some government, was the writer of the letters and other communications that distracted him time and again from mounting a serious challenge to the leaders of the Five Americas.

How much longer could she keep this up? How much longer before she became fodder for one of the steam beasts?

A statement from the Emperor interrupted her thought. He'd snuck back into the chamber to watch her while she ran through her thoughts, and his words made her blood run cold.

"Time to visit the arena, my dear."

"…the Church is not a movement but a meeting place, the trysting-place of all the truths in the world."
– GKC, *Twelve Modern Apostles and Their Creeds*, 1926

Herbert walked along the observation deck of the tiny airship for the ten-thousandth time, give or take a few hundred. Walking here was boring, pointless, annoying and cold, but better than hanging around the engine room with the steam monkeys who kept this gods-forsaken ball of tin and wire afloat. The 'recreation area' wasn't much better; two rooms with a few smelly, overstuffed couches along with a few tables that alternated as eating spaces or, for those truly desperate for distraction, games of chess or checkers.

Unfortunately, checkers had never been a game Herbert could convince himself to sink to playing since he had hit puberty. And watching the few souls who played chess grew quickly old, since the 'pieces' for either game consisted of nuts and bolts of various sizes and combinations. More than one conflict had broken out among either passengers or crew over whether a particular bolt was a rook or a bishop, or a wingnut was a pawn or a knight.

He slapped his hands against his upper arms again, trying to warm himself on the deck. It hardly seemed fair that something the size of an airship had so insanely little to do during the voyage. Clouds and the ocean below had been a thrilling sight to begin with, but had quickly become boring as the voyage had progressed. Thank G— … Thank Hea— … *Good thing* that the voyage would take under a week at this speed. Once he reached New York, he could send a telegraph asking for instructions about what to do to find Gilbert next. He hoped he survived the trip; he was only two days into the voyage, and already felt like gnawing his own arm off to escape the boredom. Going back to the sleeping quarters was out of the question. There were no single rooms, except for the one owned by the Captain. Everyone else from crew to passengers slept in communal cabins, in which the men and women were separated. Worse, his male-segregated quarters gave off a stench that made an Eastender gym locker smell like a royal rose garden.

Could he stay out here for the entire voyage? He looked over the railing, trying to let his mind wander away from the job he had somehow agreed to do. Thoughts of losing himself in the depths of

New York City and escaping his new profession had just crossed his mind when he heard a voice behind him.

"You're looking rather solitary for a man who's supposed to be chumming with his best friend."

Oh, no, thought Herbert, even as another part of him squealed with delight.

"Margaret," he said, his eyes never leaving the cloudscape.

"Of course, silly. You were expecting the Queen?"

"I was expecting to be alone."

"You're never alone, Herbert. Even when you think you are, you're not."

She leaned on the safety bar and looked out into the deep water below the cloud line, the wind whipping her black hair into a Medusa-like frenzy around her head.

"I thought you had business with Lord Musgrave."

"I did. It was concluded early, and he asked me to travel with you as a bit of insurance. Make sure you didn't lose your nerve at the last second and all."

"My nerve? I thought my name was set with him and the other blokes."

"Your name has a question mark beside it, Herbert G. Wells. And it will until your mission is completed. And completed in a timely fashion, I might add."

Herbert looked down at the water and wondered what it would be like to jump and fall for the several minutes it would likely take before he hit the water.

"How on Earth did you get aboard, anyway?" he said, trying to change the subject.

"The same way a person always gets where they want to go. I convinced the doorkeeper to let me in."

"But how did you ... no, on second thought, don't tell me. I don't want to know. Look, Margaret, I don't care where you spend your time on this tub. But when we touchdown in New York, I'm going to have to tell Musgrave that the deal's off."

"And why ever's that?"

"Why ever ... I thought you'd have noticed! Gil isn't on this boat! Ergo, there's going to be no way to convince him to join the Special Branch, or any other group. He's probably decided to take his chances back in England, perhaps moving into the sewer or something to stay out of your field of vision."

"Hut-tut-tut! No defeatist talk, Herbert. Make sure you keep that English stiff upper lip. Gilbert wouldn't be staying in London. It's so dangerous for him there, it would be against his religion to stay; Papists can't commit suicide. After our meeting, I stocked up on as much information as I could. It seems the poor scrawny thing ran afoul of a rather large side of beef in a trench coat with a metal arm and an attitude of catch-the-quarry. He now knows just how powerful Williamson is, and wants to get as far away as possible from his reach."

"But maybe he didn't *go* to New York, Margaret! Maybe he didn't bother getting on an airship at all. Maybe he hopped a train and went out to the countryside, or took a balloon to the Swiss Alps. Don't you see? He's not here, and he's not going to be found that easily."

"A little red-headed weasel told me Gilbert was assigned to travel to America, Herbert. Gilbert may be a number of things, but *he* will always complete a job he's been assigned to do. He missed this airship, but there was at least one other leaving the same day for New York from London. As he's a very resourceful fellow, I suspect he'll arrive when we do, if not sooner.

"Therefore, Herbert, dear, when we touchdown in New York, I shall complete another task for Lord Musgrave, while you will be looking at any other airships that touch down from London."

"And when we find him, you'll stay back and let me do my job?"

"It will be your job to recruit him, dear Herbert. I'm not to interfere unless you fail." She smiled, winked, and drew a finger across his chin. "But you won't fail, dear Herbert, will you?"

"Explain to me again why I fell in with you lot to begin with?"

"Herbert, you forget yourself. If you keep treating me in such a surly manner, you'll lose not only the fringe benefits of your job, but the major ones as well."

"Is that a threat, Margaret?"

"Is it working? As to why you joined our group: you remember as well as I what the Invasion was like. Do I need to draw you a picture? Do you think you were the only person who had to lie, cheat and kill to survive?"

"We lived because of Father Brown's sacrifice."

"We lived, Herbert, and that's all. Our race survived because we were superior. Period. Put all thoughts of divine providence and the special place of man in the universe out of your head. If the squids hadn't consumed Father Brown, then they would have died anyway once they reached Africa, but not before they'd destroyed civilization throughout the Northern Hemisphere!

"And," she continued, as much to herself as Herb, "Us being the survivors shows that nature has chosen us to continue the race. *Our* race, Herbert, not the Africans or the Slavs. Why do you think the aliens landed in England instead of some backwater country like Tasmania or Canada? The aliens did us a colossal favor, if you think on it. They managed to winnow out the fools and the weak, and only those strong or smart enough to live through it will be able to pass on their breeding, making a stronger, smarter generation. We have to breed a stronger race, if we want to have a chance against them in the future!"

"You've thought this through, it seems."

"Oh, I've done more than think, Herbert. We'll have to operate in the shadows for the first little while, of course. And it would be a disaster if we let anyone realize that we *Eugenicists* intend, not just to control Negroes, Slavs, Papists and the rest, but to exterminate them outright in the interests of scientific racial advancement. Still ..."

"Margaret, you know I'm still skeptical about the whole Eugenics thing. Many of the best scientists, doctors and philosophers came from what you'd call the inferior races. And as for the Papists, you're forgetting that my first job is to get one on board with us. Plus, Gil told me you can thank them for everything from the most beautiful architecture to the philosophy that everyone's worth something."

"Of course, Herbert dear! Everyone is worth something. It's just that the ordinary happen to be worth less than us. It's only wishful thinkers and the rabble in the Americas who think differently. Oh, now, cheer up! It will be easier than you think to convince him that there's no conflict whatsoever between being Catholic and favoring controlled births of undesirables. In fact, we've found that with a little fashionable persuasion, people can be trained to call themselves 'Catholic' while defying the Pope himself! That's why Gilbert is so important! Not only is he an excellent example of quality breeding, but were his mind properly turned, there's no end to the good his writings will do for our cause."

Herb paused. "Gil? A superior breed?"

"Are you jealous, Herbert? In any case, we've had this discussion before. You're willing to ignore your objections to Eugenics when it benefits you, aren't you?"

"Certainly. I just don't want Gil or me to be hurt when your lot takes over. That's all."

"Not to worry. I'll do my job and protect you both quite well, provided you both do yours. Besides," she sat in one of the rickety deck chairs and stretched out luxuriously with a sigh, "you'll witness a little demonstration of pure science and Eugenic principles when we reach the American shores."

"What's that mean?"

"Oh, you'll see. Now," she said, stretching in the rickety deck chair, "how are we to pass the time until we arrive?"

Chapter 23

"With all that we hear of American hustle and hurry, it is rather strange that Americans seem to like to linger on longer words." – GKC, *What I Saw in America*

The three men stood at the dock. Salt air, the screech of seagulls, more obnoxious noises and other, unpleasant odors all assaulted their senses when they stepped off the train.
To the casual sightseer on the docks, they looked utterly out of their element in New York City, like a bunch of slack-jawed cowboys in longcoats wasting time by staring out into the distance.

And this was fine with Colonel James H. Finn, for he'd spent a lifetime profiting from such mistaken assumptions of others. His men were undeterred and focused. Decades traveling under the Mississippi sun, riding horses in the Texas Republic or hiking through the Sierra Mountains in the Californias in pursuit of prey had made their shoulders broad, their skin leathered, their natural limbs powerfully thick and their minds alert as a flock of hawks on a sunny day.

They'd arrived in town a few days early, which also suited Finn fine. Their wealthy client was footing their hotel, food and other bills, after all.

"How long 'til the balloon gets its string tied here, boss," asked Harper, his eyes looking to the horizon.

"The manifest says three days, Corporal. We've got us a stakeout here 'til then."

"Who stays, ever-benevolent leader?" Holiday spoke this time.

"Y'all figger that out amongst yeselves," said Finn, sticking a toothpick in his mouth to gnaw on. The two remaining men faced off in an intense contest of wills that Finn completely ignored. He continued ignoring them as they began counting to three, bobbing their hands up and down, making odd gestures and shouting "axe chops wood," "wood floats on water," or "water rusts the axe," until Corporal Joseph Harper was left with an unhappy expression on his face.

"It would appear axe-wood-water just isn't your game, Corporal," Holiday drawled, a small grin under his gray handlebar mustache. "Perhaps next time we should try a spelling contest. Or maybe poker."

Harper opened his mouth to reply, but Finn cut him off.

"Corporal Joseph Harper," Finn said, "I will record in my report that it is my decision as your commanding officer that you will monitor this post, and report to us in the usual way as soon as the airship from London bearing our cargo is in sight. Are my instructions clear?"

"Yessir," said the Corporal. "Where will y'all be?"

"Right across the street at our new command post," said Finn, pointing to a tavern fifty feet from the front of the dock.

Harper fumed inside, but nodded his head and turned to face the ocean while Finn and Holiday chuckled and walked off. This wasn't the first time a game of axe-wood-water had gotten him stuck on first watch while his colleagues ran off to drink on the client's dime!

In the distance, Harper saw the tiny speck of an approaching airship. He pulled out his copy of the portrait of Gilbert Keith Chesterton. Looking for something in the picture to despise, he settled on Gilbert's large glasses. *You better not give me an ounce of trouble, boy,* he thought to himself. *Not an ounce, or those goggle-eyed glasses an' my brass leg are gonna have a real unpleasant discussion.*

"...no animal invented anything so bad as drunkenness – or
so good as drink." – GKC, *All Things Considered*

In the world of living things, a crowd of people is truly unique. Most animals typically will form crowds around sources of food. In cultures where food isn't an issue, often an unusual event such as a celebrity visit or a train wreck will draw people to a crowd out of curiosity, self-interest, or a desire not to be left out.

Such were now the reasons for the odd grouping of a crowd of small boys around Gilbert and his new chess partner, Samuel Wilks. The smaller boys completely ignored the wonder of the steam-driven artificial arm, and even the thick glass dance floor in the ballroom to their right, all in favor of the battle of skill on the chessboard in front of them.

Gilbert was mesmerized by the game tonight in a way few activities had ever fascinated him. He'd learned how to play chess long ago by his mother to while away an afternoon free of lessons. Ma and Gilbert had spent most of the morning pulling hedgehog spines out of the hide of one of the stupider farm dogs, and Ma was (thankfully) too tired to teach him more.

"Here's something every child of intelligence should learn to do, Gilbert," she'd said. "You're going to learn to play a game more complicated mentally than checkers and less difficult physically than baseball."

She had reached into one of the many hidden panels in the home that only she and Pa seemed to know about, and brought out a rectangular box. A bunch of figurines like wooden soldiers were inside.

"Are we going to play a war?" little Gilbert had asked with a cautious, excited tone in his voice. Games with toy soldiers were rare events with his school friends, who were either too distant or too disinterested in imagined warfare to play with.

"A kind of war, Gilbert. But one that relies on skill, not chance, to win. Here are the pieces."

He learned that the smallest pieces were called the pawns. They moved one square forward, could capture diagonal left or right, and became the most powerful pieces if they traveled all the way to the board's end without being taken.

Bishops moved and captured diagonally. Knights looked like

horses, moved in an L-shape and could jump over pieces blocking their paths. Rooks looked like castles and could move any number of squares up-or-down and side-to-side. The Queen could move like a Bishop or Rook, and was the most powerful piece on the board.

Child's play. Ma had begun playing the white pieces and Gilbert the black ones. Their first argument over rules began two minutes later. "Why'd you move that piece there, Ma?" Gilbert asked, pointing to the pawn she'd moved into harm's way. "I'm just gonna take him out next move."

"He's blocking the way of my better pieces, Gilbert. I'm going to sacrifice him so that I can have greater flexibility in my plans to defeat you."

Something about that strategy didn't sound right to Gilbert. But at age eight, he had difficulty explaining that he didn't like using even the pretended death of a low-ranked person as a means to victory. For now, articulating such a thought was beyond his still growing abilities of speech and persuasion.

"I'm not gonna do that."

"Suit yourself, Gilbert. But you'll see who wins."

Gilbert then had a strategy for victory appear in his mind. It was simple, but it hit with sudden and brilliant clarity. After a few more moves, it was clear his mother planned to open way in both lines of pawns through which her forces would pour in and devastate his greater pieces in the back row. Gilbert saw his mother's pieces as a coiled snake, ready to strike through an opened weak spot and pour in the venom.

How do you defeat a snake, thought Gilbert? You need something to protect against a snake's fangs. A turtle? Good, but not good enough. A turtle had good protection, but nothing to hit with. It could hide, but wouldn't win.

No. Not a turtle.

A *hedgehog.*

Yes. A hedgehog. Like a turtle, but with bristled spines that injured enemies who came too near.

Gilbert moved his pieces forward one at a time, each one protected by at least one other. Soon his forces filled the middle of the chessboard. His forward pawns acted as bristles on a hedgehog's hide, ready to spike and capture pieces that ventured too close or tried to capture them. Pawns or other defending pieces quickly closed the infrequent breaks in his line of defense. He rebuffed one attack after another, capturing piece after piece while losing nearly none himself.

Ma's looks of surprise were worth every moment of the afternoon's game. In just over twenty moves, he had battled his mother to a standstill and they'd agreed to a tied game (A "stalemate" she'd called it) so that Ma could get to making dinner before Pa came home.

Now, here at several thousand feet above the Atlantic Ocean on a luxury airship, Gilbert was again using the hedgehog strategy, and was attracting what had likely become the first cheering crowd for a chess match that any member of the passenger list had seen. The cheers were whispered, but cheers nonetheless.

Gilbert had begun the game hoping that by feigning interest in the chess match little Jack Lewis would grow bored and find someone else to be a barnacle to.

Except that something very nearly the opposite happened. Gilbert soon fell into the game, not even noticing that Jack kept disappearing from Gilbert's elbow and reappearing with steadily more adoring young chess fans his own age.

The game had begun as many chess games did, with each player bringing forward the pawn that stood in the middle of the board, directly in front of the King. But as Gilbert had moved the hedgehog up the board, Wilks was first amused at Gilbert's novel, if obviously futile, strategy. Amusement became annoyance, though, as Wilks saw how effective the strategy truly was. Wilks tried baits, tricks and traps he had learned from Singapore to Cheyenne, and he'd never seen someone play by sending a bloated group of pawns forward into the middle of the board as Gilbert was doing.

The novelty of steam-powered, insectile arm that hummed and creaked as it picked up and moved their pieces according to the controls on Wilks' left armrest had also evaporated quickly as the game progressed.

"You know, Gilbert," he said, after a dozen or so moves, "I once saw a strategy similar to yours between an English girl and a Filipino chap. Drove the poor man up the wall. He was the kind of fellow who liked to visualize the Mongol hordes sweeping down onto the Europeans at his command. When the girl managed to lock down a good third of the board doing what you're doing, he snapped and threw one of his pieces at her."

"Who won?" Gilbert asked, trying to maintain his concentration even as he hoped Wilks was losing his own.

"She won by default when the fellow was ejected from the chess club and banned for life. Women are rare enough in such places. This girl was a fairly pretty, brown-haired and sharp-minded little dear, and that made her all the more worth protecting. Sadly, she was only a year or two younger than you, putting her out of the circles of self-respecting men my age. And she claimed to be bound for the Martian colonies after they'd been revealed, going as an archaeologists' assistant or something. Such a vocation put her quite literally out of my orbits entirely."

Gilbert risked a look around and saw that Jack had not only returned, but also returned with yet another child in tow. This new one was skinnier, dressed in the blazer-and-shorts outfit that schoolboys around England wore whatever the weather, and had a head of hair as short as Jack's, but was sandy blond where Jack's was very dark.

"He looks like he's going to drive that piece right into the mouth of the beast," the new boy said to Jack.

"Like Odin against the jaws of the serpent from Hell."

"Not quite, Jack. 'Hel' was the serpent's name, not where it had come from. And it only had one 'L' at the end. And, for that matter, Odin didn't even get a chance to use his spear before he was ..."

"A little quiet, please?" Wilks' voice was tinged with a tone known by children everywhere.

"Wait here, Tollers," said Jack, and ran off. 'Tollers' looked like he didn't appreciate his new nickname, but didn't bother shouting after Jack. He turned instead to focus on the chess game.

Without Jack, Gilbert noted, it became very, very quiet in the large room.

The patrons of the nearby bar with their umbrella-capped drinks had already disappeared, leaving only a few behind. There were perhaps a dozen tables on the enclosed deck, with lights behind reflecting off the observation windows. Gilbert looked back to the face of his opponent. Wilks was studying the board intently, planning his next action several moves in advance. Gilbert was reaching for a pawn when a screechy voice at his elbow jarred him from his contemplative semi-trance.

"No!" said the voice when Gilbert's fingers were an inch from the pawn's head. "No," it repeated, "don't move the pawn again! You have a chance to castle! Castle instead!" Gilbert turned to look and saw yet another child, this one skinny with freckles and short dark hair. "You play your way, and I'll play mine, pal, 'kay?" said Gilbert with what he hoped was a pleasant yet firm tone of voice.

"My name's not pal, it's Johnny!"

"Your pal is being very right, you know, Mister Gilbert," another voice said at Gilbert's other elbow. Gilbert turned and saw that a pair of identical boys had materialized from the ether, sporting a skin tone and accent from India. "If you continue on this course without capturing something, you will finish with a stalemate, without completing a win at all."

"Maybe I don't want to win, didja think of that?" Gilbert snapped. "Maybe I'd just like to end the game without anyone getting hurt or killed, and we could all go to a pub or something and have a nice quiet drink before we all go back to our little farmhouses and get ready for the next day's work!"

"Not want to win?" Wilks said, "Do I take it, Mister Edwardson, that you are conceding this game?"

"Heck, no!" Gilbert replied, reaching for the board, but first stopping and breathing a few times. When calm, he took the pawn he had reached for initially and moved it exactly one space forward, to a square he'd protected so well any enemy piece attacking the pawn would be snapped up like a dove in a dragon's mouth.

A subdued "Ooooooh!" went up from the growing group of young chess lovers that Jack had been rounding up to view the game. Gilbert closed his eyes at the sound, and gritted his teeth as the two East Indian boys started speaking rapid Hindi to each other, as they had each time Gil had made his last few moves. Gilbert's catechist had told him suffering in this life could be offered up as a prayer for one's self or others. Gilbert offered up this game, praying for the ability to keep from losing his temper and verbally backhanding someone before it was over.

Despite these distractions, as Gilbert's strategy continued to lock down space after space, a very odd thing happened to Gilbert that had happened only rarely before:

The many directions and places his pieces could move to and conquer now appeared in his mind's eye as roads on a map. Many routes led to his defeat, a few to stalemate, but he saw one that led him to ...

He jumped his knight over the line of pawns, making an unexpected capture. Wilks' eyes grew wide, while the boys surrounding them 'Ooh'd and 'Ah'd again, as if Gilbert had just scored a devastating body blow in a boxing match. Wilks made a move, a feeble move, trying to set Gilbert up for an attack. *But*, Gilbert thought, *that leaves him wide open on his flank!* Wilks must have seen it! Couldn't everyone? All Gilbert had to do was …

Move a pawn, sit through another feeble move by Wilks, and then move another black knight.

"Checkmate," said Gilbert. He was only dimly aware of the cheering, punctuated by high-pitched squeals from a mob of nearly a dozen schoolboys Jack had mustered to cheer Gilbert on. Gilbert looked at the face of his vanquished opponent, searching Wilks' eyes to see how the older man was taking his defeat.

There was surprise on Wilks' face for a moment as he searched the board for an opening, a flaw in Gilbert's call for victory or an escape route for his trapped white king. Finding none, he looked at Gilbert and smiled. "Well done, lad," he said, his left hand tapping its armrest slightly for emphasis. "Well done! I never thought I'd see a strategy like that rule the day. What did you call it again?"

"Well," said Gilbert, leaning back and putting his thumbs in his suspenders with what he hoped looked like a casual air. "Me, I prefer callin' it the hedgehog since you'll get stuck by the spines if you come too close."

"Quite appropriate, then," he said, noting that the more excitable of the boys were nearly dancing around the room with glee at Gilbert's victory. "When you manage to get clear of your new fans, Gilbert, meet me at the bar. I'd like to buy you a drink to celebrate your victory this evening."

Gilbert turned to look at the half-dozen boys who had crowded around him since he had begun playing an hour ago. Chubby, dark-haired Jack stood at front in the leader's position, with the taller, blond Tollers at his side. Behind them were the freckled skinny boy and the East Indian twins. All wore the blazer and shorts that were common to schoolboys in the private boarding schools of the upper middle-class, though for some reason in England the private schools were called public.

"How did you do it, Mister Gilbert?" Jack asked with awe in his voice, his eyes shining behind his glasses, "None of us have ever seen a win like that before, with nearly no loss of pawns!"

"Never before!" shouted Tollers.

"Never again!" shouted the skinny boy! "That was a game for the immortals!"

"He locked down the board! The whole board! Locked it down and threw away the key, he did!"

"Could you teach us that?"

"An immortal game!"

More comments came from Jack, Tollers and the freckled boy, mixed with rapid-fire heavily accented observations from the East Indian twins.

All the voices coming at various pitches quickly got to be too much for Gilbert. "Woah," he said, putting his hands over his ears, "Woah, woah! WOAH! Quiet a second!"

Dead, sudden silence enveloped the table. Gilbert was getting more than a little unnerved at the instant obedience of these kids. "Look, boys," he said, holding his hands up in a gesture that he hoped would encourage calm as much as it would keep his personal boundaries intact, "I have had a truly difficult day. I just want to relax for a few minutes and then hit the sack, you know?"

"Certainly, Mister Chesterton," said Tollers.

"Shh," hissed Jack angrily, "d'you want him to get angry? He's going by the name of Edwardson on this trip! He's incognito!"

Nods between the boys were exchanged, the bravest ones giving Gilbert a wink or a thumbs up gesture, after first watching Jack do it to make sure it was safe.

Dear God, thought Gilbert. *You finally answered the prayer I said in high school. I'm finally popular. But it's with a group of people I can't stand to be around.*

"So, Gilbert," said Wilks, his eyes smiling, "if that is indeed your name, what is it that brought you aboard an airship bound for New York?"

Gilbert smiled, reminding himself again that he was trying to keep a low profile. He willingly followed Wilks as he wheeled from the chessboard to inside the bar proper, taking a seat next to the space where Wilks had parked his chair.

"Work really," Gilbert said. "Plus I lived in New York for a few years. Thanks for your patience, by the way, with the kids. Little Jack seems to be of the opinion that I'm a famous writer of some sort from the British Isles, and his friends have all followed suit."

"Mistaken identities can be best, my young friend, for all concerned. If you think about it, the Christian faith spent its first thirty years being formed by someone everyone assumed to be a precocious child who grew to be a carpenter peasant. Rum thing about the Resurrection, of course. Surprised everyone, and upset the whole apple cart and changed the world."

"No doubt."

"Well, as for that drink: how does a fresh Iced Tea from the Island sound to you, lad?"

"Sounds great," Gilbert said. He was tired, but memories of his mother's iced tea suddenly resurfaced, and he felt a powerful want for the sweet and tangy taste in his mouth.

Wilks looked at the barkeep and his spidery mechanical arm held up two metal fingers. "Two Long Island Iced Teas for my new friend and I," he said jovially.

The barkeep nodded with a smile born from months or years of training, and gave a slight bow as if he were overjoyed to serve them. He reached to a secret place out of sight behind the bar, pulled up a punchcard from the darkness beneath his tray, and held the card up to the gaslight like a jeweler ensuring the worth of a precious stone. The barkeep spun around suddenly, slipping the card into a slot at a machine behind him. An engine fired up somewhere as pins dropped through the holes in the card and gave information to an analytical engine, which began mixing teas, sugars and lemons.

Gilbert nodded to himself. He'd been a clacker himself once, working with punchcards and analytical engines to make a living. Someday, if he got tired of the journalist angle, the possibility still remained that he could go back to that world ...

Yeah, right. Asking him if he missed clacking was a bit like asking a freed prison inmate if he still missed his old cell. Still, it was always good to have a marketable skill to fall back on.

"Ah, here we are," Wilks said as two glasses filled with ice and an ice-tea looking mixture were served up to them. "Enjoy, Mister Edwardson! To our health and your burgeoning fame among young chess aficionados."

"Thank you kindly, Mister Wilks," said Gilbert, sipping his drink and finding the taste ... delightful! He'd give anything to make sure that no one heard him use that word to describe something outside of a newspaper, but that was the first word that came to mind. Delightful! Smoother than any iced tea he'd ever had. "Mm, that's great stuff," he said with a casual air, slurping down a gulp before he continued. "By-the-by," Gilbert continued, "how did you come to be in a wheelchair, if you don't mind me asking?"

Wilks looked at Gilbert with a slight surprise on his face as Gilbert downed the drink. "Well," he began, "it came about from the Invasion, to be precise. I had checked into a luxury hotel in London before the mollusks had even landed, intending to while away a few weeks with my fellow idle rich. And, when the Martians entered London in their machines, I was in the building when a tripod's tentacle tore open the roof. By then there were at least half a dozen of the things swarming the area, and the building I was in was swept down in a torrent of wood, metal and plaster. The last thing I recall was being hit on the left side of the head and neck so hard, I felt sure as I slipped away that my brains had been dashed out.

"The tripods ignored me in the hotel rubble, perhaps looking for more sporting prey. I lay among the rubble for days, broken but not bleeding, my injuries leaving me paralyzed from the neck onwards, with only a little movement in my right hand."

"That sounds like a nightmare."

"It was. But many such trials are blessings in disguise. During that time I came to the realization that I'd squandered a great many opportunities to do good with the gifts I'd been given, and have spent my life since funding missions in China and other nations. I am wealthy in part because of long-term investments made by my forefathers. And, I now say, if I had to lose my body to save my soul, such a trial makes me the beneficiary of the best long-term investment a man could possibly make."

He paused to take a drink from his own glass, held by his mechanical arm. After his sip, he saw Gilbert's Long Island Iced Tea sitting emptied on the bar. "By, gum, lad, you really can sock them away. Will you be having another?"

"Certainly, if you're off'ring," said Gilbert.

Except now, Gil felt ... odd. A little bleary, and tired but energized all at once. If Wilks started telling him a funny story instead of another intense one, he knew he'd begin laughing uncontrollably.

And he wanted another iced tea. And he wanted to know why they kept calling them Long Islands. But he could wait on that.

When Gilbert next looked down, he saw another iced tea in front of him. Good. Gilbert drank while Wilks told him about being rescued from under the beams of the wrecked hotel, and volunteering his nearly paralyzed self for some German firm's experiments with applied alien technology. And what did he have to lose, really? And now ...

Gilbert had finished his second iced tea. And the nice voice, it was Wilks', he was pretty sure, was asking if he'd like another?

What a great joke! Gilbert giggled. "Would I like another? Does a Martian suck blood?"

Another round, Wilks indicated with his mechanical fingers.

Gilbert looked around the deck where he had spent the last hour. The little squad of chess fans were crowded around Jack and Tollers, who were squaring off against each other trying to reenact the chess match that Gilbert and Wilks had finished an hour or so ago. One of the twins tried to comment, but kept getting cut off by the excitable freckled child finishing his sentences for him. The other twin was doing the same, but making at least semi-coherent sentences with phrases like 'rye lopez' or 'positional maneuvering.'

Gilbert's eye fell on the clock. Had it already been an hour?

There was more shouting from the table nearby. Gilbert turned to look, meaning to get back to Wilks in a moment. Just a moment, and he'd tell Wilks if he felt all right ...

A red-faced man was yelling something incoherent at a nearby table to a group of seated friends.

"Give it a rest, Turnbull," one of the red-faced man's dinner companions said.

"Never!" shouted the red-faced man, whose name was presumably Turnbull. "I cannot, and will not be silent! If the fools who've kept us in the Dark Ages with religion aren't going to be silent, then why should I?"

"What's yer beef with the Dark Ages, fella?" asked Gilbert, careful to keep his talking voice even. It had become a little difficult to speak, though thinking went just jim-dandy, thank you! "Don' forget, they were the Ages of *Faith*. They didn't call 'em the Dark Ages 'til a bunch of third-rate historians wanted to make those times look bad!"

"And you," sneered Turnbull, his face getting redder while his speech slurred, "are you going to defend an era that demanded you take everything on faith?"

"Where'd you hear people believed that? Were you there?"

"Well, no."

"Then you're taking *that* on faith! Not that you're necessarily wrong, pal. But when you only listen to the folks who hate the Church and everything it stands for, you're taking in on *faith* that the Church is a bad thing, which means you've become everything you say you hate about the Age of Faith."

"Fine, lad. If you like the Dark Ages so much, let us settle this as they would back then!"

"Oh, rot. Here it comes again," said another man at the table.

"I mean," continued Turnbull, shouting over his companion, "that I shall fight a duel, a duel of honor! There! I say that the Holy Mother Church is a mud-splatted strumpet! That Mary was a tart who blamed her unplanned pregnancy on a bird, and owes her cult today to centuries of pagan goddess worship! What say you all? Where is the courage of the martyrs which the Church so proudly proclaims as its heritage? Will anyone fight a duel for the honor of these two ladies?"

Though he didn't know it, Gilbert was now quite drunk. What he'd thought was iced tea was actually known among drinkers as a Long Island Iced Tea, a mixture of no fewer than five types of hard alcohol and a splash of cola. When combined properly it hid the taste of alcohol completely, and tasted more like flavored cola water.

Had Gilbert not put a pair of very powerful alcoholic adult beverages unintentionally in his system, he likely would have been far more apt at silencing Turnbull in a debate. He had had a great deal of practice doing so at his family dinner table growing up, and more so in the midst of newspaper reporters in the past few months.

But even though he could still speak fairly coherently, Gilbert's reaction time and ability to process information had slowed a great deal. By the time he'd realized the nature of Turnbull's challenge, another hand directed by a much more sober brain had already arisen.

"I will champion the Queen and the Mother both!"

The voice had come from behind Gilbert, from the group of young chess players.

They were all staring at little Tollers. All of eight years old, it was he who'd raised his right hand and spoken. His face and voice displayed a heroic surety and deadly earnestness that a Knight of the Round Table in its prime would have envied.

What the ... thought Gilbert through his booze-soaked brain.

Tollers, already standing, never taking his eyes off of those of the man he now called out as his opponent, moved from the chessboard and walked with the resolution of a soldier falsely accused of cowardice towards Turnbull and his cohorts.

Tollers stopped in front of the much bigger man, standing with his short legs straight. His chin quavered just a little, but still jutted out at Turnbull.

"My own mother has been shabbily treated by the likes of you in my father's family, sir," said Tollers. "For her honor, as well as that of the Blessed Virgin and the Bride of Christ, I accept your challenge!"

Turnbull laughed, made a snide remark about a Church that would allow its youngest members to go to slaughter, and turned to go.

"Yella!" shouted Gilbert, standing tall. His anger boiled over from who knew what, and his ankle throbbed from its old wound. "Yella as a flower!"

Turnbull stopped, his back still to Gilbert.

"Let it go, lad," said Wilks at his elbow, "That's the drink talking now. Don't follow its lead! Turnbull's already lost."

Turnbull now turned to face Gilbert, wound up one sleeve, and then the other. "Right, lad," he said, "I've been waiting near twenty years for someone to take me on in this fight, and I won't say no when a decent-sized second steps up."

He assumed a boxing stance, feet slightly apart with bent legs and arms raised into crooked fists.

"Turnbull," someone said, "the boy's three sheets to the wind as it is. Take a swing at him and you'll spend the rest of the trip in the brig."

"Shaddap," barked Turnbull to the nervous friend behind him, "I'm going to give one of these superstitious idiots the drubbing they need. Well, boy? Care to take the first punch?"

Gilbert stood, or made a reasonable attempt to do so. *Am I really drunk?* he thought. *Is this what it feels like?* He felt that he could, if pressed, tell the funniest joke, dance the wittiest dance, or punch the nimblest opponent. Forget the fact that he'd rarely ended a fistfight without either being rescued or pummeled to the point of saying 'Uncle' in the schoolyard. Today would be diff ...

He was never certain afterwards if he actually threw the punch. What he couldn't deny was that Turnbull's fist hit Gilbert's face, bashing his nose hard and making it bleed.

Gilbert spun 'round at the blow's impact. And the world spun around as words jammed in and steamed through his head, his *nose hurt, hurt awfully, and Ma had stripped and painted the door earlier while Pa had been away. When the door swung back after hitting him in the face, Gilbert smelled turpentine and paint, and blood gushed from his nose as he fell to the floor.*

"Where's yer maw, at?" said the voice from above. "gotta a little business offertunity ..." Gilbert was too busy screwing his eyes nearly shut while screaming in panicked pain to look up into the shadow that stood over him.

"Calvin, if you know what's good for you ..." It was Ma. She was speaking loud now, her voice booming like Gilbert had never heard it before, and Gilbert was screaming and the smells of paint and blood were in his nostrils while the shadow chuckled above him and moved

down the hall with clunking steps towards his Ma and ...

Gilbert opened his eyes, his odd dream fading. As he sank again, this time into a peaceful oblivion, Gilbert heard dim mixtures of laughter and roared anger, as a blurry face with lenses for eyes appeared above him, asking him if he was quite alright? Are you quite alright, Mister Gilbert? Quite alright ...?

Chapter 25

"To the insane man his insanity is quite prosaic, because it is quite true. A man who thinks himself a chicken is to himself as ordinary as a chicken…It is only because we see the irony of his idea that we think him even amusing…In short, oddities only strike ordinary people. Oddities do not strike odd people…"
– GKC, *Orthodoxy*

He wasn't old, he kept telling himself as he tiptoed down the hallway, his shoes making barely any noise as he made his way to the hangar bay. True, a life spent mostly indoors with his nose in Science books and his hands busy with test tubes had left him with the frail physique of a man thirty years older. He *wasn't* old, though, he said again. He was only in his early forties. He could make it to the outside and the valley floor, just as the others had done. True, they'd never been heard from again, but that didn't mean they were dead did it? Not for sure, anyway. Just a few more steps, and he'd be in the hangar, and then ...

The door! Huzzah! Now, a quick jimmying of the lock, then slide the door open, and ...

He recognized the Captain from his broad-shouldered silhouette in the doorway. His bright teeth made a pointed, crescent smile that reflected what little light there was this time of night.

He'd been waiting here. Waiting! Somehow, the Captain *knew* he'd be coming and had waited. Waited maybe for hours in the same, cross-armed, smiling position.

He gasped in fear as the Captain's silhouette walked towards him. "Evening, Samuel," the Captain said, his smile never changing, his eyes smiling too. "I thought you looked a little too much at this door today, so I followed a hunch. Thinking about a little stroll on a wind current? Or maybe you were gonna take a slide on a moonbeam?"

Samuel gulped without a sound. "I ..." he started feebly, "I just wanted to see ..."

"The stars? Why didn't you say so, good buddy? C'mon." The Captain, no longer a silhouette, reached out and put a large arm around Samuel's shoulder. Before he knew it, Samuel was inside the flight deck, looking up at the stars though a large window. The wind howled outside like a man in agony over things lost.

"Doncha like looking up there?" said the Captain, breathing in deeply. "It makes every problem in the world just disappear, doesn't it? Anything that might make us unhappy, spiteful, or ungrateful, just fritters away when you look up at the stars. Ain't that so?"

"Um ... yes?" Samuel spoke with the hesitation born of many beatings at the hands of the Captain's men, for offenses ranging from working too slowly to being near a guard when he was having a bad day.

"Yes, indeed, Samuel. You know, for a long while, I couldn't even look at the stars. Know why?"

Samuel shook his head. It was still pitch black except for the starlight, but the Captain sensed the movement.

"Because, Samuel, a little over a year ago, I was part of a team. They plucked me right out of the Federal Police, after I caught this very bad fella named Robur who thought having a flying machine made him master of the world.

"But my team, Samuel, we were from all over. France, Italy, America, England. Each of us were the best of the best at what we did. We *flew*, Samuel. They strapped those flying harnesses to us, and we flew. For training, we dropped magnetic bombs on metal targets, cheering when they blew up behind us. All the while, we couldn't wait to get into combat. All six of us. We flew, we fought, we drank a lot. But then ... then ..." The Captain let Samuel go, suddenly, and turned to look at him The Captain was a remarkably handsome man, whom all the girls in the city swooned over at one time or another (The only exception was the Emperor's assistant, but she had icewater in her veins, it was said). Now, a hint of something unpredictable had crept into those eyes that so many of the girls talked about.

"Then," continued the Captain, "the squids came, Samuel. They came in those giant tin cans, with the three legs."

"The Martians," said Samuel helpfully.

"Yes!" the Captain barked, "We got the word. '*Scramble to your Vinci Flyers, lads!*,' they said. '*This is not a drill! Scramble, lads! This is what you've trained for!*'

"And we flew, Samuel. And we dropped our bombs, and killed a few, and then they turned their rays on us, and then ... then we fell, Samuel." He stared at Samuel with a look that would have moved a stone to pity. "They turned their burning rays on us, and all of my friends, all of them! My brothers! Shuman! Cooney! Tondre! Liberty! Walker! Guys! Where are you?" He began shouting at everything and nothing, moving in a quick frenzy as he relived the moment. "Where are you? They fell, and while I'm shouting at them to dive for cover, I'm watching them, each of them, burst into flame and die screaming behind me. And you know, Samuel, you know why I lived?"

Samuel shook his head. Quickly.

"Because I messed up, Samuel!" The Captain's eyes weren't relaxed and happy anymore. They were darting around in their sockets like a pair of trapped minnows, while his arm started tightening around Samuel's neck. "They did just great, followed their training to the letter! But I lost my head! Don't you see what a joke that is? Don't you see? They were all better men than me, but I ended up in front somehow! I smacked my head on a tree branch, and they were all torched by the Martian's heat rays! They turned into ashes and blew away on the wind! Little pieces of them, flying by and getting stuck in the trees and in my clothes, burning on my skin like pinpricks. And I couldn't brush my friends out of my hair, Samuel, because I had to keep hanging on to the branch all night. All night, and all the next day until I was rescued. And then I found the army didn't even know I existed. And the base I'd come from was gone, wiped out by heat rays.

"So I was alone. Drifting. Nothing. Nothing at all. And now, now when everyone here has a chance to be part of something great, something amazing, something never done before, and I see someone trying to leave it all behind, you know how it makes me feel, Samuel?" His arm tightened around Samuel's neck further, completely unaffected by Samuel's attempts to struggle free.

"It makes me," the Captain said, his eyes squeezing shut while he gritted his teeth. "It makes me want to hang on to what I have here. Hang on, Samuel, like I did on the branch. For dear life. *Hang on*, Samuel. Can you do that for me? For all of us? Just ... hang on a little while?"

Samuel gave a gurgled, coughing excuse for a scream. The Captain's arm had tightened like a vise around the smaller man's neck, and he hadn't noticed Samuel's thin arms beating uselessly against his leather-jacketed back with the desperation of a dying man. A minute more, and Samuel wouldn't move ever again without the aid of a bolt of lightning.

"Tough times, Cap'n?" said a voice at the doorway.

Captain John Strock, age thirty-one, locked eyes with the new speaker as he released his prisoner. The older man slumped to the floor in a gasping, grateful heap and started to crawl to the doorway and its occupant.

"Nothing wrong at all, Emperor," said the Captain, snapping to attention and facing forward. "I found this citizen taking a stroll after curfew, and when he resisted I restrained him."

"I don't think that'll be a problem again, will it, Samuel?"

"No, Emperor," said Samuel from his lying position on the floor, his body wheezing like a generations-old set of blacksmith bellows.

"Good man," said the Emperor, taking another pull on his cigar and making a bright, fiery red glow on its tip. "Back to bed. You've got another long day ahead of you tomorrow."

"Yes, Emperor," he said, standing with difficulty then shambling back in the direction of his quarters.

When he was gone, Emperor Norton turned to face Jack again. "John, how many prisoners have died in your custody this month?"

"Four, Emperor."

"Tonight, you almost lost one of our scientists. It's not such a big deal when someone like that literature professor gets his neck stretched. Heck, when you sicced the steam crabs on that trade unionist who made it to the ground a few weeks back, I actually enjoyed it. But tonight, you almost lost someone *important*. D'y'see? You don't want me to toss you aside, like the army did after the Invasion?"

"Please don't send me away, Emperor! I'm sorry! I truly am! It's just ..." John sat down on the stone bench near the wall and shoved the heels of his hands into his eyes while his body began rocking back and forth.

"Now, now," said Norton, sitting beside John, reaching up and putting a comforting arm around the Captain's broad shoulders. "We'll have a new batch of citizens joining us soon, and then you'll be able to relieve your pressures and stresses then, won't you? You're a very valuable member of the team, John. There's no way that I could do all I've done as quickly as I've done without your help. You know that, don't you? Just from now on, I want you to only vent your needed frustrations on folks from the Red level. Can you do that, John?"

"I ... I don't know, Emperor. I try to. I want to. But when I see them trying to leave, I just remember how awful things were. How .. " he buried his head in his hands again.

"I believe in you, John. Do you know why?" Norton tried to make eye contact with Jack unsuccessfully. He settled for bringing his lips to the bigger man's ear instead. "Because *Archibald is my brother*, John."

The Captain's hands fell away slowly, and he sat up, blinking.

"Is ... everything's alright?"

"Yes, John. You had a nightmare and I found you here. Why not go back to your room and sleep, lad? I'll have a new job for you in the morning, one that requires a good commander who can pilot my fastest airships."

"Yes ... yes, Emperor." John Strock, looking relaxed and happy, stood and walked slowly towards the door, shutting it behind him.

Darn good job Galatea did on the boy, Norton thought and he stood up. *That one little phrase of hers always manages to calm him down when I can't do it meself. Someday, though, I gotta find out who that Archibald character is.*

Now he stood in the darkness, looking up out the large, ceiling-sized window and finishing his cigar. The subtle pleasures of life, he thought, are as irreplaceable as they are unpurchasable. Standing alone on a starlit night, smoking a good cigar, keeping powerful and capable people at your beck and call by ensuring their emotional dependence upon you. All very satisfying.

Satisfied.

A cold feeling began in his stomach. He knew that there was nothing on this Earth, ultimately, that would truly satisfy his appetites. Not forever.

And knowing that made him weak and afraid inside.

Best to cut that thought off at the knees like I always do, he thought. *A good hit of scotch and a long nap.*

Chapter 26

"Those thinkers who cannot believe in any gods often assert that the love of humanity would be in itself sufficient for them; and so, perhaps, it would, if they had it." – GKC, *Tremendous Trifles*, 1909

Herbert stood on the deck again, feeling the wind blow on his face and wondering where he had gone wrong. Or right, depending on his mood. The feeling he had gone wrong had been shrinking for some time. Now it was little more than a small, annoying twitter in the back of his head. The excitement of seeing the skyline of New York City, tantalizing in the distance, helped silence his doubts utterly.

"Good morning, darling," said a familiar voice behind him. Herb turned, and he made the smallest gasp when he saw Margaret behind him.

True, Herb hated to admit that anything could have such power over him. But today, as at their first meeting and every juncture in between, she was so captivating that resistance was of little use. He'd tried time and again to drive her off with cutting insults and unpleasant remarks. But instead of angering her, his caustic taunts often instead made her laugh. In fact, his efforts to throw off her hold on him seemed to ... interest her, even more.

"Why, hello, 'dear,'" said Herbert. She was dressed today in the fashion of a middle-class wife on holiday, complete with a yellow parasol to keep the sun out of her eyes. He was still dressed in the same sport coat, shirt and trousers he'd been packed off with at the beginning of his journey.

"Did you sleep well?" he said, making conversation.

"Terribly," she answered, stretching slightly. "Are you ready for your latest test?"

"Test?" Herb asked, "What test? I thought Gilbert was my test, and we both agreed he wasn't on board?"

"This is something completely different," she said. She looked at her watch, and then the approaching shoreline. "At our current speed, Herbert, how soon do you think we'll reach port from our current location?"

"Is this part of the test now?" Herb asked, half joking. "Fine, I'd say we're about ... three minutes away from the end of our cross-Atlantic journey. How'd I do?"

"Actually, Herbert, you did fairly well," she said, clicking open a very ladylike watch. "But the test hasn't quite started yet. Not for another ... five ... "

She paused, letting the word hang in the air.

"Well," he said, "what's the ..."

An explosion ripped through the bowels of the airship!

The ground beneath Herb's feet groaned, buckled and began making snapping noises as he reached for the useless handrail.

"This is the test, Herbert," Margaret yelled over the suddenly deafening noise. "I'll see you on the shore, if you make it!"

She dropped the parasol, hopped onto the railing and made a high-dive to the water. Herb watched in disbelief as she hit the water with a splash and disappeared from the surface, only to reappear a few seconds later and begin swimming towards the shore.

Herb looked around him. People screamed, crewmen ran, and at least one child walked about crying for her mother as another explosion ruptured another wound in the airship's belly.

"Knickers," mumbled Herb under his breath, and looked over the railing again. The water was closer now; the airship was losing altitude rapidly, rocking back and forth as its innards groaned and screeched, metal tearing and breaking around him. Lifeboats, someone was screaming! Where are the lifeboats in God's na—!

The airship hit the water, shaking the deck beneath his feet with a rough, then a gentle shudder as it started sinking. There was heat behind him—scorching heat! Herb looked back—the Zeppelin's balloon was engulfed in fire, looking like something out of the worst nightmares of Dante's Inferno. Herb ran from the light, tearing towards the railing with a will not wholly his own. He dimly heard a high-pitched screaming—a weeping child stood in front of him at the railing. She faced Herbert but didn't see him, looking past him into the firestorm sweeping through the hydrogen-laced fabric of the blimp. Her mouth was open, ready to scream again for her mother, but she'd stuck on one of the higher-pitched syllables at the sight of the inferno chasing Herbert.

Knickers, thought Herb again. The child would cost him precious seconds of escape time! From the perspective of his newfound employers, the smart thing to do would be to shove the little urchin out of the way, jump over the railing and swim like mad for shore.

And that was why Herb was so thoroughly surprised when he grabbed the child by her arm, swept her into a protective grasp and leapt into the sea, barely ahead of the angry fire now to his left and the chilling water to his right. "Hold your breath, girl," he said when he came up for air after the dive. He kicked and struggled against the sinking ship's efforts to suck him backwards towards the blazing blimp, which careened down at them like the fist of a mythic fire god.

After the gondola sank, and just before the impact of the dirigible, he inhaled and puffed out his cheeks to show the little girl what she needed to do. Herb had just enough time to hear her follow his example before he pulled them both underwater, kicking frantically down and forward while red hot pieces of metal and ash rained into the water around them, leaving trails of sizzling bubbles. Some of the smaller pieces found Herb, jabbing him like small burning pins on his back, head and legs. Still swimming, he kicked while holding onto his struggling charge. He looked down and saw the outline of the balloon in the water below, sinking in the dim rays of light that penetrated the water. Changing direction, he now kicked with his body pointed up, gasping seconds later as he broke the surface and sucked in air.

The girl sobbed uncontrollably in Herb's ear. Herb looked back and saw people treading water amidst the wreckage, all of them shouting for loved ones or shrieking in panic.

Still holding the struggling girl, Herb saw a piece of floating wreckage nearly twenty feet away with a man, woman, and two small children climbing onto it. Herb looked away to the docks, wondering how long the swim would be. Making his decision, he held the shrieking child even harder to himself with one hand, kicked out and clumsily pushed with the other hand towards the makeshift raft.

Margaret, he thought as he propelled himself and the girl towards the small family. *Margaret, this is it. As of now, chivalry is dead. But not nearly as dead as you'll be when I get my hands on you.*

Chapter 27

"I do not believe in a fate that falls on men however they act; but I do believe in a fate that falls on them unless they act." – GKC, *ILN*, April 29, 1922

K elly J. Ewing, age twenty-five, looked at his drink and wondered exactly where his life was going. He'd come to the city looking for fame, fortune and adventure as a reporter. He'd been at it for nearly five years now, but a combination of poor luck and trusting the wrong people had kept him from moving up the ranks of the New York World, a paper that had a huge readership but a reputation for poor-quality journalism. *Five years,* he thought, *and I haven't even made it off of the crime beat yet.*

He'd always been a trusting sort, unfortunately. He'd let others backstab him, scoop his stories, and hadn't retaliated when he'd had the chance. He'd nearly sobbed to his mother through the phone the other night, wondering if he'd wasted the last five years when he could have been building some other kind of life.

Ma had said she'd pray for him. Yeah, right. Like that'd help. Just like it hadn't for the past five years.

The morning after talking to her, he was told to show up at this little bar. His job today? Meet some teenage wunderkind reporter traveling from England, hand him an envelope and then go back to the office for his next assignment.

Yeah, a real step up. Not just reporting throat cuttings and burglaries. Now, he could play post office. When a couple of cowboys came in with Pinkerton badges, Kelly thought about taking the initiative and interviewing them, but decided against it. Why bother? Bold moves and brave reporting hadn't helped yet. He was taking another sip of his whiskey and feeling even sorrier for himself when the explosion sounded outside.

What, th' ...

He sat up, flipped his brown hair out of his eyes and ran outside.

A cloud of black smoke still hung in the air. The airship was sinking. Wreckage and swimming survivors floundered in the water and ...

Kelly looked around.

He'd gotten to know many other journalists in the last five years.

And not one of them was here right now. If he ran to a phone, or a telegraph, or made smoke signals or anything, he'd have the first major scoop of his career!

He flipped open his notepad and began scribbling furiously while running for the nearest phone. The reporter kid from England could wait!

Corporal Joseph Tiberius Harper Junior, age twenty-two years and about five months, liked to think of himself as the quintessential 'good soldier,' the man upon whom his superiors could confidently place their trust. Losing his leg to a well-fired Maxim gun a few months back was a tough business, true. No man liked losing a limb in the line of duty, even if you were saving a rich man's beautiful daughter in the process. But during his rare moments of unhappy angst, Corporal Harper liked to recall the most exciting moments of his time with the Pinkerton's agency, none of which would have happened if he had stayed with his Pa and run the family business in St. Petersburg.

Every mission without exception had been an exciting adventure, and each one had given Harper a new chance to marvel at Colonel Finn's ability to switch personalities and attitudes like a chameleon, putting others in states of ease or fear as the situation demanded. With criminals, Finn became harder and tougher, his words clipped, coarse and final. With the elegant set ('high-falootin,' Joe's dad had called them) like Senator Sawyer, Finn could become the perfect polished gentleman, speaking in long, flowing speeches of elegant construction that made the proper ladies swoon with admiration at all Finn's stories of adventure.

So now, Joe thought with lingering resentment, which of those adventures and lessons he'd learned about, or experienced himself, qualified Joe to be out here, cold winds blowing in from the sea, waiting for an airship filled with smelly immigrants that England didn't want? He checked his whistle and flare gun for the fortieth or fiftieth time—yep, all set.

When he saw the speck on the horizon, he wasn't sure if he should blow the whistle or not. Better to wait until it got closer, he decided, and be sure of the make of the vessel.

By the time it got close enough to see the vessel's make—yep, single engine, hydrogen-heavy base (a dangerous, but therefore inexpensive ride) in the balloon, and a gondola that could hold maybe fifty passengers and crew—Harper was ready to blow his whistle and summon Finn and Holiday from their drinking table.

Yet ... calling them from their drinks for a wild goose chase would be a sure-fire way to get stuck out here for another eight-hour shift. Better to wait until he could see the name on the airship, first.

Over the next two minutes, it grew in size as it drew closer to Harper's dock. Five airships had docked in the last hour, but none here, where Harper was stationed. With all the advances in technology since the Martians had dropped onto the British Isles, it was a wonder that the eggheads of Europe hadn't figured out a way to communicate over greater distances than could be done by heliography, but ...

Hang on a moment. That was odd. It looked like a plume of black smoke had flowered from the back of the blimp, and then someone took a swan dive over the side of the airship's gondola! Harper was just about to bring the whistle to his lips when the airship's engines exploded a *second* time, sending a rippling shockwave across the waters that hit Harper and the civilians on the docks in seconds with a warm blast of wind!

"Sweet Jesus save 'em!" gasped Harper. People were running back and forth on the dock, screaming and pointing at the burning and sinking dirigible. If only he had Doc's magic eyeball, he could see the wreckage better, maybe spot the diver ...

There! He thought he could see that the diver was now a swimmer as he made his way ... no, it was a *she* ... the long, thick dark hair gave it away, and the white skin meant it was no Indian. The girl who'd dived off the gondola was nosing her way towards the port, swimming in the midst of all the wreckage. *Odd*, thought Harper. As she got within eyesight of the folks at the dock, she ducked underwater, popping up now and again behind cooling pieces of floating wreckage flung ahead of her by the explosion, as if she didn't want to be seen. Harper himself almost lost her several times, and only his trained eye and well-developed hunting instincts were able to help him anticipate when and where her need for oxygen would cause her to resurface.

Clever girl, he thought. *Blew up a Zeppelin, and now looking to escape with the wreckage. She's had some training herself, I'll wager, or my name isn't ...*

"Corporal Harper!"

Uh oh.

Harper turned to face the stone-blank expression of Colonel Finn, which had magically appeared only six inches from his nose. Finn's large fists were balled up into rock-hard lumps at his waist.

Chapter 28

"When people impute special vices to the Christian Church, they seem entirely to forget that the world (which is the only other thing there is) has these vices much more. The Church has been cruel; but the world has been much more cruel. The Church has plotted; but the world has plotted much more. The Church has been superstitious; but it has never been so superstitious as the world is when left to itself."
– GKC, *ILN*, December 14, 1907

I t was light. There was light and it gave Gilbert great pain. Gilbert opened his eyes and feared he was going to die. His head throbbed like a thumb that had been hit with a hammer, and his gut felt it had a marching band inside, stomping double-time while playing Champs.

He tried to sit up and didn't. Instead he waited, staring at the ceiling and breathing in slow gasps. After few minutes, the sun blasted a ray of light in all its glory through the window at Gilbert's face, making him moan and throw a cover over his head. Another searing blast of pain followed his rapid movement, and he lowered his arm slowly, while wincing under the blanket.

After a half hour, he accepted that he was going to die.

A half hour after that, he found himself *hoping* he would die, and die sooner than later. No matter what Father Flambeau said, Gilbert had a hard time believing that Purgatory could be any worse than this.

Less than fifteen minutes later, Gilbert found himself silently praying for death, asking God to give him a good and courageous end like William Wallace or Saint Thomas More, rather than prolong his suffering from ...

A shot of terror went through him, pure as a vein of California gold. What if he wasn't going to die? What if he was going to live?

He hadn't moved, except to open and close his eyes and cover his head with a blanket. Crimony, but what'd happened last night? His head hadn't hurt this much since a Martian had tried to blow him apart in an English sewer.

He carefully lowered the cover, opened his eyes just a crack and gave a cautious look around his room. It was lit against his will by annoying yellow sunbeams through his window and nearly transparent curtains. The complementary clock on his nightstand ticked reproachfully, and even the little statue of Mary he'd set up beside the clock seemed to look at him with disappointment in her painted eyes.

Gilbert opened and closed his mouth slowly. It had a pasty, gummy feeling. He tried to open his eyes all the way but quickly closed them. Exquisite pain blasted into his very, very hurt brain each time he looked at light.

Gilbert stayed in bed. If left alone he would have laid there until late afternoon, moved only by hunger and the need to evacuate his bladder.

Instead a loud thumping at his cabin door forced him awake. Gilbert paused; hoping that absolute silence would make his visitor would go away.

They didn't, of course. Whoever was at the door waited exactly ten seconds and knocked again. It was a very crisp knock of exactly nine raps. Gilbert counted them after the twelfth or thirteenth pause and repetition. He counted them again after he told them to go away four or five times. Finally, he got up, shuffled across the room and opened the door.

It was Jack Lewis, flanked by the Tollers kid, and ... what was the name of the skinny freckled kid with the screechy voice? Johnny something ...

"Good morning, Mister *Edwardson*," said Jack, emphasizing the last word as he'd done last night. In his right hand, he held a glass of orange juice. His left hand had presumably done the knocking, and now pushed the door open as he and his little friends pried their way past Gilbert into his cabin. Tollers held a covered white tray held in both his hands, while Johnny held a spoon, knife and fork in one hand and had a long napkin draped over his other arm like a waiter. Jack and Tollers looked unsure, as if they knew they weren't exactly welcome at this time.

Gilbert tried hard not to look at Jack. It made him think of doing unkind things to Jack's rather large, bespectacled head that men went to jail for doing and confession for thinking about.

"We hope you don't mind, but we brought you a spot of breakfast," Jack said happily.

"Actually, Jack, I'm really not feeling ..."

"Well? Oh, no worries, sir. Say no more! I know what cook used to make us when we felt unwell, and we had the friendly proletariats in the canteen construct just the repast you'll need to put you right as rain! Here," he said, shoving the juice at Gilbert.

Gilbert, his eyes only half-open, felt grungy and dirty in the now-wrinkled and sweat-tinged clothes he'd put on yesterday morning. Worse, in his current state, every word Jack said pounded the inside of his head like a rusty steamhammer. He sat down on his bed slowly, and watched, as helpless as a sick infant, as Jack directed Johnny and Tollers to put tray, napkin and silverware on the nearby nightstand that was far too small to accommodate it.

"Will there be anything else, Mister Ches—Mister *Edwardson*," asked Johnny, his large brown eyes searching Gilbert's face.

Gilbert wanted the boys to leave. He was willing to order them out of his cabin with a voice loud enough to part the Red Sea and traumatize all in its path, headache or not. But something in the three small boys' faces made him stop.

For reasons that were an utter mystery to Gilbert, these boys saw him as their hero. What if, the thought jumped into Gilbert's head, what if he'd found out that he was sharing an airship with one of his cowboy heroes from the nickel novels? How disappointed would he have been if the fellow had been ungrateful and mean?

Besides, the kids were only guilty of ignorance. They had utter, total and complete ignorance at how annoying they were to someone who felt six kinds of sick in the morning.

Still, Gilbert reasoned, if Father Brown or Father Flambeau were here, they'd counsel Gil to…

"Well, um, thank you boys. I really don't know what to say."

"Words are not necessary, sir," said Jack, "We are happy to serve someone who is a fine example of a rational, accomplished and thoughtful human being. Apart from your Christianity, of course."

"Um, yeah," said Gilbert, letting the comment pass. Right now he felt less like taking on someone in a debate than he ever had in his life. Both Tollers and Johnny looked like they knew it was time to go.

Speaking of which…

"Well, guys," he said, picking up a cup from the tray and thanking God silently that it held coffee, "I'm really not feeling well right now, but maybe I could see you all in a little bit, after I eat and clean up?"

"By all means, sir! Lads, let's go!" Jack moved to the door, and the taller and smaller boy fell into line behind him. Gilbert lifted the lid on the tray while taking a sip of his coffee. As the scent of freshly cooked eggs wafted upwards and leapt into his nostrils, Gilbert used the last few bits of endurance he had to keep from gagging and releasing his last few meals as a large and smelly piece of abstract art on the cabin floor. Gilbert said a little prayer, gritted his teeth, smiled and somehow managed to shake each boy's hand as they left the room. He even was able to sip some coffee in front of them to show he appreciated their efforts.

"Oh, by the by," said Tollers, trying to be quick, "we're approaching the New York City dock. There's a dreadful row taking place. Based on what I decoded from the heliograph, a smaller, faster model of airship traveling from London blew up earlier this morning or some such. Would you like us to scrounge you up a book or any more information while you eat?"

Gilbert spat. The coffee made a graceful arc as it splashed in the center of the cabin's expensive carpet.

Chapter 29

"It (New York) is very much like being in hell –
pleasantly, of course."
-GKC, interview with the *Montreal Daily Star*

Herb spluttered to shore, hanging onto the side of the makeshift raft. He and the presumed father of the little family had both held onto the sides while mother and daughter had lain flat on the board, which had threatened to capsize every second they had tried to stand, even on their knees. The freezing water had begun soaking into Herb's extremities. His toes had gone numb fairly quickly and his feet and ankles were following suit. His fingers, wet but still exposed to the morning chill, were not so lucky. They'd only gotten cold, not numb, and despite the unusually warm weather for this time of year, Herb felt the exquisite pain of wind chill with every waft of air.

The rest of him fared no better. He'd once had to walk to the house in a wet bathing suit when the path had been shrouded in cool shade. As a child, going from a fairly warm water by a lakeside dock to the cool breeze of the shady path was surprisingly unpleasant, and young Herb had moved quickly as he could in bare feet through the gravel on the path back to the house where he could change into dry clothes.

Now, though, the lake was the Atlantic Ocean in late January, his uncomfortable wet swimming suit was his entire suit of clothes, and Herb's misery was compounded by a little girl's shrieks and her mother's and four sisters' alternating between louder shrieks of joy at her daughter's safety and wails of upset over their new predicament. If the father had not been present, smiling at Herb and occasionally speaking words of thanks and comfort in another language, Herb might have jumped off the raft and taken his chances with the freezing water.

After an eternity of screaming female voices and a softer, rumbling male voice, Herb and his fellow refugees touched the shoreline of the New York harbor. Crowds of people thronged the slender beaches and docks. Some had been there earlier to meet loved ones or watch the boats and airships. Almost all the rest were curiosity seekers, drawn to the site and sound of an airship's explosion. The blue-suited police were having a great deal of difficulty keeping order at the docks. Many of the survivors had to make their own way from the shore to sympathetic police or deliriously happy relatives, or lie down on the sandy shore from exhaustion. No doctors had arrived on the scene yet, though he could hear an ambulance siren in the distance.

Oh, no, thought Herb. Secrecy was supposed to be the watchword of everything done by those attached to the circle. What if a bunch of journalists snagged him and demanded an interview? Or worse, what if he were hailed as a hero for saving the little girl? The little *immigrant* girl? That would hardly bode well for him, now would it? Bad enough if Herb was simply booted out of Margaret's group. What if there were other consequences that would have to be paid for failure?

He needn't have worried. The sight of a pitiful family of European descent, barely managing to disembark with a weeping child proved an irresistible target for the photographers on the shore. By the time the ambulance workers and journalists arrived on the scene, Herb had already moved away from the group and was nowhere to be seen when the father tried to spot the young man who had saved his '*ma petite reine,*' as he called his daughter.

Herb's head was awhirl with thoughts of melting into the crowd and escaping detection when he spotted Margaret sitting on the outcropping of a rock, wrapped in a blanket, looking intently out at the wreckage in the sea with a notebook in one hand and a marking pen in the other.

Herb Wells had been trained, as many of the children of his generation of the middle-class and up, to view violence as the last solution to problems when dealing with those of your own class. An ignorant, poor Christian might need a cuffing sooner than a wealthy, educated man. Women, being the weaker sex, were never to be given a beating in public at all.

Margaret, though, had crossed a line that was as real as it was invisible. Though a woman, and though she had at least the appearances of being of the upper-class and bore no good will to anything about authentic Christianity, she had still just tried to kill Herb and likely had murdered a number of innocent people with an attitude of a schoolgirl playing a prank.

"Margaret!" he roared, storming up the hill, where she still ignored him, keeping her eyes on the shoreline.

"Yes, Hebert?" she answered, showing such total absence of fear in her voice that Herb stopped in surprise.

"Margaret, stand up. I ... I'm turning you into the police!"

"Oh, dear, Herbert," she said with mock fear, "I appear to have done it this time. What's the charge going to be? Cleaning up Eugenic grease spots without the approval of God and the President?"

"Don't toy with me, you evil little ..." He began to advance on her, his hands flexing with a will not completely his own. A red haze had dropped over her and the rest of the world.

"Uppark, Hebert dear."

Herb stopped. "What did you say?" he whispered.

"Uppark, Herbert dear," she said, going back to her note taking. She seemed immune to the cold, even though she was soaked through as much as anyone. "Uppark is the place in Sussex where your mother lives now, as a maid. Such a shame, your father leaving for parts unknown after she took that job a few years ago. You visit her an average of once a month, preferably on a weekday, likely so that it won't interfere with your carousing on the weekends. She's a very nice lady, and very, very vulnerable where she lives, Herbert."

"You wouldn't."

"You know, when people try to tell me just what I can and can't do, it makes me want to just try it all the more. Have you ever felt like that, Herbert? It's like last week, when I told Lord Musgrave that I'd like to try a series of deathtrap events, and catalog how many members of each race of humanity survive. And, looking at the survivors from my latest project," here she tapped her notebook and finally looked at him, "I think we shall definitely have irrefutable evidence over time to prove that the White European is, indeed, superior to all others."

"Margaret ..."

"Of course, we shall have to keep bits under wraps for a time."

"Margaret ..."

"After all, think of how many small-minded anti-science zealots will get all up in arms if they learned of the need for our race to exterminate the African and the Jew before we can move forward?"

"Margaret! Aren't you listening? There was a little girl on that airship! She almost died! You think that your race gives you that kind of right?"

"Herbert," she said, her mask of sweetness sliding away, and a face of ruthless efficiency taking its place, "that little girl likely has a half-dozen whining brothers and sisters living in a tenement half a world away. And each tenement building is likely filled with two-dozen of their kind, and each European city filled with dozens upon dozens of those filthy tenement rattraps breeding more and more inferior peoples at an ever-accelerating rate! And worse, now they're moving into *our* cities, dirtying up *our* lands with their poisonous, filthy offspring, polluting the pure, thoroughbred stock of *our* own children with their hereditary equivalent of pus and muck. Where does it end? So a little, immigrant girl dies in the name of science and humanity, Herbert! So what? Would you condemn her to life in a large family? The most merciful thing any large family can do to its newborn child is to kill it!"

"Merciful for the child," said Herbert, "or you? Do you really care about the child's life, or do you just care about having more comforts? The kind a child might make you sacrifice?"

"Herbert, I'm not going to argue this with you again!"

"Because you know you'd lose again."

"Herbert!" she yelled, standing with the blanket still wrapped around her, "Our race was very nearly wiped out a year ago. We can't wait for nature to weed out the undesirables, the useless eaters and the poor, grubbing mouths that take from the fit. The fit who are ..."

"You, of course."

She paused. Smiled. "I knew you'd see reason, Herbert! Yes, the fit. Like ourselves," she said, squeezing his arm.

Herb pulled away at her touch. "And what if I decide I'm done with you lot, turn you over to that mob down there, and tell them you set off the bomb that blew the airship into the water?"

"And what if you do? Who will they believe—an innocent, weeping little girl like me, or a shabbily dressed reporter? Besides: half the people in that mob don't speak English. Plus, Lord Musgrave and his set own the police in virtually every town in Western Civilization, and were you to turn on me, there would be consequences for ...other people."

"My mother."

"We do know the whereabouts of your father, too, if you decide you are interested."

Herb glared at her, clenching and re-clenching his fists twice before he spoke again. "We'll talk another time. But just know this, Margaret: if I ever get the chance, it's *your* stock and traits that I'll remove from the breeding pool, and I'll do it personally!"

Margaret smiled. "I wouldn't have it any other way, dear Herbert. Helps keep us both on our toes, doesn't it? Now, I have some information to call in, and you have to get looking about for Gilbert. Now run along!"

She stood and walked towards one of the buildings on the edge of the pier, while Herb stared after her impotently, his hands balled into fists.

Then an unexpected bright thought shone in Herb's head. *The girl,* he thought. *Margaret doesn't know about me saving the little girl. If she knew, she'd have seen that as a mistake she could have thrown up into my face at the first opportunity. That's something, at least, and it shows she and her lot aren't perfect.*

They *aren't* perfect.

He repeated the last three words a number of times as he trudged away from the still-gathering mob at the cataclysm. Each repetition kept him from losing all hope of escape, like a man treading water in the middle of the ocean even as the sharks are circling. He was so wrapped up was in his thoughts that he took no notice of a dark-haired man in a floppy cowboy hat and a longcoat who focused his very odd, brass eyepiece on Herb's retreating form.

Chapter 30

"It is not always wrong even to go, like Dante, to the brink of the lowest promontory and look down at hell. It is when you look up at hell that a serious miscalculation has probably been made."
– GKC, *Alarms and Discursions*, 1910

W ell, Holiday?"

William "Doc" Holiday had faced down gunslingers, gamblers who thought they were gunslingers, and mobs of trigger-happy farmers who thought they were gamblers or gunslingers or both. He'd had more guns pointed at him in his career than he cared to think about. And yet every time the Colonel barked a question with that particular edge in his voice, Doc had to call on every ounce of cool demeanor he had to keep from jumping half out of his skin. His being half-crocked on the whiskey he'd quaffed while waiting for the airship didn't help matters.

"Sir," said Holiday with what he hoped was a casual nod. He spun the small wheel on the side of his head, and his telescopic eyepiece sank without a sound back into its socket. "After a short investigation I have indeed confirmed that this was the airship our quarry was supposed to be on. And while he did not emerge with the survivors, I have reason to believe he was never on that particular airship to begin with."

"Explain."

"That ship primarily held immigrants coming to the American shores from Eastern Europe. Our quarry would have stuck out like a sore thumb in such a crowd, but no one I talked to can remember seeing him during the voyage. They do however, remember a young, well-dressed, dark-haired couple of British and American extraction. I espied both of them among the survivors. Now, the young man was not our job. But I'll wager a year's worth of Tennessee hooch that he was Chesterton's associate, young Wells from England. He emerged from the water yonder, and didn't even wait to dry himself before he went yelling at that pulchritudinous little piece o' dark haired flesh over there. Whatever she said took the wind fair out've his sails. He left looking like he'd swallowed a frog, then went inta that bar yonder."

"An' you didn't follow him?" Finn barked with more than a hint of menace. His eyes had been a pair of smoldering pools of anger ever since he'd learned that the doomed airship was the one supposed to be carrying Gilbert.

"Nope," answered Doc, fiddling with his mechanical eye to see if the blood vessels in Finn's cheek were flaring up the way they did when the Colonel was truly upset. "Ya'll know just how unpredictable a bar can be, 'specially if I beat them in cards or a spelling contest. But I've kept my eye on it. The Wells kid, he's in there now still. Unless he ducked out of a back door."

Colonel Finn looked at Holiday. He'd handpicked him from a life of dentistry after seeing the man play cards and shoot like a riverboat gambler born to the trade. It had been a stroke of genius for both of them, as several of Doc's family members had come down with the dreaded consumption disease after he'd left town to join the Pinkertons.

Still. Colonel Finn knew a cardinal rule about dealing with men who had made most of their living on the seamier side of life: that to remain in command, you always had to leave those under you feeling a little inferior.

"Good job, Sergeant Holiday," Finn said without smiling, as a luxury-liner airship gently pulled into the docks behind him. Finn flexed his gloved hand, touched himself briefly on the chest, and motioned for his two lieutenants to follow him to the bar. Harper walked straight, Holiday with the slightly wobbling motion of a half-drunk man trying to look sober.

If they were unlucky, there might be a fight.

If they were lucky, there'd be one for sure.

Chapter 31

"I wish we could sometimes love the characters in real life as we love the characters in romances. There are a great many human souls whom we should accept more kindly, and even appreciate more clearly, if we simply thought of them as people in a story."
– GKC, *What I Saw in America*

Afterr his ship had docked in New York, Gilbert walked with careful steps down the airship's gangplank to the wooden docks and the concrete streets. He breathed in the air that, while only marginally better than the quality of air in London, still had the most important quality of all: home. Or, at least, it was his home country.

He was, in fact, closer than he had been in nearly two years to his old school, and wondered if he had time for a trip uptown to see old chums. The airship disaster this morning had claimed surprisingly few lives, but a police investigation was still pending, and Gilbert's ship would be moored in dock for at least a few hours. Gilbert and the other passengers had been told they could explore the city if they wished, but they were strongly advised to stay either on board the vessel or close enough to listen for the boarding call every hour, unless accompanied by police or if they knew the city.

True, Gilbert had only been to the New York docks once before. But he had lived in the city for over a year. And even though he was learning to love England, he did have a desire to put his feet on American soil again. Right, that settled it. Even if he didn't visit the school, getting off the ship would feel good for a bit. Most importantly, if he were off the airship, he had better chance of avoiding Jack, Wilks, and anyone else he'd embarrassed himself in front of last night.

I guess that's what it's like to be drunk, he thought ruefully. *Next time, I'll have to make sure I know what I'm drinking, not take so much, and not get into a fight.*

Still, though he knew the fight last night was his own fault, there was in Gilbert a small sense of lingering resentment. It was a sense, though he'd never say it out loud, that Mary herself should have descended from the heavens and scooped Gilbert up in her mantle of protection in gratitude for his standing up and fighting for her.

Well ... *offering* to fight for her, anyway. Even though with his conscious mind, Gilbert could clearly understand that it would have turned out for the better had he left Tollers to 'duel' with Turnbull, Gilbert's own humiliation colored his rational mind.

Looking around, Gilbert saw a small sea of people from many different quarters. People from ships of both the sea and air variety milled around on the docks, chattering in multiple languages. A stationary group of disaster survivors sat near the beach. Some of these were in shock, others were talking excitedly to police or to each other. He passed among them like a ghost, unnoticed and insubstantial. He had no real set plans at the moment for his time off the airship other than sitting and watching the stream, ebb and flow of humanity around him.

Until something caught his eye.

Something that would have started the blood of any young man.

Gilbert had always loved reading nickel novels, small, crudely illustrated booklets detailing a single adventure of a legendary Western cowboy hero.

And now, walking away from him, towards a nearby tavern that called itself The Flying Inn, were three men dressed in cowboy hats and long, dark colored duster coats.

And all three were walking with steps that were patient, measured, confident, and relaxed.

And doing so with boots meant for riding horses.

Cowboys! thought Gilbert. Even in Minnesota, men who lived their lives on the trails were a rare sight in Gil's town of farmers. It was akin to the circus coming to town, or a congressman traipsing through while looking for the sodbuster vote. Gilbert had seen no shortage of men riding horses in his life, but these were the real, bona fide, one-hundred percent deal, the kinds of men who became badge-wearing marshals if they were good, and black-hatted desperadoes if they were bad.

Real cowboys.

Gilbert couldn't resist. Even if a part of him knew he'd hate the life if he really had to live it, the possibility of being near those who lived it drew him in, pulling him with a force as powerful as a magnet with a pile of iron filings. To hear the words and smell the tobacco, maybe even to step close to someone famous? Now there was a temptation for Gilbert that would have made the forbidden fruit in the Garden of Eden seem like a worm-ridden road-apple!

Gilbert waited a few seconds, and followed them, as stealthily as he could, into the tavern.

Chapter 32

"There is no harm in our criticizing foreigners, if only we would also criticize ourselves. In other words, the world might need even less of its new charity, if it had a little more of the old humility."
– GKC, *What I Saw in America*

H erb was enjoying life, and doing so more than he had in a long, long while.

He'd come into the bar cold and wet, looking for information on Gilbert. He slapped down his money, declaring he'd nearly been blown into smoky little bits, and wanted a drink. Within minutes, the curious formed their usual crowd, and Herb had started asking questions as beer and camaraderie loosened their tongues.

The beer was more than a little sour tasting, but he hoped that drinking it with a smile on his face would keep him from getting pummeled by the group's leader, a fellow sitting next to Herb wearing a white shirt, dark pants and a bowler hat. The bartender, encouraged by a few coins, told Herb that his new drinking buddy was known locally as 'The Black Dog.' After two beers and five minutes, if half the stories the fellow they called 'The Black Dog' had told in the last five minutes were true, then he'd committed, ordered or assisted in over two-dozen murders. And not one of them using a gun, all instead up close and personal with various hand weapons.

"Now, after that little mook tried ta sass me in front o' the Plug Uglies ... you gettin' this down?"

Herb responded by tapping his head with his index finger three times while giving a knowing look. The Black Dog, actually a handsome fellow with pale skin, jet-black hair and bright blue eyes, seemed satisfied. He pulled on the suspenders holding up his black pants and continued. "Fine," he said, "when'at little mook tried sassin' me in fronta his b'ys, well, he was a marked man. I mean, I can afford to take me time wit' someone like him. Not like if I wanted to take down a traveling man like you, Mister ... whadja say yer name was again?"

"Wells, Herbert George Wells," said Herb, feeling warmer and drier with each sip of his drink, sour as it was.

There was a pause. Black Dog held Herb's eyes for three full seconds, then tipped back his round-topped bowler hat and began to guffaw, the mouth on his unshaven face opening wide to reveal teeth that had needed a dentist since the day he was born.

Herb followed likewise, not wanting to give insult. Black Dog laughed even more heartily, standing now and slapping Herb and two fellows beside him on the back as well, both of whom had also begun laughing when Herb had given his name.

"Herb Wells, issat so?" said Black Dog, sitting down and wiping a tear or two from his eye, slapping his leg a few times. Herb noticed there was a red stripe of material stitched lengthwise on Black Dog's leg.

Looking around, Herb realized that virtually everyone else in the bar was dressed the same way—white shirts, dark pants with red stripes, suspenders.

And all of them were watching Black Dog, who knocked back another swing of his cheap beer and snapped the fingers on his right hand in the air. One of Black Dog's friends left.

Progress, thought Herb happily. He'd walked into a New York streetgang's home base, enraptured them with a thin promise of fame by being written up in a newspaper article. And rather than getting beaten up, their leader was sending away his bodyguards. Trust was developing, and that made Herb feel quite relaxed.

"My friend, yuh really don't know where you's are, do yuh?" said Black Dog, his accent a mix of Irish brogue and clipped, American twang. It was more a statement than a question.

"Sure," laughed Herb, "I'm at a dockside grog bar in New York City, having a great time, right?"

"My friend," Black Dog said, putting his arm around Herb's shoulders, "y'see that on the wall?"

Herb looked. It was one of many crudely drawn pictures of a rabbit's head he'd seen when he'd first walked in. "Looks like a rabbit," he said with a smile.

"Oh, yes, but so much more than that, me limey friend," finished Black Dog, his arm now secure around Herb's neck in a tight grip.

"Y'see," continued Black Dog, drawing a picture in the dust on the bar with his finger, "We, all of us 'ere, me, my pal Kevin over there," the remaining bodyguard smiled as Herb looked at him, "even old Cecil, there, who I've kept on as barkeep when he sold me this place, we're all from Ireland itself, or wuz born here right after our parents left the saintly soil an' touched down here in the good old you-ess-of-aye. Y'see?"

Herb nodded, hoping his smile didn't betray any of his fear. Black Dog's voice was getting an edge to it, and being called a limey by an American was rarely a good thing.

"An' in Ireland, they never spoke the King's English, nossir. They spoke the language that God on high gave to Saint Patrick 'imself. They spoke the ancient language of the Celts, the tongue known to mere mortals as *Gaelic*. And, in the ancient Gaelic language, my friend, there's a lovely little word called *raibead*. Can ye say that wid' me?"

Herb smiled wanly. "Raybeed," he said trying to play along until he could slip the grip around his neck and run. You didn't need to be six kinds of streetwise to know things were going bad, quick. Black Dog's voice was getting louder, he was shifting in his chair like a gorilla ready to pounce, and out of the corner of his eye, Herb had just seen the dismissed bodyguard return with a half-dozen more fellows, all with the rounded bowler hats and flashes of red on the pant legs.

"Good! You talk real good, for a limey. Now, a raibead means a man to be feared in ancient Gaelic. Am I right, boys?"

"Dead right, boss."

"Absolutely, boys! Dead right! When you're really right, they don't just say 'yer really right.' What do they say, Herbert me friend?"

"Dead right," Herb said.

"Exactly! Now, in this city when you're a man to really, really be feared, what do you think they call you?"

Herb paused. The bar had gotten very quiet. "Dead ... *raibead?*" Herbert said.

And then Herb understood.

Raibead. *Dead* raibead.

Sounded like Dead *Rabbit*.

Oh, no.

No. Nononono.....

Black Dog looked at Herb, and nodded his head. "Now, about a year past. I had me a gal. An English gal, an' she lived here for a few months. We got pretty close, but she moved back across the pond ta be wid her Ma and family. Right after the hoo-ha with them giant tin cans dropping outta the sky, and them squids sucking up everyone's blood, I get me a little letter from my little Maggie. An' you know what she says?"

Herb broke out in a sweat, hoping the story wasn't going to end the way he thought it might.

"It seems, that some reporter fellow named ... hmm," Black Dog said in mock forgetfulness, snapping his fingers, "Cecil, what was that fella's name again?"

"Herb Wells, Mister Aidan. A reporter for the *London Telegraph*."

"That's it!" snapped Black Dog, now known to Herb as Aidan. "Herbert G. Wells. He asks her to coffee, an' when she says she's taken, an' that her man is head of the Dead Rabbits, the toughest gang o' cutthroats on two coasts, he says something like ..."

"He's a whole ocean away," said one of Aidan's toadies in a high falsetto voice, rolling his eyes upwards and folding his hands under his chin, "we're right here."

"Right here! Thanks, Billy! We're right here!"

Aidan, aka the Black Dog, now held his face inches from Herb's. If they'd been in London, Herb would have laid his fist into Aidan's face a long time before this and run. But he was in a strange place, and knew that if he was going to pull his fat out of the very, very hot fire it was being lowered into, he'd have to not only move quick, but smart.

"Now, after all that, an' after humiliating me in a letter I hadda get someone else to read to me, the fella who made me gal think she was too good fer me strolls right inta me groggery, sits himself down, and starts chattin' wid' us! Like 'e belonged here!

"Like, he, belonged, here!" Aidan was now only one inch from Herb's face, still smiling a wide, yellow, toothful grin that would have looked right at home on a shark that had smelled blood in the water.

Strange place or not, Herb knew it was time to move.

Herb smiled, and began giggling nervously to match the nearly maniacal laughter now coming from the gang members.

Suddenly, he rammed his fist, a fist he'd made with his thumb pushing up his folded index finger, rammed it hard as he could into Aidan's chin.

Aidan roared in frenzied anger, releasing Herb just long enough to cradle his injured jaw with both hands.

Herb slipped out from under Aidan's arm and ran for the door, fast as an alley cat from a pack of junkyard dogs.

The dozen or so Dead Rabbit gangsters in the bar, shocked at their leader's screams of pain, made no move to grab Herb as he ran for the door in a bull rush with his head and eyes down.

Surprised as the Dead Rabbit gang was, Herb was even more surprised than they when he rammed head-first into something that had quietly appeared about four feet in front of the door. Something was blocking his way, something about six feet high with a torso as solid as a brick wall.

"Oof!" Herb grunted as he hit. He looked up and saw an old man's face, with an American cowboy hat on top and a blue bandanna around the neck.

"Hello, Herbert," the face said with a deep voice, grabbing him by the arm with a grip that would have been the envy of many a tripod's tentacle a year ago. "We're goin' for a little walk."

"You'll have to discuss it with my new friends, I'm afraid," Herb gasped.

"Persuasion's a gift of mine, young fella. Corporal Harper," Finn said in a loud voice, yanking Herb behind him with surprising ease. This guy was old, but strong! "Secure our new traveling companion, will you?"

"Hey!" shouted Herb and Aidan simultaneously, as a much younger cowboy grabbed Herb's arm and hand in a grip he recognized all too well. Some police called it the 'come-along,' because if you tried to escape you risked breaking your own wrist.

"We got business wit' this little punk!" roared Aidan Bourke, stomping towards Herb while pushing a clump of his dark hair out of his blazing blue eyes.

"And I've no intention of traveling anywhere with you lot!" griped Herb to the cowboys.

"You'd rather take your chances with your new friends here, Wells?" answered Harper.

Herb was silent. Never a good sign: He didn't know the young cowboy's name, but the cowboy knew Herb's.

Cowboys in front, gangsters behind? Life had gotten too interesting, fast!

"Y'all want this boy bad, do you?" The older, lead cowboy said, his blue eyes staring at Aidan's like they could burn holes in lead.

"I'm gonna give you a *three* count," Aidan said, bringing his nose within an inch of Finn's as one of his toadies pressed a length of pipe into his hand, "and if yer still here, me boys and I'll feed what's left o' ya to the hounds inna basement. *One* ..."

"We've got weapons," Finn said. On cue, the youngest cowboy tapped his leg and ... Herb blinked ... did the chap pull a gun out of his leg? These boys must be good at legerdemain, or ...

The third cowboy, as old as the leader but as skinny as the younger one and with glasses, flicked his hands like a magician conjuring a rabbit. Two pistols appeared in them, each sporting three barrels set in a deadly, steel triangle.

Herb watched as the lead cowboy held nothing but his sizable fists balled defiantly at his side.

"Yer armed, true," said Aidan. He'd interrupted his count, but his smile never wavered. "But I've got ye outnumbered a good three to one now, an' with a hundred more boys on their way here. For every one of us you so much as scratch, we'll double yer pain before ye die. Besides that, yer friend here with the funny eyepiece smells like a brewery. I'll bet he's seeing double—no, triple. *Two*."

No one saw how Doc moved so fast. Aidan had barely finished saying the 'oo' sound in 'two' before one of Doc's pistols was pressed up against the gang leader's temple.

Doc Holiday spoke, the whiskey on his breath making an invisible, odorous cloud yards in diameter. "Ah have three barrels heyah, sir," he said, his voice betraying the slightest, whiskey-induced wobble, "one for each of you I see."

Heat and tension rose in the bar. Sweat beaded on the brow of cowboy and street thug alike.

"I have other weapons besides the Doc, mick," Finn said coolly, "and I always win."

"No one calls Aidan Bourke a mick!" he said, swinging the pipe full force at Finn's head.

Finn's hand made an even quicker movement, stopping Aidan's pipe in midair.

In Finn's hand was a green wad of American dollars. And it was at least an inch thick.

And on top of the wad of bills was a shiny badge, with a stylized image of an open eye in the center.

Aidan's eyes grew wide, staring at the money like Dante at the face of Beatrice.

"Have we a deal, Aidan Bourke?" said Finn, his voice as smooth as quicksilver in a heat wave. "The Pinkertons don't forget their friends."

There was a pause of several seconds. "Well," said Aidan finally, his smile widening as he lowered his pipe, "now that you mention it, a man can't have too many friends in this world, can he?"

"Bartender!" Finn roared, holding the money above his head with an outstretched hand like a talisman, the eyes of every thug drawn to it like flies to feces on a hot day, "a round for our new friends here! And, to show there's no hard feelings, an extra twenty," he flicked the top half of a bill out of the wad for all to see, though the bottom half was firmly in his right hand, "as an apology for my crude remarks a moment ago!"

A cheer went up from the gang as pitchers of beer began to move!

" ... Plus another three twenties," his hand flicked five more times, crisp bills popped out and brought further cheers each time, "as a means of healing the intrusion my two comrades and I caused this afternoon. All we ask in return is to bring our quarry with us this day, and to say we've shared a drink with the dangerous Dead Rabbits!"

Cheers rose from nearly a hundred New York born throats as beer and money began flowing through the crowd. A song broke out in one corner in anticipation of the alcohol that would lift spirits as it dulled senses.

Gilbert opened the door.

The wave of heated, beer-scented air hit him like a warm wave. His eyes adjusted to the dim light as he saw...

"Herb?"

"Gil!" Herb shouted.

Something about the timing made the entire bar stop the festivities for a second, which was nearly three times the amount needed for Colonel Finn to recognize the face of his quarry.

"Go! Go! GO!" He yelled, pointing his gloved hand at Gilbert! "Drop Wells! Get 'im, Harper! The job! *Get the job!*"

Gilbert didn't need to hear it twice! Time to run!

He turned and ran back into the rancid smelling street as Harper and Doc pushed aside the derby-hatted gang members and gave chase to Gil.

Herb thought quickly, and stuck out his leg as Harper started running. Fortunately, he 'hooked' Harper's remaining flesh-and-blood leg. Harper tripped and hit the wooden floor with a heavy *thunk!*

Harper swore, thinking (luckily for Herb) that the trip had been an accident.

Angry voices began shouting. "Hey!" Aidan yelled, "What about the money?"

Harper scrambled to his feet and followed Doc and Finn after Gil. The cowboys were gone. The door was closed.

Herb began to breathe easier, until he looked around him.

The Dead Rabbits were staring at him.

Uh oh.

"Get him!" someone shouted!

"Get the money!" shouted someone else!

Herb didn't want to debate any more than Gil had. The way to the door was clear, and he slipped out just before the nearest Rabbit got to it.

This is not *good,* thought Herb to himself as he launched into the muddy street, *not good, not good at all!* He followed the fresh tracks made by the three pairs of expensive cowboy boots, bootprints so fresh and new they stood out in the slimy, muddy, late winter street like spoonfuls of caviar at a bangers-and-mash dinner. Herb ran, following them as best he could as the door to the bar barged open behind him. Then he ran faster, as smells of sour beer and shouts of rage invaded the street.

"*Not good!*" Herb panted, still running. He hoped Gil and company hadn't taken any quick turns; he was going too fast to do any serious tracking! "*Not good, not good, not good,*" he chanted rhythmically as he sprinted from the mob of angry Dead Rabbits behind him.

Chapter 33

"All men thirst to confess their crimes more than tired
beasts thirst for water; but they naturally object to
confessing them while other people, who have also
committed the same crimes, sit by and laugh at them."
– GKC, *ILN,* March 14, 1908

Gilbert turned down a street, pumping muscles he hadn't used
since the Martian invasion. His shoes splotched in the muddy
street and clomped on the sidewalk as he dodged a group of
young men in suspenders, red shirts, battered top hats and blue stripes
stitched on their trousers.

The older cowboys might have caught Gil, had they been a few
decades younger. Despite being in good shape for their age, the years
had taken their toll. Harper, though young and once a very good
sprinter, was so no more since his right leg had been replaced.

Instead, the younger cowboy had to stop after only a minute or so
of running. With Finn and Holiday's backs still in sight, Harper kicked
off his right shoe, and then tore open a buttoned patch below the right
side of his waist. Doing so exposed a metal panel with several small
knobs set into his brass leg. He twisted two of the knobs, and a hissing
sound gushed out of his ankle as he began running again.

And as he began to run his gait took on a loping, leaping aspect.
Each step from his right leg propelled him a foot or so further than his
last leap, until his running became a step-*jump*, step *jump*, step-*jump*,
with each jump now propelling him fifteen or more feet into the street
and a good five or six feet in the air.

People began to scream, yell and point. Harper smiled inside. At
this rate, they'd think up a nickname and be writing nickel novels about
him within the year. It almost made up for having lost his flesh-and-
blood leg.

Almost.

Gilbert had been trained never to look back when running. But
these weren't cross-country opponents; when people chased him these
days, they usually wanted to beat him to a pulp! Looking back to check
their distance behind him now would help him decide if more speed or
hiding would be the wiser move. He turned and saw the two older
cowboys behind him. They were fast for old men, but already slowing

as their long duster coats flapped in the air. *Wind resistance,* Gilbert thought. Time to use that for his advantage!

Still running and dodging casual walkers, he turned his eyes forwards again and focused on the end of the street.

He felt the first strains of a cramp, small but unmistakable, in the back of his thigh. No! He had to give them the slip and soon!

Someone screamed behind him, and he whipped around. He was making looking back into a bad habit!

What he saw made him stop.

The other cowboys were nowhere to be seen, but the third was leaping nearly over the heads of the poorly dressed people from the dockside district! The third cowboy's leg was shooting out like a pogo stick each time it touched dirt, thrusting him further up and forward with each step!

Gilbert analyzed his situation quickly, using the technique Chang had taught him: there was no way to outrun a pursuer who could move at that speed, not in the street, anyway, especially with a cramp starting in his leg. And a standard fistfight wouldn't be a real option for Gilbert against someone who punched cows or convicts for a living.

A run or a full fight wouldn't work here. There was only one other realistic option.

The cowboy was at most three bounds away. Gilbert took the stance he'd learned from Chang, indexing his body sideways, his knees bent slightly, while balancing himself on the balls of his feet. His hands were open and bobbing slightly, as if he were readying himself to catch a large medicine ball coming his way.

Just like in training! Gilbert thought, focusing on the leaping cowboy.

Harper bounded through the crowd, his wheezing companions left far behind. When it came to giving chase to a criminal, they were far more used to letting a horse or train do the running for them!

Harper focused. Gilbert's height and better clothes made him stick out like an orange in a barrel of apples among the poor and homeless in this part of the city. Harper looked into Gilbert's face, the lenses of the young job's glasses shining like a pair of tiny suns.

Only three more jumps, he thought as he blinked to clear the glare from his eyes. Now the kid was ...

Standing?

Most people went into a kind of shock when they saw Harper doing his grasshopper act. This kid looked like he was ready to take a swing at him! Colonel Finn hadn't been kidding—this fella was good!

No matter. He'd catch the job and hold him for the others, getting the bonus pay for being the first to nab the quarry. It'd be his in two leaps, one, and ...

As he reached for Gilbert with both hands, the job did something that caught Harper by surprise.

Gilbert dropped down and rolled backwards, his leg bending, catching Harper's chest and suddenly kicking up at the cowboy's midsection with a sudden push, steered by a shove from Gilbert's hands.

Oof! Harper's world turned end-over-end and stopped at a solid brick wall. Harper felt rather than heard something crunch inside him, like a pointer stick his schoolmaster had broken over Harper's back in a fit of anger over ten years ago. He was about to scream in agony, but right after his rib cracked his head smacked the wall and he lost consciousness.

Herb ran for all he was worth, trying to follow the triangular footprints left in the mud. Behind him, a mob of Irish-tinged voices roared in anger and bloodlust. Herb had seen their kind before in the scuttlegangs of London's East end; young men and boys never taught to value the life of a human being, who would commit any crime from petty robbery to murder for reasons ranging from hunger to boredom.

And now, a large group of them were very, very angry.

No trouble, Herb thought with more than a little sarcasm as the first twinge of fatigue hit. *Just ditch the angry mob of thugs, and then find your friend in a city of about a million people before a bunch of armed cowboys do. And do it fast, or Margaret kills your mother.*

When did life get so blasted complicated?

Father McGivney entered the church from the back door. Once in the sacristy, he turned ideas over in his mind again about how to bring more of his flock to confession. As he stepped on the floor of the nave, his black shoe squished in a splat of mud.

He sighed. The janitor had erred again, forgetting to clean the trail of his own muddy footprints as he mopped the church floor. No time to clean now, and Mass was supposed to start in a few more minutes.

He'd just opened the big front doors of the church when he felt the tug again.

It was quiet, subtle, and impossible to ignore. Each time he had ignored it, he'd lived to regret it. Each time he had listened to it, someone had benefited.

Or at least he'd not regretted it too much.

So, when he felt the tug to go to the confessional, he went.

He had just opened the priest's door to the confessional when the tall, goggle-faced boy charged in through the big open doorway of the church, his face the unhealthy pink shade Father had seen too many times during his time in the city. The pink came not from health, but from mixing the beet-red skin tone gotten from exertion and a pale-white fear for one's life.

Father stepped out of the confessional and opened the section next to his, meant for penitents to kneel and pray in.

"Fweet!" He whistled at the boy. Once he had Gilbert's attention, Father McGivney pointed quickly to the confessional's innards.

Gilbert, no stranger to the need for a confession booth, launched himself at the door. Once inside, he closed it behind him quickly and quietly.

As if on cue, two old cowboys appeared at the front door. Father McGivney managed a look of near-stoicism, tinged with a hint of surprise.

The largest one, breathing with less labor than the other, flashed a badge. "Where'd he go?" he barked with the smallest hint of a wheeze.

Father McGivney had worked in the seedier section of the city long enough to know the difference between a police badge and a Pinkerton shield. And he'd found that when Pinkertons were in the chase, the public good was seldom uppermost in their minds.

"Follow the prints," the priest said, holding Finn's gaze without blinking, "you'll find they go around the back and through the sacristy."

The cowboys were already halfway down the aisle. A third one, younger than the others, appeared at the door and limped after them, holding the right side of his chest and wincing. The skinnier one of the older Pinkertons stopped to kneel and cross himself before climbing the three steps near the altar.

Dear Lord, thought the priest, *please let me have done the right thing today. If I've not, help me right it. If I have done right, may I serve you the same way again, and soon.*

Another boy ran through the door, breathing heavier than the last four people combined.

"Quickest answer you've ever given me," said Father under his breath.

"What?" yelped Herb.

Father opened the other door of the confessional. "Fweet!" he hissed, sweeping his hand with an extended index finger. *Well,* Father thought, *I was wondering how to get more in confession today!*

Herb, having been baptized when close to death during the Invasion, had already gotten over most of his repugnance to the Catholic faith. Having a mob of a hundred street toughs after him broke down what little resistance Herb felt towards obeying a Father who had ordered him to run through an open door.

Herb ran into the confessional, slammed the door and slouched with his back against the wall. Breathing hard, he faced the door of his small cell. His feet rested on the door, ready to kick it against anyone who opened it.

Father McGivney inhaled again, readying himself for the boy's pursuers. He breathed a sigh of relief when the Dead Rabbits filled the back of his church, with Aidan-The-Black-Dog at their head.

"Father," said Aidan, the word coming out like 'Faddah.' He removed his hat, glaring at the others until they did the same.

"Aidan," said Father McGivney with what he hoped was a casual nod. "I missed ye at Mass this past Sunday."

"Ah, busy, Father," said Aidan, his sheepish tone getting gruff by the last syllable as the boys around him began to chuckle. "Father," continued Aidan, "where'd the limey go? We saw 'im run in here, and we gotta make him pay!"

"Pay?" barked the priest, "Pay? I finally have my confessionals full for the first time in over a year, and you interrupt me while I'm dispensing the sacraments? Pay? Pay for what?" Father asked. "Did he steal from you, Aidan? Something you'd honestly gotten?"

"No, Father."

"Did he harm or murder one of ye?"

"No, Father! We'd never let one a' the b'hoys come to harm from the likes o' him!"

"Then it seems ye've got no business chasing such a boy through the church! I'll not be helping you any sooner than I'd give aid to Long Shanks against the Scots."

"I think I can persuade ya, 'father,'" said a hulking gang member, who stepped in front of Aidan. His chest was an inch from the priest's nose.

"Boy," said the priest without a trace of anger or fear, "Boss Barker had three men yer size this close to me last week, tryin' to 'persuade' me to stop helping Catholic widows and orphans of men who disappeared after trying to form a union in one of his factories. Now, what do you have that'll scare me where he backed down? And remember, if you kill a man in a church, one day you'll have to explain your actions to Him," the priest said, still looking at the large hoodlum while pointing backwards to the crucifix that hung above the altar.

The large boy almost moved forward but pulled back, his learned instinct of killing things battling with a sense of decency towards priests, which even life in a brutal street gang hadn't managed to completely snuff out.

"As a matter of fact, I remember you eating Christmas dinner here one night, when your family was hungry, Kevin. And you, Billy," Father walked up to another boy with dark tangled hair, pale skin and an eye-patch, "I found your father a job after he lost his hand in the mill? And you, Aidan. We go way back, don't we?"

"Don't push your luck, Father."

"Or what? You'll kill a priest in his church? Columbus, boy! Knights and even kings had to do their penance for that one, *raibead*! And as for pushing luck, there's no such thing! Did luck save your mother that day, when that miscreant came at her with a cudgel? Was it luck you didn't end up being raised by Sister Perpetua in the orphanage, Aidan?"

Aidan said nothing, and tried mightily to fix his much-practiced intimidating stare on the priest.

"Oh, no," said Father, "take that evil eye of yours and use it to scare your women. Or the Plug Uglies out back. Now, since the day I saved your mother, Aidan, have I or any other man of God asked anything of you since?"

"No, Father."

"No, we haven't. In fact," he said, turning to face the group, now speaking in the Gaelic tongue foreign to most of the rest of the United States, "now that I think on it, I don't think there's a single one of you here that doesn't owe the Church for at least one of the few good things that have been part of your past. I fed and blessed all of you, and stayed the hands that would have ended some of your lives. And how do you thank me? By coming into God's house to kill someone! How dare you, and for shame! *Tume na rithe!* Do you understand me?" he said, switching from Gaelic back to English, "I am *ashamed* now, that I gave such help to young men who chose to be so malformed!"

The Dead Rabbits, one and all, swallowed and looked at the ground. It didn't matter that most of them didn't know what 'malformed' meant. All of them, even those who hadn't been to church in years, had seen Father as a smiling, happy beacon from their own childhoods. They had only seen his sterner side used when he'd had to confront 'bad' adults. Realizing that they now were those bad adults hurt more than any of them expected.

"Now," said Father McGivney again, grabbing Aidan by the shoulder and staring at him with serious, unflinching eyes, "there's one way, and one way alone you all can get back into the good graces of Our Lord. We'll now see who is truly a man, and who is only play-acting at it. Line up!"

Father shoved Aidan into the pew, and gestured the others to follow with a commanding wave of his right arm and pointed index finger. Like many children of the age, Aidan had been at least nominally trained in the faith before other adults around him had carefully steered him from it. He slid quickly into the pew and over to its edge. He knelt, folded his hands on the back of the pew and bowed his head in an action of prayer.

"Gentlemen," said Father as the other Dead Rabbits began to follow Aidan's lead. And where Aidan's example wouldn't suffice, the priest's iron will directed them as sheep from a giant shepherd armed with a loudspeaker and a shocking nancy, "I will be hearing confessions today. And I will see each and every one of you enter that booth in turn, confess your sins, and complete your penance. Bow your heads and examine your consciences!"

Young men with white sweaters and dark pants with red stripes down them neatly filled all four of the church's pews. Bowler hats had already been doffed and placed carefully on the floor. Their heads bowed in unison. More than one thought the whole business a charade, but none were willing to go against Aidan-The-Black-Dog.

"I'll be right back, boys, don't go anywhere until I call for you." Father went into the middle of the three doors in the confessional, shutting it gently but firmly.

The boy with the eye-patch next to Aidan, one of Aidan's more able lieutenants, raised his head slightly and opened his mouth to speak.

"Not a word, Billy," Aidan growled, "or I'll tell Maggie-the-Cat at the Five Points that she can use those sharpened fingernails of hers to give you a matching eyepiece."

Billy shrugged and went back to bowing his head.

Gilbert had been breathing hard for what seemed like a half hour. After hearing his pursuers leave the church, then someone else filling the confessional across from him, and a bunch of cowed bullies fill the pews, Gil tried harder than ever not to be seen or heard.

The door to the priest's portion of the confessional opened, and Gilbert could see the Father through the screen.

"May the Lord be on your heart and on your lips this day. How long has it been since your last confession, my son?"

"Is it safe, Father?"

"In here, yes. Are you Catholic, son?"

"Yes, and it's been ... hold on ... yes, three weeks since my last confession."

Father McGivney took a deep, silent breath. He always did so before hearing a confession, since painful experience had taught him to be prepared in case someone confessed the sin of murder or something of similar gravity.

"Yes, my son?" he asked.

Gilbert paused. He hadn't had a great deal of time to examine his conscience while running from a bunch of angry, steam-enhanced cowboys!

Still ...

"I ... well ..." Gilbert described the incident on board the airship, keeping it as short as he could.

"My son," said the priest, "if you didn't know the drinks held alcohol until it was too late, it's not your fault you got drunk. Now, this business about the fight, on the other hand, may be quite different. You remember it well enough, it seems. Could you tell the difference between right and wrong?"

"I think so, Father. I wouldn't have done something bad if it'd been presented to me."

"Really?" said the priest.

Ouch! thought Gilbert. This wasn't going to be a simple case of recite/redemption!

"Well, Father ..."

"Son, from what you say, the fight for Our Lady was won, but you wanted the glory for yourself. You were advised to stay back but didn't."

Gilbert was silent.

"What sin is that, then, lad?"

"Pride," Gilbert whispered after a few seconds. "I've been guilty of pride."

"Examine your conscience frequently, then, for pride is the sin from which all others flow. It's the stone that blocks the rivers of grace and makes deserts of all the virtues. For your penance, say ten Our Fathers, ten Hail Marys, and examine your conscience for pride every night before you sleep for the next year."

If the priest hadn't saved Gilbert's life a moment ago, he'd have felt more than a little miffed. Though he knew the importance of the sacrament, part of him always wished for an easy penance. This one was going to be tough!

Well, no way to argue the point. He wasn't here for a negotiation.

Gilbert finished his act of contrition and started to leave the confessional.

"Move quietly," whispered Father, "I may not be able to save you next time."

Gilbert took the hint and swung open the door to his confessional quietly, surprising himself with his own stealth as he tiptoed out of the small wooden booth. Before he could congratulate himself, though, he saw four pews in the church filled with tough-looking youths. All of them were dressed the same and kneeling with their heads bowed. Gilbert swallowed again as he made for the big double doors he'd entered through earlier, stepping with the grace and fear of a man whose path to safety led through a crowd of sleeping lions.

Herb, hearing movement from Gil's compartment, moved to leave also.

"Not so fast, lad," said the priest's voice, "let's finish what we've started, shall we?"

"Well ..." started Herb.

"Lad," said Father, "I've done this long enough to know when someone needs the sacrament. Those boys'll be out there nice and quiet for the rest of the afternoon if need be. And so: May the Lord be on your heart and on your lips. Is this your first confession?"

"Well, yes, Father. I was baptized, but I'm afraid I never was taught how to do this."

"Was that your fault or that of your parents?"

"Mine, Father."

"Well, at least you're beginning your first confession with honesty. Now, let's continue ..."

Gilbert ran down the muddy street, his feet splatting in the slimy dirt and puddles. He wished he had a watch handy—but realized it would've made little difference. He had no idea now when the airship would be taking off—was it going to be one hour, or three? He hadn't Herb speak at all in the confessional, and so didn't know where in town his friend was. Should he go back to the airship where it was safe? Or keep looking around?

Gil swallowed, and continued on to the docks. He could try to find some way of stalling the ship, maybe. Get a copper to help escort Herb, perhaps? He'd figure it out, once he knew he was safe from the cowboys.

" ... and then there was this little maid over in Germany, Father. I didn't mean to lead her on, but ..."

"Herbert, son, I'm your confessor, not your doctor. And you've got at least a couple-dozen people behind you. Just tell me what you did, not *why* you did it."

"But there were circumstances, Father."

"There always are. And there's not a one of them good enough to slide past me. Now, you hurt the girl's feelings by pretending to like her more than you really did, correct?"

"Yes ... Yes, Father, I did. I was hoping for ... well ..." Herb inhaled, then shoved the words out in a flow. "When her virtue remained ... well, virtuous, I left the country the next day without saying goodbye. I heard later that it broke her heart."

The priest paused. "Are there any more sins you need to confess today?"

"I think, Father, that I have ... I think I'm going to betray my best friend."

Father McGivney inhaled quietly before he spoke, trying hard to ignore the gunshots going off in the streets behind the church. "Son, you can't confess in advance of something you're *going* to do. You aren't fated to commit anything."

"But doing the right thing will hurt people I care about."

"That is on the conscience of those who sin, not yourself. You always have your free will. And there's always a way out of sin. It's called not sinning."

Herb was silent. "I guess you're right, Father."

"For your penance, say a rosary every day for purity of thought, word and deed. Meditate on each of the mysteries, and do not betray your friend."

Herb winced.

"Now say your act of contrition, son, and be on your way. And quietly! I've no idea how long the Rabbits will be still."

Herb, having never gone to confession before, had to be walked through the process. When he left the booth, he gulped at the sight of the praying gang members.

He stepped gingerly around the small mob of white-sweatered youths. He was halfway to the door when he felt the hand on his wrist.

Herb tried to jerk away, but the grip was too strong. The hand belonged to Aidan, The Black Dog, who hadn't even looked up as he'd clamped down on Herb's wrist.

"You got lucky today, limey," Aidan growled, his head still bowed, "but if I ever see your face in this city again, a church will be the only safe place for you. Savvy?"

"Crystal clear," said Herb.

Aidan released Herb's hand and went back to praying.

Herb felt unsettled.

Am I getting soft, Herb thought as he walked quietly to the large church doors. *He caught me so easily just now. Have I been too used to being a big fish in a small pond? What'll happen if I actually meet a shark?*

As Herb walked through the large double-doors of the church, he heard Aidan stand and enter the confessional.

Maybe churches aren't the worst things after all, Herb thought. Anything that could save his life couldn't be all bad.

Chapter 34

"I think the deeper significance of the rocking-chair may
still be found in the deeper symbolism of the rocking-horse.
I think there is behind all this fresh and facile use of wood a
certain spirit that is childish in the good sense of the word;
something that is innocent, and easily pleased."
– GKC, *What I Saw in America*

Gilbert saw the double-blimped Zeppelin moored to the dock
just as its horn sounded, and gave thanks he'd made it on time.
He ran for the ship, so intent on his goal that he took no notice
of a pair of green eyes following him as he sprinted towards the
gangplank. The eyes were framed by a face and plume of dark hair that
had begun to fill Herb's milder nightmares, and followed Gilbert until
he was very nearly out of sight.

Margaret, the eyes' owner, gave a happy sigh. She then stood,
folded the letter she'd been writing and watched Gil from the plate
glass window of the sailor bar she'd been waiting in. In Gilbert she
now saw a new quarry, a soul fresh and pure as a morning daisy. One
with exactly the kind of heart she loved; a heart she could toy with,
break, discard and gleefully dance upon like a possessed Indian dervish
when she tired of it. *Off to the Actress with this dispatch,* she thought,
as she folded and gave her small letter to a boy, who promptly ran off to
deliver it to the local heliograph operator. At least he had escaped the
Rabbits and those ridiculous cowboys.

Gilbert, blissfully unaware of his danger, jogged steadily towards
the dirigible until he heard a whistle from one of the doorways. It was
the skinny fellow with the freckles from the night before—the one they
called Johnny. "Hi, Mister Gil ... I mean, Mister Edwardson. You
wanna look at one of my family shops?"

"Oh," said Gilbert, "it's … Johnny?"

"That's right! Johnny Brainerd! Youngest son of the illustrious
Brainerd clan of American inventors!"

"Ah, I see. Well, Johnny, I don't know if you have a watch, but the
horn blasted. It's time for folks to board the airship. Plus, I've got to
keep a lookout for my friend. He's somewhere in town, and bad guys
are looking for us."

"Oh, they've aborted that take-off by now. They should have found
that there was some ... er, trouble, in the engine room."

"Trouble?" Gilbert looked the boy in front of him up and down. He couldn't have been more than twelve or thirteen, with a thatch of short, thick black hair and a face so filled with freckles that it was difficult to see skin between them. It was ludicrous to think this little squirt had anything to do with the delay of the airship, but instinct gnawing at his judgment told him otherwise.

A loud sailor bellowed from the airship boarding deck, confirming what Johnny had said—there would be at least an hour's delay until take-off.

Well, thought Gilbert, *why not?* If he spent only a few minutes in the shop, he'd be safely off the street and could keep a lookout for Herb besides.

Done, then. Gilbert walked through the shop's doorway, his path still followed by Margaret's green eyes.

If you want something done right, she thought to herself as she stepped from the window and walked to the door, *don't give it to the unfit.*

"Oi, filly," belched a voice near her as she walked to the door. She looked up briefly, just long enough to assert that the speaker was, indeed, a swarthy sailor who hadn't shaven for a few days. "Archibald is my brother," she said quietly in his ear.

"Wot?" said the sailor, looking puzzled. He'd been slapped sometimes and coddled on other occasions for his clumsy attempts at seduction, but he'd never heard a nonsense sentence like that before.

"Time to remove you from the genepool, cretin," she growled, pulling her hand up faster than most men's eyes would follow.

"Now, little lady—" His sentence ended suddenly. His speech stopped in mid-air as he stood. A trickle of blood began to run from the tearduct in his eye as Margaret pocketed something and walked away, leaving the bar to follow Gilbert through the doorway into the building he'd been led to by Johnny Brainerd. The few other patrons in the bar didn't even look up; such was the noise and bustle in the pub. When the sailor fell with a small pool of blood growing by his face, the few who had seen the exchange between the sailor and Margaret naturally assumed she'd given him a lucky slap that had drawn blood. By the time someone actually turned the dead man over and noticed the pinprick sticking out of his eye, the patrons had changed over many times already, Margaret had been long gone, and a giant robot had smashed at least half the buildings in the area.

Chapter 35

"All science, even the divine science, is a sublime detective story. Only it is not set to detect why a man is dead; but the darker secret of why he is alive."
– GKC, *The Thing. CW. III 191*

Gilbert looked around at the dingy hallway, and tried to imagine what kind of parents would buy a place like this for a workshop.

"This is amazing, Johnny," he said, trying to sound casual, "I'd love to meet your folks."

"Oh, they're not here," said Johnny, walking deeper into the building. Gilbert followed through the doorway. The floor was dusty, and looked like it hadn't been swept for a very, very long time. Light streamed in bright rays from the ceiling, which was made almost entirely of glass panels high above them.

"They're back in England, on holiday," Johnny continued. "That's why I was on board the airship with Jack, Tollers and the rest. We're all off to a school for especially smart kids, and Pa thought it'd be good to have a family holiday before I started off.

"This, though, where *we* are? This is *one* of my Pa's workshops, though," Johnny continued. "When we traveled, he always liked to keep a few unfinished projects in each city we visited. Then he'd have something to work on if he got bored."

"In each ... You're telling me your dad keeps a workshop handy in each city? Just in case he might get bored? I guess your family's pretty well off, then?"

"We do all right, I guess. I always have the best presents of any boy in town at Christmas, because Pa makes them. He's pretty smart, you know."

Johnny stopped walking, as he'd entered another doorway and turned on a switch. There was a hissing sound as lighted gas flowed into a glowing globe above them, illuminating a very large workshop indeed. They were in the main part of the warehouse/workshop now, and the building's walls were thick. The windows at street level were painted over, blocking any outside light.

"Oh ... my ...word," said Gilbert, using a phrase he'd sworn to himself a long time ago he would never use, precisely because he'd heard so many empty-headed people use it so frequently.

But the size of the 'workshop' Johnny had brought him into had that precise effect; it was so vast and filled with so many mechanical wonders that Gil's head was emptied of all thought for a few moments. There were at least thirty sets of benches and tables, each laden with engines of various sizes and degrees of disassembly. And on miscellaneous other tables and stalls were both chaotic and ordered piles, bundles of metal rods, pistons and other parts Gilbert could not have identified if his life had depended upon it. Tools both familiar and otherwise littered the benches and floors, but nothing drew Gilbert's attention as much as three odd inventions in the center of the cavernous workshop.

The first was a gigantic metal man, roughly humanoid in shape but with sheet metal and rivets instead of skin, and giant glass portholes where the eyes should have been. Coal boilers, steam gages and other technological gadgets sprouted from various points on the giant creature, whose head was topped off by a giant metallic stovepipe hat and a jaw so thick it could have been mistaken for a beard. The giant metal hat had soot around its top edge.

Gilbert breathed a sigh of relief, surprised at the effect that the large machine had had upon him. The Invasion had been over for a full year, and he still had to fight the urge to run from something similar in any way to the machines of death he'd dodged for days in the English countryside.

"Who did that?" Gilbert whispered, his voice filled with awe.

"Like it?" chirped Johnny. "I built it based on some drawings I saw from the Slave Wars. Lincoln was the tallest president we ever had, so we made him even taller! It's not all the way finished, though. I want to turn the top hat into a cannon, but Pa won't let me make weapons until I turn fourteen. So we had to settle for standard stuff."

Gilbert walked slowly down a flight of stairs to the floor of the workshop, then to the other two machines that shared the floor with the giant, steam-powered replica of Abraham Lincoln.

Closer to Gilbert's own height, the second completed invention on the factory floor was a smaller version of the Steam Lincoln, without hat or beard or even a human-like face. It was only eight-feet tall, and stared straight ahead with unseeing glass eyes as its only facial feature.

Further down from that was the third completed machine, an odd looking platform set on a high flat base at the top of another set of makeshift stairs.

The platform looked like a metal raft. It was wide enough to hold four seats, and in its center was a round metal pole with a big set of propeller blades on top, similar to what Gilbert had seen on windmills or on the posterior ends of ships. But these blades were longer, and thin, and were pointed up at an angle from the ground.

"What the heck is this?" asked Gilbert, looking at the platform, wondering how fast the propeller blades could go.

"Oh," said Johnny, clearly happy to have found someone interested in his creation, "that's my ornithopter. Pa won't let me run it more than a few feet from the ground, but when he's not around, I've been practicing and going higher each time."

"Pretty impressive," Gilbert said, utterly failing to understand what either an ornithopter was or what it did. "Do you do this all the time, Johnny?"

"No, Pa doesn't let me do this as much as I want, or I'd be in the workshops from morning to night. He limits me to four hours a day. And even then I've gotta take breaks for meals with the family. Isn't that crazy?"

"Not at all, Johnny. I used to work in a factory. You hang around machines instead of people too long, you end up being part of the machine yourself."

Johnny gave Gilbert a look that suggested he hadn't been completely convinced, climbed the stairs and moved to sit in the centered open chair on the ornithopter platform. It was the only chair in the front row, with three cushioned chairs in a neat row behind him. The central propeller-pole with gears, pulleys and other mechanical paraphernalia on the side rose out of the center of the platform, behind the pilot's chair and in front of the passenger seats. Behind the row of chairs was a small coal-and-steam burner, complete with gauges Gilbert recognized as being smaller versions of the kind in a train engineer's driving cabin. There were a number of other controls, levers and crank wheels available to Johnny at his seat, and he began to throw a number of switches there now. A small metallic claw dipped into a fastened bucket of coal and pulled it up to the burner through a small conveyor belt.

"It took me nearly a week to put the ornithopter together," he said as the conveyor belt whirred and the burner began humming softly, "but the drawings were a little easier to crank out than the ones I made for the Steam Lincoln there."

Gilbert, still more than a little in awe of Johnny's machines, stood on the edge of the platform and looked down at the wooden floor, littered with wires, tubes, gears, powdered metal and powdered drifts of sawdust. The last time he'd been on a ledge like this, in fact, he'd also been looking down at a wooden floor that smelled of sawdust. But he'd been higher up, and his mother had been below. And he'd been wearing the funny exercise suit Ma had made him.

"Take a leap, Gilbert!" Ma had shouted from below. "Your father's a good man, but he's let this part of your development linger long enough! You are seven years old now, and I am tired of you coming home with stories about how Luther has been persecuting you every time you go to school because you can't succeed at anything physical. Now jump!"

Gilbert stood on the edge of the hayloft scaffold and looked down at his mother. She had been egging him on for the last fifteen minutes.

"Ma, couldn't I just try this on a lower floor?" Gilbert's voice sounded so pathetic he wanted to hit *himself* with a heavy blunt object.

"Gilbert," said his mother quietly. Her voice chilled him for reasons he couldn't name. "I am going to count to three. If you haven't taken that leap by the time I finish, I am going to come up there and thrash you. One."

"Ma, I ..."

"Two."

"Look, Ma, it's a good how many feet ..."

"Three."

Ma began climbing the hayloft ladder. She had the same look in her eye when he'd broken her favorite sugar bowl a year ago. Memories of the consequences he'd suffered for that mistake made Gilbert do what her encouragement, humiliations and threats had failed to accomplish.

Ma had set up one of the ropes directly in front of him, expecting him to leap and catch it in mid-air. She had tied a crossbar of wood a few feet above the thick knot to 'make it easier' for him to grab. Gilbert had tried to protest that this was like giving an umbrella to a soldier facing a cannon, but Ma had ignored him.

And, when her head had gotten up to his level of the loft, Gilbert jumped. He grabbed the crossbar above the barn's dirt floor in a curled grip with his arms, more out of self-saving desperation than out of any kind of skill. His feet scrambled, eventually finding a grip in the knot his Ma had tied at the rope's bottom.

He gasped, fear sending his sense of self-preservation into overdrive. Where many children wouldn't have been worried at a ten foot drop to the floor, to Gilbert's inexperienced eye it looked like the kind of high cliff he'd read Indians drove buffaloes off of in herds to kill them more easily.

His Ma stood looking at him from the ledge, her arms folded in a gesture that was rapidly becoming annoying.

"Yes," she said calmly, looking at him while he struggled, "you might just well do."

"...how do you *do* that?" Johnny asked.

Gilbert blinked. "Sorry, Johnny. What was that?"

"I said, how do you write so many words without getting sick of them? Me, I could work on a machine for a week and not get sick of it, but if you asked me to write something? It'd be like fingernails on a chalkboard for me, you know?"

Gilbert, returning from the world of memories, looked at Johnny and then at the workshop. There were at least a half-dozen other projects in various stages of assembly or disassembly, none of which Gilbert could recognize. Could a little kid really cobble this stuff together? Could an adult?

"Well, Johnny," Gilbert said. "I guess God just makes all types, you know? Hey, I was wondering, what does your dad do? How'd he afford this place?"

Gilbert had wanted to change the subject. He was successful.

Johnny said, "He sold the designs for the metal man over there to some rich fellow in the Utah territories, along with the designs for another machine to build them. It runs on steam and difference engines. You can look at it if you like. Jack said you liked clacking."

Gilbert nodded his head. This kid was alright. Not half as annoying as Jack had been on the airship.

Airship...

Oh no!

"Johnny, the airship! What if it called again and we couldn't hear it?"

Johnny, wrapped up in the controls on the ornithopter, didn't seem to hear. "The problem in the engine room is going to take at least another hour to fix. I made sure of that so I could have some time to tinker in here."

"You ... Johnny," said Gilbert, his own voice rising over the increasing roar of the engine, "are you pulling my leg?"

"Ready, Gilbert? Watch this," Johnny yelled back, pulling a pair of goggles over his eyes that he'd gotten from the floor of his contraption. He reached forward, pulled a lever and began to turn a dial.

Gilbert watched, his sense of wonder growing as the metal blades above the ornithopter flapped up and down slowly, then quickened. As Johnny turned the dial further, the blades flapped so fast that following them with eyes alone quickly became impossible. Between the hiss of the steam gages and the roar of the engine, the noise was deafening.

But it wasn't so loud that Gilbert couldn't hear the female voice behind him say his name, followed by the soft click of a weapon cocking.

Chapter 36

"What we call emancipation is always and of necessity
simply the free choice of the soul between one set of
limitations and another."
– GKC, *Daily News*, December 21, 1905

Herb had been in tough scrapes before, but until today he'd
never been the target of an angry mob, never been to
confession, and had only once in his life been saved by a
priest. As he exited the church, he walked with the quick and quiet pace
of a person trying to escape without drawing attention. Above all, he
wanted put a safe distance between himself and the Dead Rabbit gang
before they lost their sudden religious fervor.

"WELLS!"

Herb didn't even bother turning around. It had been the kind of day
that made someone shouting his last name in a crowd into a signal to
run hard. He pelted down the street heedless of anyone in his path,
elbowing lighter people out of the way and sidestepping those too large
to knock aside. A cart filled with people wheeled slowly in front of him
on the street, and for the first time in his life, he acted like something
out of the penny dreadfuls. He leaped onto the cart, dodged around its
surprised occupants and jumped off the other side, still running down
the street towards the docks.

Hopefully the cart would delay his pursuers, unless they were good
jumpers, too. *I wish a friendly face were around right now,* he thought,
preferably one holding a weapon or two. He'd just finished the thought
when he spied a familiar female figure walking away from him and into
a building. A figure topped with a head of long, black hair.

I could do worse, he thought. *No, no. I really couldn't. But she's
always got a trick up her sleeve, and I could use one of those right now.*
He poured on an extra burst of speed, hearing more surprised yells
behind him as his pursuers shoved more people out of their way. Herb
didn't yell out her name, not wanting her to stop and perhaps slow him
down. As she walked through the entrance, he almost called out to
make sure she kept the door open. But since she didn't bother to shut it,
he flew through the open doorway only ten seconds after she did.

Finn, Holiday and Harper shook hands with the policeman and
waved goodbye. A half-dozen of the blue-uniformed officers had

materialized outside the back of the church, guns drawn against the cowboys who'd been the subject of so many disturbing reports that morning.

Finn had smiled, pulled out his money, and begun his silvertongued routine again, talking up the police while Doc Holiday and Harper made a quick exit towards the docks. It was over so fast that Finn had little trouble catching up to Holiday and Harper once he was free of the police himself.

"That was done with admirable speed, Colonel," said Holiday. "Out of idle, morbid curiosity: young Harper and I have a little wager going. Did you have to pay any money to smooth out those blue-suited wrinkles?"

"This time," Finn said, "I only used the money to get their attention. No payouts."

"How'd you get past them, then?" Harper asked, a little sore that he'd lost yet another bet to Holiday.

"Honest men are easy cons, Corporal. But dishonest men are the easiest of all. Doc knows I did a little homework on the local police chief before we rolled out here. Most men are willing to let a lot of things slide if you can make their lives easier."

"Colonel!" Holiday said with pretended shock, "You have shattered my heretofore pristine image of you! Are you telling me you really *don't* know the New York Chief of Police? And you *didn't* attend his child's christening? And you have not, in fact, ever eaten Thanksgiving dinner with him?"

"Looks like I've gotta invent a new routine," Finn said. "You're starting to get my script down a little too well."

"I know you're willing to do whatever it takes to complete a job, including lie like a flat Turkish rug in a busy shop. In fact ..."

Finn placed a hand on Doc's chest, stopping him. Finn's eyes were focused at something down the street. "You see that?" he asked.

Doc looked, as did Harper. Herb Wells, their one link to their ultimate quarry of Gilbert Keith Chesterton, was walking less than twenty yards in front of them. "That's him, that's Wells," whispered Holiday, his voice unusually surprised. He and Finn fell into step, quietly keeping pace behind the younger boy. Harper tried to keep up, but his cracked rib kept him from managing it.

"Time for us to have some fun," said Finn. "Chesterton's the real job, but we can use Wells to smoke him out. Trouble is, Wells is a fighter. But if we can tucker him out with a sprint before we nab him, we'll have an easier time of it."

Doc Holiday sighed. He was devoted to the Colonel—he'd scooped Doc and several others out of a life that really only had a happy ending to it if you died in your sleep instead of at the card table with a bullet in your chest. Still, Finn's love of the chase and capture could get tiresome sometimes. Almost as tiresome as watching him fool one of his target criminals.

"WELLS!" roared the big Colonel. True to form, the boy took off straight for the airship docks without even looking behind him.

Harper tried to start a loping jog as soon as he heard Finn shout out Wells' name, but had to slow down right away. His side hurt like the dickens from the slam he'd taken from Gilbert against the wall. No grasshopper action here! *Ouch!* He couldn't even shout without his cracked rib feeling like it was bursting on fire!

Finn and Holiday, jogging at an even trot, knew and counted on Herb's fear to blind him. They usually would tire out their quarry, then send Harper to leap overhead and come down hard on their surprised target. They'd captured this way so often it had become a routine piece of clockwork machinery in their minds, and forgot for the moment that Harper had been injured.

But when Herb jumped over the cart, he very nearly did get away. It took Doc's fancy eye to spot the boy running, not towards the airship, but instead through a doorway of a nearby warehouse.

"Excellent," growled Finn as Doc told him what Herb had done. Finn loved it when they tried to hide. Made things a lot more interesting.

Chapter 37

"For there is but an inch of difference between the
cushioned chamber and the padded cell"
– GKC, *Charles Dickens*, 1906

D on't move, Gilbert Chesterton," said a loud but steady voice
behind him. Gilbert stopped and turned, more with annoyance
than fear. He'd been chased and hunted by very large men and
murderous monsters from space. It wasn't likely at all that anything
with a girl's voice was going to worry him much ...

The girl had long black hair and green eyes that looked like a pair
of frozen emeralds. And she held a tricky-looking pistol with something
pointy sticking out from the business end.

Man alive! She was pretty, but ... wait ...

"You," said Gilbert, his mind searching frantically through his
memories like a schoolboy through a pile of index cards, "I've seen you
before."

"You and half the men in this town, little boy," she said, smiling
sweetly. "Now put your hands on your head, and follow me as I back
out of this place. You and I are going for a little ride in the country."

"Margaret!" Now the yelling voice was Johnny's. Gilbert turned to
look at the boy in his machine—the girl wasn't kidding! She did get
around! "Margaret!" Johnny yelled again, struggling to still and quiet
the flying contraption, "Pa was wondering why you skipped out on the
lab work a few weeks ago! Glad to see you're back!"

Margaret mumbled something unprintable under her breath. "Keep
walking, Gilbert," she growled, gripping the pistol, "and don't get any
ideas about rushing me, or you'll end up with a needle in your ..."

"Margaret!" yelled a third voice, this one behind her.

It was Herb! Good old Herb! He knew the girl!

And then Gilbert remembered! This was Herb's girl back in ...
"Berlin!" Gilbert said.

Margaret kept her eye on Gilbert and smiling Johnny Brainerd.
"Herbert, dear, is that you?" she said, loud enough for Herb to hear,
though he was behind her. "Look who I found skulking about an empty
warehou—oof!" Her speech was cut short by Herb grabbing her from
behind, one hand grabbing her upper arm, the other reaching for the
hand with the needle gun.

"Run, Gil!" Herb said, Margaret fighting him and screeching like a wet cat. "Run! Get on the, the," he looked at the still hovering machine Johnny was piloting, watching them with an expression of puzzlement that was visible even behind the thick goggles he was wearing. "The thing, Gil, now!" Margaret was wrestling with Herb, bringing the pistol to point at ...

No. NO! Gilbert leaped at them, knowing already it was too late. She'd twisted loose somehow, hit him twice, and then her pistol moved in a quick and deadly arc towards Herb's face.

Chapter 38

"To hurry through one's leisure is the most unbusiness-like of actions." – GKC, A Somewhat Improbable Story, *Tremendous Trifles*

When younger, Herb's family had been of lower middle-class means. What schooling he'd had had been among children from families of his own station or lower. Among such people, simple sports and fist fighting have been the most popular entertainments since children began to be educated in groups.

As a result, Herb had learned to fight early in life. Soon after, Herb's father read a stock tip over another man's shoulder as it was spit out from an analytical engine, and made an impulsive investment that paid off handsomely. The family quickly changed their homes and social station. Herbert was transplanted to a boarding school environment that was no less a Darwinian jungle as his last school had been, but at least a more socially acceptable one. At an upper-class boarding school, the fist fighting was no less vicious but used a new set of rules Herb was able to quickly master.

But now, despite his fighting experience in so many environments, Herb couldn't quite wrestle slender Margaret's pistol from her. Margaret had not only been trained somewhere how to break a hold and counter it, but after breaking his hold, she was also able to counterattack with a viciousness rivaling any predatory animal. In the very short quarter second that Margaret's hand swung towards his face with her weapon, Herb knew he was in serious trouble, and would have to come up with a fighting trick that she didn't have a quick response to.

As Gilbert ran to the pair of them, hoping to help Herb out, Herb's hand jerked up and grabbed Margaret's in mid-swing. He locked eyes with Margaret, both of them stopping for only a moment. They glared at each other with such intensity that Gilbert stopped too, braking to a halt on his tarnished shoe heels. Herb's head then darted forward, *kissing her full on the mouth.*

Gil was ... he didn't know *what* he was! He'd never seen such a thing! Pecks on the cheek or lips in England could be cause for scandal, just for being given at the wrong time of day! He looked back. Johnny'd forgotten the controls of his machine, staring at the two young people with a blush redder than an Indian sunburn.

"Je-hosephat!" said a deep man's voice that came from behind Margaret and Herb, in the doorway they'd all piled through half a minute ago. Margaret's eyes had closed at Herb's kiss, but at the sound of Finn's voice the spell was broken. Herb grabbed Margaret by the upper arms and pushed her with a rough shove. She reeled back, her arms pinwheeling as she fought for balance, shrieking with sudden anger. Her voice shot to an even higher pitch when her body hit the railing and fell over backwards, dropping a dozen feet and landing with a series of squishes and crunches in a pile of trash.

Herb didn't stop to see how she fared. Before she had even fallen backwards over the railing, he'd turned and ran towards Gilbert. "C'mon, Gil! Let's get out of here!" he shouted as he tore past Gil, grabbing Gilbert's jacket sleeve and yanking him away from the railing towards Johnny and his improbable machine.

Herb's open display of affection had also surprised the cowboys, all three of whom had been in the doorway. But seeing a lady tossed over a railing stirred something unkillably noble in them. Each cowboy, Finn included, forgot Gilbert and ran to check on the lady in distress. Even after she had landed, her screams sounded through the warehouse like a banshee with torn-out fingernails. And those screams bought precious seconds for the three boys making their escape on Brainerd's flying machine.

"Ready?" yelled Johnny to both Herb and Gil as they leaped onto the floor of his creation, hovering three feet off of the ground. Johnny pulled another lever, and the craft rose a dozen feet into the air while Johnny slipped on a pair of goggles. In two seconds, they were a dozen feet high. Some new technological wizardry made the rooftop open above them, revealing a circular window wide enough for them to fly through comfortably.

"I'll hold 'er steady, you guys get strapped in!" Johnny bellowed over the roar of the engine, holding a lever with one hand and adjusting his goggles with the other. Herb and Gilbert obeyed, mindful of the flapping metal blades above them. Gilbert and Herb sat in mismatched chairs on Johnny's ornithopter that looked like they'd been pulled from a rummage sale and nailed onto the platform. Once seated, they pulled belts attached to the chairs across their middles.

"Hang on," Johnny yelled, "this might be a little bumpy!"

An angry shriek sounded nearby. All three boys looked down. Margaret stood next to the garbage pile in her now filthy and tattered holiday dress, pointing something at them.

Chapter 39

"There is nothing that fails like success."
– GKC, *Heretics*, 1905

D own!" Herb barked, reaching out to Gil and Johnny. His left arm shoved Gil's head forward and his right hand grabbed Johnny by the scruff of the neck and pulled him sideways.

"Hey!" Johnny yelped, his hands leaving the controls for a second. None of them knew it at the time, but Herb's action likely saved all three of their lives. For Margaret had practiced enough that hitting a small, moving target was difficult, but not impossible. And Margaret had aimed her needle pistol at Johnny's throat.

But Herb's yanking Johnny's shoulder to the right jogged the flying machine in the same direction. Margaret's shot missed, embedding itself in the rim of the right lens of Johnny's goggles. Johnny yelped, squirmed free of Herb's grasp, and clutched the sticks of the control panel again, resuming their ascent.

"Whoa, there, little lady," said Finn, taking her arm in a firm grip, while Harper grabbed the other hand. Holiday trained his pistol on the impossible flapping machine that kept rising up to the ceiling. "Orders, Colonel?" Doc asked.

"Hold your fire," Finn said, keeping his eyes on Margaret, "you might hurt the job."

Margaret struggled, but quickly and correctly surmised that the men were too strong for her. At least physically.

She turned first to Finn, gazed at cold, hard eyes that had seen much, and then turned to Harper. "Are you looking to get ahold of those boys, too?" she asked, batting her eyes at Harper and letting a desperate edge enter her voice. "Them boys done me wrong," her voice now had a Southern lilt whose phoniness was obvious to the two older men, "an' I aim to take 'em down pronto! Could you, *would* y'all give me a hand?"

Harper blushed. The last time a girl had flirted with him, both his legs had been made of flesh and blood. He didn't even notice the boys and their machine rising out of the hole in the ceiling.

His comrades were a different story. "Little lady," said Finn, grabbing then squeezing her hand in his own powerful fingers until she winced and dropped the gun, "you need to work on your accent a mite more. Along with when to say 'y'all.' Now, do you know those boys?"

He pointed at the hole they'd escaped from.

She looked sharply at Finn and nodded.

"You gonna help us get 'em?"

Another nod. Time to take a different tack. She could use charm to manipulate the young one. The older ones were all about business. "Let go of my hand," she said looking at the other side of the shop, "and I'll have you snapping at their heels in three shakes of a wolf's tail."

"Why are we waiting around?" Gil yelled. "Hit that pedal a good hard one! Get us out of here!"

Johnny had been fiddling with knobs and gages for the last two minutes since they'd left through a small hatch that had opened up at their approach to the workshop's roof. Gilbert felt distinctly uncomfortable hovering above anyone who'd pointed guns in his direction, especially when their only shield was made of plate glass. Worse, now that they were outside, the glare of the sun on the glass below meant he couldn't see what Margaret or the cowboys were doing.

"Flying outside ain't like flying indoors," Johnny answered, speaking over the whipping winds while seeming to take no notice of the needle shaft sticking out of his right goggle rim. "There's a lot of adjustments to make so's we'll stay up if a stray gust of wind hits us, or we end up in a cloud and can't see straight."

"That's lovely to hear, chap," said Herb, his voice nearly cracking from the effort of trying not to scream in panic at being higher in the air than he'd ever been without a sturdy railing between him and a long fall, "but have you got anything to keep away girls with flying sewing needles?"

"Now that I'm done? You betcha," said Johnny, making a last adjustment to his controls, "speed!"

The ornithopter turned around while hovering, and its engine switched from a loud, chugging bellow to a noisome hum.

As they left the workshop behind them, Gilbert puzzled something out in his head: He was happy Margaret and her crew hadn't fired at the ornithopter, but couldn't figure out why they hadn't.

He'd just finished the thought when the Steam Lincoln's metal-hatted head smashed through the roof behind them with an explosion of breaking glass and hissing vapor.

Chapter 40

"The devil can quote Scripture for his purpose; and the text
of Scripture which he now most commonly quotes is, 'The
Kingdom of heaven is within you.'"
– GKC, *What I Saw in America*

Herb screamed when the glass roof exploded behind them,
covering his head with his arms while Gilbert looked away
from the shower of debris. Fortunately, the ornithopter's
flapping blades deflected most of the glass and metal. Johnny looked
behind. Though his eyes were hidden behind his goggle lenses, Gilbert
saw the younger boy raise his eyebrows, swallow and lick his lips
nervously.

"Pa's gonna kill me," Gil heard Johnny mumble, as the smaller boy
pulled a lever and the ornithopter swerved toward the sun, flying across
the New York skyline.

"You really know how to drive this thing, missy?"

Finn had been in more than one unusual situation in his life, but
he'd never expected to be in a giant robot. The dark-haired girl acted
with a confidence he'd never seen a woman have around a complicated
machine.

Come to think of it, he'd never seen a machine this complicated,
either.

"Just keep your boys in line, and make sure they do the jobs I set
them to," she snarled, keeping her eyes on the flying craft in front of
her while her hands flew over the switches, dials, gages and levers on
the panel before her. "I should have them in our grasp in a matter of
minutes."

"Fine. But once we catch that pigeon, we get the skinny kid with
the glasses."

Margaret hesitated for just a second, her eyes flicking back and
forth so slightly that none but Finn noticed. "That'll be fine," she said,
as the gigantic metal legs of their steam-powered replica of Abraham
Lincoln smashed through the walls of the workshop-warehouse and
stepped into the street, causing a screaming panic in the streets that
Margaret completely ignored.

"Where are we going, Johnny?" Gilbert's question was almost lost in the engine's roar and the blades' flapping.

"Looks like I was wrong; our Zeppelin's gone from the dock! I'm gonna try and go West and see if we can catch up with it."

"I thought you said it'd be at least an hour?" Gilbert shouted.

"Sorry! I'm not wrong often, but it does happen! I can catch 'em, though, if we hightail it now!"

"That's very nice," said Herb over the sound of the engine, "but how do you intend to land? I don't recall seeing a dock attached to the outside of the blimp."

"We've got two options," Johnny said matter-of-factly, seemingly oblivious to the seven-story mechanical creature stamping after them through downtown New York. "First, I could try to land right on top of the blimp, and we'll find the ladder that goes down through the blimp itself and into the gondola."

"What's the other option?"

"Remember that glass dance floor where you got into a fight last night?"

Gilbert and Herb were quiet. Neither wanted to ask Johnny if he was joking or not.

"How are you gonna catch 'em?"

"I'm about to catch them now, Finn," said Margaret, pulling a lever. A pair of spyglasses popped up from the control panel, attached by a folding arm, and she looked through them intently.

Harper looked out the wide window to his left and saw a large tube with a blunt projectile on the end of it unfold from the side of one of the Steam Lincoln's arms. "Colonel," Harper barked, pointing.

Finn's gun was out of his holster and cocked with its barrel pointed at the side of Margaret's head in a half second. "Little girl, you don't want to fire on our job, or at the contraption our job is flying in, understand?"

"And," she answered, still looking through the spyglasses while the machine carried them all forward, "how do you propose to drive this tin soldier if my brains are decorating the wall?"

"I'm not just a gunslinger—I know a little bit about machines an' how they work. Comes in handy when half your men have steam-powered limbs. This wouldn't be the first walkin' boat I've driven, and you won't be the first woman I've shot. Now stand down."

Margaret turned to face Finn. Her eyes searched his as best they could with the thick gun barrel taking up her field of vision. He held her gaze with eyes as cold and unyielding as a winter mountain on a cold, midwestern morning.

She blinked and smiled, shrugged her shoulders and pulled the lever back, retracting the missile launcher into the Steam Lincoln's arm with the sounds of hissing steam and grinding gears. While her vision was focused on the panel, Finn looked over at his men. Holiday crossed his arms and winked without changing his expression.

Harper took the hint. He'd grown up hearing stories about his father and Senator Sawyer getting in and out of trouble with Colonel Finn in St. Petersburg. The three of them had faked their own deaths and attended their own funeral, fought as some of the youngest soldiers during the Slave Wars, and helped a number of slaves escape to free territories, all before they could legally vote. But he'd never heard anything about Finn being competent with machines—much less a machine several stories tall that looked to be half Martian in origin. Harper had gone on several missions with Finn before this, but it wasn't until now that he realized he'd just knowingly seen one of the infamous bluffs of the Mighty Finn in action.

"I'd imagine a bird that small and active is going to have a spectacular appetite," drawled Holiday, looking at the flapping wings of the ornithopter. "Ah'd suggest that if we were to follow it, we could grab it once it touched down for a rest."

"How long can this thing keep walking?" Finn barked at Margaret.

That tone will one day cost you your tongue, old man, she thought to herself. "Days, if we need to. On the other hand, that flying contraption's never been in the air longer than ten minutes while I was a lab assistant here. The real trick will come in catching them before they scamper away into a building or basement."

"Grab 'em, then," Finn growled, "right out've the air."

"I can see the Zeppelin!" Herb's shout carried over the engine, which roared with more fury as Johnny pulled another level and increased the speed.

"Hang on," Johnny yelled, one hand on a lever and another on a steering wheel with a peg on the rim.

"What is that behind us?" asked Gilbert.

Herb looked behind them, a wary look on his wind-whipped face. They'd left the downtown core several minutes ago, and were flying over neighborhoods of houses clustered around smoke-belching factories. The Steam Lincoln was well behind them, though walking at a steady pace.

"When my Pa sold the plans for the metal man to that guy in Utah, he started thinking even bigger. Some king in Europe admired Lincoln, and gave us an even bigger boatload of money to make a giant version of him, weapons included. "

"What'd the king want the metal man for?" Gilbert asked.

"I dunno," said Johnny, easing up on the throttle now that they had some distance between them and their pursuers. "We'd just spent the winter burning furniture to keep warm, and Pa wasn't gonna ask any questions. Not when that job put at least a million dollars worth of gold coins in our pockets. He said he'd make a dozen Steam Lincolns if it'd help him forget that awful winter."

"That ain't gonna help," Gilbert said, remembering his own days as a poor boy in the London slums. "Poor men can forget being poor sometimes. Rich men never do."

"Look!" Herb yelled. They were getting closer to the giant, double-ballooned Zeppelin Gil and Johnny had travelled in.

"Hang on!" yelled Johnny, carefully steering their little vessel, "I'm gonna try to see if we can land on top. Brace yourselves—" Johnny continued, speaking out of the side of his mouth to Gilbert, his face pointed forward, "I've never done this before."

"You mean land on a Zeppelin?

"No. *Land*. Usually my Pa will land the 'thopter."

Gilbert's lips quickly started mumbling. "Gil, what did you say?" barked Herb.

"I'm saying he rosary. Like you should've learned when you went to catechism."

"Gil ..."

"Like you *promised* you would!"

"Gil, this isn't the place!"

"We're being chased through New York City in a flying contraption that could get knocked out've the sky by a steam-powered statue of a dead president, our pilot is young enough to need a stool to get his chin over a bar, and you *don't* think this is a good time for me to tell you to pray?"

"I heard that," said Johnny, "and my Ma just measured me last week. I'm a good four-feet and eleven inches, and more—AH!" Johnny's tirade was cut off mid-word as a large claw hooked on to the pontoon of the ornithopter's side.

"Sam Hill ..." started Gilbert, looking behind them. The giant

Steam Lincoln had somehow gained speed while they were arguing over the noise of the engine, caught up to them and now had their 'thopter hooked with a single arm that looked to be made of gears, metal beams, pullies and steam gages.

Herb's blood ran cold as he looked at the window that formed Lincoln's right eye, and saw Margaret staring out at him with calculating grin of pure evil.

Chapter 41

"It takes three to make a quarrel. There is needed a peacemaker. The full potentialities of human fury cannot be reached until a friend of both parties tactfully intervenes." – GKC, *The Thing*, 1929

Ah *hate* when this happens," Johnny grumbled. "Here, take the helm somebody." The smaller boy unbuckled his safety belt and walked with wobbly steps across the platform towards the pontoon that the Steam Lincoln's arm had hooked.

"Whoa!" Gilbert yelled, unbuckling his own belt and leaping forward at the controls. What was Johnny thinking? Gil held the levers in the same position he thought Johnny had held them, though the wind kept trying to push them up, down and sideways.

"Just hold 'er steady 'til I get back," said Johnny over his shoulder as he stretched a leg over to the Steam Lincoln's claw. "Don't worry, my Pa had me runnin' the helm all the time while he worked on stuff."

Were you both this high up? Gilbert thought as he swallowed and looked back at Herb, holding onto the arms of his chair and squeezing his eyes shut in between sneaking furtive looks at the ground.

With a grinding of metal and hissing of steam, the Steam Lincoln's arm bent and began to pull the ornithopter and its three passengers towards its metal body.

"Johnny!" Gilbert yelled, as the boy slid over the side and onto the metal claw with no more apparent concern for his safety than if he were only two feet above the ground instead of over fifty.

"Gil," whimpered Herb, "what did you call those blokes in Heaven who look out for us here on Earth?"

"Patron saints, Herb," said Gil, gulping and holding the levers in place, while looking nervously at the ground far below.

"Is there one for fellows in our position?"

"I—I think there was a monk named Joseph in Italy. He used to fly up when he prayed."

"Right," said Herb, closing his eyes and beginning to mumble desperately under his breath.

Within ten seconds, they heard a loud *POP* beneath their feet, followed by an angry hissing of steam. Johnny's hand popped up over the side, and he climbed up to them with a very large wrench latched to his belt.

"I pulled a hose on the claw," he said, patting the wrench on his belt. "We'll be able to escape once the line runs out of steam," he said as he walked back to the pilot seat and took the controls again. "Shouldn't be more 'n a few minutes."

"Johnny, the arm is still pulling us in!" Gilbert was right. They were close enough that he could make out the faces of some of the cowboys who'd chased him through the streets a half hour before.

Johnny had already seated himself and begun adjusting controls for their getaway. Looking up at the Steam Lincoln, his face went pale.

"This ain't good," he said. "There's other tubes we can cut, but you'd have to walk along the arm without falling, then swing on a tube or two like a monkey to get to 'em. I ain't never seen no one do that without a scaffolding or a safety line to catch 'em, and we don't got niether o' those here."

Gilbert looked at the Steam Lincoln's arm. His arms twitched, as if they remembered something he'd nearly forgotten he'd learned long ago …

"Nice job hookin' that group, missy," said Harper with a rakish smile. Finn gave him a cold stare that Harper took no notice of whatsoever, while Holiday chuckled to himself.

Good, thought Margaret. She'd snared the young one. She gave Harper a quiet smile and a slow wink to cement her hold on him. Harper's face shot three shades of red in five seconds.

"Thank you kindly, sir," she said with a voice slow and full of syrup. "Now, if you could help by pulling this here lever a bit? It sticks now and again."

Harper leaned forward, brushing against her just a little.

Before Finn could stop him, the girl grabbed at Harper's holster.

Harper saw her hand in the empty holster at his side, and raised his now sad eyes to meet hers.

Finn yanked her bodily from her seat and tossed her to the back of the already cramped cabin. Having trained and practiced this maneuver many times before, Harper and Holiday leaped back, each grabbing one of Margaret's arms while she was disoriented. Finn gripped a gloved hand beneath her chin and whisked a rag smelling of evil chemicals out from a container in his pocket.

With the rag in her face, her struggling slowly lost its vigor. When she stopped struggling, Finn counted to ten and released his hold on her face. Harper and Holiday seated her in the co-pilot's chair and began binding her hands and feet with a spool of twine produced from a compartment in Harper's leg, while Finn looked out the window.

The ornithopter was still hooked by one of its pontoons to the arm's hooked claw. "Now, either of you two got the knowhow to reel those fish in?"

His men gave him blank stares. "I fear I was ill the day they taught the piloting of giant mechanical automatons in our one-room schoolhouse, Colonel," Holiday said, his voice very loud in the suddenly tense and silent room.

Finn gritted his teeth and inhaled through his nose. The three boys couldn't be more than a couple-dozen feet away, but the only person he knew in the city of New York who could reel them in was unconscious. His lie to Margaret about being able to pilot the Steam Lincoln rang quite hollow, now. How the blazes were they going to nab those kids?

Just a minute, Finn thought. Why was one of the boys on the arm?

The littlest kid was undoing something on the Steam Lincoln's arm! And using a large wrench to do it!

They watched, fascinated, as the child undid something that made steam blast in a long stream from the Steam Lincoln's arm just below the claw, and then climbed back up onto the flying contraption.

"What now, Colonel?" said Harper. "I bet that this thing's gonna lose its grip quick if we don't grab 'em!"

"Hang on for a second an' let me think," Finn said, putting his hand over his eyes for a second. He thought as clearly as he could, mining his head with all its stories and experience for something that could be of use here.

For the first time in a very, very long time, he was coming up empty. Worse, he knew in a few seconds that Doc and Harper would know it, too.

"Colonel, I don't wish to add to the already considerable number of factors you're currently considering, but there's something else you should know."

"What, now, Doc?"

"I think," Holiday said, his eyescope making soft clicking noises as it extended and focused, "that another one of the boys is contemplating talking a walk along the long arm of Mr. Lincoln."

Chapter 42

"Creatures so close to each other as husband and wife, or a
mother and children, have powers of making each other
happy or miserable with which no public coercion can
deal."
— GKC, *What's Wrong with the World*

Gil, get back!" Herb's yell sounded in Gil's ear, breaking him
from his brief trip to memory lane. "Those blokes have guns,
Gil! Maybe pepperboxes! We've got to stay down if we don't
want to get filled with holes!"

"Herb, if they wanted to turn us into targets, they woulda done that
in the warehouse, doncha think? I don't even know if they're really
after us. But if they are, they want us in one piece."

"I'm not talking about the cowboys, Gil! Look down!"

Gilbert did. There were a number of bright blue uniforms visible in
the mob of people who were trying to watch from a safe distance. At
least three of the uniforms were walking slowly towards the Steam
Lincoln and its catch with pistols drawn. "Great," said Gilbert
sarcastically, "all we need to make this a perfect day is a lucky shot
from some idiots down there, trying to play-act like heroes."

Herb looked at Gilbert with an odd expression. "I've heard that
before," he said, "but not from you."

"What?" said Gilbert, annoyed.

"Never mind," Herb said, "It's stopped pulling us in for some
reason. But now how do we loosen this thing's grip so's we can fly
off?"

"Like I said before, there's a few tubes we'd have to cut," said
Johnny behind them. "The red, blue and white ones down by Lincoln's
elbow over there. One moves fuel, another steam, and a third does the
lubricant. If we could cut those three lines we could unhook Lincoln's
claw in seconds and be on our way. But they're too far and too thick for
me to do it myself. We'll have to wait here until the steam line I
reached bleeds out and the grip loosens on its own."

"But by then," said Herb, "we might be shot by the police below.
Or captured by the cowboys!"

"You got a better idea, London boy, I'll hear it. I can climb over a
few things, but you usually need a scaffold to reach those gauges. From
up here, you'd have to walk across on a metal beam like a squirrel on a

wire, then swing like a monkey in a tree on a couple of the hoses in order to get to the gauges. I'm sorry, Mister Gilbert, but even with my magnetized bag of tools here, I'm not sure I can do the first part, and I've never done the second."

Gilbert looked at the nearest of the three gear-and-pulley elbows in the arm that held their craft. The arm was still. And the craft was being held steady and level...

"Uh oh," barked Johnny, "we're low on fuel!"

That settles it, thought Gilbert. "Johnny," he said, "give me the tools! I'll do it!"

"Wot?" said Herb. "You're going to climb out there?"

"What would you suggest?"

"Throw annoying little monkey boy out there instead, what else?"

"I heard that!" Johnny yelled.

"Quiet!" Both Gil and Herb yelled at once. "Look, Gil, I don't like those cowboys, but there's no sense risking your life for this!"

"I won't be risking my life, Herb. I've been trained, both for the walking and the swinging part."

"Since when? By whom? You mean that jump you took in the underground cave last year? That was different and you know it! You at least had a river beneath you then! Miss here and you'll be like that haggis you dropped off the balcony in Scotland."

"I hate haggis. Now help Junior hold this bird steady."

"My name's not Junior!"

"Quiet!" Gil and Herb shouted again. It was becoming an automatic response.

Gilbert, oblivious to Johnny, looked and spotted a loop of cable, perfect for a handhold, sticking out from one of the many beams in the Steam Lincoln's arm. Ignoring the sudden, throbbing pain at the old wound in his ankle, he tensed his knees as he bent them, and his body at the waist, his arms held at chest height with his flat palms facing down.

"One-and-two-and-three-and-turn!"

Ma had taught Gilbert the basics of rope swinging and climbing in the space of three weeks, along with basic swing-and-bend moves on a makeshift trapeze made of a wooden dowel and two identical lengths of rope. Gilbert had been practicing for close to an hour each day now after school with Ma while the hired hands were in the field. When he mastered this, she promised to teach him how to do tricks on the balance beam.

But, in the meantime, he had to focus on the trapeze. Gilbert went into the tuck, spun and ... Success! He'd landed on his feet on the wagon full of hay that had served as a crude safety net. He'd landed for the first time as his mother had taught him to, with his feet slightly spread apart and his knees and waist both bent slightly to absorb the shock of landing. His hands were facing palm down, his arms were stretched slightly to his sides to hold his balance, and his smile felt like it had stretched only a few inches short of his fingertips.

Ma looked him up and down, her hair no longer in the severe bun that most of the Minnesota prairie mothers wore, but instead fastened with a piece of string until it pointed long down between her shoulder blades like a horse's tail.

"Form could be better," she said crisply, shooting down his sense of achievement like a pheasant with Pa's rifle. "You'll need to go into the tuck sooner. Otherwise, once we move the hay away you'll risk breaking your neck each time you land."

"Move the hay away? You joshin' me, Ma?"

"I said no slang, Gilbert. Do a lap around the barn. After that, we'll return to your exercises on the balance beam."

Gilbert grumbled in his head, jumped off the wagon and started running to the barn door, knowing from painful experience that any arguing would result in doubled punishments. He'd gotten within a few feet of the door when it swung open and Obidiah Calvin was standing in the doorway.

Calvin was in his mid-twenties, and had been hired on by Pa as a trial run two weeks before. He was the kind of drifter that appeared on farms and ranches from time to time, a man with a five o'clock shadow always on his chin and the dust of at least a dozen states caked in the crevasses of his work clothes. More dirt was lodged in a few key clumps in his dark, stringy hair. He was a slim, wiry man who no one had taken serious notice of until now. Pa had liked the man's quick eyes and easy talk. Ma hadn't liked him at all.

He spotted Gilbert and looked puzzled, then annoyed. Gilbert could tell the farmhand hadn't expected to see him in the barn.

"What seems to be the matter, Mister Calvin?"

Calvin saw Ma and Gilbert in their matching exercise suits. He whistled low, and looked Ma up and down in a way that made Gilbert shiver and want to ram his fist through the farmhand's guts. "I was just looking for a few tools to fix the wagon, ma'am," he said politely, "with your husband gone on business for a few days, I wanted to be sure it was in good shape when he got back. But it looks like I interrupted something, so I'll be ... well, those outfits are . . well, never mind. I'll be going, now. And don't worry, ma'am." He turned to leave.

"Stop," Ma said.

Calvin stopped moving, still turned away from the two of them. "Ma'am?" he asked. Gilbert could hear the smile in his voice.

"What is it you think I might have to worry about?"

"Well, ma'am ..."

"You had no need to take anything from this barn, Mister Calvin. The wagon is working quite well."

"Really? That might be a matter of opinion, ma'am. A wagon is like a family. A lot of people depend on each part workin' just right, all the time."

"The only opinions on this farm that matter are mine and my husband's."

"Well, now," said Calvin turning and giving a wide, confident smile to Ma while ignoring Gilbert, "opinions can be tricky things, ma'am. Your opinion of me decides if I eat at night. The townsfolk's opinions might decide if a family stays in a place or not. A newspaperman's opinion of a person can make or break them in a town.

"Now me, I know y'all are my bread an' butter, so's I'd be inclined, for example, to keep my mouth shut about any opinions I might have about anything that goes on here. 'Cause if I spilled my guts about something sensitive, like a wagon that wasn't as sturdy as folks might think, then my employer'd be hurt, and I'd be out of a job, wouldn't I?"

"A wagon can be fixed, with the right tools," Ma answered, keeping her eyes hard and leveled at Calvin. She made Gilbert think of a piece of iron he'd seen Smithee forge in his blacksmith shop months ago.

"True enough, ma'am. But a wagon could be broken, if the driver got careless,"

Calvin's smile was still in place. If Gilbert had a baseball bat and knew how to swing, he'd have crushed every tooth in the slimy man's smile. Along with his kneecaps. "But I don't think we've got any worries about that, do we ma'am? One thing I like about your place, Mrs. Chesterton, is that you folks take care of your own. Real good."

"We do at that." Ma looked at the wagon, then Gilbert, then at the ground. She crossed her arms, inhaled, and looked up at Calvin with a smile so fake Gilbert that saw through it more easily than a clean window pane. "I appreciate your ... concern, about our wagon, Mister Calvin. An increase in your salary by two dollars a week is, I think, in order for showing such initiative."

"Well, I thank you kindly, ma'am," said Calvin, nodding his head to her. He looked at Gilbert, gave a quick wink and headed out the door, whistling the tune to a hymn that was a favorite of the local pastor.

It was quiet in the barn for a few seconds after Calvin left.

"Ma, did I do something wrong?" Gilbert's voice was quiet, but echoed in his ears like a cannon shot in the silence of the barn.

"No, son," Ma said, "but I think we're done for today. Get changed, and I'll see you in the house for lunch."

"Yes'm."

Gilbert ducked into the alcove in the corner of the barn that had been made into a makeshift changing room and slipped out of exercise suit. He could hear his mother rustling as she did the same in the opposite corner. Through a crack in the wooden wall, Gilbert could see Calvin kicking up dust as he loped his way back to the other farmhands, who made low noises of encouragement as he approached them.

I hate, you, Obidiah Calvin, Gilbert thought quietly. *For reasons I don't entirely know or understand, you've managed to upset my mother. While Pa is away, I'll protect her from you, with whatever it takes.*

Whatever it takes.

"It's gonna take a lot more than saying you can do this, Gil!" Herb's face was in front of Gilbert, taking up his field of vision and blocking him from jumping onto the ornithopter's arm. "Herb," yelled Gilbert, partly from stress, partly in an effort to be heard over the sound of the ornithopter's flapping blades, "Herb, if I can kill a Martian in the sewers, I can climb out on an overgrown tree limb with rivets! Now get out of my way!"

"Hope you know what you're doing," Herb said in a quieter voice. Gil carefully moved past Herb over the other side. He grabbed the sides of the beam firmly with his elbows bent, his legs wrapped carefully around the beam, as Ma had taught him to begin when he was on the balance beam. Hand over hand, and avoid all the obstacles (in this case, all the tubes and hoses and wires that criss-crossed over the arm). Focus your eyes ahead about ten feet, and don't look down or you'll be afraid and freeze. Hand, foot, hand, foot ...

An annoying insect whined by his ear. Gilbert swatted at it, which made him look down.

The mob had gotten braver since the giant Steam Lincoln had stopped moving. They'd milled closer to its legs and under the ornithopter, and one of the policemen had finally gotten up the gumption to raise his triple-barreled pistol and fire at the most visible target.

Which, Gilbert thought with a blend of logic and panic, *would be me.*

"Colonel!" yelled Holiday, his normally serene voice suddenly urgent.

"What?" Finn barked back.

"I have positive identification. Our job's on the arm, and the coppers below have opened fire."

"Suggestions, gentlemen?"

"Boss," said Harper, "I been looking at these here controls, I think I know how to ..."

Finn turned at the sound of Harper's voice. The boy had jumped into the driver's seat and was reaching for one of the levers.

"Harper, don't!" yelled Finn. Holiday was already lunging for Harper's hand.

Of course, they were all too late.

"What's he trying to do?" Johnny's voice called out over the loud flapping of the ornithopter's wings.

"He looked down when the copper fired their pistols, and now he's frozen up," Herb called back from the platform's edge. His body still faced his foolish, foolish friend who wouldn't listen to reason.

The crowds were gathering below, almost all from a safe distance, or peeking around corners of buildings. There were pneumatic tubes everywhere, but so far the Steam Lincoln hadn't walked far enough to cross paths with them.

Still, even though the New York skyline hadn't been altered by their adventure, when Herb looked back down he saw yet another blue-uniformed policeman point his pistol up at Gil. A puff of smoke blasted from the triple-barreled pistol, and Gil swatted at something near his ear for the second or third time.

"We've gotta get loose! Even if those cops don't get off a lucky shot, when we run out've fuel we're gonna tip and drop! And if the claw gets loose then …"

Johnny was cut off in mid-sentence as the Steam Lincoln's arm suddenly jerked upwards, pulling the ornithopter with it a good ten feet into the air.

"Woah!" Johnny yelled as he gripped his chair arms for balance.

"Wha... Gil!" As Herb struggled to keep his balance, his voice went from a low surprise to a high-pitched screech as Gilbert fell off of the beam of the Steam Lincoln's arm and swung over the edge.

"You dad-blasted fool!"

It was rare indeed for Colonel Finn to yell at his subordinates in public, but this was a very unusual kind of day.

"Well, I was just watching her," Harper said, "and was supposed to move the arm, and …"

"GET OUTTA THAT SEAT!" Finn roared, grabbing the younger man by the shoulders and flinging him from it with no more effort than would take to move a ten year old.

Margaret, now awake, giggled from the seat she'd been tied to. "Problems, gentlemen? I can help, you know."

The arm's sudden movement surprised Gilbert so much that he wobbled, lost his balance and went over the edge. He stared at the ground as he fell with a fear that was as pure, whole and clear as the water of a mountain stream. It was a full five seconds before he realized that the ground wasn't getting any closer. He looked up—the magnetized tool bag had stuck firmly to the Steam Lincoln's arm, and Gil's right arm was hooked into the bag's two carrying straps. His other arm and legs had also hooked into a couple of the many tubes that criss-crossed the Steam Lincoln's limbs. In his fear he had drawn his limbs closer together like a baby in the womb, and it had saved his life.

Sweet Jesus, thank you! He had to say the prayer inside his head. His mouth was still afraid of making a bunch of gibbering nonsense. He tried to pull himself up to the top of the arm again, but the upper-body strength that he'd developed long ago with his mother's lessons had atrophied without practice. Doing a chin-up was out of the question, much less a full pull-up. He only managed to pull himself up halfway, trying to bring his lanky legs up to the wider rubber tubes that were gurgling with chemicals and hissing with steam.

He kicked his legs in the air, swinging, knocking, landing, and then slipping off the tubes. On his third try, Gilbert's feet landed on the largest blue and white colored tube, and he gripped it with the toes of his shoes. Well, his *shoe*, anyway. One of his shoes had fallen off, and his right foot was in a stocking. He wished he could have been bare-footed right now. Despite the cold wind coming from the ocean, it would have been easier to get a grip with his bare feet.

Still. He flexed his arms and legs together around the tubes, bringing himself close to the metal arm beam and getting a firm grip. Slowly, carefully, Gilbert moved first this hand then that leg, pulled carefully on the tool bag and moved the other leg, until he'd pulled himself back up on top of the Steam Lincoln's arm. He gripped the beam tightly with all his limbs and gasped. He didn't feel tired, but knew he didn't have an endless supply of adrenaline. He'd falter soon if he didn't free them all from this thing.

He looked to the giant metal elbow, downhill and about twenty feet away. He could pull himself down to the elbow's tubes. Maybe he could even walk it like the balance beam Ma had taught him on after the trapeze, provided he could keep his eyes off the ground.

Why not? Walking it would be quicker and take seconds instead of minutes. Johnny had said he'd just need to cut a few tubes going from the elbow motor, once he swung down to the gauges they were attached to. All he had to do was get to them.

He stood, wobbling just a little and holding the tool bag out for balance.

Margaret was conscious again and trying very hard to give a winning smile even though her face felt like it had been turned to plaster putty. She was securely fastened to the observer's chair by her wrists and ankles, as far away from the control seat as the Pinkertons could place her.

Doc had been staring hard at the girl the entire time she'd calmly, almost drolly stated how their only hope of regaining their quarry safely was to release her. "Where would that leave you dear boys with your fee?" she said innocently. "Even if the four of you are paid by the hour, I doubt if the Pinkerton detective agency would ever again look kindly upon investigators who stood by and allowed their job to splatter his guts all over Main Street, when untying me could have saved him. Wouldn't you agree?"

Finn weighed his options. He'd never shot a lady before, but he had lied more by his twelfth year on Earth than the average congressman did in a lawmaking career. Lying here could get Chesterton, the job of the day, into the cockpit safely.

Time to lie, then.

"Honey," Finn growled, pulling back the hammer on his pistol, "I am going to count to five after they pull off them ropes on your arms. If those boys ain't on their way here at a good speed by then ..."

"Oh dear, Mister cowboy," Margaret said with fake worry, "I know how men like you think. Do you mean an honorable man like you would really put a bullet through my pretty little hea—OW!"

Finn had fired, the bullet striking the thin metal wall and punching a bright, sunny hole through it to the world outside.

But the loud retort from the pistol was only part of the reason she'd screamed. Flecks of metal and powder ricocheted from the bullet hole as it made its exit, making pinprick burns on Margaret's cheek. They were small, nearly invisible, and stung like a lightning attack from a half-dozen angry wasps.

"Nope," Finn said, never taking his eyes away from Margaret even as he fired. "I've never killed a lady. Never had to. An Injun acquaintance of mine taught me most women become quite cooperative, when you go after their looks. 'Course I could notch your ears like a sow, but I think you could cover that up a little too easy with your hair. Maybe if I just put a little slice across your cheek with my knife ..."

Finn flicked a very large knife from a hidden pocket, and sliced her restraints with such speed that she hadn't time to block the knife's blade from pressing against her right cheek when he was done.

"One," said Finn.

"I'll need to get up out of this chair," she said, betraying just the tiniest bit of fear in her voice. Finn cackled to himself inside. He'd broken her. Or at least gotten a bridle about her teeth.

"Colonel," it was Harper again. Finn ground his teeth. After his little flub-up with the dark-haired flirt, and then nearly dumping the job onto the street with his attempt at running the arm, that boy had better keep quiet for the next few weeks if he didn't want to go chasing deadbeat husbands for the next year.

"What, Corporal?" growled Finn, keeping Margaret seated in case she tried her latest gambit a second time.

"You might want to rethink having her move the arm. The job's pulled himself back up, and he's walking along it now like he was a circus tightrope walker."

"WHAT?" Finn rushed over to the window.

Gilbert was walking along the arm, his eyes carefully pointed away from the ground, making his way step by step right for the elbow. Whatever goal he had in mind was anybody's guess.

"Harper," barked Finn, keeping his eyes on his prize, "your foot was built for this kind've work. Get out there and rope the boy in!"

"Easy as candy from a baby," said Joseph Harper Junior, slipping off one of his boots to reveal a thick wool sock.

"You ever tried taking candy from a baby?" drawled Holiday.

Harper chuckled and pulled a small tool from his belt. He removed his sock to show a well-shaped, brass replica of a human foot. He winced, holding his injured side as he knelt on one knee, then inserted the small wand he'd gotten from his belt and began winding it around quickly. After a few seconds he stood, and began dragging the foot behind him, as if it were sticking to the metal floor somehow. He'd just turned to face the steel-riveted door when Margaret, now freed of her restraints by Finn and unwatched by anyone when Gilbert's perilous position was announced, grinned up at Harper from her seat and gave a slow wink.

He blushed three shades of red and went out the door, as firmly caught in her emotional snare as a fly in a spider's web.

Gilbert had managed to make it to the elbow joint of the steel-and-steam behemoth. Now all he had to do was swing down, cut the tubes used to pump steam and various liquids to the needed joints and gears of the Steam Lincoln's claw, and then make his way back to Herb and Johnny.

After that, the next problem would be freeing the ornithopter from the claw's grip, and then starting the 'thopter up again before they fell to Earth.

Life could be so complicated.

He had stood, and then taken a few hesitant steps while holding the bag of tools in one of his hands for balance. But a strong gust of wind had convinced him that this wasn't a good idea, and he'd decided to take the safe route to the elbow. Ma had taught him how to walk a simple tightrope, but he'd learned only ten feet off of the ground. He'd later graduated to twice that height, but nearly always with a large amount of hay beneath him. Here, his 'rope' was a steel beam nearly a foot wide, but it was angled downwards and could spark to life again at any moment. Better by far, he thought, as he carefully knelt down again, to keep himself in a crawling position where he could grip the sides if anything unexpected happened.

He saw the miniature steam engine at the elbow that powered the ornithopter's forearm—a large, ponderous mass of clicking gears, hissing gages and gummy oil smudges. How was he gonna pull this off?

"I can do this," Gilbert mumbled under his breath as he looked for red, white and blue hoses on the elbow's steam driver engine to damage some. "I've killed Martians when other people died. I kept Herb and me alive in the collector basket by welding the lid shut. I knocked the Doctor himself down a bunch of pegs when he tried to get uppity with us. So I can pull apart a few gears when my life depends on it!"

Still, something in Gilbert's mind said he'd forgotten something, something vitally important. The small thick disk the red-head had given him was jabbing him in the side as the wind flapped his sportcoat against him.

Focus, Gilbert thought. *I'm getting too philosophical when I need to focus on the job.* He swallowed, breathed, and looked at the motor.

Johnny had said there were three tubes or hoses in the elbow assembly, tubes colored red, white and blue. "One moves fuel, another steam, and a third lubricant of some kind," Johnny had said. "Cut those three, and we can be on our way."

"Gil!" Gilbert heard the faint cry behind him and turned slightly. The voice was Herb's. "Hurry up," Herb yelled, "we've got to go!"

Gilbert nodded his head, hoping that Herb could see he understood. There was no way he was going to give up one of his precious grips on the beam in order to wave or give a thumbs up—not at this height! He carefully opened the drawstring on the bag with one hand, keeping the other firmly on the beam as much for balance as for an actual grip.

A sudden hard gust of wind hit him, moving the bag in his hand just enough to spill several of its contents over the edge with a gentle tinkling noise, including the wrench!

"Blast," said Gilbert under his breath. The bag's magnetized fibers hadn't been strong enough to hold the heavy tools in when the bag had flapped in the wind. He looked down, hoping no crowds had gathered below that might be injured or killed by falling tools.

He needn't have worried; there was no one directly below; they all were keeping themselves at a safe distance, close enough to see but far enough to avoid being stepped on. He slowly set the bag, with its remaining contents, down with one hand, waited until he heard the magnetic fibers of the bag click against the beam, then looked inside it. The bag held a measuring tape, some pliers with an odd little dial on the side, what looked like a hammer with four heads and a hand-sized set of clippers with a small steam gauge on the side.

That's the one, Gilbert decided. He had just pulled the clippers out of the bag when he heard the droning sound of propellers.

Gilbert looked up briefly.

There were Four Zeppelins in the air.

And they had surrounded him, the ornithopter and the giant metal man.

Oh, no.

Gilbert counted again. Yes, *four* of them! They were identical shades of gray, and each one sported a flag with red, white and blue stripes and a single, five-pointed star stretched across the side. Large wands, fifty feet long and several feet in diameter, sat beneath the gondolas. A long, white coil was wrapped around each wand, and ended at a silver ball at the wand's tip.

Gilbert had seen the tanks ("land ironclads," the Doctor had insisted on calling them) and similar Zeppelins fight the Tripods in the last battle against the Martians back in England. The fantastic human vehicles had managed to destroy several of the Martian machines before they had been wiped out in the Martian counterattack by the squids' heated rays and lightning cannons.

"Someone's been busy," Gil noted. The wands on the end of the Zeppelins looked a lot like the lightning cannons.

And four of those wands were glowing now, presumably in expectation of firing very large amounts of electrical energy at the metal arm Gilbert was holding onto.

"Holiday," barked Finn, "you're the high-falootin' heraldry man! Who are these guys and what're they pointing at us?"

"First," said John Henry "Doc" Holiday, sounding truly worried to Finn for the first time since they'd been trapped in that box canyon by the Wild Bunch gang, "everybody needs to get vertical in a rather quickened sort of way. Stand up I say! Make sure nothing's touching the floor but the soles of your boots, and nothing's touching the wall at all. Colonel," he continued, not even checking to see if his directions had been followed, but keeping his twitching, human eye on the two Zeppelins visible in the front windows, "I must be honest. I haven't got a blind man's chance in Death Valley to figure where those overgrown, floating saddlebags came from. Those colors and that design don't belong to any army on this continent, not to the U.S.A., C.S.A, Texarcana or either of the Californias. And those Zeppelins and the hardware they're packin' don't come cheap. Someone or some place with big money and a lot of spare time put those things together, and right now they're pointing enough 'lectricity at us to light up the whole city like an oversized Fourth-of-July sparkler."

"So if the job doesn't fall to his death, he's gonna be a crispy critter," Finn said. "This keeps getting better an' better."

Gilbert sat on the edge of the beam, wondering exactly how he was going to get out of here. It was tough enough to climb out here with the slope and the wind while the limb was still. What if it started to move again while he was traversing back? And what about the blimps?

Each of the heads of the wands sticking out from the prow of the four Zeppelins glowed brightly now. Gilbert saw one Zeppelin turn ever so gently, as the hydrogen behemoths often did when changing course. It lumbered towards Gilbert with the sound of a dozen propellers great and small, the least of which was still at least twice Gilbert's size.

Gilbert gulped, and shoved the clipper onto the nearest hose—the blue one. He'd used smaller versions of these before, when he'd had to work on clipping and re-attaching thick wires or hoses to analytical engines back in his clacker days.

He put the V-shape of the open clipper blades against the hose, and flicked a switch with his thumb. With a click and a hiss, the clipper snipped through the thick rubber of the hose, which flailed out and fell limp, black oil gurgling in a steady stream from one of the cut ends to the ground below.

He heard a metallic sound in front of him. A door had opened in the body of the Steam Lincoln, and a man stepped out confidently. One foot wore a cowboy boot, the other foot was covered in some kind of metal that stuck and slid along the metal beam.

A magnet? On your foot?

Gilbert blinked—it was the cowboy he'd kicked into the wall! The one with the jumping, pogo-stick leg!

"Hold still, Gilbert," the man said, spasms of pain creeping across his face each time he moved the right side of his body. "I'm trained to help folks in your situation!" He shouted as he walked/slid, trying to be heard over the roar of the wind. "I'll get you down safe, Gilbert, but you'll have to trust me! Now, just keep your eyes on me, and..."

Gilbert heard more noise behind him, back at the ornithopter. Gilbert turned to look. One of the Zeppelins was directly over them now, and several dark coils extended from its underbelly, hanging limply until the ends came near the 'thopter, then jumped towards it and held fast. The Zeppelin pilot was good—he'd dropped those lines where they wouldn't be clipped by the ornithopter's blades. A stray one even clamped with a metallic thunk to the arm of the Steam Lincoln, only a dozen feet from Gilbert.

Taking only a few seconds, Gilbert opened up the clipper, placed it against the red hose, and flicked the switch again. This time an acrid-smelling fluid the color of apple juice flowed out of the cut hose, soaking Gilbert's arm.

Gilbert looked back to the cowboy, who was now only a few steps away and still talking to Gilbert. Should Gilbert go with him? There were fewer hoses to grab here—escape through a trapeze-act wasn't going to happen! He was too high up, and this was way different from playing in the barn!

Gil looked back at the ornithopter again. Now men in leather suits with goggles were sliding down the attached cable from the blimps towards Herb and Johnny!

"Gilbert!" It was the metal-footed cowboy again. Gilbert turned and saw him, now barely ten feet away. Gilbert could see that they were close in age to each other. "Stay back!" Gilbert yelled, looking up from the elbow towards the cowboy. He still had the closed pipe-clipper in his hands. He might not have a pepperbox pistol, but the clipper still had a sharp, stabby point in the end that he could use to buy himself time. He waved it a bit to make his point, trying to ignore the sounds of men shouting from the ornithopter behind him.

There was a tap at his shoulder. Gilbert turned back to the ornithopter a third time.

A man stood behind Gilbert. He wore a dark leather jacket and a goggled leather helmet like the one used by the German pilots he'd seen at the Sky Palace. He was a foot or two away from the magnetized end of the cable attached to the arm of the Steam Lincoln, and stood behind Gilbert with his feet planted firmly on the Steam Lincoln's arm, his arms bent and ending at fists on his waist. His smile was wide, and set in a face that was film star handsome.

"Gilbert!" The aviator had spoken with a happy air, as if he'd found a long-lost friend passing in the street.

Over the aviator's shoulder, Gilbert saw Herb take a swing at one of the similarly dressed men from the Zeppelin who'd boarded the ornithopter. Herb connected, but the aviator swung back without a second's hesitation, clocking Herb no less than three times with some kind of black baton.

"Don't go with him, Gilbert," shouted the cowboy, still a good ten or fifteen feet away. "You'll only be safe with me!"

"Do I know you?" Gilbert asked the smiling aviator, pointing the clippers at him and trying to move away. Why wasn't this guy afraid of falling? Did he have a magnet foot, too?

"Nope!" the aviator said, still smiling. He pulled something from the back of his belt and swung at Gilbert's head.

The lights went out and Gilbert knew no more.

Chapter 43

"Children are innocent and love justice, while most adults
are wicked and prefer mercy."
– GKC, *On Household Gods and Goblins*, 1922

Gilbert awoke for the second time that day with a blistering headache and the feeling of grit in his mouth. He opened his eyes slightly. Even though the lights were dim, moving his eyelids caused him such exquisite pain that he shut them again. Which caused him more pain, which made him instinctively yank his hands to his head, which made him yelp out in even more pain.

Gilbert might have been caught in this vicious cycle for a very long time, but a small voice spoke up.

"Mister Gilbert?"

Gilbert stopped groaning and peeked between his fingers. Little Johnny Brainerd was sitting opposite him on a wooden bench, looking at him with an expression halfway between fear and puzzlement.

"Where are we?" Gilbert asked. His tongue felt three sizes too large for his mouth, and the back of his head felt like it had an ice pick lodged in it. An ice pick that had been coated in rat poison, first, and bent sideways before it'd been slammed into his noggin.

Gilbert looked around. They were in a cell made of wooden planks, perhaps ten by ten feet. Johnny's bench was actually a couple of wooden crates pushed together, as was the 'bed' Gilbert was lying on.

"The big Zeppelin," Johnny said. "One of them blackjacked you on the head, then hooked you to a winch and pulled you up. A couple of his thugs came after Herb and me before he took care of you. And ..."

"What happened to Herb?" Gilbert asked, looking very closely at Johnny. His voice had become very quiet, more from fear for the fate of his friend than fear of pain.

"I ..." Johnny started. Tears choked back his words. "Herb, he hit one of the guys hard. Real hard, Mister Gilbert. So hard I heard the glass in his goggles crack. An' Herb did it with one hand holding onto the 'thopter so he wouldn't fall!

"The guy Herb hit, he got so angry. Both the guy's hands were free, 'cause he was hooked to a safety belt. He grabbed Herb and hit him again and again and *again*. I heard Herb's body with each hit. It sounded like ... like a bag of flour I dropped on the floor once, only I heard it again and *again*. He ..."

Johnny began sobbing. Gilbert, trying hard to ignore his pain, got up from his bench, crossed the little room and sat beside Johnny. Awkwardly, he put his arm around the smaller boy's shoulders as his father and mother had done for him when he'd needed it.

"One of the guys grabbed me," Johnny continued, still sobbing. "Something clicked onto my belt, and suddenly I was flying in the air, up here. It only took a couple of seconds and I was inside. The guy who hit Herb came up a minute later.

"What happened to Herb? Did you see him?"

"No. I was too scared to say anything, or ask about Herb. When the fellow who hit Herb came back on board, he was using a lot of bad words, and he pulled his broken goggles off quick as he could.

"Then the big pilot, the guy who knocked you out? He always has that big, big smile on his face? He asked 'what happened to the other one, the friend?' Then the one who hit Herb said 'I took care of him. He hit me in the face an' nearly blinded me! So I ...' and then the smiling man, still smiling, grabbed the guy who hit Herb. He grabbed him by the shoulders and just threw him over the railing like a sack of wheat! The guy didn't even get a chance to scream.

"Then he turned around with that big, big smile, and said 'Let's go home, boys,' just like we'd won a baseball game and he was gonna treat us to ice cream sundaes."

Gilbert breathed deeply. Johnny hadn't seen Herb get captured or hit the ground. There was, Gilbert told himself, every chance that Herb had survived the encounter. Maybe even escaped.

"I want to go home," Johnny said suddenly, and started sobbing again. "I'm supposed to be going to a school for smart kids. That's why Jack, Tollers, and the twins were on the airship with me! But now I'm not there, and I don't know if I'll ever get home again!"

Gilbert looked up and out the slats from his seated position. "We'll be okay, Johnny," he said quietly. "We'll be okay."

But inside, Gilbert couldn't stop thinking the same thing as Johnny.

Chapter 44

"Reason is always a kind of brute force; those who appeal to the head rather than the heart, however pallid and polite, are necessarily men of violence. We speak of 'touching' a man's heart, but we can do nothing to his head but hit it."
– GKC, Charles II, *Twelve Types*

Colonel James "Huckleberry" Finn of the Pinkertons Investigation Agency had been in more than a few tough scrapes in his life. His earliest memories involved growing up as a homeless child on the streets of St. Petersburg, Missouri, where life taught him one cheerfully amoral lesson after another. Had he not bonded in friendship with a number of other boys who were lesser-degree outcasts in town, he might have grown to be a professional swindler.

Instead, Alan Pinkerton had recruited young Finn into the agency after the end of the Slave Wars. Finn's ability to put others at ease and either obtain or plant information had made him a valuable asset, and he'd risen in the ranks quickly while still in his teen years. Everyone he'd encountered for the better part of the last half-century, be they idle rich, street urchins, wealthy industrialists or union bosses, all had fallen to the smiles and wiles of Colonel James H. Finn of the Pinkerton Security Services.

But the English kid in front of him was posing a number of subtle challenges.

He was their only lead to find Chesterton, now that that job had disappeared into the belly of a giant, armored Zeppelin. A tough little fella, Wells had taken a swing at another one of the goggle-eyed minions that had dropped out of the bellies of the Zeppelins to grab Chesterton and the kid piloting the flappy-machine.

The English kid knew how to hit—socking his opponent hard enough to send him into a blind, punching rage, and only little Johnny Brainerd and Gilbert had been taken instead of all three.

Finn sized up Herb in a few seconds. Most of the time, Finn had found, the method used to squeeze information from a lead depended on how they'd grown up.

Folks who were poor and destitute usually cracked and gave up accomplices when he brought steaming food in the room.

Rich kids were even easier. They cracked like week-old eggshells if you threatened them with jail time among the unwashed masses, a lot of manual labor and no opportunity to sleep late for the next few years.

But the middle-class was often the trickiest, since their motivations and experiences were as different as anything could be in the world. Some feared losing their reputation, while others needed various temptations or promises of protection. Pinkerton Investigations was a private investigation firm, and there were many gray areas in the law they could exploit, which the boys in blue could not legally do.

But this kid, now. He was a tough one to size up.

Kid's lived a life of privilege, Finn thought, looking at Herb's hands and face, *for part of his life at least. Got himself an angry attitude problem a mile wide. Maybe from his Daddy's drinking or running around. Or maybe his Momma was weak and let bad stuff happen.* Finn had lived it and seen it happen at least a hundred times.

Herb looked again at Finn. The boy's chin was stuck out and his forehead pushed just a little bit down. His eyes bulged just a fraction of an inch outwards, and his fists were balled up on the table, still linked by the iron manacles. *Probably already thinking about punching the daylights out've me,* Finn thought. *Good.* Any extreme emotion could be directed to his ends like wind on a sailboat.

"Well, Mister ...Wells..." Finn pretended he'd forgotten the kid's name, looking into the dossier he'd gotten along with Gilbert's. It was stuffed with newspaper clippings and other documents with the name of Herbert G. Wells typed neatly at the top. Such a stack of papers were often all Finn needed to give a mark like Herbert a clear sense he was unimportant, outclassed and out-gunned.

"I want a lawyer," Herb cut him off, his eyes boring into Finn's.

Finn smiled. The English kid had just saved Finn the trouble of being nice. The older man snapped the dossier shut, the stiff folder shutting with a sound like a prison door.

"One," began Finn, circling behind Herb and ticking points off on his fingers, "You're not under arrest. Two, I'm not an officer of any state, federal, or city government, and so am not bound by the same dictates of the Constitution. Third, you're not an American citizen. The Constitution doesn't reach that far across the Atlantic. Fourth, I've got this," Finn plunked his heavy billfold onto the top of the table and made sure that the brass badge, with its all-seeing eye on the money clip, was plainly visible to the younger, seated man. "Do you know what that is?"

"It's an eye," Herb said. "An organ of sight very sensitive to having thumbs or sharp sticks poked in it by escaped prisoners."

"This," roared Finn, holding the eye within an inch of Herb's face, "is my own, personal passport to the wonderful world of 'I can whale the tar out of you without fear of reprisal!'"

Finn smelled something odd on the English kid.

Ah ha.

Hair cream.

The kid went through the New York Harbor, survived an exploding Zeppelin, been chased through the New York dock district by the Dead Rabbits, and been beaten by a thug twice his size.

And yet his face was free of bruises, his tie was straight, and the faintest whiff of cologne or some other scent still lingered over him.

This was a young man who cared about his appearance.

"Know why, Herbert? It's because this," said Finn, calculating his next move while he tapped his badge, "is the emblem of the Pinkertons Investigation Agency. It would take the President of the United States a good two days to get this material I have in my hands right now. With a little help from a heliograph, stipplograph, some good-old Morse code and a few well-placed smoke signals, I got this dossier together in an afternoon. *Yesterday* afternoon. You know how difficult information gathering can be, don't you Hebert? A lot more difficult than being a chemist. Or a draper. Or an amateur teacher, hm?"

Herb's eyes widened. These guys were good. He hadn't even told Gil about his ill-fated apprenticeship as a curtain maker, or as a teacher.

 Finn didn't need to be a mind reader to know just what kind of thoughts were going through the boy's head. Herb had stopped twitching in anger for a second when Finn had mentioned the drape job.

Wells had paused because he was wondering what else Finn knew. And in Finn's experience, the longer the pause, the more skeletons were in the closet.

Herb swallowed. "You've been looking at me for a while, then. What do you want from me?" he said dryly. "If you're still holding me alive, I've got something you want. Now tell me what it is so I can get back to work, or you can put a bullet in me and dump me in a ditch someplace."

"You know, Herbert Wells," said Finn, straightening up and tipping his hat back, "I've just realized why I like you. You're not like most Englishmen I've met. You don't dance around a point when you talk. You get right to it, and you're done. Now I can respect that. Just like I hope you'll respect me."

Finn stood to leave. "I'll be back in a few minutes, Herbert George Wells," he said with a tip of his hat, "but while I'm gone, I want you to think about what I've said, and what the badge lets me do." He opened the door of the improvised interrogation room they'd rustled together back at the Brainerd workshop, and sauntered out of the room without a visible care. Holiday gave a smart salute to his superior that was returned in a relaxed manner. The door was shut, and Herb was alone.

Herb counted slowly to twenty, then spent nearly every drop of energy he had left yanking and pulling at the cuffs that bound him to the table. Ignoring the flaring pain in his shoulders where the Zeppelin thug had beaten him, he grunted and gasped as he tried in vain to find a weak link in his chains.

Blast, thought Herb. He wished he'd paid more attention to that Houdini fellow when he was doing his exhibitions. What he wouldn't give for a bobby pin right now!

The door opened again. Herb looked up, ready to curse Finn, his country and family going back several generations.

But Finn hadn't entered the door.

It was the younger cowboy. The one Finn had called Harper, who didn't look more than a few years older than Herb himself.

Harper sat near Herb, perhaps two seats away on the same side of the table.

"How're you doin', Herb?" Harper said. He was giving Herb a grin that was so phony, Herb had no trouble understanding its purpose. Harper had no intention or interest in playing coy with Herb, or even in pretending to be his friend. And he cared not a whit if Herb already understood that.

"Fine," Herb said. He wasn't actually scared. More like ... unnerved, as if he were walking past a graveyard in the dark.

"Good," said Harper, smiling. "Y'see, Herb, Finn's my boss. He an' my daddy go way back. But I'm the new feller in the outfit, which means I've got something to prove. You follow me?"

Herb didn't, but nodded anyway.

"Good. So here's the way it is, Herb. We don't care 'bout you at all. Not a whit. My boss don't care if'n you turn up cut in a bunch of drippy, little pieces and fed to the birds and the fish. He'll just move on to the next lead. What we do care about, though, is your friend."

"Gilbert Chesterton," Herb said with a resigned air.

"Why, yes," said Harper, leaning in a bit. "You picked that up right quick. We got anyone one else looking for him, Herb Wells?"

"Half the world, it seems. Look, if you want me to find him, I'm trying to protect him from some very bad people myself, so if you'll just ..."

Harper knocked on the table. The door opened, but this time it was Holiday, wheeling in a large, odd contraption with hissing steam gauges and a half-dozen tubes that followed its trail through the doorway and out into the hall.

"Herb, you know why we can get buildings up in half the time it took just ten years ago?"

Herb looked warily at the young cowboy. When a captor asked him an indirect question, things had rarely gone well for Herb afterwards.

"I'm a reporter, not a builder."

"But you *were* a draper, right? How long did it take you to pound in a nail, Herbert? How many swings?"

"Too many, it's one of the many reasons I was unsuited to that noble profession."

"Oh, that's too bad. Too bad they didn't have one of these in England. Y'see ..." Harper reached over to the machine and pulled up what looked like a large gun from it. He pointed the gun at the table and pulled the trigger. There was a blast of noise from the machine, and four little shots of steam jetted sideways from the gun's nozzle. A snap sounded in the room. When Herb looked down, he saw that the head of a nail had appeared as if by magic in the tabletop, the wood around the nail's head dimpled slightly downwards.

Harper continued talking, hardly pausing while Herb's eyes grew wide looking at the nail. "Yep," said Harper with a jaunty air, "with one of these babies, Herb old boy, you can have a lot of fun. If'n you don't want to waste bullets, you can use 'em for party tricks."

As if on cue, Holiday threw a piece of thin scrap wood the size of his hand in a lazy arc over Harper's head. Harper's hand twitched without even looking at the wood, his eyes still focused on Herb's. Another nail blasted into the air, catching the wood, slamming it into the wall and pinning it like a bug on a card.

"Great for fastening wood," continued Harper, "or loosening tongues."

"Look," said Herb, "you don't need all the theatrics. I don't know where Gil is, though I wish I did. And furthermo—ook!"

With a sudden movement, Harper had grabbed Herb's tie and yanked him halfway across the table, stretching Herb with his bound hands in one direction and his neck in the other. With another quick movement, Harper fastened Herb to the table by a nail through the tip of his tie.

Herb tried to pull back, but he only succeeded in tightening his tie around his neck like a noose.

"WHAT'RE YOU DOING?" Herb roared, "That's mine!"

"Tell me where Gilbert is, and I'll buy you a dozen wholesale."

"Sod you. Buy yourself a real hat, first. And a real leg."

Harper's eyes narrowed. Herb realized he'd let his temper do the talking, and it had driven him across a very dangerous line.

"Look," said Herb, trying to back pedal, "what I meant was ..."

Harper fired another nail into Herb's tie, farther up from the first one.

"Look, I'm sorry! I just saw you limping, and I heard the squeaks and the hiss of steam, and I said something stu—"

Harper fired a third nail into Herb's tie, exactly one inch higher than the last one.

Herb yelled, and tried bobbing his head back and forth desperately, trying to help his tie dodge the muzzle of the gun. It was no use; Harper, still keeping his eyes on Herb from a safe distance of a foot or so, only had to tilt his gun slightly to fasten Herb's tie more firmly to the thick wooden table top.

"Every five seconds you make me wait, Herbert (*pop!*), I'm gonna put another nail a notch higher (*pop!*) in your tie. Know what's gonna happen when I run outta tie, pard?"

"I don't know where he is!"

Another pop. Halfway up the tie now. "Wrong answer, limey boy," the young cowboy said. "I've got about three notches left (*POP!*) make that two, before the next nail makes a nice little peg hole in your chin. (*POP!*) Make that one. It'll be difficult to get a date to your next ball with holes in your face, Herbert. What's it gonna be?"

"I ... I ..." stammered Herb. He was now pinned by his tie with his face only a few inches above the table.

"Took too long," Harper said without a trace of regret or happiness. The gun moved towards Herb's face as he screamed.

Chapter 45

"They have torn the soul of Christ into silly strips, labeled egoism and altruism, and they are equally puzzled by His insane magnificence and His insane meekness."
– GKC, *Orthodoxy*

The door to the gray, plank-walled room burst open, cutting off both Herb's scream and the pounding of the nail-blaster. Finn stomped in, disarmed Harper and set the nailgun down with one hand, then grabbed Harper by the collar and threw him to the ground with the other.

Holiday grabbed the nailgun off the table as soon as Herb's hopeful eyes landed on it.

"What in Sam Hill are you doing?" yelled Finn.

"I'm doing my job," Harper roared back, "since you're too busy visiting the hooch bottle!"

"Why, you stubborn little cuss," snarled Finn, grabbing Harper by the collar with both hands and hauling him to his feet. He gave Harper a rude shove backwards towards the door. "Get a' going," barked Finn, "get a goin' and rearrange some o' that mush in yer skull!" Harper spun sideways after being pushed, exposing his backside to a well-placed kick from Finn's boot.

Finn nodded to Holiday, disconnecting the hose from the nail gun and spiriting the tool out of the room, closing the door quietly as the hose's angry hiss died down.

Finn looked at Herb and sighed. "Sorry 'bout that, Mister Wells. Hold still," he said, reaching into a hidden pocket in his dusty longcoat and pulling out a large knife.

Herb yelped at the sight of the weapon, and tried instinctively to pull back from the sharp, shiny blade.

"Thanks," said Finn, as Herb's pull-back tightened the tie and made it easy to cut. A flick of Finn's knife and Herb was free. Another three seconds and Finn had unlocked the handcuffs from Herb's wrists. Now that he was free Herb sat back, shuddering and trying very hard to keep himself from sobbing like a little child.

"Sorry 'bout that," said Finn, "that fool Harper messes up sometimes. I'll have to kick him around a bit, remind him who's boss later."

"I should hope so," said Herb, rubbing his sore neck and wrists. "Is this how you do things in America? I heard people had rights with the police out here."

"Like I said, son, we're more of a private agency. It's complicated. Look, lemme make it up to ya. Doc!" His voice carried out at the closed door, "rustle us up some grub, will you?"

"Sure thing, Colonel Finn!" Holiday's voice carried through the closed door, followed by hurried footsteps.

Herb looked at Finn with unsure eyes. "You sent him out for worms?" he said.

"What? Oh, no," Finn chuckled, "No, Mister Wells, out here, *grub* is a word for *food*. I hope you like fried fish and potatoes. There's a little place out here Doc likes to go to that serves that kind've stuff. He'd eat it three meals a day if'n I let him."

"Fish and chips?" said Herb quietly. At the thought of familiar food, his stomach rumbled like a steam engine short on coal. He'd had nothing to eat since dinner the night before; Margaret's little adventure with blowing up the airship had taken place a few minutes before breakfast was to be served.

And it was now past mid-afternoon.

"Anyways," said Finn, "we'll just take care of a few pieces of work here, and send you on your way. That okay with you, Mister Wells?"

"Peachy," said Herb, thinking only about food.

"Good. Well, I ..." Finn was interrupted by the door opening. The smell of breaded fish and fried potatoes mixed with the tart smell of vinegar filled the air. Herb's mouth began watering.

"Well, Doc, thanks for being so prompt. You also got those forms for us?"

"Your repast, noble Colonel, sir," said Holiday, bowing like a dutiful servant, "and the forms you requested. But you may want to read the paper afore you let our guest sign 'em."

Doc dropped two wrapped packages on the table, a newspaper beneath them. Herb rubbed his neck, his eyes never leaving them.

"Oh ... um ..."

"Oh, sorry, Mister Wells, did you want some of this? Well, I think we can arrange that. Yes sir, I ..."

Finn picked up a package with grease spots staining the bottom. It was all Herb could do to keep from launching himself at the bigger, older man and tearing the package from him in a fit of Cro-Magnon like hunger.

"Well, Mister Wells, it seems you've gotten yourself a little bit of infamy, here," Finn said as he looked at the paper.

"What do you mean?" asked Herb, his nostrils twitching.

"Well," said Finn, setting the food behind him for a moment and picking up the paper, "it seems they think you had something to do with that airship exploding over the harbor this morning."

"What?"

"Yes. Here, take a look." Finn slid the paper over to Herb, his hunger forgotten for the moment.

Herb picked up the newspaper with a trembling hand, and read the headline.

"AIRSHIP DESTROYED!
MECHANICAL MAN ATTACKS!
YOUNG ENGLISHMAN SOUGHT AS CULPRIT!
By Kelly J. Ewing

As all good citizens of the city of New York can attest, our harbour was witness yet again to one of the greatest of possible human tragedies—the destruction of a mass-transportation vehicle in the skies above our fair city.

At approximately half-past eight o'clock this morning, the dirigible Tiger Moth combusted in a fireball that was visible to virtually all within sight of the harbor, and word quickly spread throughout the dock district and into the tearooms and beer halls throughout the city. While the destruction of an airship carrying immigrants to our shores is not an unheard of occurrence, fear was added to tragedy as an enormous, metal man-like mechanical creature stalked the buildings of the dock district soon after the airship's destruction.

'It's a truly horrific day,' said Police Chief Thomas Thompson, whose officers are now organized and at this writing conducting house-to-house searches for the culprit, 'but we have a sizable lead. A young, handsome Englishman was seen climbing from the waters after the blimp exploded. He was seen again minutes later running from a mob of concerned citizens, and then entering the building from which the huge mechanical monster emerged.'

"Wait," said Herb. "You *all* were on that! I remember one of your men prying me from my seat on Johnny's flying machine, and then pulling me inside the head of that Lincoln contraption! One of you put a chloroform rag in my mouth, and then I woke up in here!"

"You want to keep reading, son," Finn said softly. His attitude of deference to Herb was gone.

Herb looked down at the paper again:

Reaction to the news of a young foreigner's involvement has been swift and forceful among the New York citizenry. 'All I can say is,' claimed one citizen, 'I'm gonna keep my eye out for that fellow. He'd better hope the cops get to him before anyone in the city does!' A large crowd, hearing the man's comments, chimed in with various punishments and unpleasantness that awaited the Englishman were he found in New York City limits by civilians rather than by official police officers.

Herb swallowed.

"Things ain't looking too good for you, huh son?" Finn said with a somber air. "You still hungry?"

"You did this," Herb said, his eyes locked on the newspaper. "You said something to the reporters. You kept yourselves out of this somehow, but you kept me in it. Why?"

"Look, son, I've got no reason to lie to you. We're looking for your friend, Gilbert. We're good at what we do. The best, in fact.

"But this time we need your help. We've been hired not just to find him, but also to keep him from any kind of harm. Trouble is some pretty powerful folks've got him, and if we *do* find him he'll be more nervous'n an alligator in a handbag factory.

"But *you*, Mister Wells, are his best friend, which means if you tell him he can trust us, he's more likely to come along without a fuss."

"And just why would I help you?"

"Well, now, Herbert Wells, you don't have to. This isn't England, where a king can chop your head off because he feels like it. 'Course, there's a lot of people gunning for you right now. I reckon you'd find it a mite tricky getting from this little basement to the docks without finding someone awful sore about that airship that blow'd up real good this morning. Even if you didn't do it, people don't usually listen to reason when they're scared an' angry. Now if, on the other hand, you decide to stick around with us for a little while ..."

"You'd make sure that I was protected from mob influence, and when you've concluded your little business, the papers will learn and print that the young Englishman was innocent. Instead, the papers will blame a mad Papist or a Russian anarchist, or perhaps an angry Negro trying to draw attention to his slave-bound comrades' plight in the CSA as their annual Day of Choice approaches."

Finn leaned back in his chair, and swept the food over to Herb's side of the table with a magnanimous sweep of his thick-muscled arm. "I'm glad we can help each other, son," Finn said as Herb fell on the food. "I've got some other business to take care of, but you enjoy your grub while I get the boys to saddle up."

Herb grunted, still chewing like a feral dog.

Finn opened the door of the makeshift interrogation room and left, closing the door behind him. Harper and Holiday were seated in chairs with their guns drawn and pointed at Margaret in the center of the room.

"Well, missy, looks like you were right," Finn said softly. "He took the bait just like you said. How'd you know it'd be this easy?"

"No one knows how vicious journalists can be better than other journalists," Margaret said quietly. "He knows how a reporter will twist truth and destroy lives if it suits their agenda. The last thing any reporter wants is to be beaten with the same stick they use all the time on the little people."

"Fine," said Finn. "Now, how do we find our little googly-eyed job?"

"The insignia on the Zeppelins confirms what I already guessed. The man who commands those airships worked for my employers at one point, but his grabbing of Gilbert proves he's not following orders anymore. I'm going to have to take care of him, but to do that I'll need you boys and your firepower."

"So you use our guns to get to the feller what has Gilbert," said Finn, "and in return we snatch the boy and look the other way while you take care of your business?"

"Precisely," said Margaret with a wide, sharklike smile.

"Best you understand, deah lady," said Holiday, his triple-barreled pistol still pointed at Margaret, "that it's in your best interests to hold up your end of this bargain. Or else our agreement will likely be terminated with a bullet or three in your brains." Holiday spoke slowly. His drawl wafted through the room without hurry, yet no one mistook the nature of his threat.

"I wouldn't have it any other way," Margaret said, still smiling. She comforted herself with the thought of Doc Holiday's limbless torso turning on a spit for cannibals to eat, while the screams of Gilbert Chesterton sounded in the distance...

Chapter 46

"Those underrate Christianity who say that it discovered mercy; any one might discover mercy. In fact everyone did. But to discover a plan for being merciful and also severe — THAT was to anticipate a strange need of human nature." – GKC, *Orthodoxy*

Gilbert and Johnny sat in their cell. Nothing had changed for several days, other than a small slot opening in the bottom of the door for food to be slid under in two small dishes for each of them. The food was surprisingly good, really. Pancakes for breakfast, cold meats for lunch, and some kind of stew for dinner. Water was slid under the door in a third small dish, which Gilbert and Johnny would share.

There wasn't much to do during this time, other than hatch outlandish escape plans and tell stories of each other's adventures. After Gilbert had told the story of he and Herb meeting in London and surviving the Invasion, along with the sacrifice and death of Father Brown at the bloodsucking tentacles of the Martians, Johnny told his story.

Gilbert had heard many of the basics already, but time was something they both had lots of these days. After John Brainerd Senior, Johnny's Pa, had made a fortune from the sale of his plans for a mechanical manservant, family life had become one intriguing adventure after another. A short while after their first windfall, a messenger had arrived in a uniform of robin's-egg blue with a message rolled up as a scroll and stamped with an official-looking wax seal. Johnny had been selected for a special school, free of charge, that was being set up on the West coast to train young men like himself into *savants*, men of an emerging class of learned scientists who would steer the world on its new course of knowledge.

" ... Not only that," said Johnny, who was proving to be a far more engaging traveling companion than little Jack Lewis had been, "but the school's founder loved Pa's mechanical men. He commissioned a thousand of 'em, maybe more, for his castle. Wanted the whole shebang, he did; plans, suggestions for improvements, the whole thing. When we cashed in the gold, we had so much money it took three wagonloads to bring it all to the bank. But now, I don't know if I'll ever get to the school, or even see my folks again."

Gilbert propped himself up on his cot with his elbow. "Well, I think you will," he said. "But you'll probably have to go through a few adventures first."

"You call this an adventure?" Johnny said, "When I'm almost killed off by my Pa's own inventions? It's more of a pretty big inconvenience, to be polite about it."

"One thing I've learned, Johnny, is that an adventure is usually just an inconvenience you take on with the right attitude."

Johnny was quiet. "Does that include when you and Herb were yelling at me in the ornithopter? That wasn't real nice, you know."

"What?" said Gil, an annoyed tone suddenly creeping into his voice.

The door opened. The smiling airman who'd clocked Gil now stood in the doorway, his spit-polished boots planted firmly two feet apart. His brown trousers had been ironed to knife-edge creases, and his brown leather jacket had a thick fur collar that would have been warm even in the higher altitudes. His hands were not overly thick or small, but were wound into tight fists at his waist. His hair was slicked into place with a shine, and his smile had the kind of perfection that could have charmed nearly any woman, no matter how cynical she might be about love or romance.

"Howdy, boys," said the airman, "I'm Captain John Strock, commander of this little operation. I'm glad to say you were rescued with a minimum of difficulty, and acceptable losses in manpower. We'll be docking in a few hours, at which point you'll be able to move about the city freely."

"Who are you?" barked Gilbert. "Where are you taking us? What city are we going to?"

The Captain looked at Gilbert with his smile almost unchanged. He closed his mouth, still smiling, and gave a slight shake of his head. "I told you who I am, son. I'm Captain John Strock. And you, Gilbert, are going to *the* city. Be glad, though. When my boss heard there were other folks lookin' for you an' the trouble that airships might be in, he scrambled his best ships in the fleet. We hadda burn a lot of fuel and Cavorite to get to you in New York in time for your airship, and almost fried you with our Tesla cannons when that giant steambot showed up. But we've been able to go home at a nice, leisurely pace."

Gil just stared. Johnny stayed silent, looking up at Strock with fear.

"Stay sharp, boys," Strock said, "we'll dock soon, and then I'll come back and get you." Strock took a decisive step backwards and shut the door. The key sounded in the lock as it turned.

"Why do these things always happen to me?" Gil grumbled. "A week ago my biggest worry was learning how to dance. Now I'm thousands of feet in the air, and the prisoner of some grinning homicidal maniac."

He stopped his grumbling when he saw little Johnny's face. The boy was trying to hold back tears. Oh, no. "Johnny," Gilbert said, "what's wrong?"

"You just said what's wrong! That Captain fella looks nice, but I saw him kill a man! I wish I had ... had something to work on! That always makes me feel better!"

Gilbert, shocked out of his own self-pity at the sight of Johnny's tears, remembered something that he hadn't thought of for a while.

He dug into his jacket pocket, past the St. Christopher medal, the red rock and a couple of Frances' letters, and brought out the fat disk that the red-head had tossed to him in the Sky Palace back in Berlin.

"Johnny? Do you like puzzles? I don't know the answer to this, but maybe you can figure it out. The girl who gave it to me only said 'It opens with my love.'"

Johnny sniffled, dragged his sleeve across his nose and looked the disk over. After a few seconds, he began fiddling with it eagerly, turning it over in his hands and spinning the small dials. "So, the right combination will open it. And she said her love would open it?"

"Yep. Actually, no. She got a little flustered when I asked almost that same question. But she was in a hurry, and couldn't explain."

Johnny began trying various combinations of the dial, listening carefully to any clicks the device might make. As he worked, the smile on his face grew wider and wider.

Johnny looked hopeful, lost for the moment in happiness. Gilbert was reminded how he loved to fall into a good book when he had suffered through a particularly bad day at school. "So, what can you make of that?" he asked.

"Oh, I think this'll be pretty easy. The girl who gave this to you; did she like chemistry?"

"I've no idea, really. I don't know her that well. Why?"

"Well, see, the first clue was what she said to you. 'It opens with my love.' Well, 'my love' has six letters in it. And there are six dials on the face of this disk. Plus, each dial has numbers on it, and they're set up in no particular order that we can see, though the numbers range from one to ninety-two, see?"

Gilbert looked, still wondering what this had to do with chemistry. But it was making Johnny happy, so he kept quiet and nodded his head.

"So," Johnny continued, "my guess is that each of these dials stands for a letter in the words 'my love.' And I'd guess, too, that they'd line up here, see, this little dimple that is on the gadget, outside the numbered rings? Now," Johnny's brow furrowed as he began to figure out the puzzle. "The first dial, the smallest, has four numbers. The second dial sports seven numbers, the third has twelve numbers, the fourth has ..." Johnny paused a few seconds to count, "twenty-three, and the fifth dial has ... forty-six numbers. Quite a few combinations here, Mister Chesterton! Now, the numbers 46, 23, 12, 7 and 4. Together, they make up ninety-two. Now, ninety-two's an interesting number for someone who knows their way around a chemistry book, because that's how many elements we know about so far. The most recent additions were made to the list in 1899, and each element has a number and a one or two-letter code attached to its name."

Gilbert didn't really follow, but nodded his head anyway.

"If we look at this first dial," Johnny continued, "the one with four numbers, it has five, ten, twenty and twenty-five written on it."

"I saw that," Gilbert said, looking intently now over Johnny's shoulder. "I thought it was some number pattern, doubling it every time or something like that."

"Hah!" Johnny said, his voice triumphant and his eyes still fixed on the disk. "That's what the maker of this toy *wanted* you to think! It's a red herring, supposed to keep you running in circles when the answer's in a straight line! See, the element whose number is twenty-five is Manganese, and its two-letter code is M-n. So I set the smallest dial to twenty-five, and the second one to ... let's see ...that goes from thirty-seven to forty-four ... ah! Thirty-nine is Yttrium, and its code is Y."

"That's only one letter, Johnny."

"Yeah, but the scientists don't always follow their own grammar rules. So, the first two dials have spelled M and Y, or 'MY,' and if we fiddle with these ..."

Johnny quickly found 3, 8, 23, and 63 on each of the concentric dials, and identified them as Lithium, Oxygen, Vanadium and Europium, their codes being L, O, V, and Er. When the number sixty-three was dialed in on the outermost ring, there was a pop as the disk snapped around its edge and opened just slightly.

"Hey, it worked!" Johnny yelled, pleased with himself, his earlier sadness forgotten. "Look, Gilbert! It opened!"

"Great job, Johnny!" Gilbert said, grabbing Johnny's shoulders from behind in excitement the way his own father had done on the rare occasions Gilbert did something right in sports. "Let's see what's inside!"

They tipped the circular container open gently. Inside was a brown paper circle with a series of very small holes punched in it in circular patterns.

"What th' heck is this?" Johnny asked, scratching gently at the inner disc in a vain effort to pull it out.

"Hang on, Johnny. I think I recognize what that is. Umm ... you got any tweezers?"

"No, but I think I've got a bent pin in my pocket. I tried to pick the lock with it while you were knocked out, but no luck. Wait a sec ... yeah, here!"

Johnny brought his hand in, then out, of his pocket and opened it, revealing a bizarre collection of metal and wooden odds and ends. Gilbert took a small bent pin from the collection, unfolded it partway and delicately scraped the surface of the inner disk.

It came away and fell out of the container, floating slowly on air currents towards the floor.

"See this, Johnny?" Gilbert said as Johnny scrambled to try and scoop up the small circle of thin punched paper before it hit the dusty, dirty floor, "these are called punchcards."

"Like in a difference engine?" Johnny said, as he let the disk drift into his hand.

"Yes, although ..." he lifted up the paper disk's edge from Johnny's hand with the pin's sharp end, then used both ends of the bent pin like tweezers to gently lift the thin paper circle up to the light of the window.

"I used to work with these a while back," Gilbert said. "I hated it, but I did learn a lot about punchcards. Still, I've never seen a design like this before. The holes are too small for me to read, and why put them on such thin paper disks instead of sturdy cardstock?"

They heard footsteps coming from down the hall and looked at each other. Gilbert put the paper disk back in its container, and then Johnny snapped the container shut and stuffed it into his pocket.

The door to their makeshift prison opened again.

"Hope you're happy, sports!" Strock said, his smile still in place. "Want to see your new home?"

> "...there are no rules of architecture
> for a castle in the clouds."
> – GKC, *The Everlasting Man*

He saw a city. Gilbert was no stranger to strange sights, but this one left him as speechless as anything he'd ever seen. When Strock had directed him to the porthole, what he'd thought at first to be a cloud or floating platform quickly grew too large to be anything so commonplace.

No, it was a city. An honest-to-goodness, *floating city*.

On a train just before the beginning of the Invasion, Gilbert had read about a bizarre sighting of an enormous airship, with a witness describing it as a glowing city sitting on half of a giant baseball. He'd laughed it off, dismissing it as a made-up yarn from a 'yellow' journal.

Now Gilbert knew that whatever journalist had written that story hadn't been lying, for a change. The bottom half of the city looked like half of a ball-shaped rock, with a wide ring of buildings around the rock's midpoint. More buildings ringed the giant rock, which was perhaps two miles in diameter. The city itself sat on the top half of the rock/ball, and was made of four large, concentric rings of buildings, each set inside one another like steps on a cake. Each successive ring was smaller than the one below it, until at the center a large spire rose and pointed at the sky.

As they neared it, Gilbert saw hundreds, perhaps thousands of flags of differing colors on each of the city's levels. Red flags predominated on the first and widest level, waving out of buildings made of yellowish white stone. White flags predominated on the second level, Blue on the third, and Gold on the smallest and highest ring. The spire which rose from the middle of the highest ring had a flag waving proudly from its highest point, its colors made of three horizontal stripes of Red, White and Blue, with a white, five-pointed star imposed over all of them.

Closer still, and the city looked like two combined cities. In the outer rings, the city buildings looked to be very much like the worker apartments Gil had seen in the city of London, or in New York. The one-story white stone buildings he saw earlier jostled next to newer buildings two or three stories tall, made of dark beams and white stucco walls with wood-shuttered windows. As they drew closer, Gilbert saw several women hanging out of the windows doing laundry or tending window-box gardens.

As they flew directly over one of the city streets, Gilbert saw a long, snaky line of men of every shape and size, wearing red clothing while carrying pots or other heavy loads in their hands. They sang while they walked, and although Gilbert and Johnny were too high up to make out words, they could tell the tune's rhythm was timed to the marching feet of the workers who sang it.

Closer to the center of the city, the architecture changed dramatically. Now the buildings were exclusively of bright, polished white stone, with either flat tops or pyramid-shaped roofs. The odd buildings surrounded the spire in rings, the tallest of them next to the spire perhaps five stories high, but sporting only three windows Gilbert could see.

Chains of incredible thickness and length were set at the four compass points of the stone sphere's equator, and held the city suspended in the sky. The metal of each chainlink was at least four or five feet thick, while the chains themselves were hundreds of feet long. Each of the four chains was bound by a thick iron ring, and hung on a huge sphere at least fifty feet across and made of glowing green stone.

"A castle in the air," Johnny whispered.

There was nothing else Gilbert could say. Men had dreamed for thousands of years of seeing what both boys saw at this moment, and Gilbert thanked God for it.

As they pulled closer to the city, the only sound they heard was wind whipping through their makeshift porthole and the chugging engine of the airship. The sun shone brilliantly off the city buildings, as people-shaped shadows moved and shifted behind shaded windows, and wooden platforms and scaffolds poked out from the sides of the lower-level buildings like spiked tufts of hair on a bald man.

The airship bumped gently as they docked, and Gilbert heard dockhands shouting as they jostled with ropes and equipment. Dockworkers would have a difficult time here, Gilbert realized. A mistake when dealing with a docked boat or ocean liner meant goods or men falling a few feet into the water. But a mistake like that here meant certain death from a fall so far that the ground couldn't be seen from their perch.

After a few more minutes they heard a set of now-familiar boots stepping down the hall. There was a pause, then the sound of the door unlocking, and Captain John Strock was at the doorway again.

"Ready to go, boys?" he said, smiling so widely that his eyes squinted shut.

"So, just what is this monstrosity?" Finn asked, stepping into the room. It was the size of a large schoolhouse, perhaps thirty by thirty feet square. It had a large space in the center, with mechanical devices of varying complexities and functions against each wall. There was a bed by each of the six stations, which suited Herb just fine. If he was lucky, he'd have no duties, and during a busy moment he'd have the chance to slip away.

Herb's foot hit something that moved. He looked down and saw that a brass sculpture of a cat had gotten in the way. He was about to shove it to the side when it looked up as him, opened its mouth and meowed.

"What the ... !"

"Watch out for Nestor, Herbert," Margaret said, "he's a bit more trouble than he looks, if you get on his bad side."

Herb looked down again. The cat was gone from his feet, and already in the corner, going through the motions of cleaning itself.

"This," said Margaret, her eyes sparkling again as she addressed the four men, "is the personal living train car of Mister John Brainerd, Senior, and our collective ticket to catching Gilbert."

"Why the train? Why not horses and wagons, like most folks travel West with?" asked Harper, only partly joking. Despite his own mechanized limb, and not being in any shape with a painful rib to ride a horse over long distances, he was visibly uncomfortable with the hissing steam, huffing boilers and clicking engines coming from all the contraptions in the room. He was already inching away from Nestor's corner.

"Horses might take months," she said. "But don't fear. We won't be on the train the whole time. Plus, as I recall, you're operating with a cracked rib. A long horse ride is the last thing you'll be able to endure."

"I'm strong enough!" Harper said. He managed to keep his face straight for nearly three seconds before his lip twitched in pain.

"Gilbert," Margaret said, ignoring Harper for the moment, "is in a location that has been carefully secreted off the main train lines. Once we reach a specific mountain location, we'll disembark and continue on foot."

"Awfully nice of Mr. Brainerd to let us have the use of this box," Holiday commented with a wary tone. Nestor was purring with sounds of clicking gears as Doc scratched him behind his brass ears, "Ah wonder what he'll be asking for as payment."

"That won't be necessary," said Margaret. "I took the liberty of wiring him a message about the interruption of his son's journey. I was one of his many assistants, remember?"

"Assistant, eh?" Finn spoke this time. He'd raised one eyebrow as he'd asked the question.

"He proved remarkably oblivious to my usual charms," Margaret said as she started firing up the equipment, "and I had to rely instead on hard work and achievement to gain his trust. When he learned through Morse code transmission that felons in an airship had abducted little Johnny, he was more than happy to tell me the location of his personal living train. And, when I told him I knew where Johnny had been taken and that some very motivated Pinkertons were helping me, he was willing to put even more equipment at our disposal once we reach the California Republics."

"What about weapons?" Finn asked, sitting down in one of the swiveling chairs and looking in disbelief at the surrounding room, now brightly lit by gas-powered glowglobes. "Did he tell you where to find those?"

"He's more interested in making things that help people live better rather than die quicker. The sole exception was that Steam Lincoln, since it was designed to defend American borders against potential Martian attacks."

"So we're stuck with our peashooters?" Harper asked.

"We might upgrade you to spitballs if you remain in our good graces, Corporal Harper," Holiday said with a straight face but a twinkle in his eye. "Now please stop ogling the girl and get ready for the trip."

"I'm not..." started Harper. He shut up when he saw how futile defending himself would be. The eyes of the older men in the car were both twinkling with happy memories and holding the sadness of lost opportunities. Herb was sitting in one of the chairs with his arms folded, steadfastly refusing to take part in the conversation.

"Hang it," Harper grumbled and sat on one of the plush chairs.

"There's a thought," Finn said, and hung his hat on a coat hook protruding from the wall. Nestor leaped up with the sound of a coiled spring in a jack-in-the-box, knocking Finn's hat off its post as soon as the big man's back was turned.

"Then, gentlemen," Margaret said, "I'll feed the necessary punchcards into our automated driver. Our destination is a small town just outside the Sierra Nevada Mountains, on the Eastern border of the Southern California Republic. Make yourselves comfortable, and I'll return soon after we are underway."

Margaret slipped out the door, leaving the cowboys and Herb to themselves. Herb stared morosely at the wall.

"You trust her, Colonel?" Holiday asked, trying hard to win a staring contest with Nestor. The cat twitched much like a real animal would, but would not blink.

"Not as far as I could throw her," said Finn, "but our job just disappeared into the belly of a Zeppelin. If I went back to the office and said I let a lead slip away just cause I didn't trust her? Well, there's a lot of things I'd still like to do with my life, but most of 'em need a steady income, first."

"I've got a job for you then," grumbled Herb half to himself. "The pay is wondrous, if you don't mind giving up a little something first."

"Giving up something?" said Holiday, his eyes still locked on the clockwork cat's. "My dear boy, you preach to the choir. Haven't you been looking at us? I gave up my eye for my job. My friends Shannon and Mix gave up an arm apiece, little Joe back there gave up his leg, and I won't even begin to state the nature of our dear Colonel's sacrifice. You, on the other hand, have all your flesh-and-blood parts. What could you give up worse than that?"

"Only your soul."

Everyone was silent. The train car started with a lurch and began moving forward.

Chapter 47

"By experts in poverty I do not mean sociologists, but poor men." – GKC, *ILN*, March 25, 1911

After the airship docked on the city with a lurching, metallic bump, Gilbert and Johnny followed Strock through hallway after hallway. After a few minutes, corridors of tightly nailed wooden planks gave way to floors and walls of steel grates and plating, and then to white stone.

After one of the turns, the white stone corridor opened up to a large room with lines of people in ordinary clothes lined up in front of desks manned by men and women in red overalls. Almost all the desks had a single, simple door behind it, and people in the lineups would walk through them after the men behind the desks waved them on.

The proceedings were monitored closely on the floor by men in leather jackets, thin leather helmets and raised goggles like Strock, though none smiled like he did, and all had drawn pistols in their hands. Gilbert looked up and saw a large multi-leveled network of catwalks that stretched up to a ceiling so high that the place seemed to have its own clouds indoors. A bearded man stood silently on one of the walkways, smoking a cigar and wearing a military-style uniform with shiny medals all over the top half.

"You, over there," a voice barked at his right. Gilbert saw one of the leather-jacketed men pointing at him from maybe a dozen feet away.

"Worker line for you, kid. What's your name?"

"Chesterton. Gilbert Keith Chesterton," said Gilbert, still wondering a bit if he was in the middle of a very odd dream.

The room fell silent.

The man who'd just barked at Gilbert swallowed. "Over here," he said, pointing slowly to one of the shorter lines of people. The line stopped at a man sitting at a desk, and two separate, thick wooden doors were set in the wall behind him.

Gilbert stood at the back of the line obediently, but when Johnny tried to follow, Strock appeared from nowhere and tapped the smaller boy on the shoulder. "This way, young fella. We've got a different place for folks your age with your talents. Follow me!"

Johnny looked up at Gilbert, as if looking for approval. Gilbert looked down and nodded, but first leaned down and whispered into

Johnny's ear. "I'm sorry I snapped at you earlier, Johnny," Gilbert said. "Go with Strock, but stay sharp, keep your head down, and never stop trying to get out. If there's ways in here, there's gotta be ways out, too. And if anyone could build a gadget to get us out, I know you're the guy to do it. Okay?"

Gilbert finished the talk with a gentle slap and squeeze of Johnny's shoulder, like Gilbert's own dad had given him long ago. Johnny didn't answer, but looked up at Gilbert and nodded his head, pursing his lips slightly. He turned and followed Strock through another open doorway, as the clerks in the orange overalls began talking again to the people in line. He questioned each one, sending them through the door to his left.

When it was his turn, Gilbert turned to the clerk. "Okay, what now?" he said.

"Answer all questions," said the clerk, a man in his forties who looked like he'd never met an interviewee he'd ever liked. "I'll need your name, date and place of birth, occupation and favorite color."

Gilbert paused. Was this a joke? Were they really interested in his favorite color, after they'd abducted him and brought him to a city in the sky?

Maybe, but sometimes it paid to play along, even if the locals seemed a few drops short of an inkpot.

"Gilbert Keith Chesterton," Gilbert said crisply, as if responding to a government census-taker at his door, "May twenty-ninth, 1874. Full-time writer and journalist, part-time artist, swashbuckler and monster-slayer. Walnut Grove, Minnesota. Red."

The clerk looked up at Gilbert after he'd finished writing Gilbert's information down, but didn't bother to correct him about the wiseacre monster-killer remark. "Take this card through the door to your right," he said to Gil, handing him a punchcard, "and see the next man at the desk."

Yes! Gilbert's instincts had told him that the whole thing was likely an odd, petty sham and Gil's best option was to try to rise to the local level of lunacy. Granted, he might have instead gotten a rifle butt in the gut, but what was life without a little risk?

Gil's door led to another room exactly like the first, with another man of nearly identical age and appearance sitting at an identical desk.

And on one of the catwalks, the same fellow in the same uniform full of medals watched Gilbert and everyone else through the open-topped rooms.

"Good morning, sir!" Gil chirped, happy he had the chance to address someone as the elevator was on its way up.

"I'll need your name, date and place of birth, profession and ..."

"Let me guess, favorite color?" Gil said with a happy voice as he slid the punchcard across the desk at the clerk.

The clerk looked at Gilbert with a straight expression on his face.

"Fine," Gilbert said. "Gilbert Keith Chesterton. July the Sixteenth, the year of our Lord nineteen-hundred-and-seventy. Journalist, amateur brain surgeon and alchemist. Pale mauve."

There was a tap on his shoulder. Gilbert turned, totally unprepared for the large caliber, eight-barreled pistol that was suddenly cocked and pointed three inches from his right eye socket.

"Please answer the question accurately, Mister Chesterton," said the clerk in a droll monotone that clearly said he'd repeated the speech he was about to give on multiple occasions. "The colorful details you invent about your birth do not wholly displease us, but we most emphatically do not need or wish to hear about any amateur activities on your part. Those who fail to respect the rules or succeed in boring those of us who enforce the rules will receive consequences that are swift, certain and deadly. Is that clear?"

Gilbert, his eyes focused on the pistol, nodded quickly. The unsmiling guard holstered his weapon and turned to leave. He took three steps away, stopped, turned on his heel and stood at the side of the doorway, watching Gilbert with his arms folded.

Gilbert turned back to the clerk, still shaking.

"What do I do now?" Gilbert asked when the clerk let more seconds pass in silence.

The clerk, his eyes still on Gilbert's, waited exactly three seconds before he began speaking again. "Take this through the door behind me on your right," he said, handing another punchcard to Gilbert and throwing away the one Gilbert had handed him a moment ago. Gilbert took the new card, his hand trembling slightly, "and give it to the clerk at the next desk. If you have any questions, please keep them to yourself."

Chapter 48

"It is one way to train the tiger to imitate you, it is a shorter way to imitate the tiger. But in neither case does evolution tell you how to treat a tiger reasonably, that is, to admire his stripes while avoiding his claws." – GKC, *Orthodoxy*

I've got no idea what you're talking about," said Herb sulkily, looking up at the sober faces circling him.

"Look," said Finn, "it's very simple. You lay down the cards now, and we see what kind've hand you got."

Bored beyond words after days of steady travel, Herb had reluctantly agreed to join the circle and learn to play poker to help pass the time. He'd hoped it would be at least a little like bridge, but the rules had proved nearly incomprehensible to him. He'd just decided to quit when the train suddenly lurched and slowed. "What's happening?" Herb asked. "Have we reached the end?"

Finn's brow furrowed. "We're quite a few miles outta 'Frisco. No good reason for us to slow down yet."

The train slowed to a crawl, then a full stop. Margaret popped in through the door from her private car. "There's a minor break in the line," she said. "The driving engine's good enough it sensed a disruption in the tracks a few miles away."

"Sounds real good," Finn said quietly. "What do we do now?"

"You stay put," said Margaret. "I, on the other hand, will nip outside and see what the chances are of the line being fixed. Herbert, I'd like you to accompany me, in case bears are afoot."

"Fine," said Herb, standing. "I was getting all twitchy from sitting down the last few days anyway." Herb raised himself from his seat, rotated his shoulders a few times and walked to the door.

"Be a terribly funny thing, wouldn't it," Holiday said off-handedly, "if'n a city boy tried to run in these parts?"

"Sure would," drawled Harper, "Seein's how the nearest town's a three week horse ride. Longer, on foot. Not to mention Injuns."

"I understand perfectly, gentlemen," Herb grumbled. "I run, I die. See you in a few." As Herb exited the train car, all remaining eyes turned to Finn.

"Give 'im ten minutes. If they ain't back, we check up on 'em. I got me a feeling the tracks ain't quite as 'disrupted' as they say it is."

Chapter 49

"Aesthetes never do anything but what they are told."
– GKC, The Love of Lead, *Lunacy and Letters*

The alarm shrilled in Gilbert's ear, and he jumped from his bed to the floor. He stood at rigid attention at the end of his bunk, waiting for the inspector to clear him to dress. After he'd pulled on his red overalls, he'd jog in formation with the other workers to his day's assignment while attempting to sing the morning work song:

"Make the food, work today
For the wages that they pay.
Better than money is our pay
For we make our food today!"

It wasn't catchy, but Gilbert had to admit it did make the day go quicker. As he jogged down the cobblestoned streets, he managed quick looks at the houses. Many of them could have been from a working-class neighborhood in either London or an American city. Like the ones he'd seen on his flying tour, they were mostly two-story wood-frame and stucco walls, many with mini-gardens in the windows. *Picturesque*, was the word Gilbert's Ma probably would have used to describe them. The open sky above had been intimidating at first, but after a while it didn't bother Gilbert any more than the sky had when he'd been on the ground. There was surprisingly little wind, too, thanks to the high walls that surrounded each level of the city.

But still, gosh-all-hemlock, it was *cold* in the morning!

"Morning, Gilbert!" said Mister Smith after Gilbert had emerged from the tunnel that led from his dormitory directly to the food factory. An older father of four sons and a daughter, his words were usually hidden beneath his large mustache. He'd taken a liking to Gilbert on the first day, and hailed him now from one of the curvy stairwells that surrounded the food vats.

"Morning, Mister Smith!" Gilbert called back. "How's your wife?"

"Good as always."

"That bad, huh?"

"Bad enough I like going to work in the morning, Gilbert! Have a good day!"

Gilbert smiled. Mrs. Smith's bad temper was something of a local legend among the city workers. It had already become a friendly joke between Gilbert and Mr. Smith.

Come to think of it, he had friendly little 'in'-jokes with a number of the people in the city. It was surprising in fact how welcome he'd been made to feel since his arrival.

"Here, young Gilbert!"

Now it was Mrs. Hargen, a large woman in her forties, calling to Gilbert from a line of men who were gathering buckets of some kind of noxious-smelling goop. What they were filled with or why the men had to carry them instead of having a tube do it for them was a mystery, one that Gilbert couldn't get an answer to from anyone. Not that he tried too hard; he'd only been in the city for a few days, and still felt it prudent to keep a low profile.

Well, as low a profile as you could hope to keep, when everyone seemed to know your name and wanted to be your friend.

"Thanks, Mrs. Hargen. Where to?"

"Lead your line up to Griffin neighborhood, an' dump it in the city vat there. An' be sure you don't let none of those no-accounts in Crow neighborhood trick you, this time. They can be a sly bunch."

"No ... no problem, Mrs. Hargen." Gilbert gasped as he struggled with the large, thick-walled steel bucket, now full of the foul-smelling liquid. He hauled it, banging it against his leg and holding the handle with both hands as he struggled up the cobblestoned street. Since he was at the head of a line of twenty men with kettles the same size, he had to nod without pausing to the many people who knew his name.

"Good morning, Gilbert!"

"Top 'o the mahr-nin', Gilbert!"

"How're things, Gilbert?"

Since he knew almost none of the names of the people calling out to him, Gilbert smiled and nodded as best he could while carrying his load.

He'd been assigned to his work group soon after his gun-pointing adventure at the second bureaucrat's desk. They were a total of twenty single men living in a barracks in one of the many neighborhoods in the Red level of the city, while married members of the crew were given homes in their designated neighborhood. His own neighborhood was Eagle, and had a large red banner with a stylized bald eagle emblazoned over a red, orange, yellow and green striped flag. Each neighborhood's flag flew at the four corners of the twenty or so houses that made up the neighborhood's border. The Eagle neighborhood's name fit well, considering how many self-described patriots lived there.

"Sst!" hissed a voice near Gilbert, grabbing his attention.

"Wait," Gilbert said in a voice just as low, while looking forward. Soon another person, a few years older than Gilbert with dark-colored soot and grime filling the creases in his skin, fell into step beside him.

"The King wants you," the grimy man said, looking forward and reaching for Gilbert's bucket.

"Fine," Gilbert said, giving up his load to the older man and giving him his place in line. The men in line behind Gilbert pretended not to notice, believing instead that Gilbert's sudden departure from work detail was part of either a deeply important work summons, or a plot to overthrow the Emperor. Either one was likely to be quite harmless.

Gilbert dodged between the workers singing their songs from various stations, lines of men with full and empty pots, children clapping and cheering the men on the way to work, and women directing the human traffic with brightly colored signs or waving from the windows.

It was crazy, Gilbert knew. Tons of pointless work cheered by everyone. It was a quiet, happy, silly kind of madness, but madness just the same. He'd felt it in the air from the first day he'd stepped into the city proper. There was no way such a large number of people could be so mind-bogglingly happy for such a long and uninterrupted time.

More dodging, more quick-stepping, and more running along large cobble stones that could be felt even through the thick soles of the workboots he'd been issued.

Eventually he arrived at what looked at first to be a larger version of the many non-descript houses along the street. All that distinguished it was its larger size and an oval sign with a poorly drawn picture of a baby and a stylized eagle hanging outside over the door.

Gilbert tried the door, rattling the handle three times.

"Ministry of Contradiction," said a muffled voice from the inside.

"Don't let me in," answered Gilbert with a hurried voice. The door swung open a crack, just enough for Gilbert to slip inside, unnoticed by anyone except the thirty or so women who made it a regular practice to spy on everything in the streets.

The Emperor stood in his nightshirt, looking at one of his three favorite military-style outfits as he held it against his body and looked into the mirror.

"Well, what'm I lookin' for today?" he said to his reflection, as he sucked on the cigar with a meditative air. "Do I go for the 'I-Am-Staggeringly-More-Wealthy-Than-You' look with my white outfit, or for the 'I-Am-A-Man-Of-Immense-Possibilities' with the blue one, or the 'Today-Is-NOT-The-Day-To-Try-And-Overthrow-Me' look with my black military uniform? Sometimes I wish 'n all you empty suits could talk."

A knock at the door interrupted him. His eyebrows narrowed as he dropped his white uniform to the floor in a crumpled heap and pulled the cigar from his mouth. "Who dares disturb my meditations?" he barked.

"It's me, Galatea, Emperor Norton," said a voice that was controlled, familiar, and very female behind the door. "The young man you wanted watched, Mister Gilbert Chesterton? He has apparently made contact with one of the factions."

Norton, his irritation forgotten, clapped his hands once with glee. "Hot, dang!" he said happily, "That's m'boy! I knew he had the right stuff! Not even here a week, and he's already gettin' ready to try and topple me! Didn't I say he had it, Galatea? Didn't I?"

"Yes, Emperor," she replied.

Norton stopped. One of his ears had pricked up. He had spent a lifetime reading people's voices, faces and gestures in order to cheat and manipulate them. Dear little Galatea had let something creep into her speech that he'd never heard from her before. Barely more than a vibration on a single syllable, it was a small yet unmistakable morsel of fear.

"Galatea," Norton said, "where is he now?"

"He's entered a tavern called the Eagle and Child, Emperor. He's with the fellow who calls himself the King."

"Ah, the sybarite leader of the hookah fiends!" said the Emperor, clapping his hands in glee. "The boy certainly does like to skate on the thin ice, don't he?" He looked for a moment at his outfits, lined up carefully in the closet. "What should I wear to impress a boy such as Gilbert, Galatea dear?"

"Young men have a natural attraction to power and the military, Emperor," her voice piped through the door.

"Then the black suit it is. Ready my 'thopter, will you? The one with the three sets of blades. I want to look impressive!"

"Yes, Emperor!"

As her feet retreated down the hall, Emperor Norton picked up his cigar from his dresser and gave another pull on it with his lips. *Quite the day,* Norton thought. *Quite the day, and it's hardly begun.* His instincts had never failed him in nearly eight decades, and today they were telling him that something truly different was just around the corner.

The sudden smoky darkness in the room blinded Gilbert for a moment. He squinted and winced, trying to spot a human form somewhere in the murk.

A hand clapped on his shoulder. "Having trouble?" said an oily voice.

"Just a little," said Gilbert. "I'm supposed to meet the King."

"All in good time, all in good ... "

Someone cleared their throat nearby. Gilbert could just make out a curtain near the back of the room where the noise had come from.

"It's a good time. This way," said the oily voice's owner. His demeanor suddenly switched from slimy and toadlike to happy and warm, as he put a long, skinny arm around Gilbert's shoulder.

Gilbert didn't trust him for a moment.

"Swell," said Gilbert, smiling a little, trying hard not to instinctively recoil from the scummy doorman's touch. He followed towards the curtained door, which the doorman swept aside with a clacking of beads and rustling of thick fibers.

More smoke, pungent and spiced with unfamiliar odors, assaulted Gilbert's nostrils as he passed through the curtain. A small light beamed from a tiny window in the wall near the ceiling, and spotlit a fat boy only a few years older than Gilbert. The large boy had blond, curled locks of hair, and sat on a wooden chair set against the wall, wearing a pair of dark-lensed goggles strapped onto his forehead, and the same red overalls that Gilbert and the other workers sported. A semicircle of other workers clad in overalls sat near his feet, smoking from long tubes attached to a fancy, covered vase. Gilbert had seen one like it only once; in an illustration from Alice in Wonderland his mother had read to him when he was little, a giant caterpillar had been smoking from a similar contraption. In the book, it was called a hookah.

The boy on the chair turned slowly to look at Gilbert. The smoking boys on the floor didn't move at all.

"Is this the one?" the throned boy said with a ponderous tone. His voice reminded Gilbert of a bored, rich artist he'd met in Vienna months back.

"Yes, King," said the doorman in a reverent voice. "You were right again. He followed the directions flawlessly."

The King sighed and stood with a heavy air, as if he were

reluctantly carrying the weight of the world on his fleshy shoulders. He stepped over one of the smokers in his retinue, and approached Gilbert. "Gilbert," he said, his words sounding like stale milk, "walk with me."

"How much time before they notice I'm not at work?"

"As much as you need. The proxy who took your place in the line will not fail, for he has pledged himself to my service. And unlike my Lord Chamberlain, whom you've just met, your proxy is an honest man who never arouses suspicion. Now," He brought Gilbert back through the beaded curtain, and laid his arm on Gilbert's shoulder. As he spoke, he gestured while looking off into space. "I understand you, Gilbert, are a man of eloquent talents in the world. A man of the art of words. A man who has done great things, killed great enemies, and saved many through suffering, sacrifice, and the generous application of force."

"Well, I ..."

"Please, feel free to call me Cameron. My full name is Cameron Foggschild, and I feel too much of a kinsmanship with you as a fellow artist to have you address me as 'King,' the way so many of my sycophants do. Now, Gilbert," he said, walking the taller Gilbert with small steps around the room, "I understand you desire to leave this godforsaken, barnacle-encrusted reef among the clouds as much as I do, correct?"

"Well, now that you ..."

"Yes, it is true that the Emperor has managed to fool the poor proletariat workers into truly believing that a life of work leads to happiness. Through his songs and neighborhoods, he has mimicked the life so many wished they had to the point that many are deceived. Deceived into truly believing that labor can bring meaning to life. Do you follow me?"

"I'm afraid I ..."

"Fret not. It will come soon enough. Ours is a high and lonely destiny, Gilbert. For we are the only hope these poor, unenlightened souls have. They will live and die out their lives here if we do not rescue them from this drudgery. But while I am an exceptional leader, and a student of the arts and an experienced connoisseur of life's fineries, I need someone known, someone who can sway with *words*. And I asked the Universe, in its ever self-correcting way, to send me someone to could bring to fruition my ... I mean, *the* dream of truly free people in this city."

"You ..." Gilbert's mind was feeling more fuddled the longer he stood in the house, but not so fuddled that he couldn't smell something stupid. "Let me get this straight. You asked the *universe* for something? It's a cold black thing that goes on forever! It doesn't care about you!"

"Gilbert," said Cameron, "how could a man of your experiences have such a limited vision? How could anyone, if they had an intellectual development as advanced as my own, possibly ask a Santa-Claus-like, non-existent God for anything?"

"Maybe because God answers prayers more often than a cold cloud of rocks and hydrogen."

"To each his own, then. We may differ, Gilbert. That which you call evil I truly believe I may call good. But my point," the King said, now turning to stare at Gilbert through the dark lenses of his goggles, "is that *you* are the one needed here, a leader who can bring needed *change* to this place."

Gilbert knew something was wrong with the words he was hearing. But so far he'd seen no other way to get out of the city. He'd been approached to join other groups, but one of them consisted of three older men talking about philosophy, trying to make a revolution that would take generations. And the other was a group of angry, former university students, who would stop planning for a revolution and begin fighting each other with words, then fists when the beer ran out.

Leaving alone could possibly work, but it would also be an awful risk.

No, allying himself with a group was essential if he wanted off this giant floating rock.

Wasn't it?

"I'll say ..." Gilbert squinched his eyes shut for a second. The smoke from the other room had invaded their sitting room, and was stinging his eyes something fierce! "I'll say yes, for now. But if you mess things up, I'll jump ship on the whole bunch of you."

"Of course, Gilbert! Of course! I wouldn't have it any other way. Now," said Cameron, patting Gilbert on his shoulder as he steered Gil towards the door, "you just go on back to the line, and I'll be in touch with you for our next meeting."

"Well, I ..."

Before Gilbert knew it, he was out the door and on the cobblestoned street. He shook his head, trying to banish the fog and smoke that had occupied his mind.

A leader! The thought jumped in his head unbidden and insistent. A leader, the King had said! Gil wondered, now, if ...

He heard a noise, like a playground fight or a sporting event in his old schoolyard. Movement up ahead caught his eye. He looked. Focused. Looked again and saw two small boys with white overalls running through one of the intersections. One was shorter and plump, the other taller and thin. The shorter one looked backwards with a frightened expression on his face, and the lights above reflected off his thick glasses.

Chubby with glasses?

Oh, no.

Chapter 50

"For every engine in which these old free-thinkers firmly
and confidently trusted has itself become an engine of
oppression... Its free parliament has become an oligarchy.
Its free press has become a monopoly. If the pure Church
has been corrupted in the course of two thousand years,
what about the pure Republic that has rotted into a filthy
plutocracy in less than a hundred?" – GKC, *What I Saw in
America*

Jack and Tollers had adjusted quickly to life in the floating city.
Since both boys had already spent extended periods away from
family at boarding schools, separation from their loved ones was
not as traumatic for them as it was for some of the other boys. Johnny
Brainerd, for example, had spent all his life in the company of a loving
family, and had spent the last few weeks being tough in front of
everyone while silently crying himself to sleep at night like many of the
other boys in the savant school on the second, white-colored level of
the city.

Jack and Tollers, on the other hand, had recognized in each other
not only a bond made of similar experiences and interests, but forged
through hours of argument and debate. That Jack had already declared
himself an atheist by the age of nine made little difference to Tollers,
who was himself fiercely proud of his Catholic faith. Their arguments
served more to cement their friendship rather than to drive it apart.
Eventually, debate and comparison grew to traded stories of myths both
ancient and newly made.

And, once they'd docked at and spent some time in the city's
school for *savants*, they also shared whispered plans of escape.

That was why when Jack woke up one morning and found a map
of some kind in his white overalls' pocket, the first person he discussed
it with was the tall, skinny boy who'd quickly become his best friend in
the city.

"Doesn't it look easy, Tollers?" Jack had said, looking over the
map with him after lights out, when everyone else was asleep. Jack's
pudgy fingers played carefully over the worn and creased cloth map.
"Down here, look for the symbol of a sword, follow the tunnel, and
we're back on the Red level where the airships come and go. We stow
away on board in a cargo hold somewhere, jump ship as soon as we

dock, and run for help!"

"And what if we're caught, Jack? What then? They'll toss us over the side like so much refuse, and our trip will end there, won't it?"

"Not to worry! Alan Quartermain never gets caught, does he?"

"Alan Quartermain's adventures always took place *under*ground, not a good mile or two *above* it!"

"Details, chap. Do you want to get out of here before you're old enough to vote, or not?"

Normally, Tollers would have been up for any sort of adventure. But hearing from Johnny how a man had been tossed over the railing to his death below had made him skittish about risk. After he'd had some time to think about it, Tollers passed a note to Jack the next morning during class.

"How do you think the map got in your pocket in the first place?" he wrote, using the Dwarf Runic language he'd made up a few days earlier, when he'd had an hour of free time.

Jack had thought, and then scribbled out in the Elvish language he'd made up the night before: "Maybe someone who wasn't as bright as us owned my overalls, and outgrew them before he could remove the map from his pocket."

The escape had happened, as nearly all student escape attempts did from White level, surreptitiously and with a combination of luck and planning worthy of a vaudeville escape artist. Jack and Tollers had found a secret tunnel placed so that they, like dozens of boys before them, could find it and attempt an escape. Once found, they lit down it and ended up on Red level right outside one of the rougher factories.

They had no way of knowing that the map had, in fact, been left in Jack's pocket deliberately, as a means of encouraging their escape attempt.

They had no way of knowing that escape attempts among new student arrivals to the city were a common occurrence, and were in fact fully sanctioned by Emperor Norton himself, who liked to place wagers on how far the little escapees would get before caught.

They had no way of knowing that a bounty was placed upon the nose-bloodying or eye-blackening of a White level student like Jack or Tollers if caught on Red level, or that the bounty was large enough to keep a Red level factory worker in tobacco for a month.

Emperor Norton strode from his breakfast room with a commanding air. He had a lit cigar firmly in his mouth, along with a finger of whiskey, two scrambled eggs and several pieces of bacon in his stomach.

It was going to be a very, very good day.

"Galatea!" he barked.

"Here, Emperor!" she answered, appearing from behind a pillar. Her hair was in a perfect, bright-red bun, her glasses were straight and wide-lensed, and she'd chosen a puffed-sleeved white blouse to go with her brown skirt.

"Morning report," he said, still walking towards the landing pad for his favorite ornithopter.

"Emperor, the gossip network reports that Gilbert has just left the Eagle and Child. And there's been an escape attempt by two new students from the savant academy. They've just emerged from the secret tunnel, and are running into the Crow neighborhood of the Red level."

"Blast! Why do I have to have two interesting things happen at the same time!" he spoke without stopping his pace or turning to face Galatea.

"Sir, their path of escape will cross Gilbert's in a matter of minutes."

Norton stopped. So did Galatea.

He took the cigar from his mouth and looked at her with an air of deadly seriousness. "Can you get me there in time?"

When they'd found the entrance to the tunnel, Jack and Tollers had crept inside cautiously. They'd taken perhaps ten steps when the section of floor they stood on collapsed, dumping them onto a well-worn slide.

They flew down the slide for several spins and circles, until the slide ended abruptly, dumping them through six feet of air. They hitt the ground and kicked up identical clouds of dirt and grit. After a few seconds, Jack drew himself shakily from his stomach to all fours, and began pawing the ground for his glasses.

Tollers, already on his knees, looked up and was very silent.

"Tollers," whispered Jack, "are we dead?"

"Not yet," Tollers said quietly.

"Oh, jolly good," said Jack in his normal, booming voice as his hand found his glasses, "I was beginning to think that whatever awaited us in the afterlife was as dreary as what we see here now. Of course, I find it far more likely that the afterlife doesn't exist at all, and in fact ..."

"Jack," said Tollers quietly, looking forward as Jack fiddled with his glasses.

"Tollers, if you're going to try and talk me into that bit of Papist fancy again, I'm going to have to give you a solid, verbal drubbing," Jack continued, as he slid his own glasses onto his face.

"Jack!" Tollers barked, "Look up!"

Jack looked up. Several very large brass belt buckles attached to several Red level working-class sets of overalls stared back at him. He looked higher, and saw thick torsos attached to the belts. And grinning, grizzled heads on top of the torsos. Along with very large arms attached to the torsos just beneath the shoulders. The very large arms ended in very large hands, most of which held very large metal tools and pipes.

"Oh," said Jack, the smallest trace of fear in his voice. "Er, would you fine gentlemen have the slightest idea how to get back up to the savant schoolhouse for gifted youngsters? It's directly upon the White level, and ..."

"DIBS ON THE FAT ONE!" roared the largest workingman! A bloodcurdling scream sounded from a dozen throats belonging to Red-clad worker-class boys and young men. It startled both of the younger boys to their feet, and jolted Tollers to sprint away from their tormentors after grabbing Jack's arm.

"Come on!" Tollers yelled!

"But I'm already getting tired," Jack wheezed, trying to hold his glasses to his face with one hand while his other arm pumped frantically.

"Then you're going to have to lose weight, and quickly! I saw doors to the White level near here earlier, when we were brought in! Keep going!"

Jack, already sweating, turned back to look at the mob behind him. The red-clad workers were trotting at an easy pace, as if they knew their prey was going to tire soon enough. What could they be saving their strength for? Nothing good for the boys, that was certain!

"Is there a place to hide? Ow!" Jack yelped as he fell at a crossroads, his pudgy cheek scraping the rough gravel. Tollers helped him up, and as Jack stood up he glanced around and spotted a familiar face.

"That's ... that's ..." Jack tried to gasp.

"Come on!" Tollers shouted, looking down at Jack while grabbing him by the arm and trying to pull him to his feet, "Get up! Quickly!"

"Jack? Tollers?" The voice was Gilbert's, and it grew louder as Gil ran to the younger boys.

Gilbert arrived at the center of the crossroads and stood by the boys, exactly one second before the ten-man mob.

"Woah," said the Red leader, leaning back and stretching out his arms to hold back the rest behind him. "Who'zis?"

Gilbert had faced enough angry people in his life that he had developed a standard bag of verbal tricks that nearly always worked, if he remembered to use the right ones on the right people.

"My name's Gilbert. Gilbert Keith Chesterton, reporter for the London Times." His hand moved instinctively to his pocket for his card, and ...

Nothing. His hand patted uselessly at his side. There was no card, wallet or pocket at that spot in the overalls. All had been taken from him when he'd been given his red overalls his first day here. Oops.

The dozen workmen stood dumbly for a second, watching Gilbert fumble in his pockets, and began to chuckle softly.

"Huh," said the leader. "Chesterton. From London."

"Chester-*dumb*!" said another, "from Lon-*dumb*!" said another at the leader's left.

More chuckles from the mob, who began forming a ring around the three of them.

Gilbert swallowed, but held the gaze of the leader. Gilbert had been beaten brutally nearly two years ago by a street thug and his gang. But since then, Gilbert reminded himself, he'd learned how to fight, and even killed a ... killed *three* Martians! Well, maybe he only assisted on two of them, but was this really the time to quibble? After all ...

They were surrounded.

"If this is ... er, part of a plan, Mister Gilbert ..." Jack said with a nervous air, "I think it's a good time for the next move."

Gilbert swallowed again, and didn't answer.

Chapter 51

"The notion that cattle might fly has received sublime imaginative treatment ... And the general idea, which is that of a sort of cosmic Saturnalia or season when anything may happen, is itself an idea that has haunted humanity in a hundred forms, some of them exquisitely artistic forms."
– GKC, *Child Psychology and Nonsense*

The machine flew over the tops of the stubby buildings, held aloft by three sets of double-blades that flapped far, far faster than the eye could see. It was a thing of small majesty, large enough to carry a dozen men besides the two pilots. At the moment, its only pilot was Captain John Strock, his eyes hidden behind a pair of goggles, his smile gritted and wide, sitting perfectly above his thick-boned lantern jaw.

"Where's'e now?" the Emperor snapped. "Are we gonna miss anything?"

Galatea tried vainly to tuck a lock back behind her ear with one hand and hold her large-lensed glasses in place with the other. "The stipplograph taken just before we left suggests Gilbert is at the border between Eagle and Crow neighborhoods, Emperor," she yelled back over the roar of the flapping rotors, "at the intersection of Goose Way and Cornish Lane."

Emperor Norton sucked back on his cigar, and blew a plume of smoke that swirled out the open hatchway that looked down over the rows of houses and red flags below. "Gimme the Murphy, honey," he said, looking down at the ground from his seat.

"The worst that could possibly happen is that some workers from the nearby Crow district will sight the boys on their escape attempt, lump Gilbert in with them, and give him a solid thrashing before they turn on the boys."

"Anyone ever die at these things, sugar?"

"With ... with some frequency, Emperor."

Norton looked briefly at her, worried the cigar a bit and looked outside again. Strock, too, looked back briefly, but said nothing and focused again on coaxing more speed from the three-engined ornithopter.

Chapter 52

"In dash and hardihood, and what may be called the raw
materials of soldiership, the South, whatever it may have
had to teach the North, had little to teach the West." –
GKC, *A History of America*

SMACK! Gilbert flew backwards as the hand hit his face. He'd
tried to block the blow like Chang had taught him, but the larger
boy had faked a punch with his right hand while backhanding
Gilbert with his left. Having four or five other guys around doing the
same thing didn't help. Fighting groups was very different than a single
opponent!

Gilbert tried hard to keep quiet, but the yelp half escaped his lips.
The half-dozen workers in the group laughed harder.

"Mister Gilbert!" yelled Jack, "Mister Gilbert! Fight him! Like you
fought the Martians!"

"Heh!" said one of the small mob, smiling with yellow, dirt-caked
teeth. "Yeah, Mister Gilbert," he continued, the Southern twang in his
voice carrying over the other boy's yelling, "tell us agin' who yuh are,
an' what yuh did!"

"My name," said Gilbert. Despite feeling dazed from the punch,
his voice was even while he fixed his eyes on the Neanderthal in front
of him, "is Gilbert Keith Chesterton. I killed three Martians in the
Invasion. If you know what's good for y—"

SMUCK!

Another faked blow, this time to the gut. Cheers from the toadies.
It didn't hurt that much, and Gilbert was surprised. Either this lug nut
wasn't half as strong as he looked or he was just playing with Gilbert,
saving the real hits for when they got bored. Gilbert kept looking for an
opening, but couldn't see a weak spot with his blurring vision.

"Jack, Tollers, get outta here, now!" Gilbert barked through bloody
lips. He turned to look at them for just a second, and the largest of the
young toughs took another swing at his face, this time with a closed
fist.

The smack of the closed fist against Gilbert's face sounded very
much like the slap of a flattened palm against a brick wall. Jack's
mouth dropped as Gilbert's eyes, already locked on his own, suddenly
closed in pain as the rest of his body jerked backwards. A cheer went up
among the boys surrounding them. Jack, shocked at seeing his hero

pounded by a bully, was as stunned as Gilbert. He didn't even notice as another member of the mob grabbed his and Tollers' arms from behind.

A shadow passed overhead. Gilbert's eyes opened slightly. He was flat on his back and there was a large whale in the sky, blocking out the sun from above. The whale had noisy flapping wings attached to it, the same kind Johnny's ornithopter had. The wings were so noisy that they nearly drowned out the yelling workmen.

Gilbert turned his head a bit. Something had distracted the mob leader.

Though groggy, Gilbert remembered enough from repeated training to know what to do next. With a fluid movement, he swept the feet out from under his attacker.

Then Gilbert heard a heavy thud nearby, and readied himself for the kicks he knew would be coming from the mob.

But instead, Gilbert heard a third background sound, besides the mob and the wings. Now he heard the drumming of retreating feet clad in heavy work boots.

Gilbert blinked once. Then twice. The whale had landed barely twenty feet away in the crossroads where he'd seen Jack and Tollers running from their attackers.

The whale was ... Gilbert propped himself up on his elbows, ignoring the pain. It wasn't a whale! It looked like a metal box with three sets of flapping ornithopter blades on top. Captain Strock was in the pilot's seat, his hands hidden, but his shoulders and head visible through a pilot's window, suggesting that he was busy moving controls. The wind whipped up by the blades blasted air and loose dust in his face and those of the two boys he'd come to protect. The mob had vanished.

A flag was painted on the side of the flying machine, the same kind Gilbert had seen on the airship over New York City. As Gilbert sat up, he shielded his eyes and saw a double-doorway open up from the side of the craft.

A very odd man walked out of the doors, over a red carpet that unrolled before him like a large tongue rolling out of a huge mouth. The man was old—at least sixty or seventy if his beard and posture were any indication. He also wore a general-type uniform made of black cloth, all full of shiny buttons, polished buckles, gold-woven epaulets and a saber tied and tightened smartly to his dark leather belt.

And behind him was ... a girl ...

The girl was …

That girl!

She had glasses! Glasses this time! Glasses that almost made him forget to look at her perfect face, her beautiful blue eyes, or her exquisitely shaded red hair.

He'd first seen that hair in the office of his old undersecretary in London, right before he'd been given his job as a journalist.

He'd last seen it when a lock of it had come loose in the Sky Palace over Berlin, only then she'd been wearing a flight suit and a pair of wings.

And now she stood in front of him. Her cool eyes were locked on his surprised face, staring at him like he was a stranger.

"Gilbert, my boy!" It was the old man, now standing in front of him. Reluctantly, Gilbert leveraged his eyes away from the girl. The old fellow stood perhaps five-five, his hands were tucked with a relaxed air in his belt or resting on the pommel of his sword, and his words were spoken through the cigar planted firmly in his mouth.

"How'dja like to join us for a little midmorning refreshment?" said the general-fellow.

Gilbert raised himself to a full sitting position, crossing his legs and running his hand through his hair. He was a little hesitant to speak. He'd heard folks talk about the Emperor, of course. He'd heard many people either praising or complaining about Emperor Norton since his arrival. But if this truly was the same Emperor Norton that everyone talked about, Gilbert wasn't currently in the best physical or mental position to meet him. His face hurt, his stomach ached, and a general and a beautiful woman had just dropped out of the sky. He was confused and more than a little hesitant to trust anyone.

"And, just out of curiosity, what if I were to say no?" Gil asked.

"Well, you could spend the rest of your life working the bucket lines. Your call, son."

The air suddenly went heavy with expectation. Gilbert looked back at the girl, past the highly decorated man in front of him. She gave no hint of recognition, only staring at him from behind large-lensed glasses.

Gilbert looked back at the boys. Tollers was standing, his skinny frame holding tall with his chin sticking out. Jack was hunched over and obviously scared, but trying mightily to be as brave as his taller friend.

Gilbert looked back at the general. "What about them?" he said, keeping his eyes on the general's while tilting his head back to Jack and Tollers.

"Your friends have big dreams of escape in their little heads. They'll go back to school, until they learn how to dream a little bigger and better."

"No punishments?"

"Son," said the old man, "I like your fire and how you take care of your own. But you are not presently in a position to negotiate for anything."

The old man had a point. "Fine," Gilbert said, starting to rise.

"Strock? Help the boy, will you now?"

"NO!" barked Gilbert as the smiling pilot moved forward from the shadows inside the flying machine. "I'm fine. Really."

The general fellow waved his hand. Strock backed off, keeping his smile with a slight nod.

Gilbert stood shakily on his own, trembling from stress as much as from his recent roughing-up. "I'm ready now," he said.

The general smiled, snapped his fingers and turned back to his flying ship. As he stalked back to the gangplank, the girl followed dutifully while holding her clipboard.

Gilbert looked at Jack and Tollers. Tollers nodded at Gilbert, then nudged Jack, who did the same. Gilbert, satisfied the boys would take care of themselves, looked at Strock, and shuffled onto the gangplank.

Chapter 53

"The sword and the whip are the weapons of a privileged caste." – GKC, *The Barbarism of Berlin*

The town could hardly be called as such by any rational human being. But, Herb thought, finding rational human beings here was an unlikely prospect at best. It was the kind of place Herb had only read about in one of those dreadful nickel novels that Gil had been so fond of. Made up of two rows of house-sized buildings in an 'X' shape, the town centered on a saloon, a small bank, a church and a dry goods store. Herb guessed that the little crossroads served perhaps twenty households at most; all in the countryside, and a few hours ride by horse and cart.

But the nickel novels never talked about the smell of a place like this. The whole area reeked of old mud and horse-droppings, mingled with the odors of cut lumber and rotting stumps. Herb had spent the majority of his life in cities, raised in neighborhoods where unpleasantness was carefully screened away from the residents. If he hadn't been bunking the last few days in a large railroad car with annoyingly cheerful cowboys with clanking steam-driven machines for body parts, Herb would never have thought to get his shoes dirty by taking a hike down to the little hamlet below the railway stop.

And he certainly wouldn't have entered a saloon.

He'd swung the door open quietly and without fanfare. Commoner-types were annoying him more and more as of late, and though he'd wanted to be someplace different he also wanted to interact with as few of the rabble as possible.

Thankfully, there was only one other patron in the saloon, a lanky fellow with a thick beard and an odd air about him. He didn't seem like the other members of the town. Perhaps he might be worth talking to, perhaps not.

Of course, his only other options involved talking either to himself or the cowboys, and he was sick of doing that.

Well, why not, thought Herb, bellying up to the bar and ordering a small beer.

Once he'd gotten his drink from the silent barman, Herb saddled up to the round table where the uncomfortable patron sat, looking closely at a glass of water.

"May I join you?" Herb asked.

The man looked up with eyes that were both calm and relieved. "Of course," he said, standing politely and speaking with a slight French accent, "please, sit down."

Herb pulled out a chair and used it, the hard wood feeling strangely enjoyable after having dealt with the over-stuffed parlor chairs on the train. The fellow had spoken English well enough. Perhaps learning his story would while away at least a few minutes on this dreary trip.

"So," the Frenchman said to Herb, "what brings you to these—er, parts?"

Herb took a swig of his bottle. "I'm mucking about here looking for a dear friend. And you?"

The Frenchman looked at Herb, then back at his water, his hands still at his side. "I'm here, primarily because ... well, I would have to say now only that it is complicated."

"Boyo, I certainly understand complicated!" Herb said, taking another swig of his drink. "You have any friends out here? The Americans out here are suspicious of foreigners, I've heard."

"Ah, that type you see more in the Slave states. Here, in the mountains, everyone is from somewhere else, and no one asks about your past."

"I have a feeling I might have need of that one day."

The conversation paused.

"So, what's your story?" Herb asked. "I really don't want to have to return to the train unless I have to, and I hate drinking alone."

"I understand that. I am alone quite often, but when in this place, I much prefer it to be with a friendly face. As for my story, well ... you can call me Charles. Or Charlie, if you prefer, like so many of the locals here. I was born in France, and served in the Army. My parents were well-to-do, but were both dead by the time I was seven, and I was raised by a loving aunt. By the time I'd grown to manhood I wanted adventure and pleasure. And for a young man with money the Army offered plenty of both."

"Sounds like fun. Can you disappear into the Army as well?"

"If you have legal trouble, the Foreign Legion might be more in your vein."

"No thanks. Slogging around in a desert isn't my idea of a good time in the least. Still, please continue."

"I lived the life of a pig, really," Charlie said after a deep breath. "Actually, no, let me take that back. Saying that insults one of God's creatures. My life was so dissolute even other pleasure-seekers grew disgusted with me. I awoke one morning and realized my life had become a long, feeble attempt to fill a vacant space in my soul, and no pleasure had done that. No food, no drink, no woman, nothing satisfied me for long. I was always left empty and hungry afterwards.

"Stationed in Algeria, I witnessed evils and atrocities no civilized man would believe. Those who were supposed to protect me did so by locking us in a fortress and killing the innocents in the town around us. I ... I still, many years later, hear their cries in the night, and in my dreams."

Charlie was silent for a while, his hand touching his beard slightly as his eyes gazed into the distance.

"What happened next?" Herb whispered. Charlie's words had woven a delicate spell in the bar, one Herb feared he'd break with too loud a voice.

"I left," Charlie continued. "I resigned my commission, and gave away what was left of my inheritance. My life of pleasure had gotten me nothing, and left me fearful about how possessions could control me. I lived in Algeria for several years after that in an abandoned French fort. I took instruction from the local bishop, and was ordained a priest. But I was a priest in the middle of a town filled with Mohammedans, and made only two converts in ten years."

At one point in his life, Herb would have bristled at the thought of knowingly talking to a Catholic priest. But since then he'd come to know and revere the memory of Father Brown, the priest of Rome who'd sacrificed his life to save Herb's. The little cleric had even baptized Herb when Herb, in fear for his life, had asked for it. Such a priest could change all but the most hardened of hearts, and Herb was not yet a soul that far gone.

"What brought you here, then, all the way from Algeria?" Herb asked, the bottle of beer forgotten at his elbow.

"My bishop was also my spiritual director, and he was a perfect mix of two very contrary things: a truly holy person and one with his hand in many works around the globe. One day he had a sense that I was needed here, and appealed to the Vatican to have me begin a mission in this place."

"You mean you just picked up and moved? Just like that?"

"My vow is obedience. If I wanted comfort and predictability, I would have remained a viscount in Paris."

"You were a ... why on Earth would you leave off being a count for a place like this? Why? There's absolutely nothing you've said that would justify this! You could have done so much good with that wealth!"

Charlie was quiet. He frowned slightly, as if searching for words.

"The motivations of a student studying for an exams makes no sense to another student with no plans past Saturday night. My wealth was much better used in the service of the local church. Had the money stayed in my hands, it would have only served to enrich the local winery and servers of vice."

"But still," said Herb, "you could have ... have lived so much better! Don't you ever wonder if you did the smart thing?"

The man smiled. "I have no illusions about that. What I have done is not very smart at all. Not a whit. In the eyes of the world, I have been very foolish. I would be quite angry with myself, indeed, were I not in such good company, beginning with Saint Peter and continuing with martyrs to this day. They made choices that were stupid beyond words. They gave up joys of power, wealth or flesh. And for what, I wondered?

"Back then, I wondered what it was about such a silly, ridiculous life that it attracted men and women from the life I lived. Why would those who had everything, give it up for nothing?

"And then I looked more closely at the nothing they'd chosen, and found everything. The reality of a simple life is different and more difficult than any dream. Much as a boy will leave his toy soldiers behind once he truly becomes a soldier himself, or a girl leaves behind playing with dolls when she is ready for true love with a real, flesh-and-blood young man. Of course, a decision must be made. And a firm one, too, while willing to accept whatever consequences arise."

Charlie stopped, and Herb felt odd and different. Something in the voice of the older man had sounded with such quiet conviction that Herb had remembered his first view of an iceberg, an artist's rendition pasted into an insert in the newspaper. Only a third to a tenth of any iceberg's whole self was visible at the surface. However it might appear, any visible portion of an iceberg was really only a hint of the immense totality sitting quietly beneath.

Herb looked into Charlie's eyes, ready to bring to bear every argument against God, religion and self-denial that he had learned at school. But the priest's eyes were like warm icebergs, suggesting a rich inner life that had as little fear from Herb's arguments as an iceberg had to fear from a lighted match. In the space of a second or two, Herb looked into the eyes of the bedraggled priest who had been living in obscurity and envied him. A kind of maturity shone forth in Charlie. The kind that had begun to bloom in Gilbert, and that called out to the shallow worldliness Herb had let run his life.

Most of all, Herbert wanted the calm assuredness and sense of well being that he sensed in Charlie. All Herb's own restlessness and dissatisfaction, the aching hole in his soul that grew with each passing day, and which he tried to keep at bay with words, praise and pleasures, all became steam and ashes against the placid countenance of the bearded priest.

And he remembered Father Brown, the little priest who'd given his own life to save Herb. And done so unhesitatingly, unflinchingly, with more courage than a hundred Marxes, Engels or Huxleys had shown in the whole of their lives. Herb saw for just a moment the beauty of such a life, the exquisite joy of a life of silence, simplicity and devotion, with true hope, not faint-hearted and vague optimism of a life or society he would never see or share, but instead a whole new life, lived for something greater, calmer and more thrilling than a hundred worldly pleasures could ever offer.

And all this passed in the space of a few seconds. Herb looked down for three more seconds, then back up at Father Charlie again.

"Well … did you ever say to yourself, Charlie, that when you got to a certain age, then you'd get religion and change? That you could work with the bad guys, just for now, and escape or turn on them later?"

Charlie smiled sadly. "You can't carry a hot coal in your stomach and not be burned by it. Or can you? I've seen many men convince themselves they're blameless if they do the wrong thing for the right reasons. The good news is that even if you've traveled down the wrong road, you can change it now. The bad news is that if you wait, you won't *want* to change, even if you know you ought to."

Herb was quiet again. A rare thing, indeed, when he was faced with a religious person. "So," Herb began, faltering a little, like a child taking its first steps, "if I were to…"

The saloon's swinging door flung open, banging on the wooden frame of the doorway like an angry parent. Herb looked up, upset at the moment that had been lost.

He looked at the doorway and saw Margaret's frowning face, her dark hair swept back, her eyes staring past Herb at Charlie like two solid chips of hate.

"Herbert!" she barked, "where've you been? We've been waiting!"

"I've been here!" he shouted back. "Why're you so angry? I told you where I was going."

"Back to the train, Herbert. Now."

Herb looked back at the older man, who looked at Herb with a sad expression.

"What?" said Herb. "Why are you staring at me?"

"You know," said Charlie, "I once found a young man like yourself who was a minute, perhaps a second away from changing his life. He could have changed all with a single word."

"What word was that?" Herb said hoarsely. Margaret was striding towards them, but Herb ignored both her and the murderous expression on her face.

"Herbert!" she yelled when she was only a few feet away.

"'No,'" said Charlie, "he could have changed the whole of his life, if he'd only said 'no' when those around him insisted he say ..."

"Yes," said Margaret, her voice rising to a near shriek in Herb's left ear, "I *am* talking to you, Herbert Wells! Something told me you might jeopardize everything we've been working for! Get out, now!"

Herb tried to answer Charlie, but Margaret's face suddenly filled his field of vision. Its beauty still attracted him, but viciousness distorted her features, repulsing him at the same time. "Herbert," she said insistently, "I won't say it again! I've got too much riding on this mission to allow anyone to grow a conscience, least of all *you*! I took a risk in accepting you, pulled strings to get us this far first into the Special Branch, and then the Circle itself, and now ... " her voice dropped to a whisper as she dug her fingers into Herb's arm, turning him away from Charlie's prying eyes, "now you want put all that on a tightrope over a pit of angry lions! Herb! Chatting away with a local when we're trying to remain hidden."

"Why are we trying to hide? What's so devilishly important and breakable in your precious mission that everything has to be kept more secret and hidden than the key to a chastity belt?"

"Herbert," she said, suddenly patient, as if trying to explain the obvious to a feeble-minded orangutan, "Gilbert has proven able to upset some very powerful applecarts in his life. The men of the Circle are very, very leery of letting someone like him roam the face of the planet without some kind of leash. If I ... I mean, if *we* could possibly turn him, or at least remove him ..."

"Remove?" Herb's roar carried past the room, sailed out through the open door of the saloon and into the street where Colonel Finn and his investigators had just about convinced themselves they had a good enough reason to mosey into the saloon and have a few.

"Remove?" Herb roared a second time, standing up from his chair. "Why can't your lot just call something what it is? Is it because the real thing is too much for you? When you can't stomach the idea of killing someone, you call it *removing* them? Then you take racist snobbery, and call it breeding a race of thoroughbreds! What next? Calling infanticide a civil right?"

"Well, now that you mention it ..."

"No, Margaret!" Herb said, pounding the table, "No more! I may be a fool, but I'm not such a fool that I don't know pure evil when I see it! And right now it's looking at me with a coiffed hairstyle and a pretty, lace-frilled dress!"

"Herbert, don't you remember? Concepts like good and evil are only pretty pipe dreams that people like us use to keep people like that," she pointed at Charlie, still looking at Herb with a pleading expression, "in line and out of our way. There is no good and evil for people like us, Herbert! There's only power, and those willing to use it! It is a high and lonely destiny, but for those with the will to take it ..."

"Power," growled Herbert, "Power? Then perhaps if I used some of my own power on you, dear girl, I wouldn't have to worry about my mother's fate after all!"

"Herbert, what're you ... uk!"

Margaret's speech cut off as Herb's average-sized but powerful hands closed around her throat.

Chapter 54

Chapter 54

"... it is said that the Government must safeguard the health of the community. And the moment that is said, there ceases to be the shadow of a difference between beer and tea. People can certainly spoil their health with tea or with tobacco or with twenty other things. And there is no escape for the hygienic logician except to restrain and regulate them all. If he is to control the health of the community, he must necessarily control all the habits of all the citizens..."
– GKC, *Eugenics and Other Evils*

Gilbert's trip aboard the large ornithopter had been uneventful for the first few minutes of his journey. The fellow who'd dressed as an admiral had migrated to the front of the 'thopter with the red- haired girl in tow, leaving Gilbert seated beside three of the largest leather-jacketed thugs he'd seen since he'd come to the city.

The 'thopter's droning hum filled the cabin, which was separated from the front of the craft by a metal wall and door. Gilbert leaned over to the guard beside him and raised his voice so as to be heard over the din. "So, d'you think I'm in trouble?" he asked half-jokingly.

The guard stared ahead through the lenses of his goggles, his mouth slightly open.

The craft was only aloft for a few minutes, carrying them up several levels in the city. They passed the sections with Red, then White, then Blue flags, up to the highest level where the central building was a castle. And the highest tower of the castle rose to be a giant spire, pointing at the heavens from the city center.

A hangar door opened at the base of the spire, and the large ornithopter entered and landed. The thugs next to Gilbert let go of their strapped handholds, and motioned Gilbert to stand up and leave, after unseen hands opened the door of the craft.

After they disembarked, Gilbert's three large escorts walked Gilbert through a maze of corridors. Some of the hallways had wooden floors and paneled walls, others were white stone or marble.

Gilbert looked at the guard. "You know," he said quietly, "I've had guns pointed at me before, but never for doing something like saving a couple of kids from a bunch of bullies. Mind telling me what I've done?"

The guard, whose face showed a quiet, yet bored intelligence, answered Gilbert with a very even voice. "It would appear you've gotten the attention of Emperor Norton. That's what usually gets us mobilized like this."

"What usually happens to folks who get his attention?"

"I got his attention by winning against one of the clockwork monsters in the weekly gladiatorial games a month ago. For this I now live on the Blue level of the city, have my own room, my choice of any woman unspoken for on the Red level, or the option of requesting the attentions of a lady among the savants in the White level."

"Ah. And what about folks who get his attention my way?"

The guard shrugged. "Maybe you'll have to fight in the games. Maybe the Emperor will challenge you to a game of pinochle. He might blow your head off if you beat him. He'll do it for sure if you bore him."

Gilbert swallowed and prayed. Dimly, he realized he hadn't been praying much lately—mainly relying on his own wits and resources. *And is that working for you, Gilbert?* the thought jumped up in his head, unbidden.

They finally ended at an ominous set of double doors that looked as if they had been made out of cast iron centuries ago.

Gil kept his eyes forward as the door split down the middle, revealing a white line of light that widened as the doors swung outward.

All was quiet when the doors finished opening.

The room was a brilliant shade of white, with large, paned windows that opened up to the bright, blue sky above. There were four Doric columns that held up the ceiling of the room, and a large table set in the room's center.

As Gilbert walked in, he saw that a white tablecloth covered the table, and a number of covered, fine-smelling silver dishes were set upon it. At the head of the table facing Gilbert was the odd, old generalissimo that Gilbert had seen back at the cross street in the city.

And to the old man's right sat the red-haired girl once again, looking prim and proper as a prairie school marm, her china-blue eyes almost but not quite hidden behind her large-lensed glasses.

"Gilbert!" the old man bellowed as he stood, using the voice of a man at least thirty years younger than he actually looked, "So good to see you here, m'boy!"

The girl looked up and directly at Gilbert, but said nothing. Her face registered such a total absence of recognition that for a second

Gilbert wondered if he'd been mistaken in recognizing her.

"Thank you, sir," said Gilbert hesitantly. He heard the slightest creak of the iron doors on their hinges as they swung shut behind him.

Gilbert stood still, marveling at the size of the room, the beauty of the girl, and the smell of the food that had suddenly forced its way into his nostrils. Gilbert looked at the table and saw that there was a place set at the left-hand side of the old man, opposite the girl.

The old man pointed to the empty chair with a sweep of his hand. Gilbert walked to the table. As he walked, something caught his eye: against the far wall, nearly a hundred feet away, there was an empty white-stone chair on a raised dais.

Gilbert realized he was in a throne room of some kind.

"We'd be honored, Gilbert my boy, if you'd join us for a little refreshment. It's getting t'be lunch time, after all."

The doors locked with a barely audible click.

Chapter 55

"The modern evil, we have said, greatly turns on this: that people do not see that the exception proves the rule. And the attempt of the Eugenists and other fatalists to treat all men as irresponsible is the largest and flattest folly in philosophy. The Eugenist has to treat everybody, including himself, as an exception to a rule that isn't there."
– GKC, *Eugenics and Other Evils*

Father Charles De Foucault, once known as the Viscount De Foucault, now known to the locals as Father Charlie, stood as soon as he saw Herb's hands close around the pretty girl's throat. Herb wasn't the tallest or most muscular young man, true. But Father Charles had been in the military long enough to see many young men of apparently little brawn do incredible feats of strength when motivated by love or rage.

Herb's eyes held that kind of rage now, rage and desperation. The cowboys were outside, waiting on the young lady to emerge with Herb. The bartender was sitting with his cigarette, looking out the window with the detached air of a man who wished above all not to be involved.

A small gasp escaped Margaret's lips a half-second after Herb grabbed her, waking Charles from surprise and spurring him into action. Charles leapt from his seat so quickly that the chair was knocked back against the wall. In an instant, he had his own hands on one of Herb's. Slowly, he pulled Herb's left hand from Margaret's windpipe, freeing her enough that she wrenched away from his remaining hand with a violent twist of her body.

Herb gasped with anger, swinging at Father Charles with a blind fury not wholly his own. Had Charles been twenty years younger, Herb would have found himself flat on his back with several broken bones in ten seconds. But Charles' days of peak fighting fitness were long behind him. Herb hit Father Charles' head, his fist slamming into the priest's skull with the sound of a hammer hitting a wall.

Father Charles fell to the floor and laid still.

Herb's arms were bent, hands tightened into deadly fists. His eyes were dark pools of angry black flame, his teeth were bared and his breath came and went in wheezing, hiccupping blasts. His eyes darted around, looking for the next threat. Seeing none, he looked down at the prone figure of the priest.

Herb calmed, straightened his body and loosened his hands. The whole process took a minute or two while Margaret gasped and held her throat in the corner. When he'd regained his composure again, Herb looked at the priest on the ground and nudged him with his toe. "Look, I'm sorry about that. But ..."

Herb stopped. In a slow but steady trickle, a thin stream of bright red blood was dribbling from the priest's ear. The enormity of Herb's action began to sink in. He looked around, wild-eyed. The bartender was gone. Who knew when he'd left?

There were no witnesses, no one but Margaret, still sitting in a chair and holding her throat and sucking breath after precious breath. And even if there were, there was no way he could be caught for something this far out in the wilderness—was there?

He went to his knees and shook Charlie, called his name, but got no response. Herb put his hands over his own face, leaving his wide eyes uncovered as he began breathing in deep, terrified gasps. He'd killed a Martian in the tunnels below the town of Woking, but that had been different. He had been in the company of the Doctor, and Father Brown. They'd all fired their weapons, and ...

Father Brown.

The little, moon-faced priest had been kind to Herb. Even with all the horrid, resentful comments Herb had made about religion in general and the Catholic faith in particular. Even so, the priest had baptized Herb when they were all in danger of death, and then sacrificed his own life to save Herb's.

And how had Herb repaid him? By killing one of his brothers.

Herb tried hard not to weep, jamming the heels of his hands into his eyes in an effort to hold back the tears. Gasps that tried hard to be sobs escaped once, then twice. What would he do? What *could* he do? He'd convinced himself that his sudden belief in the Church had been an expression of the survival instinct, a desire to live on even after death. But even so, what if the instinct were only there because your soul *truly did* live forever? Gil had made that point in more than one debate. What if punishment for a wrong *could* go on forever, without hope of even death for a release from suffering? If so, what could merit such a punishment better than killing a priest?

There was a hand on his shoulder, and the well-oiled click of a weapon next to his ear. "Get up, Herbert," Margaret's voice rasped behind him. "We have work to do."

Chapter 56

"America is the only country ever founded on a creed." –
GKC, *What I Saw in America*

Gilbert sat facing Emperor Norton. Servants with white smocks and kid gloves placed food and drink in front of him after removing portions from their silver trays and putting it on his plate. Gilbert remembered another little tidbit his mother had taught him about relating to people when he was having trouble with bullies in school. A bully likes to find someone who can be intimidated, she said. It's how they make themselves feel powerful. If you fight back hard enough, it doesn't even matter if you lose. He'll think twice about trying it a second time!

Gilbert had tried to be cunning, but trying to be brazen and confident had nearly gotten him a bullet in his ear back at his first lineup in the city, and gotten him punched several times just a few minutes ago. What would be the smart thing to do now?

I've got to let him know, Gilbert realized, *got to let him know that I'm grateful for his help, but I'm not his well-kept pet.* Gilbert looked at the food warily, but didn't touch it. Not yet. "Well," he started, "do I fight for my life now, or thank you for saving it?"

"Either one as you please," said the Emperor, "but I warn ya, son: if it's a fight yer thinking of, there's a reason why my guards are the only ones allowed to carry guns in the city. If you tried anything silly now, my boys'd be in with pistols an' make you look like a piece of Swiss cheese that got caught in a needle-loom."

Gilbert paused and looked at the red-headed girl. She was staring at him with her hands folded in front of her on the white tablecloth.

"You plannin' to eat, Gilbert, or just sit there staring at my assistant?"

There was not a trace of anything negative in the voice of the Emperor, but something still told Gilbert it would be a good time to be impressive.

Well, no, not necessarily *impressive. Decisive.* "I've lost my appetite, if that's alright for now."

"Whyever's that, d'you think?"

"I'd imagine, Emperor, that most people have a difficult time eating after they've had guns pointed at 'em, nearly been chewed up by an angry mob and then rescued by a well-dressed general in a flying machine. All this while stranded in a floating city, of course."

"You do have the most interesting way of saying things, dear boy. Doesn't he, Galatea?"

The girl looked quickly at the Emperor, nodded once with perfect efficiency, and looked back at Gilbert with a steady glance. *What's she doing here?* Gilbert thought to himself. *She's popped in and out of my life for over a year now, and I can't shake the feeling there's even more to her than I think!*

Gil could tell the Emperor was watching both he and the girl, his eyes flicking quickly first to her and then back to Gilbert. "But here," the Emperor said, "I forget my manners! How can you be expected to eat when you don't even know who your host is!" The man rose to a standing position and strode around the table, past the girl. She stood as soon as he walked past her and followed Norton a pace or so behind him.

"I, sir," the man continued, "am Joshua Norton. Onetime self-declared lost-Dauphin and heir to the throne of France, now the undisputed Emperor of the seven nations of North America, protector of Mexico, ruler-in-exile of the great city of Saint Francis by the California Bay, and current ruler of this, the Floating City of the Americas." The Emperor extended his hand to Gilbert with a wide smile. Two rows of perfect white teeth were visible under the bushy white whiskers of his mustache and beard.

Gilbert stood and shook the Emperor's hand, giving the older man a firm, dry handshake as his father had taught him to do years and years before. His father ...

"Son," said Norton, before Gilbert could think any further, "let's scratch the brunch for now. I've got us a full day planned, unless my assistant Galatea here knows something I don't about our schedule. Any changes so far, dear?"

"No, Emperor," she said. They were the first words Gilbert could remember her speaking without the sound of gunfire in the background in the better part of a year. The last time he'd seen her, she was being chased by men with flying suits that looked like they belonged in the nightmares of Leonardo DaVinci. The last time he'd heard her speak a calm sentence, she was using a shocking nancy rod to restart the heart of a train engineer who'd had a heart attack ... while the train was still in motion! Between those two occasions he'd spotted her once in Paris while he was on an assignment. He'd pursued, but hadn't caught her. In fact, when he thought about it, the whole chase seemed a little blurry in his head, as if a piece of the whole episode was missing.

And now, she'd undergone yet another change, this time becoming a personal secretary for a would-be Emperor who ruled from a city in the clouds. He looked at her again. Her eyes stared back. Gilbert's face felt just a tad warmer, and he was just about to speak when Emperor Norton slapped him on the back.

"Well!" boomed the Emperor, who had a surprisingly strong arm for a man so visibly old, "Let's take us a little stroll 'round the Floating City, shall we? We can take in the sights and work up an appetite at the same time. What do you say, Gilbert? Like to take a little tour, or wouldja like to go back to pouring noxious concoctions all day?"

Gilbert paused. In a story he'd translated from Plutarch for his mother, Gilbert had learned how a Gaulish leader had waited a full day to send his reply to a dinner invitation from Caesar. 'When the fox invites the rabbit to dinner,' the Gaul had told his son, 'the rabbit should first learn what is on the menu.'

Still, Gilbert contemplated; he'd been a rabbit in a fox's lair before and survived. Besides, he thought suddenly, there was no harm in just looking over the city, was there? It certainly beat being in the worker's line!

Norton pulled out another cigar, snipped off the end with a small tool and produced a lit match as if by magic. He lit the cigar and inhaled deeply, turning the end into a brightly glowing ember and filling the air around the three of them with blue smoke. "Would you care for a cigar, son?" he asked Gilbert. "Helps me think alla time."

"I ... well, that is, I don't smoke."

"S'alright. Gotta start sometime, don't we? Here, just take one and put it in one of your pockets for later." With a snap of his fingers, another cigar identical to his own appeared in his hand. Quicker than a wink, Norton stuffed it into the breast pocket of Gilbert's red work coveralls. "On our way, son? You betcha! Galatea! Call out and let them know we are on the road! Forward! Excelsior! Excalibur! And all those other things that mean we're on our way!"

Norton spun on his heel and strode to the double doors Gilbert had entered through. As Norton approached them, the doors clicked audibly and swung open—outwards, this time. As he followed Norton and the girl, Gilbert's mind was swirling with unanswered questions. How did a quirky person like Norton ever become Emperor of anything? How had the girl ended up here? Where were they going? And, most importantly, how was Gilbert going to escape?

Chapter 57

"Nine out of ten of what we call new ideas are simply old mistakes. The Catholic Church has for one of her chief duties that of preventing people from making those old mistakes, from making them over and over again forever, as people always do if they are left to themselves." – GKC, *Twelve Modern Apostles and Their Creeds*, 1926

Herbert, like most people once they had reached the age of maturity, had some regrets in his life. There were people he wished he hadn't been so cruel to, girls he wished he hadn't broken up with quite so soon, and parties he wished he'd either stayed at longer or stayed away from completely.

But as the train moved forward with him in his seat, he knew that the events of this day would rule him forever, and cause no end of regret.

As their train car climbed higher into the mountain ranges over the tracks, he saw the snow begin collecting in tiny pools and frozen eddies against the sides of rocks and trees. Though your sins be scarlet, he thought slowly, I will make them white as snow.

Where in the Bible had that been from, he wondered. Matthew? Ignatius? Something like that. Gil would probably know.

Gil, It's no use, he thought slowly as his head lowered. *I hardly wanted to change before, when I had friends around me who wanted me to be something holy. What will they say when they hear I've killed a priest? What will be my fate, if Gil's right and there really is an afterlife? What if Hell is real? Have I no hope now of escaping it? Not bloody likely. No way I'd ever let someone on my good side again, if I were in God's shoes.*

"Redemption," Herb whispered, "no redemption."

But, if there's no way to Heaven, then what's left? Hang myself at the nearest oak tree?

There was a shadow above him. Herb looked up. Finn was standing over him. "The little lady says you two ran into some trouble back there, pard. Looks like it knocked you for a loop. You want to talk it out or suck it up?"

"I don't want to do the first, and don't understand the second. Leave me alone."

Finn sat down across from Herb and stared out the opposite

window. "You know," Finn said, "I remember the first time I killed a man."

Herb was silent, but he felt the blood drain out of his face as a shot of fear blasted through him.

Finn, still watching Herb out of the corner of his eye, leaned back in his chair. "Back about, oh, must've been over forty years ago now. I was a young buck in my teens, fresh out've the Slave Wars. I'd started out as a drummer boy, then made it through as a deal maker for the O'Hara family, selling guns to both sides. Course, the way it worked out I usually ended up giving good intelligence to the North and shoddy product to the South.

"Then one night, one 'a these fellers comes outta the forest, waving a knife big enough to give the Grim Reaper nightmares. I didn't even get a chance to see the color of his uniform. Just pulled up my pistol and darned if the thing didn't just *ke-pow!*" Finn said, pointing his finger at an imaginary opponent and then raising it in an arc as he made the sound effect.

"Well, the feller looked ... he looked surprised, he did. Then he took a step forward an' fell down. Next thing I know, old Alan Pinkerton hisself claps his hand on my shoulder, turns me to face 'im. 'Son,' he says, 'don't you be upset now. You did what you had to do. You did your job, son. *You did your job.*'

"I don't right recall what I said after that, but whatever it was musta really tugged his mustache, because the next day, I'm gettin' fitted out for my first, honest-to-goodness lawman's gunbelt, and getting my badge as a Pinkerton's marshal. And ever since then, that feller I killed ain't bothered me no more. I've been too busy with job after job, tryin' to keep one step ahead of all the ghosts in the past.

"I guess what I'm sayin' son, is that you've got that look about you. You killed someone. Not some squid from Mars, but a real human being. Maybe it was back in the bar, maybe it was six months ago. But you killed, and it's hitting you somethin' fierce."

"I ... " Herb said slowly, "I ... killed."

"See, I knew it, son. I spent too long learnin' to read faces when I was a young'n to miss that look, the one where you look like you're lookin' at something a thousand yards away. You're lookin' into a big, black pit right now, and if you don't find something else to take your eyes off've it, you're gonna be stuck looking at it forever. Find a job, or something. The kind of job you know wants you, and keep doing it. That's what life is about, son."

"I was ..." Herb began, suddenly looking down and inward. Something Finn had said made things shift in Herb's head. "I was ... I was just ... doing the job. My job. My new position requires ..."

"*Every* job requires *everything* today," Finn continued, happy that his words seemed to have brought Herb out of his trance. "You got that, son? Find the job, give it everything you've got, and you'll never be bothered by nothin' again."

Herb felt something in himself shift, as if into a perfect groove. He understood, now. There was only the job he needed to do, and the next job after that.

It was all so simple.

All the pain Herb had felt in his heart suddenly melted away. The nagging voice in the back of his head was suddenly silenced. He raised his head, now focused on his next ... job.

I must bring Gil aboard with the Special Branch, he thought, *or I must remove him.* That Gilbert was his best friend made little difference, now. What was friendship, Herbert thought? It was just another, pleasurable chemical reaction in the head of the weak. He'd make other friends, wouldn't he?

The feeble old man was still jabbering about his own useless and wasted life. A life he'd tried to give meaning to by catching criminals and making the country safer for 'decent folk.' Herb could now see, really *see*, that there was no point in making the world better for everyone. Who cared about the field beast of a commoner, roaming about the Earth, working, breeding and dying miserably?

Blessed are the strong, Herbert thought in a rare moment of poetry, *for we shall take everything. And remove those who get in our way.*

With all possible speed.

"You feelin' better, Charlie?" the farmer said, tending to the bandage over the priest's ear. "You gave us quite a start. We was afeard your brains might be leakin' out've your ears after that hit. How's that cut?"

"My head shall hurt a long time, my ear will sting. But I yet live. Where is the boy?"

"The one who crowned you? I'm afeard he got away, Charlie. Made a clean getaway."

Charlie was silent, staring into space. "I only wish he had."

Chapter 58

"The Declaration of Independence dogmatically bases all rights on the fact that God created all men equal; and it is right; for if they were not created equal, they were certainly evolved unequal. There is no basis for democracy except in a dogma about the divine origin of man."
– GKC, Chapter 19, *What I Saw in America*

Thi s is the main hallway of the highest level outside of the spire itself," Norton said as he walked with a brisk pace. "It circles the spire like a ring, and every place of significant importance branches off from the circular track towards the center."

"What's at the center?" Gilbert asked.

"All in good time, my boy, all in good time. You journalists never stop asking questions, do you? Either spoken or silent."

"Only the good ones ... Emperor," said Gilbert. He added the last words after a short pause. Norton led both Gilbert and the girl. He'd called her a weird name several times—'Gala-tay-ah,' or something like that. Where had Gilbert heard that name before? Was it historical, mythological, or something else entirely?

The Emperor looked back at Gilbert and smiled again. "You're good, son," he said with a kind air, "but if you're going to try buttering me up, you're gonna have to do better than calling me Emperor when yer heart's not in it."

"Say 'yes, Emperor,'" the girl whispered in Gilbert's ear, her warm breath sending a thrill down his arm.

"Yep! I mean, *yes, Emperor!*" said Gilbert, trying hard to change his small yelp into an efficient-sounding affirmation of the Emperor's authority and might. He had to speak louder—a roar of cheering crowds could be heard in the hallway, and was getting louder the further down the hall they walked.

Norton turned back to the front, sucked back on his glowing cigar and smiled again.

"Now, over here," said Norton, stopping by a balcony and looking down to an amphitheater, "we've got us one of my most prized possessions. An innovation that single-handedly turned around the culture of the city from one civil disturbance after another into a solid, unified, cohesive unit of pure patriotism and single-minded focus."

Gilbert stepped up beside the Emperor and looked down. There were perhaps a few hundred people seated in a rough ring, watching the conflict below. A man stood and fought in rough-looking armor made of brass and rubber, covering his right arm and leg. He also wore a shiny brass helmet, and brandished a long, black spear in his right hand.

But the warrior's opponent looked even more fearsome. Instead of another gladiator, the lone fighter faced a bizarre contraption that could best be described as a huge, brass-and-rubber crab, a creature of pipes, pincers, steel and steam, with a half-dozen squeaking, creaking legs and a series of gages leaking or blasting steam with every movement it made.

And right now, its biggest movement was the swinging of two, very large arms towards the man facing it. Each of the arms ended in a pair of very large and jagged claws with hydraulic-powered motors, opening and closing with a noise that sounded like mechanical insects.

""Welcome to the center, Gilbert. Ever seen one a' these, son?" Norton said with an absentminded air, while the fighter dodged one claw the size of his own chest, and then another.

"No," said Gilbert, remembering the horrific Martians in their scout vehicles and blood-sucking towers, "no, not recently."

"Some inventor fella over in Europe got the idea, after seein' one 'a them squid things you fought. He started showin' them off over in Germany and, well, I just had to have 'em. The fella works for me now, up with the savants."

Norton turned back to the show. The fighter was plainly tiring, but the crowd didn't seem to care. The crab swung again and again at the darting, two-legged figure in front of it, and the man moved slower and slower with each pass, trying pathetically to find an opening with the iron spear in his hands.

"Wouldn't you say the competition is a little one-sided, Emperor?" Gilbert said, trying to be both concise and diplomatic.

"Gilbert, these fellas all volunteer to fight the Clockworks. Nobody forces 'em. For most of 'em, it's the only way they'll ever get to move above the level of an everyday worker and join the elite on the White or Blue levels. Otherwise, they'd risk wearing the same red jumpsuits the rest of their lives."

"Isn't there another, fairer way to let them advance? Maybe an obstacle course or something?"

Norton turned to look at Gilbert, ignoring the fighter's screams of agony as the crab's arm connected and gave him a smack in the ribs that resounded throughout the small arena. A hundred viewers' throats called out for blood.

"Son," Norton said, ignoring the spectacle below him, "one thing I think you, above all people, should know is that life just ain't fair."

"Yes, Emperor. But does that mean you ought to make it worse? Even taking right and wrong out of the equation, you risk wasting a potentially useful person this way. You'd be better off taking folks who break the rules and dropping them down there instead."

"Really?" said Norton, suddenly intrigued. Gilbert saw a concerned look pass over Galatea's face, a lock of her perfectly coiffed hair falling over her right ear.

"Yes, really," said Gilbert, ignoring her. "I don't know who that fellow is down there, but he looks strong. I'd bet from his physique he could be one of your better workers. If you only made a person fight for their life because they've crossed the line, the people will see what happens when you break the rules and then they won't do so."

Gilbert, entranced with his own speech and the Emperor's interest in what he had to say, hardly noticed as the man was smacked yet again by the crab's other arm. This time, the worker was hit hard enough to slam into the wall with a sickening thud. His helmet spun off his head with the impact, and landed nearby as he fell face first to the ground.

"An' what about the boys who actually beat the game? What then?"

"The only way they can beat the game is to play the game. And when they get rewarded for playing the game, Emperor, you've won again. The people get to see someone who *was* a bad boy, and now benefits because they play by your rules."

"By thunder!" roared the Emperor, slapping his knee and throwing his cigar out into the crowd, "didn't I tell you this boy'd be useful, Galatea?" Norton turned back to the balcony, facing the action below. The crab was about to deliver the killing blow to its victim. The fighter could barely move, and was lying on the ground, moaning in pain. "Stop the game!" Norton roared, his voice carrying over the crowd. The crab's pincer stopped in mid-strike, pausing in midair.

Norton's hand paused in midair too, his eyes fixed on Gilbert.

"Well?" Gilbert asked. "What are you going to do?"

"Take a look down there, son," said Norton, his hand still held high while he looked at the muscular man at the bottom of the pit. His head rose briefly, and Gilbert took a quick breath of horror when he saw who the man was.

"That's Mr. Smith!" said Gilbert. "You've got to let him go! He's got a wife and kids!"

"Why?"

"Why *wouldn't* you?"

"He chose to be here, Gilbert. I told him his kids would all have higher places in the city, whether he won or lost. He knew the risks."

"But you're taking a father's love for his kids and … you're twisting it for the crowd's entertainment! You can't do this!"

The Emperor's face hardened. "Son, get this, an' get it real quick: No one, but no one tells *me* what to do in *my* city."

Gilbert thought quickly. Arguing that Norton couldn't or shouldn't do something wasn't going anywhere. But maybe a different tack?

"You're right, Emperor," Gilbert said slowly, looking very closely at Norton's raised arm, hoping he wouldn't say anything that would cause it to drop and get poor Mr. Smith killed, "you're correct that you have the *right* to do this. You have the *right* to choose if someone lives or dies in your city.

"But … well, just because you *have* the right to do something, does that mean you *are* right in doing it? Now, Emperor, I'll admit I'm new. I haven't been here long enough to know the ins and outs of your legal system. But I know that if you kill someone only because it'll make your job easier, well, that's wrong. And it's someone a lot higher than me who said so."

"You may recall a little bit in the Constitution about the separation of Church and state, son."

Gilbert swallowed. Having actually read the Constitution, he knew the phrase "separation of Church and state" didn't appear anywhere in it. That was a ploy typically used by people who wanted to remove God from public life, and so grab more power for themselves. If he had been debating with Herb or his own father back when he and Ma were alive, Gilbert would have seized on the error in Norton's statement and torn his argument to shreds like a joyful puppy with a pair of old, beloved slippers.

But Norton, Gilbert could see, Norton played by a different set of rules. Norton didn't like logic. Norton liked ...

Gilbert noted what the Emperor was wearing. Logic wouldn't convince a man like this. Norton didn't respect an argument that was logical, truthful or consistent, as Norton himself was none of these.

Norton liked flair. He liked flash. He liked to be entertained. He didn't even mind people trying to kill him, so long as it was done in an interesting way. *What if* ...Gilbert thought, *what if you presented the truth, but in a way that entertained while it was taught? What then?*

Deep breath. What did Herb say right before they went out onto the floor at the Sky Palace?

Showtime.

"Well, Emperor," Gil began, "you're right. You are absolutely, one-hundred percent right that there is a separation between Church and state in America. In America, many powerful people say that the state card should trump the Church every time. And," Gilbert continued, hardly pausing for breath, "those same people are all one-hundred percent wrong about why. Y'see ..."

Gilbert kept talking and moving quickly, like a carnival huckster he'd once seen come through his town years back.

"... y'see, the only reason there's a wall between the Church and the state is because the people who run the country now want it that way. And they only want it that way because it means they get to govern and do what they want to the people and the world. You can't have a tyrant and God share the same stage; someone's gotta go. Pull God out've any government, and then the government becomes God by filling the space. But to see what America oughta be, maybe we should look at what sets America apart from other nations, and what the men who made America meant it to be.

"Y'see, Emperor," Gilbert continued, leaping now onto the ledge where Norton and the people could see and hear him, taking the Emperor's smiling face and steady hand as a good, if not wholly dependable, sign to continue. "Y'see, I've been all over Europe and a few places besides. I've seen places most fellas my age can only dream about. And there's one thing, let me say, *one thing* that travel does for the mind of 'most any person, sir, and that's to ...'"

"Open your mind?" said Norton, as if helping Gilbert through the awkward pause.

"No!" answered Gilbert happily, suddenly bursting with inspiration. Norton needed to hear, not his *own* answer, but an *unexpected* one! "No, Emperor Norton, that is absolutely, one-hundred percent *incorrect*! Traveling for most people has the effect of closing their mind, not opening it! Because when you see a Hindoo dervish spinning around in place, or an African medicine man waving his masks, or a Catholic from the Philippines getting themselves crucified on Good Friday, you see everyone else as crazy, and it's only yourself and the people you know who are the sane ones! You may say how lovely and diverse the world is, but inside you're thanking whatever god you pray to that you aren't two napkins short of a picnic like 'those' people are!

"But on the other hand, if you open your mind too much, all you see are oddities, craziness, and weirdness. You end up loving diversity for its own sake, rather than for any real virtue in it. But that's as silly as celebrating a windstorm for its chaos, or a bomb for the lovely bit of diversity it brings to an otherwise orderly neighborhood.

"No, Emperor, and good citizens of the city in the sky," here Gil leapt onto the balcony and turned to face the audience, who'd gone silent at the sound of the young man preaching from the Emperor's seats, "the real value of seeing the world is that you see so many shadows of the truth. Shadows that point to the source of all shadows and light: the sun. Gentlemen and ladies, all the attempts of the world to find meaning find it in a particular creed, found and spread throughout the world, because it was made for all men. A creed that manages the difficult trick of being both the broadest and narrowest thing in all mankind's history. It's broad because it includes all men; rich, poor, tall, short, single, married, young and old. But it's also narrow because it states very specifically who made us and why He did so.

"And America," continued Gil, leaping from the ledge onto the back of the mechanical creature, keeping his eyes on Norton's once he landed, and addressing his speech to the crowd, "America, I can say with confidence, is the only country in the history of the world to be founded on a creed, a belief not in royalty, prosperity, raw power or geographical convenience, but on the belief that all men are created equal.

"Yes, we all have the rights to life, liberty, and the pursuit of happiness, but *not* because the people decided to give them to us. That's what they say in France, where the most powerful people decide for everyone else what is fair. No, Emperor, it is our *creator* who gives us these rights!

"But the best proof that we're a Christian nation isn't from the chapels we visit or the Bibles our government prints. No, you can see America's Christian heritage best when ...when you try to get a passport!"

Norton's brow furrowed. The slightest glimpse of fear waved over the red-head's face. Gilbert got the message: Passports are boring. Don't bore him!

"It's a simple thing, really," Gilbert continued. "If you try to get into a place like France, they ask you if you've ever planned to overthrow the government by being a Royalist. If you were to try to get into Germany, they'd want to make sure you're not a Socialist.

"But in the Five Americas, they ask if you're currently a polygamist. They ask if you're a bigamist. They ask if you are entering the United Stated for the specific purpose of doing any immoral acts, where other countries will only let you visit if you are not a threat ..."

"And the Americas are so different?" Norton growled.

"No!" Gilbert shouted happily, taking elation at the surprised look on Norton's face, "No sir, not at all! Even today, split into five nations, the Americas will bar your way if you are a threat. But *what* the Five Americas considers a threat is different!

"Y'see, America considers you a threat only if you threaten her *creed*, a creed that says all men are created equal. You'll never, ever find such a belief outside of religion, because if the Children of Darwin are right and we all just came from a bunch of soup, there's no reason at all to say we're equal! Because if God Himself didn't make us equal, then we certainly evolved unequally! If you don't believe me, look at your own city! Men have different talents and drives, but in the free Americas alone, there is a principle established (however poorly some put it into practice) that any man may go as far in life as his will and talent can take him!"

Gilbert was sweating now, and smiling as if he'd just won the spelling bee at the one-room schoolhouse he'd gone to in Minnesota.

"Last of all," said Gil, "In the Americas, especially so in the USA, there is a very different attitude towards the human person. The creed of Christianity infuses all life with a way things *ought* to be, even if the citizens are lousy at living it out!"

Gilbert's sweat and earlier nervousness was now gone, replaced by a confidence he'd never yet had before an audience. Not even when he'd spoken out against the mad scientist in Berlin had he felt such zeal! In Berlin and other places, he'd stood straight and kept his voice even. But now, strutting along the balcony's edge while he pontificated to Norton and the audience of the games below, he felt less like a lecturer or lawyer and more like a swashbuckler, a legendary pirate hunter engaging in a sword fight on the rigging of a tall ship.

Gil paused at a slight noise; it was the tittering of laughter.

Laughing *with* me or *at* me, Gil wondered.

Who cares, he realized! Laughing was better than booing. Even Emperor Norton had a smile on his bearded face, though his hand still hovered in the air.

"And this," Gilbert said, facing the audience on his improvised stage, himself again, but bigger and more aggrandized than anyone would have ever seen him. This wasn't *Gilbert*, the wallflower who'd tried his best not to be seen by the bullies. Now, he was *Gil*, the name Herb had given him! *Gilbert* was a quiet little mouse who as a child would never have willingly voiced an opinion to a crowd unless it were beaten and dragged out of him. *Gilbert* still felt the smallest tickle of fear in his stomach when he had to speak in front of an audience. And *Gilbert*, when he *did* speak, had to adopt the traditional posture of the British man speaking in a straight-postured, dignified air.

But *Gil*, now. *Gil* found himself one-part *in*former and two parts *per*former. Teaching and training while entertaining.

And he *liked* it!

"This," Gil continued, "is what separates the Americas from the rest of the nations!" He jumped from the back of the steam crab to the dirt-covered, metal-plated floor. "European nations are like oversized small towns. If you manage to move there, no one will trust you for three generations, assuming you get to be a citizen at all. Yet in the Americas, we'll take anybody in, regardless of their belief, so long as they follow the creed. You don't have to be a Protestant Christian to live well here. You can be Catholic, Jewish, even a Hindoo or a Mohammadean. You can live as a Chinaman or as an Englishman or a Northern Eskimo, if you don't mind people looking at you funny over the clothes you're wearing. No, anyone can come to live here, *as long as you agree to live by the creed*, something so important to America that if it were pulled loose, the Five Americas would become nothing more than a bunch of minor European nations, nothing special at all. And useless except to be conquered as minor fiefdoms by some bigger, nastier group that hasn't forgotten what it believes in.

"We separate Church and state," Gil continued, knowing he was running out of steam and needed to end his speech soon, "but that's to protect the Church from the state, not vice versa. Congress' first act after its founding was to publish Bibles with taxpayer money. Why was there no outcry, if this violated the Constitution? It's because while there *is* a wall, there are *doors* in the wall for the common man to walk through!"

There was a pause. Gil waited, searching first the face of the Emperor and then the red-head for some clue as to how his performance had gone over.

The applause began behind him. Only a few hands at first. Then more. Soon, the several hundred people who had gathered into the small stadium were on their feet, cheering Gilbert's speech.

Norton's right hand remained in the air, Mr. Smith's fate still undecided. He raised his left hand, palm up, a signal the crowd took for silence.

"Your speech, m'boy," he said, "has managed to put a smile on my face, something not even the last few assassination attempts could do. So if I get you right, if I let that crab down there kill Smith, I'll be violatin' his right to life. Correct?"

"Yes, Emperor. Even if he knew the risks entering the arena, he did it to further the lives of his children. But children should be able to stand or fall on their *own* merits, not based on who their father was, or what their father was killed by."

More cheers from below. The crowd began to chant Gilbert's name, it's two syllables resounding past the stadium and out into the streets.

Norton suddenly dropped both his hands silently, placing them behind his back and sucking on his cigar. As he looked past Gilbert into the crowd, he seemed deep in thought for exactly thirty seconds.

He reached up and pulled out his cigar. "Okey dokey," he said, the arena falling silent instantly, "you've convinced me. Smith doesn't have to fight the crab for his kids to advance. His kids that're old enough to go to the White savant level'll do it the old-fashioned way, by taking a pencil and paper test. And it's because I said so!"

More cheers from the audience, who threw their red worker caps into the air and at Gil in adulation. Gil beamed. The red-head clutched her writing pad with both hands and gave Gil a smile that made him want to rush over and sweep her off her feet.

A rope ladder dropped from Norton's balcony. Gil grabbed a fallen cap and climbed the rope ladder back up to Norton's balcony. Once there, he stood aloft on the balcony's railing again and waved the cap to his new, adoring fans.

Norton watched the audience cheer Gil, waiting for the cheers to die down. When they didn't, but instead nearly broke through into a frenzy of cheers and goodwill towards the youth, Norton stood forward and began speaking again.

"Yes, Gilbert lad," continued the Emperor, everyone falling suddenly silent again at the sound of his voice, "You've convinced me with your words. Words mean things, and words are how I rule. Now, for you an' Smith to go free, you'll need your talent an' drive to convince the crab."

Gilbert's and the red-head's smiles both faded. That didn't sound good ...

"Now wait a minute ..." Gil began.

"Nope," said Norton. He grabbed a pistol and a spear from one of his guards and threw them both at Gilbert. Gil caught the gun with both hands but was knocked off balance by the shaft of the spear hitting him in the head. He fell backwards, just catching his balance in time to land again on the crab, then slide down its back onto the pit floor, his feet crunching on the dirt and sand.

Gil righted himself. Mr. Smith was groaning groggily, trying to raise himself up. Gil heard a clank come from in front and above him. The crab had been still during his speech, but the engine fired up again as it began to move its pincered arms and thick, brass cased legs.

The mechanical crab was about the size of a four-wheeled growler coach, with six, sharp legs and two pincer claws the size of Gilbert's torso, all of which began moving with surprisingly quiet mechanical clankings towards Gilbert and the man he'd been suddenly and unwillingly charged to protect.

"Oops," Gilbert said, looking at the pistol in his hands. A pistol that suddenly looked very, very small.

Chapter 59

> "To have a right to do a thing is not at all the same as to be
> right in doing it."
> – GKC, *A Short History of England*

The train car chugged relentlessly, eating up mile after mile of track in its journey Westward. No engineer was visibly driving, but their way was deserted enough that this went unnoticed. Mountains with snow and occasional animals gave way to hills, then field after field with American-born African slaves—"Negroes," one cowboy had called them. The others on the train used other, cruder terms Herb could only guess the origins of.

Something in Herb had shifted since the death of the priest. It was terrifying, but felt freeing. Much like he thought he'd feel after jumping from a great height.

If there was a God, Herb was quite likely doomed and damned.

If there was no God, Herb was free.

A very ... liberating thought.

"What's on your mind, Herbert dear?" Margaret's voice was behind him again, their previous squabble seemingly forgotten. Somewhere in the back of his head, the drive he'd had to suppress for so long, the voice that told him to run from or kill her had finally been ... well, suppressed. Gone. And Herb only noticed it for its absence.

"I'm thinking about our mission, and how I could get Gil on board with us."

"That's the spirit, Herbert. Sometimes it takes a little sacrifice to help get the priorities in order, don't you think. Isn't it freeing, Herbert?" she said suddenly, her face and voice shifting from Herb to the starry sky outside.

"To think I won't suffer for what I did back there? I don't know if freeing's the word."

"Herbert, do you remember the law of the jungle? How once you said it only looked good as long as you were one of the lions?"

"Yes. It seems so long ago, now."

"Well, Hebert, now you *are* one of those lions! Better, really. You're on your way to being one of the lion tamers! Isn't that exciting?"

"To a point. There's one question that eludes me, though, Margaret. Gil and Father Brown and their ilk do what they do because they want to go to Heaven. They have a reward in mind."

"True, Hebert. But ours is a much higher and lonelier destiny. We cannot avail ourselves of fairy tales ..."

"Yes, fine. Save the speech for your next convert. What I want to know, Margaret, is this: if there is no afterlife, then why should I be concerned with building the better world you're talking about? Why bother being nice to anyone, if I can get what I want just by taking it from you?"

"We need to make the strongest species possible, Herbert! Remember? A race of thoroughbreds, free from the taint of the Negro, the Slav or the Catholic."

"But, Margaret, what if I or someone else decides they don't give a care about the race? What if I just want to please *myself*? If all right and wrong is an illusion, why shouldn't I just say, 'I'll do what I want,' and make that the whole of the law? Why not murder children, if it brings me pleasure and I can get away with it?"

"Herbert! Moving our race forward is ... is ... well, it's its own reward!"

"To you, maybe. What if to me, the thrill of murder, or other crimes against nature, are *their* own rewards? If you don't believe in God, the only reason to follow orders is because someone like you has a great, big stick waving over my head. And I wonder sometimes if that really is a better world."

"Herbert, we ..." Margaret paused. The train was slowing down. "We're almost there," she whispered.

"Where Gil is? Have we arrived?" Herb whispered back. He could hear the cowboys snoring in the back of the darkened car.

"Not quite," Margaret answered. "I'll wake the others, then set off our little homing pigeon. If the train is stopping itself gradually, it means that it's sensed we're nearing the city's location. We'll likely have to go the rest of the way on foot."

"How far will that be?"

"A few miles, perhaps. No more than a day's journey, if everything's working aright. You hop outside, and I'll see you out there in a moment. Get your long coat on, too. The night chill won't do you any good if you're still wearing that sportcoat."

Herbert sighed. The coat she'd brought for him fit well, but it was long and black. Looking at the dark swath of material made him feel more like a vampire than an adventurer.

Still, Herb rose from his sitting position, slipped on the coat and shuffled to the door. "Oh," said Margaret in a voice barely above a whisper, "there's something I'll need to give you now, too. We're in the CSA now, and we'll be crossing the border into the Southern California Republic on foot. Here—I heard you learned about these a while back?"

Herb looked down at what Margaret held out to him.

It was a pepperbox pistol, complete with a gunbelt and holster.

He'd first seen one more than a year ago, when he and Gil had had their adventures with Father Brown and the Doctor. It looked at first like a normal pistol with a fat barrel—actually, a barrel nearly three times as wide as the usual gun barrel, because the barrel of this type of gun consisted of six barrels stuck together, looking like a gray honeycomb with a gun handle when viewed from the front.

"I've never fired one of these," Herb said.

"It's easy. Pull back the safety catch, point and shoot. Repeat until your target stops breathing. The small switches on the handle control how many barrels fire at once. Now, outside with you."

Herb found himself outside the door and on the gravelly ground in short order, looking at the stars above. The sky was a huge, lit-up canopy of white pinpricks of light, all looking down on him. Herb shivered, and only partly from the chill of the night air.

The door to the train car opened behind him, and as Herb turned he saw Finn step out, fully clothed. The older man yawned, stretched and jumped down from the trestle. The one they called Doc with the eye and hand came next, followed by the young one with the leg.

"Fine night fer walking," Finn said happily. Herb shivered in the night air. What kind of person is awakened in the middle of the night for an excursion into the darkness of pure wilderness, and proclaims it a jolly holiday? No sane person Herb knew. He ignored the cowboys as best he could, and stared out over the fields of thick grass.

He knew that he had changed in the last little while. Killing the priest, even in a moment of passion, had decided his path and destiny. It would be more difficult, he knew, to alter his ways of acting and relating to others and the world around him. But it needed to be done for his survival.

He'd seen it done before. Once, in school, a close acquaintance had become more aloof to him after joining the 'Bloods,' the boys in school who were the most apt at sports. Herb had seen the young man change from an energetic, enthusiastic student into someone who ignored or tormented anyone outside his new circle of athletic friends. At the time,

Herb had resented the fellow's shallowness. But with his new set of eyes, Herb now saw this was only the cost of being popular. Those who wanted something badly enough did what was necessary to get it, and did so ...

Herb stopped the thought, then finished it. "With all possible speed," he said in a quiet voice under his breath.

Still, Margaret's way of acting wasn't for him. She seemed to revel in doing precisely the wrong thing, the evil thing, in openly defying the God she claimed not to believe in.

No, her ways weren't for him. They were as chaotic as they were evil. At least, as the world defined evil.

But perhaps ... perhaps a more detached approach. A more neutral attitude towards things.

Herb inhaled, trying on his new self for size. He was aloof, neutral, and evil. What? No. *Efficient*, he insisted, pushing the last thought away. It was the same reason Margaret was able to put aside his last attempt on her life. She had become *efficient*, able to rise above the evil around her...

No, he repeated again and again. It's *not* evil. There *is* no evil.

I'm not evil, just ... efficient.

Chapter 60

"And [Father Michael] felt as every man feels in the taut
moment of such terror that his chief danger was terror
itself…His one wild chance of coming out safely would be
in not too desperately desiring to be safe."
— GKC, *The Ball and the Cross*

Gil looked at the crab in front of him, a bizarre concoction of
pipes, rubber, copper, steam and wire, with a pair of giant
jagged pincers and a trio of metal saws for mandibles. In place
of antennae, it had a pair of reversed cones, the kind movie directors
used to make their voices heard. A loud blast sounded from a steam
whistle on top of the crab, and it began moving forward with the sound
of metal on concrete and pungent smell of burning coal in the air.

The crowd cheered, shouting Gilbert's name in unison. The crab
twitched this way and that, as if waiting for a signal. The noise from
the stands was considerable, but not deafening. Gilbert had heard
louder crowds at schoolhouse baseball games, but several comments
carried over the heads of the spectators to Gilbert's ears.

"Get 'im, Gilbert!"

"Pass the test, boy!"

"Pull them wires—it's your only chance!"

A single moan went up behind Gilbert. He turned and saw that Mr.
Smith was finally opening his eyes.

Swell. Gilbert swallowed, pointed his pistol at what looked like a
mass of cables and wires beneath the brass and steel carapace, and
pulled back the safety hammer with his thumb and forefinger. The gun
hadn't been well oiled, and squeaked as Gil pulled it back with a
grinding click!

The crab started up with a blast of steam and a clicking of gears.
Its hissing metal legs rose and stomped with squeals of smoke and
metal. The contraption's legs were pointed at the end, and where they
hit the stone floor they left dimples, cracks and small, disjointed rocks.

Gilbert backed up, instinctively trying to cover Mr. Smith as the
bigger man tried to rise. "Mister Smith," yelled Gilbert behind him, his
eyes and body still facing the steam crab, "how do you kill this thing?"

"Heck if I know," he answered groggily. "They change the weak
spot every time!"

The crab was moving slowly, but was going to corner Gilbert and

Smith in a few more steps. "Come on!" yelled Gilbert, shoving the pistol into a pocket in his overalls, then grabbing his spear in one hand and Mr. Smith's hand in the other. Gilbert pulled them both into a shambling run past the crab. A huge, clumsy pincer swung in their direction, but was too slow.

"You could dodge them all day," said Smith, still hanging on to his own spear in a limp grip with his free hand, "but they don't get tired or run out of energy before you do. If the game goes longer than ten minutes, they give weapons to the audience, and then they begin taking shots at you."

Swell, thought Gilbert, running while leading the still-staggering Mr. Smith to the opposite end of the arena. They didn't need to run far; the arena was barely a hundred feet across. The crab would catch up to them in less than a minute. "Let me try this, then, if your spear didn't work!" Gilbert pointed the pistol and fired three quick shots. There was a clever little system of tiny, squiggly silver pipes on the barrel of the pistol that flared inside when he squeezed off a shot, cutting the pistol's recoil to almost nil.

The bullets slammed into the crab. Two dents appeared in the surface, and one of the bullets hit a pipe that started hissing as steam escaped. But the creature didn't slow down by so much as an inch. Gilbert inhaled. He could run around this thing for a short while, but he'd tire, and then the audience would get into the act. He felt very much like a little David versus a very large ...

Goliath!

"Smith! Mr. Smith! How does the pilot see us?"

"I don't know, Gilbert! The fellow comes from the lower levels. They all get into the crab blindfolded!"

A-ha! Had to move fast! The crab was closing in steadily, if slowly. Gilbert had maybe a half-minute left. Gilbert stepped back and leaned over to Smith's ear. "I've got an idea—give me one of your boots," Gilbert whispered.

Smith gave an odd look at the skinny, goggle-eyed boy, but nodded and slipped the tattered leatherwork boot off his foot and gave it to Gilbert.

Gilbert shoved the pistol back into his pocket, took the spear Norton had tossed him, and aimed it at the space directly to the left of the crab.

"Gilbert, if you aim there..." shouted Smith over the roar of the crowd.

"No matter what I do or say," Gilbert hissed into his ear again, "*do not move* unless you see me run too. Got that?"

Smith nodded, though he still looked confused.

"Ready?" Gilbert roared while facing the crab, "on three follow me and run for the other side. Ready?"

The crab paused, waiting. Gilbert slid his hand down the shaft of the spear until his palm firmly gripped the butt end of the weapon. Smith watched as Gilbert counted off loudly:

"Wuhhhhhhhnnnn ..." Gilbert held the spear aloft, barely keeping it balanced as he held it by the end.

"Twooooooooooo ..." Gilbert leaned his shoulders back on Smith, reached down with his free hand and ... took off his boot?

"THREE!" Gilbert yelled, flinging the spear. The metal pole spun end over end to the crab's left, making a clattering, clanging ruckus as it bounced and ricocheted off the stone and concrete floor. Gilbert tossed his boot in the same direction a second later with his other hand, spinning it like a skimming stone. Even over the roar of the crowd, Gil could hear it as it hit the floor with a series of hollow *thunks*, scuffing and skidding as it followed the loud spear on the crab's left side.

The crowd quieted somewhat at Gil's action. They'd seen many a would-be contestant attack the crab directly, and many a shot miss, but never had any gladiator attacked their opponent with a boot as a follow up to a spear, or with such an obvious intent to miss. The crab turned to its left, legs clanking and hissing, as it followed the source of the noise.

"Now," hissed Gil into Smith's ear, "you run to its right while I take it down!"

Smith needed no convincing. He ran gingerly past the crab's right, his own footsteps barely heard as the crowd surged its approval. Gilbert said a quick prayer to St. Michael and ran forward, making for the steamwork creature's back. Knowing there was a pilot on board, Gilbert had gambled that there would be a ladder of sorts behind it for a pilot to climb up and enter.

He was right! Gilbert grabbed the first rung of the ladder and hauled himself up. It wasn't easy. Though Gil was tall, his upper body strength still left much to be desired. He grabbed with both hands and jumped up as best he could while pulling up and bending his elbows.

Now ... a hand up on the next rung, and pull. Next rung, and pull ... he had to move quickly! Once the pilot figured out what Gil was trying, he could turn Gilbert into a bloody smear of abstract art by mashing him between the ladder and a nearby wall!

The cheering in the arena jumped up a notch. Gil guessed they'd never seen something like this! Now with his feet touching the ladder, Gil scampered up and made it to the top of the crab in five seconds. Out of danger from being squished on the wall, he gripped the top rung of the ladder on the rear of the crab while surveying the hissing pipes and steaming, angry legs on the side of the beast.

"Now," Gil said to himself, mumbling just a little, "if I was a pilot, I'd come in through ..." There was a jumble of pipes and levers on top of the crab, and Gil had to try several times before he found one shaped like a hatch lever, hinged to move, and wasn't too hot to touch. When he found one after his fourth try (his hand still smarting from his third try), he twisted, pulled, and opened the hatch.

Gil was surprised. Looking down, Gil saw the pilot at the helm was younger than Gil—likely not much more than a child. At the sound of the hatch opening, the child/pilot turned around to face Gil. The blindfold over his eyes made Gil pause for a second, but only a second. Leaving the safety catch on, Gil pulled the clunky pistol out of his pocket and put the barrel on the pilot's forehead. "The game's over, pal!" Gil barked in what he hoped was an assertive voice. The pilot agreed by raising his hands and speaking rapidly in a foreign language. Gil guessed it was some form of Spanish.

The crowd had already been cheering loudly. When the pilot raised his hands they raised their voices to a roar that was nearly deafening. At least several hundred people were in the stadium now, which had been built to hold only half as many. Word must have gotten around quickly about Gil's battle, and others must have rushed to see it!

Gil, still keeping his pistol trained on his captive, raised his head and waved his free hand at the people. Now, he thought smugly, I hope those bullies who tried to beat me up can see this! *Chesterdumb* ... ha! I showed 'em all!

On the balcony, Emperor Norton stood with his hands behind his back, his cigar sticking straight out of his bearded mouth. He reached forward and pulled his cigar out, tapping the ashes onto the floor while watching Gilbert restlessly.

"He really did pull it off, didn't he?" Norton said, only half expecting an answer.

"I told you he was quite capable under pressure, Emperor," the girl said, adjusting her glasses and tucking a lock of red hair behind her ear. Only sixty seconds ago, she hadn't been nearly as confident as she now sounded.

Chapter 61

"He felt the full warmth of that pleasure from which the proud shut themselves out; the pleasure which not only goes with humiliation, but which almost is humiliation. Men who have escaped death by a hair have it, and men whose love is returned by a woman unexpectedly, and men whose sins are forgiven them."
— GKC, *The Ball and the Cross*

G ilbert sank into the cushioned chair with a wheeze. The white stone walls in his new apartment gleamed a dull yellow—the sun would be setting soon. The apartment wasn't huge, but compared the barracks it was a little corner of paradise. Clean walls, a small shower stall and bathroom, and his own bed with covers instead of a loosely padded mattress that he shared with whoever had collapsed there in the last shift.

He even had a small writing desk, a lamp, and a cushy chair to sit in. He looked down and stared at the clothes he now wore.

After beating the steam crab, Gil's adrenaline had been running high. When the audience began screaming his name in a roaring, rhythmic chant, he felt like he could have taken on an army of Martian tripods barehanded. A plank had extended from the edge of the gladiator pit, and Norton had walked to the edge of it. The audience fell silent at the sight of him. He held his hand aloft and looked steadily at Gil. Gil looked up defiantly, breathing heavily, keeping his pistol carefully pointed at the now captive pilot.

Norton smiled and gave a 'thumbs up' gesture. The crowd cheered again! Norton turned and walked back off of the plank. Three guards appeared, brandishing nasty-looking, triple-barreled rifles.

Gil looked at them warily. "You mind telling me why I should go with you guys? I do have a gun and a stadium full of pretty excitable people here."

The lead guard smiled. It was the same one who had been on the transport with him to the Emperor's home. "That may be, sir. But we've got nine barrels filled with bullets to your three. And the people won't follow a corpse."

Gilbert took the point. He pointed his pistol up and let them take him to a room with pink walls. They left him alone in the room to sit on a bench and wait. First, the girl had come in, flanked by two guards on either side. They made small talk about life in the city, until Gil realized he felt calm again. He had just noticed the soft music playing in the background when Norton entered the room again. The Emperor was all smiles and congratulations, slapping Gil on both shoulders, telling Gil how proud he was of him, and let's finish the tour, shall we?

Gil had realized that there wasn't much of a point in arguing. Not for now, anyway. It would be like trying to make a chess move when you were already mated; Norton held all the pieces and they both knew it.

At least for now.

Gil had smiled and pretended to be an aw-shucks kind of happy, sneaking peeks at the red-headed girl to see if he was doing the right or wrong thing. Her face remained blank and impassive, save for one small smile she gave him when he'd decided to accept the Emperor's praise.

The walking tour had continued. One of the first stops had been to Norton's personal tailor. Gilbert had quickly traded in his dull red factory overalls for a suit far snazzier. They had suited him up in a new white dress shirt, black suit jacket, trousers, and a charcoal-colored waistcoat. The tailor fellow had even found accessories that matched Gilbert's considerable height, giving him a walking stick, cuff links and a watch and chain that circled his chest. Gil even received a new set of glasses, trading in the special ones that he'd carried throughout his adventures for a fashionable pince-nez, a set of lenses that perched on his nose with a set of soft pincers.

Not bad, Gil thought. *I could get used to this.*

The tour had encompassed all three levels of the city, and Gil quickly learned that each level was subdivided into many sub-levels and power groups.

Among the factory workers on Red level, he'd seen firsthand how workers who were physically strong enough to compete in the gladiatorial games had the highest place socially among their peers, while workers skilled with machines and other mechanical trades had been given better beds and food than the more artistic workers, like stone carvers or woodworkers.

The White level, next highest from the Red worker's floor, was where the *savants*, or smarter people, lived. Most of the students at the savant school slept two to each white-walled room. Adult savants often had a setup similar to Gil's current apartment, particularly if they were married with children. Still, even among the smart folks, men who could create medicines or mechanical marvels were given better living spaces and enjoyments than those skilled at literature or philosophy.

Blue level, the smallest of the three rings of city buildings, housed Norton's guards. Each man had black jackets and their own rooms, and specialized in various forms of security like crowd control, Vinci flying, or interrogation.

"You got any questions, son?" Norton had said, after showing Gil the windmill power stations, the huge factories that churned out everything from chairs and bowls to the giant mechanical crabs, and the vast network of tunnels, rooms, labs and classrooms throughout the entire city.

"Well, I guess it may seem obvious, Emperor, but ... well, where did all this come from? You don't just find a floating city on the ground, dust it off and then start it flying like it was a toy balloon. One man couldn't start this, no matter how rich he was. How did you get this?"

Norton had smiled. "Pretty simple on the face of it, son. I won it in a poker bet."

Gil paused. "A poker bet?" he said, as though he'd not heard properly.

"Yep. A rather wealthy fellow from the Mormon Church was more'n a little fixated on finding a very particular South American city. Said it helped prove his Bible right, or somesuch. Ennyways, I worked with an eye to swindling him out of a good chunk of his fortune. T'waren't easy, lemme tell you! But by dropping hints that I had an 'in' with special members of his Church, along with a number of forged documents, I made my way into his confidence.

"Thanks to a smattering of knowledge about his faith and a few bits of well-placed blackmail, I was all set to have him sign over his fortune to me as a means of escaping disgrace among his fellow Churchmen. When out've the alleyway comes this ... well, a very comely young lass with dark hair, pale skin, and a smile that could melt an arctic iceberg in January. She claimed to represent gentlemen of certain business interests who wanted to acquire the city, and apply certain scientific advancements to it.

"Well, the saying goes, you can't swindle a swindler; we know all the tricks. I had my ways of checking. While they covered their tracks well, I found the young lady truly did have some very powerful friends. And they were indeed interested in getting their mitts on the city, and having me run it. Then those four giant green balls with enormous chains attached showed up on self-driven freight cars. They had those blind workmen brought in from someplace in Ecuador (a whole village of blind people, can you imagine that? Makes shiftwork easy, though, since they don't follow a day or night schedule. And where're they gonna run to, even if they could get off this rock, hey?) Ennaways, a little work, a little elbow grease and an acceptable number of worker deaths, those giant spheres got charged with a bit of electricity and pulled the whole blamed city up in the air. The whole city, Gil my boy! Now who could say no to that, I ask you?"

"It'd be hard for anyone, Emperor."

"Durned right. Taking it was easy. Holding it, now, that's been hard. Still, slicking this place out from under a moral man was easier than you might think. A man with no morals usually can win against the man with morals, since a moral man is usually afraid to play dirty, or even more afraid of getting caught if he does fight as nasty as his opponents do. Ah, here we are!" he'd said. They'd arrived at an elevator door.

And Gil, for reasons that were still a complete mystery to him, had been given an apartment at the highest level of the city, in the large, white spire that was taller than any building Gil had ever seen. Had it been set up in New York, Gil guessed it would have been at least thirty floors high, maybe as many as forty or fifty. A winch-controlled elevator had pulled Gil, Norton and the girl up to the floor. The elevator door had opened to a curved hallway, where heavy, wooden, well-made doors seemed out of place against the white stone.

"Took us weeks to polish and sand out all the silly pictures and funny writin' on the walls, so's the place could look presentable," Norton had said. "The last owners were mighty odd artists, makin' people with big lips, loincloths, an' feathers in their heads an' all." He'd opened the largest door with a grand gesture, and Gil had gaped at the new room.

"What is this?" Gilbert had asked, almost afraid of the answer.

"Yours," Norton had said. "Ta-ta for now. Make yourself at home, son. Galatea will be up later to take you to supper. Won't you, dear?"

She'd smiled. Gil had no doubt that Galatea wasn't her real name, but it'd do for now. For now, Gil thought, why not play the game? "Well, I do declare," Gil said, adopting the mannerisms of the Emperor for a moment, "that sounds right nice of you, Emperor Norton."

Norton had smiled. He took another pull on the cigar, making it glow brightly, and blew a cloud of pungent smoke into the air. "Good job, son," he said quietly, then turned and left.

The girl had followed Norton out of the apartment. Gil had hoped for a secret wink or sign from her, but no such signal had come.

And so he'd sat in the cushy chair for a while, enjoying the quiet. There was a constant rush of wind from outside, but he'd spent the last little while living in a floating city. He didn't notice the wind now, anymore than a man living by a waterfall would notice the rushing of water. His window had shutters, but they were heavy, clunky wooden things set into the white stone window frame with drills and bolts. They were difficult to open, and when he managed to pry them open a crack, the view was so high he'd felt a sick fear he'd never known. Shutting the window instantly, he returned to his seat until the fear passed.

Now he looked at his clothes again, breathing slowly. He took the pince-nez off of his nose, breathed on the lenses and polished them against the cuff of his new suit. Yep, he could learn to like this life a fair bit. Provided they didn't drop him in anymore death pits with giant mechanical crabs, of course.

There was a knock at the door. Gil, suddenly feeling very tired, gave a loud, "Come in."

The door opened. It was the red-head.

Gilbert's eyes went wide. He jumped to his feet and stood politely, his earlier fatigue utterly forgotten. He started to speak, but she held up her hand to silence him.

"Follow me," she whispered with a smile, her eyes sparkling behind her glasses.

Gilbert suddenly felt very, very docile. He swallowed and nodded his head, forgetting that he was several inches taller than she.

She swept up her long brown skirt as she turned and left Gil's apartment. Gil followed, slowing only a moment to make sure his door was shut behind him as he left. He worried for a moment about locking it, but quickly remembered he had no key, neighbors, or any possessions of his own in the place.

He followed her quick steps down the hallway, trusting her completely. The city was a gigantic maze to him, and he had no guide whatsoever other than her. Norton had been kind, mostly, but the steam crab incident had left him unable to fully trust the man who called himself the Emperor of North America.

She'd found a door and a hidden stairwell. He followed her, up and down stairs lit by gas lamps and the occasional torch. Her shoes made soft tapping noises as they traveled floor after floor of stairs. The trip gave Gilbert the feeling of descending deep into the Earth, even though he knew they were still hundreds, perhaps thousands of feet above it.

"Where are we going?" Gilbert whispered. He received no answer, and asking twice more with louder whispers achieved the same result. He was just reaching for her arm when she opened another door and led him down a long, echoing hallway. The gaslights were here too, but dimly lit, giving an eerie glow to their walk. Gilbert saw odd etchings and writings on the walls; some looked as if they may have been ancient pictures, others like they were samples of writing chiseled into the rock. The writing was puzzling, but the pictures were more than a little disturbing—many depicting humans with animal heads, people being bashed in the head with clubs, or even children dying horribly with blank expressions on their faces.

As with the shutters of his room, the brown wooden doors set into the white stone walls looked very out of place, but Gilbert held his tongue. Anyone who'd seen his own choices of clothing would know he had no good reason to judge another's sense of taste!

The floor, though, had a fairly thin rug set over it, which muffled both their steps. "Look," said Gilbert finally, "I ... Galatea, if that's your name," he stopped moving, hoping she'd do likewise, "I'd really like some answers. Ideally from someone who *hasn't* tried to kill me?"

She kept walking as if she'd never heard him. Gilbert looked around, realizing he'd never counted the number of floors they'd walked up or down, or the number of doors from his apartment to the stairwell. If he let her get away, he could be a very long while getting back to the only place he'd felt even a little safe in the city!

She stopped at another door at the hallway's end, produced a large number of keys on a key ring and opened the door with a quick, efficient turn of one of them. The door opened to a gigantic, dark chasm, blocked off from almost all sunlight. A cool wind blasted Gilbert and his guide for a second or two, then calmed down. "Stay close," she said, "and keep your hands on the rails on both sides of the bridge as you cross."

"Bridge?" said Gilbert, trying hard not to sound as nervous as he suddenly felt.

The wind from the door was already calming while she spoke. Even as she approached the doorway and stepped through it, Gilbert thought she seemed a little hesitant as she put her delicate shoe on the bridge path.

From Gilbert's perspective, it seemed as if she had stepped into nothingness. But then her shoe stopped on something with a tap just loud enough to hear, which gave Gilbert enough confidence to follow her. The bridge was flat, with a cable frame that swayed in the breeze. Its floor was made from thin planks of metal maybe four feet wide, only wide enough for one person to go across comfortably. This suited Gilbert fine, since she'd still be walking in front of him. He gripped the rail on one side as she was already doing. He then used both hands on the cable rails and followed as quickly as he could, his eyes now adjusted to seeing with the small circle of dim light above them.

"This place is the main smokestack," she called over her shoulder as they neared the halfway point of the bridge. "Almost all of the areal refuse from the factories is routed up through here and out this chimney."

"Why isn't it running now?" Gil asked.

"Coffee break," she said. "The smog normally keeps folks from exploring what's beyond the bridge, and will help afford us some privacy."

Privacy? Gilbert thought. He gulped, feeling just a little warm under the collar. For the rest of the walk down the narrow aisle, the back of her white blouse mesmerized him. He hoped he wouldn't get his new suit dirty in this place—he felt that it would make him unworthy of her somehow.

Another door, this one apparently unlocked. She reached out to it, turned a brass doorknob and stepped in just as a growling, grinding noise began from below. "Quickly," she said, motioning to him with her hand, "the machines are starting up again. The place will be filled with soot!" He stepped forward and through the door, shutting it firmly behind them.

The new room was dark. The dimming sun had barely lit the chasm they'd just left, but here nothing was visible.

"Um ... are you ... Galatea? Are you there?" he asked. He couldn't feel the walls, and reached behind him for the door he'd just shut.

"Relax," he heard her voice from a few feet away, "you're quite safe here."

There was a metallic squeak and a hiss. Yellow-orange light sprang from a half-dozen lamps on the walls.

Gilbert looked around, his eyes widening. He was now in a large, circular hall without windows, perhaps a hundred feet in diameter. Unlike the rest of the city, this room had been thickly decorated with trees, hanging plants and bushes around the edges.

A soft gurgling sound reached his ears. He turned; the sound came from a fountain made up to look like a small oasis at the far end of the hall. Gilbert let out a low whistle, wondering what would come next. Every time he'd thought he'd seen everything, something even more extraordinary happened! Now, he was in the middle of a grove in the middle of a floating factory-city in the middle of the mountains in ...

Hey, wait a minute.

"You know, I wonder just what it is you make in these fac ... *whoa!*"

He'd turned to look for her, and found her standing behind him, watching expectantly through the large lenses of her glasses.

"I'm sorry, Gilbert. Did I startle you?" she said softly.

At the sound of her voice, Gilbert suddenly calmed down a great deal. Her large, blue eyes reached into a place within him that made him feel ... well, *funny* inside. With Frances, he'd felt confident, a sense of zest, like a swashbuckler ready to take on an army of buccaneers. But now he felt a very, very exciting kind of fear. A joyful fear. One he hoped would never end, but keep on being more joyful and fearful every second.

"You ... well, you ... that is, I ... I'm, well, I'm fine. I guess."

She smiled. Gilbert melted.

"Come here," she said, taking his hand. It seemed to Gilbert that her feet didn't even touch the ground. Instead she almost floated across the dance floor to a section of wall behind one of the huge pillars that held up the ceiling.

Gilbert was silent, afraid to speak lest he break the almost sacred sense of the place. The burbling water, the smell of the plants and flowers, all coupled with the dim gaslight made the place seem like a quiet nature scene in the early morning.

"Wait just a moment," she said, and walked to the wall without any further sound.

Her shapely hand found a small circle set into the wall with a handle on it. She turned the handle, and Gilbert heard a series of linked gears turning behind the wall. Each one must have interlocked with the other, calibrated so perfectly that although she was expending no more energy than needed to turn the knob on a child's music box, a wide curtain Gilbert had mistaken for a western wall of the hall split down the middle and parted.

Now, instead of a wall, there was a curved glass window, three stories high and several dozen feet long.

And through it, Gilbert saw the most dazzling sunset of his life.

The sun looked locked in place, the same red ball he'd seen in a thousand sunsets in his seventeen years. But to see it from this height, in a sea of clouds that looked as if they were on fire...

For Gilbert, this would always and forever remain the perfect sunset. A vision he knew he would take to his grave. In his mind, it would never set, immaculate, unchanging and unaging, like a picture of a pair of lovers on a Grecian urn he'd seen in a museum back in New York.

"Magnificent," Gilbert said in an awed whisper. He had never used that word on his own to describe anything before, but nothing else did justice to the vision in front of him.

She walked back to him and stood close. She was taller than Frances, and could have just kissed him if she stood on her toes.

She stood on her toes now, stretching up as high as she could, subtly guiding his head until her lips were just outside the border of his ear.

"Will you dance with me, Gilbert?"

Her breath made him feel warm and tingly. Thrills shot from his ear to his fingers and toes.

"I'd ... I'd love to, but I don't really know how."

"I will teach you," she said, removing her glasses and placing them in a hidden pocket. She smiled at him with two perfect rows of white teeth. "Place your arm on my waist, like this," she said, taking his hand and putting it against the waistline of her skirt. Gilbert hoped his hand wouldn't sweat. Right now he was more nervous than an alligator in a handbag factory!

"And, hold my hand, so," taking his other hand in hers. Even her hand looked beautiful and perfect, the nails painted the color of summer raspberries with the new-fangled nail varnish French chemists had bragged about in Berlin.

It was getting easier to control his breathing. He wondered if she could sense how nervous he was. A dozen rational questions fired through his mind: *Why have you led me here? Why were you in the factory the day I was promoted in London? Why were you on the train with me to save the engineer's life? Why were you in Paris last year, and why did you lead me on the chase through the streets of the city?*

And, most of all, why do I feel there is so much more about you that I know, but can't say?

"When the music begins," she said, whispering in his other ear now, "I will move slowly. You need only copy my movements, and follow my directions."

He could only nod dumbly.

Now he knew the name for his feeling—calming down a little had helped him analyze that much. He was *infatuated*, he knew. Knew it as sure as he was breathing. Ma had once caught him looking a little too long at one of the local girls in the store a few years back, and sat him down the same afternoon to explain the difference between love and infatuation.

"To adore someone, Gilbert," she'd said, "is wonderful. It's how things began with your father and I. But you are reaching an age where you may be tempted to believe that a young lady who is inaccessible to you may be Helen of Troy and the Blessed Mother of the Catholics, all rolled into one. And you may be tempted to trust such a woman, to get yourself into all manner of foolishness over her. But you *must resist doing so,* Gilbert. That kind of trust and bond cannot—*must* not be given to someone who hasn't pledged their life to you first. And that kind of pledge can only be given if you've known each other long enough to see each other at your best and worst. Infatuation is *selfish,* wanting to possess another for yourself. True love is an *action,* where you do and want only what is best for the beloved."

"Marie," said Gilbert's Pa, calibrating the scopes on his rifle in the living room, "good heavens, you'll scare the boy. After all, I'd be quite a bit more worried if girls weren't filling his head at this age. Besides, foolish love never did me any lasting harm."

"You, Pa?" Gilbert had said. The idea of his father being a lovestruck youth was a difficult one for Gilbert to imagine.

"Oh, yes, son," Pa said, winking at Ma. "I fell quite hard for a pretty lass a long time back. Met her through my work, and from that moment on I could think of nothing else. She was quite invasive. Wouldn't leave me alone for a second. Even insisted on inhabiting my dreams at night. And during the day, she was even worse. Just thinking of her made my pulse quicken and my head feel light. She was my world, and I would have taken on the weight of Atlas to make her mine."

"What happened Pa?"

"I married her," he said offhandedly, "and had thr ... had a wonderful son. She gave me *a* wonderful son."

Gilbert had been a bit puzzled by his father's gaffe and the sharp look Ma had given Pa, but let it go. Ma had recovered quickly, and talked about how love was a verb, infatuation an adjective. Love was made of actions, infatuation made of changeable feelings, and so on.

But a lot of it had, for the moment, faded away.

Now, Gilbert knew that while he may have love for Frances, he was infatuated with a brilliant, mysterious red-headed girl with a name that could only be phony. *Any sane person would know the potential for tragedy in such a situation,* he thought, *but then, I'm not sane now. What's more, I'm* glad *I'm not!*

In the background, stringed instruments began to play strains and melodies that were very familiar, but Gilbert couldn't be bothered to sort them out. His throat had turned to a thick, warm paste, making speech impossible. His eyes were as securely stuck to the visage of the red-head as a dead bug to a card. He could feel every line and curve of her hand, arm, and waist against his own. And he never wanted to stop.

"Beautiful, ain't it Bilgewater?" said Norton. He was watching one of the screens set up especially in his throne room for this occasion. A series of lights, reflective lenses and mirrors beamed the image of the two young people onto the screen. The savants on White level were getting better all the time—he could even see the dizzyingly-in-love expression that Gilbert had on his face as he began to dance with her.

"Yessir," said Bilgewater, sighing and never taking his eyes off the screen. The scene made him long for the innocent days of his own youth, and for a girl whose name and face he'd never forgotten.

"If only," said Norton, mostly to himself, "look at the purity of his feeling, Bilgewater. He's fallen for her completely. If only I could go back to when I could feel that way about anything. Wouldn't that be something?"

"Yessir," sighed Bilgewater a second time.

"I agree," said Norton, smoking his cigar while his own eyes watched both Gilbert and Galatea, envying the looks of adoration the two young people gave to each other. "By the way, you're fired. Go back to Red level and turn in your uniform. I can't trust a man as easily moved to tears as you."

"Yessir," said Bilgewater, too lost in memory to be upset by his demotion. He turned and left the Emperor with his thoughts.

As she moved, showing him what he thought might be a waltz, the sunset formed a dazzling backdrop for her head through the wall-sized window. She stopped the dance for a second to pull a pin out of the bun in her hair, and with a small shake of her head her fiery locks flowed like a crimson river down her shoulders to the midpoint of her back. It made her even more radiant in Gilbert's eyes, elevating her from a beautiful, mysterious girl to a sun-goddess. She blazed in perfection like a feminine Apollo, shining in beauty like a pale-skinned Aphrodite, standing tall in stature and confidence like a red-headed Juno.

Now her face grew serious, and her eyes locked on Gilbert's own. Her eyes were deep as pale, icy seas. Had she commanded Gilbert to jump off a cliff onto a reef of razor blades, he would have done so without hesitation if it meant a few more seconds of staring into those deep, blue pools. Music piped through invisible channels to the chamber, caressing Gilbert's ears with melody.

She asked a youth who chanced a-long,
And the moral question was solved in a trice,
For he answered Oh, maid-en, it may be wrong,
But, here he proved it 'Tis very nice,
Ve-ry nice,
Ve-rrrrrrry niiiiice.

The song was reaching its end, the closing strains of the piece sounding through the hall as she stretched up to Gilbert, closing her eyes most of the way and parting her lips so slightly, he could feel and smell her breath upon his face.

Thoughts tried hard to cram into his head, but he shunted them away. He wanted to experience this without any attempt to analyze, categorize, or weigh options. He only wanted to feel, feel *now* and remember. Remember the touch of her hand, the sight of the sunset on her hair, the sound of water and whispering plants. Remember *all* of it, and never forget.

The last note of the violin sang through the air as Gilbert closed his own eyes and leaned forward slowly.

"Oh," she said when their lips were only a millimeter apart, "Oh no! It's all wrong!"

She pushed him away and ran from the hall to the doorway.

Gilbert stood in his position for a full five seconds before he realized she was gone. He straightened himself and scratched his head like a man awakening from a deep, dreamy sleep.

What happened, he thought.

Where did she ... he looked up and saw the door swinging shut.

Oh, no.

Oh *NO!*

Chapter 62

"It is not calculated to promote prosperity to have a Bull in a china shop." – GKC, *The Flying Inn*

Johnny, what on Earth are you doing?" asked Jack, holding a lit candle in the air.

Johnny looked up from his latest project to the smaller boy, putting down the pliers in his right hand and adjusting his goggles for a better look. The candle flame stood tall and almost unmoving, reflected in Jack's thick glasses. Jack could have been any chubby boy waking in the night, dressed in a blue nightshirt, robe, and a pair of battered slippers with his hair askew.

Johnny grunted something and ducked back down to his project, which looked like a large metal backpack with a series of hoses sprouting from its lower side.

"Johnny," continued Jack, "do you recall that I am the prefect for our section of the dormitory? Do you recall the forms of punishment that await those I report? Even for so simple an infraction as refusing to sleep when the lights are extinguished?"

"So report me, Jack. I told my teachers I was in a mood to tinker. Fine, they said. You can't schedule genius, they said. So if'n it's good enough for the teachers, it oughta be good enough for you. And if it isn't, maybe someone should tell about how you and Tollers are reading and editing each others' stories about talking animals, magic rings and the guys with the furry feet, all after lights out?"

Jack blinked, his mouth open slightly as if someone had poked him in his stomach. "I ... I ..." he spluttered, "That is something completely different! I was doing research!"

Johnny took off his goggles and looked at Jack. "Look, Clive, I want to finish this invention. Tonight. I won't tell about you breaking lights out if you don't turn me in either. Deal? Now I don't want to be rude, but quit distracting me, please!" he said, focusing on his machine while he reached for another crescent wrench.

"What exactly are you working on, Johnny?" Jack said, eager to change the subject. He adjusted his glasses with his left hand and walked behind Johnny's project with him, adding his candlepower to the small gaslight bulb that dangled above them both.

"Mister Gilbert told me never to stop trying to get out. In case I have to leave, this invention," said Johnny, as much to his creation as to

Jack, "is insurance to keep me and others safe."

Jack waited, holding the candle and looking at Johnny with an attitude of expectation. True, most people got annoyed when he stared at them and waited for an explanation, but that mattered little to Jack. People generally found something to be annoyed with him about anyway, and this way he could at least usually get whatever he was after.

Johnny stopped his tinkering for a moment. "You know what, Jack?" He said, pulling his goggles off his face and positioning them above his eyes.

"What's that?"

"Jack, you've brought back some memories of a few folks who worked in my father's lab. These were folks who really had no clue how irritating they could be. Others knew but didn't care, so long as they got their way. There was only one way to deal with either kind of person if you wanted a couple of minutes alone."

"Really? Do tell. I find myself often annoyed by a number of these cretins in our school."

"Well," said Johnny, "first, you turn one of these dials." Here he picked up what looked like a small rifle, and turned a metal dial on its barrel. The cords and tubes that ran from the large pack ended at the butt end of the gun.

"Johnny," Jack said with an edge of fear in his voice, "what are you doing?"

"A field test," chirped Johnny with a happy tone in his voice. He raised the mechanism to his chest level, pulled back a large lever like the string on a bow, and pointed it at Jack. "Ready, Clive?"

"Don't call me that!" Jack barked. "No one calls me that! Not even if they have a...a..."

"A gun?" Johnny said helpfully with a smile.

"I ... I do think it's time I were going. As a matter of fact, I ... AUUUUUGGHH!"

Johnny had pulled the trigger.

A spout of salty water sprang from the gun barrel, splashing Jack in the face.

"Why'd you do that?" Jack spluttered. The water was still traveling in an arc-shaped trickle, now splattering his feet.

"Oh, sorry Jack. It's really supposed to do this," Johnny said, releasing the lever he'd pulled and held on the barrel. As the lever slid back to its starting position, a bolt of electricity leapt from Johnny's gun-bow, swirling around the spout of water and striking at Jack's feet with a snap that smelled like a thunderstorm.

Jack screeched, and ran out the door of Johnny's room. His now soaked slippers left wet splotches on the white stone ground, with tiny pieces of charred cotton and leather mixed in with the footprint-sized puddles.

Johnny smiled. That had gone better than he'd hoped. Jack wasn't a mean fella, really; just clueless. He also had the loosest lips of anyone in the savant school. When word got around that Johnny had zapped Jack, he'd not only be popular among the students who despised Jack on a regular basis, but he also might even become king of the tinkering crowd, and no longer be bothered by that upperclassman with the pretentious last name of Swift.

All in a good night's work.

Chapter 63

"Slavery may be normal and even natural, in the sense that a bad habit may be second nature."
– GKC, *What I Saw in America*

Herb's walking had settled into a steady rhythm in the first five minutes. Over the next hour as the sun set, he was unusually quiet as Margaret led the way across the cooling, semi-desert wilderness. He was in second place, with the three cowboys bringing up the rear.

The squeak of Harper's leg distracted him at first, and then, after an hour, became an excruciating annoyance. Somehow everyone grew to endure it, just as they endured carrying the twenty-pound backpacks while they made the hike in the gathering darkness. Herb noted dimly that none of the cowboys had made a single complaint. Not even the old one. The closest any of them had come to making a sound about their burdens was to sigh a few times from relief when the town came into view.

As they drew closer, Herb could make out a group of buildings in sore need of repair. By the time they entered what was left of the town square, Herb and the other men in the group realized they'd been led into a ghost town. Buildings had been shattered by exploding shells, prim and proper on one side while blasted into utter ruin on the other. They could tell from the exposed and looted remains inside of each building what it had been. This had been the general store; that had been a church. The most imposing structure looked to have been a courthouse, with broken Doric columns holding up half of a triangle-shaped roof. "Where are we?" Herb whispered, though there seemed no real need for silence.

"We're in the ruins of the town of Placerville," Margaret said. "Largely forgotten in the Slave Wars, it was one of the bloodiest stalemates in the war. A fellow named Ingram led a group of Partisan Rangers to steal gold and silver for the Confederates. He became quite good at it; so good, in fact, that a Union detachment was sent to bring his head back to Washington. By the time he arrived, the Confederate press had dubbed him the Robin Hood of the Confederate cause, and volunteers and miscreants came out to join him by the hundreds.

"At the time, Placerville was so isolated from the rest of the Americas that they didn't get word of Lincoln's assassination or

Johnson's surrender until it was nearly a month old. In all the hoopla, this isolated little pimple on the edge of the Confederacy ended up being the death of nearly five thousand Union troops, Partisan Rangers and civilians. The town itself was smashed to pieces and never rebuilt."

"Why fight this much over something so far away?"

"The press, Herbert dear. In their efforts to sell more papers, they made out Ingram to be far more than he really was. The fight itself was a bloody stalemate with Ingram getting a bullet in his back. The Union commander, a drunk named Grant, was shot in his tent the night before. In the end the only real winners of that battle were a number of newspapermen who became very, very rich over the papers sold through their exaggerations. Quite funny, really."

"Yeah. A laugh riot," Finn said with a grunt. "We gonna meet your friends here, or what?"

"The forces of Emperor Norton will be passing by soon," Margaret said with a bright smile, now barely visible in the moonlight. "When they do, I will tell you what you need to do in order to hitch a ride. In the meantime you can get some rest, play poker or do whatever you wish until their arrival. Only keep your packs on; we won't have much time when I spot them."

"Wait a minute," growled Finn. "Did you say Emperor Norton?"

"Yes. Joshua Norton the First, self-declared Emperor of North America. Had you heard of him before?"

Doc Holiday rubbed his eyes with a weary gesture. "Norton an' me," Finn said, ignoring Doc, "we go way, way back. Back to when I was a young'un, and he was a two-bit con man called the Duke. If we've got the same man in mind, him and I got us a half-century's worth of scores to settle."

After an awkward silence and a signal from Finn, Holiday took a sleeping position on the ground using his arm as a pillow. Finn did likewise. Harper sat morosely with his back to a broken wall, staring first at the sky, then at his colleagues falling asleep almost instantly in a contended ring, now at Herb and Margaret, the two still standing in front of the blasted, gutted courthouse.

"You look deep in thought, Herbert. What's on your mind?"

"I was reading the inscription," he said, looking at the slab of stone set up against the wall of the courthouse. The inscription was written on the base of the blindfolded statue of Lady Justice.

"Our new government" read Margaret aloud, "...its foundations are laid, its corner-stone rests upon the great truth, that the Negro is not equal to the white man; that slavery—subordination to the superior race—is his natural and normal condition. This, our new government, is the first, in the history of the world, based upon this great scientific, philosophical, and moral truth."

Herb ignored her and read the rest aloud, "Andrew Stephens First Vice-President of the Confederate States of America and Second President of the Confederate States of America, March 21, 1861."

"President Stephens," said Margaret. "He was quite the blowhard. But it certainly did strike a chord with all who mattered in the CSA. Every schoolchild south of the Mason-Dixon line is required to memorize that speech by the end of first grade, or they aren't allowed to advance. He had some of the right ideas, of course. But in the end they've all proven far too timid. They thought that by using twisted Christianity and enslavement they could put the Negroes to good use. A bunch of nonsense, of course; they just didn't have the courage to do what needed to be done."

"And what was that again?"

"Why, the outright elimination of the Negro, of course! Why enslave them, when we can now make machines to do our work for us? Machines that will never complain or procreate unpredictably, and certainly won't infect the purer races with their own filthy bloodlines."

Herb smiled, and looked at the stars. "Margaret, this trip has opened my eyes to a number of things. Not the least of which why I'm stronger than you."

"What?" she barked.

Herb kept talking as if he hadn't heard. "I was raised without the slightest bit of religion in my life. My parents called themselves 'free-thinkers,' which only meant they were only free of any influences that challenged their worldview. Because I was raised with that kind of hypocrisy, I can see it so much more easily in you and your set. You rail against everything decent in the world, not because you think it's right, but precisely because you know it's wrong. Wrong in the eyes of those who follow God, and God Himself."

"I don't believe in God, Herbert!"

"That's funny. I hear that a lot from your lot, especially in the universities and the artist's salons. But how can you spit so much hate and venom at someone you don't believe in? I never hear of anyone acting that way towards Father Christmas."

"Father Christmas isn't holding back the human race!"

"Save it for the little children you're trying to lead astray,

Margaret. You hate that God isn't whom you wanted Him to be, or you're angry with one of His followers. You choose not to believe out of emotion and resentment, not logic.

"And that's why I'm stronger than you, Margaret. All of you. I thought at first to abandon God completely, but that's illogical. Gil's talks about Thomas Aquinas puts paid to that rot. You can't defeat an enemy by denying He exists. Instead, you admit He's there, find the source of their strength, and sap it up. Since I can't escape God, I'll convince others there's no God to dry up His supply of followers.

"Since my chance at Heaven's been lost, I'll have to hope the other side will find me useful enough to spare me the torments I deserve. If indeed I'm damned to Hell, perhaps I can lessen the pain, or avoid it altogether. I'm going to cling to the hope that the other side will win, and bring about the kind of change that will put a man like me on top of things in the next world, rather than Father Brown or Gil. It's a dim, small hope, but it's all I have now."

While Herb spoke, a subtle difference took over his demeanor. A cruel rigidity came into his speech, with an edge as keen as a headsman's axe. Worse, Herb's eyes had always had the bright quality of diamonds in the sun even when angry. Now they looked like they were nearly all pupils, with very little white visible in the darkness. The whole change chilled Margaret like nothing she could remember, though she would never admit it. "We should get some rest," she said. "I'll set up our alarum." She removed a gadget from her pack and opened it. It was a small box cage with a single pigeon inside of it. A tiny bell inside the cage was attached to a small megaphone. "Little Argus here will awaken us when our ride gets near."

"You're going to sleep, Margaret? Is that wise? Those cowboys aren't big fans of yours."

"No, but they do want to get paid. They worship their jobs, and for the moment they know their only ticket to completing it rests on my being alive. That goes for you, too, if you're entertaining any more homicidal thoughts."

Following the cowboys' example, Margaret lay down on her arm and was soon breathing heavily.

Herb looked at her sleeping form, contemplating just the sort of thoughts she'd suggested. Sighing, he laid down a few feet away and slept. The stars in the clear sky looked down on the entire group, unblinking, as they passed overhead.

Chapter 64

"The world cannot keep its own ideals. The secular order cannot make secure any one of its own noble and natural conceptions of secular perfection. That will be found, as time goes on, the ultimate argument for a Church independent of the world and the secular order." – GKC, *What I Saw in America*

I messed up somehow! The thought beat around inside Gilbert's head as he tore after her, his long legs eating up the distance between him and the door she'd left through.

He ran through the door with no memory of even turning the knob. Once in the deserted hallway, he heard her feet clacking on the hard stone floor. His feet clomped in the corridor as he followed her down the hall and through another door.

Now he was in a smaller room where a number of makeshift tables were set up. Whatever purpose the room had once served, it now appeared to be a small cantina. A bar was set up against one wall, the wood looking mismatched against the ancient stonework of the rooms and hallways.

She was standing in there with her back to him, leaning on one of the tables with both her arms and her head down, her body shaking with nearly silent sobs.

Gilbert stood still. He knew he'd just entered the emotional equivalent of a minefield; the slightest misstep could make everything blow up in both their faces.

Was she angry at him? Did she need a hug? Her accent wasn't exactly American. British people didn't hug much when they were upset. She seemed ... not British. Not exactly. What would Herb ... no, Herb's advice only helped when you wanted to manipulate someone.

What did Ma do when he came home crying?

He said a prayer, breathed twice and walked up behind her. He raised one hand. After a few false starts, he placed it gently on her shoulder.

She paused in her tears. Her head rose a bit, then bowed and started crying again.

Gilbert put his other hand on her left shoulder. She gave a kind of cough and straightened her body a bit. She crossed her right hand across her chest, resting her hand on top of his.

"Did I ..." he whispered, finding it hard to tear his eyes away from the ornate ring on her finger. It looked like a diamond surrounded by five purple stones. "If I did something wrong," he said quietly, "whatever it was ..."

"Oh, no. No, no, no," she said, shaking her head and still facing away from him. "No, you've done nothing wrong. Just the opposite. You're ... you're *good*, Gilbert. You're so good. I ... I like you a great deal. I might even say that I find myself ..."

Gilbert's heart leapt.

" ... but I can't do this. I can't do what they want me to do."

"They?"

She turned to face him, the tears staining her cheeks as her beautiful, perfect blue eyes stared into his.

"They want me to manipulate you. And they want this city for themselves, after it's served its purpose."

"Who's they? And what's the purpose they want the city for? And what is it they wanted you to do?"

She looked at him for a second, then to the side and wept again. Fresh, silent tears fell while she avoided Gilbert's gaze.

Oboy, Gilbert thought. He let her go for a second to grab a chair and put it behind her. "Please, Gal ... please, sit down for a second."

She sat, wiping her eyes with her hand. "Could you use a drink?" he asked. She nodded her head. "There's a faucet and glasses behind the bar," she said. "Just water, please."

Gilbert looked a little closer at her. "You sure you don't want anything harder? Back where I'm from, a person's under that much stress, they need a relaxant."

"Water'd be the same thing. Norton dilutes the liquor in the city so no one will get up enough liquid courage to start a mob riot."

"Okay. Wait here."

He found the faucet and glasses behind the bar. The faucet was a little tricky to figure out, until he realized he had to push a plunger a few times before it would work. He filled two goblets with water and brought one to her. She downed it in one, long gulp and set the goblet on the table. He took it and handed her the second, full goblet he'd planned to drink himself.

She sipped the second glass rather than gulping from it this time. He sat at the chair next to her, watching her with a mixture of adoration and concern. When she finished, she put down her glass and stared at him intently. "Gilbert," she said, "I think it is time I was honest with you. As honest as I can be for now, at least. Ask me any question you have, and I'll answer if I can."

Gilbert thought for a second.

"You mentioned *them*," he said. "Do you mean the Special Branch?"

"Yes." She nodded her head while biting her lip, closing her eyes and looking at the tabletop.

"Are you friends with the Doctor?"

"No. I despise him, though I have had to work with him in the past."

"I remember. I saw you and him on the train together just when the Martians landed. That time, you saved the engineer from a heart attack with the Doctor's Franklin Rod."

She fidgeted in her chair.

"He said you were a quarry of his," Gilbert said, "back when we were in the tunnels underground dodging Martians. What was that about?"

"He has desired me for his own, and arranged my *selection* for him by our masters. But I have managed to evade him by being away on assignment when he pursued me."

"Has he ever ... caught you?"

"No. He was reassigned elsewhere about a year ago. I'm not certain where. If I never see that toad again it'll be too soon."

"Who are you?"

"You've heard what Norton calls me."

"I know he calls you Galatea. But that's not your name, is it? That was the name of a girl in Greek mythology. A sculptor named Pygmalion carved a glorified doll-woman out of stone, and he fell in love with it. Aphrodite felt sorry for the guy and brought the statue to life when he kissed it. It's a good name for someone who has to keep changing who she is to match other people's illusions."

"Where in Minnesota did you go to school again?"

"At home, when I was lucky. And you didn't answer my question about who you are."

"I will later. It's in your best interests, trust me."

"Fine. What's going on here, then? Not just with you and Norton, but the whole city?"

"The city is a remarkably well-preserved piece of architecture from South America. A green-colored compound called Cavorite holds it aloft. It was discovered by a Belgian scientist, and is a compound with remarkable anti-gravitational properties. Add a large number of windmills for power, a few indoor farms, factory equipment and other amenities, and we had the basis for a self-sustaining colony in the air.

"Then, Norton came on the scene. My masters in the Special Branch had heard about the city, its unearthing and adaptation by a Utah businessman named John Jarvie several years ago. For rather arcane reasons, he felt the city and some of the more ancient symbols on its walls validated the more esoteric parts of his belief. All in all, the city has been the better part of a decade and a half in the making. It's only escaped notice because so much was done in South America, where most Americans and Europeans couldn't care less about its happenings or dealings.

"The circle of men who are my masters assigned me to work my way into Norton's confidence, seeing an opportunity to use the city at some point to control others; perhaps as a mobile base."

Gilbert furrowed his brow. "What do your people want with it? Or with me? Did you have anything to do with me being promoted here, like I think you did back at my clacker job in London?"

"Your promotion from clacker to journalist was a result of my efforts, yes. As for what Norton wants with you, I haven't the foggiest idea. As for the city, that," she said, standing with her composure returned, "I can now show you. Follow me."

"Well," he said, "about what we were going to ..."

"No time, Gilbert! We're going to be underway soon!"

She stood and walked down towards another hallway. Her agitation and amorousness of the last few minutes were both gone like an icicle in an Alabaman August. Gilbert followed her dutifully, grinding his teeth over his latest frustration. Why couldn't the unpleasant things in his life get interrupted all the time?

"Underway?" he said, his long legs still trying hard to keep up with her quickening pace. "What do you mean underway? Where are we going? Do you have an airship or something we're going to escape in?"

"Not an airship, Gilbert. The entire city will be moving soon. We're already in the air; it'll take surprisingly little energy to fire up the engines and point us to Richmond."

"Richmond? Why would you want to go to the capital of the CSA? Norton doesn't keep any slaves that I can see."

"They want enslavement of a different kind, Gilbert. Norton thinks he's going to attack the Confederate capital, and free the slaves. The punchcards used to program his metal men have all been tampered with. In short, his attack is certain to fail. And when it does, there is evidence planted here to suggest that the USA was behind the aggression. The other four Americas will break off the unification talks, and ..."

"What?" Gilbert yelped. "Unification? The Five Americas are going to unite? So *that's* why they're meeting in Richmond! My editor was talking about it!"

"Yes, and that has the Special Branch worried, Gilbert. A united America could be a threat to their plans. If they can keep America divided, they will be easier to control."

"How? Are they going to bring back slavery?"

"Not likely. There are other ways to control people, Gilbert."

"Like what?"

She didn't answer this last question, but instead opened another door while holding a finger to her lips.

Gilbert's jaw dropped.

The door had opened to a huge factory floor.

On the factory floor facing them was a row of perhaps a hundred machines, shaped roughly like humans, but with dome-shaped heads, goggle-eyes, a pincer-claw for a right hand and a pistol-like weapon for a left.

Gilbert remembered the mechanical man he'd read about in the newspaper clipping on the train, just before the Martians landed. He also remembered the half-finished models that had been in the Brainerd family lab back in New York.

Behind the first row was a second row.

Behind the second row were more rows.

Gilbert tried to count the rows, but there were too many.

And towering above the uncountable rows of metal men were even larger creatures of wood and metal, similar to the one Gilbert had dealt with over the New York City skyline.

And above them, in this truly enormous underground hanger, were over a dozen airships, several of them the two-blimp, platform-between-them kind that Gilbert had seen employed by the Special Branch's forces in their last, doomed battle against the aliens.

"Saint Michael," Gilbert whispered.

"This is the main part of his army, Gilbert," she said. "This is what the factories have been churning out. War equipment. Munitions. Mechanical automatons without the ability to disobey orders or be swayed by mercy. They are powered by steam and controlled by a combination of alien technology wedded to smaller, more potent versions of the analytical engines you once worked with. Workers like you produced parts in the city proper, and blind workers in the bowels of the city assembled them. Neither group has the slightest idea of the city's real purpose."

"What about me?" Gilbert said, still staring at the mechanical army. "Norton seems to have taken a particular interest in me. Where do I fit in to all this craziness?"

"Where indeed?" said a jolly, familiar voice behind them.

Chapter 65

"Comforts that were rare among our forefathers are now multiplied in factories and handed out wholesale; and indeed, nobody nowadays, so long as he is content to go without air, space, quiet, decency and good manners, need be without anything whatever that he wants; or at least a reasonably cheap imitation of it."
– GKC, *Commonwealth*, 1933

"Wake up, Finn," Herb said, nudging the large man with the toe of his hiking boot.

Finn moved quickly, grabbing Herb's boot before it had reached Finn's shirt. "I've been awake, kid, ever since you came within ten feet of me," Finn said with a smile. "It's a little skill you get growing up on the street. Every now and then I put myself in danger just to keep myself sharp."

"I'm very impressed. Can I have my foot back now?"

Finn smiled and let go. Herb stepped back as Finn rose up from the dirt like a dark, fairytale giant. How on Earth did a man who'd spent his early years eating out of garbage cans survive this long, let alone get to be so large? He must have made up for lost meals when he joined the army, or perhaps his parents had both been brutishly large and he'd won the hereditary lottery.

"Well, what's our next step?" Finn said, brushing the dirt off his duster jacket. "Did the little lady give us any marching orders?"

"Only that I should wake you all, and that we need to get our packs on again if they slipped off in your sleep. Whatever ride Gilbert has hitched himself to is due to pass by here in the next few minutes."

"Sounds dandy. Hang on—I've gotta take care of some business, first."

Herb rolled his eyes and turned back to the camp.

When he was alone, Finn turned his back on the group and pretended to relieve nature. What he really did, though, was unbutton his shirt and expose his chest to the sky.

Attached squarely in the middle of his chest was a small contraption that looked like a clock. Growing out of it were a dozen small pipes, two small fuses nestled in a small receptacle, and a dial with two depressed sections where fingers could hold it. Finn inhaled, gripped the dial with his index finger and thumb, and turned. After a pause, he turned it again. Pause. A third turn. Pause. A half turn and he was done. He buttoned his shirt back up, held his wrist and counted for a minute. Satisfied, he turned to rejoin his crew.

No telling how long this new mission might be, he said to himself. No way to know how long this stage of the mission might last. Since he'd taken a wound in the chest from a stray bullet two years back, he'd never let his heart wind down in the middle of a mission. Danged if he was gonna start today!

Chapter 66

"The demagogue succeeds because he makes himself understood, even if he is not worth understanding. But the mystagogue succeeds because he gets himself misunderstood; although, as a rule, he is not even worth misunderstanding. "
– GKC, *All Things Considered*

Emperor Norton had slid up behind them totally unheard. The old guy would've been a great schoolteacher!

"Where indeed," he said a second time, walking slowly between them and lighting up another cigar. Gilbert looked at Galatea. She'd already put her glasses back on, and was stealing quick glances at Gilbert that were shot full of fear.

Gilbert guessed she was thinking the same thing he was. What had the old man heard? Did they dare try to break and run, or see if they could bluff past him?

"You know, you two young rascals," he said, smiling at them as he stood back to look at them both. "I had a feeling you two might've known each other from before."

The Emperor was smiling, but Gilbert could sense that there was a test in the words. *He's sure we knew each other. He found out, either from our glances or from other sources. He's trying to find out if we'll lie about it or not,* he thought.

So, why lie?

"You're right as always, Emperor," said Gilbert, going back into the brash mode of speaking he'd used at the steam crab arena. Mirroring your audience was a technique he'd learned to help put folks at ease when he interviewed them. Maybe it would work a second time. "I figured out a little while back that Galatea and I here shared a train ride a little over a year back a'fore the squids dropped on England. Yep, we knew each other. And I'm happy to say she appears to've recovered from meeting me quite nicely."

"Indeed!" Norton chuckled. "Quite so. Heh." His laughing voice quieted. "Galatea, leave us please. Gilbert and I have business to discuss."

"Will you be needing me at all af ..."

"No, Galatea," Norton said, without looking at her. He'd used a tone that shut out any more discussion. "You may return to your rooms until I send for you. Now, Gilbert," he said, turning to Gil and giving him a light tap with his cane, "walk with me for a few minutes, son. I've got some other things to show you."

Norton closed the door to his huge mechanical army and walked Gilbert through more corridors and tunnels lit by either gas lamps or the occasional electric light. After a few minutes they came to a door with a guard in front of it. Like Norton's elite, he was dressed in a leather jacket, goggles over his forehead and a pepperbox pistol in a holster at his right side. He snapped to attention as Norton and Gilbert rounded the corner.

"One side, Ernst," Norton said. The guard moved sideways, saluting as Norton breezed through the door with Gilbert in tow.

The room was large, twenty feet on each side. It was made of the same white stone as the rest of the city, but with a lot of transplanted American furniture in it. A single gas lamp kept the room dimly lit.

In the center of the room was a young man Gilbert's age, only shorter, stockier and with stringy black hair. He was tied to the chair at his arms, waist and legs, and was blindfolded.

Norton looked at Gilbert. Smiled through the cigar in his teeth and raised his eyebrows once to give himself a knowing look. He leaned down and pulled off the blindfold.

When he could see again, the seated young man blinked, looked at Norton then at Gilbert. A sly look crossed his face, and he smiled like a fox that'd just been let into the henhouse.

"Good to see you again, Emperor," he said, in a voice that made Gilbert think of sour honey.

"How are you, Victor?" Norton said. He could have been greeting an old friend rather than a captive.

"The accommodations here are adequate," the young man said. His voice sounded like one that had been used to the finer things in life. "All the comforts of home, really. If you happen to live in a sewer."

"Look at this fellow, Gilbert," said Norton. "Trussed up like a tree at Christmas, and he's still got to act like he can put me on the defensive. Ain't he a good'un?"

Gilbert smiled. He wasn't sure if anything else was safe right now. Gilbert didn't want to say or do anything that would set Norton off. Maybe if he played along just enough.

"This feller," the Emperor continued, "tried to stage a coup. He tried to rally some of the workers of the city against me. Trouble was a different group with the same idea heard about it and turned him in.

Truly boring, really. Just a standard plan of skulk-with-knives in the dark, assassinate the leader, and then have everyone wake up with a new Emperor. How int'resting is that? Hm? Sad, really. I had such high hopes for you, Victor m'boy. Managed to sell the Eiffel Tower to scrap dealers, but couldn't keep your friends' mouths shut. I thought that in your decidedly amoral nature you could at least prove an entertaining apprentice."

"Tragic, isn't it? When is my execution, Emperor?"

Norton smiled. "Still tryin' to run the show, right to the end." Norton pulled a pistol from inside his jacket and held it to the boy's temple.

Victor's cool look evaporated like frost in a Georgia summer. He gasped, breathing faster with his eyes closed.

Then, after five seconds, when no gun went off, he opened one eye and looked sideways at Norton. Norton smiled through his whiskers.

"Are you giving me a chance at a few last words, or perhaps a last smoke?"

Norton stood and looked at the ceiling, toying with his gun with a look on his face like he was performing long division in his head.

"Well, now that you mention it ..."

"Or, perhaps, before you kill me, you could tell me what all this is about?"

"Or maybe," interrupted Gilbert. Maybe, Gil thought, he could buy some time for this poor fellow! "you could kill him a different way. After all, if someone tries to overthrow the Emperor of all of North America, isn't shooting too good for such a person?"

Norton thought a moment. "Nope," he said, pointed his pistol and fired.

Chapter 67

"None of the modern machines, none of the modern
paraphernalia... have any power except over the people
who choose to use them."
– GKC, *Daily News*, July 21, 1906

Packs on?" Margaret chirped happily. "Good. Make sure the strap across your chest is also fastened securely! All ready?"

No one answered.

"Yes, well, good. When Gilbert's ride comes by ..."

"What's he comin' in on?" Holiday asked. "I failed to notice any evidence of a stagecoach schedule at the remains of the local courthouse. We've no prospects for company here save for the man in the moon."

"Yes, well, about that... "

"And what do you think we'll do if Gilbert doesn't show, lass?" said Finn.

Holiday and Harper turned to look at Margaret. Holiday's metallic telescope eye looked more deadly in the starlight.

"Then you boys may try to shoot me. Now, here, attach this tether to your belts. When I give the signal, you'll need to pull the white ring on your packs. I'll be steering, and you'll all follow my lead, like a group of roped-together mountain climbers. And please, don't get any ideas about attacking me when we're in transit. There's only enough air to get you one way."

"Colonel, what's this little girl talkin' about?" Doc Holiday said again. His voice was relaxed, but Finn knew that tone masked a readiness to do damage to someone if his limits were pushed much further.

"Keep yer heads, boys, and do what she says. I think I've got the notion where this is goin'."

They stood quietly for five long minutes before they heard the humming.

"Wuzzat?" whispered Harper.

"It ain't horses," whispered Doc.

Confused eyes looked around. The men could see better, now that they were fully awake and their eyes were used to the dark. A brilliant canopy of stars marked by only a scattering of clouds was set above them. By marking where it began and ended, they could see they were in a gentle valley, bordered at the top by mountains, forests, or both.

Another few minutes, and the moon floated up over the edge of the valley.

It was a moon that glowed green. And floated up in a matter of seconds. Faster, in fact, than any of the cowboys had ever seen a moon rise.

"Colonel," Harper gasped, "that's ... that's ..."

"That ain't no moon," Finn said. His voice was flat, and it took every bit of will he had in him to keep his voice from shaking. "Look up top of it. Looks like a castle."

"Jehosphat," said Holiday, "it's too big to be a castle!" and crossed himself.

"Gilbert is there, gentlemen. So if you'll wait 'till I count to three and pull your cords, we can get back to the business of retrieving him. Ready? One, two, three!"

On three, each of them pulled the cord on their packs. The cloth of the packs fell away, and shiny steel-framed contraptions took their place. Herb saw large tubes on the backs of the cowboys and Margaret. Presumably, he had them himself as well.

There was a humming noise in their circle, then Herb and the rest of the little group shot into the air with a loud phhissssst! Fairylike wings popped out of Margaret's backpack flying assembly. They were identical to the creations that the flying assassins had worn on the Sky Palace in Germany, and similar to those worn by the pilots Herb had seen fighting the Martians back in England.

They were all aloft, several of the cowboys whooping with surprise as the ground dropped away and they found themselves twenty stories high in a little over a second.

Herb, more than a little nervous, focused on the back of Margaret's head.

Margaret had unfolded two levers from her pack that were shaped to her arms. Herb hadn't seen them until now, and her arms twitched as she moved the levers to steer herself in the air. Herb and the cowboys, terrified and tethered to Margaret by the cable of woven steel, had no chance to fly away, shoot her in the back, or otherwise make trouble.

There were few lights visible in the city at this distance, save for the glowing green light that came from four giant spheres of stone chained to the four corners of the city's base. As they neared the city, Herb saw dozens, hundreds, then thousands of windmills, churning at a furious pace in the high-altitude winds. Their packs kept hissing, but were eventually drowned out by the noise of turbine engines sounding at the West end of the city.

They drifted over the curved rows of flat-topped buildings made of stone, bathed in the soft green light of the glowing orbs. Herb saw lights in buildings and row after row of flags, but there wasn't enough light to see either people moving or a flag's color. Margaret's head twitched back and forth, her hair whipping about as she looked for something among the countless spires in the floating city's skyline.

After a minute, her head stopped moving. Everyone else had grown quiet, as early surprise gave way to apprehension. *Where was she taking them?* was the unasked question on their minds. *Nowhere good* would be the answer Herb would give, if asked. But he still knew that Margaret was canny enough to make sure any situation she walked into had a number of safe escape routes. And she always made sure she had some kind of hold over everyone who could be a threat to her, ready to use like a headsman's axe when needed.

In the dim green light of the spheres, they could see that one of the nearby buildings in the city skyline had a flat top. It was a kind of balcony/luxury/observation deck in the open air, and Margaret headed straight for it. A good thing, too—Herb could hear the hiss of his lift-pack getting softer. Was it running out of compressed air, or was Margaret controlling it somehow?

They touched down a few seconds later. The speed of the packs slowed dramatically, so much so that they all had just touched their toes to the floor of the rooftop when the engines stopped.

"Now, remove your packs," she said. "Don't worry about them being discovered. I'm counting on it, in fact. Leave them here and follow me."

The four men obeyed, piling the packs—which were adorned with stitched-on patches of a walking bear and a red star—facing upwards. "Any reason why these packs of ours are sporting the flags of the Northern California Republic?" Holiday asked.

Margaret only smiled and walked away, motioning for them to follow. She acted so confidently in this utterly unfamiliar place that they followed her as a broken horse would follow its master.

Even Finn, who'd had more life-threatening adventures than all the people in their group put together, seemed cowed and a little jittery from their flight. Bad enough that when the crackle of paper sounded, Finn's hand had jumped to his gun, ready to blast whatever had made the noise at his foot with all barrels. A combination of training, reflexes and Herb saying, "Wait, fool," in a calm voice kept him from pulling the trigger right away, and possibly saved Finn a few toes besides.

Herb leaned down and picked up the piece of paper from the floor where Finn's boot had pinned it down.

He held it under the combination of white starlight and green sphere light to get a closer look.

And what was written on the paper made Finn whistle low, Herb furrow his brow in disbelief, and Margaret burst out laughing.

Chapter 68

"'…I think in that case you would see a most singular effect, an effect that has generally been achieved by all those able and powerful systems which rationalism, or the religion of the ball, has produced to lead or teach mankind. You would see, I think, that thing happen which is always the ultimate embodiment and logical outcome of your logical scheme.'
'What are you talking about?' asked Lucifer …
'I mean it would fall down,' said the monk, looking wistfully into the void." – GKC, *The Ball and the Cross*

Norton had pointed the pistol with uncharacteristic slowness, and Victor had leaped out of his chair!

Gil jumped back. Victor had somehow already cut his bonds by the time they'd entered, and had only been waiting for the moment to strike! He leaped, capered and dodged around the room, easily evading Norton's feeble attempts to get a steady shot at him.

Where are the guards? thought Gilbert as he cowered near a table. Why aren't they barging in at the sound of gunfire?

Within seconds, Victor had moved in on Norton and disarmed him. In one fluid motion, he'd grabbed Norton's wrist, wrestled the gun from him and pointed it at Norton's head while standing six feet from the now feeble-looking old man.

"Hands up, cretin," Victor said, "before I remove you with all available speed."

Gilbert's ears pricked up—he'd heard that phrase before!

"You gonna spare your old mentor, Victor m'boy?" said Norton, raising his hands slowly. It looked as if doing so gave him great pain.

"Ta ta, Emperor," said Victor as he pulled the trigger.

There was a loud bang.

Norton didn't move. Victor went white.

"Blanks, son," said Norton, as he closed his left hand.

There was a second, louder blast in the room as Norton's left elbow exploded and Victor jerked backwards.

Gilbert blinked. The pungent smell of gunpowder filled the room. No, Norton's elbow hadn't exploded; the suit had exploded at the elbow.

Victor's eyes widened in panic as he looked down to his chest. The entry wound around his shirt darkened with a widening stain of blood. He looked up and locked eyes with Gilbert. "Yough," he said groggily, "Yough! Archeh ...brudda ..." Victor slumped backwards into the chair he'd sat in earlier, his eyes already dulling.

"And, Victor," Norton was talking now, as Gilbert stood looking into the dying boy's eyes, "to answer your question: no. I won't give you a last smoke, last drink, or a last kiss from your girl. Nor will I start a long monologue about my plans to take over the world, and thereby give you a chance to come up with some other smart little escape plan. After you're dead, I'm going to shoot you again, cremate your body and scatter the ashes to the winds."

It was unlikely Victor was listening to the lecture being given him, but Norton continued. "I thought I could trust you, boy," Norton shouted into Victor's ear. "I thought that I could trust a predator like you to at least be an *interesting* predator, but you disappointed me! I hope Gilbert here does me far more proud! Maybe someone with moral backbone will be a faithful apprentice, or at least not bore me when he tries to supplant me!"

Something in Gilbert's mind had snapped and shifted at the sight of Victor's death. His head felt like it was lit up and spinning inside. Not just at the violence he'd seen, but something more. He'd seen people killed before his eyes before during the Invasion. Indeed, at one point he and Herb had seen one of the Martians' victims drained of blood before their eyes.

Something, though...at the sight of Victor's death, something felt like a bubble in his head. A belch or a gut-bomb that he just wanted to vomit up but couldn't. It was...

"Gilbert, son," Norton said, holstering his pistol and adjusting his elbow-shooter, "sorry you hadda see that. I'd hoped to show you my intentions a little later, but Victor here forced my hand. Or rather, my elbow. You see," Norton wriggled out of his jacket to show Gilbert the small strapped-on pistol that ran from his left shoulder to his elbow. "it's always important to have an extra ace up your sleeve. He was gonna kill me. Then likely you. And as for Galatea, well ... I'll leave his intentions for her to your fertile imagination."

"If he was so dangerous," said Gilbert in a voice tinged with quiet shock, "why'd you bring him aboard?"

"Son, look at me," he said as he put his jacket back on. "I've got very little time left on this Earth. A lot of men in my line of work die old, broke and alone in a flophouse room. I want to leave something that'll outlast me. I thought a snake like Victor here could run the city after I died. He seemed ruthless enough. Wish he'd a-waited until the big part of the plan was finished before he did something stupid, like try to kill me in my sleep. Dagnabit, didn't he realize there's a reason a man like me lives to an old age?"

"So," said Gilbert, his eyes still staring wide with horror at Victor's lifeless body. Victor couldn't have been any older than himself. Younger, maybe. "Is that what I can expect? That if I mess up, you or someone else'll use me for close-range target practice?"

"Gilbert, son, don't feel bad for Victor. Back when you were shooting spitwads at your schoolteacher, that boy was selling people junk and bilking widows out've their life savings. Not because he needed to. His parents were rich. No, just 'cause he *wanted* to. Mean as a desert rattler who missed a week of dinners, and bad as a fallen angel. If you believe nothing else I ever tell you, believe this: the world's a less evil and much safer place without him inhabiting it.

"But what can you expect? Well, son, I'm a good judge of character. For a long while, I thought this city needed an amoral person like myself at the helm to ensure it could survive. There's other, quite terrible folks who want to pull its strings. A little while before Victor tried his clumsy coup on me, I realized we need someone who's both smart, *and* virtuous to take the helm. Someone with moral vision to guide the city day to day, but smart enough to know not everyone's your friend.

"And that person, son, I am convinced, is you. I first saw your writings a year ago, 'Here,' says I, 'here's a young man moral enough to let his faith guide him in his darkest hour, yet smart enough to fight dirty when the situation calls for it.' Now, that's true about you, ain't it?"

"Well," Gilbert said slowly, "you can't get much dirtier than a sewer."

"Precisely my point! You know the value of principled action, Gilbert, something I know that I lack. But I can appreciate it, just as a legless man can appreciate a skilled runner. The world is filled with men who are principled, but are just too stupid, weak or naive to swim with the sharks. You, on the other hand, you have faith and you're smart enough to walk into a dark alley with your Bible in one hand, but a pistol in t'other.

"So, Gilbert," continued Norton, as one of his guards finally entered the room with a new, identical and undamaged jacket for

Norton to wear, "when we march on Richmond and crush the Confederate States of America, we'll not only smash the heart of the stupidest attempt at forming a country since Napoleon tried conquering France from a little South Sea island. When we break Richmond with our steambots, we'll instantly gain ourselves a willing, human army. Millions of freed slaves, all looking to pay back. Added to that crowd of walking toasters that Galatea showed you, and we'll sweep through the rest of the CSA like a red-hot saber through a pound of butter. And after the CSA falls, then the Californian Republics, North and South. Tell the Papists they can keep their gods of bread, and they'll let you do whatever the blazes you want to the rest of the country. After that, we hit Texarcana, and maybe the boys in Mexico if we're on a winning streak. The hardest part'll be swinging the USA in the North to our side. But if they see the others fall, well, we might take them down without a shot. We can gobble up Canada as an after-dinner mint. The place is so useless, there's no way the British'll ever fight for it, no matter how many furs and trees it makes.

"Which means, Gilbert, you'll have the length of the North American campaign to learn and absorb all the lessons I have to teach. How to always get the better end of a deal, and how to bully the powerful and rabble alike into submission when you don't have time to win their hearts. And when it's over, Gilbert, you'll inherit the largest empire the world has ever known, one that'll make Alexander the Great look like a petty slumlord. How does that make you feel, son?"

Under normal circumstances, Gilbert would have reacted in one of two ways to the offer. He would have either laughed at the old man until his stomach hurt, or he would have asked for a few days to think it over until he could call the men in London who showed up at the door in white coats and a horse-drawn carriage with padded walls to take the old man away.

But the events of the last few weeks, and especially the last few minutes, had left Gilbert's brain addled. He literally couldn't think of a response to give, but stood staring at Norton in front of him while remembering the massive metallic army assembled just a little ways behind him.

"I ... don't know what to say, Emperor."

Gilbert turned away from Norton for a second and looked at the wall. He knew it made sense to be upset. The day had begun with him as a factory worker in a floating city and now seemed about to end with witnessing the cold blooded murder of someone his own age.

But even the killing couldn't explain the shakes in his legs and hands. He'd gone into shock in the tunnels after fighting Martians, but that had been a numbing tiredness. This was different. Now he felt the need to kick, scream and hide all at the same time. Most of all, he had an overall, pressing sense since seeing Victor's murder that the young man's death wasn't Norton's fault, but *Gilbert's*. He knew it was silly, and his head rejected it outright. But his heart kept hammering away at him inside, saying

... if you'd just kept quiet ... if you'd just spoken up later ... if you'd just left the door shut ... if you'd just been a good ...

What was that? What door was that ... ?

Gilbert felt cold, and yet there were beads of perspiration on his head. His knees were shaking, he felt nauseous and his nose hurt.

"Son," said Norton, "I like your caution. But I just don't see what there is to ponder. If you just say 'yes,' you'll be the heir to the Floating City, the only airborne fortress in the history of the world!"

"Wait," Gilbert said, holding up his hand while trying to stay steady. "Wait. My Pa said you should never say yes to a deal if you can sleep on it first. Would that work for you?" Gilbert said, slowly regaining his composure. "I need at least that." He sure did—he would need that to get to the conspiracy group and try to stop whatever plan Norton was going to throw in motion tonight.

And, to give himself some insurance, they had to make it interesting, too, just in case they failed.

Norton looked at Gilbert with a serious expression. For a second he felt like Norton's eyes drilled quiet holes into his skull.

Then Norton smiled again. "I think I've got it, son. I know just what it is that's holding you back."

"You do?" Gilbert said.

"Yep. Teenage boys haven't changed a whit since I was one three-score and some years back, son. What you need is right here in my pocket." With the timing of a magician he pulled out a small black locket from his trouser pocket and handed it to Gilbert.

"Open it," he said. "Go on. It's alright. Really."

Gilbert, forcing himself to breathe evenly, took the locket and figured out how to open it.

There was a picture of the red-headed girl inside, dressed as he'd seen her last with the white blouse and glasses.

"Beautiful ain't she?" Norton said while standing behind Gilbert. "You could look 'round the world for eighty years and never find a woman like her. And she's sweet on you, son."

"What?"

"Come on, now, boy! I didn't play poker all those years without learnin' a thing or two about reading faces. More'n that, you're sweet on her, too, aincha?"

Gilbert looked at Norton, then back at her picture and nodded.

"Hot diggety!" Norton said, clapping his hands and slapping Gilbert on the shoulders, "I knew it! Well, she can be *yours*, Gil. Yours real easy like! All women, son, all women love one thing in a man, and that's power. It's why they love the bullies in school and the rich boys in the world, no matter how ugly they are. And you, son, you're lookin' at being heir to the throne of the richest continent on the planet! Whaddya say?"

"There's a problem, Emperor ..."

"Hup! Lemme guess: you've got another girl? Pshaw! Not a problem! The kind of man fit to rule usually won't be sated by the love of just one woman, anyhow. What ruler didn't have a mistress or two? Or, if you insist, we could just park the city over Utah for a while, and you can marry 'em both!"

"I ... I can ..."

"And even aside of the female entertainment aspect o'things," Norton said, sweeping Gilbert out of the room and down the hallway as he took back the locket and pocketed it, "You can do good, Gilbert! That little weasel we just ended would've used my city to be a tinpot dictator. Not that I woulda minded much. But you, Gilbert, think of the good *you* can do. The wrongs you can right, when you have an entire city, and an army to do it with? How much *good* will be done, and every word of every *good* deed after I'm gone'll have your name stamped on it!"

One word Gilbert heard in Norton's latest speech had stuck with him.

No, not stuck exactly. A word had resonated in him, bouncing around in his head like an India rubber ball in a stone room.

And the word Norton had used to such massive effect was *good*.

And Gilbert liked it.

He could do *good*, and change an evil thing into ...

"Emperor!" a voice shouted a few dozen feet down the hall. It was Galatea, running towards them. She held her skirt hem in one hand while keeping her balance with the other. She must have changed her shoes, Gilbert thought, as now her steps made hardly any noise at all.

"Why, hello, sweet thing!" Norton said, looking at her. "We were just discussing you. But isn't it a tad past your bedtime?"

"Emperor, intruders have boarded the city!"

Norton's attitude shifted suddenly, from jovial and relaxed to efficient and exacting. "Galatea," he said, his words now clipped more neatly than a military cadet's haircut, "escort Gilbert back to his room and get him settled in for the night. Gilbert, you stay put in your rooms until we get this straightened out. I'm gonna send a squad of guards to keep you safe, so you cooperate with 'em 'til I or Galatea give you the all clear, you get me?"

"Yessir."

"Good, son. Now get-a-goin'!"

Gilbert shambled down the hall, propelled by the girl who now had a strong grip on his arm. Norton turned on his heel and strode in the opposite direction, never slowing or even moving his eyes from the end of the hallway when the recently fired Commissar Bilgewater rushed up to him and tried to match him step for step.

"Emperor, there's a ..."

"I know, numbskull. We're being invaded."

"More than that, Emperor, we ..."

"Bilgewater," Norton said, without breaking his stride or taking his eyes from their forward view, "this is a stressful time for me. And as such I feel an unusually strong desire to smash and kill things. If you tell me something I already know, so help me, I'll give it to you with all three barrels."

Bilgewater thrust a piece of paper into Norton's hand. Norton grabbed it without looking at it, using his other hand to first grab a funnel attached to a thin pipe and turn it towards his face.

"Strock!" he barked after flipping one switch of many on the wall.

"Yes, sir, Emperor!" Strock's smile could be heard even through the muffles of the pipe-phone.

"Report," Norton barked.

"One of the sentries spotted a small group," Strock said, "Four men, one woman. They boarded by flying in with compressed air-packs over the city skyline. The leader had a set of wings, and had the others on a long tether. They landed on one of the rooftop decks on Blue level. The packs have the emblems of the Northern California Republic on them. What do we do?"

"Mobilize everybody. Find 'em and snuff 'em. Unless," Norton paused, his eyes flashing with a keen, painful memory, "unless the woman is a pale-skinned, pretty brunette with long hair. In that case, don't kill her right away. First tell I said 'nice try,' then do the deed. Also, send a squad over to Gilbert's apartment. I want him protected until we root out these yahoos. Clear?"

"Crystal clear, Emperor."

"Don't start at White level. If they're out to overthrow the city, they've already moved up from Blue. Get the squads and start at ..."

The piece of paper caught his eye. He looked at it, and both his eyes grew very, very wide as he read the large-printed writing.

The message at the top of the handbill was written in neat, stylized, giant-sized print: "OUR LEADER! OUR SAVIOR!" it proclaimed! Below it was a hastily drawn yet fairly accurate portrait of Gilbert.

There were more words below the illustration:

"THE TIME FOR EMPERORS IS PAST! THE TIME FOR ACTION IS NOW! *Gilbert Chesterton, Eminent Slayer of Martians and Steam Crabs, Is Our Newest, Greatest Hope for a Future Free of Fear! Rally Tonight in the Worker's Square at Midnight! Come Prepared to Fight!*"

Norton spent a full five seconds reading the text and looking at the illustration.

"Another thing, Strock."

"Yes, Emperor?"

"That squad I toldja about? New orders. Galatea'll escort Gilbert to his rooms. The two of 'em aren't to be disturbed. Understand? They're not even to know they're being followed. Wait until she leaves, give the boy about a half hour to slip off into dreamland, then go in and fill him full of holes."

Strock paused. "Are you certain of this, Emperor?"

"Strock, if you go in there and strangle him, so help me, I'll set every Red in the city on you. You know you can't keep a secret from me. The boy's betrayed me, Strock. But by golly," he choked back a small sob. "By golly, man, he had me fooled. *Me!* When I thought no man could surprise me, the boy's pulled it off, understand? And that's worth giving him a good night's sleep, or at least the start of one, with the last thing you see in this world being your sweetheart. Now get-a-goin'."

"Yes, Emperor."

"An' execute those three kids from White who're always tryin' to be his lapdogs. I don't care how. They may not be involved, but I don't wanna take any chances."

Chapter 69

"How quickly revolutions grow old; and, worse still, respectable." – GKC, *The Listener*, March 6, 1935

W hat's happening?" Gilbert asked as she rushed him down the hallway while holding his hand, dragging him behind her.

"We're going to your rooms," she said without the slightest indication she was getting winded. "Once there, he'll likely send a guard to keep you safe from whoever's boarded the city. I can't believe I thought you'd be safer here than with the Pinkertons; what was I thinking with those faked messages to Norton?"

"What?" Gilbert said.

"Oh, I'll have to explain later. When I learned the Branch was after you again, I tried to have Norton grab you and bring you here, where I could watch over you. But everything's gone so wrong! For now, we're going to get you to your rooms and lock the doors tight. After the threat's removed you'll be free to roam about again."

"Wait," he said, stopping and pulling her hand to stop her as well. "I've got a better idea."

"We've no time," she said, starting to pull him down the hall again.

"Yes, we do," he said, stopping again. "Look, what if something went really wrong on this tub? Say if those big green balloon-rocks went ker-boom? How do you evacuate the place?"

"Then the people jump into the *evacuoles*, metal capsules that can transport people to the surface safely. But Gilbert, that's not an option now. Norton has them checked and heavily guarded every night, to keep people from trying just what you're thinking about. Come on!"

They started running again. Though his legs were longer, Gilbert had a hard time keeping up with her! Either she was in tremendous shape or he had let himself go slack over the past year. Or both.

"We're almost there," she said, after they'd traveled over several enclosed bridges and through several more buildings. "We'll take the shortcut through the Red square, and ..."

She opened a door in the wall.

There was a large crowd of people, several hundred at least. It was night, the wind was blowing, and the people had pulled the drawstrings tight on their red overalls and other red clothing to keep the night chill out.

Gilbert pushed through the door past Galatea into the thickly packed crowd of Red workers. Maybe one in every eight or ten carried a torch of some kind. They were cheering, raising their fists in the air and roaring some kind of chanted slogan.

And, no more than fifty yards in front of Gilbert, a crude stage had been set up. The wealthy art student named Cameron that Gilbert had met this morning, the one they called the King, was at its podium.

And behind Cameron the King was a huge, bed sheet sized poster that had a crude yet unmistakable line drawing of Gilbert's face emblazoned on it.

"Oh, my," Gilbert said.

"Oh, dear," Galatea said.

A few people turned around and saw Gilbert standing behind them. Everything was silent for several seconds.

And then the cheering started.

Chapter 70

"This great idea, then, is the backbone of all folk-lore – the idea that all happiness hangs on one thin veto; all positive joy depends on one negative…It is surely obvious that all ethics ought to be taught to this fairy-tale tune; that, if one does the thing forbidden, one imperils all the things provided."
– GKC, *All Things Considered*

How much further?" Finn asked. His voice dropped to a whisper when a group of red-overalled men walked by their doorway.

"We're going to make for the higher levels inside the spire," said Margaret, "that's where they're likely holding Gilbert."

"Does that mean he's in the White or Blue levels?" Finn asked. He'd been watching the flags flying from the buildings, and had quickly figured out Norton's little class system.

"If he's survived Norton's tests? Most likely he's past Blue, all the way at the top of the spire."

"Indeed, it appears it'll be quite a walk up that giant sewing needle," said Holiday, his eye scoping out every building window it could before they made a move.

"I've climbed higher mountains," Finn said, "and I wasn't motivated then like I am now!"

"Good for you," Herb said, "but we're not getting any closer to Norton or Gil by discussing anyone's work history. How to we get there, Margaret?"

"Wait," she said, looking at a small device in her hand. Herb looked over her shoulder. She held it in her left hand, while tuning small crank with her right. A small square on the gadget showed a flexible kind of paper-map, that moved first left to right, then up and down, depending on which dials she turned.

After a long minute she shut a flip lid on top of the map square and put the gadget in her pocket. "Follow me," she said, slipping out of the alley. "My mapper's never been wrong yet." The fine gravel crunched under her boots as she ran into another doorway, the shadows swallowing her up in a second.

"Lovely young lady," Finn said to Herb, "if you like courting sharks. How'd you get mixed up with her?"

"A very interesting costume party. She'd dressed as a fairy queen and I'd rustled up a knight outfit from someplace. By the end of the evening most of us had traded the costumes in for hooded black robes and daggers with wiggly blades."

The cowboys looked at Herb. "Let's just go," Herb said, "It's embarrassing."

"You know, Wells," said Harper in a whisper as Margaret had them follow her into the darkness, "the more I hear about your life, the more you make me into something I never thought I'd be."

"What's that?"

"A man glad he was raised in a muddy, Missouri one-horse town."

Chapter 71

"The aesthete aims at harmony rather than beauty. If his hair does not match the mauve sunset against which he is standing, he hurriedly dyes his hair another shade of mauve. If his wife does not go with the wall-paper, he gets a divorce."
– GKC, *ILN*, December 25, 1909

Cameron Foggschild considered himself an artist first above all things. For him, life existed as a support system for art. Like most such people, he had been raised in a privileged environment that was largely devoid of suffering, religion, or serious personal sacrifice. *Art* was so sacred a thing to Cameron that it was easily above holiness, happiness (well, *other* people's happiness, anyway), and humanity. Furthermore, a combination of fawning, fair-weather friends and family influences had made Cameron fully confident of his personal infallibility in producing excellent *art*. It had also convinced him that no sacrifice was too great to make if it meant achieving *art* on a grander scale than had ever previously been seen.

When captured on a pleasure barge by air pirates, Cameron saw the experience not as an unfortunate event, but instead as an opportunity to practice *art*, living *art*, in a new, vibrant and radical way.

So when the rumors circulated that Norton's latest protégé had landed in the city, a plan began forming in Cameron's self-deluded head. And upon learning that Gilbert lived in his section of the city, Cameron's plan took spontaneous root, stem, tree and branches in the space of just a few days.

Cameron had drawn a fairly accurate caricature of Gilbert within an hour after meeting him, one with Gil's bespectacled face looking out at the reader with an expression of total sincerity and security. The caption wording had been punched up in a print machine borrowed from a bureaucrat's office, and a thousand copies of a political leaflet were dashed off within the hour. The gossip network, reliable for millenias among workingmen and bored housewives alike, furnished information every hour about Gilbert's exploits, capabilities, promises, and the time and location of his leadership rally.

Foggschild had originally seen in Gilbert a simple political puppet, a living tool to be used and discarded once Norton was safely dethroned and/or assassinated. Now, with Gilbert having attained the status of folk hero since his defeat of the steam crab, Cameron saw a chance for a full-blown revolution, rather than a simple coup.

But even the revolution was going to be only a means to an end. For Foggschild, the creation and execution of a revolution, from start to finish, would be nothing less than the most brilliant piece of performance *art* the world had ever seen. Hero worship, violence, triumph, hope, change, creation and destruction all would be displayed and wrapped up in a surprisingly neat package.

There was only one problem: after he'd set the time and place for the rally, he couldn't find Gilbert.

Gilbert, the focal point of every facet of Cameron's beautiful, jewel-like plans, was gone.

Rather than panic, however, Cameron only adjusted his plans. He'd thought at some point to stage Gilbert's assassination, and thereby have the first and greatest martyr for his cause. Without Gilbert being findable and briefed upon his role in the Glorious Revolution, Cameron might have either had to find another stooge or take the risky role of frontman himself.

Then, as the starting hour of midnight approached, the shouting started in the southwest corner of the city square.

"Gil-BERT!" went up the cry, "Gil-*BERT*! Gil-*BERT*! Gil-*BERT*!"

Perfect, thought Cameron, *He must be here!*

While fascinated at first by the crowd, when the shouting started, Gilbert's instinctive reaction was to duck and hide. But eager hands seized his arms and legs, and he heard Galatea scream in anger and bodies begin to fall as she defended herself from her own group of gropers.

But Gilbert was already airborne, pulled up over the heads of the crowd and floating on a sea of waving hands. They moved him closer to the stage as Cameron shouted to the crowd through a megaphone.

"HERE HE IS," Cameron's voice bellowed above the roar of the crowd. It was like a cross between a carnival barker and a tent-camp preacher he'd heard long ago. "YOUR SAVIOR, THE ONE WHO WILL DELIVER US FROM THE EMPEROR OF NORTH AMERICA!"

Gilbert, hearing his name and the words of Cameron over the crowd, now stopped struggling and let the supportive waves of hands carry him to the stage. Lying on his back as they moved him, Gil tilted his head forward and looked at the stage between his feet.

"LADIES AND GENTLEMEN," Cameron's voice raised now to a

near shriek as the crowd's chanting voice pounded his ears and shook the city ground. "CHEER HIM!" shouted Cameron, "CHEER HIM! CHEER THE *ONE*! CHEER THE *MAN*! WE CAN DO IT! WE SURELY *CAN!*"

A few more seconds and Gil reached the stage, a hastily constructed affair made from planks of wood on top of metal oil drums. First his feet, legs, then the rest of him slid onto the stage. Someone must have grabbed his leg too hard; the scar on his calf was throbbing and hurting.

Gilbert had had few moments in his life when he was truly the center of attention for a positive reason. But now there was a huge number of people chanting his name, saying he was the man, the one.

He stood up and saw a crowd of hundreds, maybe thousands, jumping up and down in unison chanting his name and the slogan that ended with "WE SURELY CAN! WE SURELY CAN!"

"Gilbert!"

Cameron's face filled his vision.

"Gilbert, just stand back and let me handle this. I'm sorry I couldn't talk to you before, but ..."

"That's fine, Cameron. But is everything set?"

"To the last detail. The revolution will go off without a hitch. All they need is *you* to focus on while they go through it."

"Fine. I'm on a winning streak talking to crowds lately. I'll chat 'em up, then you tell me what's going on. I don't want to be the next Victor."

"Victor?"

"I'll tell you later. Where do I speak?"

Cameron smiled, only a little uncertainty showing up in his face. Gil strode to the stage, limping just a tad from the old wound in his leg, and took the megaphone that had been left standing on its large end.

"People of..." The cheers doubled in size and volume as Gil began to speak. "People of the Floating City!" Gil yelled through the megaphone, and almost had to turn away from the crushing, deafening roar of approval from the crowd.

"People of the Floating City!" Gil shouted a third time into the small end of the cone, and at least some of the adoring throngs quieted down.

Now what? Gil thought.

He didn't have to think for long. When in doubt, use what has worked before. His mother had long ago had him read Julius Caesar by

Shakespeare. How had Brutus and Antony gotten the crowd on their side?

"Some might ask: why have a revolt?" said Gil, his voice strengthening as his confidence grew. "Some might ask, 'why have a rebellion?' And others might ask, 'why have a revolution?' I say, we need all three, if we want *change* in our time!"

A wave of cheers sounded in the square. Cameron waved his hands behind Gil, which quieted all but the most enthusiastic of the crowd. It works, thought Gilbert. Asking and answering all your own questions works great!

What else had Brutus and Antony done?

"Our leader lives in the past!" Gil said, "follow me, and I promise you the future!"

The cheers became roars!

"I promise you winter, summer, spring and fall! No longer the constant wind of a mountaintop! You've been kept on a mountaintop, all fenced in! I'll *remove* that fence and make you *free*! You can have *hope* in my promise to you!"

The roar became another chanted set of slogans. Gil couldn't even hear the words, but he felt almost drunk with happiness. If the bullies from his school days could see him now! If Herb could see him now! If Father Brown could ...

The roar of the crowd jerked him out of his thoughts.

The roars became something else, something more than a simple joining of voices. It became like a single, explosive force of nature and humanity. In one of the closer rows, Gilbert saw a woman faint with a beatific smile on her face. Several people in the row behind caught her. In a different place in the crowd a clump of maybe a dozen people at Gil's right were raising their hands, closing their eyes and going into some kind of ecstatic, jerking dance.

Was *he* really doing all this?

There was a tap at his shoulder. Still holding the megaphone, Gil turned and saw Cameron's large, round face looking at him with a wide grin.

"Gil," he said, leaning in and speaking directly into his ear, "That was brilliant! Brilliant! But it's not safe here now. My men will escort you to your rooms. Wait there. Our revolution starts within the hour. When we've won, we'll come fetch you."

"Thanks, Cameron, for believing in me."

"My pleasure," Cameron replied, smiling. He waved his hand

while keeping his eyes on Gil, and four very large workers in red overalls and caps appeared at Cameron's elbows. The large leader crooked his finger at Gil. He followed with a Red guard in front, behind, and at his right and left as he walked off the stage and left the square. *Funny*, Gil thought; *that pain in my lower leg has been flaring up more and more lately, especially when I'm about to...* A guard interrupted Gil's thought as he tapped Gil's shoulder, and directed him down a darkened hallway.

Once Gil had left, Cameron gripped the megaphone by its handle with his left hand and the mouthpiece with his right. All proceeding beautifully! Before the night was out, either Norton's guards or Cameron's thug squad would execute Gilbert. Win or lose, the revolution would cause buckets of spilled blood, and exquisite tragedy flowing everywhere.

Beautiful, exquisite tragedy, Cameron thought. Mothers crying for children, wives bewailing lost husbands, tragedy greater than seen on any artist's canvas, any Shakespearean stage.

This will be true *art,* thought Cameron, *a new* kind *of art, with people taking the place of ink or paint, and an entire city as my canvas. All of it recorded in my memories, and ready to use for painting, writing, poetry or any of a hundred other mediums.*

Cameron, of course, would survive all of this. He'd long ago reasoned that the artist was the most important person in any society, and as such he must always ensure his own survival over all the other expendable people he professed to love so much.

He looked at the West globe of Cavorite, closest of the four globes to their city square and the first on the list of the night's targets.

Thinking again of his beautiful, tragic *art,* he raised the megaphone to his lips and began speaking again.

Chapter 72

"Pacifists who complained in England of the intolerance of patriotism have no notion of what patriotism can be like. If they had been in America, after America had entered the war, they would have seen something which they have always perhaps subconsciously dreaded, and would then have beyond all their worst dreams detested; and the name of it is democracy." – GKC, *What I Saw in America*

Gilbert, half in a dream, left the stage escorted by the squad of large Reds, and went back into the maze of staircases and hallways towards his rooms. Most people in of the crowd were so charged with emotion that they didn't follow Gilbert's path into the darkness of the improvised backstage.

But several pairs of eyes did.

The red-haired girl, standing alone with several men lying unconscious around her, breathed heavily from her recent combat and watched Gilbert's transformation on the stage from quiet wallflower into political revolutionary. Having participated in a few such small-scale revolutions herself, she knew what fate usually awaited puppets like Gilbert at the hands of the real forces behind a rebellion.

She couldn't chase Gilbert directly; the crowd was in a quasi-religious frenzy, only a step removed from being a violent mob. It would be more dangerous to walk through them now than through a typhoon on the open sea, even for her. Instead she ran back into the hallway she and Gilbert had emerged from, taking a different route back to Gilbert's apartment.

Margaret, Herb and the Pinkertons had watched the rally from the shadows, knowing that their lack of red clothing would signify them as outsiders, quite possibly ending their lives if the mob turned ugly. Herb's face paled as he saw first the giant poster with Gilbert's drawn face on it. Fear became resentment as the toad-like fellow whipped the crowd into a screaming, frothing mob with slogans and cheers, followed by Gil himself being carried to the stage.

That little cretin, Herb thought. *He was nothing when I met him. Now that he has confidence, this is how he uses it? Without even mentioning me?*

"Very unexpected," Margaret mumbled, "but not unworkable. Good thing we came down here first, rather than searching the spire right away."

"Where're they taking him?" Finn asked as Gilbert was hustled offstage by the red-suited thug squad.

Margaret smiled and turned to Finn. "Up to Norton's apartments in the white spire. It shouldn't be hard to find him, really. When we get to a certain level in the spire, we'll split up and find him. We might have to go through Norton, though, to get to Gilbert."

"Fine by me," Finn whispered, his hand passing over his pistol and stroking the knife sheath beside it.

In an alley just as dark on the opposite side of the square, Strock's squad of leather-clad guards watched from their own set of shadows. Despite Gilbert's open treason, they knew their dark jackets and goggles would make them targets of the mob of red-clad workers. When the workers hustled Gilbert off the stage, Strock thought briefly, then smiled wide and signaled his men to follow. Even taking the safe route through the back alleys and side streets, they'd reach Gilbert's apartment in minutes. If all went well, Gilbert would be dead before the clock in the city square's next *bong*.

"...the broad-minded are extremely bitter because a Christian who wishes to have several wives when his own promise bound him to one, is not allowed to violate his vow at the same altar at which he made it."
– GKC, *The Superstition of Divorce*

Gilbert stretched out on the bed. His hands locked fingers behind his head as a happy smile widened underneath his closed eyes. His name! The sound of his chanted name echoed in his head over and over again. He gave a sigh of joy and looked around at his rooms again. He was still dressed in his immaculate black suit and waistcoat. And one of his new, red-overalled, Neanderthal-sized servants had even brought back Gilbert's walking stick he'd gotten with his suit earlier, handing it to him as he entered his room.

After a couple of minutes, he heard a new set of voices at the door. The voices quickly moved from mumbles to angry shouts, and angry shouts turned to the sound of guns discharging and bodies falling.

Gilbert sat up to listen as the voices turned angry, then rolled off the bed at the first sound of gunshot. By the time the third shot sounded he had hidden under the bed. He waited for several minutes, hearing only silence. He was just about to emerge when he heard one of the voices speak and heard several hasty short shuffles of feet, as of several men coming to attention at the same time.

"He's inside," Gilbert heard a man's voice say.

Now Gilbert had a different idea. He scrabbled out from under the bed to his feet, and stood with his back to the wall and the closed door on his right, ready to swing his cane like a baseball bat at the first person that entered.

Granted, he'd never been especially good at baseball or any other team sport. But his apartment was too high to escape from by jumping from his window. Worse, he hadn't advanced far enough with Chang to learn how to fight a group, especially a group with guns. Maybe if he swung hard and screamed loud enough he could startle the first person to come in, and run off in the confusion.

When the knob turned and the door swung open, he made no sound as he swung his walking stick with all his might, hoping to brain whoever walked in first.

Galatea stepped in.

Fortunately, he missed her. His aim was bad, and she'd been trained to dodge superbly. Both helped her avoid the blow, and the cane smacked hard against the open door.

A very odd thing happened after that; though he'd kept a tight grip on the silvery grip-end of the stick, it flew away from Gilbert and smacked into the wall at Gilbert's right.

Gilbert did a double take and looked at his hand. The cane tip was gone. In its place was a polished sword blade that he could grip effectively at the cane's end.

"A sword cane!" Gilbert said happily as she shut the door behind her.

She stood in front of him, looking a little disheveled with a wrapped bundle under her arm. To Gilbert, though, her being less perfect only made her more beautiful.

The terrifying sounds of shouting and gunfire outside his door were instantly forgotten. But where before he'd felt he would have melted into his shoes at the sight of her, his time in front of the crowd had given him a new kind of confidence. She ran to the table in the corner of the room, removed her glasses and started unwrapping the bundle she'd brought.

Most surprisingly, she didn't seem the least bit upset that he'd just tried to cave in her skull.

"Hello, Gilbert," she said, "I'm glad to see you've been thinking ahead." She pulled a hat from the long wrap of dark material. "I couldn't find much in the time I had," she said with her back to him, "no more than a cloak and a floppy fedora, but it'll have to do. At least you've kept the sword cane."

Still standing behind her, Gilbert breathed deeply and felt something stir inside. He raked his right hand through his hair, adjusted his pince-nez glasses and smiled. "Well, thank you for coming," he said, noticing the way the room's light fell on her hair, and her eyes.

Her beautiful, blue eyes. Now, what would Herb do? Hm ... He reached out with his right hand and gently took her wrist. She spun around with a harried expression. "Gilbert, we have to move quickly here. Now what do you need?"

He gave his best Herb-like smile and winked. "We were so rudely interrupted last time. Now where were we?" He leaned in towards her face while closing his eyes.

A burst of pain sang from his right ear. He yelped and his eyes sprang open as he dropped to one knee. He looked at her through sudden tears of pain.

She had gripped his right ear with her left hand. Her lip was curled in a sneer of disgust as she used her right hand to reach over to the table and put her glasses back on while he gasped and gibbered in pain.

"That was pathetic, Gilbert," she said with a tone that could have curdled milk. Gilbert couldn't believe the amount of pressure she was putting on his ear—he heard—he felt it tearing! Was she going to tear it off? "What're you doing?" he gasped. "Stop, or I'll call the guards!"

"Norton's guards are out there now, Gilbert," she hissed, still gripping and twisting his ear. "They shot those red-suited clowns at the door, and they've been instructed to leave you utterly alone until a half hour after I've left. Then, they'll shoot *you*. Now," she growled, "we really don't have time for you to play a lothario lover-boy. We've got to get you past them somehow." With that, she released him and reached to get her bundled disguise.

"What was that all about?" Gil said as he stood, his hand jumping to his sore and swelling ear.

"Didn't you hear me? Or does your other ear need a tweaking?" she said, raising her right hand.

"No! No, no, no," Gil said, covering the sides of his head with his hands. "No. Look, I'm sorry if I moved too quickly there, but don't you think ripping half my head off is a bit much for a guy trying to steal a kiss? And why worry about time? Cameron said he would send guys to get me when they were ready to overthrow Norton."

"Cameron? Overthrow ... Gilbert Keith Chesterton, have you really fallen so far?" She was angry now. When she'd pinched his ear, she'd still been upset, but stayed calm and measured. Now her delicate hands were planted fists at her sides, her cheeks puffed out in anger, several tresses of hair flew free from her otherwise immaculate hairdo, and her eyes were chips of ice-blue fire.

"Fallen?" he said, still rubbing his ear, "I had a whole crowd *lifting* me *above* their heads to the stage! Didn't you see it?"

"Yes. And you looked like a dead leaf being swept along in a river current. Gilbert, it's all a plot! Cameron is using you as a puppet because of your popularity with the steam crab today! You aren't the brilliant leader you think you are! Don't you see?"

Gilbert bristled. "You think I'm stupid, then?"

"No, that's ..."

"You think I'm some kind've loser?"

"Gilbert, I ..."

"Well, let me tell *you* something, little lady, maybe you can hurt me when I'm not expecting it, but I took out a Martian in the sewers not too long ago! And I survived being drowned in an underground river! And that crazy Doctor friend of yours and the Special Branch group you both work for didn't manage to kill me either! So why don't you just stand back and let me have my time?"

"People will die tonight if you have 'your time,' Gilbert! This city, it's part of an Empire that's built upon the blood of innocent people, of *children*. Is that worth it to you?"

"I ... well ... " he looked away, then squarely at her face. "Yes," he said, jutting his chin out just a little. "After all, you can't make an omelet without breaking a few eggs, right? It's war. Death is part of war. And if this city is gonna be mine, I'll have to make sac ... *They'll* have to make sacrifices in the name of freedom."

She was quiet for a moment, looking at him with eyes that were sad and disappointed. "And to think," she said, "those little boys have been singing your praises at the savant school, because you wouldn't even throw away pawns on a chessboard. Is it fine, now, to throw a human being under the carriage wheels if it suits your goals?"

"But that's just it! Don't you see? It'll just be like that for a while. Once I'm in charge, it'll be different!" Gilbert, cautious but still overcome with passion, gently took both her shoulders in his hands and looked into her eyes. "Think about it, Galatea! Me running this city! I could turn it around and use it on the Special Branch, the Doctor, anyone who'd try to do the wrong thing! It'll be my city, Galatea. It could ... it could be ours!"

She broke free and went to the closed window, standing in place with her back to him and her arms crossed. "You don't understand, Gilbert. The Branch doesn't care who runs the city. They know anyone with power on this scale will be corrupted and fall into their clutches. You can't control it; *it* controls *you*. You can't fight them with armies and guns. Small people can only escape them, and hope to stay free and hidden from their notice like a rabbit dodging a hawk. Your parents knew that much; that's why they went into hiding."

"Did you ... no, I guess you didn't know my folks."

"No, but I've heard about them. Their pseudonyms are bandied about with reverence by all new agents."

"Their ... their what?"

"Pseudonyms. Fake names." Now she turned to face him. "Oh, hang it all. We have some time if we need it, thanks to those guards outside. Gilbert, field agents for the Branch are given the coded name of a simple profession that tells something about their work. The Doctor is called such because his job is to, as they say, 'cure' the 'body' of the Empire by either removing undesirables or by cutting off dead weight."

He still stood before her, very quiet. "What about you?" he said after a pause, "or my folks?"

She paused, listening. "I had wanted to move quickly. But this is important, and it doesn't sound like Foggschild is doing much damage outside yet.

"Your mother, Gilbert, was called the Maid. Since she ... killed people with knives, a lot of wet messes were left on the ground. Sometimes that was a good thing because it sent a message, but sometimes her 'wet work' needed to be cleaned, hidden from view, and the bodies disposed of."

Gilbert blinked and looked away.

"Is this difficult, Gilbert?"

"Yes," he closed his eyes, nodding. "Yes it is. Tell me about my father."

"Your father was the Groundskeeper. There was a story—your father, liking Greek history so much, likely told you this—of a new king who went to a neighboring ruler for advice. 'What must I do,' the new king asked ...'"

"'...To keep my people from rebelling against me,'" Gilbert finished, his voice half-lost in memory. "The old king said, 'Watch what I do,' and went out to a field of wheat. If he saw any sheaf of wheat with its head higher than the rest, he cut it down with his sword." Gilbert's voice drifted off as he finished the story his Pa had told him at least a dozen times.

"That was your father's job. Anytime anyone outside of the Branch became too powerful, appeared to be too intelligent, or was otherwise seen as a potential threat from school age onwards, your father was dispatched to keep all the 'plants' the same height, usually at a distance with his rifle."

"And who are you?" Gilbert said, still avoiding her eyes.

It was her turn to look down. "I am the Actress. I'm trained to play multiple roles as needed, but I've had trouble staying on task as of late. There have been too many deaths, and insane people to deal with. This city is ... it's like a corpse that's been brought out of the grave, dressed up in evening clothes and sat at a table for afternoon tea. It looks nice, but it's rotting, stinking underneath, and corrupt and vile."

"Wait ... just a second ... " he turned away and closed his eyes in pain, putting his fingers over his eyelids while his sore ear was for the moment forgotten.

"What is it? Gilbert?"

"Something you said, something about...about sitting at a table. And tea. I keep thinking there's something there, but it hurts when I try to ..."

"You have to stop," she said, her voice sharp as a carving knife. "It won't help to do that. I made a very thorough job of ..."

She stopped. Gilbert looked up at her as if her face were causing him pain. "You made a thorough job? Of what? Of *me*?"

She moved to the end table and began gathering up the cloak and hat. "We need to go," she said, "here, put these on."

"Wait, wait just a minute. How do you know so much about it? Did you..." his eyes widened and he looked at her with a mixture of anger and horror. "Did you," he said, his hands going to his temples as his eyes widened. "Did you ...what... what did you do to me?"

"I tried to protect you!"

"What did you do?"

"I kept you safe!"

"*Safe*?" he roared. Then his voice fell quiet. "D'you think I'm that weak?"

They were both silent for a moment. Then Gilbert looked down at her and spoke.

"You think you know me, don't you?" he said. His voice had a quiet edge.

"I've heard that before," she said, "but not from you."

"Who from?" he sneered, standing and feeling very tall over her for the first time. "An old boyfriend?"

"No. The last person who tried to fight the Branch by being as evil as them."

"You're judging *me*? Calling *me* evil? *Me*? How many people have *you* killed?"

"Not as many as your parents did."

The calm words stung hard. Gilbert moved back with a surprised expression, as if he'd been slapped. Then his face grew sharp.

"Now!" he said, bringing his index finger within an inch of her nose. A red haze was at the edge of his field of vision, and his leg was hurting again, his old wound throbbing insistently. "Now you've gone too far, missy! Where I come from, when you pick on a man's family ..."

Now, he tried the last move Chang taught him. Where his first move involved his hands to block and strike, and the second his feet to trip and kick, this used *both*:

He first twisted his hand free. Easier to do when fighting smart.

Then, using *both* hands, he grabbed the sleeves of her blouse just below her shoulders and tried to yank her to her right side. If it had gone well, he would have kicked her leg out from under her while she was off balance, dropping her to the floor. From there, he could restrain her without causing her any pain until they both calmed down.

But it didn't go right. When he grabbed her arms, she twisted her right arm back and out of his grip. Once free, the heel of her right hand shot out at his face. She'd been trained and conditioned when threatened to strike a person's nose at a precise angle, blasting bone splinters into the assailant's brain to kill them instantly.

But she pulled her blow at the last second. His nose *wasn't* broken, though he still felt his face explode in a blast of pain, making him yell and reel backwards. The greatest damage wasn't to Gilbert's nose, though. That wouldn't even need to be set before it healed properly, and the bleeding would stop soon enough. For Gilbert, the greatest damage came from her blouse.

Gilbert fell backwards, now an unthinking creature in his pain, seeking only to protect himself and escape in some way from a threat he couldn't beat down. His left hand still held her sleeve, and it squeezed into a fist as he pulled back his right hand to defend his injured face. She pulled back easily, and as she spun away from his grip her sleeve tore, ripping with a loud, shredding sound that lasted only a second of real time, but seemed much longer to Gilbert.

Gilbert fell backwards, now an unthinking creature in his pain, seeking only to protect himself and escape in some way from a threat he couldn't beat down. His left hand still held her sleeve, and it squeezed into a fist as he pulled back his right hand to defend his injured face. She pulled back easily, suffering only the smallest bruising. As she pulled and spun away from his grip her sleeve tore, ripping with a loud, shredding sound that lasted only a second of real time but seemed much longer to Gilbert.

The noise of her tearing sleeve, coupled with the pain in his nose, caused a number of crucial and dangerous things to happen in Gilbert's head. Had his brain been a dam, the tearing sleeve and injured nose would have caused the locks on a number of important floodgates to pop open all at the same time. He fell to the floor, breathing in odd, hissing gulps as he held his bloodied face in one hand, and a strip of her torn sleeve in the other.

She was breathing heavily herself; Gilbert had shown surprising strength and speed for someone so lightly trained in the art of fisticuffs. She, on the other hand, had been trained to escape from a hold, face her attacker and either kill them or escape. Seeing him prone on the ground, she performed a number of movements that would have seemed comical to an onlooker in the room. She pulled her foot back to give a deadly kick to the kidney with the pointed toe of her boot, but stopped and stood straight instead. She pulled back and then stopped first one arm, then the other, reason stopping instinct and deep conditioning to save Gilbert's life twice more.

I can't—I musn't! she thought desperately, turning and running out of the room. She didn't remember opening the door, could barely hear the catcalls and cruel applause of Norton's guards stationed at the entrance. Nor did she hear the screaming, shrieking speech of Cameron as she ran through the street of the Red worker level, and didn't see Herb and Margaret or the little army of cowboys as they moved towards the elevator of the white spire.

She ran, running to escape the thing that screamed in her to kill Gilbert and finish the job, hoping that by running alone she could tire out the voice in her head, as she was tired, tired of her life, and the life she'd lived since she had been pulled out of a Northeastern orphanage at the age of eleven by a sinister looking man with dark whiskers and a black top hat named the Doctor.

After running for what seemed like hours but was only a few minutes, she collapsed in a doorway and sobbed quiet tears that were drowned out by the screaming mob and Cameron's voice.

To most people, the mind is an odd and unpredictable thing. In fact, it functions according to pure rules of logic. It is only because the rules are far more complicated than most conscious human minds can fathom that the mind's workings can seem so difficult to understand.

One thing human minds are especially known for doing is causing hidden memories to arise when experiences similar to earlier ones occur. The smell of chalkdust, for example, can resurrect memories of a long-ago classroom. A piece of music can bring back a memory of a perfect romantic moment or a searing, painful rejection.

In the case of Gilbert, he'd been hit on the nose, causing spectacular pain, while simultaneously hearing the sound of tearing cloth. The combination of the two had jarred something loose that not only he, but also others, had wanted very much to keep under lock, key and cover for a very long time, ideally forever.

When he was a little boy in Minnesota, sitting home on a warm summer's evening was not unusual for young Gilbert. Having recently discovered chess, he and his mother would often play the game at night. On this particular evening, Pa had gone on a trip two towns over for supplies, and wasn't due back for another two days.

It was Saturday evening. The day's sun had hammered its simmering heat into the very dust of the prairie, and now even the moon's face couldn't banish it. The farmhands had taken their week's pay, most of them running the normally good hour's walk into town to enrich the local saloon owner. The two or three who didn't drink had gone to sleep in the small bunkhouse hours before.

But while the farmhands slept without difficulty, it was on such hot nights that seven-year-old Gilbert found his yearnings for adventure off the farm particularly intense. Too warm in his upstairs room to sleep, Gilbert would imagine himself exploring the poles with Admiral Perry, discovering the Americas with Columbus, plundering King Solomon's mines with Quartermain, or a host of other adventures where he was the plucky sidekick to the experienced hero.

He was in the middle of defeating an army of Turkish pirates in the rigging of the *Santa Maria* (Gilbert always liked to add his own twists to his historical adventures) when he heard the singing outside the house.

Singing was perhaps too kind a word. What he heard used a voice, lyrics and tunes, but the lone singer slurred his words so much and shouted them so off-key that he sounded more like the wounded moose a neighbor had shot last year while hunting with Pa.

Gilbert wasn't entirely certain, but it sounded like the noise was getting closer to his house. It was soft at first—the only reason he'd heard it was because he'd already been awake.

He thought about waking Ma, but really, he reasoned, what would Allan Quartermain do? Did Magellan check with his mother to make sure it was all right to cross the Pacific?

No, he told himself. Heroes took care of business *themselves*.

He tiptoed out of his room and down the stairs. As Gilbert neared the front door, the mangled warbling outside shot up in volume, if not in clarity. Now, it was right outside the front door, and getting close.

In the books, the hero always put their ear to the door to get important information. He first checked and saw that the front door was locked. He then crept closer, and had just turned his head to the side so he could put his ear to the door when ...

CRAM! The door burst open with a scream of splitting wood and broken metal, swinging on its hinges in a brutal arc at Gilbert's head. The heavy wooden door slammed Gilbert full on the nose, making it crunch with a sound peppermint candy canes made in his mouth when he bit down on them.

Little Gilbert screamed, as all his thoughts of adventure became so much steam and ashes. Nothing in the world now was more real and terrifying than the shaggy, mumbling, whiskey-reeking monster that had just pounded through his door and into his home.

"Shaddap, yah weak little ..." said the monster, barely looking at him as it staggered left through to the living room. Holding both hands to his battered nose, Gilbert saw between two fingers that the creature wasn't so muscular after all, and that the dark stringy hair looked familiar.

Then the monster turned, just enough that Gilbert saw it had Obidiah Calvin's face in profile, sweating and unshaven, eyes almost unseeing, lips mumbling incoherently. "Huh. Howdy, pard. Tr'peeze, huh? I won' tell, but yuh ... ya gotta pay the piper, ya gotta pay ... " Obidiah interrupted his own booze-soaked speech by heaving and soaking the floor in his own vomit.

"Heh," he said, wiping the worst of the drool and blood from a lip that was split and swollen. Gilbert, silent from fear as Obidiah spoke, saw a fresh shiner under the wiry man's right eye. "Where's yer maw, at? I gotta ... gotta a little business offertunity, an' I ..."

"Mister Calvin!"

It was Ma's voice, but different than Gilbert had ever heard it. It stopped Calvin midstep through his own puddle of vomitus, drawing his attention down the hall.

Though he could hear her, Gilbert couldn't see his mother. He whimpered as he tried to push himself back into the corner, away from the door to the outside that was slowly swinging back to its original closed position.

"Wha, h'lo, missus Ches'on!" Calvin spoke with a leering emphasis on the words. It made them more the kind Gilbert heard men use with barmaids when he'd walked past the saloon with Pa, rather than how you'd talk to your employer.

"Calvin," she said sternly, "*if you know what's good for you,* you will leave this house at once!"

Calvin hesitated for just a second. Then he blinked, shook his head, looked at Ma and smiled. "C'mere, honey!"

Gilbert, his nose flaring pain like a volcano with a migraine headache, stepped out from his alcove and readied himself. No one, but *no one* was going to talk like that to his mother!

As little Gilbert stepped into the hallway, he saw Obidiah's back slouching towards Ma, her smaller body a full head shorter than the lean farmhand, her white flannel nightgown barely visible in the moonlit corridor.

Quiet, thought Gilbert, it was important to be quiet! He could try to tackle Calvin, or brain him with a lamp. Or should he ...

Then something very strange happened.

Gilbert had seen his Ma use knives before. Ma could gut, skin and dress one of Pa's hunting kills in half the time or less than other mothers in town. She also had an odd little habit of spinning the blades in her hands twice before going to work, then doing the deed with none of the wrinkled facial expressions that other mothers (or fathers!) had used when doing the sometimes gory work.

Now, Gilbert could see the knives in Ma's hands by a sliver of moonlight that slipped through a window and glinted off the blades. It may have been a trick of the light, but the knives were different somehow, their blades at least a full foot, maybe two feet long.

Ma did something Gilbert had never seen before. The knives spun in her hands, her arms moving independently of each other in slow arcs, like a magician making mystic passes over an upcoming illusion.

"Calvin, you *want* to stay back from me!" she barked in a more commanding tone than Gilbert had ever heard her use before.

"Oh, boo'ful," he said as he staggered towards her, his long arms stretching out with crooked, dirty fingernails. "Just one li'l ...huk!"

Calvin's back jerked upward towards the ceiling, his body spasmed in surprise as he staggered back two steps.

Calvin looked down at his chest at something Gilbert could not see. "You ... you li'l *witch*... I'll kill you!" he said in a voice that sounded like he was gargling. "You'n yer skinny li'l weird kid..."

Ma's arms whirled and her knives flashed again, carving a deadly aerial ballet with Calvin and little Gilbert as its only audience. Calvin lunged at Ma three more times, and each time Calvin's body jerked with a wet *huk!*, followed by Calvin pulling back with a screech and a curse.

They were in the kitchen now, Ma and Calvin standing in profile. Calvin was bleeding freely from four red splotches on his chest, torso and arms. His right arm sagged, useless in the fight. He looked around, his eyes and head bouncing back and forth like he was searching for something. Ma was keeping a safe distance, saying something to him, trying to talk him out the back door.

Calvin's hand shot out and grabbed something, something that shone even brighter than the knives in Ma's hands. " ... Cut ya!" he roared, "Cut ya, that'll learn ya ..." He swung once, twice with his left hand, the meat cleaver he'd grabbed from the wall rack slicing a deadly arc in the air inches from Ma's face.

Ma's expression didn't change. She looked as focused and dispassionate as if she were doing a math problem in her head. "One ... two ..." she said with each of Calvin's deadly swings. Suddenly, after the third one, she ducked and lunged forward with her right hand, keeping her left blade up for defense. Gilbert had watched the entire, violent play through the doorway to the kitchen. But because Ma pushed Calvin to the side and out of Gilbert's vision, little Gilbert was spared from witnessing the killing blow.

But though he couldn't see, he still could *hear*.

Still holding his nose that was throbbing in pain, he could see Ma. Ma, who had read him bedtime stories, helped him learn math problems, bandaged his knee and made him cookies. Now he saw her lunge forward like a mix between a fencing swordsman and a picture in a book he'd seen of a Japanese Samurai.

And he heard his Ma's knife puncture Calvin's body with a sound like a pin going through writing paper. She held still for a second, then her arm made a jerk and twist. Her arm slowly pointed downwards, not stopping until Gilbert heard something heavy hit the floor like a sack of meal.

She pulled back, her knife making a long, agonizing ripping sound as it tore through the cloth of Obidiah Calvin's shirt and body.

Ma, her nightdress sprinkled with Calvin's blood, stood over him for a full minute with her long knives at the ready. Gilbert kept looking at the scene with more terror than he'd ever known, his irrational child's mind insisting that all this, all this, was *his* fault. If *he* hadn't approached the door, if *he* hadn't screamed, if *he* ...

Ma was looking at him.

Gilbert hid his eyes. His Ma, his mother, had changed in less than a minute from all things good mothers were to their sons into something dangerous, destructive and terrifying. She reached over and turned on a dim gas lamp in the hallway.

"Gilbert," she whispered, walking towards him with the knives pointing down at the ground.

Gilbert shrieked as she drew closer. She looked down at her hands and saw her knives covered in blood. She looked back at her frightened son, still backed into the corner, blood and mucus running from his nose, his eyes wide with fear at what he'd seen her become.

With one motion, her eyes never leaving his, Marie Chesterton took two large, soundless steps forward while throwing her knives to clatter on the living room floor. She crouched with Gilbert, who was sobbing uncontrollably.

"Son, Gilbert, come to Ma," she said, trying to hold him. In his fear and anger he pushed her away, shoving himself into the corner again like a trapped animal.

Then Gilbert saw something in her face that no child in the world wants to see on the face of any parent.

He saw *confusion* in Ma's face.

And he saw *fear*.

Worst of all, he could see *tears*.

"I'm not trained for this!" she said softly as she wiped her eyes, making the pinpricks of blood on her face smear into little red comets on her cheeks.

"Ma ... Momma..." he said, "why?"

She looked into his eyes, as if searching for something. She took a deep breath, looked down, and then back up again.

"Gilbert," she said, "I can explain it to you, and then I can help you. Wait here. Can you do that for a minute?"

Gilbert hesitated, and then gave two quick nods of his head.

Ma ran into the kitchen, taking large steps over Calvin's body. Gilbert heard her open a cupboard and rattle some dishes, and then heard the sound of pouring water.

She was back at his side in less than a minute. She'd washed off most of the blood, but not all.

"Now, Gilbert," she said in a slow, soothing voice, "I want you to look at this cup of water, as I pour the sugar into it. Watch the grains as they move, Gilbert, and please relax. Relax, as you watch the grains dissolve..."

Gilbert watched, the shock and fear of the night fading away with his mother's soothing voice as he began to feel very, very sleepy.

And in his waking mind, overlapping his now-conscious memory like thin paper over a picture, was another memory. Although still hazy and difficult to remember, he remembered a pretty, red-headed girl who sat in a French cafe and told Gilbert over and over again to look at the tea, Gilbert, look at the tea as the grains dissolve…

He'd awoken the next morning refreshed, happier and better rested than he'd remembered feeling in a very long time. He'd had a disturbing nightmare, but it was already fading into the murky past where all dreams go.

Bounding downstairs and full of energy, he'd barely noticed that the mirror had been removed from the bathroom. Ma was already cooking up his favorite breakfast of flapjacks and sausages. Their house was normally clean, but this morning it was especially so. In fact, the hallway and the kitchen had been scrubbed so well that the brown floorboards almost shone insistently.

"Good morning, Gilbert!" Ma said, giving him a wide, bright smile.

"'Morning, Ma!" Gilbert said happily, looking for an apple to start his day and whet his appetite.

That day was one of the best, fullest days he remembered having throughout his childhood. They took a hike together, practiced on the trapeze, and Ma introduced him to a new thing in gymnastics—a kind of balance-bar he learned to walk on and do tricks with.

Ma stayed with him nearly all day, telling him to stay away from the Western woods for the rest of the week. When pressed for a reason, she said a bear had been sighted there. Gilbert thought it odd, but didn't question her further.

They both felt unusually tired by mid-afternoon that day, and needed a rest.

When Pa returned, Ma had a serious look on her face and talked to him until far into the night, long after little Gilbert went to bed. The next few days went well, except his nose hurt for a week for some reason. His mirror was returned a week after that.

And ever after, the sound of tearing cloth was like nails on a chalkboard to his ears.

And now, Gilbert remembered it. Remembered it *all*, from being bashed in the face to his mother putting him under and telling him he would forget everything after the thing with the water and the sugar, and remembered Ma and Obidiah Calvin fighting, remembering...

He wasn't asleep; he was remembering while wide-awake. Remembering things so painful and buried so deeply for so many years that feelings of fear, guilt and anger burst and swirled as fresh and new in his mind as the day they were made. He tried to stand, but felt so sick he sat back down on his bed. More details of the horrible night played through his head, ferocious and unstoppable as a military marching band, and he slid back to the floor in a whimpering, cowering ball. He closed his eyes, mashing his hands against his eyelids as he had when he was little. Tears squeezed out slowly, then in a flood. By the time he remembered his mother hypnotizing him, there was a small puddle of saltwater on the floor and sticking to the right side of his face.

He was in this position, still dressed in like a well-to-do gentleman in his dark suit, with his sword cane out of its sheath on the floor nearby, when the noise sounded at his door.

"Johnny! Wake up!"

Johnny heard Jack's voice and wished he hadn't. It seemed he'd just closed his eyes; was the British kid gonna annoy him all night?

"What, Jack?" he asked, wishing he had a miniaturized version of his Tesla gun handy.

Hmmmm ... come to think of it, that'd be a great idea for his next invention...

"There's something happening in the city, Johnny! Something terrible! Tollers and the twins saw a group of Reds on this level!"

"So report them. You're good at that."

"Johnny, somehow they not only knew where the twins were sleeping, but they also knew about the explosive jelly they were working on!"

Johnny frowned. That sounded very, very ungood.

"Anything else?"

"Then they went after Swift, and made him give over those clockworks he's been fiddling with. There's a dreadful row outside, too. They're chanting slogans over and over in the city square on Red level like savages at a sacrifice!"

"Okay, that's it!" Johnny swung out of bed, dressed in his one-piece white coverall pajamas, and began rummaging under his bed.

"Whatever are you doing, Johnny?"

"Looking for my insurance. Haven't you been nosing around at all? Into the restricted areas, I mean?"

"Restricted areas?" Jack said, drawing himself up. "I, sir, am a prefect of this floor. It is a position of trust I take very ser ..."

"I'll take that as a no. Jack, there's a steambot army downstairs, and the city's engines are humming. Now you tell me people are tumbling smart kids' rooms looking for weapons and other toys, and some kind of revolution's underway. It's time we left this party, pronto, and take as many of our friends with us as we can!"

"Leave? How?

"There's a bunch've capsules—*evacuoles* the steam monkeys call them. You get into it and lock the door from either the outside or the inside. Once it's locked, sand runs through some little hourglass and *fwissht*! You're back on Terra Firma before they know you're gone. And there's enough of them there for you, me, Tollers, Mister Chesterton and anyone else we can grab along the way."

"Then why hasn't anyone tried to use them before? And how do you know so much about them?"

"Because the guards shoot anyone who even sees them, but I bribed a guard with a little gadget I made, lets 'im see in the dark. Now, help me get this pack on, and we can make our way to ..."

The door to the room burst open!

Up until now Jack Lewis had considered meeting Gilbert Chesterton the most wonderful event of his life. Now, standing before him was his second greatest hero, Herbert George Wells! Wearing a Western longcoat and carrying a pepperbox pistol, no less!

"Mister Herbert Wells!" Jack bellowed, more surprised than he'd been in a long time. His voice echoed down the halls of the dormitory level.

Herb's eyes snapped to look at Jack, then narrowed to razor slits.

"Not smart, Jack," Johnny said, watching Herb carefully. He was still lying on his stomach with his body only three-quarters of the way out from under his bed. His hand was on the Tesla gun. Johnny, not blinded by hero-worship, could see clearly that Herbert Wells was neither their friend nor in a mood to help them.

"And you are?" Herb said, his voice barely above a whisper, his ugly looking pepperbox pointed at both Jack and Johnny.

"I, sir," said Jack, smiling and drawing himself up into a happy, dignified pose, "am Clive Staples Lewis. And this is my colleague,

John Brainerd. You are doubtless seeking your colleague and friend, Mister Gilbert Chesterton. Correct?"

Herb smiled with a grin that gave Johnny chills. "Why, yes. Yes I am. Could you bring me to him, please? There's an awful hullabaloo about to start, and I really do need to protect him."

Herb's eye fell on a small object on the dresser. It was the small, thick disk Gilbert had gotten from the red-head, back in the floating dance hall in Berlin. He had never yet seen it, but it had been described to him.

Jack pushed his glasses back up his nose. "That may prove challenging, sir. He's indisposed at the moment."

"Yes. I'd heard something about that," Herb said dryly. "It seems he's taken it into his head to lead this revolution that's causing such a ruckus."

"Indeed," said Jack, in a voice thick with awe and hero-worship. "Are you certain of this?"

"Quite certain, Clive. Now, to help Gil, I'm first going to need that little disk on your desk, the one with all the funny letters in circles on it. Second, I'm going to need you two to help me find my friend Gil, so we can talk him out of possibly blowing up this city while I'm on it. Now come here, both of you. I plan on leaving this filthy rock post-haste."

"There's no need to be rude, Mister Wells. After all, I am a very large fan of your style of writing. In fact, I ..."

"Young man," Herb said to Johnny, while still pointing his eyes and pistol at Jack, "will you please shut your friend up before I put a number of holes in him?"

Johnny didn't answer. His eyes were too busy looking over Herb's shoulder, where the large, smiling figure of Captain Strock loomed a full head taller than the youth.

Faster than they thought possible, Strock's hand grabbed Herb's right wrist and squeezed. The pistol dropped as if by magic. Then Strock's other arm was around Herb's neck. "Did you say you were *leaving*, son?"

Still smiling, Strock squeezed.

Chapter 74

"Truth, of course, must of necessity be stranger than
fiction, for we have made fiction to suit ourselves."
– GKC, *Heretics*

After a few minutes in the doorway, she pulled herself together,
tucked her hair in place and out of her face, and stood up
again.

She'd been taught to assess situations quickly and accurately, and
it served her well here. It was obviously time to leave. Time to get
Gilbert, derail if possible the schemes of both Norton and the Special
Branch, then flee from this place like a fox with its tail on fire. Maybe
time to leave the Special Branch behind, too. Once away, she could
decide if her feelings for Gil were real or the product of stress, and
make her next move.

She ran, hiding in the shadows when necessary, and arrived back at
Gilbert's apartment in minutes. Rounding the corner of the hallway, she
stepped over the bodies of the red-clad workers that Norton's black-
jacketed thug squad had executed.

"Ma'am, I'm 'fraid you can't come through here just now. We've
got business to finish," said one of Norton's guards. Dark-rimmed
goggles were perched above his eyes on his forehead, and the muzzle
of his drawn pistol gleamed in the dim hallway gaslight. He raised his
free hand, covered in a black leather glove, signing her to stop. Though
he faced her, the other three faced the door, looking intently at the
timepiece carried by the largest of their group.

"Why ever not?" she asked with an innocent air, blinking her eyes
as best as she could. If only she'd remembered to put her glasses back
on! Something about them commanded respect from almost every
American, perhaps because they made her look like a school marm.

"We have an execution to complete, ma'am. This is no place for a
fine lady like y'self, so please walk away now."

"Indeed," she said. The squad crouched outside Gilbert's door, as
one of their number counted down from ten in an official-sounding
voice.

Gilbert was sitting up with his arms wrapped around his knees, and
his eyes scrunched shut as tears dribbled down his cheeks. Blood and
mucus had dried under his nose where she'd hit him with the heel of

her hand, but he took no notice of it. He mumbled incoherently while rocking back and forth.

It had started with small whimpers as the memories first trickled back. But then Ma's cutting of Calvin hit Gilbert's mind like a flash flood over level grassland. The whole thing made Gilbert feel sick, vulnerable, and frightened all over again in a short, violent blast of recollection. The only way he had to protect himself was to withdraw, both mentally and physically, pulling inward like a turtle into its shell where he couldn't be seen, heard or hurt in any way.

He'd become so withdrawn he didn't hear the large men counting down outside his door. When they reached five, he heard but didn't really register the sudden sounds of thumping, slamming, screaming, shooting, and finally bodies slumping lifelessly to the floor.

Nor did he notice the door to his apartment open with a slow creak. Or the red-head peek her head in for the third time that day.

"Gilbert?" she whispered, only her left eye and a lock of her hair visible.

Gilbert gave no sign he'd heard, but kept rocking back and forth while hugging his knees and burying his face into the dark trousers of his legs, moaning and mumbling incoherently. The expensive material had by now been ruined by exposure to salty tears, blood, snot and spit.

"Oh, dear," she said as she closed and locked the door. She rushed to him, tilting his head back. "Gilbert? Gilbert? Can you hear me?" she said, holding his face up to the light to see his pupils react.

Pulling him away from his bent knees made him moan, then shriek. She quickly tilted his head forward again.

"You poor, poor thing," she said, wiping away a tear from her own cheek as he continued rocking. Hesitantly, she wrapped her own arms around his huddled form and rocked him back and forth in the same rhythm he'd been using. It took nearly ten minutes before he stopped his gibbering, sobbing monologue, and another five minutes before his sobs became deep, shuddering sighs.

"Gilbert?" she said, after his voice was quiet. "Gilbert, can you hear me?" She'd softened her voice, but it sounded very loud in the silent room.

"I…" he said. It was more a breath than a word. "I…Ma. Mama. She…killed a man. He tried to…"

"Did he hurt you, Gilbert?"

"In the face. The door. If I hadn't been there, he wouldn't have hit me. Ma wouldn't have had to…then Ma got the water, and the sugar, and she told me to look at it while she stirred it. I looked, I got sleepy, and it all went away when she talked to me."

God's teeth, she thought, now holding Gilbert just a little tighter. His mother had killed an intruder, but she'd had to make the kill in front of little Gilbert in order to save him. And then she'd not only cleaned the house of the kill, but scrubbed Gilbert's young little mind, too.

"Gilbert," she said, "I will not leave you. Not while you need me. Do you understand? I am here."

Gilbert looked up at the wall with unseeing eyes.

"I got it in me to do bad things," he said, his voice a whisper.

"Shhh," she said, wrapping her arms around him, placing her cheek against his forehead and rocking him back and forth. "You're good now. You're good."

He started rubbing his hands over and over again, trying fruitlessly to remove the dried blood. "It's in me," he said, "It's all in me. All in my blood."

"You aren't your parents, Gilbert. They were good, too. Or became so. They were good to you."

"Bad things," Gilbert muttered, "Bad things. Ma did a…bad thing, but she couldn't save us any other way. But it was bad. But she saved us…"

His voice raised in pitch as he started rocking again.

I'm not trained for this, she realized. This was the first situation she'd ever encountered that she hadn't had some kind of training for.

Time to improvise.

She stood quickly and walked to Gilbert's end table. Taking a glass from the nearby sink, she half-filled it with a clear liquid from a flask she had pulled from beneath the folds of her skirt.

She flipped open a small cap under the diamond on her ring and tipped the ring sideways. A tiny amount of white powder dumped from the ring into the glass. Using her finger as a crude stir stick, she swirled the liquid until the white powder dissolved.

Back beside Gilbert, she cooed in his ear and repeated everything he said until she coaxed him to drink the concoction. "Drink, Gilbert. All will be well. This isn't tea, and there is no sugar. This will only help you sleep. And sleep well." She set the glass on the floor beside them and held him again, planning, thinking, and predicting. Slowly, Gilbert's whimpering softened and his body sagged in her arms. She set him onto his bed fully dressed, using the cloak she'd acquired earlier as a crude cover.

She'd given him enough to keep him asleep and dead to the world for perhaps a half hour. She now opened his window a crack and looked outside.

Sections of Red level had gone dark, with the only light coming from fires that couldn't burn very far in a city of stone. The darkness and firelights were climbing, though, as sections of the mob moved up into White level. She heard more noise from the streets outside. A full riot was almost certain if things weren't arrested. If so, she could count on there being no further threats to Gilbert. Both Cameron and Norton would be too busy sending their troops against each other to worry about her or the lanky, sleeping boy in the room with her.

But what if more guards *did* arrive, from either side?

She patted the two, ugly pistols in her waistband, taken from the recently deceased executioners outside. *Let them come,* she thought. She felt less like Gilbert's potential paramour now. More like a mother lion protecting her den. It was a new feeling for her, one that her years of training hadn't successfully snuffed out. *Let them come,* she repeated in her mind. *They'll find at least one person in this city who know how to defend herself, and those she...*

Those she...

She ...those I ...I ...

Those I love, she finally admitted, looking at Gilbert's sleeping form.

"…the masses are kept quiet with a fight. They are kept quiet by the fight because it is a sham-fight; thus most of us know by this time that the Party System has been popular only in the sense that a football match is popular." – GKC, *A Short History of England*

H ow much farther?" Harper asked for the dozenth time. "Just three or four floors away," Margaret said, showing the slightest bit of strain. "Norton has made Gilbert something of his pet, if my spies in the city are correct. He likely has Gilbert safe in a guarded apartment, waiting for this kerfuffle to be done with."

"Why are you so interested in Norton, all of a sudden?" Finn said. "You've been talking about him an awful lot since we got here."

"Your mission is to find Gilbert. Mine involves Gilbert, too. But I have another job in this city, one that involves finding out just what Norton is up to."

"So, you're hoping to kill two birds with one stone, then," said Harper, trying very hard not to let his attraction to her show. "Filtch this Chesterton kid after we deliver him up, and do whatever you need to do to Norton in the same breath."

"In my line of work, a number of assignments double up this way," she whispered into his ear, careful to shield her words from the cowboys. "Coupling multiple tasks is a sure way to be rewarded, for those in my line of work."

Harper swallowed hard at the feel of her breath. When she turned back to the fronthHe closed his eyes and shook his head a little.

She now looked at the door they were about to pass. To Harper it seemed no different than dozens they'd already walked by, but it meant something to Margaret.

"Through here," she said, rattling the doorknob until it opened.

"Why'd you send the English kid off a few floors back, anyways?" said Harper. It was obvious to everyone in earshot but himself that he wanted his conversation with Margaret to continue.

"We were on the level of the savant school, where Norton tries very hard to turn the best and the brightest into his little drones. There's no surer way of keeping power over a people than keeping their cultural icons in your sway. And technology is the way culture is going to be transmitted in the future. Books made in factories instead of presses in a shop. Alien technology is being harnessed as we speak to create weapons, along with entertainments that are so addictive people will riot rather than willingly surrender them. If Gil hasn't been harnessed for Norton's schemes in that area, he's going to be soon enough. He has several admirers in that group already. I gave Herbert my little map reader to find us at the location I'm taking you to, after he checks for Gilbert and tries to sway him from Norton's side."

"Norton, workin' with kids. There's a laugh," Finn said. "When I was a kid meself, Norton very nearly swindled a right nice family out of every penny they had. He sold the slaves afore he could be stopped. Separated families."

"Why should you care about the families of a few Negroes?" said Margaret.

"Missy, my Ma died bringin' me into the world, and my Pap was a vile drunk, the kind that beats on his own when he's had a few. I ain't never had no family 'til I got took in by a widow, and it learned me to hate men who break a child from the people he loves, no matter what their color.

"Ennaways, what Norton did then, that was bad, but he's done worse since. Stupid me saved him from a mob a few years back, and he slipped away from me after. He's cheated the reaper time and again, but tonight I'll make up for all the lives I wrecked by letting him live."

Finn told his story while they'd crept finished climbing the stairs and crept through a dark hallway. Suddenly, they felt a cooling breeze on their faces. The last words of Finn's monologue were swallowed up by vast space around them.

The lights came on. No longer in a tight corridor, they found themselves in a vast space of scrubbed white stone walls and a floor the size of a football arena.

They were surrounded.

On every side and on several balconies were rows of mechanical men. Each had lightbulb eyes, hinged arms and legs, bullet-shaped bodies and pipe-shaped rifles held in their three-fingered mechanical hands.

"Nice to see you again, Huckleberry m'boy," said a voice up several floors.

They looked up. The smiling, generalissimo-suited form of Emperor James Norton the First looked down at them from the highest balcony. He held his hand in the air, ready to give a signal.

> "…when we really worship anything, we love not only its
> clearness but its obscurity. We exult in its very invisibility.
> Thus, for instance, when a man is in love with a woman he
> takes special pleasure in the fact that a woman is
> unreasonable."
> – GKC, *All Things Considered*

I must insist that you release him, Captain Strock!" Jack's voice carried through the room. Johnny Brainerd was impressed, despite the desperate moment. He'd never seen Jack so assertive without some kind of rulebook to back him up.

"Not to worry, boys," Strock said, his smile still in place as small gurgles came from Herb's closed throat. "Not to worry! This fellow won't be bothering you again after tonight!"

"But he wasn't bothering us! Why won't you comprehend that? This is Herbert George Wells, the traveling companion of Mister Gilbert Chesterton! He reported on the Invasion last year, and was present when Father Brown saved the world!"

Strock's eyes grew large, his smile faltering just a bit. "What did you say, sonny?"

"I said that Herbert there," he pointed at Herb, whose eyes were bulging out of their sockets as he tried to vain to breathe, get a grip on any painful part of Strock or take back his pistol from the bigger, smiling man, "is the dear friend Mister Gilbert K. Chesterton. They traveled with Father Brown!"

Strock let go of Herb's neck. Herb hit the floor with a heavy thud and gasped for air like a newborn babe, clutching at his throat.

"Son," said Strock, still smiling, but now with a fatherly tone to his voice as he knelt next to the gasping, writhing form of Herb and grabbed him at the back of his head, "Father Brown was very special to me. I wish my daddy had been half so kind. Tell me, though, just what Church was he a priest in?"

"The Church of Rome," Herb said between gulps of air. His voice sounded like sandpaper.

"Good," said Strock, "and what was his first name?"

"I'm … It was either John or Paul, I'm not sure now."

"Good enough. Now, you tell me pard, what were his last words to you?"

Herb gave Strock a wary look. "Be watchful," Herb said, and rolled away as Strock let go of Herb.

"Not bad, son," Strock said, straightening up and tipping back his cap while Herb rolled away from Strock and gulped air on all fours. "That's what he said to us, right when it looked like we were all going to get killed by the Mau Maus in Africa. Turned out at the last second, one of the warchiefs knew the good priest's reputation and spared us an' us alone in the compound we were hiding out in.

"So, I'll spare you, Herb, the same way. As for these young'uns, though, I'm afraid that..."

Strock was interrupted by two things: a dripping column of water on his head from above that turned into a stream, followed by a bright blue flash that came out of the ceiling.

At the flash, Herb dashed to the cabinet, slipping the disk atop it into his pocket while everyone else was either distracted or blinded.

When Herb looked back, everyone else was rubbing their faces. Strock was out cold on the floor, staring at the ceiling with open, unseeing eyes. His body was making small jerking spasms on the floor, and the room had the thick smell of a summer thunderstorm.

"It works! Gilbert was right! I *can* do it!" Johnny cried, sitting happily in the rafters. The little guy had climbed up there during Strock's self-absorbed little speech, and blasted him with some weird kind of gun attached by a hose to a backpack.

"Was that truly necessary, Johnny?" said Jack, standing up from behind the bed and adjusting his glasses.

"Maybe not. But it sure was fun!" Johnny said. "Now," he swung the Tesla rifle to point at Herb, "you, Englishman, git-a-goin'! And if you try anything funny, you'll find out the hard way if anyone ever walks right again after eatin' a lightning bolt!"

"Not a problem," Herb said, carefully retrieving his pistol. "I'll try to find Gil myself, hm? That work for everyone?"

"Walk on out the door and don't hang around. We'll do just fine," said Johnny, the gun still pointed down at Herb.

Horrid little beasts, Herb thought as he backed out of the room and stomped down the hallway, hearing the door to the room slam and lock behind him. *I halfway hope they put this whole city to the sword. Because if they do I'll tell them to send you lot to the chopping block first!*

Chapter 77

"If we catch sharks for food, let them be killed most mercifully; let any one who likes love the sharks, and pet the sharks, and tie ribbons round their necks and give them sugar and teach them to dance. But if once a man suggests that a shark is to be valued against a sailor…then I would court-martial the man—he is a traitor to the ship." – GKC, *All Things Considered*

Gilbert was in the middle of the thick kind of sleep known only to the truly exhausted or the drugged. As he fell in both categories, he was mildly surprised when he opened his eyes and saw Father Brown sitting in his apartment chair.

Father Brown had been more to Gilbert than just a traveling companion. During the Martian invasion he had been a surrogate father to Gil on their journey, and his voluntary death at the hands of the aliens had infected them with his influenza, saving not only Gil and Herb but the whole world besides.

Gilbert had wept over his corpse, which upon its recent exhumation had shown no signs of decay. Other than being thinner from its being drained of blood by the Martians, of course. It had been dug up, in part, over one of the dozen or so claims by people that prayers to the good Father had resulted in miraculous cures, all of which were under investigation by the Vatican.

Gilbert had also indulged himself in a kind of hagiographic hobby over the last year, looking for people who had known, been saved by, or even been jailed by Father Brown. None had a grudge to bear against the little priest, even those who were spending time in prison as a result of his investigations. His life had been one of such unimpeachable virtue that the cause for beatification, of declaring Father Brown a saint of the Church, had been introduced and moved forward with unusual rapidity. In fact, the only reason Gilbert himself wasn't in Rome right now, testifying on Father Brown's behalf was because ...

Well, to be honest, it was fear that had made him run the other way, in the opposite direction from Rome. Fear of Williamson, and all the resources he had at his disposal. If only he hadn't given in to fear, who knows what he might have accomplished.

But what he might have done wasn't important now. For the late Fr. John Paul Brown of the Church of Rome was sitting in Gilbert's chair across the room from him.

Gilbert tried to speak, but his head felt as thick as a leaden brick. His arms and legs felt heavy and weighted down. Getting out of bed was out of the question, but perhaps, if he spoke loudly enough, he could get Father's attention?

"Father ... " Gilbert said. His mouth felt like it was stuffed with cotton.

But his words carried far enough that the little priest turned in his chair and looked at Gilbert through his large eyeglasses. As he turned, Gilbert saw that Father had been reading a breviary.

"Father Brown," Gilbert said, his voice growing stronger, "Father Brown, it's me, Gilbert!"

Father Brown now looked directly at Gil, his face had an expression of gentle disappointment.

"Gilbert," he said, "do you remember me?"

"Father Brown," Gilbert said, his voice rising, his head clearing as the smell of flowers seemed to permeate the room, though his limbs were still heavy. "Don't you remember? In the basket? In the tunnels beneath Woking village? You saved us, Father! You saved Herb and me!"

"You trusted once," Father Brown said simply, with the barest trace of sadness in his voice. He stood up, straightened his glasses, and walked a few steps closer to Gilbert.

"Father Brown!" Gilbert tried to yell, overcome with a joy he never knew he could have. With enormous effort, he raised his upper body to a near-sitting position. His arms seemed miles long, but they began to obey him.

Father Brown walked closer to Gilbert, adjusting his glasses with one hand while closing his breviary with the other.

"Gilbert, you need to *trust* again," he said, looking Gilbert squarely in the eyes. He then stood, turned and left, shutting the door behind him with a soft click.

"Wait!" Gilbert yelled, "Wait, no!" He started flailing around like a drunken man, and it was in this state that the red-head saw him as the door opened again and she entered the room.

"Gilbert!" she said, rushing to him. She holstered the pistol she'd been carrying in her right hand and took him by the shoulders.

"He was here!" Gilbert said, his speech slurred by slumber, "He was here!"

"Gilbert, I've found a clear route for us, but you have to wake up now. Wake up! I know it's difficult. Laudanum does that to the mind. But you can fight its effects. Now wake up!"

She was shaking him by the shoulders, looking down at him in the eye.

"All ... alright, alright!" he said, trying to push her arms away gently, "I'm ... I'm alright now." He inhaled, blinked and swallowed, thinking again about the memory of his mother, and his dream—or whatever it was, about Father Brown.

"Do you smell something?" he asked.

"What kind of a question is that?" she asked, sniffing the air. "Yes. *Rosaceae Rosa.* Common roses. Now, let's go. Can you walk? Can you hold your cane? Gilbert, wake up! If you want to survive the next hour, you'll need to focus. Now, can you do that?"

"I'm fine. Really, I think. I'll just ...Nevermind. Let's go."

He stood, looked around for his glasses, the one's he'd brought from England, and spied them on the coffee table. He perched them on his nose while hooking the arms of the eyeglasses behind his ears. He then took the pince-nez that Norton gave him from his jacket pocket. He looked hard at it for a few seconds, and then tossed Norton's gift on the table.

"Now," Gilbert said, after one last sigh and self check, "where are we going, exactly?"

"If all goes well? Two miles. Straight down."

"There is a corollary to the conception of being too proud
to fight. It is that the humble have to do most of the
fighting." – GKC, *The Everlasting Man*

So what happens now?" Finn said after a few seconds. "You're not
gonna shoot us, 'else you woulda done it already."

"Correct as usual, my good Pinkerton," Norton said. "I have
a few other plans for you all, first."

"Norton," Margaret snapped, "stop pretending you hold all the
cards! You know who our masters are, and they *do not* like to be trifled
with!"

"They aren't my masters, little lady!" Norton said. "And before I
kill the lot of you, you'll know that."

He paused, and looked intently at the tense expressions on the
faces of the cowboys, their hands all only an inch from their holsters.
"On second thought, I'll kill you all now," he said, and dropped his
hand.

"Run!" roared Finn, drawing his pistol and pushing Margaret to the
center of the room. The cowboys and Herb turned and made for the
door, as the steambots took their guns and ...

Pointed them at the ceiling and fired.

" ... So, you tampered with the disk, then?" Jack said, whispering
as he, Johnny, Tollers, the East Indian twins and several other savant
initiates crept down the darkened hallway. Every so often, an explosion
or scream outside made them pause their steps. Johnny had pulled back
the hammer on his Tesla gun-crossbow, and pointed it forward with his
hand on the trigger. Tollers had gotten hold of a decorative sword
somewhere, and Jack was carrying a fire ax too large for his small,
portly body.

"A little," Johnny said. "I knew it was important when I opened the
thing, and I had a feeling they'd be ransacking our rooms. So I took one
disk from the container, and put it in one of the drawers where they'd
find it. But before I did that, Tollers and me translated it and figured out
the disc was used for making punchcards, punchcards used to teach
steambots when to march an' shoot. We poked some holes in it with a
straight pin and managed to gum up the works a fair bit. A 'bot with
instructions from a punchcard made from that disk'll have a hard time

shooting straight or walking proper, if we read it right."

"We?" said Jack, looking at Tollers, who shrugged his shoulders and grinned sheepishly.

"They're going to find that their steambots' ability to hit targets has been severely compromised," Tollers said. "There was even more to that little disk, though, that I never got a chance to decipher. The language shifted, as if it were no longer a blueprint for a series of automatons, but something else entirely. I wish you could've been there then, Jack."

"Really?"

"Yes. After all the technical jabber, the text on that disk of Gilbert's began talking about temples, elder gods, a reference to the god of war, and other such interesting material—all the things you specialize in."

"And now Mister Wells seems to have stolen the rest of them," Jack said, his voice mystified. "Why ever would he do that? I'd thought he'd be even nicer than Mister Chesterton, since Mister Wells had no Christianity to cloud his vision. Mister Chesterton never stole from us, or threatened us with a weapon when we stood in his way."

As they neared one of the thick glass windows, the dark corridor was lit up by an orange burst of flame from outside. The boys cringed.

"Where exactly are we traveling to, again?" said Salim, one of the East Indian twins who had been praised for his ability in philosophy. His brother Sunil was more of a chemist.

"We're going to make for one of those little evacuoles, and hightail it out of here," Johnny said. "By-the-way, Sunil, how'd you escape the guards?"

"They made the mistake of searching my shoe after I specifically told them not to. You'd think after they found burning jelly in my room that they would heed my warning. They found the secret compartment containing my flashing-light powder. Gods willing, they should be able to see again in a week or so. As for leaving, had you considered that we might drop into the middle of the American wilderness?"

"And if you had to choose between that and being on this rock when it falls from two miles up?"

Sunil paused, but it was Salim who answered. "I am forced to agree with your thinking, my friend."

"Hold up," Johnny said, his Tesla gun at the ready. "Jack, open that door ahead of us."

"Me? Why ever would I do a thing like that?"

"Because I'm holding the gun, dum dum! How'm I gonna open a

door with one hand on the barrel, and the other on the nozzle? The twins are already carrying the water tank."

"Well, why can't Tollers do the more hazardous tasks, then? After all, one could argue that the survival skills of a linguist pale in importance to one gifted in the ability to…"

The door in front of them burst open. A tide of roaring, charging, red-clad workers charged through the doorway with such ferocity that Johnny, Jack, and everyone else in the little group froze in fear.

Gilbert was looking ahead, past his guide's bobbing head of red hair. The fog of the laudanum had largely lifted, but he was still glad he could follow instead of lead. Doing so gave him an excuse to hold her shapely hand, and grip it tightly enough that he could feel the odd little jeweled ring she wore. The tiny diamond at the top surrounded by five purple stones pressed into his hand at the fingertips, and he savored every sensation despite the desperate nature of their flight.

"How close are we to the vacu—whatsits?" he asked.

"A few more minutes at this speed, if we aren't stopped by …"

They heard a roar outside, and the lights in the darkened corridor flared orange and red. She ran to the window and looked out through the thick glass.

"Oh, no," she said, her voice filled with horror.

"What? What is it?"

"Look! Look what they've done!"

She moved so Gilbert could see. He moved close beside her, both so he could see and so he could press his cheek against hers.

What he saw dashed his romantic hopes. Outside, the night was lit up around one of the huge chains that held a green ball of Cavorite. The Cavorite itself still glowed green, but the huge explosion at the base of the chain sent a wave of slack up through the huge chain links and back again. More explosions plumed in flame at the base of the chain behind the city skyline. The glowing green ball flickered and dimmed with each explosion. At this rate, the chain would soon snap at its base.

"Come on!" she shouted, yanking his arm again.

"What …why are they doing that?" Gilbert said. "Don't they know that we're all on this tub together?"

"Mobs seldom think along those lines. Here," they'd arrived at a door that seemed as nondescript as any of the dozens they'd passed since leaving the apartment. She pulled a key ring out of her dress and began fumbling through the keys. "No, no, no, what about this one?"

While she was rifling through the keys on the ring, Gilbert noticed an odd tube near the doorway. Its end sprouted wide at the height of Gilbert's chest, making it look like a large, metal flower or a band trumpet.

"Galatea? What's this?" he asked.

"No, no, that opens the chambermaid's quarters ... that, Gilbert? That pipe flower is the public address system. Only Norton and I are allowed to use it. Why?"

"Galatea, you're going to save us; is there any way to save the rest of the city?"

"Only if you can convince the mob to listen and the guards to let them use the evacuoles on White and Blue level. Why?"

Gilbert grabbed the open end of the tube, said the quickest prayer of his life, flipped the first switch he saw on the wall and began speaking.

"Attention! Citizens of the Floating City! This is Gilbert Chesterton!"

Gilbert's voice boomed throughout the city, echoing through streets both crowded and empty, bringing even the most frustrated and hoodlum-like members of the Red level worker mobs to a halt.

Now what, thought Gilbert, getting ready to improvise.

"The Emperor no longer rules here," Gilbert continued, "but has scuttled the city in anticipation of our victory. Please proceed in an orderly fashion to the evacuoles on Blue and White level. As your new ruler, I hereby order all troopers to assist all citizens in their very orderly escape. That is all."

Outside, the roaring of the mob subsided. After a few seconds, the only loud noises were several voices carrying up from the Red level, booming directions. Gilbert looked out a nearby window, noting that most of the torches of the mob were now moving slowly but surely to other locations in the city, presumably where the evacuoles and other means of escape were located.

About time I did something right, Gilbert thought. He looked back at Galatea. She was watching him with a look of awe on her face. Gilbert felt very, very awkward all of a sudden. "Um, Galatea?" he said, trying to figure out why she was frozen in place looking at him, "Did you, ah, find the key we need?"

"What?" she said, flustered for the first time in a very, very long time.

"The key, Gilbert? Well, I ... oh, *that* key! No. Drat Norton!" she began spinning through the large number of keys on the ring again. "Norton always made the keys so similar, so that ..."

"So that people like you would have a hard time leaving," a voice rasped from behind.

They whipped around. It was Strock. His leather jacket was burned through in several places, and his hair and eyebrows were singed. There was a burned, bald circle on the left side of his head where the skin had melted and still smoked with the stench of burning meat. His eyes still sparkled, though the left one kept twitching like a hyperactive puppy in a cage. He smiled, exposing the gaps left by several missing teeth.

"You weren't thinking of leaving, were you?" he said, stepping forward with his right foot and dragging his left behind.

"Gilbert, stay back," she said, jumping in front of Strock and bringing her hand level with his face. "Strock!" she ordered, "remember! *Archibald is my brother!* And *if you know what's good for you*, you'll ..."

Strock halted for a moment, then smiled. Strock's right hand darted forward, moving faster than Gilbert had ever seen anyone move before. It grabbed her hand in a tight grip, squeezing until she winced in pain. She spun around as she had with Gil, her free hand a blur of motion as she hit him in the head, then in the gut, then even in the ...

Ow. Ow. *Ouch!* Gilbert winced wider each time she punched or kicked Strock in the place where men dread to be hit the most. But Strock ignored even these last blows, and kept smiling his multi-gap-toothed grin like a simpleton watching paint dry.

Suddenly, he folded her own hand back against her wrist, making her mouth open in a silent scream and forcing her to one knee as she'd done to Gilbert earlier.

"That used to work, little lady," Strock said with a cheerful kind of menace as she struggled against the pain in her arm and tried to rise.

"You did something to my head, so that every time you said one a' your little phrases, you could say 'jump,' and I'd only ask 'how high?' But that kinda thing don't seem work on a drunk man. You tried it on one'a my boys when he had a few, and he just laughed until you put him in the hospital fer getting fresh. And since those little bookworms hit me with a bolt a' lightning, I don't feel that lock and key inside my head neither. Matter of fact ..."

"GILBERT!" she yelled as she found her voice, turning to look at him with the side of her face, "HELP ME! PLEASE!"

Gilbert had been standing in a mixture of shock and the fading laudanum fog. Seeing her beaten by anyone in a fight was a surprise enough. Seeing her so quickly bested with no last-minute trick up her sleeve was nearly enough to put him back into shock again.

But now she needed him.

She needed *him*!

Gilbert stepped forward. He swallowed, pushed aside the fold of the cloak she'd given him and pulled the sword out of the cane's sheath.

"Strock," Gilbert said, pointing the sword at him, "let her go!"

Strock didn't move, but kept smiling his broken smile while holding her in an iron-tight grip.

"I said, let 'er go, Strock! Or I'll run ya through!"

"You haven't got the stuff, son," Strock said. His normally brash voice was now as soft as a rattlesnake's skin gliding on sand.

Gilbert moved slowly so as not to fumble, and spun the sword in his hand like a deadly silver pinwheel.

Twice.

"You really wanna try me, pal? I'll be fighting for the girl I love. But you're so shook to pieces, your teeth alone look like a Boot Hill graveyard missing a few stones."

Strock's good eye flicked at Gilbert, then at his sword. Then to his captive, then over to Gilbert again.

Then, with strength Gilbert hadn't counted on, Strock yanked her forward like a living whip, flinging her at Gilbert's blade.

Chapter 79

"A soldier, surrounded by enemies, if he is to cut his way out, needs to combine a strong desire for living with a strange carelessness about dying...But Christianity has done more: it has marked the limits of it in the awful graves of the suicide and the hero, showing the distance between him who dies for the sake of living and him who dies for the sake of dying."
– GKC, *Orthodoxy*

Margaret hadn't been surprised when Norton had formally declared his independence from their masters. She herself intended to do so someday, when she was powerful enough. Margaret *was* surprised, however, when Finn shoved her into the middle of the room, and was outraged when the steambots all trained their guns on her. *Stupid,* she chided herself as she struggled to her feet, *stupid, stupid, stupid! If I ever get out of this* ... She scrunched her eyes shut as she heard the guns go off, opening one eye cautiously as she heard glass and stone break high *above* her! They'd fired at the *ceiling!*

"Blast!" Norton roared, "I knew I shoulda tested these!"

"Shoulda, woulda, coulda," Finn growled as he brought his pistol up and fired.

The gun's blast mixed with Norton's own surprised yell, as he felt a giant sledgehammer pound him in the chest and send him flying backwards against the closed door behind him.

Norton felt something inside him crack, but not break. The bulletproof vest he had worn every day since the last assassination attempt had done its job; his sternum had cracked, but not broken.

Still ... it hurt! "You ..." said Norton, gasping, mumbling and staring at the ceiling while an invisible giant sat on his chest. "You shot me ..."

"Come on!" Finn yelled, running for the stairwell with his pistol pointed upwards in his right hand, while the steambots kept firing at the roof once every few seconds in perfect unison. Finn's eyes blazed and his right lip curled. As Finn led their little army, Herb looked at Finn and remembered Ahab, the mad sea captain who destroyed himself and those around him by chasing an indestructible white whale.

When the door burst open in front of the boys and a group of armed, Red level workers charged at them, something shifted inside Clive Staples "Jack" Lewis.

Perhaps it was the axe he held, or maybe it was being in the company of other boys too inexperienced to know just how much danger they were in. Whatever the reason, after the door opened Jack realized that Johnny's gun was a powerful weapon, but no one knew if it was powerful enough to neutralize a *group* of men.

But *one* man could at least make a group pause long enough to let the others escape.

Or one *boy*.

And Jack realized that, just as every mythological hero had a point in their lives when they were called upon to put the good of others first, now was *his* time to do so. It was *his* time to sacrifice himself for the good of the group, as any Greek hero like Horatius would have done.

Or, he was sure, as Mister Chesterton would have done.

Jack knew these thoughts in less than a half second, as the little mob of heavyset men rushed them. The mob leader held a pistol in one hand and an ugly, serrated combat knife in the other. His head was wrapped in a crude bandage and crazed a berserker fury lit up his eyes. Small rivulets of blood tracked from the Red leader's forehead down to his eye and chin.

"Run!" Jack yelled to his companions, "I'll hold them off!" Hoping it would keep their enemies at bay, he took what he hoped would be a convincing fighting stance, brandishing the oversized hatchet in his hands while facing the onslaught.

"Jack, they're ..."

"No argument, Johnny!" Jack yelled, never taking his eyes from the leader of the Red worker mob in front of him.

Jack was afraid. His insides had turned to icewater. But what had his hero done when faced with a Martian in the tunnels? Run, or fight? Jack, all nine years of him, set his jaw tight enough that he hoped that any screams he made would sound more like a battle cry instead of pure terror. "Go," he shouted behind him, "before they ..."

The squad was on them.

Then they were gone.

Jack and everyone else looked around—the small mob had run right past the boys.

In a matter of two seconds, all six of the workers had run through the corridor without the slightest look at the boys.

Jack, afraid to break his pose, still stood with his axe outstretched in his right hand and his feet planted in a clear line pointing at the door.

"Jack ..." said Johnny, his voice filled with awe. "Did you ... were you gonna die, just to cover our retreat?"

"I ... well, I had an *inkling* that you'd survive, if I annoyed them enough. They tell me I'm pretty good at that, you know. Speaking of which," his voice grew stronger, though he didn't know it. "Which way to those escape evacuoles?"

Johnny looked at the others, who nodded their agreement. "Forward, Jack, about twenty paces, and then a right turn."

"Follow me, boys!" Jack said with a jaunty air, waving his hatchet. "And if you get scared, just think about what a great story this'll make when we're done!"

Jack strode forward, whistling a happy tune. His high spirits were infectious, and spread to the boys behind him. Such was their confidence that when they heard another mob down the hall, they waited nearly a whole second before scurrying into the nearest side room to hide.

Twice in life, Strock had seen most of his friends die in one night, first, at the hands of natives in Africa, and later by Martian heat rays. The traumatic events had convinced him that few things were more valuable than friendship. And, for Strock, helping those *connected* to friends who'd passed on was a way of honoring the dead.

Strock had long known that Gilbert was a friend of Father Brown, the priest who'd saved Strock's life and calmed his fears on a night when more than nine of every ten of the men in his platoon had been butchered. As such, Gilbert would have to do something truly stupid to merit death at Strock's hands.

Unfortunately, those Strock needed kept leaving him, either by choice or by death. In the twisted labyrinth his mind had become since fighting Martians in a DaVinci flyer a year ago, Strock had become utterly intolerant of anyone leaving him, for any reason.

Thus the conundrum before him: Gilbert and Galatea were obviously attempting to leave, and therefore needed to die.

But Gilbert was a friend of Father Brown, and could not die by Strock's hand.

And Galatea was a friend of Gilbert's, and thus could not die by Strock's hand either.

Strock's powers of reason rattled and bounced in his brain, and in seconds formed a solution acceptable to his very addled mind.

He took that snobby little assistant of Norton's, and tossed her at the blade that the little boy had been waving at him.

After all, that toothpick in Gilbert's hand wasn't enough to kill a person right away. If they didn't leave, but looked for help, she might survive.

Gripping her hand tightly, Strock flung her, and was mildly surprised when Gil's sword didn't run her right through the midsection. The kid was quicker than Strock had thought he would be! Gilbert had managed to dodge just enough that the sword stuck her through her side, right above the hip bone, puncturing blouse and skin with almost no sound at all.

There was silence for a second or two. The kid looked in horror at what he thought he'd done. The girl didn't realize what had happened either, until she followed his gaze and saw his sword blade and hilt apparently growing from her hip.

"Oh, bother!" she said with a mixture of annoyance, surprise and horror.

Strock gave his smile to the both of them as best he could. "You two kids take care now. I'd put off leaving and get to a doctor if I were you, missy!"

Strock gave a jaunty salute, turned on his good heel and shuffled off down the opposite end of the hallway.

Gilbert, trembling with fear, focused again on the girl.

"Oh, no!" he said several times, each with increasing horror, "Oh no! Oh NO!"

"Gilbert," she said, her eyes locked on his, "I know what to do. Please let go of the sword."

Gilbert blinked. Wasn't she supposed to scream or something? He obeyed her, and watched with disbelief as she gritted her teeth and yanked the sword out of her side, letting it clatter to the floor.

Blood flowed freely, and she pressed her hands on the wound to staunch the bleeding. She looked herself up and down, then at Gilbert.

"My sash," she rasped, "Gilbert, untie my sash and give me your tie. I have to halt the bleeding before I faint."

Gilbert, knowing that fumbling could cost her her life, was already undoing her long, ribbony sash and his bow tie before she'd finished her second sentence.

She took his tie, bunched it up into a neat, folded package, then had Gilbert re-tie the sash so that it held the folded tie against her exit wound. The bleeding slowed, but didn't stop.

"Are you gonna be alright?" he asked, feeling five kinds of stupid but hoping for reassurance anyway.

"Yes," she said, looking worried at the still growing red splotch on her side. "But Gilbert, I'm going to need your help in one more thing to make sure I won't faint from loss of blood."

"Anything. Name it."

"First, give me the strap of your cummerbund." She winced as she lowered herself first to a kneeling position, then laid flat on her back.

Gilbert quickly undid the decorative belt from his waist, handed it to her, and watched as she draped it over her neck.

"Now, remove my right boot," she said, grunting a little as she sat on the floor. Her hands were still pressed to her wound. "You'll find a small rectangle of scented material in the heel."

Gilbert did as she asked. The stick was more like thick paper, with a thick yellow substance like dried wax at the top.

"It's silver nitrate," she continued. "You'll need to strike it on the floor like a matchstick, then give it to me when it lights up."

"Lights?"

"The wound won't stop with pressure alone, and I don't have sutures."

Gilbert, still kneeling, scratched the tip on the floorboard. The end of the stick began glowing, but with neither smoke nor flame.

"Now, Gilbert, you're going to have to hold the sides of my wound together with one hand, and with the other you'll use the flare to burn the wound closed."

Gilbert breathed. He'd seen farmers do basic types of emergency surgery and first aid of the type he was being asked to do here, but doing so to a loved one was another matter entirely.

His hands went to the tear in the fabric of her dress at her hip as she put the cummerbund between her teeth with one hand, and held the glowing flare in the other. When she told him to do so, he loosened the sash and exposed the entry wound.

"Ready?" she asked through the belt, looking down her side at her cut.

Gilbert looked at her side. The wound at least was a clean cut; he'd seen bayonets that were made to leave diamond-shaped holes in their targets precisely so that the wounds couldn't be burned closed on the battlefield. He pushed the separated flesh together with his left thumb and forefinger as he'd seen Mr. McGinty do to one of his farmhands when he'd been sliced up by a harvester's scythe. His fingers were an inch or two away from the cut itself, so that when the glowing ember hit the wound his digits wouldn't be crisped along with it. "Yep," he answered, trying to make his voice sound strong and capable. "Are you?"

She nodded. She then closed her eyes and bit down on the cummerbund, while gripping a pair of pipes growing out of the wall. Gilbert said a quick prayer and brought down the burning flare.

The glowing stick touched her skin, making it sizzle, crackle and burn. Gilbert held his breath and wished he could plug his ears to block out the noise. She inhaled with a hiss but made no other sound.

He hated being there all of a sudden, hated that she'd been hurt, hated Strock for hurting her, hated Norton for employing Strock *and* her, hated the tears that squeezed out of his eyes that he couldn't wipe away and hated the Special Branch both for making her into something she should never have been and ruining his life.

Most of all, he hated himself, for feeling sorry for himself while she was in so much more pain than he was, but enduring it with quick breaths and quieted screams through the fabric of his cummerbund.

It lasted for the longest sixty seconds of his life.

Then, after they were done, they began work on the exit wound.

It was much worse. They were only halfway through it when the second round of explosions rocked the city, snapping the Western globe of Cavorite from the city completely.

Chapter 80

"The unconscious democracy of America is a very fine thing. It is a true and deep and instinctive assumption of the equality of citizens, which even voting and elections have not destroyed."
– GKC, *What I Saw in America*, 1922

The old man looked at the papers on his desk and sighed, wishing for the ten-thousandth time that day that he could be a child again. Back then, in a world over a half-century past, the biggest consequences for failure were a whuppin' from either his Aunt Polly or the schoolmaster with the funny shoes that pointed upwards.

Now, he mused, even the simplest error in judgment would cost lives, land and money. Always, always money. He looked out the window of the opulent hotel room he and his wife had been given for the conference, and thought about how beautiful even a corrupt city like Richmond could be at night. Had he known what the life of a senator would entail when he first agreed to run over a quarter-century before, he might have gone into hunting criminals like his childhood friend, known to mere mortals as Colonel Finn of the Pinkertons.

"Sugar?" a voice said from the next room.

He sighed and took off his reading glasses. "Yes, dearest."

"Do you plan to sleep tonight, honey?"

"The Five Americas won't unite themselves, sweetheart."

"True. But unless you sleep, you'll be facing those vultures from the North with a mind slower than molasses going uphill in January."

He sighed and stood, arching his back while his hands pushed that small place at the base of his spine. "You're right again, Becky, as usual. It'll be hard enough taking on the Yankees, the Texans and the Papists. Tomorrow I'll have members of my own gov'ment trying to crucify me." For years, now, he'd been something of a lightning rod among southern politicians. His ability to get favored treatment for his constituents had gotten him re-elected for decades, but his hardline stance against slavery in any form had gotten him labeled 'judgmental' and 'inflexible' by the papers, along with other unprintable names among various pro slave-choice factions.

He let loose a yawn that could have come from an upset Grizzly bear, and looked again at the glittering lights in the city skyline. *How peaceful a city can look at night,* he thought, *no matter what went on beneath its rooftops.* Another yawn and then…

What he saw made him pause in mid-yawn. He looked almost comical, his mouth frozen open, closing only slowly as his eyes widened.

"Thomas," his wife said, emerging from the hallway in her nightgown, "they will only best you if you insist on negotiating with half your brain tied behind your…"

She stopped too. Both Senator Thomas A. Sawyer and his wife, Rebecca, had been childhood sweethearts in a town in Missouri that had been almost wiped off the map during the War of Northern Aggression. Neither had seen anything in their skies more technical than a Zeppelin airship.

Now a city sat *above* the city of Richmond, Virginia, capital city of the Confederate States of America.

Three large, glowing green globes held this new city high in the air, and several fires were visible on it.

And while the Sawyers watched in awe, one of the three globes winked in color from green to solid black.

"Tom," she said, "What … what is it?"

"I don't know, Becky. I … we need to …"

When the second globe went out, it fell towards the lake, snapping its giant chain and causing the city above to tip.

Chapter 81

"A change of opinions is almost unknown in an elderly military man." – GKC, *A Utopia of Usurers*

Huckleberry!" the voice called out in the dimly lit warehouse. "Huckleberry, m'boy! It's so good to see you again!"

Finn tried to pinpoint where the voice was coming from. Norton was still fast despite his age, and had dodged into a huge room filled with crates and boxes. Somewhere in the distance, Finn could hear engines whirring.

"Yeah, you better keep your scrawny carcass hidden, old man," Finn yelled back in no particular direction, "'Cause when I see you I'm gonna fill you so full of holes that when you drink water people'll think you're a Lessler lawn sprinkler."

"That's not one of your better insults, Huckleberry," Norton's voice sounded from everywhere and nowhere at once. "You never were good at insults under pressure. Only at lying your way out of trouble."

There, thought Finn. Though old by most standards, Finn's hearing was as good as it ever had been. There was a small trace of an echo that said Norton was to Finn's right.

"My lies only got me food an' shelter as a young'un from folks who could spare it," Finn said before he moved. "You wrecked people's lives, Duke. That's why they ran you out on a rail and tried to tar an' feather you."

"I can't be caught or killed by the likes of you, *Huck*," Norton said with a heavy emphasis on the slightly younger man's ancient nickname. "I pulled a switch with a stewbum before they got me. He died, I lived. Natural selection at its finest."

There was a muffled roar from outside as the chain tethering the second Cavorite globe exploded and broke. The city lurched to Finn's right, throwing him against a stack of crates. He heard Norton shout in fear and surprise. Now the self-declared Emperor sounded very un-regal almost directly above Finn, calling for help on an upper balcony.

Finn knew he might likely die in this crazy place. But it would be worth it and a fitting capstone to his life if Norton met Lady Justice first, one way or another.

The city tilted, but was right enough that Finn could almost walk straight. When in doubt, move forward, Finn thought. Forward and silently. Moving down the hallway in search of another stairwell, he checked his pepperbox and kept an eye out for Norton.

"That you, Huckleberry?" Norton said suddenly.

Finn paused; was Norton talking to him? The old confidence man's voice sounded too far away to have heard Finn over the noise and ruckus.

"I'll be your Huckleberry, now!" It was Doc Holiday's voice, casually spoken, and followed by the click of his pistol's safety hammer and the snap of a gunshot.

Finn ran towards Norton's voice with fear gripping his chest. Fear that the prey he'd stalked for over a half-century would be taken from him when it was right in his grasp!

"Is this it?" Gilbert said, still holding her arm with mixed feelings. Having been raised on a prairie, he was no stranger to tough women. But after cauterizing her wound, she had surprised him yet again by standing up after saying just a few words to herself through clenched teeth. He couldn't imagine the degree of pain she must be in, but if she was still hurting, she managed not to show it. She asked only for Gilbert to hand his cane to her once the sword had been placed back inside it, and to hold her arm in case her strength gave out.

It occurred to him that she was using another of her mind tricks to block the pain and keep moving forward. Strock's speech and her earlier words had gotten him thinking again about something else: this wasn't the place or the time to ask, but when they touched down on Terra Firma Gilbert was going to grill her something fierce about any little locks she might have placed in *his* head, and what was behind the doors inside.

They had arrived at another corridor that Gilbert had never seen before. It stretched down at least a hundred feet before it curved around to the right. Steel doors lined the hallway, and each door had a round window set at eye-level.

"Is this where we escape?"

"No," she said, "this is where you will get into an evacuole and drop down to Earth."

"You're coming with me!"

"No," she was limping with greater urgency to the closest of the closed circular doors. Several doors were already open, freezing cold air blasting through, smelling of morning chill. Gilbert could see the lights of a city below them through the open holes. Each door also had a large red button set into the wall beside it, surrounded by a small cage made of brass rods. By each door that was open, the cage had been flipped up and the button had been pressed into the wall.

"There's information secreted in Norton's command center," she said, using her cane to walk to the nearest closed door. "It's hidden so well even he doesn't know of its existence. It won't be discovered until he's attacked Richmond and failed. It frames the Californian Republics for founding the city and trying to start a war. The Special Branch wants to keep the Americas fragmented and fighting each other, but if I can destroy or alter that evidence, the Americas may be united again. And *that's* something, maybe the *only* thing, that could counter the Branch." She stopped at the closed door, her right hand holding the cane and her left hand motioning to the door and the button beside it.

"Right. Get in, Gilbert."

"You're coming with me, I said! And don't try any tricks. You're not strong enough to beat me up this time and we both know it."

"No! You're too important to die here!"

"You're too important for me to lose you!"

"Gilbert, the *world* needs you!"

"I don't *care* about the world! You hear me? I don't care about being rich, or famous, or anything like that anymore! The world can go hang! I just want a little farm with three acres and a cow! And I want that *with you!* Now, you go through that door! Or so help me, wound or no wound, I'll grab you and stuff you inside myself!"

Another explosion sounded outside. The gaslights went dark, while the buttons next to the doors glowed red, bathing the hallway in crimson light as sirens began wailing throughout the city.

"You can't have me, Gilbert!" She was screaming now, louder than the sirens and with tears tracking down her cheeks. "I'm not going to escape! You've got to let me go, leave me behind!"

"I can't leave you! How could I? I don't even know your name!" he yelled, reaching for her arms.

Before he could hold her, she let go of the cane and grabbed the sides of his head with her hands. She looked deeply into his eyes, and he was silenced.

Pulling his head down to hers, she kissed him. Her lips were warm, and fit more perfectly than he could have imagined in his happiest fantasies. His eyes closed and the world flowed away. Sirens, lights, threats of death and imminent destruction of the Five Americas all faded away into a warm and happy puddle in an unimportant and easily ignored corner of his brain. *I'm doing this,* his mind screamed joyfully,

I'm actually... Then, for a few seconds, Gilbert felt everywhere and nowhere at once. Bliss, joy, happiness, none of the words of description he would have normally used did justice to the moment. Thoughts or words would have brought him out of joy, and none formed after the first second.

And their kiss lasted *five* beautiful and eternal seconds. To him it could have lasted forever. She pulled back, her eyes dancing but sad. Gilbert looked as if he were in the midst of a dream he hoped he would never wake from.

"It's Anne," she said, and slammed her forehead into his face.

Gilbert's world exploded in colored lights.

"Spelled with an e," she said as he reeled, stunned. She grabbed his right shoulder with her left hand, and opened the small brass cage over the escape button with her right. The door slid open, down into the floor. Using all the strength she had left, she grabbed him by both shoulders, pushed on her left leg and sent the taller boy toppling through the door into a room hardly bigger than a broom closet.

Gilbert, still halfway in dreamland, was utterly unprepared for her attack. By the time he'd blinked twice, she'd tossed him into the evacuole and slammed her hand on the red button. He tried to stand, but the door slid shut again with a hiss of steam. A loud series of clicks sounded in the room, the kind a large clock might make, and the room dropped like a screaming elevator. There was another porthole in the wall opposite the door, and as the floor dropped beneath him, the view in the little circled window blurred and disappeared, replaced by a view of the starry night sky.

Gilbert screamed in frustration, pounding his fists against the floor of his escape room. And as propellers and parachutes popped open from the roof above him outside, Gilbert cussed, well and truly *cussed* for the first time in his life at all the horrible turns of events his life had become.

Cameron Foggschild looked over several fires burning freely in the city, as worker mobs battled vastly overwhelmed guards. Somewhere, the order had been given to mobilize Norton's steambot army. Cameron could feel the ground tremble as Zeppelins loaded with mechanical cargo slowly lumbered out of their docking bay and into the air, searching in a vain hope of finding a viable landing spot from which to dig in and take over the city.

This, he realized, was pure beauty. Beauty as his new wave of art would make it known to the world. The fire, death, destruction and despair in the air brought a tear to his eye. Perfection of Despair. Yes, that's what he would call the musical piece he would name for this night.

"Isn't it beautiful, Aristodemus?" he asked the large bodyguard behind him. "It will be hard to leave, once I've completed this piece."

Aristodemus grunted and scratched his large chin. Greek by birth, he had far more in common with his dockworker father than the Spartan warrior Foggschild had renamed him after.

Cameron now brought out a flute from a sheath at his waist where most men would have carried a sword. Once at his lips, he began to play. It was not a composition that any critic would have hailed, but it held many long, low notes and wavering high ones, and so pleased its owner.

He stopped his latest composition in the middle of a note when the base of the chain for the second globe exploded. He was so enthralled with the spectacle at his feet that he hardly heard Aristodemus' mutters behind him. "The city will tip, soon," Foggschild said, "dumping much of its precious human cargo into the river."

Then, Cameron heard a new noise. Blasting from every speaker in the Floating City, Gilbert's voice ordered the mob's rampage to cease and everyone to leave in an orderly fashion. Cameron was angry; angrier, in fact, than he could remember being in a very, very long while. He felt that what Gilbert had done to Cameron's beautiful, live tragedy was the equivalent of spitting in the eye of the Mona Lisa as its last brush stroke was being applied.

He would wreak bloody vengeance upon that skinny, closed-minded, anti-art zealot, Cameron vowed, as soon as he escaped. Yes! Gilbert would be a delightful new little canvas of pain for Cameron to experiment upon, once they were safe.

"Let us leave now," he said coldly, studiously avoiding the use of contractions, just as his heroes did in classic Greek literature.

Cameron Foggschild then turned and saw the first thing in a long, long time that could frighten him.

Cameron himself had picked Aristodemus as a bodyguard. The big oaf had been chosen for his fighting skill from hundreds of similar oafs who wore the red overalls. He was now splayed on the floor of the observation deck, his unseeing eyes bulging and his neck twisted at an impossible angle.

Captain Strock stood over Aristodemus' body. His once handsome features and uniform were shattered, melted or twisted, yet his feet were planted confidently over Aristodemus' cooling remains, and his sizable fists were squared against his hips. "Sorry, son," Strock said, "but what did you say you were gonna do?"

Finn's legs devoured the stairs as he flew up them. "Norton!" he roared at the top of his lungs, feeling the strain. He could barely hear himself over the grinding of huge iron gears and Zeppelin engines, and some voice over the loudspeaker system calling for folks to leave. As the enormous door of the docking bay opened, an armored Zeppelin, now filled with hundreds of steambots, along with huge cannons and Tesla guns mounted on its side and belly, floated up and out of the city.

It was suddenly quiet. Well, quieter than it had been. There was only the sound of metal, pounding in unison as steambots tramped onto the second Zeppelin in perfect lines, while making right and left turns that would have made any drill sergeant envious.

Finn waited. His eyes and ears were on high alert for anything that was even remotely threatening.

There was something slippery under his boot. Finn looked down. Blood was on the ground, flowing from around the corner and puddling near Finn's feet.

No. No, no ... oh, no...

When he rounded the corner, his second-worst fears were confirmed. Doc Holiday, whom none other than Wyatt Earp called the most dangerous gun in the West, was lying gasping in a pool of blood. A neat, dark hole stained with a trickle of blood marred his white-ruffle shirt in the center of his chest.

"Doc!" yelled Finn, still looking around for Norton or snipers, "Doc, where'd he go? Where's Norton?"

"It's ..." Holiday's white goatee and mustache were flecked with blood, "it's funny, James. Did I ever tell you my cousin was a nun ...?"

"Hold on, Doc," said Finn, going on one knee and cradling Doc's head. "You're gonna be alright. You're gonna live forever, Doc. Just hold on ..."

"She was a woman of singular beauty, James ... she said ... oh, my," Doc said, his eyes staring at something past Finn, "this ... this is funny ... Filius aspicio vestri matris..."

"Quit talkin' Doc. You'll tire yeself out too much. Just rest. Remember back when we nabbed the Wild Bunch ...?" Finn kept on talking, holding Doc's head, knowing the routine and the drill. He wondered if Doc remembered it, too, and knew he was dying.

And then after a few minutes, Doc stopped talking. Another minute and he stopped sucking air. Finn was talking to himself.

Finn scrunched shut his eyes, and inhaled deeply, twice.

What had he heard Doc say to someone he'd taken down?

"Wreck-weezat Apache, Doc," he said quietly, hoping his mangled Latin would do.

Then, James 'Huckleberry' Finn went very quiet, and tried to listen very, very hard.

There! A footstep! Higher up! He sprang up like a man one-third his age and stomped up four more flights of steps with his sizable boots. At the top, he saw Norton's fleeing figure darting in and out between columns of steambots as they marched in perfect formation, rifle-arms at the ready, towards the drawbridges of gondolas beneath the giant Zeppelins.

"Je-hosephat!" Finn said in a low voice, distracted by the mechanical regiments and the three giant war machines only for a second from his prey.

Finn charged again, following the same path he'd marked Norton take. It was a bouncing, zig-zagging track. Had Finn been raised in the woods, Norton would have gotten away clean by now. But Finn had raised himself on small town streets. The faintest outline of mud on stone, the slight scraping of boot against plank wood floor, a cooling fingerprint on a wall, these were tracks as blatant to Finn as blood drops and bear tracks would have been to a Blackfoot Indian or a road sign to a city-born white man.

A confident hunch surged in Finn's gut. Every time he'd ever felt this way, his quarry was his in a matter of seconds, minutes at most. "Coming to get you, Norton! You hear me, old man? An' this time nothing's gonna save you from me!"

Finn had just finished this last sentence when Norton leapt at him from above, shrieking like an angry banshee. His curved officer's saber was unsheathed and swung in a deadly arc at the top of Finn's skull.

The steambots had turned and filed out of the room in the same direction as Norton and Finn, leaving Herb, Harper and Margaret behind. Holiday had slipped away unnoticed.

"What now?" Herb yelled over the sound of tramping metal boots.

"This," mouthed Margaret without a sound, bringing her pistol to the back of the young cowboy's head and tapping him on the shoulder.

"You know," Harper said as he turned around.

Margaret pulled the trigger.

As fast and as hard as any bullet, the needle hit him squarely between the eyes.

"I don't care if the President *is* asleep, you numbskull!" roared Senator Sawyer into the telephone, "Look out your window! Do you want to go down in history as the Secret Service agent who let the President sleep through a city falling into the James River, right outside his house?"

Becky Sawyer heard her husband's conversation partner speak several words loud enough to be heard halfway across the room. The Secret Service agent had presumably looked out his window and seen the floating city tipping like an unbalanced plate, since his volume increased while his coherency decreased at roughly the same rate.

"You do that, bright boy!" Sawyer barked into the phone, banging the mouthpiece into the cradle and rushing back to the window. "Any change, Sugar?"

"Nothing, dear." Becky was looking through a pair of opera glasses at the floating metropolis, now held aloft by only two giant globes. "Every now and again I think I can see people scurrying back and forth, but it may be a trick of the light. It keeps tipping one way, then another. Oh!"

"What's happened?"

"Something just flew off the ship, like a cannonball! No, no ... it's ..." she looked closer with her opera glasses. "It's too big to be a cannonball. Propellers of some kind sprouted from its top, and it's coming down for a landing in the river."

A dark look swept over Sawyer's face. He grabbed his gun and holster along with the work clothes he was taking from his trunk. He took off his robe, pulled on his trousers, shirt and suspenders, and then his boots with the efficiency of a fireman heading out to a call. Lastly, he strapped his Colt .45 to his waist and tied the bottom of the holster to his thigh. "I'm going outside. It's early enough a lot of folks won't even know what's happening unless someone does a Paul Revere."

"Just don't make yourself into a Johnny Booth!"

"No, dear. I'll not be dying tonight for any causes. You just keep those lovely eyes of yours on that monstrosity. It's not traveling this way, but if it does ..."

"I'll run, leave everything behind and meet you at the Capitol building. I wouldn't worry—it looks like it's turning towards the river."

"Good girl."

As he left, Rebecca turned to look out the window again. Nearly half a century of marriage, half-a-dozen children, and a career as a Confederate States Senator, and he still liked to run off to tell news to the world and fight a fire! Shouts were just starting from the street. She could also see the horizon getting brighter with the early morning light. Her husband had been up later than she'd thought, the rascal!

She was still thinking about him when the airships started flying and more of the oddly shaped 'cannonballs' started lobbing from the floating city.

Finn didn't even look up at Norton's sword. Dangerous objects had been aimed at his head before, and training and instinct took over.

Moreover, this was a fight he'd been ready to wage for half a century. Keeping his eyes locked on Norton's, Finn switched his pistol from his right to his left hand with a deft movement worthy of Victorian stage magic. He then brought his pistol up, opening his hand wide just before the saber hit to keep his fingers from getting chopped off. The sword hit Finn's pistol, making a loud *clink* that both men still heard over the sound of the steambots marching into the second Zeppelin. Finn deflected Norton's saber with a parry that was fluid, fast and perfect as he leaned forward with his left foot.

Since Finn had only deflected Norton's sword instead of stopping it outright, Norton didn't stop in place either, but fell forward towards Finn himself. And as Norton fell, Finn pulled back a large right fist that had been planted on the jaw of many a famous criminal. Though he'd pounded many a dangerous lawbreaker, he'd never had the sense of destiny this punch had behind it, a sense of fate fueled by a chase and grudge that had criss-crossed half-a-dozen countries and been burtured fir nearly five decades. Norton had always been his fish to catch, and the one job that had always eluded Finn one way or another.

Until now. Finn's powerful right fist swung at the elderly man's bearded face like an angry meteor, curving up and down in a deadly arc, his right thumb pushing his middle knuckle into a deadly hoodlum punch. When it connected with a meaty crack, Finn didn't even feel his own middle knuckle break. And he barely felt Norton's cheekbone crumple beneath his powerful blow like a woven lattice of cheap toothpicks. Norton didn't scream. He gave a kind of sigh, spun halfway around and fell down on the steps, his sword clattering as it fell and bounced down the stairwell.

Finn felt more satisfied than he'd been when he'd captured the head of the Wild Bunch gang.

Had it been nearly any other capture, Finn might have tried to grab Norton's sword as a trophy. But he didn't want to take his eyes off of the wily snake he'd just dropped in front of him. He flipped Norton roughly to his stomach, jammed his knee into the elderly man's spine, pulled out a set of manacles and cuffed Norton's hands behind his back.

"Joshua Norton," Finn said, grunting slightly as he cuffed the old man's wrists behind his back, "also-known-as the Duke, the Dauphin, and the Emperor of North America, you're under citizen arrest under charges of fraud, theft, multiple counts of murder, and high treason against the governments of the USA, CSA, and the Republics of the Californias and Texas."

"Go spit."

"Now, how'd I know you'd say just that?"

"You'll never take me alive, *Huckleberry*!"

"I just did, *Josh*." He hauled Norton to his feet. "Now, just to make sure you don't get any ideas about picking those manacles," he pulled out a large knife. Ignoring how large Norton's eyes became, his knife darted at Norton's arms with the speed of a master tailor. When he was finished, Norton's once immaculate General's uniform was without sleeves from the elbows on down. Finn whistled when he saw Norton's elbow-gun, and cut its straps from Norton's body as well.

"Pity these things only carry one shot, isn't it, Josh? You might've killed *two* officers today. Now," Finn continued, shoving Norton roughly ahead, "if you've any thoughts of escape, you'd better save them for the prison they're talking about putting on that island in the 'Frisco bay. If you give me the slip now, you'll die when this city of yours hits the James River, and drown with your hands cuffed behind you. You think on that. No tales sung about a disappearance into a watery grave, no Nickel Novel written about a valiant last shootout with the lawmen. Just dying stupid with your hands buckled down behind you. You got me?"

Norton glared at Finn. Finn smiled. "You have no idea just how happy your anger is making me, old man. Now, how's about we both get off of this rock?"

Chapter 82

"It is true that I am of an older fashion; much that I love has been destroyed or sent into exile."
– GKC, *The Judgment of Dr. Johnson, Act III*

Gilbert's little escape pod had fired out of the city at a speed faster than any earthly transportation machine he'd travelled on in his life. Once out, he heard the now familiar sound of whirring propeller props above his head on the roof of the evacuole.

It was dark inside. The only light came in from the stars and the rising sun outside through the small porthole window. He searched for any kind of control panel that he could use to steer the craft back to the city, to get back to...

Anne. Spelled with an E.

He had to get back! He just had to!

He was still thinking this when his little pod touched down, and began bobbing.

Bobbing?

He stood on his tiptoes and looked out the porthole. The sun wasn't visible, but by the dim morning light he could see he was on a lake or a river. And there was a city, a real, earthbound city, just at the edge of it! Maybe he could use the pod like a rowboat, and ...

His toes felt cold. He looked down. There were two inches of water at the flat bottom.

"Uh oh," he said. Either the evacuole had been designed to touch down lightly on solid ground, or something had jarred loose when it was fired out of the city. Either way, he'd have to get out quickly or risk eating river bottom sand for breakfast!

There was a lever on the ceiling of the craft. He pulled it and it moved with the sound of a rusty nail pulling out of wood. The top of his ship opened and water began spilling and seeping in over the rim.

Gilbert moved quickly, scrambling out through the open hatch as more water flooded in. In three seconds, he was engulfed in icy river water, swimming as best he could in the suit and dress shoes he'd been given hours before.

He heard a slurp and gurgles behind him as his craft took a last drink of river water and went under. He looked back, and saw it submerge.

There was a noise above him.

Gilbert looked up and saw many more pods dropping into the water, hitting with loud splashes and opening with similar rusty sounds. In seconds there were shouts for help, screams of panic and splashes of people swimming for their lives. Gilbert also saw more metal globes the size of the evacuole he'd escaped in, but instead of flying out of the city, they were being lowered quickly on long ropes to the ground.

I can't help any of them, Gilbert thought, spluttering. *I need a boat, or these folks'll pull me under, too!*

He was about to swim for shore when a louder noise sounded overhead.

Another one of the evacuoles had launched from the underbelly of the city. It was directly above Gilbert, dropping down quickly.

After firing Gilbert off to safety in the evacuole, she'd grabbed the cane again and was hobbling as fast as she could to the command center. She wondered if anyone would be there, or if they'd all disobeyed orders and run for the evacuoles like rats from a sinking ship.

The corridor lurched to the side as another muffled explosion tore through the city. Foggschild's mobs were doing a frightening amount of damage in quick order! She staggered forward through a corridor that was slowly but definitely tilting further to the left as the city shook itself to pieces.

A quick, pain-filled check with her hands after leaving Gilbert had confirmed it: she'd been pierced just above her hip bone, with only her flesh being wounded, her major organs very likely spared. Still, she had to keep repeating the litany she'd been taught to control the pain.

And the pain was still there, and it was getting harder and harder to concentrate. Nothing she'd experienced before this compared to a puncture wound, an assisted self-cauterization, and then having to walk afterwards.

She was at the door to the control room. Normally this door was the most heavily armored piece of flat metal in the whole city. But now the heavy door's opening mechanism had been blown inwards from the outside.

She drew one of her pistols, stood beside the doorframe with her face and body hidden from any who could be inside and sniffed the air.

Charcoal, saltpeter, sulfur … all in the wrong ratios, too, by the smell of the residue. What had blown off the door had been cooked up in a kitchen, not the munitions factory. Reds had been here, either to try and wrestle control of the city at the source or as part of their rampage.

Having been the one who'd set the evidence to begin with, Anne moved with quick surety, even considering her recent handicap. After reaching the main control panel, she started pushing several buttons and throwing levers from completely unrelated areas on the panel. She pointedly ignored the difference engines that were frantically stipple-printing status reports no one would ever read. She also ignored the view from the forward windows, which showed the city tipping even further to the side.

One last dial, then ... a panel slid opened with very little fanfare. She reached in and her hand found another container disk similar to the one she'd given Gilbert in the floating dance palace in Germany. She spun several dials on it, holding the lid down slightly with her thumb when the device sprang open like a clam.

There were several disc-shaped punchcards in the container, punchcards that could be easily read by the more modern difference engines. She took them out and looked at them carefully against the firelight from outside. Satisfied, she stuffed them in her mouth.

She chewed quickly, swallowing only when the disk was thoroughly soaked by her saliva and reduced to unrecognizable mush.

"Is there a food shortage in the city, Actress?"

Anne looked behind her, even though she recognized the voice.

"Hello, Farmer," she said to Margaret. "Good job keeping us informed of Gilbert's whereabouts."

"I always aim to please. You did a sparkling job of letting us know Norton's plans and whereabouts. Don't those new heliographs and telegraph lines make it so much easier?"

"I didn't expect you here until the attack," Anne said, brushing back a red lock of her hair while trying to keep a casual voice. Perhaps she could talk her way out of this one.

"It shows, Actress. Where is the Salesman?" Margaret's smile was wider, more lethal than Anne had ever seen it before.

"Victor? He's dead. Norton shot him through the heart a few hours ago."

"Such a pity. It's disappointing, but not unexpected. Now ..." There was a click near Margaret's hand as she cocked her small magnetic arrow/pistol, and carefully tucked back a lock of her dark hair, "in the few minutes we have left until this place crashes, let's discuss your performance on this mission."

Gilbert gulped air and ducked under the water, kicking and flapping his legs in an effort to put watery distance between himself and the very large-looking evacuole only a few seconds above him.

He'd thought of swimming sideways, but instantly analyzed and discarded the option. The craft had air in it, his own had only sunk a few feet when it first hit the water, and swimming down at least kept his head away from the thick metal of the ship.

It turned out to be a good choice. He felt the bottom of the craft smack into his feet with a surprising thud, shoving them forward until they almost jackknifed.

His body already craved air, but he wasn't in a bad way yet. His eyes ... he'd lost his glasses! They must have been knocked off when the ... when Anne had smacked him in the head! No wonder he could barely see anything down here! Being underwater was blurry enough when your vision was *good*!

There was enough light now that he could at least see the bubbles rising, even without his glasses. That was another lesson he'd remembered from his traipsing about in underground rivers! Swimming and kicking, he pointed himself upwards, following the bubbles.

His head was only six feet from breaking the surface when another pod slammed into the water right above him, knocking him unconscious and pushing him further down into the cold river.

Herb was tired of looking for Gil. After leaving Margaret and the dead cowboy, he'd followed Margaret's instructions of the likely route to follow. And while he'd found the empty, furnished apartment Gil had apparently been given, there was blood on the floor and the door had been left open, and there was no sign of Gil himself.

He paused in the room. There was a funny smell in the air. Something that made him feel ... guilty, somehow. No matter! After a few seconds of searching, he then followed the small map-contraption she'd lent him up the nearest flight of stairs to the metal door of Norton's control room.

Margaret's mapper had been set to direct him from Gil's room to the control center, but he'd traveled up only two floors when another explosion had sounded, tilting the city like a ship slowly spun on its axis. Nearer to the outside at this point in the spindle, he could hear cries for help, crumbling buildings and alarms sounding off at chaotic intervals outside. The whole thing reminded him too much of the Martian death pits at the end of the Invasion. He shuddered and kept climbing the stairs.

By the time he reached the top of the stairs, Herb heard the sounds of a struggle coming from the end of the hallway, where the map said Norton's control room was. He heard thumps, slams and the sound of a pained grunt or two coming from the control room itself.

Margaret must be in there, Herb thought, now walking even more slowly towards the door. He'd gotten maybe ten steps when a loud crash sounded from the control room, followed by a flash of light and showers of sparks.

He arrived at the end of the long hallway after a walk of nearly a full minute. He was still eight feet from the door when Margaret emerged from the room.

There was a fresh cut along the side of her chin, her sleeve was torn, and there was a bloody spot with a small red river flowing down the side of her pant leg. Her eyes had the wild look of a person who'd spent the last few minutes fighting for her life. Her pistol holster was empty, but she had a knife in one hand and a small bundle wrapped in red and white rags in the other.

"An early Christmas present for me?" Herb asked, keeping a cool exterior while pointing to the bundle.

"Shut up and turn around," she said. "We're getting out of here now, and in style."

Herb shrugged and turned his back to her. Even with the noise of the city descending and falling to pieces around them, he knew he could stop her if she tried knifing him in the back. For the last little while, he'd felt more powerful, more able, and more *aware* of things than he'd ever been before.

And right now he was most aware of the venomous, killing hatred coursing through every fiber of Margaret's soul.

Gilbert felt like he was floating serenely in a happy soup of relaxation, right until he tried to breathe and got a noseful of water.

His nose hurt again. A *lot.*

Then there were two strong arms pulling him from the soup and into a loud, screaming mass, where blurry fires burned far and near, smells of the dead and the dying were mixed with the stench of machine oils and grease, and he heard shouts and screams everywhere.

"This one's awake an' breathing!" roared the owner of the big, dark, calloused hands that had grabbed him.

"Put 'im on the beach, face up!" another voice yelled as Gilbert spluttered, still disoriented, though the morning chill was waking him from his beating and dousing. The big man dragged him like a small child, and soon his feet no longer floated but touched the bottom of the watery bed he'd been lying in. His nose was still throbbing, and now his leg and head were singing in his little concert of pain, too.

Then his well-shoed heels dragged on sand alone as he coughed and spit up swallowed river water that reeked of blood and oil. The large man laid Gilbert out in the morning light on the river shore, sand sticking to his once nice suit and ruining it further. "Can yuh unnerstand me?"

Gilbert looked at him and nodded his head dazedly.

"Good. Look, we gots to save the rest, or's many's we can. There'll be doctors along soon, I'm sure. You stay here and wait, 'kay?" Without waiting for an answer, the big laborer ran off back to the lake and began grabbing at other bodies floating or struggling to the shore. Off behind his field of vision, Gilbert heard a loud explosion, followed by a snap louder than any thunder he'd ever heard. "It's crashed!" he heard an excited voice say outside his field of vision, "It's crashed in the river and snapped in two!"

Gilbert wet his lips and looked at the sky. There were red wisps of clouds up there in the sunrise, as delicate as fairy dancers. He had just begun singing a small nursery rhyme his mother used to sing when he blacked out for the second time that day.

"Strapped in?" Margaret said, putting on her goggles and checking the steering wheel.

"What's this contraption do?" Herb said, adjusting the belt on his seat. "It'd better fly, somehow." They were pointed at a ramp in the hangar, and out through it, he could clearly see the twilight-lit ground with people running and screaming below.

"Just hold on," she said. "This motorcar has quite a few tricks up its sleeve." She revved the engine and the boiler hissed. The steamcar lunged forward on its four oversized wheels, drove off the ramp and into the open air.

"Margaret …" Herb's voice was on edge as the ground rushed up to meet them.

Margaret giggled and pulled a lever. Several large parachutes puffed out of the steamcar's backside and midsection. There was enough confusion on the ground between floating evacuoles, sputtering robots and a giant city crashing into the dirt and water that a steam-driven horseless carriage parachuting in the midst of screaming refugees received very little notice.

"Wait here," Herb said when they'd landed, trying to sound calm as his heart raced.

"How do you plan to find him in this mob?" she'd said.

"I've been able to do a lot of things lately I couldn't before. Putting up with you is just the worst of them," said Herb. He opened the passenger door and stalked off into the milling group of onlookers, survivors and wreckage. Margaret had been about to speak, but instead slouched in the driver's seat and sulked.

Gilbert was dreaming about walking along a grassy field outside his old house in Minnesota when the voice called him. "Gilbert," the voice said. It was a male voice, a voice he knew he could trust. It was a voice whose owner had never done him a wrong in his life.

He opened his eyes, and even without his glasses on he could tell it was Herb standing over him. "Herb!" Gilbert said, through a mouth that felt like it was full of mud. All around were the cries of the wounded, frightened and confused. He blinked and saw other people walking around, looking like trees moving to and fro. Gilbert had somehow been moved far up the shoreline, near the outskirts of the city of Richmond. "How'd I get here?" Gilbert managed to ask.

"Half the city broke off, like the Titanic did when it sank," said Herb. "You've been out for a little while, I'd guess. The river's started flowing around the chunks of the city in it, but it looks like the waves pushed folks like you and the first bunch of escapees up to the edge here, where you were rescued."

"Amazing," Gilbert said. He took Herb's offered hand and stood up, wincing. Gilbert checked himself. Other than his head feeling like a baseball team had used it for batting practice, he was sore virtually everywhere but not in massive amounts of pain. He winced and held his temples while squinting in Herb's direction. "How did you get here, Herb? And where'd you get that crazy black longcoat?"

Herb looked at him and smiled. "I've come looking for you, old bean," he said.

Joy welled in Gilbert, pure joy at the devotion of his faithful friend. "You're kidding, right? No? Herb … I … I don't know what to say."

"Well, you don't have to say anything, do you? What are friends for, after all?"

"In our case, friends are for getting us out've crazy messes. Well, you could've come earlier, but it looks like you're here now, so that's what counts, right?"

"Right," said Herb, struggling to be heard over the noise and confusion on the beach. "You've saved me more than once, old chum," he said, drawing his pistol quietly from its holster, out of Gilbert's sight. "First from that dying Martian, and later you distracted those flying Neanderthals in Berlin. Seems a long, long time ago, doesn't it, Gil?" Herb paused in thought, closed his eyes and breathed deeply several times. A single tear rolled down the corner of his cheek as he looked at the lanky, relaxed form of his friend.

"And I think it's time I saved you from something for a change, Gil," Herb said, backing away several quiet steps.

"Herb, what're you talking abou—"

Herb raised his hand and shot Gilbert. He'd pointed at Gilbert's heart, but at the last second he'd moved the pistol a fraction of a degree's angle. Gilbert heard, not the familiar explosion of a pistol's retort, but a kind of *pop*! More like the cork in a wine bottle. Being shot didn't feel like he'd thought it would. There was a rude poke in his ribs, then pain and burning. When he looked down, the now-shabby waistcoat had a stain already growing darker by the second. "You ... Herb!" Gilbert felt more indignant than panicky, more like he'd been pranked or insulted than shot.

"Look, Gil," Herb babbled, running up to him and pushing the taller boy to the ground. Gilbert yelped in pain as he hit the crumbly soil, and a tree root dug into his back.

"You shot me!" Gilbert yelled, his voice now rising above even the incoherent screams and wailing sirens from the town and the beach. "Of all the dirty, low-down ..."

"Gil!" Herb barked while pressing Gil's mouth shut with his free hand and looking in Gil's eyes. "Gil, look, stop screaming! I had to be able to truthfully say I shot you, or they'd know I was lying! Look, Gil, *Aagh*!"

It was Herb's turn to yell as Gilbert clamped near frantic teeth down on Herb's palm. Herb jumped away, looking at his injured hand as Gilbert gave a feeble kick at Herb's legs.

Gilbert winced as he tried to fell Herb as he'd done to the agent back in London. But the *pain*! The pain in his chest! This wasn't what being shot was like in the nickel novels! Jehosephat, this *hurt*!

"You turned nose, didn't you?" Gilbert said, using the term he'd heard the British use for someone who'd switched sides. "What'd they buy you with, pal? Money? Girls, maybe? What was worth shooting me for? "

"It's ... Don't judge me, Gilbert! It's more complicated than that!"

"Sure it is. It always is, isn't it? Are you one of ...?"

Now Herb was in Gilbert's face, crouching with a wild look in his eyes as he held the pistol to Gilbert's head and pulled back the hammer.

Gilbert stopped mid-sentence and inhaled deeply through his nose. His mouth was silent while he said a weak prayer for forgiveness for all he'd messed up in the last few weeks.

"Now, Gilbert, you, you *listen* to me, understand? I'm *damned*, now. There's no going back. But you, you I can save. Here's what you have to do. Are you listening?"

Gilbert nodded his head. Herb sounded as if a few of the more important strings that held his head together had snapped. His speech sounded a little like a skipping phonograph record.

"Gil, now, I'm going to walk away from here. When they ask me, I'm going to say I shot you, and that should be enough. But if they question me further, I'm going to say that I *removed you as a threat*. Do you understand? You've got to *stay down*, Gil. If you have to write or speak, talk about the price of ginger or the state of the theater, or how awfully Americans make tea. But don't get in their way, Gil! Don't become a threat or they'll kill us both. You *can't* fight them, Gil. You'll only be crushed, understand?"

"And what makes you think I won't keep fighting you?" Gilbert was speaking through gritted teeth. "What makes you think I'll be bought by a threat? What're you gonna do? Threaten my family? I travel light these days. If you kill me I'll die a martyr, fighting the most evil people in the world."

Herb stood up, his right hand still pointing the pistol at Gilbert.

"Gil, I have something in my pocket that will break you, just as I was broken. Every man has his price, and what I have will buy your despair."

"Oh, really? And what's that? You think a gun or a girl is gonna get me to join the other side?"

"No, Gil," said Herb, reaching into his pocket and pulling out a red and white bundle of cloth, about a half-foot wide. He tossed it to Gilbert, who caught it with a clumsy left hand against his chest. "No guns, blonds or brunettes. Not this time. Unwrap that after I go. If all goes well, you'll never see me again."

Herb turned and disappeared over the edge of the hill.

Gilbert, still dazed, looked at the bundle Herb had thrown in his lap. The rags weren't tied together. It wasn't difficult to unwrap at all. It was close enough to his eyes that he could see the strands of rag and cloth to pull and unwrap. And when he saw the hand in the bundle he ...

The hand in the bundle ... The hand ... It was a hand.

A human hand.

Even without his glasses, in the growing morning light he could see it was a dead, sickly yellow hand that had been tied tight at the wrist with a cord. The wrist had been cut haphazardly, and left a jagged edge with two pieces of bone sticking out. It had fingernails painted the color of summer raspberries, and on the finger next to the pinky was a ring with a diamond in the center surrounded by five purple stones.

The diamond in the middle of the ring was flipped up, revealing a small hidden compartment. Whatever had once been inside the ring was now gone.

Gilbert stared at the hand, the nails, and the ring. Deaf now to the activity surrounding him, he could barely hear the screaming in the far distance. He still took no notice even when he realized *he* was the one screaming, louder and longer than any person ought to be able to scream. He was still screaming when the stretcher-bearers finally worked their way to him through the crowds of dead, dying and wounded. He screamed in the horse-drawn ambulance all the way to the makeshift hospital tent. He screamed himself into a louder kind of hoarseness when they tried to pry the hand from him. He took no notice when an unsympathetic passenger clouted him several times in the head in a fruitless effort to shut him up. Gilbert kept screaming in a thin, raspy voice as the memories from another time in his life began to crash, froth and dance inside his mind like jumping beans in a frypan.

He screamed when they strapped him in a hospital bed to ensure he wasn't a danger to himself or others. He screamed until his fellow patients in the beds neighboring his begged the harried doctors to give a precious shot of morphine to Gilbert, anything to make him sleep and be quiet!

When he finally slept, Gilbert fell into a dark, dreamless land without voice or thought. He didn't even notice when a stray soldier took the hand from Gilbert and slipped the ring into his own pocket, throwing the hand into a nearby trashcan.

Margaret sat for ten minutes after Herbert left. She'd lost her needle gun in the fight with the Actress, but brandishing the jagged, bloody knife she'd taken from the wreckage of the city convinced any would-be attackers to find other prey. She was just considering driving off and leaving Herbert to his fate when she saw him return.

She pulled her goggles and black gloves on and fired up the engine as he rounded the car and opened the passenger door.

Herb walked with his eyes facing forward, trying with every grain of will he possessed to leave behind the friend he'd just shot and whose spirit he'd crushed.

He saw Margaret waiting for him in the driver's seat of the steam car, looking down over the fat rubber tires that would treat almost any terrain, short of boiling lava, as a paved roadway. The boiler hissed and belched steam behind her like a pet dragon. Margaret herself had been busy; there was no sign of the parachutes.

"I take it Gilbert was not interested in joining our little group?" she said as he took his seat.

"I shot him," Herb growled, staring forward with a blank expression on his face.

Margaret tilted her head slightly as another steam-powered ambulance charged past them, followed by a wooden wagon piled with at least a dozen dead bodies.

"You killed him, then?"

"I removed him as a threat, yes. Get us out of here, Margaret, before I remove you next."

She looked at a gauge on the instrument panel below the steering wheel. Satisfied, she pulled a lever and began driving forward, nearly running over a pregnant woman who staggered and groaned while holding the arm of her husband.

"I'm halfway surprised you didn't flatten her, Margaret."

"She has blond hair. She might be among the fit."

Herb rolled his eyes and slouched in his chair. "By-the-by," he said, with a voice tinged with the need for sleep, "did you really kill that red-head? The one who'd been following Gilbert all this time?"

"What say you do your job and I'll do mine, and never the twain shall meet?" she said, her goggled eyes focused on the approaching road.

"Fine with me," he yawned, "you just didn't strike me as the type to leave a jagged cut when you remove a hand, is all."

"Shut up, Herbert."

Herb shrugged. Closing his eyes, he fell into a light sleep and didn't wake up until she stopped.

Chapter 83

"A man imagines a happy marriage as a marriage of love;
even if he makes fun of marriages that are without love, or
feels sorry for lovers who are without marriage."
– GKC, *Chaucer*

Gilbert's universe worked differently now. For most people, life progressed as a series of linked moments. Each one was attached to the last, building and constructing a stable experience known the world over as reality.

For Gilbert, life was now disjointed, a series of surrealistic dreams punctuated by short stints when he felt imprisoned in a large white bed in a larger white room. In the white room, something held his head still, facing always forward at a cross mounted on the wall.

For Gilbert, there now seemed little difference between dream and reality, except that his dreams were usually more pleasant. Dreams often saw Gilbert sitting under a large tree in a meadow, talking with people he'd loved about peaceful things, all past conflicts forgotten. Sometimes he was with his Ma or Pa, sometimes with Herb. Sometimes with a pretty, brown haired girl, or sometimes Anne.

Anne was the one he dreamed about the least, his heart leaping when he saw her, then falling when she shifted position to reveal the dark, bloody stump on the end of her arm.

He never dreamed of Father Brown, though when awake, he wished he would.

Waking in the hospital brought different sights each time. Sometimes a nurse came to change linen or other sundries in the room. Once he heard a beautiful, quiet voice speaking to him from outside his field of vision. His head, fixed in place, couldn't turn to see who it was. Another time an older face, seamed and lined with sadness, pain and regret underneath a cowboy hat, stared at him from the foot of the bed.

Over time that could have been minutes, days or weeks, his open eyes began remembering familiar faces while analyzing new ones. The voice that read to him belonged to the beautiful girl from his dreams with brown hair and eyes. Her name was Frances, and she was kind. The sad and sometimes angry face that stared at him belonged to a tall, muscular older man he did not recognize who wore a long gray coat with a silver badge that sported an eye in the middle instead of a star.

Other odd people appeared after that. Two young boys, one short and chubby, the other slim and bespectacled, stood in front him beside a well-to-do looking man and a pretty woman of more modest means.

"Things are going well, Mister Chesterton," whispered the chubby one. "Tollers and I have been working diligently to help our parents see the best in one another. It may mean a house of six children, and that my father becomes a Papist like Tollers and his mother, but sacrifices have to be made, don't they?"

"Johnny's been picked up by his father already," Tollers said, his thin face nodding happily. "And Jack's father has been quite taken by my mother! He's even willing to convert if it means marrying her! Isn't that wonderful, Mister Gilbert? "

Gilbert nodded, and fell into a stupor again. More time passed. The older face appeared in front of him one more time, at the foot of his bed.

"I knew you were gonna be trouble, kid," he said to Gilbert, "right from when I saw your picture. But I didn't think chasing you would cost the life of a friend, or of Joe Harper's son. It ain't your fault, I know. It won't be a pleasure going to Joe with his son's badge. But, when you've got nothin' left, revenge is a good way to keep yourself goin'. And now I've got that little dark-haired chicken and your English friend. I'll hunt them all the way back to Europe, if'n I hafta." He was speaking to himself more than Gilbert now, who was still staring straight ahead.

He saw someone at the door, and moved right, out Gilbert's field of vision. Gilbert, his head still fixed in place by the restraints, kept staring forward. Fortunately for him, boredom was impossible. In his current state, he was like a drunk man who could gain total satisfaction and pleasure staring at the patterns on a stucco wall for hours on end.

"Howdy, ma'am." Gilbert heard Finn speaking in the hallway. Frances' pretty voice was there, too.

"I've had my people deliver your fee in the wagons outside, Colonel Finn."

"It's Mister Finn now, Miss Blogg. I resigned by telegraph this morning. And might I say that this young man cost you a mighty pretty penny."

"It was worth it to me, Mister Finn. Have you ever been in love?"

"Yes ma'am. Well, I wish a happy life to the pair of you. I say he's a truly lucky man."

"You're very kind, Mister Finn. God bless you."

"Likewise."

Silence. The door to his room opened and closed again.

His world slipped and slid as a girl stood in front of him. For a crazy moment he thought it was Anne again.

But Anne had red hair, and this girl had brown hair swept into a bun on top. Her dress was immaculate, as if she'd spent a very long time trying to look her best for Gilbert.

Frances looked beautiful.

Frances.

"Frances," he croaked. He tried to turn his head to face her, but his head was held in place. He moved hardly a millimeter, but even that sent sharp spines of pain shooting up and down from his ribs, leg, head, and numerous other places in and on his body.

"Gilbert! Oh, Gilbert, my dear, sweet, sweet Gilbert!" she said, running first to him, then into the hallway. She shouted for a doctor, a nurse, anyone, for Gilbert was awake! Awake and lucid again!

She was by his bedside, looking into his eyes and waiting for him to speak.

"Frances," he said again.

"Don't tire yourself, my sweet love! Oh my dear! My darling! We'd received word you were dead! Blown to atoms in that terrible airship explosion over New York! But I knew they'd find you! I *knew* it! It cost me my dowry to hire the Pinkertons to find you! Sending the stipplograph across the Atlantic alone cost more than most lawyers' salaries! But Father doesn't know yet. And they did find you, eventually. The interest on Father's investments will cover the whole of the amount probably in a few years. Oh, but do you know me, Gilbert? They said you'd taken some kind of trauma, something beyond your concussion and the grazing on your ribs. But best of all, Gilbert, look! Look!"

She grabbed a newspaper from the nearby table and held it so he could read it.

His picture was on the front page. The date on it was meaningless.

"Your role in saving the Americas, Gilbert! That reporter you were supposed to meet in New York? A Mister Kelly Ewing? He first wrote about your death, now he's going to win some prize for being the first to write about your heroic exploits, phenomenal luck and bravery in defeating that horrible Emperor! Everyone knows that *you* were the one who started the revolution! Were it not for your heroism, all those steam-driven metal men would have been marching on the capital city here, instead of into the river from a great height. You've accomplished great things, Gilbert! You're a hero!"

"I ..."

Frances waited, excited by the single syllable Gilbert had uttered. "Yes! That's it my love! It's true! They examined that terrible Emperor's control room, his personal living quarters, everything, and found his plans of conquest! As a result, they made public their plans to *unify* the Five Americas! Perhaps even Canada, too! Well, the Queen isn't happy at that prospect, of course. But still! You saved the Americas, Gilbert!"

Gilbert looked back and forth, understanding her, but only barely able to form his thoughts. His head was immobilized, and he couldn't turn away from the stipplographed picture of him on the paper's front page.

He closed his eyes. "No," he whispered, his voice feeling as thick as molasses. "I'm not ... not a ..."

"Oh, don't be so modest, my dear! This is wonderful! They were worried that with all the injuries you sustained, you'd never be the same afterwards! A concussion, broken nose, a bullet grazing your ribs, and goodness knows what else! Gilbert, you must promise that when we're married you'll stop running about on these terribly silly crusades! Or at least take me with you! I couldn't bear to be at home with the children, constantly wondering about your safety."

Gilbert's eyes began to go dull again. Frances noticed and stood back.

"Oh, my Gilbert! I'm ... I'm sorry that I must have tired you! I am so sorry, please forgive me. You just rest, now. Rest and let me tell the doctor this wonderful news!"

She took careful, quiet steps out the door. Once she was in the hallway, Gilbert heard her feet clacking against the wooden planks of the floor.

They think I am a hero, Gilbert thought. *They think I am a hero, when really I was only a puppet. And as soon as my strings were cut, I fell.*

He was no hero. Not on this adventure. Had he taken better control, could he have ...?

No.

He hadn't taken control of himself.

A thought jumped in his head. Probing. Insistent.

Why were you there in the first place? The thought went. *You've tried to do the right thing your whole life. And you tried to be the right kind of person in the city. You've been beaten down since you were a child. Who wouldn't say yes to all that attention? Sure, you ran out on Father Brown's canonization, but so what? He's already dead! That wasn't cowardice—it was ... it was ... self-preservation! Yes, that's it!*

Thoughts of the red-head, of *Anne*, spelled with an *e*, came back to him. Had he caused her death? Had he caused death in the city on a grand scale? Had he botched things?

Yes! No! He could see reasons for and against the idea. What was the truth?

What was the truth? The question made his head hurt until he blacked out again.

And now Gilbert was running, running in snow and ice as a dark, nameless horror of immense size bore down on him from behind.

He looked around again. There was only flat, level powder as far as he could see in any direction. The wind whipped the snow in circuitous swirls into drifts and pools, cold and pitiless as a winter mountain range.

Running was pointless—where to? But staying in place was a sure way to be caught! He started running again, holding his arms around himself to keep warm and hoping the thing chasing him would lose his trail. He tried turning his face away from the knife-edged wind, but whichever way he turned, the angry blasts of air found a place to cut into him.

"Help," he whispered, trying to scream. "Help ..."

"Gilbert?"

Gilbert opened his eyes. Frances was there, looking at him with a worried expression.

"Frances," he said. His voice was weak.

"Yes, Gilbert! It's me! You recognize me! I'm so glad, so very happy!" She wiped a tear from her face, breathing deeply to keep her joy under control. "The doctor wanted me to call him as soon as you awoke, but I want you all to myself for just a few seconds first."

Gilbert knew he should be happy to see her, but something inside him had died since he'd left Frances on the docks in London.

Frances either didn't notice his lack of enthusiasm, or didn't care. She leaned forward and kissed him gently on the cheek.

"A kiss for the gallant sir knight, for slaying the evil Emperor and freeing the enslaved workers!"

"I'm not a hero," he said in a quiet voice.

"Oh, but my dear, dear one! You *are*! Who knows what might have happened if you hadn't ..."

"I'm *not* a *hero*!" Gilbert said louder, his head held stationary by the restraints. "I didn't do anything but get swept along by a current! I saved someone's life, but she died anyway! You understand? Everything I did has come to nothing! Nothing!"

"Gilbert, I ..."

"And another thing! You think I'm something special? You think I'm some kind of a holy-holy fella? Lemme tell you something! Lemme tell you how it really is! God just looks over everyone He's gonna make, and then He decides who He's gonna bless and who He's gonna curse. People like you'n yours, you couldn't mess up your lives if you tried! There'd always be more money if you needed it! More guards to keep out riff raff like me, more of everything!

"But people like me, Frances, *it just keeps hitting us!* My folks got pulled out've a normal life by a bunch of guys who run the world and they were made into a couple of killers! And then *they* got killed! And I got stuck in a factory, and then the Martians landed, and then I met Father Brown but he *died*, and I finally made a best friend and he *shot* me, and then a girl saved my life, but *she* died, and now *you're* here and I don't even know if *God's* there, or if He's abandoned me, or if I even wanna be with Him after *what He's put me through!*"

Gilbert scrunched his eyes shut. Halfway through his speech, Gilbert stopped looking at Frances and began staring at the cross on the wall. After a few more sentences, his eyes were closed and his words were running together in a long trail that made sense only to him. By the time he was finished, Frances' eyes were full of tears and she'd run for the doctor.

"Frances," he said the empty room, "Frances I'm sorry, I ... I'm so, so sorry ..." Finally, Gilbert's breathing slowed. His speech became a series of mumbles as his eyes opened, but looked glassed over.

Once in his room, the doctor looked at Gilbert with his instruments. Satisfied, he glared at Frances with a stern expression, frowning eyes looking at her over a handlebar mustache.

"Ma'am, I specifically instructed you to call me the moment he woke up!" His voice was calm with the slightest Confederate twang to it, but there was no mistaking its angry undercurrents.

"I'm so terribly sorry. But—what's wrong with him?"

"He's had a fair bit of trauma, and not just to his head or his side. It can make a man funny, and a boy often ain't never the same afterwards.

He's been raving in his sleep so much, I wondered if this was his first concussion after all. Or if maybe he got hit harder'n we thought."

Frances blinked, looked inward, straightened her back and held the doctor's gaze. Her hands were clutched just below her breastbone. "How long then, until he will be well?" she said calmly.

"If you mean for you two to get married? Only you can answer that, really. If you mean well enough to where he was before? Well, the mind's a tricky thing. I really can't say. He's lucky he's a hero—that's what got him his own room, and quiet's probably doing him the best good right now, along with you bein' here readin' to him."

"How long," she repeated.

"Little lady, he could be goin' in and out of the real world for days, weeks or months. Years, maybe. He's seen things that've hurt'im bad. Real bad. Unless something in him gets right, he might be like this forever."

"But he's a hero! The talks are back on because of him! There's even rumblings that the Americas will join again over the threat! Can't someone be found in this entire country to help him? To fix him?"

"Helpin' him's easy. It's fixin' him that's gonna be hard, Miss Blogg."

As the world melted away, Gilbert felt, rather than saw, Frances look at him with worry and tears in her eyes, and the doctor with her look at him from beneath gray eyebrows with little expression at all.

Chapter 84

"The way to love anything is to realize that it may be lost."
— GKC, *Tremendous Trifles*, 1909

Gilbert awoke again. Typically, he awoke only long enough to eat and reply dumbly to what people said to him. And then he remembered the argument. *Please*, thought Gilbert, *please let her come back.*

She was at the door, and then in front of him again.

"Frances," Gilbert whispered. "Frances, I'm sorry, I'm really, really sorry about yesterday!"

"Gilbert," she said, holding up her hand, "I wasn't going to bring this up until after we were ... well, until later. I have spent a sizable sum on the Pinkerton private detective agency in an effort to see you protected from Fortescue Williamson and his father. Yet, even after this, yesterday you were very cruel to me. And you need to know I was raised to accept criticism where it was earned, but never to bear cruelty. Is that clear?"

"Crystal, Frances."

She walked closer to his side. "Gilbert, while we were apart. Did you ..." she took a deep breath with her eyes closed, "... has someone taken my place in your heart?"

Gilbert swallowed and thought. "There was someone who I met before I knew you, Frances. I saw her again in the floating city. I didn't betray you, Frances. I did not ... she's dead now, Frances. Dead and gone."

Frances sat in the nearby chair. At first she'd seemed different, somehow. More ... more *formal*. Her back had been straight, her hands folded in her lap.

Now she relaxed, her breathing returning to normal. "When I mentioned heroes, Gilbert, you mentioned God and became angry. Is that who you were really angry with?"

"I don't think I could get angry with you, Frances. So, yeah, it's God I'm mad at."

"Gilbert, the whole time you've been away, I thought of nothing else but you. Your poems, your face, your eyes, they brought me peace and joy inside each time I thought of them."

"The same for me, Frances. When I thought about you, that is. There's just something ... well, something I need to tell you."

Slightly, almost imperceptibly, Frances' back stiffened again.

"Frances, I still care for you. I still love you, and I still would marry you."

He paused.

"But?" said Frances.

"Frances, I saw a different side of myself on this trip. One I didn't like. And doing that taught me I've got a ways to go before I'm ready to get married, and to be the kind of man you want and deserve. Plus, they tell me it's gonna be a while before I can walk down the hall, much less a church aisle."

Frances relaxed again. "You wish to … postpone our betrothal, then?"

"Just for a while, Frances. I'm not a hero, honey. I don't know if I could've stopped the city, or saved the people who died. But I know I made a lot of mistakes this trip, and I coulda done better. And most of all," it was his turn to breathe deeply, "I know I *should* have gone to Rome. I was supposed to testify at Father Brown's canonization, but I got afraid and ran all the way here to the West coast, instead. I … I did the wrong thing. I know that now, even though it took having that giant city swallow me up and spit me out for me to understand that. Maybe I can put it right, but I know I won't be ready to be your husband until I at least try. And maybe while I'm doing that I can put things right between God and me again, too. Does that make sense?"

Frances, overwhelmed with emotion, smiled through her tears. She stood up and reached for Gilbert, gently hugging him with a great, relieved sigh. "I was … I was so worried, Gilbert, dear, that you would say you didn't want me anymore! Or worse, that *I* might have to leave *you*!"

"Frances …"

"I could wait for you, Gilbert. Do you have you an idea how long, though?"

"I'd … I'd hope you could wait, Frances. I can't ask you to wait forever for me, though. Could you wait maybe...?"

"A year?" Frances said.

Gilbert, his head still fixed to face the front, looked at the cross on the wall. He'd have been happy to have a month! "Okay," he said. "But I don't want you to feel trapped, Frances. I've realized that I have to give some things up in my life. I don't want you to be one of them, but if you ever find you'll be happy with, well, someone else, I'll understand."

She smiled. Looking over her shoulder first, she gave him a quick, gentle kiss on the lips. "Never, my dear, dear one," she whispered in his ear, as a thrill ran through him.

From his hidden spot in the doorway, Doctor Johnson looked at the young people in front of him and sighed without sound. Even though Gilbert was scheduled for a few more tests, the doctor instead turned and silently left the room to check on his newest patient down the hall: a gal who'd come in looking like she'd been beaten within an inch of her life by an angry steamhammer.

Funny, Doc thought as his feet made crisp steps down the nearly silent corridor. Even though there was no shortage of hurt folks like that in the city these days, the patient Doc was about to visit had won a place in the elite ward almost by luck of the draw. He wondered, though, if the expensive-looking gown she'd been wearing when she'd been found had anything to do with it.

He entered her room and looked at her chart. The tissue was apparently responding to treatment, with surprisingly little infection. Dad-gum if those squids who'd invaded England hadn't known a thing or two! He looked at the prosthesis that had been molded to her missing limb. Made from a melding of Earth and Martian technology, it promised to be the wave of the future. Perhaps even a means for countless cripples to live normal lives again.

He looked at the half of her face that hadn't been burned and covered in bandages. Such a shame! She'd been so pretty! But even the Martians hadn't left behind any secrets of healing scar tissue. "Wish you could talk, little missy," Doc whispered. Her eyes hadn't opened since she'd been rushed in here. "I'd like to at least know yer name."

"Ah ..."

Doc blinked. The noise had come from her! She'd spoken!

"Hang on, honey," he said, reaching down to examine her. If she were getting conscious, there were a number of folks who'd want to know, pronto! He'd just leaned down to look in her good eye when he felt the crushing grip on his left wrist.

Oh, no! He tried hard not to scream; that would've disturbed too many patients. But he had to use every bit of his considerable inner strength to call out for an orderly's help in a normal voice. Then he gasped in pain as the bones in his wrist begin to crack. Je-hosephat! The girl'd gotten *strong*!

Grimacing in tremendous pain, he looked with widening eyes at his wrist. It was enveloped like a child's arm in the three, large fingers of hinged brass as the steam-hand creaked and hissed like a waking dragon. She pulled his injured arm towards her. He scrunched his eyes shut and opened his mouth in a silent scream as burly orderlies, strong but often worse than useless, appeared in the room and tried to pry him loose.

"Ah ... *Ahnnnnnn*," she whispered in his ear, the words slurred by pain and morphine, while a lock of her red hair tickled his nose, "*spuhld whiv ahn eeeeeeee ...*"

The five-sided table had not been used for some time. It had lain idle for months while the members pursued their respective projects. The oldest man at the table looked at his cohorts. Each one knew their place. More importantly, he knew each of their movements and plans even more intimately than his own.

He began. No one needed to tell him to report. "Our plan with the Floating City has failed. The attempt to use it to divide the Five Americas has had the opposite effect."

"The Salesman was reportedly captured and executed," said the Second man, hiding his discomfort expertly in the sizable folds of skin around his sunken eyes. "But the Farmer managed to ensure that Norton was punished for his overtures. Norton was captured by the Pinkertons and hanged within the week at a show trial."

Now the Third man, who was perhaps even heavier than he'd been before, removed the cigar from his mouth and spoke. "Young Chesterton was not successfully turned to us. However, the Wells boy managed to remove him as a threat. He also managed to obtain the disk with the most important portion of its information intact. While I remain less than wholly convinced of Wells' usefulness, he might be suited to lesser assignments. Perhaps assisting the Doctor on Mars?"

"The Doctor has been busying himself writing those absurd detective romances, with himself as the secondary character. I'd suggest ..." The Fourth man's thin, waspy voice now carried across the table with a tang of disgust.

"We must maximize the advantage that the Doctor presents us with." The Fifth man, his voice like milk, had interrupted the Fourth man's.

There was a pause around the table. Interruption of one's better was an act of war. And they all responded in the customary fashion, which was to show no response at all. "Do you propose ... an alternative to liquidating Wells or the Doctor?" The First man had spoken. All eyes moved from him to the Fifth man. The Fifth man smiled. Though his hair was gray, he was the youngest at this table, his face as smooth as a baby's. "I propose instead to encourage the scribblings of both the Doctor and Wells. Both are apt at creating fictional heroes who have no use for authentic religious faith. A hero with no God creates followers of no God. And, as we all know, people with no God are far easier to manipulate than a people who would hold their leaders to a celestial standard of behavior."

The First man leaned back, looking carefully at the youngest man in the Fifth place. "And, if the Doctor shows any of his previous ... ambitions? What then?"

"While young Wells has proven reluctant to remove a friend, perhaps assigning him to remove an enemy? If the Doctor was truly unstable, and Wells were ordered to clean up such a mess, he would enjoy it and become even more useful."

"A *Cleaner*," said the First man, his aging, liver-spotted skin pulsing with each word.

"We have enough agents," the Fourth man said, his knuckles going white, heedless of the breach of etiquette he'd committed.

"We can never have enough agents, in truth," said the Third man, his double chins moving in and out while he spoke. "It is my understanding that in this fiasco we have, regrettably, suffered the loss of the Actress. Now this event, while unfortunate, demonstrates that replacements are *always* needed," he said, looking pointedly at the Fourth man.

"I believe this matter can now be considered settled," the First man said, also looking coolly at the now shaking hands of the Fourth man across the table.

"Or," said the Second man, "at the very least, tabled for a later date." His voice was a death knell throughout the hall.

The clock ticked, suddenly very loud in the silence. The First man rose to go, followed by the Second, Third and Fifth.

Mortimer, the butler who was the fourth generation of his family to serve in this hall, waited at the door. He bowed slightly as each man left. After the table and hall had emptied, his eyes fell on the Fourth man seated alone. Mortimer's face sprouted a slight smile, in anticipation of his evening's enjoyment.

The Fourth man looked up from his folded hands, a look of resignation, sadness and fear upon his face. Mortimer closed the door with a soft and perfectly timed click.

Gilbert waved good-bye to Frances in the darkness from behind the window of his train compartment. She blew him kiss after kiss, her breath making clouds of steam in the night air. He surprised himself at how hard it was to hold back tears as she began receding on the train platform behind clouds of steam.

She'd been a wonderful support the past few weeks. Even if her brother had begun frothing at the mouth over the news of their ... well, just what was their status, now? Definitely not engaged ... not exactly courting ... maybe, they were just ...

Waiting?

Waiting. Waiting was good.

They'd spent hours and hours together in the hospital, and Gilbert had told her each one of his adventures, minus a few key points with Anne, of course. There are some things, Gilbert decided, that even Frances didn't need to know just yet, if ever.

Doc Johnson had been very helpful, too. He hadn't concealed his surprise at the rapidity of Gilbert's recovery, but he hadn't belittled it either. "Love's got a funny way of doing things to a man. Bad love can drop you lower than the devil's doormat, but good love can heal better 'n quicker than an angel's kiss."

"By the way, you never told us what happened to your arm," Gilbert had asked as Frances had blushed. The Doc had sported a cast on his left lower arm for over a week now.

"Well, it coulda been worse. A patient down the hall from you got a mite pestiferous while I was examining her, and the orderlies we had on security were 'bout as useful as a back pocket on a vest. I'll be right as rain in a few weeks, though. More'n I can say for her, poor thing."

Doc wouldn't say more about the patient, but he had seen Gilbert off at the hospital door when he'd left for the train after supper that evening. Please God (as Father Flambeau liked to say), Gilbert'd be back in New York in several days, and back in Rome another couple of weeks after that courtesy of the taxpayers of each of the Five Americas.

He still felt funny about the five medals he'd been given yesterday, one from each of the presidents of the Five Americas, all of whom had been in town for the unification talks. It was true that he'd come around in time to save many lives, but he still felt he could've done better. At least they'd been given in private ceremonies in his hospital room. He wasn't sure if he could've handled people cheering him again for heroism he felt was undeserved. Senator Sawyer had been particularly enjoyable, looking at him as if he could read in Gilbert's face the private shame he felt over the awards. "There's many who get what they don't think they oughta, son," the Senator had said, and somehow it'd made Gilbert feel better.

Also, he had a new set of glasses and a new satchel the size of a large dictionary, filled with a few dozen letters from various well-wishers. He'd saved them for the trip, knowing that leaving Frances behind would leave him in need of cheering up. One of those letters had been a sealed envelope given to Gil by courier just as he'd arrived at the station.

He tore through the first three at the top of the pile, discarding a lucrative job offer (he was going to Rome now, *period*) and two marriage proposals. He was ready to throw the satchel back under his seat and try for a nap when the lettering on a fourth piece of mail caught his eye.

The writing was on the letter he'd gotten just before stepping on the train. It looked official, like the kind he'd seen soldiers and government workers send to each other by transcribing Morse code, which was transmitted by the flashing lights of a heliograph. Or maybe like a governess would write for a child in their care.

Gilbert tore it open and read. The letter was written in the same blocky print as the address, and his blood ran cold before he'd finished reading two lines.

Gilbert, it said, *I lived through the Invasion. I cannot write well, not since they took my right arm in the basket. Do you remember that?*

The *Doctor*, Gilbert whispered.

He was *alive.*

No on else on Earth but Gilbert and Herb knew those details. He'd been edited out of Gilbert's stories, right before the editor disappeared.

They tell me you saved Earth. Good lad. I hope you liked the red stone I had put into your desk.

Gilbert remembered. The red stone had been in his desk drawer at the London Times, right before his hasty exit from England.

There are two stipplographs in this envelope, the Doctor's letter continued. Look at them before you read further.

Gilbert, his mouth suddenly very dry, probed inside the envelope with a shaking hand. As the letter said, there were two pictures inside, dotted stipplograph portraits of a young man and a young woman, both looking to the left with smiles on their faces. About his age, they had several of his facial features. The young man in particular looked so like Gilbert on the forehead, in his smile and around the eyes that he could have been ...

They are Cecil and Beatrice, continued the letter, *your younger brother and sister. They are with me here on Mars. Would you like to meet them? Come and see us. We have things to finish.*

Your Servant,

The Doctor.

Gilbert struggled to his feet, ignoring the screaming pain in his head, right leg and chest. He needed to move, to do something besides sit in place. Clutching the paper in a white-knuckled, dead-man's grip, he staggered to the door at the end of the train car. *Got to get another one of those walking canes,* he thought as he gripped nearby seats of sleeping passengers for support, *one with a hidden sword inside.*

Once at the end of the car, he opened the door and stepped out. In the air, with his hand on the railing, he looked up and saw stars again. The constellations were full of life and light, and he hadn't seen them that way since he'd left the Minnesota prairie, nearly two years and a lifetime ago.

He stood for several minutes, looking up at the night sky until he found a speck of red in the sea of blackness and white pinpricks. *I'm coming for you, Doctor,* he said to himself, not knowing or caring if it was Mars he was looking at or a distant red star. *You've gone and done the stupidest thing possible. You've given me a reason to track you down and save a sibling, even if I have to wring your scrawny neck to do it.*

Gilbert looked again at the letter, hobbled to his seat and picked up his satchel. He then went to his bed in the sleeping car and slept well for the first time since the World's Fair.

Mars, thought Gilbert, as he slipped into the land of dreams, *when I am healed and whole and finished in Rome, I will travel again, and I will go to...*

He slept for nearly fourteen hours, woke up and ate two breakfasts in the dining car.

It was a new day, and the rain outside couldn't change that.

THE END

Acknowledgements

Stephen King once likened the writing of a fiction novel to crossing the Atlantic Ocean in a bathtub; without adequate guidance, there's quite a bit of room for self-doubt and wandering astray. As such it would be a grievous wrong if I didn't thank those who patiently donated their time and advice to me on this project. *Amicus certus in re incerta cernitur.*

First and foremost, I am thankful to God for my gift of life and the life I now have, and for His family in the Catholic Church.

I am very, very thankful for the forbearance of my publishers and editors, who were willing to guide me through my first book and wait for the completion of this, my second.

Thanks go to my father-in-Law, Gerry Reiner, who has been most patient with me in my vain attempts to prove worthy of his daughter's hand these past two decades. He is also an extraordinary chess player, and showed me the Hedgehog strategy that served Gilbert so well on the Zeppelin.

Father Charles Gordon, C.S.C., a true Chestertonian Scholar, has been both a good friend and a wonderful resource of Chesterton's life and thought. He's also been a steady presence at every book signing I've held. Thanks, Father! Let's get together and grab another slice at Rocco's Pizza.

My ideal readers have been invaluable to me for their friendship, warmth, and willingness to improve the manuscript without pulling punches. This has been especially true for my Franciscan University college classmates Kathleen McKusker, David McCarthy and Edward Shuman, along with the members of the Saint John the Apostle School community. Thank you, all.

Very special thanks go out to DeOna Bridgeman, MD. A patient and wonderful consultant and school parent, she described injuries, procedures for field surgeries, and other details of the medical profession in ways even a career English major like myself could understand. This book would have taken far longer to complete without her assistance, and been far less accurate in a number of areas. Thank you, DeOna.

Most of all on this Earth, I wish to thank my wife and my family, for once again believing in and encouraging me through this process. I love you, Jeanna!

If I have missed anyone, please don't be angry with me, as it is through personal stupidity and not malice that I have erred.

Mistakes in the story, though, are mine alone. Those, you can be angry with me for. *Mea Culpa!*

CPSIA information can be obtained at www.ICGtesting.com
Printed in the USA
BVOW081942030713

324985BV00001B/72/P